FANNIE FLAGG

# The All-Girl Filling Station's Last Reunion

VINTAGE BOOKS
London

Published by Vintage 2015

2 4 6 8 10 9 7 5 3 1



First published in Great Britain in 2014 by Chatto & Windus

Vintage
20 Vauxhall Bridge Road,
London SW1V 2SA

www.vintage-books.co.uk

A Penguin Random House Company

global.penguinrandomhouse.com

A CIP catalogue record for this book is available from the British Library

ISBN 9780099593140

Penguin Random House is committed to a sustainable future for our business, our readers and our planet. This book is made from Forest Stewardship Council® certified paper.

Printed and bound by CPI Group (UK) Ltd, Croydon, CR0 4YY

# THE ALL-GIRL FILLING STATION'S LAST REUNION

Fannie Flagg began writing and producing television specials at nineteen and went on to distinguish herself as an actress and writer in television, films and the theatre. She is the author of the international bestsellers *Fried Green Tomatoes at the Whistle Stop Cafe*, *Welcome to the World, Baby Girl!* and *A Redbird Christmas*. Flagg's script for *Fried Green Tomatoes* was nominated for both the Academy and Writers Guild of America awards and won the highly regarded Scripters Award. She lives in Alabama and California.

ALSO BY FANNIE FLAGG

*Daisy Fay and the Miracle Man*
(originally published as *Coming Attractions*)

*Fried Green Tomatoes at the Whistle Stop Cafe*

*Fannie Flagg's Original Whistle Stop Cafe Cookbook*

*Welcome to the World, Baby Girl!*

*Standing in the Rainbow*

*A Red Bird Christmas*

*Can't Wait to Get to Heaven*

*I Still Dream About You*

*For Sam Vaughan*

# PULASKI, WISCONSIN

June 28, 2010

*A few years ago, if someone had told me that*
*I would be at this reunion today,*
*I wouldn't have believed them in*
*a million years. . . . And yet, here I am!*

—Mrs. Earle Poole, Jr.

*Prologue*

# THE BEGINNING

Lwów, Poland
April 1, 1909

In the year 1908, Stanislaw Ludic Jurdabralinski, a tall, raw-boned boy of fourteen, was facing a future of uncertainty. Life in Poland under Russian rule was bleak and dangerous. Polish men and boys were being conscripted to serve in the czar's army, and in an attempt to destroy Polish unity, Catholics and priests had been jailed for anti-Russian sentiments. Churches were shut down and Stanislaw's father and three uncles had been sent to prison camps for speaking out.

But with encouragement from his older brother Wencent, who had escaped Poland five years earlier, Stanislaw arrived in New York with nothing but the ill-fitting plaid woolen suit he was wearing, a photograph of his mother and sisters, and the promise of a job. With the help of a Polish stevedore who he had befriended on the ship, he managed to hop a freight train.

Five days later, Stanislaw arrived on his brother's doorstep in Chicago, excited and ready to begin his brand-new life. He had been told that in America, if you worked hard, anything was possible.

# The All-Girl FILLING STATION'S Last Reunion

# A MOST UNUSUAL WEEK

POINT CLEAR, ALABAMA
MONDAY, JUNE 6, 2005
76° AND SUNNY

MRS. EARLE POOLE, JR., BETTER KNOWN TO FRIENDS AND FAMILY AS Sookie, was driving home from the Birds-R-Us store out on Highway 98 with one ten-pound bag of sunflower seeds and one ten-pound bag of wild bird seed and not her usual weekly purchase for the past fifteen years of one twenty-pound bag of the Pretty Boy Wild Bird Seed and Sunflower Mix. As she had explained to Mr. Nadleshaft, she was worried that the smaller birds were still not getting enough to eat. Every morning lately, the minute she filled her feeders, the larger, more aggressive blue jays would swoop in and scare the little birds all away.

She noticed that the blue jays always ate the sunflower seeds first, and so tomorrow, she was going to try putting just plain sunflower seeds in her backyard feeders, and while the blue jays were busy eating them, she would run around the house as fast as she could and put the wild bird seed in the feeders in the front yard. That way, her poor finches and titmice might be able to get a little something, at least.

AS SHE DROVE OVER the Mobile Bay Bridge, she looked out at the big white puffy clouds and saw a long row of pelicans flying low over the water. The bay was sparkling in the bright sun and already dotted with red, white, and blue sailboats headed out for the day. A few people fishing alongside the bridge waved as she passed by, and she smiled and waved back. She was almost to the other side when she suddenly began to experience some sort of a vague and unusual sense of well-being. And with good reason.

Against all odds, she had just survived the last wedding of their three daughters, Dee Dee, Ce Ce, and Le Le. Their only unmarried child now was their twenty-five-year-old son, Carter, who lived in Atlanta. And some other poor (God help her), beleaguered mother of the bride would be in charge of planning that happy occasion. All she and Earle would have to do for Carter's wedding was show up and smile. And today, other than one short stop at the bank and picking up a couple of pork chops for dinner, she didn't have another single thing she had to do. She was almost giddy with relief.

Of course, Sookie absolutely worshipped and adored her girls, but having to plan three large weddings in fewer than two years had been a grueling, never-ending, twenty-four-hours-a-day job, with all the bridal showers, picking out patterns, shopping, fittings, writing invitations, meeting with caterers, figuring out seating arrangements, ordering flowers, etc. And between dealing with out-of-town guests and new in-laws, figuring out where to put everyone, plus last-minute bridal hysteria, at this point, she was simply weddinged out.

And no wonder. If you counted Dee Dee's last one, technically there had really been four large weddings, which meant shopping and being fitted for four different mother-of-the-bride dresses (you can't wear the same one twice) in less than two years.

Dee Dee had married, then promptly divorced. And after they had spent weeks returning all the wedding gifts, she had turned around and remarried the exact same husband. Her second wedding hadn't been quite as expensive as the first, but every bit as stressful.

When she and Earle had married in 1968, it had been just a typical church affair: white wedding gown, bridesmaids in matching pastel dresses and shoes, ring bearer, best man, reception, over and out. But now everybody had to have some kind of a theme.

Dee Dee had insisted on having an authentic Old South *Gone with the Wind* wedding, complete with a Scarlett O'Hara dress, large hoop skirt and all, and at the last minute, she had to be driven to the church standing up in the back of a small moving van.

Le Le and her groom wanted an entirely red and white wedding, including the invitations, food, drinks, and all the decorations, in honor of the University of Alabama football team.

And Ce Ce, Le Le's twin sister, the last girl to marry, had carried her ten-pound Persian cat, Peek-a-Boo, down the aisle instead of a wedding bouquet, and the groom's German shepherd, dressed in a tux, had served as best man. And if that wasn't bad enough, someone's turtle was the ring bearer. The entire thing had just been excruciating. You can't hurry a turtle.

Looking back on it now, Sookie realized she really should have put her foot down when Ce Ce and James invited all their friends to bring their pets to the reception, but she had made a sacred vow to never bully her children. Nevertheless, having to replace an entire banquet room's wall-to-wall carpeting at the Grand Hotel was going to cost them a fortune. Oh, well. Too late now. Hopefully, all that was behind her, and evidently not a minute too soon.

Two days ago, when Ce Ce left for her honeymoon, Sookie had broken down and sobbed uncontrollably. She didn't know if she was experiencing empty-nest syndrome or just plain exhaustion. She knew she must be tired. At the reception, she had introduced a man to his own wife. Twice.

The truth was, as sad as she was to see Ce Ce and James drive off, she had been secretly looking forward to going home, taking off all her clothes, and crawling into bed for about five years, but even that had been put on hold. At the last minute, James's parents, his sister, and her husband had decided to stay over an extra night, so she had to quickly try and whip up a little "going away" brunch for them.

Granted, it wasn't much: Earle's coconut margaritas, an assortment of crackers, cream cheese and pepper jelly, shrimp and grits, crab cakes with coleslaw, and tomato aspic on the side. But still, it had taken some effort.

* * *

WHEN SOOKIE DROVE INTO the little town of Point Clear and passed the Page and Palette bookstore, it occurred to her that maybe tomorrow, she would stop in and pick up a good book. She hadn't had time to read anything other than her daily horoscope, the Kappa newsletter, and an occasional *Birds and Blooms* magazine. We could be at war for all she knew. But now, she was actually going to be able to read an entire book again.

She suddenly felt like doing the twist right there in the front seat, which only reminded her how long it had been since she and Earle had learned a new dance step. She had probably even forgotten how to do the hokey pokey.

All she really had left to deal with was her eighty-eight-year-old mother, the formidable Mrs. Lenore Simmons Krackenberry, who absolutely refused to move to the perfectly lovely assisted-living facility right across town. And it would be so much easier on everybody if she would. The maintenance on her mother's yard alone was extremely expensive, not to mention the yearly insurance. Since the hurricane, the insurance on everybody's house on the Mobile Bay had gone sky-high. But Lenore was adamant about never leaving her home and had announced with a dramatic gesture, "Until they carry me out feet-first."

Sookie couldn't imagine her mother leaving anywhere feetfirst. As long as she and her brother, Buck, could remember, Lenore, a large imposing woman who wore lots of scatter pins and long, flowing scarves, and had her silver hair teased and sprayed into a perfect winged-back flip, had always rushed into a room headfirst. Buck said she looked like something that should be on the hood of a car, and they had secretly referred to her as "Winged Victory" ever since. And Winged Victory never just left a room; she whisked out with a flourish, leaving a cloud of expensive perfume in her wake. Never a quiet woman in any sense of the word, much like a show horse in the Rose Parade, she could be heard coming a mile away, due to the loud jingling of the numerous bracelets, bangles, and beads she always wore. And she was usually speaking long before she came in sight. Lenore had a loud booming voice and had studied "Expression" while attending Judson College for women, and to the family's everlasting regret, the teacher had encouraged her.

Now, due to certain recent events, including her setting her own kitchen on fire, they had been forced to hire a twenty-four-hour live-in nurse for Lenore. Earle was a successful dentist with a nice practice, but they were by no means rich, and certainly not now, with all the money they had spent sending the children to college, the weddings, Lenore's mortgage, and now the nurse. Poor Earle might not be able to retire until he was ninety, but the nurse was a definite necessity.

Lenore, who was not only loud but also extremely opinionated and voiced her opinion to everyone within earshot, had suddenly started calling total strangers long-distance. Last year, she had called the pope in Rome, and that call alone had cost them more than three hundred dollars. When confronted with the bill, Lenore had been incensed and said that she shouldn't have to pay a dime because she had been on hold the entire time. Try telling that to the phone company. And there was no reasoning with her. When Sookie asked why she had called the pope, considering that she was a sixth-generation dyed-in-the-wool Methodist, Lenore had thought for a moment and said, "Oh . . . just to chat."

"To chat?"

"Yes, and you mustn't be so closed-minded, Sookie. One can certainly be on speaking terms with Catholics. You don't want to marry one, but a friendly chat can't hurt."

And there had been other incidents. At a chamber of commerce meeting, Lenore had called the mayor a pointy-headed little carpetbagger and a horse thief and was sued for defamation of character. Sookie had been worried to death, but Lenore remained unfazed. "They have to prove what I said was not true, and no jury in their right mind would dare convict me!" In the end, the judge had thrown the case out, but still, it had been very embarrassing. All last year, Sookie had to try to avoid running into the mayor and his wife, and in such a small town, it had been almost impossible. They were just everywhere.

Since the lawsuit, they had been through three different nurses. Two quit, and one left in the middle of the night, along with one of Lenore's dinner rings and a frozen turkey. But now, after months of searching, Sookie felt she had finally found the perfect nurse, a darling older Filipino lady named Angel, who was so patient and so sweet, even though Lenore continued to call her Conchita, because she said she looked exactly like the Mexican woman who had worked for her in Texas in the forties, when Sookie's father had been stationed there.

The good news was, now that Lenore had Angel, Sookie was finally going to be able to attend the Kappa reunion in Dallas, and her old college roommate, Dena Nordstrom, had promised to meet her there. They talked on the phone regularly, but she hadn't seen Dena in a long time, and she couldn't wait.

AS SOOKIE SAT AT the intersection waiting for the red light to change, she pulled down the visor and looked at herself in the mirror. Good God, that was a mistake. She guessed that after fifty, nobody looked good in the bright sun, but even so, she really had neglected herself. She hadn't seen her eye doctor in over three years, and she clearly needed a new prescription.

Last month at church, she had embarrassed herself half to death. The correct quote was, "I am a vessel for God's love," but she had read out loud in front of the entire congregation, "I am a weasel for God's love." Earle had said that no one had noticed, but of course, they had.

Sookie glanced at herself in the mirror again. Oh, Lord, no wonder she looked so terrible. She had run out the door this morning without a stitch of makeup. Now she was going to have to drive all the way home and throw some on. She always tried to look somewhat presentable. Thankfully, she wasn't as vain as her mother, or she would never have left home at all. Outward appearances meant everything to Lenore. She was particularly proud of what she called "the Simmons foot" and her small, slightly turned-up nose. Sookie had gotten her father's longer nose, and wouldn't you know it, Buck got the cute one. Oh, well. At least she got the Simmons foot.

JUST AS THE LIGHT changed, Netta Verp, Sookie's next-door neighbor, whizzed by in her huge 1989 Ford Fairlane, probably on her way out to Costco, and tooted her horn. Sookie tooted back. Sookie loved Netta. She was a good old soul. She and Netta were both Leos.

Netta's house was in between their house and Lenore's. Poor thing. She had been stuck in the middle, with all the Poole children and animals on one side and Lenore on the other, calling her night and day, but she never complained. She said, "Hell, I'm a widow. What else am I going to do for fun?"

Sookie supposed she shouldn't have been surprised that Ce Ce's wedding theme had been "Pets Are People, Too." At one point, there had been eleven animals living in the Poole house, including an alligator that had crawled out of the bay and up the back-porch stairs, three cats, and four dogs, one being Earle's beloved Great Dane, Tiny, who was the size of a small horse.

All the dogs, cats, and hamsters—and the one blind raccoon—were fine, but she had drawn the line with the alligator and insisted that it stay in the basement. She loved animals, too, but when you're scared to get up at night and go to the bathroom, it's time to put your foot down, and hopefully not on top of something that could bite it off.

The hard part of having animals, for her, was losing them. Two years before, Mr. Henry, their eighteen-year-old cat, had died, and she still couldn't see an orange cat without going to pieces. After Mr. Henry died she told Earle no more pets. She just couldn't take the heartbreak.

Sookie drove straight on through town, waved at Doris, the tomato lady on the corner, then headed down the hill, toward her house on the bay.

The old historic scenic route was lined on both sides with large oak trees planted before the Civil War. On the right side, facing the water, were miles of old wooden bay houses built mostly by people from Mobile as summer homes. Sookie guessed that if she had a penny for every time she had driven on this road over the years, she would be a millionaire by now.

She had been eight the first time her father had brought the family down from Selma to spend the summer. They had arrived in Point Clear on a warm, balmy evening, and the air had been filled with the scent of honeysuckle and wisteria.

She could still remember coming down the hill and seeing the lights of Mobile, sparkling and twinkling across the water, just like a jeweled necklace. It was as if they had just entered into a fairyland. The Spanish moss hanging from the trees had looked bright silver in the moonlight and made dancing shadows all along the road. And the shrimp boats out in the bay, with their little blinking green lights, had looked just like Christmas to Sookie. For her, there had always been something magical about Point Clear, and there still was.

ABOUT A MILE PAST the Grand Hotel, Sookie turned in and drove up her long crushed-oyster-shell driveway and pulled into the carport. Netta's house was almost identical to theirs, but Netta's yard was much prettier. As soon as she could get rested enough, one of the first things Sookie was going to do was prune. Her azalea bushes were a disgrace, and her limelight hydrangeas had just gone completely wild.

Their house, like most of the others along the scenic route, was a large white wooden home with dark green shutters. Most of the bay houses had been built long before air-conditioning and had a wide center hall that ran all the way to a large screened-in porch in back overlooking the bay. And like their neighbors, they had a long gray wooden pier with a small seating area with a tin roof on the end. When the kids had been much younger, she and Earle used to go sit there almost every evening to watch the sunset and listen to the church bells that rang up and down the bay. They hadn't done that in years. She was so looking forward to being alone with Earle again.

Sookie took the two bags of seeds out of the car and put them in the little greenhouse Earle had built for her, where she kept her bird supplies. A few minutes later, after she went inside, Sookie suddenly noticed how quiet the house was. Almost eerily quiet. As she stood there, all she could hear was the ticking of the kitchen clock and the cry of the seagulls out on the bay. It was so strange not to hear a door slamming or someone running up and down the stairs. How pleasant to have peace and quiet, and not hear loud music blaring from someone's room. So pleasant, in fact, she thought maybe she would fix herself a cup of tea and sit and relax a few minutes before she headed out again.

Just as she was reaching for a tea bag, the kitchen phone rang. Now that the house was empty, it sounded like a fire alarm going off. She picked it up and looked at the caller ID number. It was a long-distance call, but not from an area code she recognized, so she just let it ring. She was too tired to talk to anyone if she didn't have to. In the past few days she'd had to smile and talk to so many people that her face still hurt.

Sookie stuck a cup of water in the microwave, grabbed her tea bag, and went out on the screened-in porch to enjoy it. She sat down in her big white wicker chair. The bay was as smooth as glass, not a ripple in sight.

She noticed that her gardenia bushes were still in bloom and thought she might cut off a few and float them in a dish in the living room. They always made the house smell so sweet. She took a deep breath of fresh air and was about to have her first sip of tea when the phone started ringing again. Oh, Lord, it was obviously somebody calling the wrong number or a solicitor trying to sell her something, and if she didn't answer they would probably drive her crazy all day. She got up and went back to the kitchen and picked up. It was her mother.

"Sookie, I need you to come over here right now."

"Mother, is something wrong?"

"I have something extremely important to discuss with you."

"Oh, Mother, can't it wait? I just got home."

"No, it cannot!"

"Oh, well . . . all right. I'll be there as soon as I can."

Sookie frowned as she hung up. That particular tone in her mother's voice always made her a little anxious. Had Lenore found out she had spoken to the woman at Westminster Village about assisted living? She had just been inquiring about the price, and it had only been one short call. But if someone had told Lenore she would be furious.

A few minutes later, Sookie walked over, and the nurse, who was in the front yard cutting fresh flowers, looked up and said, "Oh, good morning, Mrs. Poole," then added with a sympathetic little smile, "God bless you."

"Thank you, Angel," said Sookie.

Oh, Lord . . . it must be worse than she thought. As Sookie walked into the house, she called out, "Mother?"

"I'm here."

"Where's 'here'?"

"In the dining room, Sookie."

Sookie went in and saw her mother seated at the large Georgian dining room table with the twelve Queen Anne chairs. On the table, placed in front of her, was the large leather box with the maroon velvet inside that held her set of the Francis I silverware. Next to the box was the large Simmons family Bible.

"What's going on, Mother?"

"Sit down."

Sookie sat down and waited for whatever was coming. Lenore looked at her and said, "Sookie, I called you here today because I am not entirely convinced that you fully appreciate what you will be receiving upon my demise. As my only daughter, you will be inheriting the entire set of the Simmons family silver . . . and before I can die in peace, I want you to swear on this Bible that you will never, under any circumstances, break up the set."

Sookie was so relieved it wasn't about the call to Westminster Village, and said, "Oh, Mother . . . I do appreciate it . . . but really, why don't you leave it all to Bunny? She and Buck entertain much more than I do."

"What?" Lenore gasped and clutched at her pearls. "Bunny? Leave it to Bunny? Oh, Sookie," she said with wounded eyes. "Do you have any idea what was sacrificed to keep it in the family?" Sookie sighed. She had heard the story a thousand times before, but Lenore loved to tell it over and over, with large dramatic gestures included. "Grandmother Simmons said that at one point during the war, all that stood between them and the entire family going hungry was your great-grandmother's silver. And do you know what she did?"

"No, Mother, what?"

"She chose to go hungry, that's what! Why, she said there were days when all they had to eat was a pitiful little handful of pecans. And they had to bury the silver in a different spot every night to keep the Yankee soldiers from finding it, but she saved the silver! And now you say, 'Oh, just give it to Bunny'? Who's not even a Simmons—and not even from Alabama? Why don't you just cut my heart out and throw it out in the yard?"

"Oh, God. All right. . . . I'm sorry, Mother. It's just . . . well, if you want me to have it, then thank you."

Sookie certainly hadn't meant to hurt her mother's feelings about the silverware, but she really had no use for it. She didn't know anybody who used a pickle fork or a grapefruit spoon anymore, and you can't put real silver in the dishwasher. You have to wash each piece by hand. And she certainly didn't want to have to polish silver all day. The Francis I pattern had twenty-eight pieces of carved fruit on the knife handle alone, not to mention the tea service, the coffee service, and the two sets of formal candlesticks.

Sookie realized she probably should care more about the silver. After all, it had come all the way from England and had been in the family for generations. But she just wasn't as formal as her mother. Winged Victory would die of epilepsy if she knew her daughter sometimes used paper plates and plastic knives and forks and just hated polishing silverware.

Lenore dearly loved to polish silver and, once a month, would sit at the dining room table wearing white cotton gloves with all of it spread out before her. "Nothing relaxes me more than cleaning my silver."

Oh, well. Too late now. The die was cast. Sookie was stuck with it. She swore on the Bible that not only would she never break up the set, but that she personally would polish it regularly. "Don't ever let tarnish get a head start on you," Lenore said.

What could she do? Being Lenore's daughter meant she had come into the world with preordained duties. First, to proudly carry on the Simmons family line that, according to Lenore, could be traced all the way back to fifteenth-century England. Second, to protect the family silver.

It was such a beautiful warm day, and after Sookie left her mother's house, she took her shoes off and walked back home along the bay.

As she strolled along, she suddenly wondered how many times she and the children had walked back and forth to Lenore's house over the years. It seemed like only yesterday when all day long, the kids were running back and forth to her house and theirs.

Time was so strange. When the children were younger, she used to marvel at the tiny little footsteps they left in the sand, but those days were gone forever. They were all grown up now . . . and, bless their hearts, not a one of them had the Simmons foot, and three had the Poole ears. But that was another story.

A FEW MINUTES LATER, after she had thrown on a little makeup, Sookie drove back to town and was sitting in line at the drive-in bank waiting to make a deposit to cover yet another one of Lenore's unexpected expenses. About ten years ago, Lenore had suddenly started bouncing checks all over town and hadn't seemed the least bit concerned. "I hate fiddling with figures," she said. So now all Lenore's mail was delivered to Sookie to handle, including all her bills. Lenore's letters alone were almost a full-time job. She was always firing off editorials to the newspaper. The last one, suggesting that we do away with the vote for people under fifty-five, had brought in more than one hundred letters that Sookie had to answer. Lenore never looked at her own mail. "Just tell me if something is important," she said. The woman ordered almost everything she saw on television, and Sookie always had to send it back. Why would anybody over eighty want a ThighMaster?

Lenore was her mother, and she loved her, but *Lord,* she was a lot of trouble. When Earle had first bought the dental practice and they had moved down to Point Clear for good, Lenore insisted that before she would move with the family from Selma, Sookie's Great-Grandfather Simmons must be moved from the Selma Cemetery and transferred down to the Soldier's Rest Cemetery in Point Clear. "I would just die if I didn't have Grandfather Simmons to decorate. He was a general, Sookie!" And, naturally, Sookie was the one who ended up having to deal with all the endless red tape of trying to arrange it. After weeks of hassling back and forth with the cemetery people, having to sign paper after paper, she finally just begged them to please dig up anything—dog, cat, or horse—and send it on. At that point, she was so tired, she didn't care.

The car in front of Sookie moved one space closer to the teller, and she moved up with it. She looked at herself in the mirror again. She looked a little better with her makeup on, but, of course, she had forgotten to put on her earrings. Honestly, between the weddings and dealing with her mother, it really was a miracle she was still sane at all.

She had always had a delicate nervous system and a tendency to faint under pressure. And it was very stressful never knowing what her mother was going to do next. Lenore had shown up at Ce Ce's wedding wearing a large yellow hat with two live lovebirds in a cage sitting on top. God only knows where she got that.

Thank heavens, all Sookie's kids had been good kids, because when they were growing up, she had let them do pretty much what they pleased. She had wanted them to have a carefree childhood. Hers certainly hadn't been, with Lenore pushing her into everything. She had always been basically shy. She never wanted to be a Magnolia Trail Maiden or a cheerleader or to join all those organizations. But she had had no choice. Lenore ruled with an iron hand. "You owe it to the Simmons name to be a leader in society, Sookie!" she said.

Well . . . that certainly hadn't worked out. She knew she was a disappointment to her mother, but what could she do? She didn't know why, but in school, as hard as she tried, she had never been able to get more than a C average while Buck had made all A's. And those ballet lessons Lenore had pushed her into had been a complete disaster.

Sookie was finally at the drive-through window and handed the bank teller her deposit and suddenly noticed that she had developed a strange tic in her right eye, probably some leftover stress from the wedding. Thankfully, Earle had finally just picked the turtle up and handed it to James or they would probably all still be sitting there. The girl in the window pushed the drawer back out with her receipt and said over the speakerphone, "Thank you, Mrs. Poole, have a nice day."

"Oh, thank you, Susie. You, too."

"Tell your mother I said hello."

"I will."

After she left the bank, Sookie ran into the market and picked up a few pork chops and, as an afterthought, a can of sliced pineapple. Earle said he had a big surprise for her tonight, so she thought she might spice up the chops a bit.

SOOKIE WAS STANDING IN the "less than six items" checkout line when she heard someone call out her name. It was Janice, a pretty blond girl and one of Ce Ce's bridesmaids, who rushed over from the produce department, still holding a head of lettuce, and hugged her. "Oh, Mrs. Poole, I'm so happy to see you! How are you? You must be exhausted from all the excitement . . . but I just had to tell you, that was one of the nicest weddings I have ever been in. And such fun, too! Ce Ce and Peek-a-Boo looked so cute coming up the aisle—and it's always so wonderful to see your precious mother. I swear she never changes. She's still the prettiest thing . . . and funny. I wish you could have been at our table—she had us all just screaming with laughter. And that hat with those birds! How does she come up with these things?"

"I have no idea," said Sookie.

"What a character, and she was so sweet to bring her little Mexican nurse with her."

As Sookie moved one person closer to the checkout girl, Janice moved with her. "Oh, and listen, Mrs. Poole, I was going to drop you a note and apologize for Tinker Bell's terrible behavior at the reception. I don't know what got into him. He usually just loves cats to death."

Sookie said, "Oh, don't worry about it, honey. . . . After all, dogs will be dogs."

Janice thought about it for a second and said, "Yes, I guess you're right. They just can't help themselves, can they?" Then she made a sad face. "How are you holding up? You must be so blue with Carter and all the girls gone—but thank heavens, you still have your mother to keep you company . . . and I'll bet she just keeps you entertained twenty-four hours a day doesn't she?"

"Oh, yes, she certainly does," said Sookie.

Finally, it was Sookie's turn at the cash register, and Janice said, "Well, I'd better run. 'Bye, Mrs. Poole, so nice to see you. Be sure and tell your mother I said hey."

"I sure will, honey."

When she came out of the market, she saw that the Elks Club ladies had set up a bake sale, so she walked over to see what they had. Dot Yeager, sitting behind the table, said, "Don't they all look good?"

"Oh, they do."

"Your mother looked so pretty at church yesterday in that bright blue dress with her silver hair. I wish I could wear that shade of blue, but it just fades me out to nothing. I had my colors done, and I'm a fall, but Lenore is definitely a spring, isn't she?"

"Yes, I believe she is."

Sookie was standing there, trying to decide between the lemon icebox and the pecan pie, when her friend Marvaleen walked up. "Oh, hi, Marvaleen. What do you think would go better with pork chops? The pecan or the lemon icebox?"

"If it were me, I'd go for the key lime, but then, I'm a fool for key lime." Sookie bought the key lime.

Sookie was glad she had run into Marvaleen. She seemed so much calmer now. Marvaleen had recently gone through a divorce and, for a time, had been quite intense. She had been seeing a life coach over in Mobile named Edna Yorba Zorbra, and all she wanted to do when you saw her was tell you in great detail what Edna Yorba Zorbra had just said.

A few months ago, Sookie had been at the store and in a hurry, and she had tried to hide, but Marvaleen had spotted her and cornered her in the frozen food department. "Sookie, do you journal?"

"What?"

"Do you journal? Write things down?"

"Oh, like lists. Yes, I have to. I went to the store four times before I remembered to buy Parmesan cheese."

"No, Sookie, I mean seriously journal. Write down your innermost thoughts. Edna Yorba Zorbra says it's essential to maintain a healthy psyche. I can't tell you what a difference it's made in my life. I would never have divorced Ralph if I hadn't started journaling. I didn't realize how much I hated him until I saw it written down in black and white. Oh, you must journal, Sookie. I didn't know who I really was until I started journaling."

Well . . . that was fine for Marvaleen, she guessed, but she couldn't imagine anything she would rather not do than write about her innermost feelings. And besides, she already knew exactly who she was and, unfortunately, so did everyone else within a five-hundred-mile radius.

Driving home, Sookie passed by the cemetery, and sure enough, there was Lenore's car parked at the entrance. Every Monday, she put fresh flowers on her Grandfather Simmons's grave and inspected the grounds and made sure to call anyone whose relative's blooms were fading and lecture them about honoring the dead. Most people had moved on and were more interested in the recent dead. But not Lenore. The woman was obsessed with her ancestors.

Lenore's own mother had died in childbirth, and she had been raised by her grandmother. That probably explained a lot about Lenore and her propensity to live not just in the past, but in the distant past. Sookie's Great-Grandmother Simmons had been born during the Civil War, and her memories of that time were still raw and somewhat bitter. From early childhood, the message given to Lenore almost daily at her grandmother's knee was that in order to survive in this world, she was to remain strong and proud. The South had been bloodied and defeated, yes, but never bowed. They had lost everything but their pride and their good name.

At seventeen, Lenore was sent to Judson College and became president of her sorority, Kappa Kappa Gamma, and valedictorian of her class. It was at Judson where Lenore had met Sookie's father, Alton Carter Krackenberry. He had been a cadet attending the Marion Military Institute nearby. And from the first moment he met her in the receiving line, he had been blinded by love for life.

During World War II, Sookie's father had commanded an entire unit of men in Brownsville, Texas. But at home, Lenore always ruled the roost. He spoiled her terribly and did pretty much whatever Lenore wanted him to do. No matter how many insane things she did, he would just look at her and exclaim to his children, "Look at her—isn't she just wonderful?" To the day he died, he said that Lenore had been the most beautiful girl at the Senior Military Ball, a fact that Lenore had agreed with most wholeheartedly. And often.

* * *

After Sookie got home and put the groceries away, she went into the sunroom with the paper and sat down to read when Peek-a-Boo jumped up in her lap. Oh, dear. She was perfectly happy to keep her until Ce Ce came back from her honeymoon, but she didn't want to get attached to her, so she picked her up and put her down on the floor. But the cat jumped right back up again. Sookie sighed and said, "Oh, Peek-a-Boo. Honey . . . don't make me like you. Go on now," and she put her back down again. But she jumped right back up. The poor thing was obviously starved for affection, and so against her better judgment, Sookie started to pet her. After a minute, Peek-a-Boo was purring and kneading Sookie's legs, looking up at her, happy and content. "Oh, well, bless your heart. . . . You miss your mother, don't you? But she'll be back, don't you worry. Do you want me to get you some more bites? Is that what you want, precious? Do you want to play with your little toy?"

Oh, Lord. She had only had the cat forty-eight hours, and she was already talking baby talk to it. But what could she do? She couldn't just ignore the poor thing . . . and she was so cute.

When Earle came home from work, Peek-a-Boo was happily chasing her mouse on a string that Sookie was pulling all through the house. Earle said, "Hi, sweetie. What did you do today?"

Sookie had been waiting for years to say this: "Nothing. Absolutely nothing."

That night in bed, Earle was fast asleep, and so was Peek-a-Boo, who was now cuddled up next to her, but as usual, Sookie was still wide awake. Earle's big surprise was that he was going to take her on a second honeymoon and she was so happy about it. She wanted to spend as much time with Earle as she possibly could, while she still could. With her future being as uncertain as it was, Sookie really didn't know how much time she had left.

It was the curse of the Simmonses. When they reached a certain age, some of them (her Aunt Lily and Uncle Baby) had to be sent to Pleasant Hill Sanitarium. As the doctor said, "When a fifty-eight-year-old man goes downtown dressed up in a Dale Evans cowgirl outfit, complete with a skirt with fringe, it's time," and after Aunt Lily's unfortunate incident with the paperboy, it was obvious she needed to be committed. But with Lenore, it was hard to tell. When Sookie had called Dr. Childress in Selma about her mother's latest exploits and asked what he thought, he sighed and said, "Sookie, honey, I've known your mother all my life, and the problem with Lenore has always been trying to figure out what behavior is just 'delightfully eccentric' and what's 'as batty as hell.' I know it's not an official diagnosis, but every Simmons I ever knew had a loose screw somewhere."

Dr. Childress had been the family doctor for years, and Sookie wished he had told her this before, not after, she had had four children. Who knows what wacko genes she may have passed on? Being second-generation, the children could be safe, but she was a genetic time bomb waiting to go off any minute. She lived in fear and dread of one day embarrassing her husband and children, and at one of the weddings, having someone point at her and say, "That lady in the corner talking to herself and batting at imaginary flies is the mother of the bride."

When she tried to tell Earle how worried she was about the Simmons curse, he had always dismissed it. "Oh, Sookie, don't be silly. You're not going to lose your mind. You're as sane as I am." She hoped he was right. But a few weeks ago, she had gone for a dress fitting in Mobile and had left the dress at home. Hopefully, now that she was almost sixty, it was just a normal senior moment and not the beginning of something worse. She didn't know, but she had written her family a letter and put it in the safety-deposit box at the bank, just in case.

She also wished Carter would get married sooner rather than later. He had always been popular. A couple of his old girlfriends still called her, wanting to know about him, so she was hopeful. The other day, he had said, "Mom, I want to get married . . . it's just that I haven't found anybody, yet, and it's getting pretty discouraging."

"Oh, I know, darling, but I promise one day, you'll meet the exact right one, and when you do, you will know it."

"How?"

"You just will, that's all."

Sookie knew it was a stupid answer, but it had happened to her, sort of. She'd known Earle Poole, Jr., since grammar school. She just hadn't known he was the right one until years later. Granted, her life had not always been a bowl of cherries—but then, whose had? Even if her life were to end tomorrow, she still had so much to be grateful for. First and foremost, for Earle.

And her children had mostly been a joy. The twins, Ce Ce and Le Le, had never given her a minute's trouble. They had always been happy, probably because they had each other. From the moment they could talk, they just chattered away together. They were like their own separate little unit, and she was amazed at how well they got along. She had read that some twins hated to dress alike, but not hers. They loved it and had to have matching underwear and pajamas. They even spoke in stereo. One would start a sentence, and the other would finish it.

Raising Carter had been easy. He was just like her brother, Buck. Send him outside with a ball to play with, and he was fine. Dee Dee was the one she worried about the most. She had never been a particularly happy young girl, and her teenage years had been especially painful. She had always been a little on the chunky side, and unlike the twins and Carter, who had inherited Lenore's perfect complexion, she'd had terrible acne all through high school. Each new pimple brought on a new set of histrionics. Almost every afternoon, Dee Dee would come home from school, run to her room, and fling herself across her bed in tears, because some boy hadn't spoken to her or she hadn't been invited to some party or something equally as devastating. Sookie had spent hours sitting with her, holding her hand, while she cried and sobbed about how terrible her life was. "Oh, Mother," she would sob. "You just don't know how it feels to be me. Everybody's always telling me how cute and darling the twins are. All my life, people have fallen all over them and just ignored me." Then, inevitably, she would wail, "Oh, Mother . . . why did you have to have twins? Why couldn't you have just *one* like a normal person!"

Sookie tried to explain. "I'm sorry, honey. It wasn't anything I planned. It just happened. It was a surprise to me, too. They are the first twins on either side of the family. It was just a fluke."

"Well, I hope you're happy! You've ruined my entire life. I will always be some ugly fat lump with bad skin that nobody wants." And so it went, on and on. She tried to give Dee Dee special attention and be patient with her, because, unfortunately, what she said was true. Whenever the girls went anywhere, especially when they were younger, people made a huge fuss over the twins and left poor Dee Dee standing there, having to listen to them ooh and aah about how absolutely adorable they were. It broke Sookie's heart to see her suffer so. And she did know how it felt. Growing up with Lenore, she had always felt like a little brown wren, hopping along behind a huge colorful peacock.

# TUESDAY

June 7, 2005

The next morning, Sookie woke up early, prepared to try to solve her bird problem. Earle had just walked out the door when the phone in the kitchen started ringing, and she wondered who in the world was calling her so early. It couldn't be Lenore; she was on her way to water therapy at the senior center. Oh, dear God, please don't let it be Dee Dee saying she was moving back home. She knew she was having marital problems again and today's horoscope had warned her to "Expect the unexpected." Sookie looked at the phone with trepidation and read the number on the readout. It wasn't Dee Dee. It was that same area code as yesterday, probably the same phone solicitor, so she didn't pick up. She didn't have time to talk to anybody now. She had to concentrate on her bird-feeding plan. It was going to be tricky. She'd seen how those blue jays could go through all their food in just a matter of minutes, so she was going to have to move very fast.

Sookie quickly rinsed off the breakfast dishes and stuck them in the dishwasher, but whoever was calling wouldn't hang up, and it was distracting. They used to have an answering machine, but Lenore thought it was an open mike for her to speak into on any subject at any time and had left fifteen- and twenty-minute messages on it, sometimes in the middle of the night, so they had to get rid of it.

As she finished up in the kitchen, she debated whether to put the sunflower seeds for the blue jays in the front yard or the back. If she put the sunflower seeds in the front, someone driving by might see her and want to stop and talk, and she didn't have a second to spare. So she decided she would start at the back and run to the front. Her success depended on how long it would take the blue jays to finish the sunflower seeds before they discovered the bird seed in front and how fast she could run from one yard to the other.

But what shoes should she wear? She looked down and realized she shouldn't try and run in her flip-flops; it was too dangerous. She went to her closet and found nothing suitable—practically every shoe she owned had a little heel.

She went down the hall to the twins' bedroom closet and started rummaging through a box of their old shoes. She found a pair of worn-out pink sneakers with pom-poms. Unfortunately, they were two sizes too large, but they'd be better than trying to run in flip-flops and breaking an ankle.

She put them on and laced them up as tightly as she could and went out to her greenhouse and filled her two large ceramic polka-dotted bird seed containers, one with sunflower seeds and the other with the wild bird seed. She went out and placed the container with the wild bird seed on the side of the house, ready to be picked up as she ran by, headed to the front yard. She then went back to the greenhouse, picked up the container with the sunflower seeds, took a deep breath, and ran to the backyard, filling up the feeders as fast as she could.

After Sookie finished filling the feeders in the backyard, she dropped the container on the ground and ran to the side of the house and picked up the other polka-dotted seed container and was running toward the front yard when she stepped in a gopher hole and lost her left shoe. She couldn't stop so she just went on without it.

And of course, the very same moment she hit the front yard, the new Methodist minister and his wife were driving by the house and saw Sookie, wearing one pink shoe with tassels, hopping around on one foot, throwing seeds from a large polka-dotted container at her feeders. They slowed down and, as a matter of courtesy, were going to stop and say hello, but thankfully for Sookie, decided against it and quickly drove on. They were from Scotland and didn't know if running around wearing one pink shoe with tassels while carrying a large polka-dotted container and throwing seeds was some kind of Southern bird-feeding ritual or not, but they were afraid to ask.

Sookie's neighbor Netta Verp was sitting out on her side porch in her robe, having her morning coffee, when she suddenly saw Sookie flying around the yard like a bat out of hell, with her polka-dotted bird seed container, slinging seeds every which way, and she wondered what in the world she was doing. Netta had never seen anyone in such a hurry to feed their birds in her life.

After Sookie had filled all the front yard feeders, she ran back into the house and stood looking out the living room window, waiting to see if her smaller birds would come to feed. She waited, but none came. Where were they? There was not a bird to be seen anywhere. She then ran down the hall and looked out the kitchen window and saw the blue jays happily gobbling up all the sunflower seeds in back, while as usual, all of her smaller birds flittered around in the bushes below. Oh, no. Those little birds didn't know what was waiting for them in the front yard. Oh, Lord. She hadn't planned on this. Now she didn't know what to do. She ran out on the back porch and started waving her arms and yelling at the top of her lungs, "Go to the front, little birds—go around to the front! Hurry up, little birds!" But how do you communicate with birds? It was so frustrating. Now not only were her little birds not getting anything to eat; all those sunflower seeds seemed to have attracted every blue jay in the entire area, and more were flying in by the minute.

Netta observed her neighbor out on her back porch, jumping up and down and waving her arms around like a crazy person, and she didn't know what to think. It was certainly peculiar behavior. She just hoped poor Sookie hadn't flipped overnight, but with the Simmons family you never knew.

After a moment, Sookie ran back to the living room window to see if, by chance, any little birds were there, but now a whole new gang of big blue jays were in the front yard, eating all the bird seed. It was so frustrating. The only other thing she could think of to do was to get Carter's old baseball bat and run out and try to scare the blue jays off. But she didn't want to get reported to the humane society for cruelty to animals, especially since she was on the board. Oh, God, the phone was still ringing off the hook. Whoever it was must have her on some computer redial. Between the blue jays and the phone, she was getting a headache, so she went in and picked it up.

"Hello!"

The person on the other end seemed surprised that someone had finally answered and said, "Oh, hello! Ahh . . . to whom am I speaking, please?"

"Well, whom were you trying to reach?" asked Sookie, as she saw three more blue jays swoop in.

"I'm trying to locate a Mrs. Earle Poole, Jr."

"Yes, this is she." As soon as she said it, she knew she had made a mistake. She should have pretended she was the maid and said Mrs. Poole wasn't home. She was stuck now. As she stood watching more and more blue jays show up at the little birds' feeder, she suddenly remembered that old BB gun of Carter's in the closet and wondered if she could fire off just a few warning shots from the porch without being seen.

The man on the phone was asking another question. "Are you the former Sarah Jane Krackenberry?"

"Yes, I was . . . am." Sookie realized that the idea that she would even think about shooting a gun at a helpless bird was not her normal way of thinking, but those blue jays made her so mad—the way they pushed the smaller ones around.

"Was your mother's maiden name Simmons, middle name Marion, first name Lenore?"

"Yes, that's right."

"Did your family live in Brownsville, Texas, from the years 1942 to 1945?"

"Yes, uh-huh."

"Is the current mailing address for Mrs. Lenore Simmons Krackenberry 526 Bay Street, Point Clear, Alabama?"

"Yes, all her mail and bills are sent to me." Sookie was still thinking whether or not she should get Carter's old BB gun and try and scare the blue jays away, but decided not to. If she were to accidentally hit one, she would never be able to forgive herself.

"Is your zip code 36564?"

Peek-a-Boo walked over and rubbed up against her leg. Then it suddenly occurred to her: Maybe Peek-a-Boo would like a big fat blue jay for breakfast. She could let her out. But on the other hand, if Peek-a-Boo ran away and anything happened to her, Ce Ce would have a fit.

"Ma'am? Are you still there?"

"Oh, I'm sorry, what was it?"

"Is your current zip code 36564?"

"Uh, yes. That's correct. You have to forgive me. I'm a little distracted. I'm having a little bird problem at the moment." Sookie sat down, held the phone against her ear, and retied her pink sneaker. She felt a dull pain start up in her right ankle. Oh, no. She knew as soon as she had stepped in that gopher hole, she had twisted something. She just hoped it wasn't sprained. She needed to put ice on it right away, before it could swell up, and she also had to get the man off the phone, but in a nice way. "Sir, I'm so sorry, but I think I've sprained my ankle, so I'm going to have to hang up now."

"I see . . . uh . . . Mrs. Poole, one more thing before you go. Will you be home tomorrow between ten A.M. and twelve P.M.?"

"Pardon me?"

"Will you be at this address tomorrow?"

"Yes, I guess so. I might go to the travel agency later. Why?"

"We are sending a letter to Mrs. Lenore Simmons Krackenberry—and we need to know if you will be home to sign for it."

It suddenly occurred to Sookie that this was certainly a weird call. Why did this man want to know where she would be tomorrow and at what time? She began to get a little suspicious and wondered if he might be some sex pervert or a burglar. So she quickly said, "Yes, I will be home, and so will my husband, the police chief. May I ask where you are calling from?"

"I'm calling from Texas, ma'am."

"Texas? Where in Texas?"

"I'm in the Austin area."

"Austin, Texas?"

"Yes, ma'am. And Mrs. Poole, the letter should arrive at your address tomorrow, sometime between ten and twelve."

Now Sookie really was baffled. Why would anybody in Texas be sending Lenore a letter? "Is this from the Gem Shopping Network? Are they in Texas? Has she ordered more scatter pins? I hope not. She has over a hundred now."

"No, ma'am."

"Is it from Barbara Bush? My mother thinks they have a lot in common, and she's always writing the poor woman, asking her to come down for a visit. I said, 'Mother, Barbara Bush is far too busy to come all the way down here, just to go to lunch with you.'"

"No, ma'am, it's not from Mrs. Bush."

"Oh . . . well, is it a telephone bill? Has she called somebody and reversed the charges again? If so, I apologize in advance. We have a wonderful nurse watching her, but she must have turned her back for five minutes. Anyway, I'm so sorry, and tell whoever she's called that we will be happy to pay for it."

There was a pause, and then the man said, "Mrs. Poole, we have a registered letter we are sending out overnight, and I just need to confirm that someone will be home tomorrow who is authorized to sign for it."

Sookie's heart stopped. A *registered* letter! Oh, no. That always meant something legal. Sookie winced as she asked the dreaded question. "Sir, when you use the term, 'we,' are you by chance a law firm?"

"I'm sorry, Mrs. Poole, but I'm not at liberty to discuss it over the phone."

Oh, God, it must be something serious, if the man can't even discuss it over the phone. "Listen . . . I'm so sorry. What is your name?"

"Harold, ma'am."

"Listen, Harold, is it about some editorial she's written? She watches the news and gets herself all riled up, and she's always spouting off about something. But believe me, if my mother has made any threats against the government or said anything stupid, I can assure you that she's a perfectly harmless old lady. Well, harmless as far as not being armed or anything. She's just not quite right, if you know what I mean. It's a family trait. You just have to know the Simmonses. They are all a little off. She has a brother and sister that are really off. You have no idea how much trouble the woman has caused. She's almost eighty-nine years old, and she won't go to assisted living, and she refuses to let us put in a walk-in tub for her, and I worry to death about her falling and breaking a hip." She sighed. "I'm sorry to be so upset. It's just that my poor husband and I have just gone through four weddings, and my little birds won't go around to the front yard. I'm just being overrun by blue jays, and another lawsuit is just not what I need right now. My nerves are all a jangle as it is. Can't you tell me what it's about?"

"I'm sorry, ma'am. I'm not authorized to give out any information over the phone."

"Oh, please, Harold, don't drag this out. You don't know me, but I really could go off the deep end at any moment. It's the Simmons family curse. It hit Uncle Baby overnight. One day, president of a bank, and the next, off weaving baskets over at Pleasant Hill. And Aunt Lily was perfectly fine and then for no reason, she shot at the paperboy. Thank God, she didn't hit him or she could be sitting in jail right now, instead of where she is."

"As I said, Mrs. Poole, you will be receiving the letter in the morning."

"Oh, Harold, can't you just open it up and read it to me now? I don't need to know all the details, just how much she's being sued for. We just went through our entire retirement account for a down payment for a house for our daughter Le Le and her husband. He's perfectly nice, but he plays the zither for a living."

"Oh . . ."

"Yes . . . that's what we said. But she loves him, so what can you do? Anyhow, we are mortgaged up to the hilt. Can't you at least tell me how much my mother is being sued for, so I can be prepared? I won't tell anyone. I promise."

"I'm so sorry, ma'am, but I don't have the authority to do that. I was instructed to locate the current mailing address and send it on, that's all. This is not even my department. I'm just filling in."

"Oh, I see. Well, couldn't you just take one quick little peek and tell me if it's over a hundred thousand dollars?"

Then she heard his muffled voice, obviously whispering behind his hand, "Mrs. Poole, the wife and I just married off our daughter, so I know what you've been through. Don't worry, she's not getting sued."

"No? Oh, thank God! Oh, bless you, Harold. I don't know why, but with Mother, I always assume it's going to be bad news, but then again, it could be good news, right?"

Harold didn't say anything, so Sookie's mood suddenly brightened. "Hey, wait a minute. Did she win a contest or something? Are you from Publishers Clearing House? Should I have her over here at the house in the morning, dressed and made-up or anything? I need to know, because she'll want to have her hair done. Will there be photographs? Or news people?"

"No, ma'am."

"Oh . . . well . . . can you give me just a little hint of what to expect?"

There was a long silence on the other end, then Harold said, "Mrs. Poole, all I can say is . . . you are not who you think you are," and then he abruptly hung up.

Sookie sat there with his last words ringing in her ear, and now there was someone banging away on her back door. As Sookie stood up, her ankle throbbed even worse than before, but she hobbled down the hall and opened the door, and there stood Netta in her robe, who looked at her strangely. "Honey, are you all right? I saw you running around the yard like you were in some kind of distress. I tried to call you, but your line was busy. You left one of your shoes out in the yard." Sookie took the shoe and said, "Oh, thank you, Netta."

"Are you okay?"

"I'm fine, Netta. I was just trying something new with feeding the birds, and this man just called about some registered letter for Lenore and I think I've sprained my ankle. Come on in."

"No, I can't, I'm still in my robe. I better get back home, but call me if you need me."

A FEW SECONDS AFTER Netta left, Sookie went and looked out in the front yard to check on her birds and, to her dismay, saw that her entire yard was now a veritable sea of blue. It looked like she was running a blue jay reserve. She'd been so distracted by the phone call that she didn't know if the little birds had gotten anything to eat at all. Oh, drat. She would just have to try again tomorrow.

She hobbled back into the kitchen and put some ice cubes in a hand towel and wrapped it around her ankle. As she sat there with Peek-a-Boo in her lap, she thought more about the phone call and what the man had said. "You are not who you think you are." Then it suddenly dawned on her. That man had probably been calling from the Jehovah's Witnesses or some other religious group. They were always leaving pamphlets at her door asking, "Do you know who you are?" or "Do you know who your father is?" Oh, Lord. Now she felt like a fool. What a complete idiot she had been, telling him all that personal stuff about the family.

But on the other hand, knowing her mother, he could be calling from ancestor.com or some other genealogy-tracing company. She'd also seen ads for them that said, "Who are you?" or "Who do you think you are?"

The more she thought about it, she thought that it must be Lenore trying to trace the Simmons family line again. "I just know we're related to the royal family in some way. I just feel it in my bones," she said. For as long as Sookie could remember, she had been tracing and retracing, but so far, no connection. Now even Dee Dee was obsessed with it and had the Simmons family crest hanging over the mantel in her condo.

AS THE MORNING WORE on, Sookie tried to relax and just forget about the call, but she was still feeling a little uneasy. It was the word "registered" that bothered her. She hated to call Earle at work but she dialed the number anyway, and his receptionist answered. "Dr. Poole's office, may I help you?"

"Hi, Sherry, it's me. Could you get him to pick up? I need to ask him a quick question."

"Sure, hold on. I'll buzz him. How's your mother?"

"Fine, thank you."

"Well, good. Hold on."

A few seconds later, Earle picked up. "Hi, are you okay?"

"I'm fine. I just need to ask you something."

"Honey, I'm right in the middle of a root canal."

"Okay, I'll make it fast. A man from Texas just called and said he was sending Lenore a registered letter tomorrow. Should I be worried? He said he wasn't a lawyer."

"Well, then, no."

"What do you think it's about?"

"Oh, I don't know. It's probably just some come-on, trying to sell something or get her to join something."

"Then I shouldn't worry?"

"No, just forget about it."

"But it's registered."

"Well, honey. Just don't sign for it."

"Isn't that against the law?"

"*No.* Just tell Pete you don't want it. That's all. Sweetie pie, I've really got to go. I'll see you at home, okay?"

"Earle, maybe . . . I just won't go to the door."

"Fine."

"But won't he leave a note and try and redeliver it?"

"Honey, do whatever you want. Don't go to the door or just sign for it and throw it away. It's probably just junk. Okay?"

"Then I shouldn't worry?"

"No."

"And I don't have to accept it."

"No. Forget about it. I gotta go. Love you."

Sookie hung up and smiled. Earle always knew how to make her feel better. Even her ankle felt better.

# WEDNESDAY

June 8, 2005

Sookie woke up and planned her day. She decided that this morning she would try a slight variation on yesterday's bird plan and put sunflower seeds into every other feeder. She hoped the little birds would figure it out and eat a little while the blue jays were still at the sunflower seeds. Then after she fed the birds, she was going downtown to the travel agency and check out trips and cruises. A second honeymoon—what fun! Her brother, Buck, and his wife were always going on cruises, so yesterday afternoon she had called Bunny in North Carolina and asked her advice. Bunny said that Prague was "the new Paris," but Sookie hadn't seen the old Paris, yet. She hadn't really been anywhere, except to college and to the store and back, so anywhere Earle wanted to go would be fine with her.

At 8:10, Sookie had filled all the feeders and was out in the backyard in the pink tennis shoes, hiding behind a tree with her binoculars, when suddenly someone walked up behind her and tapped her on the shoulder. She nearly jumped five feet in the air. It was Pete, the mailman. "Oh, my God, Pete," she said. "You nearly scared me to death!"

Pete, a tall skinny man in gray shorts, said, "I'm sorry. I knocked on the front door, but you didn't answer." He then reached into his bag and said, "I have a certified letter for you, but first I have to ask you, 'Are you Mrs. Earle Poole, Jr.?' "

Sookie sighed. Pete had only been her mailman for the past thirty years. "No, Pete, I'm the queen of Romania. Of course, it's me. You know who I am."

Pete took his job very seriously. "Oh, I know who you are, but it's an official letter, and I have to ask. Do you have power of attorney to sign for Mrs. Krackenberry?"

"Yes. What I want to know," Sookie said, "is *why* you are here so early? Don't you usually start your deliveries on the other side of the pier?"

"Yes, but I thought the letter might be important, so I came here first. I just need for you to sign right here on this line."

"Oh, Pete, I'm sorry you came all this way, but I don't want to sign for it."

He was completely taken aback. "But . . . it's a registered letter."

"I know, but Earle said I didn't have to sign for it, if I don't want to."

"Oh . . . well . . . huh . . . I've never had this happen before . . . so I guess I'll just write out a first attempt slip and try again tomorrow, then."

"But I won't want it tomorrow, either."

"Well, officially, I'm required to make three attempts to deliver it."

"Pete, I don't want it. I don't even know who it's from."

"Huh . . . well, that's up to you. But it does seem a shame—somebody sure went to a lot of trouble and expense to make sure you got it. And it could be important. . . . It looks like it's some kind of medical records."

"Pete! I really don't want to know. Right now, I'm busy trying to plan a vacation. Did you know that Earle and I have not been anywhere alone since 1970? And what makes you think it's medical records?"

"It's from the Texas Board of Health, so I just figured it had something to do with health information."

"Texas Board of Health? How weird. What could they want?"

"I don't know," he said, looking at the large envelope. "Did someone ever get sick in Texas or hospitalized for anything there?"

"No. I was born in Texas . . . but . . ."

"Well, there you go. Maybe it's an outstanding hospital bill or something."

"Oh, I can't imagine it could be a bill at this late date. You knew Daddy. He always paid his bills."

"Yeah, that's true. Maybe it's a refund."

"Fifty-nine years later? I don't think so."

"Well, if you're sure you don't want it, I'll just leave you the attempted delivery slip on the door and go on then."

"Okay, thank you, Pete. Sorry."

As soon as Pete walked away, Sookie looked out in the backyard. Once again, it was full of blue jays. Not one little bird to be seen. Her plan was clearly a failure—not only a failure, but she might have made things worse. She wouldn't blame the little birds if they all just packed up and never came back. And it was so sad, because they were her favorites, and they didn't even know it.

Later, as she sat in the tub, she tried her best to forget about the letter, but it was still on her mind. It wouldn't have been so hard if Pete hadn't waved it around in her face and hadn't blurted out who it was from. It was so irritating. All she had wanted to do today was relax and not have to think about any more problems. She knew the letter had something to do with her mother, but what? She couldn't imagine. Had Lenore been sick or hospitalized when she was living in Texas? She had never said anything. Was there something her mother didn't want her to know? Everyone always said how young and beautiful she looked for her age. Maybe she had had a major face-lift in Texas. Or she could have hit somebody and put them in the hospital. Lenore was a terrible driver, and she had run into almost everybody in Point Clear at one time or another. Or maybe she had had some sort of mental break, like Aunt Lily, and been committed at some point. Could Lenore have been in a mental hospital? Oh, dear.

By the time Sookie had dressed and put on her makeup, her imagination had completely run away with her. The next thing she knew, she was downtown at the post office with the pink slip and had picked up the letter and was on the way home with it. She never did make it to the bookstore or the travel agency. She stared at the envelope it on the seat next to her all the way home. Sure enough, it had TEXAS BOARD OF HEALTH written across it, and stamped in big black bold letters across the front was PERSONAL AND CONFIDENTIAL MATERIAL ENCLOSED.

At 5:15 that afternoon, Earle walked in the house. "Hi, sweetheart. I'm home."

"Hi, honey," she said, not giving him a chance to sit down. "Earle, I know you think I'm silly, but I've been waiting for you to come home all day. Would you sit with me while I open this letter?"

"What letter?"

"The registered letter."

"Oh. I thought you weren't going to sign for it."

"Well . . . I tried not to . . . but anyhow . . . I wanted you to be here."

He smiled at her. "Okay, sweetie. Let me fix a drink, and I'll be right there."

Sookie sat down on the sofa in the sunroom and waited until he came back in and sat down across from her. "Okay, open her up, and let's see what we got."

Sookie took a deep breath and opened it and read the cover letter.

Attention: Mrs. Lenore Simmons Krackenberry
c/o Mrs. Earle Poole, Jr.
526 Bay Street
Point Clear, AL 36564

Our office has received the following, and as requested, we are forwarding to your present address.

H. Wilson

The envelope attached was postmarked Matamoros, Mexico, and handwritten in an almost uneven and childlike scrawl. Sookie read the letter inside, which was in the same handwriting.

May 20, 2005

Dear Mrs. Krackenberry,

Hello. I am the daughter of Conchita Alvarez, who worked for you in Brownsville, Texas, during the war. I am sorry to say my mother passed away last spring at the age of eighty-five. When we were going through her things, we found these papers she was keeping for you. They look important. They look like you might need them. I do not know where you live. I am mailing them back to where they came from so they can send them to you. My mother liked you very much. She said you were so pretty.

Sincerely,

Mrs. Veronica Gonzales

"Oh, for heaven's sake," said Sookie.

"What?"

"A lady in Texas that used to work for mother died and her daughter found some of Lenore's old papers and is sending them back. Well, that's very sweet of her."

"What kind of papers?"

"I don't know, yet. Let me see." Sookie picked up another piece of paper.

The next thing Sookie knew, she was lying on the floor, and Earle was standing over her, fanning her with a newspaper.

"It's okay, honey, you just fainted. Just relax and breathe. Don't talk."

Lying on the floor beside her was what she had just read.

October 8, 1952

Dear Mrs. Krackenberry,

Due to the military's recent lifting of certain restrictions in the Children's Medical Privacy Act, and in reply to your request of January 6, 1949, we are now at liberty to release photocopies of your daughter's original birth certificate, including all birth mother medical records in our possession, up to the date of her adoption from the Texas Children's Home. We hope this information will assist you and your daughter's health care professionals in determining her risk of any hereditary conditions. Please contact this office if you have any further questions.

Sincerely,

Cathy Quijano

Director of Public Health Services

Please find enclosed the following:

Birth certificate
Medical records
Adoption papers

A few minutes later, Earle had helped Sookie to the couch, and she was lying there with a cold rag on her head, trying to comprehend what she had just read. All she remembered were the words "her adoption."

Earle came back with a brown paper bag for her to breathe into, and a glass of brandy. "Here, honey, drink a little of this." He looked very concerned and kept patting her hand.

"Did you read it?" she asked.

He nodded. "Yes, honey, I read it. What a hell of a thing to spring on somebody."

"But what does it mean?"

He picked up the letter and read it again. "Well, sweetie . . . I'm afraid it means just what it says. Evidently, you were adopted from the . . . here are the papers . . . the Texas Children's Home . . . on July 31, 1945."

"But Earle, that can't be true. It has to be a mistake."

Earle looked at the papers again and shook his head. "No, honey . . . I don't think so. It looks pretty official, and they have all the right information."

"But it has to be a mistake. I can't be adopted. I've got the Simmons foot and Daddy's nose."

"Well . . . maybe not."

"Why? What else does it say? I don't understand."

"Honey . . . just keep breathing, and let me look at this again." He sat there reading the papers while Sookie continued breathing into the brown paper bag, but she didn't like the look on his face.

"Well?" she asked, between breaths.

He looked at her. "Are you sure you're up for this? This is a lot of information to get in one day."

"Yes . . . of course, I'm sure."

"I'm not going to read anymore, unless you promise me you won't get too upset and faint again."

"I promise."

"Well . . . your medical records look good. You were a very healthy baby."

"What else?"

Earle picked up the birth certificate. "According to this, it says that your mother's name was Fritzi Willinka . . . and I think the last name is . . . it looks like Juraaablalinskie. Or something like that."

"What?"

He spelled it out.

"Good Lord! What kind of a name is that?"

"Uh . . . let's see. Oh, nationality of mother . . . Polish."

"What?"

"Polish."

"Polish? I don't even know anyone Polish."

"Hold on . . . it says . . . birthplace of mother . . . Pulaski, Wisconsin . . . November 9, 1918. Religion of mother: Catholic."

"Catholic? Oh, my God. What does it say about the father?"

Earle looked again and then said quietly, "Uh . . . it says here, father unknown."

"Unknown? How can it be unknown? What does that mean?"

"I'm not sure. It could mean a lot of things. Maybe she didn't want to say or . . . I don't know."

Then Sookie said, "Oh, my God, Earle . . . I'm illegitimate. I'm an illegitimate Catholic Polish person!"

"Now, honey . . . calm down. We don't know that. We can't jump to any conclusions."

"Well, Earle, if you were married to someone, he certainly wouldn't be unknown, would he? Did she even give me a name?"

"Wait a minute. Yes, here it is. Your birth name is . . . Ginger Jaberwisnske or however you pronounce it . . . and you were born at 12:08 P.M., October fourteenth, 1944, weight . . . eight pounds, seven ounces."

Sookie slowly sat straight up and said, "Earle, that's not right."

"What?"

"1944."

"Well, honey, that's what it says. October fourteenth, 1944. Look . . . there it is in black and white."

Sookie looked stricken. "Earle, do you know what that means? Oh, my God, I'm sixty years old! Oh, my God—I'm older than you are! Oh, my God!"

"Okay, honey, now just calm down . . . that's no big thing."

"No big thing! No big thing? *You* go to bed thinking you are a fifty-nine-year-old woman, and the next day, find out you're sixty!" Sookie felt the blood slowly begin to drain from her face. Earle caught her just before she fell off the couch and hit the floor again.

A few minutes later, after she had come to again and had had a little more brandy, Sookie, who almost never cursed in her life, looked at Earle and said, "And *who* in bloody hell are the Jerkalawinskies?!"

# WHO INDEED!

## Pulaski, Wisconsin

Stanislaw Ludic Jurdabralinski had arrived in Chicago on January 5, 1909. During his first few years in America, he had worked hauling beer barrels for a local brewery and learned English at night. Sometime later, Stanislaw got a better job building the Chicago and North Western railroad that went from Green Bay, Wisconsin, through a small town called Pulaski.

At the time, Pulaski, Wisconsin, was a tiny village of Polish immigrants who had been lured there by a savvy German landowner. After purchasing the land, he had spread brochures throughout the predominantly Polish neighborhoods in Chicago, Milwaukee, and the Pennsylvania mining regions, hoping to sell plots of land to the large number of Polish immigrants wanting to establish a "little Poland" in America, complete with churches and schools. He had even named the town after Count Casimir Pulaski, the Polish nobleman who fought with the American patriots in the War for Independence, as an added incentive. When the first group of new landowners arrived in Pulaski, they found that the churches and schools the man had advertised in his brochures were yet to be built, so they got busy and built them.

In the year 1916, Stanislaw Jurdabralinski arrived in Pulaski, working for the railroad, laying tracks. While he was there, he boarded with a nice Polish family who had a pretty eighteen-year-old red-headed daughter. In a few weeks, when the railroad moved on, Stanislaw did not. He stayed and settled down in Pulaski with his brand-new wife, Linka Marie.

Stanislaw, never afraid of hard work and always in a hurry to make money, held down a job at the local sawmill in the daytime and one at the pickle-canning factory at night. On Sundays after church, he began studying to become a citizen of the United States. As he sat in their little rented room above Glinski's Bakery, studying the Constitution and the Declaration of Independence, he would get so excited and would read out loud to his wife. "Linka, listen to this. It says, 'life, liberty, and the pursuit of happiness.' Imagine that, Linka. Our country wants us to be happy . . . and you will be. As soon as I get rich, I'll buy you a fur coat."

Linka laughed. "We have to buy a house first."

"And after I become a citizen, I can say anything I want, and they can't arrest me, and I can buy a house, and they can't take it ever away from me never."

Linka corrected his English. "Away from me, ever."

"That's right. And I can own my own business, like Mr. Spierpinski. Oh, just think, Linka, from now on, all our children are going to be Americans, and our grandchildren and their children, too."

Linka, who at the time was two months pregnant with their first child, said, "Stanislaw . . . slow down, and study."

THE PROUDEST DAY OF his life was the day Stanislaw went to Green Bay to be naturalized as a U.S. citizen. As soon as he was sworn in, he immediately grabbed his wife's hand and ran over to the big courthouse next door so he could apply for his American passport. Linka, trying to keep up with him, asked, "Why do you need a passport so fast, Stanislaw? We're not going anywhere for a long time."

"I know," he said. "But when I get back to Poland, I want them to see how long I've been a citizen."

A few weeks later, when his passport finally arrived in the mail with his smiling photograph inside, he walked all around town, showing it to everyone he met. He would point to his height listed and ask, "Do you know who else was six foot four? Mr. Abraham Lincoln, that's who."

A few weeks later, Linka gave birth to their first child, a dark-eyed little girl with black curly hair they named Fritzi Willinka Jurdabralinski, who was her father's pride and joy. To Linka's dismay, he would sometimes come home from work, pick her up from her baby bed, and take her to town to the Tick Tock Tavern and show her off.

Two years later came a son they named Wencent Stanislaw Zdislaw Jurdabralinski, and then a year later, twin daughters. One was born a few seconds before midnight on May 31, and the other thirty seconds later on June 1, so they named the first Gertrude May and the other Tula June. Two years later, their youngest, another baby girl, Sophie Marie, was born.

The twins and their baby sister had red hair like their mother, and Wencent, who they nicknamed Wink, was a sturdy little blond boy. Stanislaw was proud of all his children, but his firstborn, Fritzi, remained the apple of his eye. When she was five, he put her up on his shoulders, and they walked up and down Main Street, showing everyone they saw the deed to the land he had worked so hard to buy. "Look at this," he would say. " 'Sold to Stanislaw Jurdabralinski, two acres of land.' So I own land now . . . what do you think?" People in town liked Stanislaw. He was always cheerful and was a good man and could be counted on.

A few years later, with a loan from the bank and the help of his friends, Stanislaw built a large two-story brick house with a big kitchen and a long, wide front porch. Within a few years, in order to make a little more money, Linka, who was a wonderful cook, started selling her Polish pastries and sausages to lunchrooms and catering for big church events, while raising her children at the same time. And it wasn't easy. Her eldest girl, Fritzi, was turning out to be a handful. Always on the go, jumping and running here and there, playing ball with the boys, hanging from trees, jumping off twenty-foot ladders on a dare, she was, in fact, a show-off. But in her father's eyes, she could do no wrong. He would laugh when Linka told him what Fritzi had done that day. Even when the nuns called them in to speak about Fritzi's habit of getting into fights with the older boys on the playground, Stanislaw, being a good Catholic man, had nodded and looked serious. But later, he had said nothing to Fritzi.

So, what if she was a little wild? He had a feeling this girl of his was going to be something one day. He knew Linka was hoping one of the girls would be a nun, but Stanislaw was fairly certain it would not be Fritzi.

## MEANWHILE, BACK IN POINT CLEAR

Earle was still sitting with Sookie, trying his best to calm her down, but he was having no luck.

"Oh, Earle . . . my life is over. I'll never be the same as long as I live."

"Oh, honey . . ."

"I'm not who I thought I was . . . and I never will be again."

"I know it's a big shock. It was to me, too, honey. But let's try to look on the bright side."

"What bright side?"

"Well, for one thing, aren't you just a little bit glad that you are not a Simmons?"

"No, I'm not glad! At least when I was a Simmons, I knew who I was and what I had to worry about. Now I don't know who I am . . . or what I have to worry about. I feel like I've just been abducted by aliens." Sookie suddenly became short of breath and clutched her chest. "Oh, my God . . . I think I'm having a heart attack. Oh, my God . . . I'm going to die and never know who I am!"

"Sookie, just calm down. You are not having a heart attack. You are just fine."

"No, Earle, I'm not just fine . . . . I'm a stranger in my own home!"

Earle had her breathe into the paper bag for a few minutes, and she calmed down a little, but her heart was still pounding, and she still felt dizzy. She suddenly grabbed his hand. "Oh, Earle, now that you know I'm not me . . . will you stop loving me?"

"No! You're my wife, and I love you. You'll always be the same wonderful person you always were. Nothing has changed."

"How can you say that? Everything has changed. I'm an entirely different person than I was, even a few minutes ago."

"No, you're not."

"I am so! Yesterday, I was a Southern Methodist English person, and today, I'm a Polish Catholic person with an unknown father."

"Oh, honey, think about it. If you hadn't found out anything, wouldn't you still be the same person?"

"But I did . . . and now I know I'm not myself. How can I ever be myself again? I was never myself in the first place! And I don't know why you're so calm about it. You've been married to me all these years, and you have no idea who I am or who my parents were."

"Sweetheart, it doesn't matter. You're the one I'm in love with. Not your parents."

"But . . . what about the children? I could be the daughter of a criminal or a mass murderer. You don't know." Earle laughed. "It's not funny, Earle. You can laugh, but I'm the one with two complete strangers' genes running all through my body. I know about DNA, and it does matter."

"Oh, honey . . ."

"No, really, how would you feel if you didn't know who you were?"

"But, sweetie . . . we do know. It says right here that you are the daughter of Fritzi—I can't pronounce the last name—but that's who your mother was."

"Yes, but I don't know her. I wouldn't know who she was if I fell over her. She could be Doris, the tomato lady, for all I know!"

LATER, EARLE WAS FINALLY able to get Sookie to sit up and eat a little hot soup and a piece of toast, but she cried and blew her nose all through dinner. "I can't believe I'm not a Simmons. No wonder I've never been pretty."

"Sookie . . . you are very pretty."

"Not like Lenore . . ."

"No, in a different way . . . but just as pretty, if not more so. I don't know why you never believed me."

But Sookie was not listening. "I'm not even a Krackenberry. No wonder I was never as smart as Buck."

"Sookie, honey, you are smart."

"No, I'm not. I failed algebra three years in a row. How smart is that, Earle?"

After she had her soup, Sookie sat up for hours reading and rereading the papers, feeling just like she was in the Twilight Zone. It all seemed so unreal. She knew that the baby girl with the strange name listed on the birth certificate was supposed to be her, but she still couldn't quite believe it. Earle felt terrible and kept walking in and out of the room, asking what he could do, but there was nothing.

At about three-thirty, Earle came in and insisted that she come to bed. But even after Earle turned off the light, her mind was still racing a mile a minute. They say when you are dying, your whole life passes before your eyes. She supposed that was what was happening to her now. Every time she tried to calm down and sleep, something else from her childhood flashed before her eyes, and she'd think about all the things she had done to try and please her mother, trying to be what Lenore thought a Simmons should be. Her hair had always been dark red and straight, and she remembered all those mornings when Lenore had tried to fix her hair for school and how she always looked at it with disappointment and would say, "You don't have an ounce of curl." She thought about those hours she had spent at the beauty shop, getting all those horribly smelly permanents, having her hair fried into one big red frizz, trying to please her mother, or else her mother would get discouraged and have it cut in a short straight bob with bangs. All her life, she had either looked like Little Orphan Annie or the little Dutch boy on the can of paint.

Lenore hadn't liked how dark Sookie's hair was, either, and at least once a week, would always look at it and say somewhat wistfully, "Of course, when I was your age, I was more of a strawberry blond. I don't know why your hair turned so dark. It was blond when you were a baby . . . ."

Sookie had even tried dying her hair strawberry blond, but it had turned a really unattractive shade of pink. She had spent a good part of her freshman year of high school with bright pink hair, long before it was fashionable to have bright pink hair. And for what?

Surely, this was just some terrible nightmare she was having, and she would wake up tomorrow, and things would be normal again. It just *couldn't* be true.

# LIFE CONTINUES

Pulaski, Wisconsin
1928

In the years following World War I, the sleepy bucolic world of rural America was beginning to change, and a man named Henry Ford was to blame. When he invented the first Model T automobile, he put America on wheels, and as more roads were built and cars were improved, people who had never traveled farther than the outskirts of their own towns started traveling by the thousands. Roads couldn't be built fast enough, and suddenly, family motor trips were all the rage. Americans were of pioneer stock and naturally adventurous and soon began driving all over the country. And if they could have built roads across the ocean, they would have driven all the way to Europe and on down to South America.

New businesses started popping up all over the country: auto courts, tourist camps, hotels, motels, and restaurants to accommodate the traveler along the way.

In 1920, there were 15,000 gas stations in the entire country, but by 1933, the number had jumped to 170,000.

It was clear the automobile was the future, and what better business to get in than owning a gas station? Gas companies were selling franchises left and right. And Stanislaw Jurdabralinski had the perfect spot for a filling station, on the empty lot right beside his house. So using their savings and another loan from the bank, and after finishing a two-week course in service station management, Stanislaw received his Phillips 66 uniform, complete with hat and black leather bow tie, and soon, a brand-new twenty-four-hour full-service filling station opened in Pulaski.

Stanislaw was so proud to have a family business at last, but when they were naming the station, he thought Jurdabralinski's Phillips 66 was too long, so he just named it Wink's Phillips 66, after his son, who would inherit it someday.

The first night the station opened, when the pump topper with the big, round, illuminated glass globe lit up, the entire family stayed up for hours and watched it glow in the dark. Poppa, who would now be sleeping on a cot in the back of the station, flicked the neon OPEN ALL NIGHT light in the front window on and off for them to say good night.

From then on, their lives revolved around the filling station on the side of the house. The cheerful ding of cars and trucks coming into the station day and night meant that Poppa was busy, and that was good. Wink and the girls grew up playing with hubcaps, air hoses, old spark plugs, and rubber tires, and the smell of gasoline. It seemed like fun to them. By the time Fritzi was eleven and Wink was nine, they already knew how to change a tire and pump gas and make change at the cash register. Soon the Jurdabralinskis were simply known as the Gas Station Family. Every town had one . . . or soon would.

IN 1936, AFTER THE Depression had hit the country, it had been devastating, but the Jurdabralinskis did better than most, with milk and cheese from the nearby farms and eggs from the chickens that Momma kept in the backyard. And thanks to Wink, who had grown into a big, strong guy, who loved to hunt and fish, there was always food on the table.

Stanislaw had worked out a contract with the county to supply all the official vehicles—fire trucks, police cars, snowplows, and all the school buses—with gas and repair service, so when many stations across the country had been forced to close, Wink's Phillips 66 managed to stay open.

In the summer of 1937, life at the Jurdabralinski house was anything but depressed. Momma played in the Thursday night Ladies Accordion Band of Pulaski, and they practiced in the living room four nights a week. The younger girls were all in the school accordion band, so they played along as well, and on most afternoons, the boys and girls from the high school would gather upstairs in the huge third-floor attic with the big record player on a table in the corner and dance and play Ping-Pong.

Fritzi and her sisters were of an age when boys were always either hanging around the station or sitting on the front porch of the big two-story brick house next door.

Even Wink, who worked at the station with his father after school, had female admirers who would pile into their cars and drive over to watch and giggle as he walked around and did a full service on their cars, washing the windows, checking the oil, water, antifreeze, and battery, and filling up the tires. They usually had only enough money for a fourteen-cent gallon of gas, sometimes just a half gallon. One local girl, Angie Broukowski, who was younger than Wink, borrowed her father's car, and she and her friends seemed to come in more than usual, even when she didn't have money for gas. Poppa said Old Man Broukowski's tires had been checked more than any other car's in the state of Wisconsin.

But at the Jurdabralinski house, Fritzi was the main attraction for both the boys and girls. She had just graduated from high school, and in her senior year, she had been voted most popular, best dancer, most athletic, biggest cutup, and most likely to succeed. Fritzi was definitely the personality kid of Pulaski High. Poppa was proud of her, but Momma worried that if Fritzi didn't slow down for five minutes, she was never going to get a husband. If she wasn't swimming, she was bowling or skating all night at the Rainbow Skating Rink or running up and down the roads to see how fast some car would go or running to the movies, and if she wasn't doing that, she was busy smoking cigarettes. Momma found a half-full pack of Chesterfields hidden in her top drawer. And as usual, when he was told what his daughter was up to, Poppa just shrugged. "She's a modern girl, Momma. They all smoke." Momma hoped that in the fall, when Fritzi went to work at the pickle factory, she would settle down with one of the local boys, so she wouldn't have to worry about her so much. Momma had already said a novena and prayed to Saint Jude about it.

# NOW WHAT?

Point Clear, Alabama
Thursday, June 9, 2005

The next morning, Earle brought Sookie breakfast in bed and sat down beside her and said, "Honey, do you want me to cancel my appointments and stay home with you today? I will. I just don't think you should be alone."

"No, I want you to go to work. I need to think this out and decide what I'm going to do."

"Okay, whatever you want . . . but call me and let me know how you're doing."

After Earle left, Sookie did fall asleep for an hour, but when she woke up, she was still so devastated, she couldn't get up. She called Netta and told her she had the flu and asked her if she would feed the birds. She lay in bed and cried all morning. She knew she had to talk to someone else about this—someone she could trust not to tell Lenore—so she rolled over and called her old college roommate, Dena Nordstrom, in Missouri. Dena picked up right away.

"Dena, it's Sookie."

"Sookie! Hello—"

"Thank God you're home. Oh, Dena, something terrible has just happened."

"Oh, no, has something happened to Earle?"

"No."

"The children?"

"No."

"Your mother?"

"No . . . it's me!"

"Oh, honey, what's wrong? Are you sick?"

"No," she sobbed. "I'm Polish!"

"What?"

"Oh, it's a long story . . . but . . . oh, Dena . . . this man from Texas called and said I wasn't who I thought I was and at the time, I thought I knew who I was. But yesterday, I got a letter and found out that I was adopted—that Lenore is not my real mother and Daddy is not my real daddy either. And not only that . . . I'm a year older than I thought I was. I'm not even a Leo. All my life, I've been reading the wrong horoscope."

"Wait a minute . . . are you sure about this?"

"Yes, I'm sure. October is Libra."

"No . . . no . . . about being adopted?"

"Yes, it's all written down. I have it right in front of me. It says that on July 31, 1945, Mr. and Mrs. Alton Krackenberry adopted a baby girl named Ginger . . . Jurdbberlnske or something or other Polish. Anyhow . . . that's me. Or who I was supposed to be. Anyway, my real mother was born in Wisconsin, and I'm probably a Catholic to boot. You know how quick they are to baptize."

"Oh, wow . . . oh . . . what does Lenore say about it?"

"I haven't told her."

"Oh . . . well, have you said anything to the kids, yet?"

"No, you're the first person, besides Earle, that knows, and I knew you, being married to a psychiatrist, would understand. I just feel so confused and betrayed. Lenore knew I wasn't her real daughter, and she went ahead and pushed me into all these things . . . and all under false pretenses. She always made me feel so bad because I wasn't just like her. And I wasn't just like her, because I wasn't just like her! And now, thanks to her, I've been a card-carrying member of the Daughters of the Confederacy since I was sixteen, and I'm not even a Southerner. I'm a Yankee. And, Dena . . . here's the worst part," she sobbed. "I'm not even a Kappa."

"What do you mean? Of course, you're a Kappa."

"No, I'm not. I'm a fraud. I can't go to the Kappa reunion. I'll just have to resign. The only reason I got in was because I was a legacy through Lenore. I'll have to turn in my pin and everything."

"Oh, don't be silly, Sookie, you're a Kappa because everyone loved you. I went through rush with you, remember?"

But Sookie wasn't listening and continued to ramble on. "Oh, my God. I even made my debut at the Selma Country Club under false pretenses. I told Lenore I didn't want to be a debutante, and she went ahead and let me make a fool of myself. What will people think when they find out I'm not a Krackenberry or a Simmons—that I'm an illegitimate Yankee Polish orphan?"

"Wait a minute. What makes you think you are illegitimate?"

"Because . . . it's written on my birth certificate: father unknown."

"Oh . . . well, Sookie, people don't really care about that kind of thing, anymore."

"Well, I do. I'll feel like an imposter, like some kind of social climber. Oh, I could just die of shame. I'm looking at myself in the mirror right now, and I have turned beet red with shame."

"But why, Sookie? You didn't do anything wrong. What are you ashamed about?"

"Because you know me, I have always prided myself on being honest and open and then to find out you are a fraud—that your entire life has been one big lie? I can never hold my head up again. I'm sure I need serious medication. I'm probably having a psychic break right now. Is Gerry at home? I might need him to send me some pills. How much are they?"

"Oh, Sookie, honey, you're not having a psychic break. You've had a shock. That's all. I'm shocked. It's understandable that you are upset. I mean, my God . . . who wouldn't be? What does Earle think?"

"Oh, he's being very sweet about it . . . but I'll tell you who is going to have a fit when she finds out: Dee Dee. She's always running out to the cemetery to help decorate Great-Granddaddy Simmons's grave . . . and then to find out the man is a total stranger. Oh, my God. And Dena, no wonder I didn't get Lenore's nose. I didn't get Daddy's nose, either. I got a total stranger's nose. I don't know why I thought I looked just like Daddy. I went through the photo albums last night, and I don't look a thing like any of them. I didn't get the Simmons foot. I got the Jaberwisnski's foot!"

"Well, what are you going to do now?"

"I don't know. I just feel all wicky-wacky. I'm just thrown for a loop and back. I can't even think about what to do. What can I do at this late date? I should have been told this when I was six, not sixty. All those Polish people I'm related to are probably all dead by now. And who would name their child Ginger? We had a golden retriever named Ginger. Anyhow, it's very upsetting."

"I know it is. And as upsetting as it is right now, you always told me you never wanted to be like your mother, and you're really not. Isn't that kind of good news?"

"That's what Earle said. And I guess it is, but right now, I feel like I've been hit by a train. Why couldn't I be a year younger? But no. Yesterday, I was only fifty-nine, and today, I'm already sixty, going on sixty-one! No wonder I look so old and tired. I am! I'm the world's oldest living orphan. Oh, God, how embarrassing. I feel like walking out and jumping off the end of the pier."

"Sookie, do you want me to come down there and be with you? I will. Just say the word."

"Oh, that's so sweet, but no, there's nothing anybody can do. I'll just have to figure this out by myself."

"Well, all right, but in the meantime, you won't do anything foolish, will you?"

"No, I've got to get Carter married and settled before I do anything foolish."

"Sookie, this is a lot to handle by yourself. Maybe it would be a good idea to seek out a professional to help you through this."

"Well, you're the lucky one. You married a psychiatrist. I married a dentist."

"Would you like me to ask Gerry to try to find someone for you?"

"No. This is not the kind of thing I would talk to a stranger about."

"But, Sookie . . . that's the point."

"Well, I'll think about it, but right now, I really don't want to tell anyone but you."

"All right, but I want you to call me and let me know what's going on, okay?"

"I will."

After she hung up, Dena thought about just getting on a plane and going down to Alabama, but Sookie had said she wanted to try and work it out by herself, and maybe she was right. Dena knew Lenore and had always gotten a big kick out of her, but she had also felt kind of sorry for Sookie, and finding out that she was adopted was going to be hard. Sookie had always viewed herself through Lenore's eyes. No matter how many times Dena had tried to tell her, Sookie had never understood what a great gal she was on her own. She had been one of the funniest and best-liked girls on campus, but she had never quite believed it. Everybody seemed to love Sookie but Sookie.

AFTER SOOKIE HAD SPOKEN to Dena, she realized that Peek-a-Boo needed to be fed, so she got up out of bed and went downstairs. As she opened a can of tuna, she thought about what Dena had advised. She was probably right, but there was only one psychiatrist in Point Clear, and it was obvious that Dr. Shapiro had never practiced in a small town before. His office was right next to the Just Teazzing hair salon, and you couldn't go in or out without everyone seeing you. She certainly couldn't go, or it would be all over town in less than five minutes.

Even Mobile was not far enough away for that, thanks to Lenore knowing so many people. At one time or another Winged Victory had been the chairman of every committee known to man, and was a club-woman to the bone. If they didn't have one she liked, she started one, and she was always elected president. But as Netta said, "Lenore's damned good at running things, so why not?" Netta was right, of course. The woman seemed to have been born with a gavel in her hand.

The rest of the day, Sookie kept catching glimpses of herself in the mirror. She knew she looked the same on the outside. She walked and talked like the same person. But she didn't know who or what she was on the inside.

Finally, she called Earle, who came to the phone right away. "Earle, my ears are ringing. Does that mean I'm going to have a stroke? I feel like I might be having a stroke."

"No, honey, it's just stress."

"Yes, but my heart is racing. I could be having some kind of attack. Should I call an ambulance?"

"No, you're fine. Just breathe, sweetheart. Listen, my last patient cancelled, I'll be there as soon as I can."

She sure was glad to see him when he walked in the door. Later, she managed to fix dinner, but she still felt disoriented. Earle didn't leave her side.

When they got in bed, she tried to sleep, but she tossed and turned all night. Even Peek-a-Boo got fed up and went over to Earle's side of the bed. But she couldn't help it. All she could think about was that person she used to be . . . that woman in the mirror.

Earle finally rolled over and said, "Honey, it's four-twenty. Close your eyes, and get some sleep."

"I will, but Earle, are you sure I'm not having a heart attack? I can still hear it beating. Here, can you feel it? Shouldn't I go to the emergency room?"

Earle felt her heart and patted her hand. "No, baby, it's just anxiety. Try to get some sleep, and you'll feel better. I promise you."

Earle was right. After a few minutes, her heart did slow down. Thank God she had married Earle. He had been her strength and her rock through thick and thin. But with Lenore, even that hadn't been easy.

After she graduated from high school, her grades had not been good enough to get into a top college like Lenore had wanted, but not to be deterred, at the last minute, Lenore had pulled some strings with an old Kappa sorority friend of hers, and two weeks later, Sookie had been sent off to Southern Methodist University in Dallas with a new wardrobe and a note in her pocket.

Sookie, Dear,

If you can't be smart, be perky. Men love a happy girl, and date, date, date! Men love a popular girl.

Love,

Mother

The minute she hit SMU, she started rush week and, thanks to her being Lenore's legacy, had pledged Kappa right away. And, per her mother's instructions, she joined almost everything else in sight, as well. And God knows she had dated morning, noon, and night. By her sophomore year, she had almost wrecked her health trying to be popular, and it didn't help matters when her roommate, Dena Nordstrom, was voted the most beautiful girl on campus. All Lenore ever said after that was, "Oh, Sookie, why can't you be more like Dena? That girl is going to make something of herself." And as Lenore had predicted, Dena left college early and became one of the first female newscasters on television, while Sookie still struggled to make a passing grade.

At Christmas during her senior year at SMU, she had come home a complete nervous wreck and sick as a dog. And then two weeks later, when she had informed her parents that she was going to marry Earle Poole, Jr., from Selma, Lenore had thrown a complete fit.

The Pooles were a perfectly nice family. Earle's father was a doctor. But unfortunately, all the Poole men had big ears that stuck out a little on the side. "If you don't care about me, think of your future," Lenore had cried, waving her handkerchief in the air. "Those ears may be fine on a boy, but dear Lord in heaven, Sookie, think of those ears on a girl! You can't hide a thing like that. I've waited all my life to have granddaughters to dress up and to have their portraits painted, and I certainly don't want the Poole ears in the picture!"

Lenore had then flung herself onto the sofa sobbing. "I don't understand you. With your family background, you could have anybody you wanted. I sold my soul to get you into Kappa, so you would only meet the very nicest boys from the finest families, and this is how you reward me? By marrying Earle Poole, Jr.? Some dental student with big ears? Someone you went to grammar school with? Oh, why did your father and I bother to spend all that money on your debut and college? When I think of all those contacts wasted, oh, I just can't bear it. I feel like getting Granddaddy Simmons's sword off the wall right now and just falling on it."

It was usually at this point that Sookie had always given in to her, but probably because she was sick and still had a high fever, for the first time in her life, Sookie had stood her ground.

"Mother, I know you don't want to hear this, but I couldn't have married any boy I wanted. Don't you think I tried to find someone you would approve of? I dated everybody that asked me out. I had six dates in one day. Do you know how hard it is to be perky six times a day? I'm not pretty like you, Mother. The boys didn't fall all over me like they did you. I can't do it anymore. Earle loves me just the way I am, and no, we are not perfect. He has big ears, and I'm not smart or beautiful, and if you can't bear it, I'll go and get the sword, and you can do what you want with it. But I am going to marry Earle Poole, Jr."

Lenore had been so stunned at her daughter's sudden strength that she stared at her for a moment. Then she sat up and said, "Well, I can see that you are becoming more like your father every day." She sniffed a wounded little sniff. "This stubborn streak is certainly not from my side of the family. And if you refuse to listen to reason, there's nothing more I can do, but when you give birth to Howdy Doody, don't say I didn't warn you."

She had married Earle, but she had never heard the end of it. After Dee Dee, their first girl, was born, as Sookie was being taken back to her room, she had heard Lenore from all the way down the hall, standing at the hospital nursery window and wailing at the top of her lungs, "Oh, my God, Alton, she has the Poole ears! I knew it! I just knew it!" Unfortunately, the Pooles, who were in the waiting area around the corner, had heard Lenore as well. After that, family holidays were never pleasant.

When she told her mother she was expecting again, Lenore's reaction had been less than enthusiastic. "Oh, no," she sighed. "Well, let's just hope and pray it's a boy."

Eight months later, as Sookie was being rolled down the hall, exhausted and groggy from delivering not just one, but two more, baby girls, Lenore had come up alongside the gurney and whispered to her, "Mother doesn't want you to worry. I've checked into it, and my friend Pearl Jeff knows the very best plastic surgeon in New Orleans. She says it's a simple little procedure, and who's to know the difference?" My God . . . if Earle had not stepped in and stopped it, she might have let Lenore push her children into plastic surgery!

* * *

As for Earle, he had loved Sookie all through grammar school, and they had dated a little in high school, but he knew her mother had higher hopes for Sookie's future than him. So when Sookie had gone off to SMU, he had more or less given up.

But that Christmas in 1966, when he heard she was home for Christmas and was sick in bed, he screwed up his courage and went over to see her. Lenore had come to her door and begrudgingly let him in. "You can only stay for a short while, Earle, she needs her rest."

"Yes, ma'am."

Sookie had been propped up in bed, dozing on and off all day, when she thought she heard a knock on her door. A second later, there stood Earle Poole, Jr., wearing a blue suit and holding a bouquet of flowers and a box of candy. He said, "Hi, Sookie. I heard you were home, and I just wanted to say hello." The minute she saw him, Sookie suddenly burst into tears. He looked so goofy standing there in that bow tie and that bad haircut. She had always liked Earle, but it wasn't until that moment that she began to love him.

# POINT CLEAR, ALABAMA

Friday, June 10, 2005

The next morning, while Sookie was feeding Peek-a-Boo, the phone rang, and Sookie almost jumped out of her skin. She looked to see if it was Lenore calling. If it was, she would not pick up, but she saw that it was Ce Ce calling from her honeymoon at Callaway Gardens in Pine Mountain, Georgia.

"Hi, sweetheart," she said as cheerfully as she could possibly manage.

"Hi, Mother, how are you?"

"Oh, just fine, honey."

"I just called to let you know that we got here safe and sound, and we are just loving it. How's Dad?"

"Just wonderful."

"Is Peek-a-Boo giving you any trouble?"

"No, not at all. She's right here, honey, having her breakfast, and we're having a good time."

"Oh, great. Well, I love you. Tell Dad hey."

"Okay, darling. We love you. Have fun, and we'll see you when you get home."

After she hung up, she realized that at some point, she was going to have to tell the children that their grandmother was not really their grandmother. But it certainly wasn't the kind of thing you would tell someone on their honeymoon.

That afternoon, she took her binoculars upstairs and waited until she saw Lenore heading out to the end of the pier with her tea cart to have her usual five o'clock cocktails with her Sunset Club friends. Sookie then called Lenore's nurse, Angel, and told her that she had just come down with a terrible flu that the doctor said was highly contagious and could be fatal to older people, and he had advised her not to get anywhere near her mother for at least two weeks. She felt terrible about lying to Angel, but at this point, she didn't care if she ever saw or talked to Lenore again.

Just seeing Lenore from a distance was upsetting. All she really wanted to do was go downstairs and pull out a bottle of vodka and drink the entire thing. She thought about it, and it was very tempting, but she also had a big fear of becoming completely unruly and disgracing her husband and children in public. Unfortunately, she had always had a tendency to fall apart under stress and do something stupid. At her coming-out party, she had been so nervous, she had way too much to drink, and at the formal dinner afterward, she wound up flipping ice cream across the table with a spoon and had hit a good friend of her mother's in the back of the head. That same night, she had stepped on an olive and had skidded across the dance floor and wound up under someone's table.

And it wasn't just alcohol. In college, she had been heartbroken when some boy didn't ask her to the big fraternity party, and she had eaten two dozen Krispy Kreme doughnuts she had pilfered from the Kappa house kitchen pantry. Her roommate had come back from a date and found her passed out in the bed with a half-eaten jelly doughnut still stuck in her hair.

And she had always been accident prone. Coming down the aisle at her own wedding she had somehow managed to trip over her wedding veil, and she was the only person she knew who had broken a leg falling off a merry-go-round that was standing still at the time. Why Lenore ever thought she could become a ballerina was still a mystery to her.

As Sookie sat in her bed petting Peek-a-Boo, something suddenly occurred to her. All those years of feeling bad about herself, and it might not even be her fault! Polish people might not even be good dancers.

EARLE HAD BEEN ALMOST as surprised at the news as Sookie was, but driving to work that next day, he suddenly remembered a conversation he had once had with Sookie's father. And thinking back now, he wondered if Mr. Krackenberry had been trying to tell him in a roundabout way that Sookie was adopted.

That night, Earle and his future father-in-law had just escaped the huge engagement party given for them at the country club and had gone out to the back patio overlooking the golf course to have a smoke.

As they stood there listening to the crickets, Mr. Krackenberry, a tall distinguished-looking man, had felt sorry for the boy. He could tell that Earle was scared to death of Lenore, but to his credit, Earle had hung in there, even after Lenore had thrown such a fit and continued to stare at his ears.

After a long moment, Mr. Krackenberry had cleared his throat and said, "Earle."

"Yes, sir?"

"You and Sookie are about to take a mighty big step. However, before you do, there's something about her that you should know."

"About Sookie?"

"Yes . . . and it could make a difference about how you feel."

Earle took a deep breath and faced him. "With all due respect, sir, I know her mother doesn't approve of me, but there's nothing you could tell me about Sookie that would make me change my mind. I love her, and I intend to marry her."

"I'm glad to hear it, son . . . but . . . how can I put this? You've heard the old saying, 'If you want to know what your wife will be like in twenty years, just look at the mother'?"

"Yes, sir. I've heard that . . . but I still love her. Oh, no offense, sir."

"No, none taken. And I assume you're aware that my wife has a brother and sister at Pleasant Hill and the family history."

"Yes, sir. Sookie told me."

"Ah . . . and so, naturally, you might have some concerns about

Sookie and any future children. But, if I were you . . . I wouldn't worry about it."

"Oh, I don't. Why?"

"Do you trust me, son?"

"Yes, sir."

"And do I have your word as a gentleman that this conversation will never be repeated to anyone—especially to Sookie's mother?"

"Yes, sir."

"Well, then . . . don't ask how I know, but I give you my word. Sookie is not a thing like her mother, or any of the Simmonses, for that matter. Do you understand?"

"Yes, sir. I think so. Oh . . . wow . . . well, that's a relief."

"Yes, I thought it would be."

"Oh, no offense, sir."

He laughed. "Again, none taken. I realize that Lenore may seem a little odd to you now and then, but I'll tell you, son . . . to me, she's still the most beautiful girl in the world. I haven't had a dull moment since the day I met her."

At that very moment, Lenore had whisked out on the porch in a tizzy, scarves flying behind her, and called out, "Alton . . . where are you? Oh, there you are. I need you. We have a tragedy. I just dropped my good ring in the punch. I just pray no one's swallowed it. It was Great-Grandmother's! Hurry!" Mr. Krackenberry looked at Earle and said, "See what I mean?" and started rolling up his sleeves as he followed Lenore back inside.

It's funny, but somehow, after that conversation, Earle had not worried about Sookie, nor had he ever really questioned what Mr. Krackenberry knew. But now he understood what the man had been trying to tell him.

THAT NIGHT, WHEN EARLE came home, he told Sookie about the conversation he'd had with her father at their engagement party.

Sookie was surprised. "Why didn't you tell me this before?"

"Well, honey . . . to tell you the truth . . . I just forgot."

"You *forgot*? Earle, do you have *any* idea how many sleepless nights I've spent wondering if I was going to wind up at Pleasant Hill?"

"No."

"No . . . you didn't! Because I didn't want to worry you. And now I find out you were never worried in the first place. I even wrote you and the children a good-bye letter with instructions, and now you say, 'I *forgot*?' "

"Well, honey, I also gave your father my word as a gentleman not to say anything. And he didn't tell me *why* you were not like Lenore."

"But why didn't Daddy ever tell me?"

"I guess he thought it would be better for you not to know."

"I wonder if Buck knows I'm adopted. I wonder if he knew all along and didn't tell me—"

"Oh, I would doubt it, honey . . ."

Now Sookie was even more shook up. What *else* did she not know that nobody had ever told her?

It was all so strange, and none of it made any sense. Buck was clearly related to Lenore, and yet, growing up, Lenore had always looked at him like he was something that had just dropped out of a tree. Whenever he would run through the house, she would exclaim, "Who is that odd creature that just ran through my living room with filthy feet? Surely, it can't be related to me!" Lenore had always paid much more attention to her than she had to Buck. And Sookie had always felt somewhat guilty about it. She had even asked Buck if he didn't resent her because of it, and he had said, "Are you kidding me? I'm just glad she has you to push around and not me." But why had she pushed her so hard? Was it because she was a girl? Lenore always said, "Men are necessary up to a point, but women are the natural leaders in society and in the home." Or was Lenore trying to make her into something *she* was not? Had Lenore almost wrecked Sookie's life just so she would look good?

Sookie realized she shouldn't be upset with Earle about not telling her about the conversation with her father. He thought he was doing the right thing at the time, and she could see he just felt terrible about it. But she was still confused about what she should do now, or if she should do anything at all.

# WINK'S PHILLIPS 66

1937

Besides Wink Jurdabralinski, the six-foot blond dreamboat who filled your tank and cleaned your windshields, there was another reason Wink's Phillips 66 had more than its share of female customers. Clean restrooms! Momma had been ahead of the national mind-set on that score.

At the beginning, the care and maintenance of the station was mostly a male-dominated affair and as a result, most filling station restrooms were poorly maintained. The sinks and toilets were rarely cleaned, and the floors were usually filthy. As one horrified woman said upon leaving one in Deer Park, Michigan, "You could grow a garden in the dirt on the floor in there!" Women rarely felt safe using one and did so only in emergencies.

But at Wink's Phillips 66, Momma always insisted that both the men's and women's restrooms were kept as clean as the bathrooms inside her home. All four girls took turns making sure there was a fresh cake of white soap on the basin and a clean white towel, and that each customer that walked in would be greeted with gleaming white sinks and toilets and a white tile floor that had just been scrubbed with Lysol. A germ would not stand a chance at Wink's. All day long, you would see one of the Jurdabralinski girls scurrying to and from the house with a pail and scrub brush and a towel over her arm. Naturally, there were squabbles about whose turn it was to clean, but it was always done. Wink and Poppa and the other mechanics were never allowed to use the customers' bathrooms. "I don't want you and your greasy hands getting everything all dirty," Momma said.

As more and more women and girls were starting to drive cars, the gas companies finally caught up and started to compete with one another for female customers. A well-known nurse and nationally known health lecturer, Matilda Passmore, had said, "What better way to lure them into the stations than offering them a clean bathroom?" Texaco formed the White Patrol and maintained a fleet of White Patrol Chevrolets that carried trained cleanliness inspectors around the country looking for dirt in every corner. Texaco station owners hoped to pass inspection and win a White Cross of Cleanliness award and be allowed to add to their sign the words REGISTERED RESTROOMS. Soon, another company started sending out a group known as the Sparkle Patrol. And Phillips Petroleum Company, not to be outdone, came up with its own cleanliness campaign and hired a crew of attractive young registered nurses known as Highway Hostesses, dressed in light blue uniforms, white shoes and stockings, and a smart military-styled hat. Phillips executives hoped the Highway Hostesses would promote goodwill for the company by their "courteous manner, pleasing personality, and willingness to aid anyone in distress." They also gave directions, suggested restaurants and hotels, and found time to discuss infant hygiene with traveling mothers.

The hostesses started roaming the highways and byways in large cream-colored sedans with dark green fenders and the Phillips 66 logo on the door. Their job was to make sure each Phillips 66 bathroom lived up to the standards of Certified Restrooms. Unfortunately for the filling station owners, they picked stations for inspection at random, so you never knew when one might show up, a further incentive to "keep 'em clean" at all times.

WINK SAW IT FIRST. And as the huge cream-colored sedan with the dark green fenders quietly drove up and turned into the station, it might as well have been a shark. Wink felt the hair on the back of his head stand up. He blinked to make sure he was not seeing things, but no—it was real all right, and it looked exactly like the photograph in the Phillips 66 magazine. He walked over and asked, "May I help you, miss?"

The woman with a long, pointy nose said, "Yes, young man, I'd like to speak with the owner. Tell him that Registered Nurse Dorothy Frakes is here for restroom inspection."

"Yes, ma'am," he said and ran in the back and got Poppa.

Gertrude May, who happened to be looking out the window of the second floor, saw it next. "Oh, geez," she said and started running downstairs to get her twin sister, Tula June, and Momma.

By the time Momma looked out the kitchen window, the woman was out of the car, and Poppa was already talking to her. Momma had never been nervous before, but when she saw how official the woman looked, standing there in her crisp uniform, holding her clipboard under her arm, she suddenly panicked. "Oh, dear Blessed Mother of God," she said. "Whose turn was it to clean last?"

"Fritzi's," said the youngest girl, Sophie Marie, and Fritzi could have killed her.

"Oh, no!" Now Momma was really scared. Fritzi was terrible at cleaning. Momma grabbed her by the shoulders. "Fritzi, look at me. Did you remember the soap?"

"Sure, I did."

"Did you scrub the sink?"

"Yes, and it wasn't all that dirty anyway."

Momma looked out at Poppa, still standing there doing a lot of nodding. What was he saying? Then, suddenly, the nurse briskly turned on her heel and marched toward the women's bathroom with her clipboard held high, like she was headed for battle.

In the windows of the house, five pairs of eyes were fixed on the door, waiting for the nurse to reappear, but after several minutes, she still had not come out. Momma twisted her apron. "Oh, I wonder what's taking her so long?"

Tula June said, "Maybe she had to go to the bathroom or something."

Another minute went by and then they got a quick glimpse of her leaving the women's bathroom and entering the men's room. Momma said, "Sophie Marie, go and get my rosary. I'm a nervous wreck."

A short while later, Momma was still staring at the station and working her beads when the nurse came out of the men's room and spoke to Poppa. Again, there was lots of nodding, and he kept looking over and pointing at the house. "Oh, geez . . . what's he doing . . . for gosh sake," said Momma.

The nurse turned and walked over to the house, climbed up the steps, and knocked on the door. Sophie said, "She's at the door, Momma. Should we hide?"

"No, no—just stay where you are, girls," she said, as she took her apron off and smoothed her hair. She took a deep breath and opened the door.

"Are you Mrs. Jurdabralinski?"

"Yes, I am."

"Hello, I'm Nurse Dorothy Frakes from Phillips Petroleum. Congratulations on having scored a perfect 100 and having the cleanest restrooms I have ever had the pleasure to inspect. Why, you could eat off the floor in there, Mrs. Jurdabralinski, and so, at this time, I would like to personally present your official Certified Restroom emblem."

Momma was so overwhelmed, she burst into tears while Fritzi nattered in the background. "One hundred. I told you so. Ha-ha-ha," Fritzi said. "I don't know why people don't believe me."

After that day, Registered Nurse Dorothy Frakes became just plain Dottie, and the whole family loved it when she stopped by. She never bothered to inspect the bathrooms again. She just liked to go to the house and sit down, put her feet up, smoke a cigarette, relax a bit, chat with Momma and find out how all the girls and Wink were doing, and then head on out on her appointed rounds. "I'll tell you, Linka," she said one day. "I know being a Phillips Highway Hostess may seem glamorous to a lot of people, but it can get mighty monotonous at times. If you've seen one bathroom, you've seen them all. And if it weren't for nice people like you, I'd turn in my uniform tomorrow."

# THE NEXT DAY

## Saturday, June 11, 2005

Sookie decided to close all the shades and lock all the doors, and other than feeding Peek-a-Boo, she stayed upstairs. Her nerves were so on edge, every time the phone rang, her heart would start to pound, especially when she saw it was Lenore's number, so she finally took the phone off the hook.

At around twelve-thirty, she went downstairs. Lenore had her DAR meeting from twelve to one, so she was safe on that account. She was headed back upstairs when suddenly the doorbell started ringing. She heard someone calling out her name, and it wasn't Lenore. It was Marvaleen. Oh, Lord . . . just what she didn't need right now—a visitor.

She went over and unlocked the door and said, "Hi, Marvaleen."

"Oh, there you are. I was just about to leave. I was on my way to yoga, and I thought I might take a chance on finding you at home." Then Marvaleen looked at her intently and asked, "Sookie, do you get colonics?"

"What?"

"Colonics."

"No . . . I don't know what it is."

"They're like a very high-powered enema."

Sookie made a face. "Oh, Lord . . ."

"Oh, no, Sookie!" she said. "I've already had six high colonics, and I've never felt better in my life. Edna Yorba Zorbra says that before you can ever move forward with your emotional healing, having a clean colon is absolutely necessary. It's all part of learning to release the old negativity you've been holding on to."

"I see."

"Anyhow, I go to this terrific gal in Mobile." She opened her purse. "Let me give you her card. I'm telling everybody I know about her. And when you do call, be sure and tell her that I recommended you. She's giving all my friends a ten percent discount and a fifty percent discount on a series of ten. And you really need ten. Hey, maybe we can go together sometime . . . and then have lunch afterward. Call me."

"Oh, okay, Marvaleen. I sure will." She took the card and waved good-bye to her friend, but she couldn't imagine anything more she would rather not do than have a high-powered enema and then lunch with Marvaleen afterward. She would just stick with her two tablespoons of sugar-free orange-flavored Metamucil at night.

Marvaleen had always been somewhat of a spiritual seeker and was still seeking. Ten years ago, she had talked Sookie into going to a women's Bible study group, and Sookie had gone through a very short born-again period. She had been so happy, but Lenore had been horrified. "My stars, Sookie . . . you can believe in God, but you don't have to go around town telling everyone! You're embarrassing the family. The next thing I know, you will be handling snakes and speaking in tongues!" Eventually, Sookie told Marvaleen and the group she couldn't come anymore. She still went to church and still believed in something, she guessed, but she wasn't sure what.

But now after what had just happened, she wasn't sure of anything. She had always just assumed that a person's life was planned out somewhere, and that someone was in charge and paying attention. But the more she thought about it, the more Sookie came to realize just how random the events in her life had been. And in her particular case, alarmingly precarious!

As a baby, she had been just like some cat or dog at the pound put up for adoption, and the people in charge of her had quite obviously given her to a crazy person. Don't they check people out first, before they just hand over a baby? If they had known about Lenore's brother and sister, surely they would have found someone else. Sookie had a good mind to call those people in Texas and tell them they should have been more careful.

It was particularly upsetting when she realized that throughout her entire life, her every move had been controlled by Lenore saying, "Oh Sookie, a Simmons would never do this" or "a Simmons would never do that." She had no idea what a Jurdabralinski would or would not do.

She knew everybody had to have a mother, they even gave poor little motherless monkeys a ticking clock wrapped in a towel as a substitute. But now, thinking back on her life with Lenore, she wondered if she wouldn't have been better off with just the clock.

# NEVER THE SAME AGAIN

PULASKI, WISCONSIN
AUGUST 1938

IT'S FUNNY HOW ONE EVENT CAN CHANGE THE ENTIRE COURSE OF A family's future. For the Jurdabralinski family of Pulaski, Wisconsin, that event took take place on August 9, 1938.

In the 1930s, hero worshipping and movie star crushes were in full bloom. Pictures of glamorous movie stars were plastered on the bedroom walls of most teenage girls, but a new craze hit when a tall, lanky flier named Charles Lindbergh had flown across the Atlantic Ocean. His picture had appeared everywhere. He was in the movies and on billboards, and every boy wanted to grow up and fly a plane like Lindy. All of America had fallen in love with the handsome young Charles Lindbergh, and a year later, they fell in love all over again with his female counterpart, Amelia Earhart, so bold and dashing with her auburn tousled hair and dressed in men's trousers. Girls sent off for her pictures and added them to their photos of their favorite movie stars.

Hoping to cash in on what Lindbergh and Earhart had started and take advantage of the new flying craze that was sweeping the country, Phillips Petroleum came up with an advertising promotion that was sure to be noticed. In a bold move, they hired skywriters to fly over their gas stations and write "Phillips 66" in the air. Most of the skywriters were old World War I pilots or barnstormers, the name given to the men who flew around the country performing aerial stunts, picking up a little extra cash on the weekends. But the pilot assigned to fly over Wink's Phillips 66 filling station in Pulaski, Wisconsin, picked up more than a little extra cash.

Billy Bevins's uncle had been a flier in World War I. He started his own flying school when he came home and taught Billy to fly when he was fifteen. Billy had been flying ever since. It was a good way to make a living, and in Billy's case, a good way to meet girls. He had done it all, from barnstorming to crop dusting, and had even flown a Davis Waco with the Baby Ruth Flying Circus. It was an advertising blitz unlike anything the country had ever seen. Billy would fly over county and state fairs, racetracks, and crowded beaches in his red and white plane, dropping hundreds of tiny rice paper parachutes—each one bearing a small Baby Ruth candy bar—on the crowds below.

It was a great job; however, one day, after too many drinks, Billy took it upon himself to fly in between the buildings in downtown Pittsburgh and it caused a riot in the streets. Several people almost fell out of office windows trying to grab the candy bars as they floated by. Traffic was snarled for the next two hours as people left their cars sitting in the streets to look for Baby Ruths. The next day, Billy was fired. Now he was back to barnstorming around the county and skywriting on the side.

The people in Pulaski had been waiting for weeks for the skywriter to fly in. In preparation, Poppa and some of his farmer friends had brought in tractors and cleared out the large field in the back of the house, and Wink and all his friends got busy and cleared out all the rocks and made a long, smooth runway where the plane could land. When word got out that he was coming one Saturday morning, the entire town went out into their yards or stood waiting in the empty lot behind the filling station. Pretty soon, they heard the sound of a faraway motor. Fritzi was the first to see the plane and shouted for everyone to look up. Soon, a large white "P" was being formed in the sky. The entire crowd stood looking up in awe as the word "Phillips" was spelled out, then the number "66." As the icing on the cake, the pilot flew the plane straight down toward the ground and then back up and formed an arrow that pointed right down at the station. He then made a large circle in the sky, came back around, and landed the plane to wild applause from the waiting crowd.

But the pilot who opened the door and jumped down from the plane was not like anything they expected and a far cry from Charles Lindbergh. Billy was a short and stocky young man with a wide grin who clearly loved his work. "Hiya, pals!" he said as he made his way over to the filling station with the crowd following behind him. Fritzi was blown away. She had never seen anyone so confident, so self-assured, and she loved the way he had said "Hiya, pals!" with such flair. It was as if he had stepped right out of a movie.

Billy walked over to the station and posed for pictures and gave radio and newspaper interviews for about an hour. Later, he waved good-bye to the crowd with a "So long, pals," and went inside the house next door and was treated to lunch with the Jurdabralinski family.

During his visit, they learned that he had flown over that morning from Grand Rapids. Wink was enthralled as he sat and listened to Billy tell tales about his flying exploits as a barnstormer and stunt flier. After lunch, they walked him back to his plane and waved as he took off to the east. They all agreed it had been the most exciting day of their lives.

It had also been a very good day for Billy. He had flown away with a large paper bag full of good Polish sausage and homemade candy that the mother had packed for him, plus something else. He had learned the names of all four daughters.

NOT LONG AFTER BILLY'S first visit, someone heard the sound of a plane circling above the town. They all came out and looked up and saw that it was the skywriter back again, but this time, after he had finished, they saw he had written in large white letters across the sky,

HEY, FRITZI, HOW ABOUT A DATE?

Billy had a hunch. Fritzi was not the prettiest sister. Sophie, the youngest, was the beauty, and the other two girls were swell looking, too, but there was something about Fritzi that he liked. She had real spirit, and he was looking for a gal with spirit.

When Momma stepped out and looked up and saw the message in the sky, she shook her head. She had been concerned about something like this happening. She was afraid that of all her children, Fritzi would be the one who would run off from home, looking for some wild new adventure. And she could tell by the way Fritzi had pushed her way past everybody to sit by Billy Bevins at lunch and how she had hung on to his every word, this might be it.

Two days later, when the family was having dinner, Billy Bevins called the phone number at the filling station, and Wink ran over to the house to get Fritzi.

After a few minutes, Fritzi came back to the kitchen looking flushed and excited and announced to the table, "Billy's coming to get me on Saturday and fly me to Milwaukee for dinner and dancing!"

Momma turned to her husband, waiting for him to put his foot down and say no, but he just nodded and kept eating. Wink and the other girls were as excited as Fritzi and started jumping up and down. Wink asked, "Can I go, too?" so Momma knew she was outnumbered. And, besides, what could she do? Stanislaw was right. Fritzi was a new breed of American girl with a mind of her own, and nothing she could say would stop her anyway. All Momma could do was go to Saint Mary's and light a candle to the Blessed Mother and pray Fritzi didn't fall out of the plane.

The next day, when Fritzi told her friends about it, one girl said, "Oh, Fritzi, I'd be scared to go off with a stranger like that." The other girl said, "Yeah, aren't you afraid he might get you up in the air and then try to get fresh?" But Fritzi wasn't worried. She had been on too many hayrides with over-six-foot-tall Wisconsin farm boys, and if she could handle them, she surely could handle him. Billy wasn't much taller than she was.

The following Saturday afternoon, Fritzi, dressed in a blue suit, white blouse, white shoes, and a white hat, climbed into the backseat of the plane and waved good-bye to her family, while Momma stood there making the sign of the cross over and over again. "Oh, dear Mother of God, let her live through this." But Momma knew, even if Fritzi did live, they were in danger of losing her. They always said that "Once you've been to Milwaukee, you're never the same."

# THE LETTERS

Point Clear, Alabama

In the past week, Sookie had gone through all the food she had stashed away in case of an emergency. She hadn't stepped out of the house. But now even she couldn't face another frozen shrimp. She really had to do a little grocery shopping. So she waited until noon, when she knew Lenore was safely at the Red Hat Society ladies luncheon. After she finished her shopping, she thought of something else she needed to do while she was out, so she whipped around the corner and parked in the back of the bank.

She went in and opened up their security box and removed the two letters she had written almost three years ago and reread them.

Dear Family,

If anything should happen to me as far as my mental health, I am saying good-bye to you now while I am still of sound mind. I want you to know that you are the very best thing that ever happened to me and that you have always been my constant joy and pride. I don't know what I ever did to deserve such a wonderful husband and children. Take good care of each other, and try and remember me when I was well.

I will love you forever,

Mother

Then, she opened up the one to Earle.

To My Darling Earle,

Promise me if something should happen, please feel free to divorce me and remarry. I want you to be happy, and you need someone to take care of you. Sweetheart, thank you for all the wonderful years we did have. When I'm gone, take care of Mother as best you can, and let Dee Dee help you. She is devoted to Lenore and will be happy to take over the paperwork.

Always,

Your loving wife,

Sookie

P.S. Pleasant Hill has recently raised their prices, so I have checked around for places a little less expensive. Try Brice's Institution in Tuscaloosa first. I think they may take Blue Cross.

P.P.S. Marvaleen told me on the QT that she thinks you are very handsome. Just a thought . . .

When Sookie reread the last letter, she was so glad Earle had not seen it. Marvaleen? What had she been thinking? Marvaleen was far too new age for Earle. Marvaleen wore thong underwear—not that there was anything wrong with that, but it would be a little too much for Earle. Sookie knew she really was the perfect wife for Earle. He had always said so, and now she could clearly see he was right. She knew exactly how he liked his corn bread: thin and crispy. He wouldn't be happy with anyone else but her. She tore both letters up and threw them away.

Sookie realized that starting today, she was going to have to reset her thinking. For years, she had lived with the fear of the Simmons gene, but now that was a worry she didn't have anymore. Of course, she didn't know about the Jurdabralinski genes, but she was fairly certain nobody could be crazier than the Simmonses.

As Sookie drove home from the bank, she suddenly remembered it was Monday and ducked down in her seat and hid as she drove past the cemetery. Her mother's car was there, but thank heavens, she hadn't spotted Sookie's car. That was another thing Lenore had put her through. It was so irritating to think that she had gone to all that hassle and trouble to move her great-grandfather there, and now it turns out she wasn't even related to him. The man was a complete stranger!

She felt like such a fool. Lenore had made her do all that stuff, knowing full well she wasn't a Simmons. Honestly!

And it wouldn't be so bad if the woman had ever once said thank you or even appreciated it. Lenore didn't even seem to have a clue or notice what all she had put her through.

Last year, after the mayor's lawsuit, when she was driving her mother home from the courthouse, Sookie had asked, "Mother, do you have any idea how hard it is to be your daughter?"

Lenore had looked at her completely puzzled. "Why, what an odd question. Hard? In what way, hard? I think I have been a wonderful mother. I would have loved to have been my daughter. Haven't I done everything humanly possible to see that you have every advantage?"

"Yes, Mother, you have. It's just that you come with an awful lot of drama, and you are never quiet."

"Well, I'm sorry if I'm not some dull and boring Sally-sit-by-the-fire. Yes, I talk a lot, but I happen to excel in the art of conversation."

"It's not just talking, Mother. It's just that you always have an opinion."

"Well, I should hope so."

"But it's always such a strong opinion."

"How can you expect me to have a weak opinion? Would you go into a restaurant and order a weak cup of coffee?"

"Yes, as a matter of fact, I would."

"You know what I mean, Sookie. Why have an opinion, if it's not a strong opinion? Oh, I know the Good Book says the meek shall inherit the earth, but I don't believe it for one minute."

"But, Mother, surely there is something in between meek and overpowering. Like . . . just normal." Sookie knew the minute she said it, she had said the wrong word.

Lenore's eyes suddenly got very big. "Are you suggesting that I am not normal? Granted, your Uncle Baby and Aunt Lily have their little quirks, but I'm as normal as they come. Really, Sookie, you hurt me to the quick."

If Lenore thought shooting at the paperboy was just "a little quirk," then there was no point in expecting her to ever think anything was wrong with her. Lenore had never been normal in her life. She certainly hadn't been a normal mother or a normal grandmother, either.

One Christmas Eve, when the children had been quite young, she and Earle had left them with Lenore while they ran out and did a little last-minute shopping, and Lenore had served each child several cups of the Simmons eggnog, which was 75 percent rum and 25 percent nog. When they came to pick the children up, all four were stumbling around her living room in a drunken stupor. "I don't know why you're so upset, Sookie," Lenore had said. "My word, a little eggnog never hurt anybody, and if we can't celebrate the birth of our Lord on Christmas Eve, then I don't know what the world is coming to."

That year, they had been the only children in town who had opened their presents on Christmas morning with a hangover. And, of course, no matter what Lenore did, the children just adored her. Especially Dee Dee. Whenever she was punished for doing something at home, she would exclaim, "I'm going to live with Grandmother. She understands me!"

Lenore had been so hard on her own children, but to Sookie's great surprise, with her grandchildren, she thought whatever they did or said was "Just darling! Just precious!" or "The cutest thing in the world!" She had given them all the candy they wanted, even though Earle, being a dentist, had asked her not to. So, of course, the children loved being with her. Why not?

But then, they hadn't been raised by a woman who thought that Sookie and Buck were the only two things that had stood between her and winning an Oscar. She had said, "Oh, Sookie, when I saw Barbara Stanwyck in the movie *Stella Dallas,* I just cried my eyes out. I could have played that part to a T. Oh, well," she sighed. "Barbara Stanwyck had the career I should have, but it's all water under the bridge now." Oh, brother.

## MILWAUKEE, WISCONSIN

1938

Fritzi didn't let on, but she had actually been terrified as Billy taxied the plane over to the edge of the field. She had never been in an airplane in her life, and when he revved the motor, ready for takeoff, she shut her eyes and held on to her hat for dear life. As the plane started rumbling down the field, her heart was pounding so hard she could hardly breathe, but if this is what it took to impress Billy, she would do it. She had been dazzled by Billy at first sight, the way he had jumped down out of the plane and sauntered through the crowd. Besides, she wanted to see something of the world before she settled down. She didn't want to marry one of the hometown boys and have five or six children before she was twenty-five. A lot of her friends had dropped out of high school, married, and already had a baby on the way. So when Billy had flown into her life, it seemed to her that she was to be rescued, not by a man on a white horse, but by one in a bright yellow plane.

After a bumpy ride, the plane lifted off the ground, and, suddenly, Fritzi felt the most amazing sensation. The loud roar of the engine became more of a hum, and she felt as if she were floating. When she opened her eyes, she was way up in the air and looking down at the small world below. Her family, still standing by the fence waving, became smaller and smaller as she and Billy flew up way above the town, headed over to Milwaukee.

Flying to Milwaukee was a revelation to Fritzi. Billy followed the railroad tracks all the way, and from up above looking down, the silos and water towers looked like some of Wink's old toys sitting on top of a patchwork quilt. Tiny tractors moved slowly through rows of corn and wheat, and the lakes that spotted the countryside looked like little round mirrors. The farmhouses, with sheets and overalls hanging from the clotheslines in the backyard, looked no bigger than the little wooden house pieces on a Monopoly set.

Fritzi didn't want Billy to know, but she had never been more than a few miles away from home before. When they landed in Milwaukee, they picked up Billy's car, and he drove her downtown for an evening of dining and dancing at the Oriental Room atop the Hotel Ambassador. Fritzi had never been in such a big city before, and as streetcars, taxis, and cars whizzed by, she felt as excited as she had ever been in her entire life.

Pulaski had pretty much shut down after dark, except for the roller rink and Friday night bingo at the church and an occasional polka night out at Zielinski's Ballroom. But here, everybody was wide awake and going somewhere. All the department stores, some a block long, were still open, and the windows were filled with smartly dressed mannequins wearing fancy clothes. Fritzi was amazed as they drove past flower shops, candy shops with little pink neon signs, and at least six or seven movie theaters with huge marquees.

Geez . . . if this was Milwaukee, what must Chicago or New York be like? She couldn't imagine, but she knew one thing: After this, she could never be happy just staying home and working at the pickle factory.

* * *

ONCE THEY ENTERED THE hotel, she did get a little nervous. This was the first time she had ever been to a hotel with a man. She hoped there really was a supper club, and she was not going to wind up in a hotel room. But she needn't have worried. As soon as the elevator doors opened on the twenty-second floor, they heard the music. And when they walked into the Oriental Room, Fritzi was overwhelmed. She felt as if she had just stepped inside a movie set, and she half-expected to see Fred Astaire and Ginger Rogers at any minute. She had never seen anything so glamorous. The room was lined with lime green leather booths. Little oriental red and green lanterns hung over the dance floor, and waiters dressed in yellow and black silk Chinese pajamas scurried around, serving drinks with tiny paper umbrellas. The dance floor was packed with people dancing to the Speed Hooper Orchestra. Fritzi noticed that there was not one accordion player. The girl singer, dressed in a long white sequined gown, wore a gardenia in her hair and just oozed sophistication.

As they were escorted to their booth and made their way through the crowd, everybody seemed to know Billy and would call out, "Hiya, Billy!" and he would say, "Hiya, pals!" Fritzi suddenly felt like a rube among all the beautifully dressed women in the room. When they sat down, Billy ordered her a champagne cocktail and a double scotch for himself.

Later, after Billy and Fritzi came back from the dance floor, a cute girl in a short skirt carrying a camera came up and asked Billy if he wanted a picture of the two of them. Another had a tray full of cigarettes and cigars and corsages for sale. Billy bought her a wrist corsage. All through the evening, Fritzi remained calm and pretended she had done this kind of thing before. She tried not to let Billy see it, but inside, she was impressed out of her mind. It was true. Once she had seen Milwaukee, she knew she would never be the same again.

THAT NIGHT, WHEN BILLY flew her back home to Pulaski, Fritzi looked down and saw the lights of the filling station below, and she was sorry the date was over. She wished it could have gone on forever. Long after they had landed and Billy was already back in Grand Rapids, Fritzi Jurdabralinski was still up in the air, in more ways than one. Somewhere along the way, she had lost her hat, but she didn't care. She had lost more than her hat; she had lost her heart. That night, Fritzi had fallen hopelessly in love with flying . . . and with Billy Bevins.

# WHERE DID I GET MY TRAITS?

Point Clear, Alabama

When she woke up that morning, Sookie realized she really needed to find out more about her ethnic background. She had always assumed that she had inherited either the Simmons or the Krackenberry traits. Now she wanted to try and figure out what behavior was from her Polish DNA and what was learned behavior. She wished she had paid more attention to world geography. She wasn't even sure exactly where Poland was. She knew it was in Europe somewhere, close to Russia or France, maybe? And she didn't know a thing about Polish people. As far as she knew, her only encounter with anything remotely Polish was eating those little Polish sausages they served at the Waffle House. And so after her bath, she fed Peek-a-Boo and turned on the computer. She typed up the words "Polish Traits," and clicked.

"The Poles are generally a fun-loving and hardworking people." Well, that was good so far, but she was curious about what they looked like, so she typed in "Famous Polish People." The first two names that came up were Frédéric Chopin and Liberace, both piano players. And she could see from Liberace's picture that they had similar noses. When she read on and saw that Martha Stewart was also Polish, she began to cheer up just a tiny bit.

* * *

Later, Sookie waited until she knew Lenore was in water therapy and went outside and walked around her yard for the first time in days. When she saw Netta out in her front yard, pruning her azaleas, she wandered over and said, "Hi, Netta."

Netta looked up. "Well, hey there, gal . . . feeling any better?"

"Yes, I am. But don't tell Mother, okay?"

"I won't."

"Thanks, Netta. And thanks so much for feeding my birds."

"No problem, hon. Happy to do it anytime."

"Netta, let me ask you something. What do you know about Polish people?"

"Polish people?"

"Yes."

"Oh, well . . . let me think," Netta said, snapping off a dead branch in one of her bushes. "I know they like sauerkraut. And they love to sing, but they are not very good singers."

"Really?"

"Yeah. I heard that somewhere, but I've forgotten where. And, oh, they like their accordions and like to do the polka."

"Have you ever met any Polish people in person?"

"Not that I recall, no . . . or if I did, I didn't know it. Why?"

"Oh, no reason, I was just wondering. Well, I'll see you later."

Netta watched as Sookie slowly wandered back over to her house like she was in some kind of a daze. Between the pink sneakers and now this, she was getting worried. Maybe it was the flu, but Sookie just didn't seem like herself.

# A FINE ROMANCE

PULASKI, WISCONSIN

BILLY BEVINS THOUGHT FRITZI WAS A GREAT GAL. BUT AS IT TURNED out, he had had motives other than romance for taking her out. He hadn't told her yet, but he was really just looking for a new gal to join him in his flying act. The big draw at air shows were the female wing walkers, and Fritzi filled the bill. She had a terrific figure, a great smile, and a lot of confidence.

After they had gone out a few more times, and he had flown her over to see a performance of the Billy Bevins Flying Circus, he asked Fritzi whether she would ever be interested in joining his flying act if he trained her to do a few stunts. She answered with an emphatic "Yes!"

"Great!" he said, patting her on the back, then added, "Fritzi, gal, I'm going to show you how to do things in a plane you never dreamed about."

Fritzi shot him a look and said, "Yeah, I'll just bet you will!"

He had laughed when she said it, but to Fritzi's disappointment, and as much as she wished he would, he never so much as kissed her good night.

As time went by, Fritzi felt baffled. She knew he liked her, but something was wrong. She had never had a guy not try and get fresh with her. Maybe he thought she was too young or not worldly enough for him. So Fritzi tried acting a little older and tougher. She even plucked her eyebrows like Jean Harlow, but so far, nothing. She ordered a pair of tan jodhpurs, a white silk shirt, a leather cap, and a long white scarf. She put them on and strolled around town looking very much like a real pilot. Or so people in Pulaski said.

Every Monday, Billy would fly over to Pulaski and give Fritzi a flying lesson. He needed his wing walkers to be trained pilots, and as a favor to Fritzi, he threw in a few lessons for Wink as well.

Wink hero-worshipped Billy and started to walk like him and follow him around like a puppy. Wink did very well with his lessons, but Fritzi was the one whose progress Billy was interested in, and she didn't disappoint him. She was strong, athletic, coordinated, and—most important of all—as he had found on their first date, she was a damn good dancer. Before he trained any girl, he always took them dancing first.

Billy knew from experience, people with no rhythm made lousy pilots. Not only was Fritzi a good student and a fast learner, unlike a lot of girls, she was not afraid to get her hands dirty. After having watched her father work at the filling station all those years, Fritzi could take a motor apart and put it back together and change a tire in three minutes flat.

A few months later, when Billy flew in, Fritzi came running out, ready for another lesson, and he started off with his usual drill. "So, pal . . . what's your first rule?"

"Safety."

"Who's your best friend?"

"My mechanic."

"What do you do before you take off?"

"Check everything."

"How many times?"

"Twice."

"Right!" Billy was a highly skilled pilot, but he was also a real stickler on safety. That day, after they had landed, Billy turned to her and said, "Okay, kid. You're ready to solo. She's all yours. Take her up, do your stuff, then bring her on in. See you later," and he walked away and left her standing there.

Fritzi had no idea this was going to happen so soon, and she panicked, but she knew that if she didn't do it, she might not ever see Billy again. She walked around the plane with her heart pounding and did her safety check, twice. When she finally got in the plane, she was so nervous that her legs started to shake, and she wanted to jump out and run, but she took a deep breath and started the motor and taxied out, with her mind full of all the things Billy had taught her. To her amazement, before she knew it, she was up in the air, looking down at Billy, who gave her a thumbs-up. She stayed up in the air for about twenty-five minutes, flying in circles, and practiced landing in the air ten times, like Billy had taught her. "Go up and give yourself plenty of altitude, and envision that your runway is laid right out in front of you. Then, go through all your landing procedures, so when you do land, you've already done it so many times, landing for real will be a piece of cake."

And, sure enough, on her first solo landing, she did pretty well. The next week, Poppa drove her up to Grand Rapids to get her pilot's license. Poppa was so proud and showed it to everyone who came in the station. Fritzi was happy to have her license, but privately, her heart was broken. When she had gone to Grand Rapids, after she had gotten her license, she made Poppa drive her over to the hotel where Billy lived and had knocked on Billy's door to surprise him. A tough-looking woman with frizzy red hair had come to the door in her nightgown. She found out that the whole time she had known him, Billy had been living with Gussie Mintz, his second-string wing walker from Altoona.

What a fool she had been. He had never been the slightest bit interested in her and probably never would be. It was hard being around him after that, but Billy had never led her on, nor had he made any promises, so what could she do?

After that Fritzi started doing a few shows now and then. Billy would call her whenever Lillian Bass, his first-string wing walker, was not available and Gussie was too drunk to go on.

Soon, Billy began to see that not only had Fritzi taken to flying and performing stunts, she'd invented a few of her own. She didn't do the usual girl stunts. She went out on the wing and stood on her head, jumped through hoops, and did the jitterbug five hundred feet up in the air. As Billy told his mechanic one night at the hotel bar, "That crazy kid has more guts than brains. Damn," he said. "She reminds me of me at that age, and that ain't good." Billy took a swig of his drink, then said, "Now if I was a nice guy, I would send her packing, but I ain't a nice guy, I guess."

The mechanic, who had been with Billy for eleven years, said, "You'd better watch out, buddy. The next thing you know, that little gal is liable to have *you* jumping through hoops."

A few months later, when Lillian quit wing walking for good to get married, Billy called Fritzi in Pulaski and told her the first-string job was hers permanently, if she wanted it.

Did she want it? She jumped at the chance. Momma did not want her to go, but she could also see how unhappy she was. Her other three girls were homebodies, but not Fritzi.

Fritzi gave her notice at the pickle factory. One week later, Billy got her a hotel room where he lived and she moved to Grand Rapids for good and started traveling with the Flying Circus. To Poppa's delight, the move was headline news in Pulaski.

**MISS FRITZI JURDABRALINSKI,**
**PULASKI'S OWN AMELIA EARHART,**
**JOINS FLYING CIRCUS**

# WHERE *IS* PULASKI?

Point Clear, Alabama

The next morning, after Earle left for the office, Sookie was sitting at her kitchen table, looking at Earle's big road atlas of the United States, trying to find the town of Pulaski, when Netta knocked on the back door. Sookie got up and went to the door.

"Hey, Sookie, I saw Dr. Poole leave a little while ago, so I thought I'd run over and see if you needed anything from the store."

"Oh, thank you, Netta. I'm fine, but come in, and have some coffee."

"No, I can't stay. I'm still in my hairnet." Netta looked over at the table and said, "I see you've got your road maps out. Are you going on a trip?"

"No, I was just looking at a map of Wisconsin. Have you ever been to Wisconsin, Netta?"

"Nope, sure haven't. Have you?"

"No, I don't know anything about it. Do you?"

"Nothing much, except . . . isn't that where the horses with the big feet come from? I think they're pulling a wagon of Budweiser beer. Don't they call it Milwaukee's Finest?"

"I think you're right."

"And they like their cheese. And Wisconsin may be where Daisy the Contented Cow comes from, but I could be wrong. But if you're not going there, why are you looking at it on the map?"

"Oh, no reason. I just woke up and was curious about where it was, that's all. I'm surprised at how far up it is, almost as far up as Canada. I wonder how cold it gets in the winter?"

"I wouldn't know, honey. Well, I'll leave you to your map. Call me if you need me."

As Netta walked across the yard back to her house, she wondered why anyone in their right mind would just wake up one day and be curious about Wisconsin. But maybe Sookie wasn't in her right mind. Maybe poor Sookie had flipped. Oh, Lord. Another Simmons over at Pleasant Hill. Once that gene gets in there, it just hits them like a hammer, and off they go. Bless her heart. One day sane, the next day looking at maps of Wisconsin for no reason. Her poor kids are going to be very upset, and no telling what will happen to Dr. Poole. She never saw a man so devoted to his wife as he was. But it was to be expected, she guessed. With Lenore for a mother, that girl was probably driven to the brink. She liked Lenore, but she was glad she wasn't related to her.

Sookie sat back down and continued looking for Pulaski and finally found it. "Pulaski: Home of the largest polka celebration in the country." It was close to Green Bay, she could see that. Oh, dear, that was where those people painted themselves green and sat in the football stands in the freezing cold with wedges of cheese on their heads. Oh, well. Who was she to pass judgment? Carter and the girls had all gone to the University of Alabama, and Carter and his friends wore elephant hats to the games. To each his own, she supposed, but still, it was very strange to think that some of those people sitting in the stands with wedges of cheese on their heads might be her own relatives. Then another thought hit her. She had always liked cheese, especially pimento cheese sandwiches. Could that have come from her genetic background, or did she just love cheese? When Earle came home, she asked, "Earle, have you ever noticed that I eat a lot of cheese, or is it just my imagination?"

"Cheese? No, I haven't noticed you eating more cheese than anybody else. Why?"

"I was just wondering."

The next day, when she knew Lenore was busy playing bridge and that there was no danger that she would run into her, Sookie hurried downtown to the bookstore and spoke to the owner.

"Hi, Karin, how are you?"

"I'm fine, Mrs. Poole. You just missed your mother. She was here earlier with her little Mexican nurse, buying some birthday cards."

Oh, for heaven's sake. "Well, listen, Karin, I was wondering . . . where should I look for a book on Poland?"

"The country, Poland?"

"Yes. Or Wisconsin."

"Okay. Well, both of those would be in the travel section, but if you don't find what you want, let me know. I can always order it. Are you taking a trip now that all the weddings are over?"

"Well, you know, I just might be. I'm just not sure where, yet."

"Let me know if I can help you."

As Sookie searched through the books, it dawned on her that her mother always bought her greeting cards there, so she was probably in there earlier buying a birthday card for her, knowing full well that July 31 was not her real birthday. *Honestly!*

# PULASKI, WISCONSIN

## 1939

In 1939, most Americans, especially the young, were blissfully unaware of what was happening outside of their own little world. But the citizens of Pulaski, young and old, were painfully aware of the horrible war that was raging across Europe. Every night, families sat glued to the radio, listening to the news of Poland. Most still had relatives and friends there, and each day, the men would gather at the bulletin board at the drugstore, reading the news of the day in disbelief. The Poles were fighting bravely, hoping to hold out for England or France to come and help. Stanislaw had a cousin who worked in the telegraph room at the Grand Hotel Europejski in Warsaw, and he had managed to send news of the bombing of the city by the Germans. He reported that each night, the Nazis sent more bombers, and each morning, whole new sections of the city were destroyed. Men, women, and children were being killed by the hundreds and left in the streets, along with the dead horses. And then, after September 1, the news abruptly stopped, and nothing more came out of Poland.

September the ninth was a cold, gray day, and the entire town of Pulaski was suddenly deadly quiet as the news was announced.

Father Sobieski, whose family was still in Warsaw, walked slowly up to the bell tower of Saint Mary's and rang the bell over and over with tears streaming down his face. Poland had fallen to the Nazis. Like so many, he had dreamed he would return home one day, but that dream was over. The Poland they loved was gone.

After a while, stunned people slowly began coming out of their homes into the streets, and, not knowing what else to do, they all walked over to the church, where a special mass was said entirely in Polish. When it was over, they all stood and sang the Polish national anthem.

Several weeks later, at the Pulaski movie theater, when they ran the weekly *Eyes and Ears of the World* newsreel, they showed films of the fall of Warsaw, and one woman screamed when she thought she recognized the man with his arms over his head being brutally shoved through the war-torn streets by a Nazi soldier. "That's my brother!" she screamed over and over, and she had to be taken home.

Poland had fallen, but life in America carried on as usual. Kids still played baseball, and the 1939 World's Fair in New York was being mobbed by people thrilled about seeing all the marvelous inventions that were in the works. The World of Tomorrow exhibit promised nothing but an exciting future. Elsewhere, across the country, women and girls sat in movie houses, swooning over Clark Gable in *Gone with the Wind*, while men and boys were enthralled watching John Wayne ride shotgun across the West in *Stagecoach*. At night, people were still laughing at their favorite radio shows, *Charlie McCarthy* and *Fibber McGee and Molly*. Teenagers everywhere were jitterbugging to Glenn Miller's "Little Brown Jug," and the Andrews Sisters had a big hit with "Beer Barrel Polka," a song that was especially popular in Pulaski.

BY THE SUMMER, GERTRUDE May and Tula June had graduated from high school. Both were well-liked and were members of the Thursday night Ladies Accordion Band of Pulaski and marched with them that year in the Polka Days parade. Tula and Gertrude both had steady boyfriends, lived at home, and helped Momma in the kitchen. The youngest girl, Sophie, was in her junior year at high school. The three girls were a joy to Momma. Gertrude was a big-boned, good-natured girl with a big laugh like her father. Tula was just plain silly and loved to giggle. Sophie was very pretty, and the boys liked her a lot, but she was shy and quiet and very much a homebody, which pleased Momma. She had already lost Fritzi, and she wanted to keep her last three little chickens close by, where she could keep an eye on them.

Momma hadn't said anything, but she had noticed that of all her children, Sophie Marie was the most devout and never missed mass, and she said her rosary every night. Momma would not be surprised if she turned out to have a religious vocation. She hoped so. It would be wonderful to have a nun in the family. She knew that with the way Wink fooled around with all the girls, particularly Angie Broukowski, he was never going to be a priest. Girls were now driving all the way over from Green Bay to the filling station just to flirt with him.

By the end of 1939, those in Washington, including Franklin Roosevelt, fearing that the United States would eventually be drawn into war, became concerned that the country was not prepared. The Army Air Corps was turning out only three hundred pilots annually, and so the government quietly and without much fanfare set up a new program, offered at colleges, called the Civilian Pilot Training Program, which turned out to be good news for the Jurdabralinskis. They already had the little airstrip they had built for Billy, and the local college needed a place to keep small planes and train students. When they asked Stanislaw if they could build a small hangar on the property and rent the land, he saw an opportunity for Wink and the girls and told the college they could use it rent-free. The only stipulation was that the instructor give Wink and his girls flying lessons in his spare time. The girls were thrilled. They idolized Fritzi and wanted to be just like her. But Momma was not happy. Having Fritzi flying all over the place was enough.

Dear Goofballs,

Poppa wrote and told me about your new venture. Can't wait for you to take me for a ride into the wild blue yonder. Billy says, "Be careful, be safe, have fun."

Fritzi

All three girls did fairly well—all except Tula. When she soloed, she came in far too low on the landing and brought an awful lot of cornstalks down with her. After that, Tula decided to just stick to playing the accordion and roller-skating.

# THE INVISIBLE WOMAN

## Point Clear, Alabama

The minute Ce Ce got back from her honeymoon, she ran over to see her mother and pick up Peek-a-Boo. "Oh, Mother, the honeymoon was just wonderful. And thanks again for taking such good care of Peek-a-Boo."

"Oh, honey, I was happy to do it."

After they had visited awhile and caught up on Ce Ce's trip, Ce Ce looked at her and asked, "Mother, is there something the matter? You just don't seem like yourself today."

"Oh, no. It's . . . well . . . with all my children gone, I've been doing a little reevaluating, that's all."

"About what?"

"Oh, how proud I am of all my girls. Le Le and Dee Dee have such good careers, and now you're studying to be a veterinarian. And I guess I'm just feeling a little bit like a failure. I never did anything with my life."

"Mother, what are you talking about? You worked and helped put Daddy through dental school."

"Oh . . . not for that long, and I just did a little simple filing."

"And you raised four children. You were always there when any of us needed you. You cooked and cleaned and made sure we all had clean clothes. I don't know how you did it at all."

"Oh, honey, that's just housewife stuff. Anybody can do that."

"No, they can't. I can't. Grandmother sure couldn't. I don't know why you never give yourself any credit for all you did every day. And you never complained."

"Oh, yes, I did."

"Well, not to us. We never heard you complain about anything."

"No?"

"No. You were always so easygoing, so sweet. You just went along with everything."

"I did?"

"Oh, yes."

THAT AFTERNOON, SOOKIE CALLED Dena. "Dena, I want you to tell me the truth and feel free to be brutally frank. You were my best friend in college."

"Yes, I was."

"What would you say were my main personality traits?"

"Oh . . . well, you had a *great* personality. Everybody liked you, Sookie."

"But why?"

"Why? You were fun to be with and always so—"

"Agreeable?"

"Yes . . . and you always went along with everything."

"I knew it!"

"What?"

"I am a nonperson. I never had any real personality traits of my own. I'm traitless. I've just picked up things. If I hadn't been pushed into a personality by Lenore, everyone would have seen that underneath, I am nothing but a dull, traitless blob."

"Oh, Sookie, that's not true."

"Yes, it is. All these years, I've just been imitating other people. I'm just an empty suit."

"Sookie, what happened? You don't sound like yourself."

"That's just it. I'm *not* myself. I'm just one big piece of plasma floating around in space . . . the Invisible Woman. Why couldn't I have found all this out when I was young and still had a chance to change? Now it's too late. I'm already formed. I'm just a second-banana kind of person, and I always will be."

"Oh, Sookie, it's not true. And it's never too late to change, and do something different."

"Yes, it is. For me, at least. I don't think I've changed one bit since high school. I'm just older on the outside, that's all."

"Oh, honey."

"No, it's true, Dena. And there's nothing more unattractive than a sixty-year-old ex-cheerleader still trying to be perky. I just make myself sick. I don't even know if I really like people or if I'm just a big phony. Anyhow, thank you for being my friend."

Dena hung up the phone and felt so bad for Sookie, but she could understand how she felt. She had always thought that Lenore was hilarious and a lot of fun, but then she wasn't her daughter. And with Lenore, everybody was a second banana.

# GRAND RAPIDS, WISCONSIN

Billy Bevins had met plenty of girls, but never one like Fritzi. He was twelve years older, but pretty soon, when they all went out after the show, she could match him drink for drink, cuss word for cuss word—and lately, she had added a few new ones he had never heard of. Best of all, she had become almost as good a pilot as he was.

For the first few months in Grand Rapids, Fritzi had her own room at the hotel, and everything had been on the up and up. But as time went by, Gussie Mintz, the wing walker from Altoona that Billy was living with, had seen the handwriting on the wall. She saw how Billy looked at Fritzi and vice versa. He denied it, of course, but Gussie was not a fool. So one Saturday, while Billy and Fritzi were off doing the show, she up and packed her bags and moved back to Altoona. But she did leave Fritzi a note.

> Dear Fritzi,
>
> Well, I'm off. Good luck, and be careful. They say once flying gets in your blood, you can't ever get it out. I'm getting out while I still can.
>
> Yours truly,
>
> Gussie Mintz

P.S. I ain't mad at you, Fritzi, but you tell Billy I think he's a real shit.

Gussie may not have been the most refined of girls, but Fritzi had always liked her. When you got past all the makeup, booze, crying jags, and bad grammar, there had been something kind of noble about old Gussie, and Fritzi would miss her.

And no matter what Gussie had called Billy, Gussie was clearly still in love with him. She hadn't left because she *wanted* to. But, after all, she herself had kicked some other gal out before she and Billy had gotten together. Just the same, if she had had a gun, Gussie would have shot him right where it counted. It would have made her feel better and probably saved Fritzi a lot of heartache down the line. Billy was not the marrying kind, and he never would be.

As Gussie had predicted, things with Billy and Fritzi progressed, and a few months later, she was spending more time in Billy's room than her own. He said, "Why pay for two rooms when you are only using one?" It was as close to a proposal as she was ever going to get. She knew by now there was never going to be a wedding. Billy didn't believe in marriage. The choice was hers. She knew it was a sin, but she had stopped going to church a long time ago, so she moved in with Billy. She only worried about two things: Momma and Poppa finding out, and getting pregnant. As Lillian, the other wing walker, had told her, "Honey, be careful. Once you get pregnant, your flying days are over."

# WHO AM I?

Point Clear, Alabama

Sookie really was in a dilemma. She knew who she believed she was for the past sixty (dear God) years. But it had all been a lie. The real question now was, if she wasn't that person . . . then who was she? And then she suddenly remembered something. She picked up the phone and dialed.

"Marvaleen, it's Sookie."

They chatted for a few minutes and then Sookie asked her, "So how are things going with your life coach, Marvaleen? Still going well?"

"Oh, yes. I see her for a private session twice a week and then once a week at her Goddess Within group. Oh, Sookie, I wish you would come with me to the group. It will just change your life. We meet every Tuesday in her backyard, in a yurt."

"A yurt?"

"Yes. She had it sent from all the way from Outer Mongolia, and I swear, Sookie, it has special powers. I feel it the minute we enter. We all enter the yurt completely naked in order to free ourselves of the superficial trappings of Western culture, then we drum and chant to awaken the female goddess within. And after just a few sessions, it's raised my consciousness to a higher level."

"I see. Well, let me think about it. What I was really wondering was . . . do you still journal?"

"Of course. It's a lifetime journey. Have you started, yet?"

"Not yet. But you said it really helped you find out who you were."

"Oh, it did, Sookie. You've just *got* to journal! First of all, Edna Yorba Zorbra says that all females have been raised in an oppressive society, and so our self-esteem is low, and so we start by doing an Appreciation Journal and build from there, then we go on to our Rage Journal. You can't get to primal scream until you do."

"I see."

"And it really works. At first, all my rage was at Ralph, and then it moved on to things I didn't know I was mad about—personally and globally—and after you release all your rage, you can begin to lift into a yin state of being. But, Sookie, I wish you would come to group or, at least, yoga."

"Well, let me see how the journaling goes first. How do you start?"

"Well, you start every morning making a list of ten things you like about yourself."

"Oh . . ."

"For instance, like . . . 'I like my breasts' or 'I like my feet'—things like that."

Later that afternoon, Marvaleen had printed out instructions and dropped them by for Sookie with a note.

Sookie,

I am thrilled you are embarking on this magical journey to your interior and honored to be your guide to self-realization and mindfulness. First, it is imperative that you create a private Sacred Space and set up an altar with a photo of yourself as a child, a candle, or anything else that speaks to you. I have a picture of the Dalai Lama and Oprah Winfrey. As a beginner, I would start with this simple self-esteem and appreciation journal. It helps open your chakras for more intensive work later. Each morning, write ten things you like about yourself and five things you would like to change. And, Sookie, be kind to your inner child. Remember, she needs reassurance from the adult you. Tell her you love her and that everything will be all right. Edna Yorba Zorbra says we must learn to parent ourselves as we trudge the road to Happy Destiny.

Blessings and White Light,

M

P.S. Just so you know, Edna Yorba Zorbra is doing a chant and meditation study this Thursday night, including a vegetarian potluck. Would you like to come? Let me know.

The next morning, Sookie went about creating her Sacred Space. She decided to set up her altar out in the greenhouse. She found a school picture of herself from the third grade and a candle and headed out with her journal in hand. She lit her candle and placed her photograph on the shelf. Lord, she really had looked like Little Orphan Annie. How pitiful. And then she sat down in her big rocking chair, opened her journal, and started to write.

Ten Things I Like About Myself

1. My husband
2. My children
3. My house

She had never even thought about body parts, one way or another, except her hair, and she had never liked her hair, but she needed seven more things. Earle always said she had pretty skin, but she had always hated her freckles. An hour later, she still had only three things. This wasn't going well at all.

Maybe she should just skip this and start with five things she hated. Aha—she had one.

1. Blue jays

Well, no . . . she really didn't hate them. She was just mad at them at the moment. And they couldn't help being how they were. And she couldn't be mad at nature, could she? Oh, Lord.

Two hours later, her candle had gone out, and Sookie was still sitting out in the greenhouse. It was clear the "journaling" wasn't working. As hard as she tried, she had not been able to get past number three on her "Ten Things I Like About Myself" list. Maybe tomorrow, she would try and reread some of the codependent books Marvaleen had given her.

A few years ago, before she had found the life coach, Marvaleen had been attending a twelve-step program for codependents and had dropped some books by. Sookie had read them and for a time she'd really tried to be a little more assertive where her mother was concerned, but it was hard to make any progress. Lenore was just so darned overpowering. And no matter what was going on, she always had to be the center of attention.

Every Mother's Day was a command performance, and it was all about Lenore. Never mind that Sookie was a mother herself and had four children. Lenore said, "Sookie, you may be a mother now, but remember, I was a mother first!"

God, when she thought about all those years she'd been sure to buy her a Mother's Day corsage and made sure all the kids had presents for her and had them get all dressed up, because they had to look just perfect for Grandmother, and they always had to go to the big Mother's Day buffet at the hotel, because it was where all Lenore's friends went, and she wanted to show off her grandchildren. As usual, Sookie had just been another person at the table while Lenore had held court.

On Lenore's birthday, Sookie always had to plan a huge celebration somewhere and make sure she received lots of presents. Even on Sookie's birthday, Lenore had hogged the spotlight, and they all had to hear about how she had been in labor with Sookie for over forty-eight hours and how Sookie had been such a large baby. But that was Lenore: the bride at every wedding, the corpse at every funeral.

Maybe the fact that Lenore hadn't had a mother herself was one of the reasons she had such poor parenting skills. Or maybe, as Buck said, she was as crazy as a loon. But whatever the problem was, Sookie was convinced that a lifetime with Lenore had wrecked her nervous system. Thank God, Earle had built her the greenhouse, where she could go out and sit and be quiet for a couple of hours.

Whenever she had complained to Buck about something Lenore

had done, he would say, “Oh, Sis, don’t let her bother you. Just ignore her like I do.” But Sookie couldn’t just ignore her. She was far too close to ignore. Even now, she could hear Lenore sitting out on her pier and talking. No surprise. If the wind was right, people in Mobile could probably hear her all the way across the bay.

It wasn’t fair. Her real mother was probably some nice, quiet, little Polish woman.

# A STAR IS BORN

For the next few years, Billy and Fritzi performed almost every weekend all through the Midwest and did a few shows as far away as Canada. And because of Billy, Fritzi had met a lot of the great old-time barnstormers. She even took a plane ride with the most famous of all, Clyde "Upside Down" Pangborn, who taught her how to improve her spins and loops and how to pull out of a stall.

Sure, it was dangerous, and as she found out, flying with the circus was a hard-living, hard-drinking life. But it was also fun and exciting, and as Fritzi always said, "A hell of a lot better than my old job working at the pickle factory."

On most Monday mornings, after doing their show on the weekend, Billy was usually too hungover to fly, so Fritzi would have to fly by herself to the next town where they were performing and drop the flyers advertising their upcoming show. But she didn't mind. There was something thrilling about being up in the air all alone, just her and the plane, flying with the wind in her face. Sometimes, when she didn't get back until after dark, and it was just her and the stars, she felt like she could stay up there forever. She loved flying in and out of the silver clouds and seeing the lights of the little towns below. Of course, she missed her family something awful, but other than that, life was good and getting better all the time. After only a short while, she was already a headliner.

*Come See*
THE BILLY BEVINS FLYING CIRCUS

*Featuring*
FRITZI
*The Most Famous Female in the Air Today*

*Performing*
*Death-Defying Aerial Stunts*
*&*
THRILLS AND CHILLS!

*See Famed Aviator Billy Bevins & Fritzi, the Female Daredevil*
*Perform Spectacular Stunts & Flying Demonstrations*
*&*
BE AMAZED!

*This Saturday at Legion Field*
*Starting at 2 p.m.*
*Fun for the Whole Family*

*Rides: $5.00 for 10 minutes*

And they were spectacular stunts. Fritzi, dressed in her purple leather flying outfit with her long white scarf, tall boots, and helmet, would crawl out on the wings and do her stunts and dance for a while. Then, at a certain point, Billy, who was wearing a parachute, would level the plane and crawl out of the cockpit onto the other wing and walk to the end and jump off. People on the ground would scream in terror. "Oh, no! He's left the girl up there all alone! She'll be killed!" In the meantime, Fritzi would crawl back into the cockpit and take over the controls. And then, to the audience's surprise, she would perform rolls, loops, and tumbling spins almost all the way down, then, at the very last second, pull up and do the same thing again, leaving the audience screaming and breathless, thinking she would crash at any minute while Billy slowly floated to the ground in his parachute.

The crossover in the air looked dangerous to the crowd, but Billy, who left nothing to chance, had timed it to the last second.

When Fritzi would finally come in for a landing, her plane would be mobbed with fans. She liked that, and so did Billy. While Fritzi was still out on the field, signing autographs and posing for pictures and taking people up for ten-minute rides at five dollars a pop, Billy would be over at the airport bar, having drinks and "counting the gate." Some weekends, Fritzi's cut was almost seventy-five dollars.

Fritzi was glad she could send a little money home to help out. Momma still worried about her night and day, but Poppa said, "She's happy, Linka."

"Yes, she's happy she's showing off," Momma would say with a sigh. "But at least she's showing off for money."

## POINT CLEAR, ALABAMA

SOOKIE WAS WORRIED ABOUT TELLING THE CHILDREN AND WAS TRYING to figure out the best way to do it. What could she do to soften the blow? She picked up her new cookbook, *Polish Cuisine*. Maybe she would have them all over for dinner and fix nothing but traditional Polish dishes, and if they liked it, she could say something like, "Well, I'm glad, because as it turns out, you all have Polish DNA." She read the recipes to see what she could do, but everything had too many beets and too much sauerkraut.

She knew her kids, and they would definitely not like golonka, pork knuckles cooked with vegetables, or zrazy, stuffed slices of beef and tripe. Besides, she didn't know what tripe was. She tried her best to find something fun she could make, but it was no use. She finally just gave up trying when she came to something called czernina, duck blood soup. Oh, dear. This was not going to work at all. She would just have to find another way. She supposed that when she did tell the children, she should probably start with Dee Dee first. And that was going to be very hard.

Lenore had filled Dee Dee's head with the Simmons family history and all that silly First Families of Virginia nonsense, and at times, Dee Dee could be a little snobbish. When Dee Dee was thirteen, Sookie overheard her saying to a new little girl in the neighborhood, "My grandmother is a sixth-generation Simmons from England. Who are your people?" She had made Dee Dee immediately apologize to the little girl. She also asked Lenore to please stop telling Dee Dee that she was better than everyone else. But, as usual, Lenore was absolutely no help. "Well, Sookie," she said. "Do you want me to lie to the child? Breeding counts in animals. Why not in people as well?"

As the days went by, Sookie started feeling a little steadier than she had. And, thankfully, after that one close call when she had driven by the cemetery, she had been able to successfully avoid seeing her mother. Then one morning she ran downtown for just a second to pick up the dry-cleaning and ran smack into her.

Sookie managed a pleasant hello, but Lenore just stared at her and said not, "How are you?" or "Are you feeling any better?" but "Good Lord, Sookie, your skin looks terrible. How long has it been since you've had a facial?" It was all Sookie could do not to strangle her right in front of the hardware store. As she walked away, her heart was pounding, and her hands felt all sweaty. It was at that moment she realized she must be more upset than she knew.

When she got home she called Dena.

"Sookie! I'm so glad you called. How are you, honey?"

"Terrible."

"Oh, no. Are you having problems?"

"Well, if you consider wanting to murder someone in broad daylight, only a half block from the police station, problematic, then yes."

"Oh, honey, that doesn't sound like you."

"No, it doesn't. I could be right in the middle of a nervous breakdown and not even know it."

"Are you concerned?"

"Yes, I'm concerned. Considering the fact that I don't know about my real genetic makeup, who knows what I might be capable of doing? I could have relatives sitting in jail right now. I could be a danger to myself and others."

"Oh, Sookie, I'm sure that's not true."

"Really?"

"No, of course not. I'm sure that you come from a lovely, sweet family. You wouldn't be you if you hadn't."

After they hung up, Sookie hoped what Dena had said was true. She had done a little research on the subject and she knew that there were twenty-three chromosomes from each parent. She may never know about the unknown father, but she supposed for the kids' sake, for health reasons alone, she should try and find out a little something about her mother's side of the family—and for her sake as well. If by any slight chance she did have homicidal tendencies, she needed to know now, rather than later.

AFTER A FEW HOURS, Sookie finally got up her nerve and called information and got the number for the Pulaski, Wisconsin, Chamber of Commerce. She grabbed a small paper bag just in case she started to hyperventilate. When she dialed area code 920 and the number, a woman with a very blunt and definite accent that was alien to Sookie's ears answered and said, "This is Marian. Can I help you?"

"Oh . . . hello. You don't know me, but I'm calling to inquire about a family there named Jurdabralinski?"

"Who?"

She spelled the name for her. "J-U-R-D-A-B-R-A-L-I-N-S-K-I."

"Oh, the Jurdabralinskis. The Gas Station Family."

"Pardon me?"

"They used to run the gas station in town."

"Oh, I see. . . . Well, do you happen to know if the family was healthy?"

"Healthy?"

"Yes. Any history of diabetes, heart problems, any mental issues, cancer, or alcoholism?"

"Oh, geez. I never heard anything about that. My mom went to school with a couple of the Jurdabralinski gals, and as I recall, there were four girls and a boy, and two of the girls were twins."

"Twins? Really? Oh for heaven's sake."

"Oh, yeah. And one of the girls became a nun. And they were all healthy as far as I know."

"Do you know if any of them are still around?"

"Oh, let's see. . . . I think Tula Tanawaski was a Jurdabralinski before she married Norbert, but they moved to Madison. Are you a relative?"

"Oh, no. I'm just a college student doing some research on old Polish families."

"Well, we've sure got a lot of them in Pulaski. Now, I can find out more about the Jurdabralinskis for you, where they are and so forth, but it'll take a few days. We're awful busy here this week. We've got the Pulaski Polka Days going on, and we're up to our ears in activities, with the parade and all."

"Oh, well, I won't keep you, then. I'll call back next week."

"Give me your name, hon."

"My name?" Sookie panicked. "Oh, it's Alice. Alice Finch."

"Well, okay, Alice. I'll talk to ya next week, then."

She hated to lie to the woman, and she was sure she didn't sound like a college student, but she had to protect her real mother and Lenore as well. As she was quickly finding out, one deception begets a hundred others. At least she had gotten a little information. The woman said the Jurdabralinskis were healthy as far as she knew. That was all the information she really needed. Her hands were shaking as it was. What if her mother was the one who became a nun? Then she really wouldn't want me showing up. And if she found out that her child had not been raised Catholic, she wouldn't like that, either. She had enough information. Too much really. She was afraid to call back. Who knows what else she might find out?

Oh, dear. Dena was right. She really did need professional help.

# HELP

Point Clear, Alabama

"Hello, Dr. Shapiro?"

"Yes?"

"You don't know me, but I was wondering. I just live ten minutes from your office. Do you ever make house calls?"

"Oh, are you housebound?" he asked with some concern.

"Yes . . . well, sort of. I have a problem that, for many reasons, needs to remain anonymous."

"I understand, but I assure you that anything we discuss in session is confidential. Would you like to set up an appointment?"

"I would, but I can't. I know it's probably hard for you to understand, but my problem has to do with my mother. And if anybody saw me going in or coming out of your office, she would hear about it. She just knows everybody."

"I see. And are you still living at home with your parents?"

"Oh, no. I'm a fifty . . . uh . . . sixty-year-old woman with a husband and four grown children."

"I'm sorry. You sounded younger. Well, could you go into a little more detail?"

"This phone call isn't being recorded, is it?"

"No."

"Well, I've just had a terrible shock. I just found out I could be the daughter of a Polish nun from Wisconsin and that I am not who I thought I was at all. Dena, my friend, said I need professional help. She's married to a psychiatrist. Then today, when I wanted to strangle my mother, I realized she was right. Dena had already suggested that I call you, but I didn't. But now I'm worried that I could be having a nervous breakdown. I might need medication, but I'm not sure. Can you prescribe something over the phone?"

"No, I would need to see you first."

"Oh . . . darn."

"But I guess I could see you at your house, if you'd like."

"You could?"

"Yes."

"Wonderful. When?"

"Just a second . . . uh . . . I have an hour open at four o'clock tomorrow afternoon. Would that work?"

"Absolutely. Let me give you my address. It's . . . oh . . . you know, Dr. Shapiro, on second thought, that might not be a good idea. My mother lives just one house down from me, and she could just pop in any minute. And she never knocks. I know it's a lot to ask, but could we possibly meet somewhere else?"

"All right. If that would make you more comfortable. Where?"

"Uh, let's see—oh I know. How about the Waffle House on Highway 98?"

"Fine. And could you give me your name?"

There was a pause. "I'd really rather not . . . if you don't mind. I would prefer it not get around that I was seeing a psychiatrist."

"Okay, then. But how will I recognize you?"

"Oh, dear. Well, I'll tell you what. I'll be wearing a hat—and pink sneakers with pom-poms. Is that all right?"

"Okay."

"Oh, and how much will it be?"

"Well, let's just meet first and see where we need to go from there."

After Dr. Shapiro hung up, he was a little apprehensive. He had never met a patient outside of his office before and certainly never at a Waffle House, but the poor lady on the phone was either a paranoid schizophrenic or one of the craziest people he had ever talked to. Either way, she obviously needed help.

## PULASKI, WISCONSIN

MAY 1941

WINK HAD GRADUATED FROM HIGH SCHOOL AND WAS NOW WORKING full-time at the filling station with his cousin Florian. He knew his parents needed him at home. His father was slowing down a bit and was not as strong as he used to be. Years of sleeping on a cot in the back of the filling station, being up and down all night, and going out in the freezing cold had started to take its toll. But secretly, Wink, who had his pilot's license, was chomping at the bit to get into the fight overseas. A few of his friends had snuck into Canada and joined the RAF and had been sent to England and were already in the thick of the fighting. But he had promised his girlfriend, Angie, who was two years younger, that he would take her to the senior prom, and at this point, anything Angie wanted, she got, and he didn't want to go off and leave her still single in a town full of bohunks like himself. He was not sure what to do, so he called Fritzi and asked her what she thought. She said, "Well, Wink-a-Dink, the old ball-and-chain bit's not for me, but if that's what you want, you've got yourself a great gal. You know I've always liked Angie, so I say full speed ahead."

"Okay! Thanks, Fritzi."

"Hey, do you have enough to buy a ring?"

"Oh . . . I forgot about that."

"Well, don't worry. I happen to be a little flush right now. Had some luck at a poker game up in Des Moines last week, so I'll send you a little when she says yes—and she will."

"Oh, thanks, Fritzi. But I don't know. I may have waited too long. She's been getting pretty popular lately."

"Well, get off the phone, knucklehead, and get over there."

WINK NEEDN'T HAVE WORRIED. Angie Broukowski had been madly in love with him since she was in the eighth grade. To her, Wink was the most handsome, most wonderful, sweetest boy in the world. She had only one goal in life: to become Mrs. Wencent Jurdabralinski, so of course she said yes, and they set a date in June. Between both families, there were to be more than two hundred relatives at the actual wedding, and the number of people coming to the reception afterward was so large that it had to be held at Zeilinski's Ballroom outside of town.

FRITZI CAME HOME A few days before the ceremony to help out with the festivities, and everybody in town was glad to see her. Since she'd started flying with the Billy Bevins Flying Circus, she'd had several write-ups in the local paper, and everybody was so proud of her. They felt like she was their very own Polish movie star. Her younger sisters, who had never been out of Pulaski and had grown up wearing mostly handmade dresses that Momma made, could hardly believe they had such a glamorous sister who had actually been to Chicago.

They sat in her room and stared at her in awe as she put on clothes that they had seen only in magazines. Fritzi even wore a tiny gold ankle bracelet, the height of sophistication, they thought, and just when they thought they had seen it all, the little white frilly cocktail hat she pulled out of a box was so elegant and saucy, they all screamed.

The next morning, Wink came into the kitchen and asked where Fritzi was, and Momma said, "Oh, you know your sister. She and your dad are already out walking around town, big-shotting it." Momma said it like she didn't approve, but she was really glad about it. She hadn't seen Poppa this happy in a long time.

Fritzi had tried to get Billy to come home for the wedding with her, but he'd refused. He said he was allergic to anything that involved church or him having to wear a tie.

However, on the day of the wedding, Fritzi figured that he either felt bad because he hadn't come or else he was drunk or both, because as the bride and groom came out of the church, Billy was flying around up above and had written inside a big heart "Congratulations, Wink and Angie," and then flew on back to Grand Rapids. As mad as she was at him, Fritzi had to laugh at the fool. He must have hijacked the plane right off the field, because he wasn't working that weekend. But that was Billy.

## THE WAFFLE HOUSE

Dr. Shapiro, a nice-looking young man in glasses, was there a few minutes early and now wondered if the lady would even show up. But, suddenly, a woman wearing pink tennis shoes with pom-poms, large white plastic sunglasses in the shape of two hearts, and a man's fishing hat with lures all over it appeared at the plate glass window and was peering in. She then came in the door and quickly looked around the room, spotted him, hurried back to the booth, and said, "Dr. Shapiro?"

"Yes."

"It's me. Your patient."

He had the urge to say, "I never would have guessed," but his wife said people in the South didn't like his New York humor, so he said, "Please sit down."

She took her seat and slumped way down in the booth. The minute she did so, a large waitress in a pink uniform came over and said cheerfully, "Oh, hi, Mrs. Poole, I haven't seen you in here in a long time."

"Well, so much for anonymity," thought Sookie. "Oh, hello, Jewel," she said.

Jewel looked at Dr. Shapiro and asked Sookie, "Is this your cute son, the one your mother's always talking about?"

"No . . . just a friend."

"Oh. Well, what y'all gonna have today?"

"Just coffee, please. Decaf," said Sookie.

Dr. Shapiro added, "Make that two."

After Jewel walked away, Sookie said, "First of all, thank you so much for meeting me."

"Of course. How can I help you? You say you have a problem?"

"Yes, I do. And it's a very long story. Well, let me start at the beginning. A few weeks ago, I was feeding my birds. I have a terrible blue jay problem. I had thought I would try just putting sunflower seeds in the backyard and just the plain Pretty Boy small-bird seed in the front. . . ."

Thirty minutes and three cups of coffee later, when she finally got around to telling him just who her mother was, he suddenly understood. No wonder this lady was a nervous wreck. He'd met the mother. Who wouldn't be?

At eight A.M. the first morning after Dr. Shapiro and his wife had moved into their new house, they were awakened by what he thought sounded like a band of Hare Krishnas jingling up the front stairs. When he opened the door, he was greeted by a large, imposing-looking woman in a cape, holding a huge basket with a ribbon on it, who announced in a loud voice, "Good morning. I am Lenore Simmons Krackenberry, president of the Point Clear Welcome Wagon Committee, and on behalf of the entire committee, I want to say . . ." and then she sang at the top of her voice to the tune of "Shuffle Off to Buffalo," "Welcome! Welcome! Welcome! May we help ya, help ya, help ya! With your brand-new move!" Then she shoved the basket at him and said, "The rest of the girls will be along in a minute, but I wanted to get here first." And with that, she stormed right past him and into the house, calling out, "Oh, Mrs. Shapirooo . . . put the coffee on. You've got company!" He had spent only one hour with her, but it seemed obvious that the mother was the one who needed medication, not this poor woman. But he let Sookie continue to talk, because she seemed to be in such distress.

"So as I told Dena, I just feel all wicky-wacky. One minute, I'm mad at my mother and then I feel guilty and then I get mad at her all over again. So do you think I'm having a nervous breakdown?"

"I think under the circumstances, anger and confusion are perfectly natural."

"You do? You think it's *natural* to want to strangle your mother?"

"Under certain circumstances, yes. You feel betrayed and hurt and, naturally, you want to lash out."

"That's right. Yes, I do."

"Nobody likes to be lied to."

"No, they don't, do they? Oh, I feel so much better already. Dr. Shapiro, you're a professional, so you would know if someone was having a breakdown, wouldn't you?"

"Yes."

"So in your opinion, I'm not getting ready to flip out or anything?"

"I think it's highly unlikely."

Sookie sighed a huge sigh of relief. "Well, I just can't thank you enough. And this wasn't nearly as scary as I thought it would be. I'm sure you've heard this before, but you're such a good listener."

"Well, thank you."

"And you must think I'm very rude. Here I am going on and on about my problems, and I haven't asked you a thing about yourself."

"That's perfectly fine, Mrs. Poole. I'm here to listen to you."

"Oh, before I forget, how much do I owe you for this? And do you mind if I pay you in cash? I don't want the people at the bank to know that I had to see a psychiatrist. They might not say anything, but you never know. I've enjoyed this so much, could we do it again? Same time next week, same booth?"

To his surprise, Dr. Shapiro found himself agreeing.

After Dr. Shapiro got back to his office, he jotted down a few notes.

*New patient: Mild situational anxiety and very nice lady.*
*Mother of patient: Narcissist with mild to severe illusions of grandeur.*

# WAR

Pulaski, Wisconsin
Sunday, December 7, 1941

Before the Sunday mass started, Father Sobieski had gone to the side door of the vestry and motioned for Stanislaw Jurdabralinski, who always sat in the first row, to come around to the back of the church. His altar boy had not shown up, and he needed him to fill in. It was kind of funny to see the five-foot-nine-inch priest enter the altar with the six-foot-four Stanislaw, wearing a black-and-white altar boy vestment that, on him, looked more like a blouse, but the mass came off without a hitch. After mass, the Jurdabralinskis walked home together, except for the youngest, Sophie, who always stayed and helped the nuns wash and iron the vestments for the next week's service.

Later that day, Gertrude and Tula were over at the Rainbow Skating Rink, practicing their routine for the big skating contest that was coming up, when Mrs. Wanda Glinski, the organist, abruptly stopped playing, right in the middle of "Blue Skies," and everyone wondered what had happened. A few seconds later, an announcement was made over the loudspeaker that the Japanese had just attacked Pearl Harbor and that the rink was closing. As stunned skaters slowly started heading off the floor, Mrs. Glinski began playing "God Bless America."

A few blocks away at the Pulaski theater, people were watching *How Green Was My Valley,* starring Maureen O'Hara and Walter Pidgeon. Wink's wife, Angie, and a girlfriend were seeing it for the second time, when the screen began to slowly fade, and the house lights came on. The theater manager walked out on the stage and said, "Ladies and gentlemen, we just got word that the Japanese have attacked Pearl Harbor, and all servicemen are to report to their bases immediately." As confused people got up out of their seats, gathering their things and silently beginning to file out down the aisles, a picture of the American flag suddenly appeared on the screen.

Most of them had no idea where Pearl Harbor was or why it had anything to do with them, but those few who did were somber. One man said, "Well, we're all in it now."

Over at the church, one of the nuns came in and told Sophie that she was to go home to her family right away, but did not tell her why. When Sophie got to the house, Momma and the other girls had all gathered in the kitchen, and the minute she saw her, Momma grabbed her and held her close. Poppa was sitting at the table with his ear to the radio and kept shaking his head in disbelief as he listened to the same report repeated over and over. After a moment, he looked up at his wife with a stricken expression on his face. "Oh, Linka, we can't lose America. If we lose America . . ." Then his voice cracked and the big strong man, who had always been their tower of strength, put his head down on the table and sobbed. All the girls quickly gathered around their father and hugged him, while his wife stood by, helpless and unable to do anything. She knew he was right. If America was lost, then there was no hope—not only for them, but also for the world.

FRITZI AND BILLY HAD just done an air show outside of Akron, Ohio, on Saturday, and as usual on Sunday morning, Billy stayed in bed with a hangover. Fritzi was up and already downstairs in the hotel coffee shop when she heard the news from a bellboy who ran in the door and yelled, "The Japs just bombed Pearl Harbor! It looks like war!" and ran back out, on his way to tell everyone in the hotel and up and down the street.

When Fritzi got back upstairs with his coffee, Billy was wide awake and sitting up. She sat down on the bed and handed the coffee to him. "Honey, have you heard?"

He nodded. "Yeah, some kid just ran down the hall, so I guess it's true, then?"

Fritzi said, "Yeah, it seems to be."

He took a few more sips of his coffee, then looked at her and said, "Well, that's it for me." He got up, showered and shaved, put his clothes on, and headed out to find the nearest recruiting office. Fritzi tried to call her family back home, but all the circuits were busy.

By the time Billy got downtown, he saw that a line had already formed, and the office had not yet opened, but one of the guys said someone was on the way. Billy was older than most in line, but he was more than willing to go. In fact, he couldn't wait. Like all the other guys that day, he was mad. How dare those bastards attack America. Just who the hell did they think they were fooling with?

That Sunday, as the news spread across the country, people who hadn't thought much about it suddenly felt things they hadn't just a day before. At the big hockey game at Madison Square Garden, after the announcement was made and as all the men in uniform stood up and started filing out of the stadium, headed back to their bases, everyone suddenly stood and gave them an ovation that didn't stop until the last man had left the stadium.

From that day forward, the National Anthem was not just something Americans had to get through before a game started. Now hats came off, hands were held over hearts, and the cheer at the end was heartfelt. They had just gone through one war and a Depression, and nobody wanted war, but now that it was here, there was nothing more to do, except get in there and win it as fast as possible.

Sunday night, Wink came over to the house with a teary-eyed Angie beside him. They sat in the living room with Momma and Poppa, and Wink, just a year out of high school and for the first time looking like a grown man, said, "Poppa, I hate to leave you to run the station, but you know I'm going to be drafted sooner or later, and if I sign up now, I have a shot at getting into the Army Air Corps."

Momma said, "But, Wink, Angie is going to have a baby."

Angie looked at Momma. "I tried to talk him out of it, but he won't listen to me."

Poppa looked at Wink. "You do what you think is right, son. Don't worry about the station. We'll get by."

"Thanks, Poppa, and listen, while I'm gone, can Angie move into my old room upstairs and stay with you guys until I get back?"

"Of course," said Momma. "We would love to have her."

"I can help with the cooking," said Angie. "I just don't want to move back home. I think I won't miss him so much if I'm here."

AT SIX A.M. THE next morning, Wink, along with almost every boy in his senior class, stood outside the drugstore in the snow, waiting to be picked up by the school buses that were driving them to Green Bay to sign up.

Billy took his army physical in Grand Rapids and would have been 4F because of his liver, but they needed all the experienced pilots they could get and as fast as they could get them, so he and his bad liver were ordered to report to Pensacola, Florida, on December 15. In the next few days, he officially disbanded the Flying Circus and, luckily, was able to sell the planes to a flying school.

On the afternoon of December 12, Fritzi saw him off at the train station, and when he stepped up on the train, he said, "I don't know when I'll see you again, pal, so take care of yourself, and write me a letter every once in a while, okay?"

"I will."

As the train started pulling out, he shouted over the noise of the engine, "Hey, who's your best friend?"

"You are!" she yelled.

He gave her a thumbs-up, and that was the last glimpse she had of him. When she left the train station, the streets were packed, and she couldn't get a cab, so she had to walk back to the hotel in the snow. As she walked, she noticed a lot of the store windows had already been decorated for Christmas, and some had been left only half done.

She and Billy had been together for a long time but had made no commitments. She had realized that Billy was not the marrying kind, and evidently, neither was she. But still, she was already feeling a little lost without him. When she got back up to the hotel room, she saw the envelope on the dresser he had left. Inside was a hundred-dollar bill and a note.

Merry Christmas, Squirt. Buy yourself a new hat.

Billy

Fritzi sat on the bed, wondering what she was going to do now. She didn't want to just hang around, waiting and doing nothing. And damn it to hell, it wasn't fair. She could fly as well as most of the guys she knew. She had tried to enlist in the army and showed her pilot's license to the man at the recruiting office, but he informed her that neither the Army Air Corps nor any of the armed services would take female fliers.

"Why not?" she asked. "The plane doesn't know if it's a man or a woman flying it."

"Regulations," he said. "Now, if you could just step aside and let me get on with my business. We're at war, little lady, and war's no place for women."

One guy standing behind her piped up. "I've got a place for you, honey, anytime," as the other guys laughed.

Fritzi picked up her license and stuck it back in her purse and said, "Well, okay, if that's how you feel. It's your loss." As she walked out, she said, "So long, knuckleheads, see you in the funny papers." But she was mad and hurt, and when she got back to her room, she sat down and cried her eyes out.

She knew from the magazines that England and Russia were using female pilots to ferry planes, but here, it was a no-go. So that afternoon, she packed up her purple leather flying suit and the rest of her clothes and went home to Pulaski, just in time to say good-bye to Wink. He had been accepted into the Army Air Corps and was being sent to Scott Field in Illinois for training.

Now she had even more reasons to hate the Japs. They had knocked her out of a swell career, Billy and Wink were gone, and she was stuck on the ground for the duration. It was quite a comedown. But flying and doing stunts was all she knew how to do, so after a while, she signed up for the job on the canning line, back at the pickle factory.

# LUNCH WITH LENORE

## Point Clear, Alabama

It was going to be a very hard day. In the past, Sookie and Lenore had a standing lunch date every Wednesday, and Sookie really couldn't put it off any longer without causing even more trouble. Lenore had already left a picture of herself in Sookie's mailbox with a note attached. "In case you have forgotten, this is your mother. Where are you?!"

Sookie sighed and looked at the clock and dialed the phone. After a moment, her mother picked up. "Hello, this is Lenore. To whom do I have the pleasure of speaking, please?"

"It's me, Mother."

"Oh . . . hello, you."

"How was your water therapy?"

"Very wet. Where are you?"

"I'm at home, why?"

"I thought maybe you had moved to China. Are we finally going to lunch today? Or have you called to tell me you have suddenly come down with some other mysterious disease?"

"No, Mother, we are going to lunch. Where do you want to go?"

"Oh, I don't care. You pick."

"Well, how about the Fairhope Inn?"

"No, I'm tired of that."

"Okay. The Bay Café?"

"No, let's go to the Colony. I'm in the mood for crab cakes."

"Fine. I'll pick you up."

When Sookie hung up, she noticed her stomach was hurting. Just the tone of Lenore's voice was already irking her last nerve.

LENORE SWEPT INTO THE restaurant and waved at everybody she knew. And as usual, if there was someone there she didn't know, she went over and introduced herself. As head of the Welcome Wagon Committee, she was sure they wanted to meet her.

When she sat back down, she said, "That cute couple over in the corner are visiting all the way from Canada, can you imagine? Anyhow, she was very nice and said she loved the color of my hair, and I said, 'Well, if one must go gray, it's just as easy to go silver.' I gave her Jo Ellen's number. Did you order my crab cakes?"

"Yes."

Lenore waved at the couple again and turned back to Sookie. "She really could use a new rinse. But look at you, Sookie. You're fifty-nine years old, and you don't have a gray hair on your head. Count yourself lucky, my girl. When I was your age, I was already completely white, but I think it's an English trait. Queen Elizabeth went gray early as well."

"So you said."

"As you know, I used to be a strawberry blonde."

"Yes, Mother, you have told me that almost every day of my life."

"Well, it's true. I was known far and wide for being the only strawberry blonde in south Alabama. At the Senior Military Ball, when they played, 'Casey Would Waltz with a Strawberry Blonde and the Band Played On,' everyone in the room stopped and stared at us. Your father was a wonderful dancer. We both were, and they played it over and over again. And all the other boys would cut in, and I remember one said, 'Lenore, dancing with you is like dancing with a feather.' But, then, I was always light on my feet." She looked over at Sookie and sighed. "Oh, Sookie, I wish you just hadn't given up on your dancing lessons."

"I didn't *just* give up on them, Mother. If you remember, Miss Wheasly told me it would be best for the class if I pursued other interests—something I had a natural talent for."

Lenore made a face and looked away. "Mrs. Bushnell's daughter, Gage, is a prima ballerina in New York. That could have been you, Sookie."

"When every time I went up on a point, I fell over? I don't think so, Mother."

"I don't think you tried, that's all."

Sookie looked at her. "What?"

"Well, I'm very sorry, but it wasn't me that gave up a promising career to marry Earle Poole, Jr."

"Mother, what promising career? As what?"

"Oh, Sookie, you could have been anything in the world if you had wanted to. You had a real chance to be something, but no. You threw it all away to marry Earle Poole, Jr. I didn't have the opportunity like you did. When I was at Judson, I excelled in dramatics. Dr. Howell said that I could have been a professional actress if I had wanted to, and he taught Tallulah Bankhead, so I guess he knew a talented actress when he saw one. Of course, Tallulah's daddy let her do what she wanted, but Daddy wouldn't let me go on the stage. And it's a shame, really, because I always wondered what would have happened if I had. There's no telling what I could have done if I had been allowed to follow my natural bent. I might have gone straight from the stage to the movies, but I married your father and settled for being just a housewife."

"Mother, you were never just a housewife."

"Well, I was so. I cooked and cleaned and raised two children, and if that wasn't me, then who was it?"

"Mother, you never cooked, and you never cleaned."

"Well, I oversaw everything, and anyhow, that's not the point. That's why I pushed you to be something. But you just never had any ambition, and I don't understand it. You are descended from a long line of leaders. Your great-grandmother single-handedly saved the family home from the Yankees, and you are just content to sit around all day and fiddle with those birds. You will be sixty years old soon, and what have you done? If I told you once, I have told you a hundred times. You need to think about your duty as a Simmons, and at least try to accomplish something to be proud of before it's too late."

Sookie had heard this same speech a hundred times, but today was obviously one time too many. "Mother, just stop it. All that Simmons stuff is just a bunch of baloney, and you know it!" Sookie was stunned at her own outburst.

Lenore was shocked as well and just looked at her for what seemed to be a long time and then said, "I don't know what you mean, Sookie. It's obvious that you are just not yourself today, and so I am going home." Lenore stood up, walked out, and got into the car and waited.

Sookie, still a little shaken, paid the bill and went out, and drove her mother home in silence. When they arrived at her house, Lenore got out of the car and said, "Call me if and when you regain your senses."

Sookie felt terrible about snapping at her mother like that and immediately called Dr. Shapiro, and he met her for an emergency meeting. But he did not find her behavior alarming at all. "It's to be expected," he said.

Sookie understood that that kind of behavior might be expected somewhere else, but in Point Clear, Alabama, upset or not, she should never have raised her voice in public. It just wasn't ladylike, and besides, she was married to a dentist, and a certain amount of decorum was expected.

# CHRISTMAS

Pulaski, Wisconsin
1941

Momma had tried. She still baked the oplatki—Polish Christmas wafers—as usual, but it was a bleak old Christmas in 1941. All of the songs about peace on earth and goodwill toward men that played in between the grim news of the war rang a little hollow that year. It seemed the whole country was preoccupied with one thing. Every large company in America was busy changing over, mobilizing, and gearing up to put all their resources toward the war effort. Everybody wanted to do something to try to help win the war and get the boys home again.

Fritzi had been home for only about a month when their old friend, bathroom inspector and nurse Dottie Frakes, came by for a visit and informed them that after today, she was taking a leave of absence from Phillips Petroleum to become an army nurse. After a big lunch, Poppa went back to work, and Momma and the other girls started to clean the kitchen. Dottie offered to help clean up, but Momma said, "No, you two just go relax."

Dottie got up and said, "All right, then, Fritzi, let's you and me go sit in the parlor and have a little catch-up chat."

As they went in, Dottie turned and pulled the wooden sliding doors shut and turned to Fritzi with a concerned look. "How long has your father had that cough?"

"Oh, quite a while, I think. He's had a bad cold. Why?"

"I didn't want to alarm your mother or the girls, but I don't like the sound of that cough."

"What do you mean?"

"I've worked in hospitals, and I know what that sound means."

"Oh . . . what?"

"He needs to see a doctor as soon as possible."

That afternoon, Fritzi tried to get her father to go see the doctor, but he said, "Oh, Fritzi, I can't leave the station for that kind of foolishness. You know how shorthanded we are now. I'm fine. I'll be better tomorrow."

She put her hands on his shoulders and pleaded with him. "Please, Poppa. Just go for me."

He laughed. "If I'm not better in a week, I'll go. I promise."

When she had first arrived home, Fritzi had noticed how thin and tired her father looked, but when she felt his shoulders now, there was nothing there but skin and bones.

She hated to do it to Poppa, but she had to tell Momma what Dottie had said and see if Momma could talk some sense into him. Before she even finished the sentence, Momma had her apron off and her hat and coat on and was headed next door to the filling station. Five minutes later, she and Poppa were downtown, sitting in Dr. Renschoske's office. Momma was an old-fashioned wife and rarely questioned her husband in any way, but not this time.

The tests came back, and the diagnosis was as Dottie had suspected: advanced tuberculosis that had to be treated right away. But when the doctor started talking to him about the different sanitariums that specialized in TB treatments, Stanislaw would have no part of it. "Just give me some medicine. I have a business to run."

"Stanislaw, you won't be alive to run anything if you don't do what I tell you. You will go home and get in bed and rest until Linka and I work out where you are going and when."

He did, and in the meantime, his nineteen-year-old nephew Florian was put in charge of running the station. Three days later, the arrangements for Stanislaw had been made at the sanitarium. The hard part was getting him there. All the trains and buses were full of servicemen trying to get to bases. So Fritzi called a flying pal of hers and Billy's in Grand Rapids, who flew over and picked up Poppa to fly him all the way down to Hot Springs, Arkansas. Poor Poppa. He had flown off with two sets of clean pajamas, a sack full of sausages, and a rosary that Sophie had slipped into his pocket. When the plane had taken off, Momma, who had never been separated from him for even one night, had stood and cried into her apron and wondered if she would ever see him again.

AND AS IF THINGS couldn't get worse, Florian soon received his draft notice, as did Poppa's mechanic. The other fellow they had just hired to fill in quit to work in Sturgeon Bay, where he could make more money, and Momma was worried to death.

A week later, after Fritzi came home from work, Momma went into her room and closed the door behind her and told her about an offer she had received from a man in Oshkosh to buy the station. Fritzi was stunned that her mother would even think about selling. "You can't do that, Momma."

"But Fritzi, what will we do when Florian and the boys leave for good? We have to close down. There will be no one left to run the station. When I think how hard Poppa worked to get this place . . . it will kill him for sure."

"You can't sell it, Momma."

"But Fritzi, the hospital costs so much. We have to. Who knows how long Poppa will have to stay away or how long the war will last. And there are no men left to hire. They will be all gone—either to the service or working at the factories. We have no choice."

Fritzi said, "Yes, we do."

"What?"

"I'll run it!"

"Oh, Fritzi, by yourself? You can't do that."

"No, not by myself. The whole family—all of us. Now that you have Angie to help cook, Gertrude, Tula, and Sophie can help."

"But, Fritzi, you can't have all girls running a filling station. Nobody would come."

When Momma said that, something suddenly clicked in Fritzi's mind, and she said, "Momma, you just wait and see."

Later, Fritzi called a meeting in the kitchen with all the girls and told them her idea. They seemed skeptical. "But we don't know how to fix a motor or anything about carburetors and things like that," said Gertrude.

"No, but I do."

Tula said, "But it's so dirty over there. I don't want to get grease all over me."

"Oh, come on, girls. We can't let Poppa down now or Wink. We've all worked at the station at one time or another, and what we don't know, we can learn. Florian isn't leaving for a couple of weeks. He can teach you what you need to know, and I can teach you the rest. I know we can do it. Whatta ya say?"

The sisters all turned to Momma. "What do you think, Momma?"

Momma said, "I think you should listen to what Fritzi says. She's the man of the house now."

THE NEXT DAY, FRITZI gave her notice at the pickle factory. That night, she rooted around in the gas station files and found Poppa's old study materials from the service station management course he had taken. She sat down and studied all night long. It didn't look too hard. All you had to do was follow instructions.

1. Welcome greetings and windshield service
2. Gasoline solicitation
3. Radiator check, oil check, battery test, tire pressure check—including spare tire—lubrication check, vacuum service offered
4. Itemized collection and friendly farewell and thanks for stopping
5. Attendants must be neat and clean at all times, fingernails, uniforms, etc.

"Oh, hell," thought Fritzi. This was going to be easy. She knew most of this stuff already.

The gals would need uniforms, so Momma took all of Wink's and

Poppa's old uniform pants and shirts and cut them down to fit the girls. Just for an extra added touch, she embroidered in red on each individual shirt the words "Hi, I'm Fritzi" or "Hi, I'm Gertrude," and so on.

Fritzi had learned a little about organizing a work team from her old Flying Circus days, so she sat down and worked out a plan. And at the end of the week, everybody had a designated assignment.

Tula would do most of the mechanical work. Gertrude, the strongest girl, would be in charge of changing tires and fixing flats. Fritzi would pump gas and check under the hood and drive the tow truck when needed. Sophie was good at math, so she would work as the cashier. Inside the station, they sold candy, potato chips, cold drinks, hot coffee, and Momma's sausages and homemade sandwiches and pastries. They also sold trinkets, key chains, lighters, glass ashtrays, and toys and gave away free maps and free postcards.

In three weeks' time, Fritzi and her sisters, wearing brand-new uniforms with hats and cute little black bow ties, were ready to start. When word got out that four good-looking sisters were now running a filling station, business suddenly started to pick up. Doing the air shows with Billy, Fritzi had learned a lot about advertising, and pretty soon, ads started appearing in local newspapers that featured a photo of the four smiling girls standing in front of the station with a caption above it that said:

WHEN IN PULASKI, STOP AT WINK'S PHILLIPS 66
THE ALL-GIRL FILLING STATION

They had signs put up along the highway that, underneath their logo, said:

*Is your car ailing? Let us kiss it and make it better.*
*Car dirty? Let us houseclean your car.*
*The prettiest mechanics in the state of Wisconsin.*
*Let us put the spark back in your plugs.*

*Fresh coffee, sandwiches, homemade candy, and Polish sausage inside. Mothers, we'll change your wipers and your baby's diapers.*

As an added attraction, a day before he left for the navy, Gertrude's boyfriend, Nard Tanawaski, had come to the station and rigged up the record player to four big outside speakers. After that, they played big-band swing music all day long. It added some cheer to the cold winter days.

As word continued to spread about the "All-Girl Filling Station," long-haul truck drivers suddenly made it a point to reroute their runs through Pulaski, and a lot of men all the way from Green Bay and as far away as Madison mysteriously developed car trouble.

Carloads of guys and gals carpooling to factories stopped in to fill up on their way to work. The music made them feel happy, and so did the four friendly girls with the big smiles. Before long, they even had big logging trucks swinging down across the border of Canada just to get a look.

Secretly, Fritzi had been worried whether her sisters would be able to handle it, but they surprised her at how they had jumped in and helped. Even though Sophie Marie was still a little shy, she was very pretty and, therefore, a big asset. Nothing helped sales faster than a pretty girl, and the All-Girl Filling Station had *four*.

Dear Wink-a-Dink,

I am sure you know by now that yours truly and your sisters are running the station, so don't worry. We will hold the fort down until that happy day when you come back and take over for good. Soon, I hope.

It's sure hard to look pretty and get dates with grease under your fingernails and with your hair smelling like gasoline. Momma and Angie are cooking almost day and night. We are selling sausages as fast as they can make them. But with the sugar rationing starting . . . no more paczkis or pastries of any kind, and Gertrude is not happy about it.

Love,

Fritzi

P.S. Heard from Billy. He's down in Pensacola instructing naval cadets and says they are scaring the hell out of him. Sure do miss him and wish I was in Florida today enjoying the sunshine, that's for sure. I am sending you a photo of the four of us taken at the station for the newspaper. Don't we look cute?

# THE WAFFLE HOUSE

POINT CLEAR, ALABAMA

SOOKIE WAS DEEP IN THOUGHT IN BOOTH NO. 4 AND THEN LEANED IN and said, "The thing is, Dr. Shapiro, I can understand her not wanting me to know I was adopted, but all those years of her telling not only me, but my poor children, how lucky we were to be a Simmons. All that was a lie, and she's put us in a terrible position. I can't tell the Daughters of the Confederacy or the Kappas that Dee Dee and I are not really Simmonses without Lenore finding out. I hate being a fraud, but I don't want to upset her, either. You don't know me, but I've never really been this mad at anybody before, and it makes me feel so bad, but I just don't know how to get over it. I seem to be stuck."

"Well, first of all, as we've said, your anger and hurt at your mother are perfectly normal, and yes, it was a terrible thing to do to a child, but I think it might help you to know that most of her behavior was probably unintentional. Think of a person being born without a foot. In other words, your mother has a little something missing, and in her case, it's the ability to see or feel beyond oneself or empathize with another person's feelings, even one's own children. And in most cases they're not even aware they are doing it."

"Maybe . . . but I still just don't understand how she could keep on lying to me all these years."

"I'm not so sure she was lying—at least not in her own mind—and as you have said, when your mother believes something, facts don't mean a thing."

"Well that's true. She's convinced she's related to the queen of England."

"Exactly, and sometimes this kind of delusional thinking is a survival skill gone wrong. What do you know about her childhood?"

"Not much . . . just that she was raised by her grandmother. Her mother died in childbirth, and she said that when she was growing up, her daddy was hardly ever home. He was a state senator so he spent most of his time in Montgomery."

"I see. And has she ever mentioned her mother?"

"Only one time . . ."

"Just once?"

"Yes."

After Sookie left the Waffle House, she realized it was strange. As obsessive and preoccupied as Lenore had been about the Simmons family line, she had never discussed anything about her mother, where she was from, or how old she was when she died. Her name hadn't even shown up in the family Bible. And whenever Sookie had asked about her, Lenore had made it quite clear she didn't want to talk about her. Lenore had never even mentioned her mother at all until that one day after the twins were born. Sookie had been exhausted, and all she wanted to do was stay in bed and rest, but Lenore had stormed into her room and thrown open the blinds. "I'm here to announce the good news. You are going to get up, and we are going out to lunch."

"Mother, not today, please. I'm too tired."

"Oh, come on, Sookie. You'll feel so much better if you do."

"But I don't feel like it. I don't think I ever want to get up again."

"Oh, don't be such a baby. I'm your mother, and you have to do what I say. It would be rude not to. Besides, haven't I always been right? You're just lucky to have a mother who cares. And don't forget you come from a long line of military leaders, and we always advance. We never retreat."

This was a conversation they had had many times, but on this particular day, for some reason, right in the middle of it, a strange faraway look had crossed over Lenore's face—one that Sookie had never seen before. It was as if she suddenly remembered something. Then she said rather sadly, "Oh, Sookie, you just don't know what it's like growing up without a mother. I even used to envy those poor little white-trash sharecropper families that lived out in the country. As poor as they were, at least they had a mother. We only get one chance in life, and I missed mine, and once you miss it . . ." Just for a split second, Sookie thought she saw tears start to well up in her mother's eyes, but then Lenore quickly changed the subject.

Sookie tried to get her to talk more about it, but Lenore said, "There's nothing more to say, except that you and Buck need to get down on your hands and knees and thank your lucky stars you have me. Nothing stings more than an ungrateful child, you know. Now you get up out of that bed and get dressed, and put on something nice. We are going out to lunch, and let there be no ifs, ands, or buts about it. Your life awaits you out in the world, my girl, and you're not lollygagging your life away in bed."

# PULASKI, WISCONSIN

Fritzi had been home for only a short while, but she soon found out that old Gussie Mintz back in Grand Rapids had been right. Flying was now in her blood, and as busy as she was running the station, she was becoming restless. She missed Billy, but there were still a few good-looking guys left who were doing war jobs. And that big Irish redheaded trucker, Joe O'Connor, from Manitowoc, who was always trying to get her to go out with him, *was* a good-looking son of a gun. She liked him a lot, but she was not in love, and she certainly had no interest in getting married or, God forbid, ever having children. She and Billy had too much to do after the war was over, but Joe was a great dancer, and she was not against having a little fun. After all, she had been to Milwaukee, and knew the score. And as Billy said, "Life is too short for regrets."

As the days went on, the filling station became the center of the war-drive effort in Pulaski. Uncle Sam needed all the supplies he could get for the troops. As an incentive, Fritzi set up a kissing booth outside, and anything that Uncle Sam needed, from a bundle of paper to tin cans, would get you a kiss from one of the girls. And like all filling stations, theirs was an official drop-off place for the huge rubber drive, and considering the reward, all the guys from near and wide collected all the rubber they could—everything from old tires and water hoses to sink stoppers and canning jar tops. One man, eager to get a kiss from one of the girls, even stole his wife's rubber girdle and brought it down, and Mrs. Luczak wasn't happy about it, either. She marched down to the station and got it right back. She said, "Fritzi, I'm as patriotic as the next one. They can have everything else, but I *need* my girdle."

That night, Momma sat down as she always did and wrote to her husband at the sanitarium.

Dear Poppa,

We miss you, but we know you are busy getting well, and we can't wait for you to come home. Oh, Poppa, you would be so proud of your girls. They are all working so hard to help win this old war as fast as possible so Wink and all the boys can come back home soon. They all seem so grown-up now. Even Sophie Marie is such a different girl now. She has realized how pretty she is. All the boys want a kiss from her, but she is the same sweet girl who never misses mass. Wish I could say the same for the other girls, but I know God will forgive them for sleeping in on Sunday. They work so hard during the week. I may have gotten good news about Fritzi. She has been seeing a lot more of that nice Irish boy I told you about. I just pray she will get all that flying planes out of her head and marry him and stay home. We got a nice long letter from Nurse Dorothy Frakes today. She is overseas somewhere and says so many of our poor boys are being killed and hurt, but she says all the nurses are working as hard as they can to save as many as they can. Rest up, Poppa, and don't worry about a thing. We are all fine.

Love,

Momma

# THE WAFFLE HOUSE

## Point Clear, Alabama

This week, Dr. Shapiro had a cancellation, and they were meeting earlier than usual. Jewel greeted them with a big smile. "Here you two are again. Two coffees?"

Dr. Shapiro said, "Yes, and you don't happen to have a bagel, do you?"

"A what?"

"A bagel?" He could tell by her expression that she didn't and said, "Just give me an English muffin."

"Okay. You want anything, Mrs. Poole?"

"No, thank you, Jewel, I'm fine. I just had breakfast."

After Jewel left, Dr. Shapiro asked, "How are you doing?"

"Oh, a little better, I think, but every time Lenore starts on the Simmons stuff, it's hard not to say anything. It makes me remember all those years growing up and how bad she made me feel. The woman never let me forget anything. She always brought up everything I did wrong."

Dr. Shapiro said, "I understand, but you know, those are your mother's behavioral patterns."

"And then I start to think that I'm just remembering only the bad things."

"Do you have any positive memories about your mother?"

Sookie sat there racking her brain, but nothing came to her.

Jewel brought the coffee and muffin. "Thank you," said Dr. Shapiro.

Sookie put cream and Sweet'N Low in her coffee and frowned. "Hmmm . . . positive memories. Well, I had a wonderful father and brother, and in high school, we were the state football champions my senior year."

"No, I mean positive memories about your mother."

"Well, life with Lenore was never dull, I'll say that. And she is funny. I have to admit she can say and do some of the funniest things. When Buck and I were little and lost a tooth, we would put it under our pillow for the tooth fairy to find, and later, Lenore would always dress up as the tooth fairy, with a tall hat and a wand, and come in our room and dance all around and sing some silly little song and leave us a present under our pillow. And I remember feeling good when everybody said that Buck and I had the prettiest mother in school. And she always smelled so wonderful. One time, I must have been four or five, I was sick with a terrible fever, and I remember she sat by my bed all night and petted my head. Every time I woke up, she was right there. And she would say, 'Don't worry, Mother's right here.' " Suddenly, tears welled up in her eyes, and she was embarrassed and grabbed a napkin. "Oh, Lord, I'm sorry. I don't know why I'm crying."

"Why do you think you are?"

"I guess I just remembered how happy I was to wake up and see her sitting there. I just wish I hadn't disappointed her so much. What about you, Dr. Shapiro, did you have a happy childhood?"

"Let's go back to your last statement for a moment, about disappointing your mother. Did your brother ever disappoint her?"

"Oh, yes, but in a different way. She didn't particularly like Bunny, the girl he married."

"What about earlier? When you were younger?"

"She more or less let him alone. I think the problem was that I was a girl, and she wanted me to be more like her, but I couldn't. And now we know why."

"And if your mother had had a biological daughter, do you think she would have lived up to all her expectations?"

"I think so. Yes."

"How?"

"Well, she probably would have been prettier and smarter. Not had straight hair. She probably would have had talent and certainly been more ambitious."

"*Or* she could have been none of those things. Just because she would be related by blood doesn't guarantee she would have any of these attributes. Did it ever occur to you that Lenore was lucky to have you? I'm amazed you turned out as strong and sane as you did."

"*Me?* I don't feel very strong . . ."

"But why would you? Your mother formed an incorrect opinion of you and, naturally, you agreed with her. Children always think their parents are right. But in this case, your mother was entirely wrong. Think about it. Your mother is an overpowering individual, and yet, you managed to have a stable marriage and raise four children."

Sookie said, "Well, yes, I did, didn't I? And knock on wood, not one of them got on dope that I know of. At least, that's something, isn't it?"

"Yes, it is. You may not be the person your mother wants you to be, but you are you. Our job here is to try and separate the wheat from the chaff and figure out who *you* are and not who your mother thinks you are."

Sookie looked concerned and said, "Oh. And will that require me having to journal?"

"Not unless you want to," he said.

"No. I like just talking."

"Good. Same time next week?"

"I'll be here."

That afternoon, Sookie called her friend Dena. "I'm so sorry. I know I promised, but I can't go to the Kappa reunion this year."

"Oh, no . . . why?"

"Well, first of all, I just couldn't face everybody, knowing that I am an imposter."

"Oh, Sookie. You know that's not true."

"Well, even so. I can't leave now. I really need to keep seeing Dr. Shapiro, the poor thing. He's so sweet and, honestly, Dena, I think I may be his only patient, and I can't let him down. He depends on me to show up."

## THE ALL-GIRL FILLING STATION

PULASKI, WISCONSIN

THAT SPRING, WHEN THE STATION GOT BUSY, GERTRUDE AND TULA came up with an idea of their own to help speed up customer service. They presented it to Fritzi, and she approved.

After that, the minute a car pulled in, Gertrude and Tula, wearing cute little caps and short skirts with fringe on them, would fly out of the station on roller skates, and while Fritzi was filling the car with gas, they would clean all the windows, the lights, and the tag in less than two minutes. And, sometimes, if the boys inside the car were cute, they added extra little twists and twirls and skated backward as they cleaned.

Momma watched them out the window one day and later said to Fritzi, "Don't you think that all that skating around is a little too show-offy?"

"No, I don't."

Momma laughed. "No, you wouldn't."

"And it brings in the customers like crazy."

"Well, whatever you think, Fritzi. I don't know what we would have done without you. If anything happens to me or Poppa, I can die happy, because I know you'll take care of the girls."

"Sure, Momma."

"But I worry about you sleeping in the station all night. Are you sure you want to do that?"

"Sure, I'm sure. Don't you worry about a thing, Momma."

Fritzi didn't tell Momma, but being on roller skates at a gas station could be dangerous. One day, Tula had shot out of the station to the tune of "Boogie Woogie Bugle Boy" with a rag in her hand and had hit a grease spot. To everyone's amazement, she skidded underneath a big eighteen-wheeler truck, came out the other side, and ended up all the way across the street. Without missing a beat, she had skated back across the street to the station and finished cleaning the windows of a Packard.

After all their initial bellyaching, Gertrude and Tula came to love working at the filling station. Gertrude's boyfriend, Nard, had proposed to her in a letter, and she had written back and accepted, so she wasn't dating, and all the boys Tula had been dating were in the service, so there wasn't much else to do but work. And Fritzi always made sure there was something fun going on all the time, including weekly Friday night dances out on the big platform on the side of the filling station. One week, Fritzi got Quiren Kohlbeck and his Orange Crush Orchestra to come all the way from Manitowoc, Wisconsin, and play on the back of a truck, and that night, the town of Pulaski bought more war bonds than the next five towns over combined, and they were very proud of that fact.

It was mostly girls jitterbugging with other girls, but they did have a good turnout from the guys still home working at the factories nearby and some of the Coast Guard boys stationed over in Sturgeon Bay. Sometimes the music went on until after midnight, but nobody in town complained. Everybody was working hard, and they deserved a little recreation. Even the nuns from Saint Mary's came over and sat with Momma on the porch and watched the fun.

It was a busy time for everyone. When Momma and Angie weren't cooking, they were rolling bandages for the Red Cross or tending to the big victory garden in the back. In their spare time, all the girls wrote to the servicemen and sent packages of good Polish food to all the boys from Pulaski.

The youngest girl, Sophie Marie, had just graduated from high school and was still torn about what to do. She felt she had a religious vocation, and she had planned on entering the convent right away, but she also knew her sisters needed her at home to help at the filling station. She cried when she told Sister Mary Patricia that she would have to wait until her brother, Wink, came home after the war to take over. Sister Mary Patricia was very understanding. She said, "Sophie, it could be for the best. I entered at seventeen, and not that I regret my decision, but I often wish I had lived a little more out in the world. I think it might have helped me understand more what the girls are going through. And, sometimes, we can serve Him best by serving our families and our country."

Fritzi hadn't said anything, because she hadn't wanted to be a bad influence on the kid, but she was glad Sophie was staying. She was a big draw with the customers. And as Fritzi figured it, after the war, none of the girls would ever have the chance to run a gas station again. Besides, Sophie had the rest of her life to be a nun, so why not have a little fun while you can? The only downside with Sophie was that Fritzi had to watch her language around her, and she hated that. She just loved to cuss a blue streak and shock the truck drivers.

All the Jurdabralinski girls, including Momma and Angie, were kept busy morning, noon, and night, but they were not too busy not to be worried about Wink. They had not heard from him in a while. When they finally received a V-mail letter from him, they were so relieved they called Poppa in Hot Springs and read it to him over the phone.

Dear Folks,

Guess what? I am writing this letter to you from the deck of a troop ship. Our entire unit is being shipped overseas. Don't know where we're going yet, but I am sure it will be where Uncle Sam thinks we can do the most good.

This ocean is something else. I didn't know there was that much water in the world. A lot of the guys are pretty seasick, but I am OK so far. Sure wish I had my rod and reel with me. There must be some pretty big fish swimming around under there. Don't worry about me. I am in good hands and the grub is pretty good. Not as good as Momma's, though. I think this war will be over soon and I will be home again before you know it.

Love,

Wink

P.S. I really appreciate you girls taking over the station for Poppa and me. I have shown the guys in my unit the photo you sent, and they all say I sure have some swell sisters. And pretty, too. A few of them said after the war, they were headed to Pulaski to see you in person.

# PULASKI, WISCONSIN

Dear Wink,

Don't know where you've ended up, but we all really miss you, buddy. Momma is still keeping that candle lit for you over at church, and she and Sophie never miss daily mass, so you are in good hands on that score.

I just wish I was there with you so I could keep an eye on you. I know you are a big-shot flyboy now, but I can't help it. You're still my little brother you know, and, despite it all, I am quite fond of you, so don't go being a hero on me. OK?

Fritzi

P.S. We hear that Poppa might be coming home soon. Not too soon, I hope. It was eight below zero here today, and the pumps froze again. Well, gotta go. Take good care of yourself, Winks. We are so proud of you . . . and give them Krauts hell for me, will ya?

# HAPPY BIRTHDAY

POINT CLEAR, ALABAMA

Every morning, Sookie walked around and filled her bird feeders. She couldn't let the blue jays go hungry, but she still missed her small birds. They wouldn't come to the small-bird feeders she'd tried, either. Every once in a while, one or two would come and feed on the seeds that had fallen on the ground, but she still had more blue jays than anything. Mr. Nadleshaft at the Birds-R-Us store said it was a common problem, but so far, nobody seemed to have an answer.

When Sookie came in from the yard, the phone in the kitchen was ringing. It was Lenore, who sang into the phone, "I know a little girl who's having a big birthday on the thirty-first."

Sookie wanted to sing back, "No, I'm not," but she didn't.

"What I want to know is where are we going this year? Have you thought about it? I know where I think we should go."

"Mother, I have thought about it, and I really don't want to do anything this year. I just want to skip it."

"What? Skip your birthday? Don't be silly."

"I'm not being silly. I really just want to be with Earle and spend a quiet evening at home."

"A quiet evening at home? On your birthday? Sookie, what in the world is wrong with you? Are you over there drinking? I swear, you are just getting more peculiar every day. You can have a quiet evening alone with Earle anytime, but you are not going to skip your birthday, for heaven's sake. And, anyhow, it's not just about you. I'm the one who gave birth to you. So don't make me have to come over there and spank you. Besides, I've already written the funniest poem, and I've set it to music. 'Roses are red, my dear, violets are blue, after forty-eight hours, then there was you!' Oh, and it goes on and on."

A thousand smart replies went through Sookie's mind, but what was the use? No matter what she said, the woman was determined to continue perpetuating this lie to the grave.

"Sookie, are you still there?"

"Yes, Mother."

"I think we should have the party out on my pier this year."

"I see. Are you going to cook?"

"Of course not. We'll have it catered. And you need to start thinking about who all you want to invite."

She supposed she would just have to go along with the charade. She was still confused about how to handle the situation and she wasn't up for a fight with Lenore over it. And so once again, she would be celebrating the wrong birthday. Oh, Lord what a mess.

Sookie found herself in a strange position. She was grateful to Lenore for adopting her, but now that she knew she was not a Simmons, it was hard for her to keep on pretending. She went back and forth between being grateful and wanting to kill her, but as Dr. Shapiro had said, it was natural to feel that way. Still, it did make it hard when Lenore blathered on and on about how proud she was to have the small and delicate Simmons foot.

Lenore hadn't had the Simmons foot for years. She just didn't know it. Lenore was so vain she wouldn't wear her glasses, and so when Sookie took her shopping and she would ask to see a shoe in a size 6, Sookie would quietly walk back to the storeroom and ask the clerk to bring her mother the same shoe, only in a size 7½. It was a small white lie, but Sookie knew that any other way Winged Victory would cause a scene and insist they were all wrong. Once Lenore believed in something, you could never convince her otherwise.

She believed she was perfectly self-sufficient, too, but she wasn't. Lenore wouldn't even be going to water therapy three times a week if she had let them get her a walk-in tub. "Those are for invalids," she had said, and then she proceeded to fall getting out of her bath, knocked herself out, nearly broke her hip, and wound up at the emergency room. When she woke up in the hospital, Lenore thought she was dying and called everyone and told them if they wanted to see her alive, they needed to get there right away. "I doubt I will live through the night," she said. All the kids had dropped everything and run home from college, and Buck and Bunny had flown in all the way from North Carolina. The next day, when she woke up alive, Lenore turned to Sookie and said, "Sookie, call Jo Ellen and tell her I need her to come over here and fix my hair, and tell that orderly she needs to water these flowers."

That afternoon, when everyone had gone home, Sookie had asked her, "Mother, do you know how much trouble you caused? You scared everybody half to death, calling them like that. Carter almost killed himself speeding to get here in time."

Lenore said, "Well, you're just lucky I survived, but if I had died, they needed to be here." Then she added, "Good heavens, Sookie, you sound like you're *sorry* I didn't die."

"That's not what I meant, Mother, and you know it."

But Lenore wasn't listening. "I don't think I like this room. Sookie, go down the hall and ask them if they have something with a better view."

## THE MISHAP

PULASKI, WISCONSIN

WORKING AT A FILLING STATION COULD BE REALLY DANGEROUS. GAS was highly flammable. Hubcaps could pop off and hit you in the face. You could burn yourself on overheated engines. Tires could blow up if you put too much air in them. And when slamming down hoods, if you weren't careful, fingers could be broken.

Fritzi had told the girls a hundred times that they needed to keep their minds on what they were doing. So far, there had been only one serious mishap at the station. And, of course, a man was involved.

TULA WAS ALL ATWITTER, because Arty Kowalinowski, the handsome six-foot star football player from Pulaski High, was home on a four-day furlough from the army. And thrill of thrills, he had asked her out to the movies that Friday night. He had not known it, but Tula had spent most of her junior and senior years writing "Mrs. Arty Kowalinowski" all over her notebooks and dreaming about him at night. But this was the first time he had asked her out, and so she was over the moon. Tula had not even gone on the date yet, but she was already hearing wedding bells and planning what she would wear. Something with a lot of white netting, she thought.

That Thursday night, she spent hours washing her hair over and over again—trying her best to get the gasoline smell out—scraping the grease out from under her fingernails, and picking out her outfit. The next morning, she didn't want to chip one of her newly painted bright red fingernails, so she showed up at work wearing big, thick workman gloves.

She was in such a daze all day that it was hard for Fritzi to get her to do much of anything. And Tula was not happy when late that afternoon, a huge black 1936 Chevy with transmission problems came in for service. Tula wanted to wait and do it the next day, but Fritzi wouldn't let her. Tula was their main mechanic, so she rolled under the car on the wooden dolly, grumbling about it, but she still wouldn't take her gloves off.

Tula was an excellent mechanic, but that day, she must have been thinking about her date with Arty Kowalinowski, because when she was underneath the car working, she somehow unscrewed the wrong valve, and suddenly an entire pint of thick five-year-old filthy oil gushed out and landed all over her face.

Tula screamed so loudly that Momma heard her all the way over at the house. Gertrude got to her first and grabbed her by the legs and pulled her out sputtering and spitting out black oil.

Her screams were so loud that the fire truck and the police showed up. Five minutes later, Tula was still hysterical and dripping oil as they led her over to the house to try to clean her up.

It was already five o'clock, and she had a date in two hours. She knew Arty was leaving the next day, and she might not ever get another date with him again.

But the oil was everywhere: in her hair, her eyelashes, up her nose, and in her ears. After being scrubbed for at least an hour, her face was still stained a strange gray color. She and Momma had shampooed her hair three times with Oxydol soap, but even so, she still reeked of old, rancid oil. Tula looked in the mirror and realized it was no use. She couldn't possibly go. "I look like a dead rat," she said.

THIRTY MINUTES LATER, ARTY Kowalinowski was standing in front of the Pulaski theater waiting for his date, when Fritzi and Gertrude showed up instead. Tula had threatened to kill both of them if they told him what had happened, so all they said was, "Tula's not coming."

He was disappointed, but they all went inside anyway and had popcorn and saw the movie *Kitty Foyle* with Ginger Rogers and a cartoon.

While they were sitting in the theater enjoying the movie, Tula was upstairs at home, sitting in the big claw-foot tub, soaking her hair and bemoaning her fate to her mother and Sophie. "I begged Fritzi to let me wait until tomorrow, but she's so bossy. She wouldn't let me. She said, 'No, it has to be done today.' I hate her. I just hate her."

"Now, Tula, she's your sister. You don't hate her. That's a sin."

"I don't care. Arty Kowalinowski is the only boy I ever really loved, and she made me miss my one chance to go out with him. Now he'll probably meet some other girl, and I'll wind up an old maid, and it's all her fault."

When Gertrude and Fritzi got home later that night, they went upstairs to see Tula, who unfortunately, still looked gray. "We brought you some popcorn," said Gertrude. "And Arty said to tell you he was just heartbroken not to get to see you this time."

"He did?"

"Yes," added Fritzi. "And when we gave him your picture, he said he would be looking at it and thinking about you every day until he got back."

"He did?" said Tula, reaching for the popcorn.

"Oh, yes . . ."

It was a bold-faced lie, but it made Tula feel better.

# THE WAFFLE HOUSE

## Booth No. 7

At their next session, Dr. Shapiro suddenly looked up from his notes and asked Sookie a question that surprised her.

"What about your father?"

"What about him?"

"I've heard a lot about your mother, but you haven't mentioned him."

"I haven't?"

"No."

"Oh . . . well, he was so sweet, bless his heart."

"He must have seen your mother's behavior. Did he ever try and stop it?"

"No. But you didn't know Daddy. He thought she was the most wonderful woman in the world. And when I would complain that she was pushing me around, he would say, 'Oh, honey, I know you don't want to join that club or do whatever, but she's only pushing you because she loves you, and it means so much to her,' so no, he was never very much help."

"How did you feel about that?"

"You mean, did it make me mad? Oh no. He couldn't help it. Poor Daddy always had a blind spot when it came to Mother. When they met she had evidently been the belle of the ball . . . and I don't think Daddy ever got over the fact that she married him. Every year on their anniversary, he would play the song they had danced to at the Senior Military Ball . . . and they would waltz all around the living room."

"So in other words, you and your brother grew up in a house with a domineering mother and a father who gave you little or no protection."

Driving home, Sookie thought about what Dr. Shapiro had said. It was true. Her father had seen how unhappy Lenore had made her, and he really had not stood up for her. Should she be mad at Lenore for that or mad at Daddy? Or mad at both? Oh, Lord. She didn't want to be mad at anybody. There was a part of her that just hated sitting around, whining about her childhood. It was embarrassing at her age. But Dr. Shapiro said it was important. Still, it made her feel creepy, like she was doing something bad, betraying the Simmons family secrets, and there were a few.

The Simmonses, like most families in the South, had lost everything during the war, and all they had left was their pride and stories of the "glorious past." Her grandmother told tales of how her mother, Sookie's namesake, Sarah Jane Simmons, had single-handedly saved Greenleaves, the family plantation, by charming the Yankee soldiers and dazzling them with her beauty, and how after the war, three Yankee officers had written and begged her to marry them, which was, of course, out of the question . . . and on and on.

As a child, all these stories had enthralled Lenore. But in Lenore's case, with each passing year, the "glorious past" had become more and more glorious until in 1939, she had confided to a friend, "I could have written *Gone with the Wind* about Greenleaves, but Margaret Mitchell beat me to it."

When Buck and Sookie were growing up, Lenore had waxed poetic, ad nauseam, all about the grandeur of the old Simmons family plantation, "almost a complete replica of Tara," she said, "only much better furnished." But when he was in high school Buck had looked it up in the Selma Civil War Archives over at the courthouse.

The truth was that Greenleaves was never a plantation. It was just a nice two-story farmhouse located on a few acres of land, and the Simmons family's only encounter with the enemy during the war was when one little skinny half-starved Union soldier, who was lost, stopped by and asked for directions. But to hear Lenore tell it, hundreds of Yankee soldiers had marched through the county, looting and stealing and digging up every inch of their land, looking for buried silver and gold. The fact that the man her grandmother later married got drunk and burned the place down was somehow never mentioned.

## GOOD-BYE, MR. HATCHETT

PULASKI, WISCONSIN
1942

ALL THAT YEAR, EVERYBODY IN TOWN WAS BUSY PITCHING IN TO HELP with the war effort. Housewives were saving grease for bullets, and were collecting all the rubber and aluminum and scrap metal they could scare up. The Jurdabralinski girls, like all the others, had given up their nylon stockings, which were needed for parachutes, and now everybody had a victory garden.

The good news was that Poppa had come home from the hospital, and they all celebrated. But the war news was not good. Pulaski had already lost three of their boys, and Fritzi was worried about Wink and all the other guys she knew who were now in the thick of it.

They got another letter from their friend Dottie Frakes, who was tending to wounded soldiers in the Pacific. It made Fritzi feel so damn useless. Momma and Sophie went to mass every morning and prayed for the boys overseas, Gertrude and Tula rolled bandages for the Red Cross in their spare time, and all she did was pump gas. And since gasoline was now being rationed, she pumped less and less of it every day. The posters down at the post office had a picture of a soldier and read "They do the fighting, you do the writing." Fritzi had written to all the guys she knew, but she wanted to do more.

So a few weeks later, when Mr. Hatchett, the Civilian Pilot Training instructor over at the college, was drafted, and they asked Fritzi if she would step in and take over his job while he was gone, Fritzi said she was more than glad to do it.

Teaching would give her a chance to fly again. The college knew they were taking a chance on trusting a former female stunt pilot with their students; however, they needed a replacement for Mr. Hatchett. But Fritzi turned out to be an excellent instructor, and her students loved her—especially the boys. Between running the gas station and teaching, she was pretty busy, but sometimes after a lesson, she would take off and fly for a while by herself. It was wonderful to be up in the air again, even if it was in a Piper Cub.

## PULASKI, WISCONSIN

Dear Wink,

We are OK here. Hope you are the same. Not much news except that the CPT instructor you and the girls took lessons from was drafted. And yours truly has taken over his job. Just for a laugh, I gave Sophie and Gertrude a few lessons, and I was surprised. They've both gotten pretty good, especially Sophie. She aces her landings like a pro. It almost put me to shame . . . but not quite. Ha-ha! But it makes me wonder if after this is over, you and me and the two girls and Billy might start our own Flying Circus? But I'm just dreaming, I guess. I have a feeling when you get home, your bride is going to nail your feet to the ground and never let you go upstairs again. Can't say as I blame her. There is not a man left here that's not under 16 or over 60. They're either too young or too old. And it sure is lonesome here. So come home soon.

Fritzi

P.S. How does it feel to be a daddy? He's a fine little boy, Winks. Looks like you.

## PULASKI, WISCONSIN

My Darling Husband,

I hope you got the package I sent. I knitted them all myself. I am over at the station filling in for Fritzi for a few hours and things are pretty slow. I'd rather be busy. It seems if I have time on my hands I do too much thinking. I know we are told our letters must always be cheery and gay but, honey, sometimes I do wonder, why us? We were so happy for such a short time. Why did this war have to happen now? Why couldn't we have been born five years earlier or even five years later? It isn't fair. I had you for such a short time and I'm scared I'm not the same girl you left and when you come home, you won't love me anymore, and I'm scared this war will change you, too, Wink. We can never get back to those two kids we used to be, and that's what hurts. It's hard to believe that just last year I was a silly teenage girl playing house, and now I'm a grown woman with a baby to raise and my husband is across the world, and I don't know when I'll see him again. Oh, honey, please don't be brave and take any chances. Just do what you have to do and come home to me. I kiss your picture every night. Do you feel it? Everybody here asks about you.

All my love,

Angie

# PULASKI, WISCONSIN

Dear Wink-a-Dink,

Woke up on the wrong side of the world this morning, grumpy as hell. Was a bear all day until I figured out what was wrong. I forgot to say thank you to the man upstairs today for being born in the good old USA, for Momma and Pop, the rest of the girls, and especially for you, Wink, the grandest guy I know and who is my very own brother. After I had a good talking to myself, I felt better. Anyhoo, pal, things here are status quo. With all this darn gas rationing, folks are just dribbling into the station, not more than one or two a day now, and then not spending much. Had a kid come in the other day who could only afford to buy a nickel's worth, but your Angie, with the big heart, shot him a little more.

Angie's holding up pretty well, Wink, but do write her when you can. I swear, that gal just lives from letter to letter. She's fighting this war with you, Wink, and is being brave. The whole town is fighting this war with you. You should see the kids. They have collected everything but their Momma's kitchen sink, no joke, and Poppa and Mr. Rususki are now in the home guard, helmets and all. We had a blackout drill the other night, and Poppa was so excited he walked off the back stairs and fell in the bushes. Momma was in the kitchen and heard him cussing in Polish and ran out and fell off right on top of him. Before it was over, all of us girls wound up in the bushes, laughing our heads off. Nothing was hurt but Poppa's pride. Good thing it was just a drill. Don't know what would happen if it was the real thing.

Fritzi

# LONDON, ENGLAND

December 25, 1942

Hi, Gang,

Merry Christmas all the way from England. Sure was strange not being home at Christmas. It really stirs up a lot of memories, especially today. I sure have learned something in these last months. All the guys here are very quiet tonight, including big-mouth me. We had a special Christmas Day broadcast from the States, and it sure was good to hear their voices, especially Frances Langford. At the end, when she sang, "I'll Be Home for Christmas," a lot of the guys had to leave the auditorium pronto, including me. The British people have been swell to us. Last night, every family here invited two or three of us to spend Christmas Eve at their house with them. My family was not Catholic, but the father drove me and Kracheck over to the next town for midnight mass and waited, then drove us back to the base. There sure are a lot of nice people here, but it's not home. I know after we clean up all this stuff over here, I will be back next year to enjoy Christmas with you for real.

Winks

# THE END OF AN ERA

1943

WINK'S PHILLIPS 66 WASN'T THE ONLY STATION THAT WAS HIT HARD BY gas and rubber rationing. People just weren't driving much anymore, and filling stations all over the country were closing down every day. Fritzi and the girls kept theirs going longer than most, but finally, Poppa and Fritzi came to the same conclusion. It was costing them more to stay open than they were making, so the decision was made that at the end of the week, they would close down. It had been snowing on that last day the station was open. The weather outside was cold and gray and more or less matched the mood inside. The girls were sad as they cleaned out the counters and took down the pictures on the walls. Sophie packed up all the old maps and postcards and took them over to the house. Poppa said it was only temporary. He was sure that after the war, they would open right back up, and everything would go back to normal. But the girls wondered if anything would ever be the same.

Running the all-girl filling station had been a lot of hard work, but now that it had come to an end, they began to realize just how much they would miss it. For a short while, thanks to Fritzi, they had sort of been famous, and now it was all over.

It was around five when they finished and already dark outside.

The girls had gone home, and Fritzi walked around and locked all the doors and turned the lights off for the last time. When she came back over to the house and handed Poppa the keys, Gertrude said what they had all been thinking: "Oh, Fritzi, I wonder if we'll ever have as much fun again."

# SHOULD SHE OR SHOULD SHE NOT?

POINT CLEAR, ALABAMA

SOOKIE FELT SHE HAD MADE SOME PROGRESS SINCE HER FIRST THERAPY session. She was finally able to be around Lenore without having such a strong emotional reaction (like wanting to strangle her), but it was still so strange seeing Lenore in a brand-new light—not as her mother, but as a total stranger—and she was torn about what to do.

Sometimes she'd wonder whether she should she tell Lenore she knew she was adopted. If she did, what good would it do? The woman was eighty-eight years old, and she obviously didn't want her to know. She had gone to great lengths to keep it from Sookie, and telling her now would only upset her. And it's not like they could work anything out at this late date. The damage had already been done. Sookie still felt hurt and angry, but at the same time, she was also beginning to feel grateful to her. Other than Lenore pushing her into everything known to man, her family life had been wonderful. She couldn't have asked for a better father or brother. She had grown up in a lovely home and certainly had never gone without a thing. And if she hadn't been adopted by them, who knows where she might have ended up? A Texas family could have adopted her, and she could have grown up on a ranch, and that would have been a disaster. She was absolutely terrified of horses. Or she might not have been adopted at all and never left the orphanage, just sat there until she was eighteen and then been kicked out with nowhere to go. And if she hadn't grown up where she had, she certainly would never have met Earle Poole, Jr. She would have been a totally different person with a completely different husband and an entirely different set of children, or maybe she wouldn't have married at all. It was mind-boggling to think about just how random her life had really been.

If her real mother had kept her, she might have grown up in Wisconsin speaking Polish or at least speaking with a Yankee accent. She may have even played the accordion or, who knows, she might have become a nun. And if she had been that other person and had passed herself on the street, she probably wouldn't even have recognized her. She supposed she would have still looked like herself on the outside, but she would have been someone entirely different on the inside. She would have been herself, but an entirely different version of herself. Of course, she might not have been as nervous, or she might have been just the same. Maybe her bad nerves had nothing to do with Lenore. It was hard to know what parts of her personality had been formed by DNA and what parts had been the result of her environment. She had always assumed she had gotten her height and her nose from her father and the Simmons foot from Lenore, but now who knew where anything came from?

Oh, Lord. Just when she thought she was going to be able to relax and enjoy her life, this had to happen. How could she relax with all these questions running around in her head all day and night?

As the days went by, she found herself thinking more and more about her real mother. One night, in the middle of dinner, she said to Earle, "I wonder what she looked like."

"Who?"

"That lady. Fritzi. My real mother. I wonder if she had red hair?"

"I don't know, honey, but I'm sure we could find out."

"Oh, it's probably too late. If I'm sixty, she would be at least eighty-something. She's probably dead by now."

"Well, honey, maybe not. We could at least try to find out, and if she is still alive, I'm sure she would love to meet you. Think about that."

Sookie thought about it for a minute. "Oh, I don't know, Earle. Even if she is still alive, you wonder why would she just give up a baby like that."

Earle shrugged. "I don't know, honey, but I'm sure she had a very good reason. We don't know the circumstances."

"No, you're right. But still, I think I might be too scared to meet her."

"Well, you could always just talk to her on the phone."

"That's true. But what would I say? 'Oh, hello, this is the daughter you gave away sixty years ago, just calling to say hi,' or 'Hi, guess who this is.' "

"No, sweetie, just tell her the truth. That you just found out and you wanted to make contact; you could do that, couldn't you?"

"Yes, I suppose, but I could give the woman a heart attack, calling out of the blue like that. And don't forget she's never tried to find me. And it's been so many years, she might have even forgotten she had me."

"Well, just think about it. But if it were me, I'd want to at least try to find out."

THAT NIGHT IN BED, she did think about it. And it occurred to her that even if the woman was still alive, she might not want to hear from her. She could have married and had a completely new family and might not want them to know anything about her. The woman was Catholic and, who knows, she could have seven or eight or even more half brothers and sisters out there somewhere! Oh, my God . . . and if she did find her mother, and they all wanted to meet her, the entire family might come out to Point Clear and bring all their children and grandchildren. She could have hundreds of Polish relatives piling in on her from all over the country. Where would they stay? You couldn't keep a thing like that quiet. If all those Polish people hit town all at once, Lenore would be sure to hear about it in five minutes. So, no, she'd better just leave well enough alone. Who knows what a hornet's nest she might stir up?

But still, she was curious, and it really was a mystery. Why had Fritzi Jurdabralinski, who was from Wisconsin, wound up all the way across the country? And what was she doing in Texas? Had she married a cowboy? Or a soldier? Or had she married at all?

# RESTLESS IN PULASKI

PULASKI, WISCONSIN
1943

SINCE MOST OF THE BOYS FRITZI HAD BEEN TEACHING WERE NOW going into the service, the Civilian Pilots Training program at the college was shut down and the plane was sold to the military.

And now that the filling station had closed, Fritzi had nothing to occupy her time and she just hated to sit around doing nothing.

That good-looking Irishman had been somewhat of a distraction, but he had joined the marines and was off in North Carolina. She was not content to just be a sideline spectator in the war. She wanted to do something other than roll bandages and write soldiers. She could apply for a job at one of the big airplane factories out in California like a few of her friends had, but even that wasn't enough for Fritzi. She didn't want to build planes. Hell, she wanted to fly them. Day after day, she paced back and forth on the airstrip in the back and cussed a blue streak where Momma and the girls couldn't hear her. Damn it to hell and back, there were times she just hated being a female.

FRITZI DIDN'T KNOW IT, yet, but things were starting to move in her direction. Even before the war started, two highly skilled American women flyers, Jackie Cochran and Nancy Harkness Love, had started to plant the idea with the military higher-ups that if war came, the United States should seriously consider training women to fly military planes so that they could perform ferrying missions, flying new planes from the factories where they were built to the military bases. This would free the men up for combat service. England already had women flying ferrying missions and were successfully completing assignments. Russia even had female combat pilots. Eleanor Roosevelt said publicly, "Women pilots . . . are a weapon waiting to be used."

But in the United States, when the subject was approached with the top brass, they said that the idea of women ever flying planes for the military was absurd and completely out of the question. Women were far too high-strung and emotional. Flying was and always would be a man's job. This was their attitude, until the war actually started, aircraft production increased, and a shortage of male pilots ensued. In late 1942, these very same men suddenly had a change of heart and had to admit that maybe it was not such a bad idea after all.

A list was compiled of all the women in America with flying experience and a pilot's license, and telegrams were sent out asking if they would be interested in flying military planes for the U.S. government, and if so, to please report to the Howard Hughes Airport in Houston, Texas.

Fritzi opened her telegram and read it. Was she interested? She was not only interested, she couldn't wait. She talked it over with Poppa, and he gave her his blessing. Momma cried in her apron again and said, "It's all Billy Bevins's fault that Fritzi won't stay home."

When she told the girls she was leaving, they were sad to see her go. But they were also proud and excited to think that their big sister was going to be flying planes for the United States of America government.

## PULASKI, WISCONSIN

Dear Winks,

A great big yahoo! Looks like you won't be the only Jurdabralinski flying for the good ol' USA. I passed all my preliminary tests with flying colors, and it's now official. Excuse me, but I am writing this letter while jumping up and down with excitement. A bunch of us have been chosen to train the army way, so we can ferry airplanes in the States and free up more of the guys for combat duty, and so, my boy, have no fear. More help is on the way. I am headed out for Houston in two days to begin training. We are starting out as civilian volunteers, but the scuttlebutt is that as soon as we get up and going, we will be military for real, and I am hoping to outrank you, buddy . . . so watch out. Texas, here I come!

Fritzi

# AN OLD FRIEND

## Houston, Texas

Fritzi arrived at the train station in Houston and was picked up, along with a bunch of other girls from all over the country. They were driven over to either the Bluebonnet Hotel or the Oleander Motor Court, where they would be staying until they could get into the new barracks out at Avenger Field in Sweetwater, Texas.

The next morning, they were all out at the base for orientation. On their first break, Fritzi walked into the rec room to get a Coke, and she suddenly heard a familiar voice say, "Well, lookie at what the cat done drug in."

Fritzi looked over, and she couldn't believe her eyes. Sitting over in the corner at a table was Gussie Mintz, Billy's old girlfriend from the Grand Rapids days. "I heard you were coming in today," she said.

"Well, my God . . . Gussie! How are you?"

"Honey, I feel like a tired old poker chip, but don't you look smart and sassy. You haven't changed a bit. Have a seat, gal."

Fritz threw her bag down and joined her at the table. Gussie poured her a Coke and shoved it over.

"Well, is that son of a bitch Billy Bevins still alive?"

Fritzi laughed. "Oh, yeah, he's still with us."

"Well, shit, and I was hoping to hear some good news. Where is he? In jail, I hope."

"No. He's down in Pensacola, teaching cadets."

"Really? Well, they must be desperate if they took that fool. You two ever get hitched?"

"No. You know Billy."

"Yeah, I know Billy. But still together?"

Fritzi nodded. "On and off. You know Billy."

"Well, at least you hung in there. But enough about him. What do you think about the gals getting to fly? Isn't it great?"

"It's terrific. Finally, they came to their senses."

"Too bad they won't let us go military officially, yet. Hell, if they did, them Japs and Krauts wouldn't last a day between me and you. If nothing else, I could cuss them to death."

Fritzi laughed. "You could for sure, but from what I heard on the bus coming in, it could be happening any day now. Are you down here training?"

Gussie shook her head sadly. "Naw . . . I still have my pilot's license, but I can't fly no more, Fritzi. I lost my nerve."

"Oh, no."

"Yeah, after I left the act and sobered up a little, I just couldn't do it no more. When I got the letter, I told them I couldn't fly, but that I wanted in on it even if it ain't no more than sweeping out hangars or cleaning toilets, so here I am . . . a lot older and not one damn bit wiser, but still here."

"I'm glad you are, pal," said Fritzi.

"Yeah, me too. After all these years, I wound up right back where I started out. I'm slinging hash over at the mess hall, but I'm doing it for Uncle Sam and the gals, so it ain't so bad."

# TELLING THE CHILDREN

## Point Clear, Alabama

After talking it over with Earle, and as much as she was dreading it, Sookie decided she really had to tell the children. They had a right to know about their genetic background. As planned, she would start with Dee Dee, and it was not going to be easy. Dee Dee was devoted to her grandmother and had always dined out on being a Simmons. Sookie was afraid that when she found out the news, she would throw a complete hysterical hissy fit. So she decided that Miss Busby's Pink Tea Room in downtown Mobile, near Dee Dee's office, would be the perfect place. Nobody ever raised their voices in there. At least she hoped not.

Sookie screwed her courage to the wall and called Dee Dee at work. Two days later, they were seated in a lovely little pink booth over in the corner. After they had been served their tea, Sookie said, "I haven't been here in a long time. I forgot what a pleasant place it is."

"Yes, Grandmother loves it here."

"I can see why. Such lovely little watercress sandwiches. We should meet like this more often. I think it's important that mothers and daughters stay close, don't you? Speaking of that, I was doing a little reading, and did you know that as a rule, Polish people are good-natured, hardworking, and loyal?"

"Really?" said Dee Dee, clearly not engaged.

"Yes, I thought it was very interesting. And were you aware that Chopin and Liberace were of Polish descent?"

"Yes, I know."

"And here's another little fun fact. The Poles excel not only at the piano, but on the accordion as well."

"Yes, so? Who cares, Mother?"

Sookie paused. "Well . . . you might."

Dee Dee looked at her. "Mother, why are you talking about all this stuff? You're beginning to worry me. Are you all right? You just don't seem like yourself today."

"Well, it's funny you should say that, Dee Dee . . . because that's exactly what I wanted to talk to you about. The truth is, honey, I really am not myself—or at least who I thought I was—and here's the bad news: Unfortunately, neither are you."

"What?"

"Oh, Dee Dee, this is so hard for me. And believe me, it was a shock to me as well, and I thought about not telling you . . . but you need to know, especially if you have children."

"Mother, what are you talking about?"

"Well . . . a few months ago, Lenore received a letter, and naturally I read it, thinking it was a bill or something."

"Yes?"

"Well, it was from the Texas Board of Health, and I found out that your grandmother—now promise me you won't get upset."

"Okay, you found out that . . . what?"

"That my mother—your grandmother—is not really my real mother, and when I say 'real,' I mean that we are not related to her . . . that, in fact . . . I was adopted."

Dee Dee smiled. "You are kidding me. This is a joke, right?"

"No. I have the letter right here and my birth certificate. And you can read it if you want—but only if you promise not to scream and make a scene. Do you promise?"

"Okay, I promise. Let me see it."

Dee Dee took it and read it, and her mouth dropped open. "Oh, my God! Oh, my God!"

"Honey, keep your voice down."

"Mother, do you realize what this means?"

"Yes, among other things, it means we are not related by blood to either Uncle Baby or Aunt Lily. At least that's some consolation."

"No, Mother! It means that if you are not a Simmons, then I'm not a Simmons!"

"That's true, but considering the heredity factor in—"

"But it can't be true—I've *always* been a Simmons!"

"I know . . . it's very shocking, and I'm still having a hard time believing it. But evidently, it's true."

"Have you told Daddy?"

"Of course."

"What did Daddy say? Was he upset?"

"Well, he was surprised . . . but not upset."

Dee Dee suddenly looked ashen. "But how can I not be a Simmons? I feel like a Simmons. I've *always* felt like a Simmons."

"I know you have, honey, and I also know how much that has always meant to you, and that's why I hated to tell you."

Dee Dee continued staring at the birth certificate. "Your real name is Ginger Jurdabralinski? Like our *dog*, Ginger?"

"Yes."

Dee Dee looked at her with horror, and her voice was getting louder and louder with each new discovery. "Your real mother's name was Fritzi Willinka Jurdabralinski?"

"Evidently."

"Your mother was *Polish*? Born in Pulaski, Wisconsin? Oh, my God!" After she continued to read on, Dee Dee almost yelled, "Father unknown?" Three ladies at the next table turned and looked over at them.

Oh, dear, Sookie knew Dee Dee was not going to like that part. "Honey, please . . . try and keep your voice down."

Dee Dee dropped her voice level down to a whisper. "Oh, my God, Mother. That means you are a—you haven't told anyone about this, have you?"

"No, no. You and your father are the only two people that know. And I wanted to tell you first, before I tell the other children."

Sookie knew Dee Dee would be upset, but she had no idea how much. Dee Dee had just come completely undone, and so they left the tea room and made their way to a bar down the street. Dee Dee was on her second drink, still rattled to the bone by the news, when she said, "And Grandmother knew about this all along—and she let us all think we were real Simmonses. My God, Mother, I'm the recording secretary of the Alabama chapter of the Daughters of the Confederacy."

"I know."

"Why . . . *why* would she do such a thing?"

"Oh, sweetie, why does she do anything she does? Your father thinks she just wanted us to feel like we really belonged to her."

"What did she say when you told her you knew?"

"I haven't told her. And Dee Dee, I've given a lot of thought to this, and I don't think we can ever let her know that we know. I'm afraid it would kill her. Remember, she is eighty-eight years old."

Dee Dee's eyes suddenly filled with tears. "But she always said I was her favorite. Why wouldn't she have at least told me?"

"Sweetheart, I don't know. But I'm so sorry. I knew you would be upset."

"Upset? I'm just thinking about staging my own death is all. My life is over. I hope you know that. Why live?"

"Oh now, sweetheart, I think you're making too much of this. After all, we're talking about my parents, not yours. You know who your real mother and father are. And don't forget, you know for sure that you are half a Poole. That's something, isn't it?"

Dee Dee sighed. "Oh, the Pooles are all right, I guess. But what about my Simmons family coat of honor? And who are these people anyway—the Jurdabralinskis? Or however you say it. Do you know anything about them?"

"Well, a little . . . yes."

"What?"

"Well, I know that they were evidently a very nice family, four girls and a boy, and two of the girls were twins, just like ours. Isn't that funny?"

"Were they cheese farmers or what?"

"Oh, no . . . no, honey. The father was a very well-respected businessman."

"What did he do?"

Sookie knew Dee Dee really wasn't going to like this, so she soft-pedaled it for a moment. "He was in the automobile business." She didn't dare tell her he ran a gas station.

She was going to tell the twins next, but she wanted to wait until Ce Ce had been home from her honeymoon for a while so she could tell them together.

After she told them, they were surprised, but they took it very well. Ce Ce said, "We love you, Mother. We don't care that you are adopted, do we?"

Le Le shook her head. "No, we don't care if we're not really related to Grandmother."

"No," said Ce Ce. "We don't care."

"Yes, but I know how much you both love Grandmother, so I hope it won't change how you feel about her."

"No, not at all," said Le Le. "She's still our grandmother, and we will always love her."

"But you're our mother, Mother. You're the one we love the most," added Ce Ce.

"Yes," said Le Le, "and we always wondered why you let her push you around so much."

"You did?"

"Yes," Le Le said.

"We did," said Ce Ce. "She was always nice to us, but she pushed you around something awful."

"And it made us mad, too," said Le Le.

"It *did*?"

"Yes, it did," said Ce Ce. And they both nodded in agreement.

She waited to tell Carter until the following weekend, when he came home from Atlanta with a guy friend of his. They were going to go deep-sea fishing with Earle and watch the Alabama game. That Sunday, a few hours before he was supposed to leave, she took him in the den and told him. After he got over his initial shock, Carter said, "Wow . . . Mom. From the look on your face when you said you had something you wanted to talk to me about, I thought it was really serious, like you and Dad were getting a divorce or something." Then he looked at her with wide eyes. "Wow . . . so you were adopted. How about that."

"I know it's pretty shocking to find out after all these years that none of us are related to Grandmother. How do you feel about it?"

He sat there for a moment and then said, "Well . . . I think it's really kind of great news. Now none of us have to worry about winding up over at Pleasant Hill."

Sookie was surprised to hear him say that. "Oh, honey. I never knew that ever worried you."

"Sure it did, Mom. You know I love old Winged Victory to death and always will . . . but let's face it. She is as nutty as a fruitcake. I was always afraid that one day, you might wind up just like her."

Sookie smiled. "Well, honey, it could still happen. And I'll tell you, if I get any more big shocks like this one, who knows?"

"So," said Carter, "your real mother worked at an all-girl filling station? How cool is that?" Then he grinned. "Oh, boy, I'll bet Miss Dee Dee had a flying fit when you told her."

"Pretty much," said Sookie. "But you know, honey, your sister really surprised me. She seems to be coming along pretty well."

IN THE PAST WEEKS, all her children had surprised her in some way. She found out things she never knew about them. Dee Dee even called her a few days after her meltdown at Miss Busby's Pink Tea Room and said, "Mother, I just want you to know that no matter what your background is, I still love you."

"Well, thank you, Dee Dee. I appreciate that."

"After all, it's not your fault you are not a Simmons. You can't help it, and you must be as disappointed as I am. So if you need to talk, call me anytime, night or day. I'm here for you . . . and Mother, I just want you to know that I've taken down the Simmons coat of arms."

"Ah . . . well, I know how hard that must have been for you."

"Yes, it was. But I've ordered the Poole family coat of arms, and I'll put it up as soon as it arrives."

"Oh, how nice. I'm sure your father will be so pleased."

"And Mother, just so you know . . . about your people. I've looked them up, and the Polish are considered to be extremely intelligent and good-looking people, so you mustn't feel too bad about yourself, okay?"

"Okay, honey, I'll try not to, and thanks for the information. I feel better already."

Poor Dee Dee. At least she was trying to move on, and much faster than Sookie had expected.

# AVENGER FIELD

Sweetwater, Texas

Billy Boy,

Sorry I haven't written for a while, but we left Houston and arrived at our new base in Sweetwater and have been kept busy twenty-four hours a day. This is the hottest place I have ever been. If hell is this hot, then I ain't going. It hasn't been under a hundred degrees since I've been here, and the dust storms are terrible. I have red dust in my hair, teeth, ears, and everywhere the sun doesn't shine. I don't know if I'll ever be clean again. And, oh, have I mentioned the snakes and scorpions and the bugs? It's so hot, a lot of us gals pulled our cots outside to sleep, but you never know what might crawl in bed with you. These damn snakes even try to get in the planes for a little shade . . . not happy about that. I make them do a good check on mine—don't want any snake copilot.

And they don't make it easy on us girlies. We are doing everything the army way. We train like the big boys, including calisthenics, and we march everywhere . . . I'm even marching in my sleep. No fun, but we do it. My new pal Willy says it's just more proof that they will be taking us in the Army Air

Corps for real pretty soon. The grub is pretty good. Had my first hominy grits. Mmmm . . .

Other than dodging tumbleweeds and spiders and water bugs, I'm just fine. The other girls I have met here are all swell as far as I can tell. We have six girls to a bay. I'm in with Pinks, this real cute little Jewish gal from New York. Her dad runs a big brassiere factory, and we are all sporting new undies, compliments of Mr. Pinksel. I really get a kick out of her and Bea Wallace from Oklahoma, who wears steel-toed cowboy boots and carries a .45 on her hip. What a snazzy-looking dame she is . . . brunette, about five foot nine with a million-dollar smile and all legs. She is the only one of us who still looks good in these god-awful overalls they gave us. None of them fit worth a damn. The crotch in mine hits me at the knees, but when she walks by, all the guys' eyes pop out of their heads. And no, you ain't meeting her, so stop drooling. Anyhoo, she must be loaded. She started flying so she could check out the cattle on her family's ranch. Her dad was a great pal of Will Rogers, so we call her "Willy" just to razz her. The other three gals in my bay are nice, but kinda not in my league: girls finishing school, rich debutante types, all college grads, one from Vassar and two from Smith, and they sorta have a snooty air about them, always talking about their la-di-da schools.

Anyhoo, the other night, when we were all sitting around chewing the fat, did I pull a good one. Willy and Pinks were in on the joke, and I casually let it drop that I was a recent graduate of the Phillips School for Young Ladies.

One of the Smith gals looked puzzled and was about to say something when Pinks piped up and said, "Oh, Phillips. Why, I heard Phillips was so exclusive it was almost impossible to get in. How did you ever manage to do it?" And I said, "Daddy did have to pull a lot of strings." Well, that shut them up.

Boy, did the three of us have a big laugh later. Quite a feat for someone who barely made it out of high school, eh?

Fritzi

P.S. I see what you mean about cadets. We have a lot of ninety-day wonder boys flying around Texas now. They just got out of flight school and don't have near the flight time hours that the gals do, but they still feel superior to us and like to hotdog it and show off in front of the girls, and it's pretty damn dangerous. Some of the boys have been buzzing the gals, playing fighter pilot and trying to scare them. None of us have been given formation training, and a plane flying that close does scare them. When they complained, their CO said, "Boys will be boys, and some of them may be tempted to fly on your wing and horse around a bit with the gals, but it's to be expected." But after a few close calls, he ordered that they were to stay five hundred feet away from us at all times. That rule applies on the ground as well. Our barracks are off-limits to all males. Mrs. Van de Kamp is a nice local lady who acts as a house mother to all the girls here and she makes sure that law is strictly enforced!

# AVENGER FIELD

## Sweetwater, Texas

Dear Billy,

We are training every day now. I saw my first real live Mexican and had my first tamale. Pretty good. I am sending you a ceramic sombrero ashtray and a picture of me in the flying rig. They have issued us men's flight suits—they look more like zoot suits on us. Took your advice and made friends with the mechanics. Have a swell one by the name of Elroy Leefers who is looking out for me. I miss you, and congrats on your new commission. Guess I'll have to salute you now.

Fritzi

P.S. The town of Sweetwater gave us gals a barbecue—sure was fun. These Texans are some of the friendliest people I ever met.

# AVENGER FIELD

Sweetwater, Texas

Billy Boy,

I thought I was a tough guy, but from now on, you have my permission to call me a sissy. Yesterday, Willy and I took off and were in the air no more than five minutes when I look over and see the biggest rattlesnake I have ever seen crawling right toward me. It must have been sleeping in the side compartment, and the vibration of the plane woke him up in a hurry.

Well, you always wonder how brave you will be in a crisis. I've pulled planes out of spins, I've danced on wings in a windstorm, I've done a lot of things . . . but Billy . . . when I saw that damn snake headed toward me, I froze as stiff as a starched collar. My head was telling me . . . jump out . . . move . . . do something . . . but I just sat there with my eyes as big as two platters. Then Willy looks over, sees it, calmly reaches across me, grabs that thing by the tail, and slings it out the window into the wild blue yonder. When I could breathe again, I see that Willy is as calm as a cucumber. She looks at me and starts laughing. She says she never saw a person turn green before. She tried to make me feel better and said I did the right thing by not moving—little did she know it wasn't planned. If I could have moved, I would have. Willy is one swell gal and my hero, but I didn't tell her that.

Fritzi

P.S. I'll bet that snake was surprised to find itself flying.

# AVENGER FIELD

SWEETWATER, TEXAS

Billy Boy,

Long time no hear from. Hope you're sending lots of good pilots over the pond to kick their asses. We are busier than hell here. By the way, remember those three college gals I told you about? I have to take it all back. After being around them for a while, I found out they are regular fellers. In fact, they really have the goods. Damn good fliers. They work hard. Don't complain. And can slug it out with the best of them. Ain't this old war funny? Here I am living and flying with gals that I would never have met in a million years, and I was wrong about thinking they were snooty. I think it was me that had my nose out of joint. Oh, well, wouldn't be the first time . . . eh? Anyhow, after a few bars, I finally broke down and told them about Phillips being the name of my old man's filling station back in Pulaski, where the Jurdabralinski sisters majored in grease monkeying, and they had a good laugh. Turns out they were fascinated and made me tell them all about it. Go figure. I think this war is going to change a lot of people's thinking. It's changed mine already. Okay, Billy Boy, time for me to hit the hay. Take care of yourself, and I'll see you real soon, if I get anywhere near you. Even if it is only for a night, and you know what I mean.

Me

P.S. I read that in Pensacola the boys outnumber the girls about a thousand to one. No wonder you are lonesome for me. I hate to report that the opposite here is true. Five thousand men to one girl. We sure don't lack for dancing partners. But don't worry, I am being good. Well, as good as I can be.

# HELLO, ALICE

Point Clear, Alabama

Sookie had already fed the birds, still mostly blue jays, and done a little gardening before it got too hot. August was deadly, and by eight A.M., it was already so hot and humid outside, you wound up soaking wet. It was Monday, and she thought she would get dressed and run out to the Walmart and do her weekly shopping early and get it over with.

She had just stepped out of the tub when she heard the phone in the bedroom ringing. Her mother was at her garden club meeting, so it was probably Netta. She usually wanted Sookie to pick something up for her at Walmart, so she wrapped herself in a towel and ran in and picked up.

"Hello."

"Alice?"

"Pardon me?"

"Is this Alice? I'm trying to reach Alice Finch."

Sookie suddenly recognized the voice and quickly said, "Oh, yes! This is Miss Finch, yes."

"This is the lady from Wisconsin calling, from the chamber? You called a while ago wanting to know about the Jurdabralinskis. I kept waiting for you to call back, but you never did, so I got your phone number off the phone bill. Where is area code 251?"

Sookie panicked and lied and said, "Georgia," and immediately realized that was stupid, but it was too late.

"Oh, well, listen, I have some information for ya, hon. Real interesting tidbits about the Jurdabralinskis. Mom says that three of the Jurdabralinskis were WASPs. How about that?"

"WASPs?"

"Yeah, kinda unusual, don't you think?"

"Yes, I thought they were Catholic."

"They were Catholic, but they were WASPs—ya know, girl fliers during the Second World War?"

"Girl fliers?"

"Oh, yeah. Mom says there were a bunch of write-ups in the paper back then. They were known as the Flying Jurdabralinski Girls of Pulaski. She says at one time, three of the Jurdabralinski girls were in the service, and the one girl that was killed . . . died in a plane crash."

"Oh, no."

"Oh, yeah. They had a big funeral for her over at the cathedral and everything, and she was a big hero and all."

Sookie felt her heart sink. "Which sister was it? Do you know . . . was her first name Fritzi?"

"Hold on, I've got all the stuff written down. Okay. Hmmm . . ." As Sookie waited for her to find it, she felt her heart start to pound. "No . . . that's not it. Wait a minute. Oh, here it is . . . no, it was another Jurdabralinski sister who died."

Sookie suddenly felt strangely relieved. "Do you have any information on the sister named Fritzi—about what ever happened to her?"

"Hold on . . . let me ask Mom. She's right here. Hey, Mom, do you know what ever happened to Fritzi Jurdabralinski?" Sookie heard mumbling in the background. "Mom says she moved off years ago. She thinks to somewhere in California."

"Does she know where?"

"Hold on. Mom . . . Mom! Alice wants to know where she moved to in California . . . . She says she doesn't remember, but it was a Danish town."

"A Danish town?"

"Mom, a Danish town? . . . Yeah, she says she got a postcard from her sometime in the fifties, and it had windmills on it."

"I see. Does your mother happen to know if she's still alive?"

"Is she still alive, Mom?" More mumbling in the background. "She says she must be or it would have been in the papers. Mom reads all the obituaries. But now here's the other really interesting tidbit. One of the girls went on to become quite a celebrity in her own right. She and her twin sister. They had an accordion act and used to play locally, and Mom says she wrote an awful lot of good polkas. I know she wrote 'I'm Too Fat to Polka' and 'The Wink-a-Dink Polka' and a lot of others. I can get you a list. I can go down to the newspaper and look up those articles and send you a packet of what all I find."

"Oh, that would be wonderful."

"Okay, then. I'll dig up what I can and send it on to ya. What's your address, hon?"

Oh, dear, now she was caught. "Uh . . . send it to Alice Finch, in care of Mrs. Earle Poole, Jr. 526 Bayview Street, Point Clear, Alabama."

"Huh. I thought you said you lived in Georgia."

"Yes, but it's very close to the state line, and I get my mail in Alabama."

"Oh. Well, okay, then. I'll get this off to you as soon as I can get it all gathered up. Nice talking to you, Alice."

"You, too. Thank you."

AFTER SHE HUNG UP, Sookie sat there and noticed her hands were shaking. She knew the woman was talking about her real mother and her real family, but it still seemed so unreal and scary. She didn't even know that women flew planes during World War II. She thought there had only been men pilots.

The phone rang again, and she picked it up. This time, it was Netta. "Are you going to Walmart?"

"Yes, I sure am."

"Could you pick me up a six-pack of paper towels and a carton of Diet Dr Pepper?"

"Of course."

"And a pound of frozen shrimp. If you're coming right back."

"I sure will. No problem."

"Are you okay? You sound funny."

"No, I'm fine. Listen, Netta, do you know anything about the WASPs?"

"What wasps?"

"The girl WASPs that flew planes during the Second World War."

Netta thought to herself, "Uh-oh, here she goes again." "No, honey, I didn't know wasps flew planes."

"Well, I didn't either . . . until just now . . . isn't that strange?"

"Yes . . . I would say so."

"Have you ever heard of a town in California that's Danish and has a lot of windmills?"

"No, honey, sure haven't." After Netta hung up, she was worried again. She had thought Sookie was getting better, but evidently not.

Later, as she wheeled through Walmart, Sookie asked a few people if they had ever heard about the WASPs, and not one person had. Mr. Lennon, one of the Walmart greeters, said he thought he remembered something about them, but he wasn't sure. But then, he was ninety-two. Sookie couldn't wait for Earle to get home.

The minute Earle walked in the door, Sookie said, "Earle, you won't believe this, but I just found out my mother was a WASP and flew planes in the Second World War!"

"What?"

"A woman from Wisconsin called and told me. And her sisters did, too."

"Hold on. Slow down. Now what?"

"My mother was a WASP. Like a WAC, only they flew planes. Have you ever heard of them?"

"No. I knew there were WACs and WAVES, but no."

"Can you look them up on the Internet for me? I'm too nervous."

"Sure, honey." They walked back to the den, and Earle sat down and turned on the computer. He typed in "Women Fliers," "World War II," and the word "WASPs," and suddenly, something came up. "Here it is," Earle said.

> The Women Air Force Service Pilots (WASPs) were the first women to serve as pilots and fly military aircraft for the United States Army Air Forces during World War II. The original twenty-eight women were under the direction of Nancy Harkness Love, who was an advocate of using experienced women fliers in domestic service to ferry airplanes in order to free up male pilots for combat or overseas ferrying.

WASP FACTS

1. The WASPs served in the Army Air Forces from September 1942 to December 20, 1944.
2. More than 33,000 women applied. 1,830 were accepted. 1,074 graduated from the training program.
3. Governed by the Civil Service Commission, although under military discipline order, the WASPs were originally stationed at the Howard Hughes Airport in Houston, Texas, but were transferred to Avenger Field, Sweetwater, Texas, in February 1943.
4. WASPs received seven months of training, the same as male cadets.
5. WASPs were stationed at 120 Army Air Bases within the United States.
6. WASPs flew 78 different types of aircraft, every plane the Army Air Corps flew, including the B-29.
7. WASPs flew sixty million miles of operation flights.
8. Types of flying duties included ferrying aircraft from factory to bases, flight instruction (basic and instrument), towing targets for antiaircraft, towing targets for aerial gunnery, tracking and searchlight missions, simulated strafing, and radio-controlled flights.
9. Thirty-eight died while flying for the Army Air Corps.

"Wow," said Earle. "This is pretty impressive. I had no idea. This is really something, isn't it?"

"Yes, and now I know why she was in Texas, and my two aunts were there, too. One of those girls that died was my aunt."

"Oh, no. Really?"

"Yes. The lady is sending me newspaper articles."

"Really? Does she know if she's still alive?"

"She thinks so. The last time she heard from her, she was in California. Look up a town in California that's Danish and has windmills."

"Oh, okay, but could you get me a drink? An iced tea or something?"

Sookie was in the kitchen when she heard Earle call out. "I found it!" Sookie brought him his iced tea, and he pointed to the screen, and sure enough, there was a picture of a town with lots of big windmills everywhere. "Here it is. It says, 'Solvang, California. Two hours north of Los Angeles, nestled in the beautiful Santa Ynez Valley. Come and discover the charming little town of Solvang, California. History: In January 1911, the Danish-American Colony Corporation, looking for farmland and impressed by the area's abundant year-round sunshine, bought nine thousand plus acres of land. The new settlement was named Solvang, which means "Sunny Field" in Danish. The corporation advertised in Danish-language newspapers, and soon both U.S. Danish immigrants and those still in Denmark bought land in the colony. Many descendants of the original settlers still populate the area today.' This has to be it."

"I'm sure it is. But I doubt if she's still there."

"Don't you want to find out?"

"Oh, I don't know, Earle. I'm not sure. Even if I did meet her, what good would it do? What if she's just horrible, and I hated her? Or what if, after she met me, she decided to move here with us? And I couldn't say no, and then Lenore would find out. I don't know, Earle. I still think it might be better to just leave well enough alone."

"You do what you want, but if you don't, and she dies, you might regret not meeting her when you still had the chance, or at least talking to her on the phone."

"But why?"

"Well, you could find out why she gave you up. Don't you think she at least deserves a chance? Don't forget you just found out about her, but I'm sure she has been wondering about you for fifty-nine years."

"Sixty," added Sookie.

LATER IN BED, SOOKIE said, "Just imagine, Earle, I'm scared to go on a Ferris wheel, and my real mother actually flew a plane."

Earle smiled. "It's pretty exciting."

"Yes . . . I guess it really is."

Earle was glad to see Sookie start to take some sort of an interest. He hoped she would change her mind after reading about the WASPs and all that they did. He would like to meet the old gal himself. But it was Sookie's decision.

NOW, THINKING MORE ABOUT it, Sookie realized that another reason not to meet her real mother was that when she found out that her daughter had never really accomplished anything and was just a housewife, she could be terribly disappointed in her. Good Lord. She had already disappointed one mother, and that was bad enough. She didn't know if she wanted to take a chance on disappointing two.

# AVENGER FIELD

## Sweetwater, Texas

Billy,

What's wrong with the damn male race? We are getting a lot of flack from a bunch of disgruntled flyboys. As if things weren't tough enough, a group of them here are not happy that girls are doing the same thing they are, and in some cases (mine), doing it better. We could ignore it, but they have started enough rumors about us to sink our entire program. They are telling people that we are a bunch of man-hungry females who joined up just so we could sleep around with the male pilots and are generally a no-good lot that should be sent home. Two weeks ago, we found out that they brought in a group of prostitutes and put them up at the Sweetwater Hotel and told everybody they were WASPs. I can tell you that didn't endear us to the townsfolk.

Finally, it got straightened out, but we are now being forced to live like nuns. Our director Jackie Cochran says we can't afford a hint of scandal. No dating instructors, no cussing, and ladylike behavior at all times while the flyboys do what they want. But Cochran says that our morals are to be above reproach. It's hell being a guinea pig, but as our house mother Mrs. Van de Kamp said, if we can prove ourselves, it will all be worth it in the end. Then maybe the next group won't have it so bad.

I know you are not reading about it in the paper. They don't want it getting out, but we lost three girls this month, and one was a bay mate of mine and a really nice gal. She was married to a marine serving in Guadalcanal and has two kids at home. A few days ago, she came in too low and crashed on landing right outside the barracks.

I know you see a lot of this, and it's all just part of training, but I am still not used to it and hope I never will be. It makes me so mad when all the newspaper reporters that come here only want to show the gals putting on lipstick or posing like models . . . all this phony baloney stuff. If anybody thinks this is a glamorous job and that we are just in it for the fun, they haven't watched them pull a friend out of a burning plane and die right in front of them. Nobody here is saying much, but the mood is pretty glum.

Fritzi

# THE CHECK RIDE

Sweetwater, Texas
1943

Most of the male instructors at Avenger Field were nice, but some bitterly resented being assigned to Sweetwater, and they went out of their way to make the girls' lives miserable. They would yell at them, call them "stupid" and "incompetent," and do everything in their power to try to make them wash out. One, a surly lieutenant named Miller, was particularly rough on them. Day after day, girls would come in after their lessons with him in tears. One girl had been so devastated by his bullying, she quit and went home. And he made no bones about how he felt. It was clear he thought women had no business flying planes.

One afternoon, over at the club, he was sitting at the bar, talking to the bartender in a loud voice, so he was sure to be heard by the girls that were there. "God, I hate this job. When people ask me what I did in the war, what am I gonna say? That all I did was teach a bunch of Goddamned women? Shit . . ."

Fritzi was standing around, waiting to go up and take her first military check ride, when Miller walked up and said, "Okay, Jurdabralinski, let's go. I'm gonna take you up and see what you can do. And when I tell you something, don't talk, just do it."

"Yes, sir," she said.

As she was climbing up to her altitude, he reached over her from behind and yelled at her, "Jesus Christ, pull the damn stick back . . . don't ease it back," and he grabbed it and jammed it against her leg as hard as he could. "You're not in some powder puff derby. Pull the damn thing. Jesus Christ, what idiot taught you to fly?"

Fritzi desperately wanted to pass this inspection, but something snapped. She gunned the engines and as soon as she got her altitude, she suddenly flipped the plane over and flew upside down while Miller, who was now suspended in midair and hanging on to his shoulder straps, screamed for dear life, "Turn over! Turn over! God-damn it!" When she did, Fritzi did a barrel roll, shot straight up, and then did her famous death drop into fifteen spins straight down. She then pulled up at the last second, shot back up, and went into a hammerhead stall just for good measure.

DOWN BELOW AT AVENGER Field, all the ground crew was standing there and looking up and watching what was happening and yelling. Pretty soon, everyone on the ground was looking up, and people were running out of the hangars and barracks to see what all the noise was about.

Gussie Mintz came out of the mess hall with a cigarette hanging out of her mouth to see, and she looked up just as Fritzi did another barrel roll, and she started to laugh. "You show 'em how to do it, gal," she said.

After another series of amazing spirals and loops, mechanic Elroy Leefers started grinning. "Give him hell, Fritzi!" After a few more minutes, she did a double loop, came in for a perfect landing, drove the plane to the main hangar, and stopped. She turned around and said to Miller, who was red-faced and fuming with rage, "Compliments of Billy Bevins, the greatest flight instructor alive."

"Get out of the plane!" he said.

"Yes, sir! Right away, sir!" she said as she jumped down. She undid her parachute and left it lying on the ground. Fritzi knew she had washed out, but nobody called Billy Bevins an idiot and got away with it, not while she was alive.

As Fritzi walked away, Willy and Pinks ran up to walk with her, and when Pinks looked back, Miller was still sitting in the plane. Fritzi went straight to the barracks and started packing her things. Once a girl washed out, they left as soon as possible. It was too painful an ordeal for everyone to drag it out.

Her bay mates who had witnessed her flight were not happy and stood there and watched her pack. Pinks said, "The bastard had it coming, but damn, Fritzi . . . what are we going to do without you?"

After Fritzi had packed, Willy and Pinks walked with her to the gate. Just as Fritzi was about to get on the truck, a girl came running up, panting, "The captain wants to see you in his office right away." Damn. She was hoping to get out before the report was finished and she had to face the music, but she hadn't made it.

A few minutes later, when she walked into the commanding officer's office, she saw Captain Wheeler sitting at his desk with an extremely grim expression on his face. Mrs. Van de Kamp sat in a chair behind him and looked as if she had been crying. Captain Wheeler glanced up from the report, looking furious, as he barked at her, "Young woman, that was one of the most reckless and irresponsible displays of complete disregard of rules and safety that I have ever witnessed. Do you realize you endangered the life of an instructor and yourself and risked destroying a military plane?"

"Yes, sir."

"And if that wasn't bad enough, you also put the reputation and the future of the entire WASP program in jeopardy today. You, of all people, know how hard Mrs. Love and Mrs. Cochran are working to ensure that this program continues, and then to pull a stunt like that."

"I understand. I'm sorry, sir. I wasn't thinking. I lost my head."

"This program is not about you. It's about all the girls and the ones that will follow them."

"Yes, sir."

He picked up the report from Lieutenant Miller and said, "You obviously didn't pass the inspection."

"No, sir."

"Mrs. Van de Kamp has informed me of some of the problems you girls have had with Lieutenant Miller, but that's no excuse, and according to official military protocol, you should be court-martialed."

"Yes, sir."

Captain Wheeler put the report down on his desk, leaned back in his chair, and looked out the window. After a long minute, he turned back around and looked at her and said, "I know military rules, and by all rights, I should throw you out on your ear." Then he sighed, "But I think anybody that can make that sour little son of a bitch Miller mess his pants deserves another chance, so I'm grounding you for two weeks or until we can ship Miller out of here. But if you ever pull a stunt like that again, you are out. And I will personally make sure you never fly another plane as long as you live. Do you understand?"

"Yes, sir."

"Now get out of here."

"Yes, sir. Thank you, sir."

"And Jurdabralinski . . ."

"Yes, sir?"

"Tell Billy I said hello."

NOW SHE KNEW WHY Miller didn't get out of the plane. They told her later, Miller made the mechanic taxi the plane over to another hangar and then ordered everyone out. But word got around. The mechanic was Elroy Leefers. As for Fritzi, she didn't know how much she really loved being a WASP until she almost wasn't.

# THE AFFAIR

Winged Victory was at the Just Teazzing beauty shop having her hair done when her friend Pearl Jeff came in looking for her. Pearl had just heard something from a friend, and she couldn't wait to tell Lenore.

Thirty minutes later, Lenore came storming in Sookie's front door and marched back to the kitchen where Sookie was sitting and having her lunch. "I want to talk to you, young lady, and I mean right now. I am just appalled at your obvious complete lack of discretion. Have you forgotten you're a married woman?"

Sookie looked up. "What?"

"I wondered why you were never home anymore and why I could never get you on the phone, and now I know."

"What?"

"You know what. Word has just reached my ears about what's been going on between you and that Dr. Shapiro, and I want you to put a stop to this nonsense right now."

"But, Mother—"

"Don't you 'But, Mother' me. Why, the very idea of you having . . . whatever you are having . . . is disgraceful. Earle Poole, Jr., is one of the finest men I have ever known in my life, and now you do this?"

"Do what? What are you talking about?"

"Everybody knows you two have been meeting all over town. I simply will not allow you to treat Earle this way. Earle has been nothing but an ideal husband and father, and you're lucky to have him. I just hope and pray I'm not too late, and he doesn't find out. Remember, what's good for the goose is good for the gander, and with his looks, why, he could have any woman he wanted, so I would suggest you just nip this little thing in the bud right now, before you wake up and find yourself a divorced woman."

Sookie sat there completely flabbergasted. "I don't believe what I am hearing. First of all, it's not true. I am not having an affair with anybody, and I can't believe you would even think that of me. And secondly, I thought you didn't like Earle."

"What do you mean? I've always liked Earle, and you know it. And if it isn't true, why are you meeting this man all over town? It certainly looks suspicious to me. Nobody's that crazy about waffles!"

"All right, Mother, since you insist on knowing everything, yes, I am meeting Dr. Shapiro all over town. And do you know why? Because I happen to be a patient of his, and I was trying to keep it a secret, so I wouldn't embarrass you or, God forbid, besmirch the precious Simmons family name, even though two of them are sitting over in the loony bin right this minute!"

Lenore looked at her with shock. "Sookie, Pleasant Hill is not a loony bin. And they are being treated for a simple nervous disorder. Why would you say such a terrible thing?"

"Okay, Mother, have it your own way. You always do."

"And, anyhow, why are you seeing a psychiatrist? Is this one of Marvaleen's ideas?"

"No, it isn't. I'm sure it's hard for you to imagine, Mother, but every once in a while, I actually have an idea of my own."

"Well, it's just plain silliness, and I want you to stop it right now. Do you hear me, young lady?"

"Mother, you do understand that I am a grown woman?"

"I don't care how grown you are. You're still my daughter, and I won't have you causing a scandal."

There was long pause while Sookie debated whether to just let her have it once and for all . . . but she didn't. "Okay, Mother."

"Good. I just hope and pray that Earle doesn't hear about this. That poor man is under enough strain as it is, having to fiddle with all those teeth all day, without you acting a fool in public."

"Yes, Mother."

"Well, now that we have settled that . . . I'll take a cup of coffee."

Lenore sat down and stared at Sookie while she made the coffee, then said, "I must say, Sookie, I am very concerned about your behavior lately. Has that doctor been giving you pills?"

"No, Mother."

"Hmmm . . . well . . . something's wrong with you. He could be hypnotizing you, and you just don't know it. You've never been very smart about your friends. I always said if Marvaleen said, 'Let's jump off a building,' you'd be right behind her. Don't forget what happened when she drug you to that Bible study."

"No, Mother."

A few days later, Marvaleen heard the rumor about Sookie and had an entirely different reaction. When she saw Sookie get in her car at the parking lot at Walgreens, she ran over and knocked on her car window. Sookie rolled down the window. "Hi, Marvaleen, how are you?"

"Open the door," she said, pulling on the handle. Sookie unlocked the door, and Marvaleen jumped in and playfully slapped her on the leg. "Oh, you sly dog, you devil you. They always say it's the quiet ones you have to watch out for. Why didn't you tell me? I think it's all just so exciting, and he is sooo cute."

It suddenly dawned on Sookie what she was talking about. "And young, too. I told you journaling would change your life, and I was right. What is he—thirty?"

"Oh, Lord, Marvaleen, whatever you've heard is not true. I am not having an affair."

Marvaleen winked at her. "Uh-huh, of course not, but honey, you don't have to be embarrassed with me. I approve wholeheartedly. Edna Yorba Zorbra says it's really what nature intended. We should all be with younger men. She says it's only fair. She says we don't hit our sexual peak until sixty. Our sex drive is going up while the men our age are going down."

"But, really, Marvaleen, Dr. Shapiro is just a friend."

"Uh-huh, well, do me a favor. See if your friend has a friend."

"Marvaleen, believe me. I am not having an affair. I'm only seeing him professionally. He's helping me with a few issues, that's all."

"Sure you are, and of course, that's what I'll say if anyone asks. You can trust me. But between us, I'm so proud of you. I always thought you were just one of those dull little housewife types that would never change."

"What? Do you think I'm *dull*?"

"Not anymore."

"But you used to think I was dull?"

"Yes, but not in a bad way. Just conventional. You know—"

"I see, and what else did you think? Don't be afraid to hurt my feelings. I really want to know. Seriously, if you were to describe me to someone, what would you say?"

"Oh, well, I would say you were just as nice and sweet as you could be, that's all."

"That's all. Is that what most people think?"

"Well, yes . . . I guess so. But it's all positive."

"But isn't there something about me that's negative? I have to have some bad faults."

"No, I really can't think of anything, except . . . but even that's not bad."

"No, no—tell me. Except what?"

"Oh, I suppose if you had any fault, I guess it would be that you let people push you around."

"You mean Mother."

Marvaleen nodded. "And me, too. But Sookie, that's not a bad thing. Edna Yorba Zorbra says there are leaders and followers, and the secret to happiness is to embrace your role in life."

"I see."

"Edna Yorba Zorbra says that I'm a perfect combo of student and teacher combined."

"Really?"

"Yes. She says I could morph into becoming a professional life coach any day now if I followed my goddess within. But anyhow, what I really wanted to tell you was that if you and—you know who—ever need a little privacy, I do have that guesthouse in back, and the key is under the mat. Feel free to use it anytime. After all, we cougars have to stick together."

Sookie realized there was no convincing her otherwise, so she said, "Well, thanks, Marvaleen, I just might take you up on it. A couple of sailor friends of mine are shipping in next week."

"Sailors?"

"Uh-huh. Twins."

"Twins?"

"Uh-huh. They do everything together." Sookie winked at Marvaleen. "If you know what I mean."

Marvaleen opened the car door in a daze and got out, stood in the parking lot, and stared at Sookie as she drove away. "Wow. Talk about still waters running deep."

After Sookie drove off, she realized she really shouldn't have said that about the sailors. She would call Marvaleen when she got home and tell her she had made it up. But at least she had found out that people thought she was dull, and what she had suspected all along was true. She had heard of a man without a country. She was a woman without a personality. She had absolutely no personality.

How *do* you get a personality after sixty? She didn't even know where to begin. And why didn't she have one? Had Lenore squashed it? Or had she just been born that way? Her kids all had their own unique personalities—where did they get them? Now she wondered what her personality would be like if she had been raised in Wisconsin by Polish people. She might have been a whole lot of more fun . . . and played the accordion, done the polka, and everything.

When she got home, Sookie was still upset to think that anyone would believe that she, of all people, would be having an affair. Honestly. It was so embarrassing. But obviously, the Waffle House was out. She picked up the phone and made a call. "Dr. Shapiro, do you by any chance know where the Ruby Tuesday out on the four-lane is?"

# GRADUATION DAY

## Avenger Field

Winter of 1943 had been rough. A bitter battle was raging in Europe, and Uncle Sam needed all the gas it could get to help fuel the necessary planes and military vehicles. After talking it over with Poppa, Gertrude was the next Jurdabralinski girl to sign up for the WASPs.

Momma wasn't happy, but there was nothing she could do, so Gertrude arrived in Sweetwater, Texas, on May 4 with sacks filled with homemade bread and sausages and two large jars of sauerkraut for Fritzi. The next day, Willy, Pinks, and Gertrude had a picnic on Fritzi's bed with six bottles of Jax beer that Gussie Mintz had smuggled out of the officers' mess.

Fritzi was in her final phase of training and anxious to finish and get her assignment. The girls had hoped that by the time they graduated, they would be taken in the Army Air Corps and get their real wings, but it had not happened. At the last minute, Jackie Cochran, at her own expense, had Neiman Marcus in Dallas make up special wings for the girls. Graduation Day was pretty special. A lot of the top military brass flew in from Washington, and the entire town of Sweetwater turned out to cheer them on as they marched in. As disappointed as they were not to have real Army Air Corps wings, it was pretty funny for all of them to watch General Hap Arnold try to pin the wings on each girl's chest. He got pretty flustered trying to figure out what was chest and what was not. And on some of the girls, especially Pinks, there was an awful lot of what wasn't chest. Before it was over, the general was red-faced and sweating, And it wasn't from the heat.

That night, before she went to bed, Fritzi sat down and wrote her brother a letter.

Dear Wink,

I got your last letter, but it was mostly blacked out. Those censor boys are really on a tear, so I don't know where you are now or what you are up to, but I get the idea that you are in it pretty good. Not much news is coming out of Europe, but we know our guys are letting them have it.

Just so you know, I graduated today, and we got our assignments, and my pal Willy and I sure are happy. We found out we will both be stationed at Long Beach, California, and will be ferrying planes straight from the factory for shipment overseas. Our pal Pinks has been kicked upstairs and is staying on here at Avenger Field to assist Captain Wheeler. And she is going to make one hell of an administrator. Pinks had never mentioned it to us until today, but she has a law degree. I didn't even know there were women lawyers. Those New York gals are smart as hell. We sure will miss her, but we will be stopping in at Sweetwater from time to time to check up on her and Gertrude and the rest of the gals.

Well, gotta go. Keep 'em flying! California, here I come!

Fritzi

# LONG BEACH, CALIFORNIA

Dear Billy Boy,

Flew over to Palm Springs, California, headed back to Long Beach, air smooth as glass. I never knew there were so many mountains and oil wells in California. Just for fun, flew with one wing in Mexico and one in California. Wow.

When this thing is over, I'm thinking about pulling up roots and heading out west. Billy, this place was made for flying. And the rest ain't so bad, either. Palm trees, movie stars, and you can pick an orange or a lemon right off a tree. Everybody here has a tan and the whitest teeth I have ever seen. And speaking of movie stars, I was walking down Hollywood Boulevard, headed for the canteen, when I heard someone tooting their horn at me. I looked over, expecting to see some fresh guy, but it was this snazzy-looking blonde in sunglasses driving a big blue convertible who pulls over to the curb and says, "Hi, soldier, need a ride?" And when I jumped in, Billy, I'll be darned if it wasn't Ginger Rogers, my favorite actress, and I said, "Hey, the last time I saw you was at the Pulaski theater in *Kitty Foyle,* and you were swell in it, too." "Thanks," she says and then looks at my wings and wants to know all about it, and despite being so famous, is real down to earth. When I got out of the car, I said, "So long, Kitty, thanks for the ride," and she got a laugh out of that. She is one sweet gal, but then everybody here is just swell to us. I haven't paid for a drink or a meal since I've been here. And the place is crawling with famous people. Willy and I went to the Brown Derby for lunch, and when we asked for the check, the waiter said, "The two gentlemen in the corner have already taken care of it." We looked over and there sat Mr. Bob Hope and Mr. Bing Crosby. Then Bob Hope comes over and gives us two free tickets to his radio show and invites us to come to dinner at his house in Toluca Lake after the broadcast. All strictly on the up and up. His wife and kids were there, and so was Martha Raye, and after dinner, the doorbell rang, and I swear, Willy and I about died. It was Edgar Bergen and Charlie McCarthy, and old Charlie said, "I hear there are some beautiful pilots here." Anyhow, we had one swell time. They sure make us feel appreciated, and it's not only here, it's everywhere. People bend over backward to make you feel at home. I know it's not me, it's the uniform, but it still feels good. Billy, after the war is over, you need to come out here and look into doing some stunt flying for the movies. We met a few of the guys here, and they say the pay is great.

Fritzi

P.S. An hour later.

Billy, I just read this letter. Yikes! Boy, do I sound like one big jerk going on and on about Hollywood. When I think about the gals that got killed, I feel ashamed of myself for still being alive and having such a swell time. But I don't know what else to do, and I still miss them like crazy.

## PENSACOLA, FLORIDA

Fritzi Gal,

Great to hear about Hollywood. I sure will put the stunt-flying idea in the hopper. Sounds good to stay in one place. I am getting too old for barnstorming anymore. These kids here are scaring the living hell out of me. A little training, and they think they are hot shots. They are cracking up planes left and right, and a lot of them are determined to take me down with them. You tell that guy bellyaching about teaching a bunch of women, I'd be happy to swap places with him. I would rather fly with a woman anytime.

Listen, Fritzi, I know it's a rough deal losing your pals, but you just enjoy every minute you have, and that's an order.

Billy

# LONG BEACH, CALIFORNIA

Dear Billy,

Your pigeon landed back in Long Beach, tired and happy. It sure was great to see you, honey, even if it was for just two days. Maybe next time, we will actually leave the room for some sightseeing. Ha-ha. I doubt it. I'll tell you, Billy, when I saw you standing there at the gate in Newark, I almost fainted. A visit with you was just what the doctor ordered. But the next time you have a few days off, let me know, so a gal can at least throw on a little lipstick and comb her hair. I must have looked terrible, but it's hard to look pretty after ten hours of flying. You look great. The navy must agree with you, and those stripes you are sporting don't hurt, either.

The P-38 I picked up in Newark today had parts falling off of it, but tonight, all the way across the desert, the stars twinkled like diamonds in a dark blue velvet sky, and coming in and seeing all the lights of L.A. spread out for miles, whew! So beautiful. Foul weather, bad gas that funked up the engines, mechanical problems . . . all forgotten.

Love,

Fritzi

## RUBY TUESDAY

POINT CLEAR, ALABAMA

DR. SHAPIRO GOT A LITTLE LOST ON THE WAY AND WAS LATE FOR THEIR appointment. And when he did find the restaurant and walked in, he almost didn't recognize Sookie. She was wearing a long blond wig and big black sunglasses. "It's me," she said. He sat down and apologized for being late. "Oh, that's all right. It's my fault. I should have given you better directions." After the waitress had taken their order, Sookie leaned in and said, "Dr. Shapiro, I'm sure you're wondering why I asked you to meet me here and not at the Waffle House."

"Well . . ."

"I didn't want to tell you this over the phone in case your wife or someone was listening."

"Ah."

"But the thing is—we have somewhat of a sticky situation. It seems we have been spotted by somebody. This is such a small town. Anyhow, my mother's friend Pearl Jeff has evidently heard a rumor . . . about us . . . and told Lenore, and she had a fit."

"Oh?"

"Yes, I know it sounds ridiculous, but someone must have seen us together a few times, I guess, and now Mother has the idea that I am running around town, having an affair with a younger man behind my husband's back. Can you believe it? And it's not only my mother, but Marvaleen has heard it, too. Of course, she was thrilled about it. She thinks I'm dull. Anyhow, she even offered me her guesthouse, for an illicit tryst, I guess. Anyhow, I don't want you to worry about it. They have no idea who you are. It's me they are talking about. But isn't it just the silliest thing you ever heard of? I told them it wasn't true, but they wouldn't believe me. And, of course, the first thing I did was tell Earle."

"Oh?"

"Yes, and he thought it was the funniest thing he had ever heard, you and me having an affair."

"Really?"

"Oh, not that he thinks you're funny. It's me. I've always been sort of a prude about these kinds of things. Marvaleen had always been the racy one. Anyhow, Earle said that I should let them go on thinking it. Of course, I didn't tell him about the twin sailors I mentioned to Marvaleen, either, but as I said to Earle, I have Dr. Shapiro's reputation to think about, too. Anyhow, that's why I'm wearing this wig and the reason I asked you to meet me way out here, in case you wondered."

"I see."

"Lenore said that I had to stop seeing you or I would ruin my reputation, but I certainly don't want to stop being your patient. But after hearing this, if you feel we should not go on, I will certainly understand."

"No, I don't want to stop. I'm still game, if you are. And I think the fact that you're here at all shows great progress."

"You do?"

"Yes, you are not allowing what someone may or may not think deter you from doing what you want."

"Even though I wore the wig?"

"Yes."

Sookie sat back in the booth and thought about what he just said. "Well, I guess that's true, isn't it?"

"Yes. Under the same circumstances, some people might not have the courage to continue."

"No, they wouldn't, would they?"

Sookie drove home feeling really good about herself. She really must be doing better. But still, just to be on the safe side, next week, she and Dr. Shapiro were meeting at Mrs. Minor's Café and Truck Stop on Highway 98.

# NEW CASTLE ARMY AIR BASE

## Wilmington, Delaware

Dear Billy,

How's by you? Excuse the handwriting. It is 3 A.M., and I am sitting in the nurses' quarters john, where they put us for the night. Stopped in at Sweetwater the other day to check up on all the gals, and Gertrude is doing just fine. She says she got a letter from Sophie, and Sophie is thinking about joining up as well, but I am going to discourage her. This rough-and-tumble life is not for her. Too bad, though, because she is a damn good pilot.

In the meantime, yours truly is busy. Made six deliveries in five days, setting a record. Ahem, gloat, gloat. I did have a laugh along the way. Had one woman ask me if I was in the Mexican Army. Best yet, people still don't know what to make of the uniform. We have been taken for everything from Girl Scout leaders to stewardesses to Red Cross volunteers. And most good restaurants won't let us in. When we arrived in Wilmington, looking forward to a steak with all the trimmings, one snooty puffball says to us, "We don't accept women in trousers," to which Willy says, "Would you accept a boot in your behind?"

But she said it to us, not him. We are to be on our best behavior, damn it.

Worst of all, the other day when a few of the gals had to land on a base in Georgia, they were held at gunpoint by an eager MP. This yo-yo thought they had stolen a U.S. military plane. When they finally got it straightened out, he said, "Nobody told me about no women flying." We still seem to be the best-kept secret in the country, even to the army.

Fritzi

# LONG BEACH, CALIFORNIA

Dear Sophie,

I hear from home there are still some rumblings about you threatening to sign up for the WASPs. Hmmm . . . I know you didn't ask for my advice, but you are getting it anyway.

Here's the deal. It ain't easy. Once you get to Avenger Field, you will be sharing a room with six other girls and a bathroom with twelve others. No privacy. They will work you until you drop. The instructors here are strictly army and tough, and if you don't wash out and do start delivering, it is worse. You are up before dawn and head out in the cold so you can get to the airport, ready to take off at light. You will most likely be flying in an open cockpit in snowstorms, sleet, and rain or in weather so hot you are a baked potato when you land. And not to be crude, but these planes are designed for men with a built-in tube. Once you're up, there is no way we can wiggle out of forty pounds of heavy flying suits and parachute, and go to the bathroom, and on those four- and five-hour trips, this can be hell.

Once you deliver, you are on your own to get back to base. Now, because they don't want any talk about fraternization, they won't let us hop a ride back on a military plane with the guys, so we have to go commercial or any way we can. And here is my other big worry. Guys. As good-looking as you are, you are bound to be swamped by every guy here wanting to date you. We are outnumbered by the guys about five thousand to one, and I'm not sure you are ready to handle that. Gertrude is a big gal, and as you know, I have a big mouth, so we can take care of ourselves. But knowing you? You are a sucker for a sob story. In other words, I don't think this is the place for you. You have always been on the delicate side, and I am not sure you could even get through the physical training. I know you want to help out, but there are a lot of other things you can do. You mean too much to Mom and Pop and all of us, and if anything ever happened to you, I would never forgive myself. Okay?

I've had my say and told you the worst, and you have to make your own decisions, but at least you have been warned.

Love you, kid,

Fritzi

## THE DECISION

Pulaski, Wisconsin

Sophie had read the letter she received from Fritzi, but each day, as she sat in the kitchen with her father listening to the war news, she felt more and more that she had to do something. She knew she was a good enough pilot to at least try to join up at Sweetwater.

Besides, working at the filling station with Fritzi, she had heard bad language and had guys make passes at her. She assured her mother that nothing could change her mind about her religious vocation. "But, Momma, I really believe they need me. I can fly as well as Gertrude, and she went. And if I can free up just one man to fight overseas, it could make a difference."

Momma sighed. "Well, if you think so, then I guess you should go. It means that now I'll be lighting four candles, instead of three. Oh, dear Jesus in heaven, I hate this war. It's taking all my children. Thank God, your sister Tula doesn't fly or I'd be losing her, too."

Five days later, when Sophie Marie arrived in Sweetwater, Gertrude was waiting for her as she got off the bus. Gertrude was so happy to see Sophie, even though it meant she would have to start getting up early on Sunday mornings again. Since Gertrude had been away from home, she had been slacking off on going to mass every week, but she had promised Momma to take good care of Sophie. Now that Fritzi had left, she was the oldest sister, so she was going to be on her best behavior, but oh she had loved sleeping in on Sundays.

# LENORE'S AT IT AGAIN

POINT CLEAR, ALABAMA

AFTER SHE HAD REPEATEDLY BEEN ASKED NOT TO, LENORE STARTED watching the local late-night television news again. "It only upsets you, Mother," said Sookie. And sure enough, a few mornings later, Lenore called Netta and woke her up out of a sound sleep.

"Hello," said a groggy Netta.

"It's Lenore. Listen, dear, I want to run something by you before I call the newspaper."

Netta looked at the clock. It was 6:18 A.M. "All right, go ahead, Lenore."

"This country is a mess, and it's not getting any better."

"I agree with you there, hon, but what can you do?"

"That's just it. I know exactly what we can do and where we went wrong."

"Well, good for you, Lenore," said Netta, as she slowly got up out of bed and put Lenore on speakerphone and headed to the bathroom.

"Looking back now, it is clear that our first big mistake was ever doing away with the monarchy. This democracy thing is just not working. And we've certainly given it a fair chance for how many years now?"

"Two hundred and something, at least," called out Netta from the other room.

"More than a fair chance, wouldn't you agree?"

"Oh, yes, more than fair."

"It sounded like a good idea at the time, and I hate to say it, but the majority of people in this country are simply just not capable of governing themselves. My Lord, look who they just reelected mayor. That man doesn't have enough sense to tell time, much less run an entire town."

"You're right about that," said Netta as she flushed the toilet.

"I know I am! And something has to be done before he runs us all into the ground. Nobody wants to spend all that money for those stupid bicycle paths."

Netta came back to her bedside table and took Lenore off speakerphone. "I agree, hon, but what do you propose?"

"People just have to step aside, and let someone who knows what's best for them take over."

"Sounds good, but who?"

"Well, this is where I need your feedback, Netta. Not to toot my own horn, but you know I have excellent organizational skills."

"You wouldn't be president of all those clubs if you didn't, Lenore."

"Right. So I'm thinking about just stepping in, bypassing the entire election thing, declaring myself mayor, and just be done with it."

"Well, I don't know why not, Lenore. You sure couldn't do any worse."

"That's right. I say throw the bums out. Start small, on a local level, and then we can decide where to go from there. I don't see where we have any other choice *except* absolute rule. Do you?"

A FEW SECONDS LATER, at 6:21, Sookie picked up her phone. "Hey, Sookie, it's Netta. I'm sorry to call so early, but your mother's at it again."

"Oh, no. What's she done now?"

Netta chuckled. "Nothing yet, but she says she wants to declare absolute rule, appoint herself mayor, and overthrow the city government."

"Oh, *God* . . . is she serious?"

"I don't know. It could be just one of her whims, but just in case, you'd better get over there and stop her, before she calls the newspaper."

"Thanks, Netta. I'm so sorry she bothered you again."

"Oh, that's all right, I'm used to it by now. But you know, Sookie, as crazy as it sounds, she just might have a point."

Sookie dressed and headed straight over to her mother's house. She found Lenore in the kitchen.

"Good gracious, what brings you over so early in the morning?"

"Mother, I am here because you cannot be calling up the newspaper and causing any more trouble."

"Trouble? What are you talking about?"

"Netta just called me."

"Oh, well. You know I'm right."

"Mother, you may be right, but let me remind you one more time. Earle has to practice in this town, and I cannot have you stirring up another hornet's nest. We haven't finished paying for the last lawsuit."

"But somebody has to do something. The man is going to ruin us all."

"Fine, Mother. Just let someone *else* do it. Please—let's just try and get through Thanksgiving without some big drama. Promise?" Lenore looked pained. "Please, Mother? For the family's sake?"

Lenore sighed. "Well, all right. I promise. But you know I could whip that city council into shape in twenty-four hours."

"I'm sure you could, but just let it be."

"All right, Sookie. If you insist on interfering with my freedom of speech, then I have no choice but to be muted. But I must say you have certainly become very demanding of late. Are you sure that doctor didn't give you pills?"

"No, Mother, he didn't give me pills. I wish to God he had."

Later, Sookie stood in the kitchen, thinking about what all she had to do to get ready for Thanksgiving. She had never been a particularly good cook, and yet, for the past twenty-something years, she had somehow managed to prepare three meals a day plus meals for all the dogs, cats, hamsters, and—for a short while—the alligator. She had always tried her best to provide good nutrition and balanced meals, but there were times when she had given in and let them all eat pizza. After all, when some boy with a lit "Pizza" sign on top of his car would deliver it right to the door, who was she to object? Her girls were not very good cooks, either. Her only hope was that Carter would marry a girl who cooked. Not only cooked, but who would just love to do Thanksgiving for the entire family.

Thanksgiving was always stressful. This year, Buck's wife, Bunny, had invited the family to come up to their house in North Carolina for Thanksgiving, but Lenore had refused to go. She said, "Sookie, I don't even like to have to write the word 'North' on a letter. Why would I go there?"

"Mother, please tell me you're kidding."

Lenore laughed and said, "Oh, I suppose I am . . . but I'm not sure." Nevertheless, they didn't go to North Carolina.

So, once again, Sookie was cooking. And, as usual, Lenore would arrive shortly before the meal, looking fresh and beautiful in some lovely outfit and sit and hold court all through the meal. It was so irritating. But one thing Sookie vowed she was not going to do this year was make the stuffing for the turkey from scratch. It took too much time, and it never turned out right. This year, she was going to order it from Bates House of Turkey, and she didn't care who knew it. And if Lenore said one word about it, she would say, "Well, Mother, if you don't like the stuffing, then next year, you can bring your own."

# NEWARK, NEW JERSEY

Dear Billy,

Hit Newark late Monday night, rain, sleet, zero visibility, and had to land at alternative airstrip in Tenafly. Landed in mud up to our you-know-whats. We had some damage, but at least we landed. The guys in the two planes before us flipped over, and one hit a fence. Whew. Anyhow, we were stuck here for a few days, and Pinks found out and called her dad and managed to get us tickets to a Broadway show called *Oklahoma,* and boy, was Willy happy about that. She sat up all night polishing her boots.

It was our first Broadway show, and what a show! Being from Oklahoma, Willy got pretty excited about the whole thing, and every time anybody on stage said, "Oklahoma," Willy stood up and yelled, "Hee-haw!" It was pretty funny. I'm just glad she didn't shoot off her gun. We went backstage afterward and met the cast, and Alfred Drake, the leading man, took one look at long tall Willy and asked her out, and I got to go along for the ride.

He is one snappy dresser. Offstage, he is strictly Fifth Avenue. He took us to Sardi's, where all the big shots go, and we got a table right up front. And pretty soon, in walks George

Raft with six feet of blond bombshell in gold lamé hanging on his arm. Then on to the Rainbow Room and the Copacabana. What a night. And the next day, we went ice-skating at Rockefeller Center. I skated. Willy watched. They don't ice-skate in Wapanucka, Oklahoma. Rode on a bus and a subway and had drinks at the Plaza Hotel. Oh, brother. How are you gonna keep Willy down on the ranch after she's seen New York? She took to that town like hot cakes, and it took to her. Cabbies almost wrecked their cabs, waving and honking their horns at her.

Miss you,

Fritzi

# AVENGER FIELD

## Sweetwater, Texas

Dear Wink-a-Dink,

On a trip across, Willy and I stopped in at Avenger Field, and just so you know, after all my warnings, it seems our little sister Sophie showed up here a few weeks ago and is now in training. I was not happy about it, but Pinks said not to worry about her and that Gertrude and Sophie were both doing great. And I guess she is right. My mechanic, Elroy, said he overheard another mechanic say that "those Jurdabralinski girls sure know their motors. They can tell you what's wrong, even before we check it out." Our grease monkeying days are sure paying off here. I heard all the instructors are pretty impressed with them as well. One told me Sophie was a natural fly-by-the-seat-of-her-pants pilot. I wanted to tell him I taught her everything she knows, but for once, Miss Show-Off didn't. Momma would be surprised.

I am sending you an article that was in the newspaper telling how our family now has four pilots flying for the good ol' USA. Momma says Poppa is so proud, he is about to bust. Me, too!

I have no idea what you are up to, so the next time you write, tell the censor boys to lay off for just a line or two, will ya? Get this war over with and come home soon. I need to see your ugly face.

Fritzi

P.S. Gertrude brought her accordion and is pretty popular around the barracks. My pal Willy from Oklahoma said she had never even heard a polka in her life and is teaching Gertrude some country western tunes. Ever heard "Back in the Saddle Again?" Ouch. Pretty corny, but I didn't tell Willy this.

# LONG BEACH, CALIFORNIA

Dear Billy!

Now the tale can be told. It seems that the new big B-29 was having a lot of problems with engine fires, and a lot of the boys were afraid and refusing to fly the thing. It seems like Lieutenant Colonel Paul Tibbets must be anxious to get it up and going, because he secretly trained a few WASPs to fly it. He then painted "Lady Bird" on the side along with the WASP symbol, and they toured it all around the country to air bases. When they landed and the boys gathered around the plane and saw two females step out of the cockpit, it shamed them into flying it. No more refusals. I am proud as punch to tell you that those two little gals were bay mates of mine. Don't know what Tibbets has in mind with the B-29, but it must be something pretty darned important.

Love,

Fritzi

# THANKSGIVING DAY

POINT CLEAR, ALABAMA

HAVING EVERYBODY HOME FOR THANKSGIVING WAS WONDERFUL, AND Sookie was glad to see all her children and Buck and Bunny, of course. But it was also a strain. When Lenore found out that Carter was bringing a girl home, she insisted that Sookie use the Simmons silver. "We don't want her to think we don't know better."

ON THANKSGIVING DAY, SOOKIE watched as Lenore took her first bite of the Bates House of Turkey stuffing, and she was ready with her rehearsed reply, but Lenore didn't even seem to notice the difference. Next year, she just might order the turkey from there as well.

After dinner, when all the dishes were done and everyone else was busy watching football, she asked her brother, Buck, if he would come and take a walk with her outside. "Sure," he said. "I need to walk off some of the turkey," so they headed out the back door and down the stairs into the yard. As usual, the weather on Thanksgiving Day was warm and balmy. People in Point Clear were often still in their short sleeves until at least December, sometimes later. And today was just perfect. They walked out to the end of the pier and sat down.

Buck took a deep breath and smiled as he looked out at the water and the big white clouds floating over the bay. "God, I love this place. Sis, do you remember all those summers when we slept out on the screen porch and listened to that old radio?"

"Oh, yes."

"And remember those big thunderstorms and watching the lightning over Mobile? What a show. I sure miss this old bay, but"—he sighed—"Bunny loves North Carolina, so what are you gonna do? But it's sure nice to come home once in a while. I know it's a pain in the behind to have all of us and have to do all that cooking."

"Oh, no. Not at all. I'm just glad you could come."

Buck suddenly looked over at Sookie. "Sis, are you okay? You seem worried about something. Is Winged Victory being sued again?"

"No, thank God. But I do need to ask you something."

"Sure, what?"

"Well, it's something that might come as quite a shock to you . . . or maybe not . . . I don't know."

"What?"

"Buck, did you know that I was adopted?"

Buck blinked and looked out at the water again and thought awhile before he answered. "Oh, I might have heard something about it. Why?"

"Then you knew?"

"Yeah, I guess so . . ."

"You knew that I was adopted? It didn't bother you?"

"No. Not a bit. Why should it?"

"You didn't resent me?"

Buck looked shocked. "Resent you? Good Lord, no. Like I said, I was always just glad you were there to help keep Lenore off my case."

"But, Buck . . . we were always so close. Why didn't you ever tell me?"

He sighed. "Well, Sis, I didn't find out myself until I was in high school. And Dad said not to tell you, because he thought it might upset you or make you feel bad. So I didn't. But when did you find out?"

"About five months ago. The Texas Board of Health sent Lenore a letter and I opened it. My adoption papers were inside."

"Oh, I see. Did you tell Lenore?"

"No, I didn't."

"Are you going to?"

"I don't know yet. But why did Daddy tell you?"

"Oh, I guess he was worried. It was after he had his first heart attack. He said that just in case anything were to happen to him, he wanted me to have a letter he had written. He said if anybody ever came around asking anything about your birth certificate in the future, I should give the letter to them."

"Why would anybody ask about it?"

"Well, it seems after you were adopted Lenore wanted to make sure you had a birth certificate with her listed as the mother, so she and the Mexican lady who worked for her drove over the border and had a fake one printed up in Mexico. The thing had been done illegally, and I guess Dad was worried that if somebody ever found out, Lenore might be hauled off to jail or something, so he wrote out a confession saying that he did it."

"Oh, no."

"Yeah, poor guy. He was going to take the rap for her. Anyhow, Sis, I'm sorry you had to find out like that. But honestly, I'd really forgotten all about it. To me, you were always just my sister, and I just felt lucky to have you."

Sookie looked at her brother and smiled. "Buck, you may just be one of the nicest guys in the world."

"Yeah, I probably am."

He put his arm around her, and they strolled back to the house. Suddenly he laughed. "You know, the thought of Winged Victory being thrown in the slammer is pretty funny."

"Yes, can you imagine? I'll bet after two days, they would be begging us to take her back."

"Yeah," said Buck. "And after three days, she'd be running the joint." They both laughed.

* * *

The next morning at breakfast, Bunny looked at Sookie and said, "Well, all I can say is that Buck sure can keep a secret. In all these years, he never told me you were not his real sister."

"Bunny, for God's sake," Buck said. "She is my real sister!"

"Oh, you know what I mean. Sookie, he never said one single word to me about you being adopted, so I can tell you it makes no difference to him, or I would have known it. But I still can't believe it. It's just amazing how you two act so much alike, and yet you're not even related."

Buck rolled his eyes. "Bunny, I think you just need to drop it, okay?"

Buck was upset with Bunny, but Sookie wasn't. After all, what she said was absolutely true. They were not related by blood, but it really didn't matter. They would always be brother and sister, no matter what.

They were two different people thrown together for life by some odd twist of fate and random coincidence. In 1945, Lenore had wanted a daughter, and Sookie had been available. And as to what had caused her to be there on the exact day that Lenore had walked in, she didn't know. Lenore could just as easily have picked out another little girl, or if she had even come a day later, she might have already been adopted by somebody else. She guessed it was just supposed to be.

A few days after everyone left, Sookie got a letter from Buck.

Sis,

Thanks for having us. We had a great time, and Bunny and I are still full of turkey. Honey, here is the letter Dad gave me. Thought you should have it. It might come in handy if you ever wanted to blackmail Winged Victory.

I love you, Sis.

Buck

Enclosed was a note written in her father's hand.

To Whom It May Concern:

This is to verify that I, Alton Carter Krackenberry, am fully responsible for the illegal forgery of my daughter's birth certificate.

A. C. Krackenberry

## BROWNSVILLE, TEXAS

JULY 1945

LENORE SIMMONS HAD RARELY FAILED AT ANYTHING IN HER LIFE, BUT after eleven years of marriage, she had failed to have a child. She had hoped that something would happen while they were stationed in Texas during the war, but it hadn't. And now with the war almost over, the thought of returning home to Selma, where all her friends were now happily raising children, was humiliating. It was actually her housekeeper, Conchita, in whom she had confided this, who had suggested she go to Dallas to the Gladney Home and just take a look. On the first day Alton could get away, they flew to Dallas.

The staff was very nice, and there were plenty of wartime one-, two-, and three-year-old children to see, and Lenore saw them all, but at the end of the day, when the lady came back in the room, Lenore said, "Well, they are all really darling, but I was wondering . . . do you have anything smaller?"

"Excuse me?"

"I was really looking for a baby, preferably a little girl."

"Oh, I see."

"Do you have any more in the back that we haven't seen?"

"No."

"No little babies at *all*?"

"Well, we do have one little nine-month-old girl, but we already have an interested couple that are coming back to see her tomorrow."

Lenore's eyes lit up. "You mean she's on hold?"

"Well, I guess you could say that. Yes."

"Oh, couldn't we just look at her? Just in case the other couple doesn't work out? Please? Sometimes people change their mind."

"Well, I suppose I can show her to you if you like, but remember . . . she's pretty well spoken for."

"Oh, I understand, don't we, Alton? We'll just take a quick little peek."

FIVE MINUTES LATER, AS Lenore held the baby, she exclaimed, "Oh, Alton, look at these eyes. Why, if she isn't the spitting image of myself at that age, I don't know who is. And look," she said, when she pulled back the blanket, "she even has the Simmons foot!" From the first moment Lenore saw her, she was in love, and the other couple never stood a chance.

# THE FORGERY

BROWNSVILLE, TEXAS

ALTON KRACKENBERRY HAD BEEN VERY UPSET WHEN HE FOUND OUT about the baby's forged birth certificate. "I can't believe you did something like this behind my back. My God, Lenore, what were you thinking? I'm an officer in the United States Army. I could get court-martialed over a thing like this. You tear that up right now."

Lenore clutched it to her breast. "No, I can't. Oh, please, Alton . . . it's just a little white lie, and it will mean so much to Sarah Jane down the line to carry the Simmons family name. Think about *her*. And imagine that poor little thing having to go through life with a birth certificate with 'father unknown' written on it. It would destroy her self-confidence forever."

"Do you realize that this is an illegal document? If people found out you paid for it, you could be arrested for forgery."

"But nobody is going to find out. Oh, Alton, think about your daughter's future. I did it for her sake, not mine. What nice boy from a nice family is going to marry a girl with an unknown father? She could never be a Kappa or make her debut, and, really, what girl wouldn't want to be a year younger, if she had the chance?"

"What?"

"You want her to have all the advantages she can, don't you? It's hard enough for a young girl to succeed in society—and then to burden her with this stigma, over something she can't help? Yes, it may be bending the law just a tiny bit, but this little piece of paper will make all the difference in the world to her."

"But Lenore, it's a lie—"

"Yes, but it *could* have been true. She could have been our daughter. And you have to admit, she looks more and more like a Simmons every day. Don't you believe in predestination? I think God meant for us to have her."

"Lenore, don't bring God into this. This is a criminal offense."

After more pleading, ending with Lenore flinging herself onto the sofa sobbing and screaming, "You don't love me!" Alton, against his better judgment, finally agreed, but with one stipulation. "Lenore, if we get caught, don't say I didn't warn you."

"Oh, I won't." She smiled and dried her tears. "And don't worry, Alton, I'll take full responsibility. As her mother, I would gladly serve time sitting in a lonely prison cell if it meant protecting my daughter's future. A mother's love knows no sacrifice." This last sentence was delivered while looking at herself in the mirror.

TWO MONTHS LATER, WHEN Lenore and Alton arrived back home in Alabama with their new daughter, Sarah Jane, everyone noticed she was rather large for a two-month-old baby, but Lenore had wanted the baby's official birthday to be the day she was adopted. And so it was, with the help of a rather good fake birth certificate that Lenore had bought in Mexico, thanks to Conchita, who had a friend who specialized in these things. Lenore had really wanted only one child, and a year later, Buck had been a complete surprise. Oh, well.

LENORE HAD NO QUALMS about making things up. Her father and grandmother had done the exact same thing. Lenore's mother had not died in childbirth. The truth was that when Lenore was five, her mother, whom she had adored, had come home from a trip to New Orleans and announced to her husband that she hated him and Selma, Alabama, and was leaving for good.

As the carriage had driven away, Lenore ran after it, calling out to her mother to stop, but she had not turned around, and the carriage kept going. She had never seen her mother again. Lenore never knew why she had left. She could have been unstable or had simply not loved her children enough to stay. Either way, it was easier to pretend it had never happened. As far as she was concerned, Sookie was her daughter, and she really had been in labor for over forty-eight hours.

# THE IRISHMAN

Scott Field, Illinois
1944

It was late when Fritzi arrived on base, but she sat down and wrote a letter to Billy. He had been on her mind.

Dear Billy,

Landed at Scott Field a few hours ago, and the place was packed. Finally got a bed in the nurses' quarters, so am dropping you a quick line before I hit the sack. I'm feeling a little worse for the wear tonight, after flying all day in headwinds and fighting with a faulty odometer that I had to kick all the way across the country.

Also, too much fun the night before. When I was in Wilmington, I ran into two old flying pals, Nancy Batson and Teresa James, who were headed to Orlando. Boy, did we do that place up good. Nancy is the beautiful blonde from Alabama I told you about, so we didn't lack for dancing partners . . . mostly guys waiting to dance with "Alabama." And Jamsie's from Pittsburgh and a real kick in the pants . . . and she can hold her liquor. I was doing okay until we went to some joint and Jamsie ordered us some concoction called a gin rickey.

Don't remember much after that. Didn't get in until four A.M. and had to leave at six. But it sure was great to see those gals again. Besides Sharpie, they are two of the best fliers in the entire outfit, and when we go military for real, I wouldn't be surprised if both don't turn out to be generals. As for me, I'll be happy just being a plain private. Wouldn't know what to do if I couldn't go on cussing officers.

Me

What Fritzi failed to mention to Billy was at one of the last bar stops, she had run into that big redheaded Irishman Joe O'Connor from home. He was now in the marines and was shipping out the next day on his way overseas. It really was good to see him again. She just wished they hadn't wound up at the Pink Cloud Motel. But as he said, the way the war was going, he might not ever see her again.

# WARTIME ROMANCE

Long Beach, California

As the war progressed, Fritzi started delivering the P-47, the heaviest fighter plane that the WASPs flew. It weighed 12,500 pounds and had a 2,400 horsepower engine. It was twice the size of a British Spitfire. The cockpit had enough room for only a single pilot, so her first flight had to be solo. She had flown the smaller AT-6, but it had a much smaller 450 horsepower engine, and so she was a little nervous the first time she flew the P-47. It had so much power on takeoff that it pushed her back in the seat. But after she got the gear up and leveled out, she found that it was actually easy to handle. She had heard so many tales from the guys about how hard the P-47 was to fly, but to her, the thing was a pussycat. From then on, it was her favorite plane.

In Long Beach and Newark and at all the stops at the air bases in between, Fritzi and Willy met a lot of cute guys. Many of the fellows they met and danced with were headed overseas, and a few thought they were in love and tried to get serious, but Willy was engaged to her hometown boyfriend, who was a captain in the army, and Fritzi had decided no more Pink Cloud Motel situations. Even so, the guys really got a kick out of them. Word got back to the states that a lot of the bombs being dropped over Germany had either "Willy" or "Fritzi" written on them.

It seemed that romance was in the air that year, even back home in Pulaski. The next time Fritzi landed in Long Beach, she had four letters waiting for her: three from Tula and one from Momma.

# LONG BEACH, CALIFORNIA

Dear Billy,

How's by you, honey? Sorry I haven't written much lately, but have been up to my ears. Then we had a love crisis going on back at home, and I got stuck right in the middle. It was touch and go there, and it could have blown up into a pretty serious situation.

A few months ago, Nard Tanawaski, Gertrude's fiancé, came back home from the army on a hardship leave and was missing Gertrude so much, he started hanging around our house all day. They said they hadn't meant for it to happen, but he and Tula fell madly in love with each other and want to get married. What a big mess! And everybody, even Momma, was afraid to tell poor Gertrude. So you guessed it. They tapped yours truly to do it the next time I stopped in at Sweetwater. I sure was dreading giving the poor kid the bad news, but when I told her, it turns out she was as happy as could be about it. She says she realized she wasn't in love with Nard a long time ago and had been trying to think of a way to let him down easy, and if Tula wants him, that's just fine with her. So it looks like it will be the same brother-in-law, just a different sister.

Whew! I'm glad that's all over, but speaking of love, it looks like Sophie has it bad for some English pilot she met. Sure surprised me. I didn't know she had any interest in guys at all. Oh, well, we'll see. In the meantime, I'm not telling Momma.

I'm a little tired, so I will sign off for now. I need to hit the hay. Hughes Aircraft had a backlog, so I am making three or four deliveries a day to San Francisco from Long Beach. I know each one is headed out to our boys in the Pacific, so I leave a little good luck note for the lucky pilot. I swear, Billy, those planes are flying off the assembly line every ten minutes now, but we need them, so no complaints.

Love,

Fritzi

# YOGA SOUP

POINT CLEAR, ALABAMA

MARVALEEN WAS TERRIBLY DISAPPOINTED WHEN SOOKIE TOLD HER the truth. "You mean all that stuff about the sailors wasn't true, either?"

"No, honey, and the young man I'm meeting every week is not my boyfriend."

"Well, who is he then?"

"If I tell you, will you promise not to tell anyone?"

"Of course."

"Well, I've started seeing a psychiatrist."

"At the Waffle House?"

"Yes, among other places. It's not that I'm ashamed, it's just that I'd rather not have it get around town. And there is no way we could meet at his office without being seen. So he agreed to meet me outside for my sessions."

"Oh. But why are you, of all people, seeing a psychiatrist?"

"Well . . . uh . . . I've just been under a lot of stress."

"Childhood issues?"

Sookie said, "Yes, that's right. Childhood issues."

"You know, Sookie, when I first started seeing Edna Yorba Zorbra, I had a stiff knee, and she said that sometimes the body holds stress from early childhood trauma and that yoga is one of the best ways she knows to release it. And, really, it's done wonders for me."

After that, Marvaleen started dropping brochures by the house from Yoga Soup, the yoga studio she went to. Sookie usually threw them out, but lately she had been feeling a little stiff, and she wondered if maybe it *was* a holdover from early childhood trauma. Lord knows she'd had her share.

And it had started at a very early age. Sookie remembered being only seven when Lenore, true to form and ignoring all facts, had taken it upon herself to write, direct, produce, and star in an original historical pageant entitled *The Saga of the Simmons of Selma*. The opening scene had taken place on a large Southern veranda where Lenore (playing her own grandmother) was discovered with her two grandchildren (played by Sookie and Buck) at her feet. To this very day, Sookie could still remember how terrified she had been when the curtain had gone up at the big auditorium. She had only one line, "Oh, Grandmother, you fought off all those Yankees all by yourself. How brave." But when the time came for her to speak, she had such a bad case of stage fright, she froze. Luckily, Buck had said the line for her. And then there was the Junior League Mother-Daughter Beauty Pageant. That hadn't gone very well, either. No wonder she was so stiff. So she thought she might give yoga a try. She bought a mat and leotards and signed up for Yin Flow for Beginners.

Bright and early the next morning, she showed up for class ready to begin. She did just fine during the sun salutations part, but she must have done something wrong during the hip opening stretch, because that afternoon when she went for her session with Dr. Shapiro, she could hardly walk.

Dr. Shapiro was already waiting for her at the new spot she had found called A.J.'s Steak and Ale House, located on U.S. Route 78. He was alarmed when she limped in the door and over to the table. "Are you all right?"

"Oh, yes." She sat down and winced in pain. "Have you ever done yoga?"

"No."

"Well, if you ever do, take my advice, and watch out for the hip opening stretches."

"Thanks, I'll keep that in mind," he said.

# LONG BEACH, CALIFORNIA

Dear Wink,

Sorry I haven't thanked you for the great Brown Betty teapot you sent all the way from merry old England. You will be happy to know that it arrived here safe and sound. I would have written sooner, but time's just gotten away from me. The last few months have gone by so fast, I even forgot to send something for Poppa's birthday, and I could kick myself around the block and back for that.

Speaking of time going by, Angie sent me the latest photo of little Wink. What happened? In the last one she sent six months ago, he was still a baby, and now he is a little boy in short pants. We all sure miss you over here, buddy. Momma said that Angie is just counting the days until you get back. Me, too. And if we have our way, it shouldn't be too much longer. The whole country is throwing everything they have behind the war effort.

Seriously, Wink, I wish you could see with your own eyes how hard people at the factories are working around the clock to get as many planes to you boys as possible. Tell your guys that they would be proud to see how the whole country is pulling together and doing everything they can to help get this war over and get you boys home safe and sound.

All of us in uniform get all the glory, but my hat's off to all those guys and gals showing up day after day, working on an assembly line, doing their job. And you never hear a complaint. Poppa always said this was the greatest country in the world, and now I see how right he is.

Fritzi

# LONG BEACH, CALIFORNIA

Dear Billy,

It is late here, but I can't seem to sleep tonight. Flew through a big rainbow today. Was delivering another sweet new P-59 to San Francisco, and it was foggy and gray all the way down, until I hit the Santa Ynez Valley, north of Santa Barbara, and then bang, all of a sudden, the sun comes out. I looked down, and the hills below me have turned a bright lemon yellow, and there was a big rainbow right in front of me, and when I flew through it, I swear, Billy, I looked out, and my wings were glowing pink and green and blue, and I felt so damn happy I wanted to stay up there all day.

I feel sorry for the poor people that don't fly, don't you? Anyhoo, this sure is beautiful country. After my ride on the rainbow, I circled around a bit and saw some windmills and scared a few cows, but what a sight. I just wish you could have been there to see it with me. You have been on my mind so much lately, Billy, and I wonder if you ever feel that way. Things that used to seem important to me, like being famous and just having a good time, don't seem to matter all that much anymore. I used to laugh at all those gals who talked about wanting to put down roots and settle down somewhere. But lately, it doesn't seem like such a bad idea at all. Didn't mean to get all corny on you. Guess I might still be up there flying around in that rainbow or it could have been all those damn cows. Anyhow, honey, as you might have noticed, I miss you.

Fritzi

# LONG BEACH, CALIFORNIA

Hi, Momma,

All is well. Still busy as ever. Stopped in at Sweetwater the other day to see Sophie and Gertrude, just in time to share the box of goodies you sent from home. Sure do miss your cooking. All the girls in Sophie and Gertrude's bay started hanging around, hoping to get a homemade doughnut. We shared some, but hid the rest.

Sophie says to tell you not to worry. Seems like she caught a bug down here. Got a little run-down and needs to take it easy for a while. Darn it all, why couldn't I have caught that bug, so I could loll around in bed and be waited on hand and foot? That gal gets all the luck. But the docs say it shouldn't be too long till she's up and at 'em again.

Also, Gertrude won't tell you, but she has been chosen to go to Camp Davis and fly tow target, so the boys on the ground can practice their shooting. Don't worry. They won't be shooting at her, just at the target she will be pulling behind her. A pretty swell job, and only the best gals were chosen. Tell Poppa hello for me. Gotta run.

Fritzi

P.S. Don't know if it's all this Mexican food out here in California, but you will be happy to know that I am gaining weight. If I don't slow down, I could give Gertrude a run for her money.

## LONG BEACH, CALIFORNIA

Dear Billy,

I just got word that I am coming out your way. On the fourteenth, I am taking a B-24 Liberator across to Biloxi, Mississippi, and will have a few days off before I have to pick up another and fly it back. Can you meet me somewhere in between? I know you are busy, but I sure do need to see you, honey. Let me know.

Fritzi

# THE BUBBA GUMP SHRIMP CO.

Sookie and Dr. Shapiro were meeting in the back room of the Bubba Gump Shrimp Co. restaurant out on the Causeway. After he came in and sat down, she looked at him and asked somewhat apologetically, "Dr. Shapiro, would you think I was terribly rude if I ordered something to eat? I don't know if it's all right to eat a meal during a session or not."

"Of course it is. Order anything you want."

"Oh, thank you. I was so busy working out in my yard all morning, I lost track of time and completely forgot to eat breakfast, and I'm just starving. I got so behind I didn't even have time to change."

The waitress who took their order informed her that, unfortunately, it was too late to order breakfast.

"The grill's already off, hon. We just have what's on the luncheon menu."

Sookie looked it over. She knew shrimp was their specialty, but she had just made shrimp and grits last night, so she ordered the fried oysters, hush puppies, coleslaw, and a side order of fried zucchini sticks.

Dr. Shapiro stuck with his usual cup of decaffeinated coffee. He had not quite come to terms with Southern cuisine. You could hardly get a thing that wasn't fried.

After Sookie's food came she took a few bites and was in the middle of telling him what she had said to Marvaleen about the twin sailors. "Honestly, Dr. Shapiro, I just don't know what possessed me to say a crazy thing like that. I've never even dated a sailor, much less—" Suddenly Sookie's eyes flew wide open and she turned white as a sheet. "Oh, my God," she said. "I've got to go." She then jumped up from the table and ran back to the ladies' room as fast as she could.

Dr. Shapiro had no idea what was wrong, and she didn't have time to tell him. Sookie was sitting facing the door and had suddenly spotted Pearl Jeff, her mother's friend, coming in the door with a group of ladies. Other than her mother, Pearl Jeff was the last person in the world she wanted to run in to.

When Sookie did not return to the table after fifteen minutes, Dr. Shapiro became concerned. She must have eaten a bad oyster, and it could be a case of seafood poisoning, because it had certainly hit her fast. He waited a little while longer, then walked over to the table of women sitting in the corner. "Excuse me," he said. "My friend is in the ladies' room and I think she may be ill. Could one of you please do me a favor and check and see if she is all right?"

"Why, certainly," said Pearl Jeff, as she picked up her purse and headed back to the restrooms. One door was marked "Buoys," and the other said "Gulls." She entered the door marked "Gulls."

Sookie was hiding in a stall, and the minute Pearl spoke she recognized the voice.

"Hello," she called out. "Is there a lady in here?" When she didn't get an answer, Pearl marched over to the stall where she saw two feet and banged on the door. "Hello? Are you all right in there? Your gentleman friend is worried about you."

Sookie panicked. She didn't know what to do, so she just kept flushing the toilet over and over again.

A FEW MINUTES LATER, Pearl came back out and asked Dr. Shapiro, "Was your friend wearing pink tennis shoes with pom-poms?"

"Yes, I think so," said an anxious Dr. Shapiro.

"Well, she's in there all right, but from the sound of things, I don't think she'll be out for quite a while." Now he didn't know what to do. He couldn't just leave, so he sat there and waited.

Finally, after the table of women left, he went up to the counter and asked the waitress if she would go in and check on his friend. After a moment the waitress came out and handed him a note that Sookie had just scribbled on her check pad.

Dear Dr. Shapiro,

I am so sorry! I know my time is up for today, but I will see you next week and explain. Don't worry. I am not sick.

The waitress had informed Sookie that the table of ladies had left, but she was afraid to come out too soon. Pearl and her friends could still be out in the parking lot.

By the time Sookie did think it was safe to come out, the place was empty. Her lunch was ice cold and she had missed her session. Sookie sat in the booth almost in tears. There was just no escaping, no matter how hard she tried. Being Lenore Simmons Krackenberry's daughter in a small town was like having a tracking device attached to your body. Somebody was always going to know where she was at all times. She had always felt so sorry for poor Princess Anne of England. No wonder she lay low. Sookie knew just how she felt.

# A SAD DAY

LONG BEACH, CALIFORNIA
1944

It was a Tuesday in October. Fritzi walked into the barracks and greeted everyone as usual. "Hiya, pals, I'm back and ready to eat. Who wants to—" She stopped talking when she noticed that they had barely looked up, and some of the gals looked like they had been crying. "What's the matter?" Willy pointed to the letter on Fritzi's bed.

She picked it up and saw that it was from the Army Air Forces headquarters in Washington. She quickly opened it and read the news that General Hap Arnold had directed that the WASP program was to be deactivated on the twentieth of December. Fritzi was stunned. "Is this a joke?"

"No, read on."

Fritzi sat down on the bed and read the letter. "When we needed you, you came through, and you served most commendably. Blah blah blah." Then she cut to the end. "But now the war situation has changed, and the time has come when your volunteer services are no longer needed. If you were to continue in service, you would be replacing, instead of releasing, our young men. I know the WASP wouldn't want that. Blah blah blah. My sincerest thanks, and happy landings always." That day, WASPs stationed on ninety different bases all over the country received the letter.

It seemed that thousands of civilian male flight instructors had been excused from joining the army as long as they trained military pilots. But now that the army had all the pilots they needed, they had started closing down flight schools across the country. However, the army didn't have enough infantry troops for the ongoing war in the Pacific and in Nazi-controlled Europe. Suddenly, these civilian flight instructors found themselves subject to the draft and could end up in combat not as fliers, but as regular foot soldiers. And just as suddenly, a lot of these same instructors wanted to take over the WASPs' jobs, so they could remain in the States.

Many would have to be trained at great expense to the government to handle the advanced planes the women were now flying, but, nevertheless, the men got together and organized a huge publicity blitz to try to defeat the bill that was now in front of Congress that would militarize the WASPs and keep them flying.

The public was told that it wasn't patriotic for women to be military pilots if they would be taking jobs away from men, and it was suggested that if they wanted to serve in the military, the women could join the WAC and become nurses, where they were really needed. And then the VFW and the American Legion jumped on board, and the bill to militarize the WASPs was defeated. This meant that the families of the girls who had been killed would be receiving no death benefits, and at the end of the war, the WASPs, unlike all other discharged veterans, would be left with no GI Bill, no medical, no nothing.

## PENSACOLA, FLORIDA

Fritzi,

Honey, just heard what happened. What a raw deal. And what a damn stupid move on the army's part. It's gonna cost the army a fortune to train all those guys to replace you. Arnold says the main flack was caused by those guys that didn't want to be drafted and have to go into combat, and they did a bang-up letter-writing blitz. He said they even got their mommies to write Congress. What a bunch of pantywaists. My friend Barry, who trained some of the WASPs, says there wasn't a thing wrong with you gals, except that you were gals. Wish I was running this man's army and could help, but dammit, I ain't. Anyway, I know how bad you must be feeling right now, but the hell with them. Go out and get yourself a stiff drink. Oh, hell, get as many as you want, and know that I am always in your corner.

Love you, pal,

Billy

It was the first time he'd ever said he loved her, and she really needed to hear that right now. It softened the blow a little. And she did take his advice about the drinks.

# HAPPY LANDINGS

DECEMBER 17, 1944, FRITZI LANDED THE BIG FOUR-ENGINE BOMBER for the last time, and before she walked away, she stopped and gave it a pat. "Well, good-bye, old gal. You're one hell of a plane."

On December 20, all the WASPs who were stationed all over the country were called back to Sweetwater, and after they had turned over their equipment—gas masks, goggles, leather flying suits, and boots—the government gave the women a dinner to say "Thanks again for your service, good luck, and happy landings." Fritzi sat there and thought to herself, "Well, that's a hell of a note." After the dinner was over, when she'd said all her good-byes, she wandered out on the field and found a plane, gassed and ready to go, and decided if she was being kicked out, the government owed her at least a free ride home.

Fritzi knew she was drunk, but she didn't care. She had done something she would never be able to forgive herself for. And now that the WASPs had been disbanded and she wasn't needed anymore, it really didn't matter to her one way or the other if she lived or died, so she started the motors, took off to the left, and headed in the direction of Wisconsin. She didn't really want to go home, but she had no other place to go.

She made three or four stops along the way, and the army finally found the missing plane a week later, parked outside a hangar at Blesch Field in Green Bay. After calling a cab, Fritzi was home. A little hungover, but home. Hijacking a military plane was a serious offense, but no charges were ever filed.

Pinks had been left in charge of cleaning up inventory back in Sweetwater and agreed with her. She knew what Fritzi had been through. And Pinks figured that after what all those gals had done, the government should have flown all of them home.

After the war was over, the WASP records were sealed, and it was pretty much forgotten that they had ever existed at all.

It would be another thirty years before another woman would fly a military plane.

# VICTORY

PULASKI, WISCONSIN
1945

ON VJ DAY, A NEIGHBOR RAN OUT IN THE STREET AND WAVED HIS arms and shouted, "The war is over!" Suddenly, there were church bells ringing all over town and horns blowing and kids running around banging pots and pans. They knew it was the end of an era for the entire world.

But most people who had been in it, like Fritzi, just sighed a big sigh of relief. For her, it meant that Winks had made it through alive and would be coming home for good.

The war was over, but it had taken its toll. More than 400,000 Americans had been killed and 1.7 million had been hurt in some way. And most people didn't know about the 39 WASPs who had been killed or that 16 Army nurses had died by enemy fire, and 67 had been taken prisoner, including Nurse Dottie Frakes, who was held in a Japanese concentration camp for more than three years.

But in August 1945, Americans were in a jubilant mood. Finally, their world could get back to normal. As the headlines said, "Hooray! Rosie the Riveter can finally go home and be Rosie the Housewife again!"

The problem was that a lot of women didn't want to be just housewives again. Fritzi was hoping to join Billy and go to California for employment, and Gertrude hoped to get a good, high-paying job at the big Ford Motor Company plant in Willow Run, Michigan. But in the summer of 1945, Kaiser-Frazer Corporation took over the plant to prepare for the postwar years, and it had no room for women. It wanted the best of the jobs to go to the returning GIs. Wink came back home and reopened the filling station, and Angie was happy to go back to being a housewife and mother again. But Gertrude still wanted to work. She tried to get a job flying, but quickly found out that the only job open for women in aviation was that of a stewardess, and when she applied she was told she was too fat to be a stewardess, so she wound up teaching accordion over at Saint Mary's school.

## SOOKIE HAS THE BLUES

Sookie and Dr. Shapiro still met once a week, despite the fact that they had almost run out of meeting places. But even with all the hassle of having to change restaurants, she knew it was doing her a lot of good. However, she was finding out that self-examination was not easy. They say the truth can set you free, but sometimes it can really depress the hell out of you. Sookie woke up one morning feeling a little blue, and when Dee Dee came to pick her up for lunch that day, Sookie was still in her nightgown.

When she answered the door, she said, "Oh, honey, come on in for a minute. I'm sorry. I didn't realize how late it was. I should have called you sooner, but I don't think I'm up for lunch today."

"Why?"

"Oh, I don't know. I just feel a little down today. Do you mind?"

"No, I guess not. But what's the matter with you? Are you sick?"

Sookie sat down in her chair and shook her head. "No, I'm not sick."

"Then, what is it?"

"Oh, sweetheart, I don't want to bother you. It's nothing. I've just been thinking too much lately is all."

"Thinking about what?"

"Oh, stupid things . . . about my life . . . things like that."

"What about your life?"

"Oh, sometimes I think maybe your grandmother was right about me all along. I've had two fantastic mothers—one a hero who flew planes—and I turned out to be just a big nothingburger with no courage at all."

Dee Dee looked at her in utter disbelief. "What? You must be kidding. You were our hero. Don't you know that? You were the best mother in the world. And you did so have courage."

"Me? I don't think so."

"Yes, you did. Don't you remember that day when we were little when Daddy's Great Dane fell off the end of the pier? You're not a good swimmer, but you jumped right in the bay and pulled him out. Don't you remember that?"

"Yes, I guess so—but your daddy loved that stupid dog."

"And that time we went to Disney World, and you were scared to death, but you got on that roller coaster, just so you could ride with us?"

"Yes, I do remember that. And I wouldn't do it again, I'll tell you that."

"But you did it once. That's something, isn't it? And I don't care what you say, it takes great courage to have four children and sit by and watch them make mistakes. Look at me. I've obviously married the wrong man twice, and you never made me feel bad or said a word about it. And when I needed you, you were always there. So I won't have you thinking you are a nothingburger. Nothing could be further from the truth. Now, Mother, don't make me have to spank you. You just get up out of that chair right now and get dressed, because we are going to lunch. Do you hear me? The world awaits!"

Sookie looked at her daughter and smiled. It was at that moment that she realized that her little girl, the one she had been worried about the most, had quietly grown up.

Sookie got up and did what Dee Dee said. As she was upstairs getting dressed, she had to laugh. Dee Dee may not be a Simmons by birth, but she was certainly Lenore's granddaughter, all right. They went to lunch and had a marvelous time.

# LENORE'S BIG DAY

POINT CLEAR, ALABAMA
JANUARY 2006

LENORE HAD A BIRTHDAY COMING UP, SO IT WAS TIME TO START PLANNING, and she always had a list of instructions for Sookie about how she wanted to celebrate.

Sookie got out her notebook and walked over to her house. Angel told her Lenore was back in her little den off the alcove. When she went inside, she found her mother fully made up but still in her floral dressing gown, sitting at her desk looking forlorn. "Hey, what are you doing? I came over to find out what you wanted to do this year to celebrate your birthday."

"Nothing. Absolutely nothing. When you're my age, there's nothing to celebrate."

"Why? What's the matter?"

"I'm so upset."

"Why?"

"Oh, Sookie, it's so awful to be old. Look at my phone book. Almost everyone I know is dead. Nobody is left that remembers me when I was young. I don't have anybody left to reminisce with. If it weren't for you and Buck, nobody would remember me at all. I'm being pushed into the past. Oh, it's terrible when you don't have a future or anything to look forward to. I used to think that after you and Buck were grown, I'd go on the stage, but then your daddy got sick, and I had so many club obligations, I guess I just misjudged time. And when your daddy died, it was too late. Oh, I could write a book. I'd call it *A Life of Regret* or *The Things I Didn't Do*. And I could have done so many things. I was always good at anything I put my mind to, you know that."

"That's true. You could do anything and do it better than anybody else. But you know, Mother, I have always wondered: Did it make you happy?"

"What?"

"Have you ever been happy?"

"Oh, Sookie, why do you ask me these silly questions? I must say I liked you better when you were busy raising children. Lord, all you do now is sit around and think, and thinking is not good for you, Sookie."

"Thank you, Mother."

"Well, Sookie, your mother is the only one who will ever tell you the truth. You know I'm right, Sookie."

"Okay, Mother. Whatever you say. But what do you want to do about your birthday this year?"

"Oh, I suppose I owe it to the children to have some sort of celebration. It means so much to them, and who knows? I may not be here next year, so maybe we should do a little something."

Sookie sighed. "How many people?"

"Oh, no more than thirty. I'm just not up to it this year."

"Yes, Mother."

"And if we do go to Lakewood, don't let them talk you into putting us in the smaller room."

"Yes, Mother."

That meant she wanted to go to Lakewood and be in the big room. And knowing Lenore, she would start adding more and more people as it got closer.

But that was Lenore. Her birthday was a big thing to her and she assumed it was for everyone else in town as well.

As Sookie walked back home, she began to think about the situation regarding her own birthday. Her real birthday, in October, had quietly come and gone. She wondered about the woman listed on her birth certificate. It was strange to think that somewhere out there, someone she had never met might have been remembering that day too.

# GETTING TO KNOW YOU

Point Clear, Alabama

Sookie had always worried that she and Dee Dee had never been as close as she would have liked, but Dee Dee had started calling and asking her to meet for lunch almost every week now. And it was nice getting to know her daughter just a little better.

They were sitting outside at Sandra's Sidewalk Café one afternoon, when Dee Dee said, "Oh, Mother, did I tell you that I finally got the Poole family crest reframed?"

"No, you didn't. Are you pleased with how it looks?"

"Oh, yes. I think I like the gold even better than the red."

"Oh, good." Sookie took a sip of her iced tea and said, "You know, Dee Dee, I just realized something."

"What?"

"Well, just think, you are a Poole by blood, and I only married a Poole, so you are even more related to your father than I am. And none of us are related to the Simmonses at all. Isn't that strange? I mean, what is genetics, and what is environment? And why am I the way I am?"

"Oh, Mother, who cares? We certainly don't. The only thing that matters is who you are now. And besides, this is America, and you are free to be anybody you want to be. You can even change your name legally, if you want to, and not be a Simmons or a Jurdabralinski. You can be whoever you want to be."

Sookie smiled. "Can I be Queen Latifah?"

Dee Dee laughed. "No, but you could call yourself Lucille Flypaper or Tiddly Winks McGee, if you want."

"I know you're kidding, but you know, it might be fun to be someone different, just for a change. 'Sookie' is way too babyish for a sixty-one-year-old woman, don't you think?" Sookie took a bite of her salad and then said, "Virginia Meadowood."

"What?"

"From now on, I want to be known as Virginia Meadowood."

"Yes, Mother."

"Do you think I'm too old to start over?"

"No, Mother, sixty-one is young."

"I wish I could start over. I would do things so differently if I had the chance."

"Oh, what?"

"Oh, I wouldn't have let so many things bother me, and I would have stood up to your grandmother more, of course. But then if I were someone else, I might never have been a Kappa, and I wouldn't have married your father. You would have had a completely different father or else you might not have been born at all or I could have had four totally different children. I can't imagine. It just boggles my mind thinking about all the what-ifs, wondering why things turned out how they did and if it was supposed to be that way or is your life just an accident."

"It's a mystery, isn't it? But, Mother, you may want to change and be someone different, and we will support you in anything you want to do, but we've all talked about it, and we're really glad you married Daddy, and we admire you for having so much patience with us and with Grandmother."

"Really?"

"Oh, yes. But seriously, Mother, you are not who you think you are."

Sookie had heard that before. "How so?"

"Well, it's true that Grandmother is flashy and flamboyant and all that, but she's a little shallow. You think you're not important, but you are. You have heart, Mother. You are a real human being."

Sookie was suddenly overwhelmed to be hearing this from her daughter, and tears sprang up in her eyes. "Well, thank you, honey. That means a lot to me."

LATER THAT AFTERNOON, SOOKIE called Dena. "I'm telling you, Dena, when you live long enough to see your children begin to look at you with different eyes, and you can look at them not as your children, but as people, it's worth getting older with all the creaks and wrinkles."

# PACKAGE FOR ALICE

Point Clear, Alabama

Pete the mailman walked to Sookie's door and knocked just as Lenore was coming up the stairs with a sack of B & B pecans she had picked up for Sookie. When Sookie opened the door, she saw them both and said, "Well, good morning!"

Pete said, "Good morning. I've got another package for Alice Finch."

"Oh, thank you, Pete. I'll take it."

"She's been here for quite a while now. She must like it here."

"Yes, she does. Thank you, Pete," Sookie said. "Have a nice day."

As Lenore walked in the door, she asked, "Who's Alice Finch?"

"Just a friend."

"What friend?"

"You don't know her, Mother."

"Why not?"

"I don't know."

"I know everybody who's moved here. I've never heard of anyone named Alice Finch."

"She's a friend of Marvaleen's."

"Oh, well, no wonder. Why are you getting her mail?"

"Mother, do you have to know everything?"

"Yes, I do. Here are your pecans."

"Thank you."

"Do you have any of Earle's coffee left? I need a little more. Conchita makes the weakest cup of coffee known to man."

"No, but I can make some. Did I tell you I spoke to Carter?"

"No."

"He has a new girlfriend, but he isn't serious about her, he says."

"Well I certainly didn't like the last one he brought home. She was far too loud and aggressive for my taste."

ALTHOUGH SOOKIE REMAINED PLEASANT on the outside, the next hour and a half was sheer torture. She was dying for her mother to leave so she could open her package, and the minute she heard the front door shut, she tore into it.

> Dear Alice,
>
> Here are a few articles and other stuff. Some of the pictures are a little faded, but I thought you might want to see them. Will send more when I find it.

She opened the folder and saw a newspaper clipping with a picture of a slender young woman wearing jodhpurs, lace-up leather boots, and a white shirt standing by a plane with her hands in her pockets.

Sookie knew this was a special moment in her life. She was looking at a picture of her real mother for the very first time. The pretty dark-haired girl smiling at the camera couldn't have been more than seventeen or eighteen, but she looked so confident and self-assured. Underneath the picture was the headline:

> MISS FRITZI JURDABRALINSKI OF PULASKI
> BECOMES WISCONSIN'S FIRST GIRL PILOT
> *Pulaski News*
> *1939*
>
> Miss Fritzi Jurdabralinaki, Pulaski's own Amelia Earhart, will be appearing with the famous Billy Bevins Flying Circus.

Then Sookie saw a clipping with another photo of Fritzi.

SISTER JOINS HER BROTHER IN THE AIR, FLYING FOR THE USA
*Green Bay Journal*
*1943*

Miss Fritzi Jurdabralinski, a licensed pilot, has joined a group of women fliers who have volunteered their flying services to the United States government. She will be going to Houston, Texas, for training. "I am very happy and hopefully, with women taking over the domestic ferrying of planes, we will be able to get this war over sooner." Fritzi is the daughter of Mr. and Mrs. Stanislaw Jurdabralinski of Pulaski, Wisconsin.

Sookie sat staring at the glamorous girl in the photos. She liked her face and the way she stood, looking like she was ready to go out and conquer the world.

Before that, Fritzi had just been a name on a piece of paper, but now that Sookie saw that she was a real person, the enormity of it all hit her. This was her mother, who had carried her for nine months. This pretty girl was the one who had given birth to her. Had she held her, she wondered? Or had she not even looked at her? Why had she handed her over to strangers? Had she done something wrong? Had her mother not liked her? Earle was right. She had to try to find her. She might not like the answers, but she couldn't go on not knowing. Now she was worried she had waited too long.

When Earle came home, he was glad about the decision. "I know it's a hard thing to do, but like I said, if you don't try, you will always regret it."

Earle went to the computer and started searching for websites pertaining to former WASP pilots and found one. After a few days, he had an answer and a telephone number. Mrs. Fritzi Bevins of Solvang, California, was still very much alive.

SOOKIE SAT THERE WITH the number in her hand. "Earle, could you call her?"

"No, sweetie, that wouldn't be right. You're the one she wants to hear from, not me. Do you want me to dial the number?"

"No."

"Do you want me to be here with you?"

"No, it would make me too nervous."

"All right, but I'll be right outside on the porch, okay?"

"But Earle, what if she hangs up on me?"

"Honey, she's not going to hang up on you."

"Okay, but what if I faint?"

"You're not going to faint."

"I feel like I might."

"All right, I'll tell you what. I'll go and get the smelling salts, and if you start to feel funny, just take a few whiffs. But you're not going to faint." He came back and handed her a small bottle. "You can do this, sweetheart. And you'll be so glad you did. I'll be right outside."

Earle left, and she stared at the phone. She had the same feeling she had when she was eight and had climbed up on the high diving board at the swimming pool and had looked down. It had been so embarrassing. She'd had to turn around and crawl back down the ladder and make her way past all the other kids who just couldn't wait to jump.

She went over all of Earle's pep talk points in her head. Okay, you have nothing to lose . . . everything to gain. She will be glad to hear from you, and even if she isn't, you at least tried.

She closed her eyes and dialed. 805-555-0726. Oh, God. As the phone was ringing, she suddenly felt her mouth go dry. She might not be able to speak. Should she hang up?

"Hello."

"Hello . . . is this Mrs. Fritzi Bevins?"

"Yes, it is."

"From Pulaski, Wisconsin?"

"Yes."

"Uh . . . you don't know me, but I recently received some papers. From Texas. And, well . . . I think I might be your daughter?"

There was a long silence on the other end, and then after a moment, the woman in a softer voice said, "Hiya, pal. I've been waiting for this call for a long time."

* * *

A FEW MINUTES LATER, after she hung up, Sookie screamed, "Earle!" He jumped up and ran in, and Sookie said, "I just talked to her."

"You're kidding."

"No!"

"How did she sound?"

"Very nice. And she's invited me to come to see her."

"No! Wow."

"Can you believe it? She said she would love to meet me."

"See? Now, aren't you proud of yourself?"

"Yes."

"Are you going to go?"

"Well, maybe . . ."

A FEW DAYS LATER, Sookie went up and knocked on Lenore's door, and Lenore opened it just a tiny crack. "Mother, it's me. I just wanted you to know that I will be gone for a little while, so if you need me to do anything before I leave, let me know."

"Well, come in, don't stand out on the porch. You're letting all the air-conditioning out."

"Okay, but I can't stay."

"Come in. Now, what do you mean you're going to be gone? Where are you going?"

"To a health spa."

"A health spa? What for?"

"Earle thinks I've put on a few pounds, and I just need a little rest . . . after the weddings."

"Where?"

"Oh, I guess my hips."

"No, where is the spa?"

"California."

"*California?* What's the matter with the hotel spa right up the street?"

"Nothing. I just need a change of scenery."

"You don't look fat to me."

"Mother, please!"

"All right, all right. But I just hope this trip is not another one of Marvaleen's harebrained ideas."

"No, Mother, she has nothing to do with it."

"Well, good. That girl is just not up to you, socially or otherwise. Don't forget you have your reputation to think about. When will you be back?"

"I'm not sure, but call Earle if you need anything."

Lenore looked at her as she walked toward the door and called out, "Sookie!"

"Yes?"

"Make sure your luggage matches." Lenore had not said anything to anybody, but she was still concerned about her daughter. She just hadn't seemed herself lately.

## MEETING MOTHER

SOLVANG, CALIFORNIA

THE CAR PICKED SOOKIE UP AT THE SANTA BARBARA AIRPORT AND drove her about forty-five minutes up the 101 Freeway and into the small Danish town of Solvang. Sure enough, there were windmills everywhere. She had never been to Europe, but she felt like she was there. The driver, who had the address, went through town and made a right turn on Alisal Road and drove about three blocks, and there was the sign, RANCHO ALISAL ESTATES. As he turned right on the street, she suddenly said, "Stop! Please, may I just sit here for a minute?"

"Yes, ma'am," he said and pulled over to the side of the road.

She took her small bottle of smelling salts out and took a few sniffs and sat and waited. There was a moment when she just wanted to turn around and go home. But she pulled herself together and said, "All right, I'm ready."

FRITZI HAD SAID SHE lived in a trailer park, but this was no ordinary trailer park. This one was beautiful, with a lovely little golf course in the middle. They found her street and pulled up to a pretty light blue mobile home, and the driver said, "This is it."

Sookie got out and walked up the three steps covered with green felt leading to the front door with her heart pounding, but before she could knock, an older woman with dyed blond hair worn up on her head in curls, wearing a sleeveless striped cotton dress and white plastic earrings, opened the door. And after all the mental rehearsing of just what she would say, at this very moment, all Sookie could manage was a weak little, "Are you Mrs. Bevins?"

"You bet I am," said the woman in a definite Midwestern twang. "You must be Sarah Jane. Come on in. I was kinda worried you wouldn't find me, but here you are."

"Yes, well, I had someone drive me."

"Ah, smart. Come on in the living room, and have a seat. You must be tired coming all this way."

Sookie walked over and sat down on the brown plaid sofa and placed her purse by her side.

The woman sat across from her and said, "Well . . . you made it."

"Yes," and after an awkward silence, Sookie said, "Uh . . . you have a lovely place here."

"Thanks. It's not much, but it's paid for. You need to use the facilities?"

"Pardon me?"

"The bathroom."

"Oh, no, I'm fine. Thank you." Sookie couldn't help but stare at her. The lady was older, but she still recognized her from the old photos. And now seeing her in person, she could see a definite similarity to her own face. "Well . . . so here we are, after all these years," said Sookie.

"Yeah, here we are."

"Yes."

"Is this your first time in California?"

"Yes."

"Would you like some coffee or a drink? I've got some beer or wine and some hard stuff in there, I think."

"No, thank you, but I would love some water, if you have it."

"Oh, sure. It's not bottled, though. Is that all right?"

"That's fine." Sookie looked around and noticed the photographs that almost filled the fake brown wooden walls in the living room and all the way down the hall. "This certainly is a lovely spot, Mrs. Bevins.

Driving in from Santa Barbara was just beautiful. All the mountains and trees."

"Call me Fritzi, honey, everybody does. Yeah, I'm from Wisconsin, but hell, after you've seen California, I couldn't live anywhere else." She walked over and handed Sookie a glass of water.

Sookie took it, but her hands were shaking so much she spilled some of it on the rug. "I'm so sorry. I think I'm just a little nervous."

"Don't worry about it, kid. We both are. Don't forget the last time I saw you, you had no hair or teeth and weighed eight pounds, and now look at you. A grown woman with four kids. And good-looking, too."

"Really? Well, thank you."

"I know I'm not much to look at now, but believe it or not, I used to be somewhat of a looker."

"Oh, you were. Absolutely. I've seen pictures of you. You were wonderful looking and still are. Your hair is different, but I would have recognized you anywhere."

"Yeah? Well, I guess I look pretty good for an old bag. Where did you see my picture?"

"In the newspaper articles. I read all about you, and I'm just in awe of what you did during the war. You were so brave."

"Well, honey, it was a job that needed to be done, and we did it, that's all. What about you? Have you had a good life?"

"Oh, yes, and as I mentioned, I have a wonderful husband and four wonderful children, and well, you have four wonderful grandchildren."

"And the people who adopted you, were they good to you?"

"Oh, yes, just wonderful. I have no complaints."

"Are they still alive?"

"Just my mother—well, the lady who adopted me. My father passed away in 1984."

"I'm sorry to hear it. Does your mother know you're here?"

"No. She doesn't know that I know I was adopted."

"Ah."

"I didn't see any reason to upset her. She's not . . . well, anyhow . . . no, I didn't tell her. I hope you don't mind that I came. I can understand that meeting me must be very difficult for you, but I really needed to see you in person and, well, come to terms with . . . well, as you can imagine, it was quite a surprise to find out after all these years."

"Ah, yeah, and I'll bet you have a lot of questions you need me to answer. So ask away."

"Well, yes I do. I have a list somewhere here." Sookie fished in her purse. "Oh, here it is. I guess I need to know about family health issues. If there was anything genetic we should be worried about, any heart or diabetes or mental issues. Things like that."

"No, everybody mostly died of old age. Everybody was pretty hardy." She laughed. "Some a little too hardy. Momma and Gertrude got pretty fat in their old age."

"Oh, well, that could explain my oldest daughter, Dee Dee. She's always had a tendency to put on weight. So, umm . . . no dementia or Alzheimer's?"

"No, everybody—Momma, Poppa—were as sharp as tacks right up until the day they died. And just so you know, all of us Polacks are pretty healthy."

"Well, that's certainly good to know." Of course, the elephant in the living room was who her father was. Fritzi didn't seem to be forthcoming with that information, and Sookie thought it might be rude just to ask her outright so soon. "I guess I have so many things I've wondered about."

"Yes?"

"I guess I wondered, during all these years, did you ever think about me?"

Fritzi nodded. "Oh, sure, kid. All the time. I always wondered how you turned out. What you looked like, what you were up to. Things like that."

"I see . . . and did you ever think about trying to find me?"

"No, I never did. I figured it was best not to. To tell you the truth, after the war, I went through a pretty rough patch. Drank too much, stuff like that."

"Oh."

"Did you bring pictures of your kids?"

"Oh, yes."

After Fritzi looked at all the pictures, she said, "Great-looking kids. And your husband looks like a regular nice guy."

"Oh, he is. And he said to be sure and tell you that he would love to meet you one day, but he thought that maybe I should come by myself the first time. And, of course, if you ever need any dental work, he'd be glad to do it. To tell you the truth, I really wanted him to come with me. I was kind of scared to come by myself, but I'm so glad I did. I'd love to see some photographs of your . . . well, *my* family."

"Oh, sure, kid. I got all of them hung up." As they walked down the hall, Sookie saw a picture of the four sisters standing in front of the all-girl filling station taken in 1942. Sookie was surprised at how much her girls looked like the Jurdabralinski sisters.

Sookie said, "I just can't imagine how hard it must have been to run a gas station."

Fritzi nodded. "It was, but it was also a hell of a lot of fun. And this is your Uncle Wink when he was in the Air Corps over in England."

"Oh, wow, he looks a little like my son, Carter."

"Yeah?"

"He has the same smile."

Then Fritzi pointed to another photograph. "And here's a picture of your grandmother standing in front of the house. You can't tell here, but Momma was the one with the really red hair."

"Really?"

"You bet. Even redder than yours."

"Is this the house where you grew up?"

"Yep. Poppa built it for us in the twenties. But after Wink died, Angie sold it to a real nice family in town."

"Is the filling station still open?"

"No, it closed down a long time ago. I think they just use it for storage or something now, but it's still there."

After they had visited for a while and Fritzi had made them a cup of coffee, Fritzi picked up the pictures of Sookie's family and looked at them again. "Real nice house. Right on the water."

"Oh, yes. Our backyard is the Mobile Bay."

"You're not far from Pensacola or the Gulf of Mexico."

"No."

"I know that area. Very pretty. I used to fly around there."

Fritzi placed the photos down and nodded. "Yeah," said Fritzi. "I can see that after having such a nice quiet settled life all these years, finding out about this must have knocked you for a loop."

"Well, yes, it did. You can imagine my shock after all these years. I mean at age sixty, to meet your real mother for the very first time is pretty extraordinary."

Fritzi reached over and took a cigarette out of a pack, lit it, and looked at her for a long time, then said, "Damn, I hate to do this to you, pal, but I'm afraid I have another shock for you."

"Oh? What?"

"I'm not your mother."

Sookie was not quite sure she heard right. "Pardon me?"

"I'm not your mother."

"But . . . your name is on my birth certificate."

"Yeah, I know. But just the same I'm not your mother." Sookie felt herself suddenly getting lightheaded. Fritzi looked at her. "Hey, are you all right? Sarah Jane?"

Sookie realized she must have blacked out for a second, but said, "Yes, I guess so, but I don't understand. If you're not my mother, then who was?"

"Well, it's a long story, kid. You probably should have a drink; you don't look so good." Sookie did slug down a scotch and took her smelling salts out of her purse, just in case, and waited with her heart still pounding for Fritzi to continue.

# AVENGER FIELD

SWEETWATER, TEXAS
JANUARY 1944

FRITZI WAS IN SWEETWATER FOR A FEW DAYS TO CATCH UP WITH PINKS and Gussie Mintz and have a little visit with her sisters. The first night she was there, Sophie came in from her date with her cheeks flushed and her eyes glowing, smiling and laughing to herself. Fritzi was sitting in a chair, painting her toenails. She looked at Sophie and said, "Somebody must have had a good time. If I didn't know better, I'd say you were as boiled as an owl."

Sophie sat on the other cot and smiled at her. "No, I haven't had a drop to drink. Oh, Fritzi, I never knew I could be so happy. I'm in love with the whole world. He's so wonderful!"

"Who?"

"Jimmy. Jimmy Brunston. He's the RAF pilot here on special assignment I introduced you to."

"Oh yeah. I remember."

"Well anyway, he's picking me up late Friday night, and we're going to Houston for the weekend."

"Whoa. Oh, no, you're not."

"Oh, Fritzi, it's all on the up and up. I promise you. He's already booked a room for me at the Shamrock Hotel, and he's staying with some English friends across town. It's our last weekend together. He's going back overseas next Tuesday. Oh, Fritzi, I've just *got* to go. He's gone to so much trouble to arrange everything, and he's so wonderful."

"Well, all right, if you're so crazy about him, go on, but look, kid, don't do anything you shouldn't. These guys will say anything. Just remember, they're all here today and gone tomorrow. Have fun, but be careful."

"You don't understand, Fritzi. Jimmy's not like that. He's a perfect gentleman. He really loves me, Fritzi. He's asked me to marry him, and he said the minute the war's over, he's coming back to get me."

"Does he know your family ran a filling station? He seemed like the snooty English type to me."

"Of course, he knows. I've told him everything, and he thinks it's just charming. That's what he said. He's not snooty at all. He's told me all about his parents, and they're just regular people, and he said as soon as they met me, they would love me."

"Fine, but tell Lieutenant Brunston if he does anything he shouldn't, he'll have to answer to me."

THE NIGHT JIMMY AND Sophie flew over to Houston was warm and clear. The clouds below them were like huge silver balls of cotton. When they were halfway there, Jimmy switched channels on the radio and picked up a big band station. As they listened to the Glenn Miller Orchestra play "Moonlight Serenade," Sophie felt like they were the only two people in the world, all alone up in the clouds, so much in love.

SOPHIE DIDN'T UNDERSTAND WHEN, after a couple of months, Jimmy's letters from overseas became less and less frequent, and then they stopped altogether. It wasn't like him not to write. He had written her every day. Something must be wrong. She knew he was going on bombing raids over Germany almost every night and that there had been losses. She held her breath every time the casualty report with the names of the pilots came in, but it wasn't until after three of her letters were returned unopened that she started to panic. She was desperate and sick with worry. He had to come back.

The next morning, she went to the Red Cross office in Sweetwater and spoke to Mrs. Gilchrist, a nice older woman, and showed her the returned letters. She gave Mrs. Gilchrist his regiment number, where he was born, the names of his parents, the name of the town they lived in, and the date he had last called her.

Mrs. Gilchrist wrote it all down and said, "I'll do my best, but I can't promise anything. As you can well imagine, overseas communications are very difficult right now. But try not to worry. I can't tell you how many girls have come here expecting to find out the worst, and it was all a mix-up. So don't give up hope. Tomorrow, you may get five letters."

Two days later, back in the bay, Sophie heard someone yell across the room. "Sophie Jurdabralinski! Phone call!"

Sophie ran over to the phone, hoping it might be Jimmy, but the girl made a face and said, "It's a female."

"Oh . . . . Hello."

"Sophie?"

"Yes?"

"This is Mrs. Gilchrist from the Red Cross. Can you come by my office? I have some good news for you."

"Have you located Jimmy?"

"No, but we contacted our office in London, and we have his parents' phone number, and I have arranged a transatlantic call for you. I'm sure they know where he is and will be happy to hear from you, so come to my office when you can."

Sophie immediately went to Mrs. Gilchrist's office. The Red Cross operator on the switchboard placed the call for her and then motioned for her to pick up.

After a few rings, a woman answered, "Hello?"

"Is this Mrs. Brunston?"

"Yes?"

"Oh, hello. This is Sophie Marie, and I'm calling from America."

"Oh, hello."

"I don't know if he has mentioned me or not, but I'm a friend of your son's, and I haven't heard from him for quite a while. I was wondering if you knew where I could contact him."

"Oh, yes, I see, but I'm afraid you've reached the wrong number. James's mother's line was bombed out."

"Oh, no."

"Yes, but not to worry. No injuries. She's quite safe with friends in Hampshire. But this is his wife speaking, and he's due home on a short furlough any day now. Hush, darling, Mummy's on the phone. I'm sorry. Is there a message or a number where you can be reached? Hello? Are you still on the line?"

"Yes, I'm here. Uh . . . no message."

"I'll be happy to tell him you called. Was it Sallie?"

"No, Sophie, but it really wasn't important. Thank you anyway."

After she hung up the phone, she just sat at the desk, and when Mrs. Gilchrist walked back in the office, she assumed by the look on the girl's face that her young man had been killed. She went over, sat down beside her, and took her hand. This was the heartbreaking part of the job she hated. "I'm so terribly, terribly sorry, dear. I was hoping . . . well. Oh, how I hate this old war, so many young people lost. Is there anything I can do—anyone I can call for you?"

"No, but thank you." Sophie went back to the barracks and said nothing to anybody for three weeks. But when Fritzi came through Sweetwater again, Sophie knew she was going to have to tell her.

FRITZI WAS QUIET FOR a moment, then sighed. "How long?"

"Three months."

"Damn. I know some people, but it's too late to do anything now. Why didn't you tell me sooner?"

"I guess I thought if I told him, maybe he could get a leave, and we could get married. I don't know. I guess I was just too ashamed. I don't know what to do."

"Well, you're not the first or the last gal that this has happened to. I figured that guy was up to no good." Fritzi lit a cigarette and blew the smoke up in the air and then said, "You know this kind of thing is not good for the WASPs. We have a reputation to uphold. How soon will you start showing?"

"I don't know. Another couple of months, I guess."

"Well, the good news is the way those flying suits fit, nobody will be able to tell for quite a while, so you can keep flying. But at the first sign, when you reach the point you think you can't go anymore, call me. And let me take it from there."

Fritzi walked into the office of a friend, who was the head nurse of the base hospital. Nurse Joan Speirs looked up, happy to see her. "Fritzi! Hello, you old slug. How are you?"

"Hiya, pal," Fritzi said, then she closed the door behind her and sat down. "Listen, I've got a situation, and I need a little help."

A year earlier, before Joan's husband, Don, was shipped overseas, Fritzi had taken a big chance and smuggled him on a flight from Grand Rapids to Dallas and had gotten Joan and Don a room off base so they could spend the weekend together before he left. He had been killed a month later. She was more than glad to do Fritzi a favor.

About three and a half months later, after a visit to Nurse Speirs, Sophie was officially put on sick leave. Diagnosis: unknown viral infection. Nurse Speirs arranged for her to stay in a private clinic in Amarillo until the baby girl was born.

A couple weeks later, Gussie Mintz asked around and found a couple in Sweetwater who would keep the baby, and as soon as she could, Sophie returned to flying. But every free second she had, she spent with her baby. She said after the WASPs were disbanded, she would probably just go somewhere and get a job. She knew she couldn't go home, but she couldn't give up her baby, either. As she told her sister, "Oh, Fritzi! I've never loved anything so much in my life."

Then, just three weeks before the WASPs were to be sent home for good, the accident happened. It was a midair collision, and Sophie Marie had been killed instantly.

# SOLVANG, CALIFORNIA

Fritzi could see that Sookie was upset at the news. "I'm sorry to have to tell you this, but you needed to know."

"Yes."

"And I did wonder about you a lot. But to come totally clean with you, I guess the other reason I didn't look for you was that I didn't want to have to face you. The truth is, your mother should never have been in Sweetwater in the first place, and it really was my fault that she was there at all. Oh, I wrote her a letter and told her how rough it all would be, but I could have stopped her if I had tried hard enough, and I didn't. And I should have. I always knew deep down she didn't belong there, but I think there was another part of me that thought it would be great to have three Jurdabralinski girls flying for the WASPs. It was a show-off kind of a thing. I was always such a damn show-off. If I had been thinking about her, instead of me, she might be alive today.

"Anyway, after I got back to Sweetwater from your mother's funeral, I found out that the couple that had been taking care of you were moving back to Ohio, and I couldn't take you home. I had promised Sophie I would never tell our parents what happened. She was always Momma's good girl. Hell, we always thought she was going to be a nun, and it would've broken Momma's heart if she had found out. So I didn't know what to do. God knows I couldn't take care of you, and I wanted you to have a shot at a good life with a real family, ya know?

"Anyhow, my pal Pinks had just seen some movie called *Blossoms in the Dust* about some woman in Texas that ran an orphanage, so she checked it out. They were full up, but they gave us the name of another place, so she called and set it up, but they told her she had to get there as soon as possible, because they only had room for one more. So that night around two A.M., a friend of mine named Gussie Mintz picked you up and smuggled you onto the base. It was freezing that night, so Pinks and I wrapped you up in a leather flying suit, and Elroy gassed up a plane and had it ready to go. The two of us flew you over to Houston and got back before anyone noticed a plane was missing. I won't lie to you. I was going to walk in and hand you over and say we didn't know who you belonged to—that we'd just found you somewhere—but when the time came, I couldn't do it. You were just so damn little, ya know, and I guess I wanted you to know that you had belonged to somebody, so I put my name down on the birth certificate. I figured if for any reason Momma and Poppa ever did find out about you, it wouldn't have been such a shock. I was always a wild hare. It's kinda funny now, because I was never the maternal type, you know? Did I hate to leave you? You're darn tootin'. But the way things were going, I didn't know what else to do, so for better or worse, I did what I thought was best. And there you have it."

"I see."

"Oh, pal, believe me. You were better off. Maybe if it had been a different time, things might have been . . . different. But I tried to do the best I could for you."

"Oh, I'm sure you did. And I've had a wonderful life. So . . . you're really my aunt."

"That's right. I didn't know if I was going to tell you. But after meeting you, and seeing what a nice sweet kid you are . . . you deserve to know the truth."

"I see."

"Your adopted parents were nice? You liked them?"

"Oh, yes, very much."

"Took you to church, did they?"

"Oh, yes. And that was another question. Am I Catholic?"

"No. Your mother and I tried to have you baptized, but that damned Irish priest said he wouldn't do it unless we had a marriage certificate. I've been a lapsed Catholic ever since, but now that I'm older, I go every now and then. Take what you like and leave the rest behind, you know. I'm sorry to have thrown so much at you. I could have let you go on believing I was your mother, but you need to know about your real mother. She wasn't a tough old broad like me. And I'll bet you're just like her. A true-blue lady to the core."

"Oh, I don't know. I've tried to be a lady, whatever that means."

"No, you're a good girl. I can tell. You're more like your mother than you know. She never tooted her own horn, and as pretty as she was, she was never stuck up. If she had a fault, it was that she was too tenderhearted. We used to call her Saint Francis of Pulaski. She was always bringing stray cats and dogs home, taking care of sick birds . . ."

"Oh, did she like birds?"

"Oh, yeah. One time, she had this old crow that used to eat right out of her hand."

"Really? I like birds, too."

"See? And I want you to know something else about your mother. She loved you."

"She did?"

"Oh yes. You were her entire world, and if she had not had the accident, she would have kept you. She never for one moment thought of giving you up."

"Really?"

"Absolutely. No question about it. Your mother loved you more than you will ever know."

LATER, SOOKIE CHECKED INTO her room at the little Solvang Gardens Hotel, not far from Fritzi. It was a sweet little room with a small kitchen, and it had a small garden in the back. That night, she looked at the photograph of Sophie that Fritzi had given her. My God, she was, as Fritzi said, the prettiest sister, and she did look shy. Sookie knew that look so well. She had seen it on her own face so many times before.

Fritzi had let her take some books that had been written about the WASPs back to the hotel, and she sat up that night and read all about them and what they had done, and she was in awe of all of them.

When she finished, she gave them back and said, "Thank you for letting me read these. Wow, I had no idea. Just think, Fritzi, you are all legends."

Fritzi laughed. "Well, I don't know about that."

"But you are. It must have been quite an exciting time in your life."

"Oh, yeah, it was, but you ask any veteran of World War II, and they will tell you the same thing. I try not to live in the past like some of these old geezers. I'm pretty happy with the present. But looking back now, I can tell you, those years were pretty damn special. I used to hate it when I heard all that talk about us being the greatest generation. But now, looking back at how young we all were, and when you think about how we started the war with almost nothing, and how everybody pulled together . . . the soldiers got most of the glory, but it was also those gals and guys working day and night, cranking out all those planes and tanks and ships that won the war. And you know, it's funny. It never occurred to any of us that we wouldn't win. So now when I think about all we accomplished in just four years, I have to agree, we were great. We didn't know it at the time, of course. I was one of the lucky ones. I got to do what I loved and serve my country, too. None of us felt like a hero. We were just doing what everybody else was doing, only we were doing it in the air.

"It was a magic bubble of time. You knew you had to live for the moment, and we all felt so alive. The music seemed like it was written just for us. Hell, we thought we were saving the world, and in a way, we did. Who can say what would have happened if we hadn't come into the war when we did? We could all be speaking German or Japanese right now. Who knows? But as hard as it was, I wouldn't have missed it for the world.

"It seems like we were always moving. I don't remember ever getting more than two or three hours' sleep. None of us did. I think we lived on adrenaline. We were too excited to sleep. None of us thought much about what would happen after the war, and then when we were told the WASPs were being disbanded, and it was all over, it was tough. Of course, it wasn't only us. It was all the gals that had stepped in during wartime and gone to work at the factories and everywhere else where they were needed. And now we were being told to go home and be happy to be housewives again. Some of them were glad to go home, but a lot of the gals found out they liked being independent and on their own and wanted to keep working, but they were told that it was unpatriotic to take a job away from a returning soldier. It was quite a kick in the teeth, particularly for the WASPs. All that we did to prove ourselves didn't mean a thing. They just wanted us to go away and pretend it never happened. Even our records were classified.

"Then back in 1976, when ten women began flight training for the U.S. Air Force, a Pentagon press release touted them as 'the first women military pilots,' and I called Jamsie and Nancy and Dinks and they hit the roof. 'Hell, no. We were the first.' None of us were whiners, but we knew what was fair. So a group of us got together again and decided we weren't going to let all those gals who died, your mother or any of them, just be forgotten."

THE NEXT DAY, FRITZI picked Sookie up and took her to lunch at the Alisal River Grill, where Fritzi often played golf. After they had ordered, Sookie asked her if she had ever met her real father.

"Just once. A real quick hello and good-bye. But I can tell you his name. It was James Brunston. I don't know his middle name."

"What did he look like?"

"He looked very healthy, if that's what you're worried about."

Sookie laughed. "No, I mean was he tall? Short?"

"Geez, honey, it was over sixty years ago now, but I remember that he was a tall, good-looking blond guy with blue eyes. You got your mother's hair, but I think you got his nose."

"What was he like?"

"Oh, he seemed nice enough. Of course, later when I found out what he had pulled on Sophie, I changed my mind.

"But you know, looking back on it now, I realize that it was a different time. People were scared, and all bets were off. We all sort of lived for the moment. We had to. That's all we had. None of us knew if we even had a future, so we grabbed for every little slice of happiness we could. I know I did. And who's to say? He could have loved your mother, and maybe he would have come back. Who knows? Not to excuse him, but this kind of thing happened. Boys fell madly in love with girls they didn't even know. Boys were desperate to get married. Hell, I could have married a hundred different boys if I had wanted to. All they knew was that they could be killed any day, and I guess they wanted to leave something or someone behind to prove that at least they had been here.

"Me, I got lucky. After the war, me and Billy moved out here and started a little flight school, and we had forty good years together. After we retired, we traveled. We had a little plane, and I flew us wherever we wanted to go. I can't complain. I've had a damn good life, and I've lived long enough to see the gals fly jets and finally get a chance. And it feels good to know you helped open up a little window for them, ya know?"

Sookie stayed on in Solvang for a week and visited with Fritzi every day. They usually had either lunch or dinner together, and the rest of the time, she just wandered around town, talking to people, and it was wonderful. Here in Solvang, she wasn't Lenore Simmons's daughter. For the first time in years, she was just herself. She met a lot of Fritzi's friends, and she even made some friends of her own. Two nice ladies visiting from Japan invited her to have dinner with them, and she had breakfast with the sweetest couple, Susan and Michael Beckman from Tenafly, New Jersey. And she met the cutest lady, named Linda Peckham, in the hotel spa.

She called Earle every night, and in one conversation, he said, "Honey, I haven't heard you sound so happy in a long time." And it was true.

On her last day in California, she and Fritzi went to the old Spanish mission for mass and had dinner at Bit o' Denmark restaurant.

When they had finished dinner, Sookie said, "Uh . . . Fritzi, before I go home, could I ask you one more question? I'm really curious about the name Ginger. Did you name me after someone in your family?"

Fritzi laughed. "No, sorry about that, kid. The night we took you in, when they were filling out the birth certificate, and they asked me what your name was, it was the first name I came up with. I was a big fan of Ginger Rogers."

"Oh, as in Fred Astaire and Ginger Rogers?"

"That's right."

"Oh, how nice. I love her."

"Yeah? Me, too. I met her once, and she was a pretty swell dame on the screen and off. But you did have a real name—the name your mother gave you."

"Oh?"

"Yeah, and you're probably not gonna like it, but she named you after me."

"My real name is Fritzi?"

"Yeah. Fritzi Willinka Jurdabralinski. Can you take it?"

Sookie smiled. "Yes, I can. And not only that, I am honored to be named after you."

THE NEXT MORNING, WHEN Sookie was leaving to go home, Fritzi walked her to the car, and Sookie said, "Thank you for a wonderful time."

Fritzi said, "Kid, I wouldn't have missed meeting you for the world. And oh, before you go, here's a little present for you."

"Oh, thank you."

"You keep in touch, ya hear?"

"I will."

AS SOOKIE'S CAR DROVE away, Fritzi walked back in the house and thought to herself, "That poor kid. Such a nice sweet gal, and she's been lied to all her life. And now I'm doing the same damn thing." She hadn't told her what had really happened to her mother. Sookie had been through enough already, and what good would it do for her to know anyway? Nothing could be proved.

In the car, Sookie opened the little package that Fritzi had handed to her. Inside was a small blue rosary and a note.

Dear Sarah Jane,

This belonged to your mother, and I know she would want you to have it.

Fritzi

# THE ACCIDENT

November 23, 1944

Although the WASPs had only a few more weeks before they would be officially disbanded and would return to civilian life, there were still a lot of guys wanting to get a date with Sophie. But dating was the last thing on her mind. All she wanted to do was fly the remainder of her ferrying trips and, in between, spend time with her baby.

None of the fliers were having any luck with her. But one guy in particular was having a hard time taking no for an answer. He wasn't used to it. Bud Harris had a certain reputation to uphold. He was known as the Lady Killer. He was handsome, was a smooth talker, and had always had success. He'd been so sure he could get a date with Sophie, he made a bet with his buddies that not only would he go out with her, but he would have her in the sack in two weeks.

He tried everything he knew, including the old "Oh, honey, I may never come back alive. Won't you give me just one date?" line. He sent flowers, he wrote notes, he used all of his tricks of the trade. But she still had no interest, and he wasn't happy about it.

He wasn't about to lose his bet over some dumb little Polack bitch who didn't know how lucky she was that he'd even looked at her. One evening, when he was sitting around having a few drinks, he found out that Sophie was doing a cross-country that day and was bringing in a plane later that night. After another drink, he decided he would go over and meet her and try to talk a little sense into her—tell her to stop playing so hard to get. He knew she wanted it. Besides, that's why most of them were here anyway.

Sophie was tired when she pulled in and just wanted to get back to her bay, crawl into bed, and go to sleep. She walked out of the hangar, headed over to make her flight report, when Harris was suddenly beside her. He grabbed her by the arm and slammed her up against a wall. "Hey, baby, what's your hurry? Come here, I wanna talk to you. Why are you being so damn snooty? You don't even know what you are missing yet."

Sophie tried to get away and push past him, but he pinned her arms down and kissed her roughly on the mouth. "Stop it! Please . . . don't!" she said, but he wouldn't stop, and before she knew it, he had ripped open the top of her flight suit and was groping her. She fought him off as hard as she could, but he was over six feet tall and strong. She screamed "No! Stop!" She tried to scream again, but he put his hand over her mouth, and pushed himself up against her even harder. He was going to win that bet one way or another. And it would always be her word against his.

Suddenly a man's voice said, "Hey, what's going on out here?" And he aimed a flashlight at them. It was Elroy Leefers, the mechanic, who had heard her calling out. Harris looked around, saw the scrawny little mechanic, and said, "Get lost, Hayseed, we're busy here."

From the look of terror in Sophie's eyes, Elroy quickly figured out what was about to happen, and he reached into his belt and pulled out a heavy metal wrench. "Let go of her, Harris, or I'll knock your brains out all over this tarmac."

Harris loosened his grip on Sophie for just a split second and she managed to break loose and run toward Elroy. When she got there Elroy put her behind him and looked at Harris. "Come on, flyboy. I dare you. Let's see what you've got."

Harris stood there and thought about it, but figured it wasn't worth the trouble. He was out of the mood now, anyway. As Harris walked away, Sophie collapsed in Elroy's arms. "Oh, thank you, Elroy."

"Aw, it's all right, honey, don't let it get to you. He's just a bad apple is all." Sophie didn't tell anyone what had happened. She had only a little more time left and didn't want any trouble. She just wanted to get on with life and raise her baby. She managed to avoid seeing Harris for a little while.

But a few days later, the guys in Harris's unit were flying formation, and one spotted the plane below them and recognized the red hair and he said over the radio, "Hey, lover boy, look downstairs. There's that redheaded gal who's so crazy about you. Why don't you go and say hello?" Harris heard the guys laughing, and he broke formation. That was the last time the guys saw him that day.

When they arrived back at base two hours later without him, they were told that he had been forced to make an emergency landing because of a mechanical malfunction, but that he was fine. It wasn't until later that night that they heard that another plane had crashed and that the female pilot had been killed.

At the investigative hearing, Bud Harris testified that they had, in fact, by mutual consent, been flying in formation, when the WASP pilot suddenly—and for no apparent reason and without warning—pulled up, causing the tip of her right wing to scrape the underside of his plane, ripping into his landing gear. He assumed she had pulled up and away and was in control and did not see her crash.

There was just one witness. A farmer said he was out in the field and heard a loud roaring noise. When he looked up, he saw two planes flying close together, and then the smaller one suddenly flew off to the right and went into a spin. He watched it spiral slowly down and crash. The plane exploded on impact and burned, and there was little left to determine the exact cause. After an investigation, the crash was declared accidental, and no charges were filed.

He hadn't meant to do it. Harris had thought that now that Sophie was alone and didn't have that hayseed looking out for her, it might be fun to throw a little scare into her—let her know just who she was dealing with. He would teach her a lesson about flying she wouldn't forget in a hurry.

So he circled around and flew in behind her and pulled up beside her. But in his zeal to have her see who he was, he'd pulled in too close, too fast. When she suddenly saw the plane right up on her, she pulled up sharply, trying to get out of his way. As she pulled up, the tip of her wing scraped the bottom of his plane, and he heard the sickening sound of metal meeting metal.

Harris worried that the scrape might have done some damage to his landing gear, so he did not stick around to see her plane spiral down to the ground and crash.

One of the other fliers in the air that day was a friend of Fritzi's and told her what he suspected had happened. Harris had been known to be pretty reckless.

Fritzi had flown into the base on the day of the hearing and tracked Harris down in the waiting room, just outside the inquiry room.

She threw the door open, and when she saw Harris sitting there with his feet up on a desk casually smoking a cigarette, her eyes filled with tears of rage.

"You no-good, lousy bastard! You just killed my sister, you sorry no good son of a bitch. I ought to kick your ass all the way to hell and back. Was it worth it? Showing off for your pals?"

He looked up at her. "I don't know what you're talking about."

"No? I swear to God, Harris, if I had a gun right now, I'd blow your Goddamned head off."

"Hey, lady, it wasn't my fault. She pulled up."

"Keep telling yourself that, Harris. You know damn well whose fault it was," Fritzi said. "You're not worth killing. I hope you *don't* die. I hope they throw you in the brig for life, and that you remember what you did every day for the rest of your lousy, stinking life."

An officer opened the door, motioned for Harris, and said, "They're ready for you in the other room." Harris put out his cigarette, stood up, and walked out.

A collection was taken up among the other girls to take Sophie home, and Fritzi rode all the way to Pulaski with her coffin. Gertrude May flew in from Camp Davis in North Carolina, and Wink got a leave of absence and flew in from England.

The entire town—every man, woman, and child—attended the funeral that day. And even though Sophie wasn't officially in the army, the local VFW draped the American flag over her coffin anyway, rules be damned. As far as they were concerned, she had died while serving her country.

As a tribute, they had this inscribed in bronze and placed on her tombstone:

*She has climbed to the peaks above storm and cloud*
*She has found the light of son and of God,*
*I cannot say, I will not say*
*That she is dead.*
*She is merely flown away.*

*—James Whitcomb Riley*

# NEW YORK CITY

March 1945

After the WASPs disbanded, Fritzi's friend Willy had gone home to Oklahoma, but like all the girls, she found herself restless and took off for a trip to New York to see Pinks and catch some shows. One night, while having drinks with some friends, she looked over and happened to see Bud Harris sitting at a table across the room with a bunch of other pilots. She excused herself and walked over to the table. "Hi, good-looking. Wanna dance?"

A few hours later, in a very exclusive hotel room, Harris had done exactly what he had been told to do by the sexy dame from Oklahoma. After he had removed all of his clothes, he smirked at her. "Will I do?"

Willy, still fully dressed in her steel-tipped cowboy boots, smiled and said, "Oh, yes. Come here, big boy." As soon as he got close enough, she hauled off and kicked him as hard as she could, and Harris fell to the floor, clutching his pride and joy and screaming in pain. Willy calmly strolled over and picked up his shoes and all of his clothes and threw them out the twenty-second-floor window. She left him lying on the floor, naked and writhing in agony.

Willy never told a soul what she had done, but she figured it was the least she could do for Fritzi.

# POINT CLEAR, ALABAMA

Sookie was glad to be home. She was even happy to see crazy old Lenore and actually called and asked her to lunch.

Lenore showed up at the restaurant looking radiant in a beautiful lime green dress with a long white scarf flowing behind her. "The prodigal daughter returns!"

"Hello, Mother. Don't you look pretty."

"Why, thank you. I think this is one of my best colors, don't you?" she said as she waved to a friend across the room.

Lenore must have missed Sookie when she was gone, because she was pleasant all through lunch, until the very end when she said, "I don't mean to burst your bubble, Sookie, but I don't think you lost a pound at that spa. I'd ask them for my money back if I were you."

After Sookie had been back for a few days and had time to think about everything that had happened, she realized that this had been the most important trip of her life. She had learned so much that she never knew, and mostly about herself.

She was a lot more than Lenore Simmons's daughter. She was beginning to be somebody else, and she liked who she was turning out to be. Thank God, Earle had urged her to go. He was right. She wouldn't have missed this trip for the world.

Just a few months ago, she had been ready to sit back and take it easy, and now her life was just beginning again. She was learning so much—about Wisconsin, California, the WASPs, Polish food, Danish food.

Sookie ordered five copies of *A History of Poland,* and gave one to each of her four children. Then she sat down and read it herself. She was just in awe of how brave the Poles had been and at all the hardships they had endured.

Why hadn't she known all this before? She looked down at her arm and thought to herself, I have proud and brave Polish blood running up and down in all my veins. How wonderful! The next time she and Earle went over to the Oyster House, she did something that she had never done before in her life. She ordered a dozen raw oysters—and not only that, she ate them! She would probably never do it again, but at least she had done it once. Mrs. Poole was beginning to branch out in the world.

OF COURSE, WHEN SHE got back from Solvang and told Dee Dee her real father's name, Dee Dee immediately hired a professional genealogist to trace the Brunston family in England and find out if James Brunston was still alive. The lady found out that they had all died, except for one of his daughters.

Dee Dee wanted her mother to contact her. "She's your half sister, Mother!" But Sookie decided that there was really no point in contacting the poor lady at this late date. It would only mean having to divulge unpleasant information about the woman's father. Why upset her? She would just let that be. But they did find out that James Brunston had lived to be almost ninety and had died of natural causes. That was all she really needed to know.

Since meeting Fritzi and studying so much about history, Sookie had begun to look at Lenore with different eyes. She began to see how being a female and growing up when she had, with so many restrictions, must have been very frustrating for her. If she had been allowed to go on the stage, she probably would have been a star. And given all of Lenore's organizational skills and her ambition and drive, had she been a man, she most likely would have been a CEO of some big company. It really was sad to think that if Lenore had been born just a little later and gone into politics, who knows where the woman might have wound up?

Thank heavens, Sookie's girls could be almost anything they wanted to be. And it made her happy to think that her birth mother and two aunts had helped open doors for the women who came after them. As Carter said, "How cool is that?"

# BLUE JAY AWAY

Life was finally back to normal again, with one exception. Dr. Shapiro was very pleased with Sookie's progress and said he felt she was well on the way to making a new life for herself, but his practice in Point Clear was not growing. It seemed nobody wanted to see a psychiatrist, and if they did, they certainly didn't tell anybody about it. And so he and his wife had decided to move back to New York, where seeing a psychiatrist was a status symbol. His only regret in leaving was that he would miss Sookie. He would never have told her, of course, and she was an older lady, but in the past months, he had developed a little crush on her. She was probably the nicest person he had ever met, patient or not.

Sookie was feeling better, but she still missed seeing her smaller birds. She hadn't seen a nuthatch or a chickadee all spring. Day after day, she sat in her greenhouse and watched the blue jays. She studied their feet and the way they landed on the rim, and she began to do sketches of bird feeders and try to figure out the measurements.

She was trying to come up with a better smaller feeder with wire mesh, so just the tiny bird seeds would filter through, with a smaller ledge that curved up just enough for the smaller birds to land.

Walter Dempsey was a handyman they used from time to time,

and he could fix almost anything. He had a small carpentry shop where he made all kinds of gadgets. After Sookie had drawn a sketch with what she hoped were the correct measurements, she drove over to his shop and walked in. "Hey, Walter. I have a little drawing of a bird feeder. Do you think you could make this for me?"

He looked at it for a moment, then said, "I think I can do this up for you. When do you need it?"

"As soon as possible." It wasn't as if she didn't like blue jays. She did, but she felt she had to do something or else the little ones would just stop coming altogether.

ONE WEEK LATER, SOOKIE sat in her greenhouse and waited. In about five seconds, a big fat blue jay swooped in and tried to land on the rim of her new bird feeder. He kept fluttering around, trying to balance himself and eat the bird seed at the same time, but eureka! He couldn't do it, and after about three or four more attempts, he finally gave up and flew away. Soon several more blue jays tried to land, but because the ledge was so narrow, they, too, had a hard time balancing themselves, and they gave up and eventually flew over to the sunflower seed feeder.

It took a while for the little birds to understand, but the next afternoon she received a visit from a tiny titmouse, and as she watched, he was able to perch on the rim and feed. Success! She immediately called Mr. Dempsey and ordered five more bird feeders.

The following Monday morning, Sookie ran into the house and called Mr. Dempsey. "Oh, Walter, we had three more house finches, an indigo bunting, *and* a chickadee! I just can't thank you enough."

"Well, you're welcome, but it was really your idea. I just followed the plan. I think you may have invented a really useful thing, Mrs. Poole."

"Really?"

"Yes, ma'am, and you know, Mrs. Poole, I was thinking. Maybe you should get a patent on that design. I figure I could knock out at least twenty of these a week. I talked to Mr. Nadleshaft over at Birds-R-Us and told him about the success you'd been having with your feeder, and he said if I made some more, he'd be happy to try and sell them for us."

Sookie was delighted. She and Walter took her design to a lawyer in town, and they drew up a business agreement for their new company that Sookie named Blue Jay Away. They would split the profits fifty–fifty. Within a month, Sookie and Mr. Dempsey were so busy they could hardly keep up with the orders. In just six months, they hired an assistant and a bookkeeper, and the business grew from there.

A year later, they branched out even more and hired an advertising company. Pretty soon, they had ads running in *Southern Living* magazine and in all the bird-watcher magazines, featuring a photo of the feeder.

> "Tired of all those pesky blue jays eating your smaller birds' feed? I know I was. But with the Blue Jay Away feeder, finches, titmice, and all my small bird visitors can now feed in peace."
>
> —Mrs. Earle Poole, Jr.
> Point Clear, Alabama

Pretty soon, the company had its own website, www.BlueJayAway.com, and much to their surprise orders started coming in from all over the world. As Sookie said to Earle, "I didn't even know they had blue jays in China. Did you?"

When the local paper did an article on her, they referred to her as "Mrs. Earle Poole, Jr., housewife and inventor," and she couldn't have been more pleased. Life was so amazing and full of surprises. All of her life, she had thought she was stupid, and now she was an "inventor."

Not only that, but with the way sales were going, Earle started considering retirement. As the next few years went by, the company pretty much started running itself, and she and Earle had time to enjoy being alone again.

Sookie did have one big scare. One Sunday afternoon, Earle had been on the phone talking to a friend of his, and as she passed by the den, she overheard him say, “Yes, but deep down, I really would like to have another Great Dane.”

Oh, dear God, she thought. Why not a small horse or a cow in the house? Please, dear God, let this just be a passing fancy. She loved Earle, but having one Great Dane was enough for a lifetime.

## THE STRAWBERRY BLONDE

Both Uncle Baby and Aunt Lily had died at Pleasant Hill in their late eighties, but at ninety-three, Lenore was still going strong. Unfortunately she had outlived Angel, her live-in nurse. After much pleading, she finally agreed to go to Westminster Village, but only temporarily, until Sookie and Earle could find another nurse. However, to Sookie's surprise, during her last visit, Lenore seemed pretty happy. "I have to say, Sookie, I am enjoying my step-in tub, and the food here is quite adequate, but I could just kill Conchita for up and dying on me."

A week later, Sookie had just come in from the store when the phone rang, and when she picked up, she heard a woman's voice. "Mrs. Poole? This is Molly from Westminster Village, and I'm calling because your mother has just had what the doctor thinks might be a slight stroke, and he thought maybe you should come over."

When she arrived, she was told that her mother was in the intensive care unit, but that she was to wait before she went in. Dr. Hindman came out and said, "Mrs. Poole, before you go in, I just want to warn you: She's still very disoriented, so don't be surprised if she doesn't recognize you." He entered the room before her, walked over to the bed, and indicated for her to follow. Sookie walked over to her bed, and the doctor said, "You have a visitor, Mrs. Simmons. Do you know who this is?"

Lenore opened her eyes and looked up. She smiled, then took Sookie's hand and said, "Well, of course I do. This is my daughter, Sarah Jane, and she's the best daughter in the whole world, and I love her."

Sookie looked down at the old woman lying there, so small and helpless, and squeezed her hand and said, "I love you, too, Mother." And she meant it from the bottom of her heart. Lenore squeezed her hand and dozed off again.

Sookie sat by her bed as Lenore slept, and she didn't know if her mother could hear her, but as she sat there, she quietly sang to her, "Casey would waltz with a strawberry blonde, and the band played on. . . ." As Sookie watched Lenore sleep, she was amazed that even now, as old and as helpless as she was, she was still so pretty.

THE DOCTOR CAME BACK a few hours later and told Sookie to go on home and get some rest, and he would call if there were any changes.

That night, they called with the news that her mother was gone.

THE NEXT MORNING, LENORE'S lawyer knocked on the door and said, "Mrs. Poole, I'm so sorry about your loss, but your mother said I was to deliver this to you in person within twenty-four hours of her passing." She opened the envelope, and inside was a letter.

> Sookie,
>
> Not that I am planning on going anywhere anytime soon, but just in case, I thought this might be helpful.
>
> OBIT
>
> LENORE SIMMONS KRACKENBERRY
> Born January 20, 1917, Selma, Alabama
> Passed (Date and time to be filled in), Point Clear, Alabama
> She was the daughter of the late Mr. and Mrs. William Jenkins Simmons of Selma.

Grieving survivors include: (to be filled in).
She was a member of (list clubs, organizations, etc.). She is to be remembered for her devotion to family, her innate Southern charm, and for her high degree of integrity in all of her volunteer tasks.
Memorials would be appreciated. Please send to:
Point Clear Soldier's Rest Cemetery Care Fund
Point Clear, Alabama

MEMORIAL FAMILY AND FRIENDS RECEPTION:

SITE CHOICES

1. Grand Ballroom, Grand Hotel
2. Lakewood Country Club (in the big room)

*Day: Saturday or Sunday, 3 P.M. to 5 P.M.*

- Food and beverages: Coffee, iced tea, a light punch, finger sandwiches, assorted sweets, cheese straws, nuts, etc. (Mrs. Busby has the list.)
- Seasonal, tasteful flowers at each table.
- Greeters to arrive at 2:30 for assignments from Mrs. Poole.
- Greeters are to be stationed at entry doors and/or lobby and stairs area.
- A simple white lapel flower should be worn by each greeter.
- Guestbook(s) to be placed in the room, NOT entry area.
- I do not want people just running by and signing the book—only serious mourners.
- Greeters are to move about and mingle with the guests.

Sookie, don't bother with the church service. Rev. George already has all of his instructions. You will busy enough with out-of-town guests, arranging special parking, etc.

Mother

At three o'clock that afternoon, the phone rang, and it was a man from the local monument company. "Mrs. Poole, I have instructions to deliver the headstone. Where would you like it placed?"

"What?"

"Your mother ordered a headstone . . . and it's pretty large."

"How large?"

The man told her that Lenore had ordered a five-foot white marble statue of a weeping angel for her gravestone and said, "to bill her in care of you."

"My God, when did she do this?"

"Oh, about ten years ago now, although she came in every so often and made changes. She was quite specific. It had to be carved out of Alabama marble only and had to have absolutely no flaws."

Sookie nodded. Of course. That was Lenore. Gone for good, but still calling the shots. Sookie thought, "Well, okay, old gal. Why change now?" As usual, Lenore got her way in the end, just as it should be.

SOOKIE WAS AMAZED AT all the flowers and tributes that were paid to her mother at the funeral. So many people said such lovely things about her. But the one that meant the most to her was sweet old Netta, who took her hand and said, "She was a lot of trouble, but it's going to be a dull old world without her."

It was a beautiful service, just as Lenore had wished. Of course, it all cost more than they thought it would. The weeping angel statue was so large, they had to buy two full cemetery plots. As Sookie stood at the graveside, she had many mixed feelings, but she realized the woman they were now lowering in the ground would always be a huge part of her life. Whom the heart first loves does not know or care if they are related by blood. The fact was that her mother—the only mother she had ever known—was dead. That impossible woman had driven her crazy and caused her much heartbreak, and yet, despite it all, she would miss her every day for the rest of her life.

*Lenore Simmons Krackenberry*
*1917–2010*
*A true daughter of the South,*
*gone home.*

# LENORE'S LEGACY

Point Clear, Alabama

A few weeks after the funeral, Sookie walked over to the house to start the process of cleaning out all her mother's things. When she unlocked the front door and walked in, the faint fragrance of her mother's perfume was still lingering in the air. She half-expected to hear Lenore's voice calling out from another room at any second, but it was eerily quiet. As she made her way back to the kitchen and looked around, it was so strange to see all the small things left behind—little objects that once would have meant nothing, but now seemed so important. She looked at the notepad on the wall and saw her mother's handwriting. "Tell Sookie I need more coffee." The sight of the handwritten note made her realize what a cruel trick death really was. One moment, a person is here, alive and talking, and the next, presto, she's vanished into thin air. Death was still the great mystery, the question that no one can really answer. She wandered around the house and wound up in the dining room. She opened the large mahogany breakfront drawer, and there it was: all that silver . . . just waiting.

She sighed and walked into the kitchen and came back with a rag, her mother's white cotton gloves, and the silver polish and sat down at the dining room table. What else could she do? She could almost hear Lenore's voice as she polished: "Remember, Sookie, nothing says more about a family than good silver and real pearls. The rest is just fluff." It was such a big house, but Lenore had filled every room. Now without Lenore, she felt so small, but she kept polishing.

That afternoon, Sookie picked up the phone. "Dee Dee, it's Mother calling. Honey, I've been cleaning a few things out, and I wondered if you would like to have Grandmother's silver?"

"The Francis the First?"

"Yes."

There was a pause, then she said, "No, not really. It would be kind of useless to me, and I'd never use it. Unless, of course, you'd let me sell it and buy something else, and I know you won't let me do that."

"No, Grandmother was insistent that it be handed down to someone in the family."

"Why don't you ask the twins? Maybe they want it."

"I can't. I promised her that I would never split it up, and I can't give it all to just one of them."

"That's true, and you know Carter doesn't want it."

"No. Anyhow, I was thinking that if you really don't want it, would you mind very much if I offered it to Buck and Bunny?"

"No, not at all. I think that's a great idea. Knowing Bunny, she'd love to have it."

Sookie was not a real Simmons, nor were any of her children, and so by rights, Buck and Bunny were the ones it should go to. Besides, Bunny was now the most Southern person she knew. In the past few years, she had developed more of a Southern accent than Sookie had.

A week later, Sookie packed the car and drove up to North Carolina. Bunny, as expected, was over the moon. "Oh, Sookie, you just don't know how happy I am to have it, and, of course, you can always borrow it anytime, but I can't tell you how much I've always loved it," she said, caressing the large soup ladle. "I think it was one of the reasons I first fell in love with Buck. I had never met anyone whose mother had a complete set of Francis the First. And now that it's ours, I feel like a real Simmons at last." Bunny gasped when she realized what she had said. "Oh, Sookie, I didn't mean it like that. I just mean . . . well, of course, you are a real Simmons. Oh, I could just kill myself for saying that."

Sookie shrugged it off. "Oh, Bunny, don't worry about it. Believe me, I'm so happy you have it."

"Really?"

"Oh, yes, and all I ask is that you promise me one thing."

"Oh, of course, anything. Anything at all."

"Promise me you won't break up the set."

Bunny suddenly recoiled in horror. "Break up the set? Break up the set? I would never ever think of doing a thing like that! Why, it would be a total sacrilege. I would sooner starve to death than break up a complete set of Francis the First." Sookie laughed and walked over and hugged her.

As Sookie was driving home, she smiled. She didn't know how it happened, but a little part of Winged Victory must have latched on to Bunny and was hanging on for dear life. Sookie had done the right thing. The Simmons torch and all that damn silverware had been officially passed on, and she suddenly felt about twenty pounds lighter.

On Sookie's first morning home from North Carolina, she was out in her garden working and looked over and saw a beautiful bright blue dragonfly with silver wings flittering all around in her flowers. That had to be a sign. If Lenore had come back to say hello, it would be just like her to be a bright blue dragonfly. Lenore was a spring, and blue was one of her colors.

A few weeks later, Sookie picked up the phone and heard Dee Dee almost screaming with excitement. "Mother! Are you sitting down?"

"No, but I will—"

"You are not going to believe this!"

"Okay . . ."

"You know that woman I contacted in London to look up the Brunston family tree?"

"Yes?"

"Well, she just found a wedding announcement in the London *Times* for your father's grandparents published in 1881, and it says that on that June twenty-second, Reginald James Brunston married the former Miss Victoria Anne Simmons at Saint James Cathedral."

"That's nice."

"Mother! Don't you understand what this means? Your real great-grandmother's maiden name was Simmons, so we are Simmonses after all!

"Oh. Well, I don't know if that's good news or bad news."

"It's *great* news, Mother. Thank God I didn't throw out the Simmons family crest. And not only that, she also found out that your real father's grandmother, my great-grandmother, was a fifth cousin, twice removed, of Queen Victoria!"

Oh, dear. Bless Dee Dee's heart. It was probably not the same Simmons family at all, but she was obviously thrilled to pieces with this information and would no doubt tell everyone she knew.

SHE WAS GLAD DEE Dee was so happy. It didn't make all that much difference to her except that at least now, she didn't have to feel too bad about the Kappa legacy. At least there was a Simmons somewhere in her background. She guessed her only regret was that Winged Victory never knew, and it would have pleased her so to know she had been right all along.

## MARVALEEN STRIKES AGAIN

A few weeks later, Sookie ran into Marvaleen at the store, and she said, "You are not going to believe this Sookie, but Ralph and I are dating again."

"Oh, really?"

"Yes, I realized that I really didn't hate him as much as I thought I did. It was the institution of marriage I hated."

"I see. And what does Edna Yorba Zorbra say about it?"

"Oh, I haven't seen her since she moved to Las Vegas. She doesn't do life coaching anymore."

"Oh, well, that's a shame."

"Yes, she's promoting a new line of jewelry now, made entirely of feathers."

"Really?"

"Yes, she's one-quarter Native American, you know, and they just love their feathers. Anyway, so far, it's been going pretty well with Ralph, so we're thinking about just moving in together and having sex. That's the only reason I married him in the first place. He was always great in bed. Of course, he's not as young as he used to be, but being a doctor, he can get all the Viagra he wants."

"Ah. Well, I'm glad things are working out for you. I've got to run, but great to see you."

"Yeah, me, too. I'll keep you posted. See you later."

Oh, Lord, Marvaleen. She always offered far too much personal information, or at least more than Sookie wanted to know. Ralph was Sookie's gynecologist, and now she would never feel the same way having a pelvic again.

BUT THE GOOD NEWS was that she and Dena finally did get to the Kappa reunion, and to her surprise, even after she told them the truth, they elected her chairman of the following year's reunion committee.

But then, so many surprising things had happened. The town mayor who had once sued Lenore for calling him a carpetbagger and a horse thief had been convicted and sentenced to jail for embezzlement. Dee Dee finally left her husband for good, and had promised Sookie that if she ever did marry again, it would be only a small courthouse affair. Both Ce Ce and Le Le were pregnant. And Fritzi had just sent her a photograph of herself that had appeared in the Solvang paper. She had won the senior's cup at the Alisal Golf Tournament.

Later, when Earle and Carter went on their once-a-year camping trip, she missed Earle, but it gave her a little time to reflect. She realized that thanks to Dr. Shapiro, she had learned that being a successful person is not necessarily defined by what you have achieved, but by what you have overcome. And she had overcome something that, for her, was huge. She had overcome her fear of displeasing her mother and had married the right man. And no, she wasn't a leader in society, or a rich and famous ballerina, but her husband and her children loved her. And, really, what more could a person ask for?

That night Sookie sat out on the pier all by herself and smiled. She sat there until all the stars came out, and the church bells from town rang up and down the bay.

## ALBUQUERQUE, NEW MEXICO

Dee Dee had become so fascinated with the history of the WASPs that when she found out that they were having a World War II military plane exhibit in New Mexico, she bought two plane tickets, and she and Sookie went.

Sookie told the man at the gate, "My daughter and I have come all the way from Alabama to see this today. Thank you so much for having this exhibition."

"You're welcome, ma'am. Glad you could come."

Sookie and Dee Dee stood in line to tour the B-17 Flying Fortress, the last one flying in the world. First of all, she couldn't get over the size of the thing. It was huge. As they walked around it, she read all the names written on the sides of the plane of the pilots who had flown it. She looked for her mother's name, but did not find it. There were only men's names.

Dee Dee was snapping pictures and called to her to get in line to go inside the plane. As they stood there waiting, a man affiliated with the exhibit was holding court, explaining to another group of men how he had flown one just like it at the end of the war, when most of them were sold to Russia. Sookie walked over and listened for a while, and then she said, "You know, women flew this plane, too. My mother and aunt flew this model right from the factory."

The group of men looked at her in surprise, and one said, "Really? A *woman* flew one of these?"

The man with the exhibit who was lecturing looked at her and, without much enthusiasm, said, "Yeah, a few of them did," then continued his speech to the men.

As Sookie and Dee Dee climbed the stairs and entered the plane, she could not believe how raw and stark it was inside—nothing but open sides of dark green metal and corrugated metal floors. They moved through the plane, and she was amazed that everything was so hard, with no softness anywhere. This might have been the same plane she had been flown to Houston in that night with Fritzi and Pinks.

When they reached the front of the plane and looked in at the crude cockpit and what looked to her like a hundred levers, instruments, and dials and the huge metal pedals on the floor, she was completely awestruck. My God, how could a 120-pound girl possibly fly this thing? Where did she ever get the nerve? Sookie couldn't imagine what it must have been like flying in the blistering heat of the day and in the freezing cold.

As she stood there, she suddenly became overwhelmed with the enormity of courage it must have taken, and she burst into tears. It was one thing to read about it and see photos, but to be standing inside the exact plane the girls had flown gave her a sense of overwhelming pride.

IT HAD NOT BEEN easy getting in and crawling from the front to the back of the plane and climbing down the narrow, hot metal steps. When they came out the other side, both Dee Dee and Sookie had grease all over their hands from holding on to the metal sides. There sure weren't any frills or comforts on this plane.

Later, a few people who had paid a lot of money were able to go up in the B-17. The noise was deafening as it taxied down the runway and took off, and Sookie was nervous that it would never get off the ground. But at the last minute, it lifted up and flew out, headed over the mountains. If she had had any courage at all, she could have gone for a ride in it, but she was not brave enough for that.

As they left the exhibit, they stopped by the man seated at the long table who had taken their money and stamped their hands, and Sookie thanked him. "Oh, it was just wonderful to see those planes in person and actually get inside one."

The man smiled. "I'm glad you enjoyed it."

Sookie looked back at the plane for the last time. "I'm just in awe at the bravery and skill those fliers must have had."

Then Dee Dee piped up and said, "You know, you really should tell people going through that women flew these planes as well, especially the little girls. I think they would like to know that."

The man's smile hardened ever so slightly, and he looked right past her, as if he hadn't heard a word, and motioned for the next person in line to step up. It was quite obvious that he had no intention of mentioning that fact.

Then Dee Dee did something that shocked her mother. Dee Dee looked at the man and said, "Asshole," and turned around and walked away.

Sookie did not like bad language, but she heard herself add, "Macho asshole," and followed her daughter, and they both burst out laughing.

They left the airport that day with a feeling of tremendous pride and with a deeper appreciation of what the WASPs had done. And now she had a clue as to what it must have felt like, risking your life day after day, and not even being appreciated. No wonder some of the gals were bitter.

Dear God, thought Sookie. Even after all these years, after so many of these women died flying for their country, these men still didn't want to acknowledge it ever happened. Some things never change. Thank heavens for the younger generation.

# THE REUNION

Point Clear, Alabama

The moment Sookie picked up the phone, she recognized the voice.

"Hiya, kid!"

"Hello!"

"I'm calling to see if you want to come home with me."

"When? Where?"

"To Pulaski."

"Oh . . ."

"I just got off the phone with Pinks, who's organizing it. This year, we're having the WASP reunion in Pulaski. Can you come? There's going to be a parade, and yours truly is grand marshal, and I want you to ride with me."

"Oh, my gosh . . . well, yes! Of course! When?"

"August fourteenth."

"I'll be there."

Sookie was so excited. She had wanted to go to Pulaski, but she hadn't wanted to embarrass anyone by just showing up. Now she had an official invitation from Fritzi.

* * *

ON AUGUST FOURTEENTH, SOOKIE flew into Green Bay. Everybody was staying at the big Hyatt, and Sookie's plane was late, so she was told to meet them at the hotel dining room, where they would be having lunch. As she walked in the door, she looked over and saw a group of women at a table in the corner and stood and watched them for a moment.

She realized that to a stranger, they would look like any group of old ladies having lunch. One would have no idea who they were or what they had done. The maître d' came over and took Sookie over to the table, and Fritzi looked up and said, "Here she is! Pinks, Willy, this is Sarah Jane."

She would have known them anywhere. Pinks looked just like her photos, and Willy was, of course, older but still a beauty. Later, she met her Aunt Gertrude, now a nun called Sister Mary Jude, for the first time. She had a face like a chubby angel on a tree, and she grabbed Sookie and hugged her. "Oh, you look just like her. Oh, you darling girl. Oh, if only Momma could have seen you!"

Someone sent over a bottle of champagne, and Fritzi lifted her glass and said, "Well, now that we are all here, here's to all the great gals who have already gone upstairs, and here's to us. We may not be as young and spry as we once were, but by God, as the song says, 'We're still here.' "

"Hear, hear," they said as they all drank a toast.

"And here's to Sophie's girl, Sarah Jane. Welcome home."

The next day, Sookie and all the ladies in their uniforms were picked up early in the morning and driven to Pulaski. As they drove into town, they were greeted by crowds of excited people, lined up on both sides of the streets, waving little American flags, yelling and applauding as they passed by. After the parade was over, they all went to the large auditorium at the Knights of Columbus Hall, where the official ceremony was to take place, and both walls were filled with large photographs of Avenger Field in Sweetwater and the girls and the planes they flew. Right in the front, on the right, was a large photograph of Sookie's mother, Sophie, smiling, standing by her plane.

* * *

AFTER EVERYONE WAS SEATED, Fritzi got up and welcomed all the WASPs and their families to Pulaski and then sat down by Sookie in the front row.

There were a number of speeches from the mayor, the governor of Wisconsin, a few senators, and other dignitaries. After the governor spoke, everyone assumed it was over, but, suddenly, Pinks came out onstage with a twinkle in her eye. She looked like she was trying her best not to smile and said, "Ladies and gentlemen, there is someone backstage who has flown here today in order to deliver a special message."

They all looked down at the program, but this speaker was not listed, so they wondered who it could be. As soon as the woman walked out onstage, there was a loud gasp and then spontaneous applause. They all recognized the U.S. astronaut immediately. She smiled, looked out at the crowd, and then said:

"Good morning, I'm Sally Ride. I came here today to say something long overdue on behalf of all the women in the military who are flying today, and that is . . . thank you. At a time when your country needed you, you stepped up to the task and proved that women could fly and do it magnificently. You faced and overcame seemingly insurmountable obstacles with grace, bravery, and courage. Your sacrifices, determination, and refusal-to-fail attitude opened doors that now allow women like myself to fly higher than we ever dared to dream. And so as those of us in the space program today and in the future head off for the moon and the stars and beyond, know that you and all the WASPs were truly the wind beneath our wings. God bless you."

As she walked off and waved good-bye, the recording of Bette Midler singing "Wind Beneath My Wings" started playing over the loudspeaker.

What a day!

That night, the town threw a huge party for the WASPs out at Zeilinski's Ballroom. The place was packed, and when the band leader saw Fritzi walk in, he stopped the music, and everyone applauded as she made her way through the crowd. "Hiya, pals!" Sookie didn't know if they knew who she was or if they were just the friendliest people in the world, but she had never been hugged so much in her life. Pretty soon, the music started up again, and a large, jolly woman with a gold tooth grabbed Sookie, and off they went on the dance floor, dancing the polka. She *guessed* that's what it was.

Later, after Sookie had a chance to catch her breath, she noticed the long table laden from one end to the other with food. And she thought Southerners ate a lot! She grabbed a plate and started eating the most delicious something with mustard and sauerkraut. She didn't know what it was, but it was all good. She watched as Fritzi and all the others danced. They looked like they were having the time of their lives.

After being grabbed and whisked around the room by at least a hundred different people, including one eight-year-old boy, Sookie realized she couldn't blame her failure at ballet on her genetics. The Polish were very good dancers.

About an hour later, a man approached the bandstand and said something to the bandleader, and after the next song, the bandleader went up to the microphone and said, "Ladies and gentlemen, we have a special request for a song. Where is Sister Mary Jude?" The crowd roared and applauded. Sister Mary Jude was eating, but being a good sport, went up to the stage, took the accordion, and started a rousing rendition of "The Wink-a-Dink Polka." The next thing she knew, Sookie was out on the floor again, dancing to "The Oh, Geez, You Betcha Polka."

# FRITZI'S SURPRISE

The next day, after the former WASPs had gone home and all the banners were taken down, Fritzi called Sookie at the hotel, sounding as chipper as ever.

"Hiya, pal, did you survive the evening?"

"Oh, yes, but I'm still in bed. What a party!"

"Well, get your duds on and come on downstairs, because I have another little surprise for you."

When Sookie reached the lobby, Fritzi was outside in a car waiting for her. "Get in," she said.

Sookie said, "Where are we going?"

"Ah-ha. That's for me to know and you to find out."

The old Phillips 66 filling station had been closed for years, and all that was left was the shell of a building and the cement ramp where the gas pumps had once stood, but as they drove up to the front, Sookie suddenly heard the Andrews Sisters singing "Boogie Woogie Bugle Boy." Then she saw the huge banner draped across the front:

WELCOME TO THE ALL-GIRL FILLING STATION

Then the three women and one lone man who had been waiting for them came over to the car, all talking at once. As Fritzi and Sookie got out, Fritzi was grinning from ear to ear and said, "Sarah Jane, I want you to meet your Aunt Tula. This is Wink's wife, Angie, and you know Sister Jude, and this one old geezer is Nard, Tula's husband. He just came over to set up the speakers. He's not staying. No men allowed."

Nard laughed. "Okay, Fritzi, I'm leaving, but it sure was nice to meet you."

Tula just stared at Sarah Jane and then burst into tears. "Oh, honey," she said. "You look so much like Sophie." Then she grabbed her and almost squeezed the life out of her. Fritzi said, "Don't kill her, for God's sake."

When they walked around to the back of the station, Sookie saw that the ladies had set up a big table full of more food. Fritzi explained, "Every three or four years, the gals and I try to get together for a little reunion."

Tula chimed in, "And this year is so special, because you're with us, Sarah Jane."

Fritzi looked at the table. "Yeah, usually we don't get Tula's homemade sausages or her cabbage rolls."

"Or her paczki . . . oh, boy," said Gertrude, eyeing the plate piled high with homemade Polish doughnuts.

After Sookie sat down, she said, "I just want you to know I'm honored to be here, and thank you so much for inviting me. Life is so strange. A few years ago, if someone had told me that I would be at this reunion today, I wouldn't have believed them in a million years. . . . And yet, here I am!"

"And we're so glad you are here. When Fritzi told us about you, we were all just dying to meet you, but she didn't tell us how much you look like your mother," Angie said. "Oh, Sarah Jane, I wish you could have known her. She was so pretty."

"And she was twice as sweet," said Tula.

As they sat and ate, they told Sookie all about what it was like when the station had been up and running. Tula said, "I know it's hard for you to believe now, Sarah Jane, but God, this place used to be so busy. The house was right on that lot over there, and all you would hear day and night was ding, ding, ding . . . people in and out. Momma said no wonder we were all a little ding-y. That's all we heard."

Angie said, "I'll tell you something else you wouldn't believe. Gertrude and Tula used to fit into the cutest little roller-skating outfits, and what a show. They would come flying out of that station, and boy oh boy, they would whip around those cars so fast, those poor customers didn't know what hit them."

Gertrude laughed. "That's true. We were pretty fast."

All afternoon, Sookie heard the most vivid and wonderful stories about what those war years had been like, the dances and the kissing booth, and how all the boys used to hang around. Sookie said, "Oh, it sounds like it must have been wonderful fun."

"Oh, it was," said Tula. "I never knew how much until it was over. But you know, life goes on. Then the boys came back home, and after that, it was a whole different life."

Later, as she and Fritzi were driving away, Sookie turned around and took one last look at the old station, and just for a split second, she could have sworn that she heard a bell dinging, and she saw the station as it used to be, with all the girls moving around happy and busy, young and pretty again.

THE NEXT MORNING, BEFORE they left for the airport, Fritzi drove her by the church and the school that her mother and all the family had attended. It was so strange for Sookie to think that she might have been brought up here and gone to that same school. Then they went to the cemetery, and she saw her mother's grave. And she saw those of all the other Jurdabralinskis she never knew.

WHEN THEY SAID GOOD-BYES at the airport, Sookie said, "Fritzi, you will never know how much this trip meant to me."

"Well, I wanted you to see where you came from and know that you had a family. Hell, you still do. You've always got me, kid, and don't you ever forget it."

"No, I never will."

# WHAT?

Point Clear, Alabama

Sookie had just come home from her Pulaski trip and was looking forward to a nice long rest when the phone rang. It was Carter.

"Hi, darling, how are you?"

"Fine, Mom. Is Daddy home?"

"No, honey."

"Well, good, because I really wanted to tell you first. Are you sitting down?"

Oh, Lord, she hated when people said that. "No, but should I? Is it bad news?"

"No, it's good news, I hope."

"What?"

"Well, you know how you always said that someday I would meet the One?"

"Yes?"

"Well, I have."

"Oh, honey, how wonderful!"

"Yes, it is, and the thing is, we're getting married, and I want you and Daddy to come."

"Well, of course. Oh, my God, I can't believe it. Do we know her? What's her name?"

There was a long pause. "That's just it. Mom, his name is David."

"What?"

"I know this must come as a terrible shock to you, but I wanted you to know."

"Your friend David? The one you brought home that time?"

"Yes. I didn't tell you about it before, because I didn't want to upset you." Sookie sat there preparing to faint at any moment. "And it's not just a spur-of-the-moment thing. We've been together for quite a while, and you liked him, didn't you?"

"Well, yes, he was a perfectly nice person, but . . ."

At that moment, Earle walked in the door accompanied by a large black-and-white Harlequin Great Dane, who proceeded to leap up on her good Baker sofa, walk across her lap, and jump over the other side, with Earle looking at him with eyes of love. "Isn't he wonderful, honey? He's a rescue dog, and his name is Rufus," he called out over his shoulder as he followed Rufus, who went galloping through the dining room, knocking over one of her mother's good Queen Anne chairs, headed for the kitchen area.

"Mother, are you still there? I am so sorry to tell you over the phone. I should have come home and told you in person. Are you just terribly shocked?"

Sookie sat there, phone in hand, and thought for a moment. She took a deep breath and realized that, to her amazement, she was not shocked.

"No, honey. I'm surprised, of course. But I've had so many shocks in the last few years, I can honestly say that nothing shocks me too much anymore. And if you are happy, then I'm happy."

"Oh, Mother, you are the very best. Could you tell Dad? I just hope he understands and won't be too upset."

After she hung up, she sat there in a daze. She heard the back door slam and saw Earle wave at her as he and the dog ran by the front window, off to romp and play in the yard. She would have to tell Earle about Carter, and that would certainly not be easy, but she knew he would come around eventually. The girls would not be a problem. They adored Carter. Then a terrible thought hit her. She liked to think of herself as a modern and accepting woman. She had watched *Oprah* and read articles about these things, but she had absolutely no idea about protocol. When it's two grooms getting married, just who pays for the wedding, and most important to her, just who is considered the official mother of the bride? Oh, God. She suddenly wished Winged Victory was here. She would have known exactly what to do. Oh, well, onward and upward, and next year, on to Poland to see the family home. As she sat fingering Lenore's pearls, watching Earle throw a ball for Rufus, she had to admit, he certainly was a *pretty* dog.

# EPILOGUE

From the Greenhouse
2014

Sookie had to laugh. It was ironic. After all of her worrying, she had just turned seventy, and she still had all her marbles. Now and then, she had a few little aches and pains, but as Earle had said to her that morning, "Honey, the good news about hitting seventy is at least you know you didn't die young."

No, she had not died young, and that was good, because she now had five darling grandchildren she was busy spoiling and Rufus the Great Dane and her birds.

After Lenore and Fritzi died, Sookie had experienced some moments of regret, wondering about how different things might have been and who she might have become if she had known the truth about herself earlier.

But now, after all these past years, sitting in her greenhouse, trying to figure out all the reasons, whys, and wherefores of life, she had finally come to a conclusion: No matter how crazy her life had been, she was exactly the person she was always meant to be and living exactly where she belonged.

Now, as to whether or not her theory was true really didn't matter to Sookie. All that mattered was that she was happy. And *yes*, she was still decorating Great-Grandfather Simmons's grave every Memorial Day. She knew it was probably silly, but it was the least she could do for Lenore.

As for her real mother, the one she'd never had a chance to know, some sixty years after the WASPs were disbanded, something wonderful happened. And today Sookie's most precious possession, now proudly displayed over the mantel in the living room, was the framed Congressional Medal of Honor awarded to Sophie Marie Jurdabralinski for service to her country.

This book was written in loving memory of Nancy Batson Crews, Teresa James, Elizabeth Sharp, and B. J. Erickson and all the other WASPs who came to the aid of their country in a time of need.

And also with my very special thanks to the four fabulous women, Joni Evans, Jennifer Rudolph Walsh, Kate Medina, and Gina Centrello, who made this book possible.

—*Fannie Flagg*

# ABOUT THE TYPE

This book was set in Garamond, a typeface originally designed by the Parisian typecutter Claude Garamond (1480–1561). This version of Garamond was modeled on a 1592 specimen sheet from the Egenolff-Berner foundry, which was produced from types assumed to have been brought to Frankfurt by the punchcutter Jacques Sabon.

Claude Garamond's distinguished romans and italics first appeared in *Opera Ciceronis* in 1543–44. The Garamond types are clear, open, and elegant.

www.vintage-books.co.uk

I have written many novels over the last ten years and am probably best known for my comedies under the name Sophie Kinsella. However, long before I dreamed up the *Shopaholic* series I wrote seven books under the name Madeleine Wickham (my real name).

I'm often asked why I write under two names and the reason is that these books are in a different style from my Sophie Kinsella books.

Although I have not written as Madeleine Wickham for several years, I am immensely fond of these novels and hope you enjoy this one!

Madeleine Wickham

aka Sophie Kinsella

**Madeleine Wickham** was born in London and published her first novel, *The Tennis Party*, while working as a financial journalist. Under the name of Sophie Kinsella she is the author of many number one bestselling novels including the *Shopaholic* series, now filmed as *Confessions of a Shopaholic*. She lives in London with her husband and children.

Her **Madeleine Wickham** novels:

THE TENNIS PARTY

A DESIRABLE RESIDENCE

SWIMMING POOL SUNDAY

THE GATECRASHER

THE WEDDING GIRL

COCKTAILS FOR THREE

SLEEPING ARRANGEMENTS

Her **Sophie Kinsella** novels:

THE SECRET DREAMWORLD OF A SHOPAHOLIC
(also published as CONFESSIONS OF A SHOPAHOLIC)

SHOPAHOLIC ABROAD

SHOPAHOLIC TIES THE KNOT

SHOPAHOLIC & SISTER

SHOPAHOLIC & BABY

MINI SHOPAHOLIC

CAN YOU KEEP A SECRET?

THE UNDOMESTIC GODDESS

REMEMBER ME?

TWENTIES GIRL

For more information on Sophie Kinsella and her books, see her website at **www.sophiekinsella.co.uk**

# THE GATECRASHER

Madeleine Wickham

TRANSWORLD PUBLISHERS
61–63 Uxbridge Road, London W5 5SA
A Random House Group Company
www.rbooks.co.uk

**THE GATECRASHER**
**A BLACK SWAN BOOK: 9780552776721**

First publication in Great Britain
Black Swan edition published 1998
Black Swan edition reissued 2010



A CIP catalogue record for this book is available from the British Library.



Addresses for Random House Group Ltd companies outside the UK can be found at: www.randomhouse.co.uk
The Random House Group Ltd Reg. No. 954009

The Random House Group Limited supports The Forest Stewardship Council (FSC), the leading international forest certification organisation. All our titles that are printed on Greenpeace approved FSC certified paper carry the FSC logo. Our paper procurement policy can be found at www.rbooks.co.uk/environment

Typeset in 11/14.5pt Giovanni Book by
Falcon Oast Graphic Art Ltd.
Printed in the UK by CPI Cox & Wyman, Reading, RG1 8EX.

2 4 6 8 10 9 7 5 3 1

For Freddy

# ONE

Fleur Daxeny wrinkled her nose. She bit her lip, and put her head on one side, and gazed at her reflection silently for a few seconds. Then she gave a gurgle of laughter.

'I still can't decide,' she exclaimed. 'They're all fabulous.'

The saleswoman from Take Hat! exchanged weary glances with the nervous young hairdresser sitting on a gilt stool in the corner. The hairdresser had arrived at Fleur's hotel suite half an hour ago and had been waiting to start ever since. The saleswoman was meanwhile beginning to wonder whether she was wasting her time completely.

'I love this one with the veil,' said Fleur suddenly, reaching for a tiny creation of black satin and wispy netting. 'Isn't it elegant?'

'Very elegant,' said the saleswoman. She hurried forward just in time to catch a black silk topper which Fleur was discarding onto the floor.

'Very,' echoed the hairdresser in the corner. Surreptitiously he glanced at his watch. He was supposed to be back down in the salon in forty minutes. Trevor wouldn't be pleased. Perhaps he should phone down to explain the situation. Perhaps . . .

'All right!' said Fleur. 'I've decided.' She pushed up the veil and beamed around the room. 'I'm going to wear this one today.'

'A very wise choice, madam,' said the saleswoman in relieved tones. 'It's a lovely hat.'

'Lovely,' whispered the hairdresser.

'So if you could just pack the other five into boxes for me . . .' Fleur smiled mysteriously at her reflection and pulled the dark silk gauze down over her face again. The woman from Take Hat! gaped at her.

'You're going to buy them all?'

'Of course I am. I simply can't choose between them. They're all too perfect.' Fleur turned to the hairdresser. 'Now, my sweet. Can you come up with something special for my hair which will go under this hat?' The young man stared back at her and felt a dark pink colour begin to rise up his neck.

'Oh. Yes. I should think so. I mean . . .' But Fleur had already turned away.

'If you could just put it all onto my hotel bill,' she was saying to the saleswoman. 'That's all right, isn't it?'

'Perfectly all right, madam,' said the saleswoman eagerly. 'As a guest of the hotel, you're entitled to a fifteen per cent concession on all our prices.'

'Whatever,' said Fleur. She gave a little yawn. 'As long as it can all go on the bill.'

'I'll go and sort it out for you straight away.'

'Good,' said Fleur. As the saleswoman hurried out of the room, she turned and gave the young hairdresser a ravishing smile. 'I'm all yours.'

Her voice was low and melodious and curiously accentless. To the hairdresser's ears it was now also faintly mocking, and he flushed slightly as he came over to where Fleur was sitting. He stood behind her, gathered together the ends of her hair in one hand and let them fall down in a heavy, red-gold movement.

'Your hair's in very good condition,' he said awkwardly.

'Isn't it lovely?' said Fleur complacently. 'I've always had good hair. And good skin, of course.' She tilted her head, pushed her hotel robe aside slightly, and rubbed her cheek tenderly against the pale, creamy skin of her shoulder. 'How old would you say I was?' she added abruptly.

'I don't . . . I wouldn't . . .' the young man began to flounder.

'I'm forty,' she said lazily. She closed her eyes. 'Forty,' she repeated, as though meditating. 'It makes you think, doesn't it?'

'You don't look . . .' began the hairdresser in awkward politeness. Fleur opened one glinting, pussycat-green eye.

'I don't look forty? How old do I look, then?'

The hairdresser stared back at her uncomfortably. He

opened his mouth to speak, then closed it again. The truth was, he thought suddenly, that this incredible woman didn't look any age. She seemed ageless, classless, indefinable. As he met her eyes he felt a thrill run through him; a dart-like conviction that this moment was somehow significant. His hands trembling slightly, he reached for her hair and let it run like slippery flames through his fingers.

'You look as old as you look,' he whispered huskily. 'Numbers don't come into it.'

'Sweet,' said Fleur dismissively. 'Now, my pet, before you start on my hair, how about ordering me a nice glass of champagne?'

The hairdresser's fingers drooped in slight disappointment, and he went obediently over to the telephone. As he dialled, the door opened and the woman from Take Hat! came back in, carrying a pile of hat boxes. 'Here we are,' she exclaimed breathlessly. 'If you could just sign here . . .'

'A glass of champagne, please,' the hairdresser was saying. 'Room 301.'

'I was wondering,' began the saleswoman cautiously to Fleur. 'You're quite sure that you want all six hats in black? We do have some other super colours this season.' She tapped her teeth thoughtfully. 'There's a lovely emerald green which would look stunning with your hair . . .'

'Black,' said Fleur decisively. 'I'm only interested in black.'

* * *

An hour later, Fleur looked at herself in the mirror, smiled and nodded. She was dressed in a simple black suit which had been cut to fit her figure precisely. Her legs shimmered in sheer black stockings; her feet were unobtrusive in discreet black shoes. Her hair had been smoothed into an exemplary chignon, on which the little black hat sat to perfection.

The only hint of brightness about her figure was a glimpse of salmon-pink silk underneath her jacket. It was Fleur's rule always to wear some colour no matter how sombre the outfit or the occasion. In a crowd of dispirited black suits, a tiny splash of salmon-pink would draw the eye unconsciously towards her. People would notice her but wouldn't be quite sure why. Which was just as she liked it.

Still watching her reflection, Fleur pulled the gauzy veil down over her face. The smug expression disappeared from her face, to be replaced by one of grave, inscrutable sadness. For a few moments she stared silently at herself. She picked up her black leather Osprey bag and held it soberly by her side. She nodded slowly a few times, noticing how the veil cast hazy, mysterious shadows over her pale face.

Then, suddenly, the telephone rang, and she sprang back into life.

'Hello?'

'Fleur, where have you been? I have tried to call you.' The heavy Greek voice was unmistakable. A frown of irritation creased Fleur's face.

'Sakis! Sweetheart, I'm in a bit of a hurry . . .'

'Where are you going?'

'Nowhere. Just shopping.'

'Why do you need to shop? I bought you clothes in Paris.'

'I know you did, darling. But I wanted to surprise you with something new for this evening.' Her voice rippled with convincing affection down the phone. 'Something elegant, sexy . . .' As she spoke, she had a sudden inspiration. 'And you know, Sakis,' she added carefully, 'I was wondering whether it wouldn't be a good idea to pay in cash, so that I get a good price. I can draw money out from the hotel, can't I? On your account?'

'A certain amount. Up to ten thousand pounds, I think.'

'I won't need *nearly* that much!' Her voice bubbled over with amusement. 'I only want one outfit! Five hundred maximum.'

'And when you have bought it you will return straight to the hotel.'

'Of course, sweetheart.'

'There is no of course. This time, Fleur, you must not be late. Do you understand? You-must-not-be-late.' The words were barked out like a military order and Fleur flinched silently in annoyance. 'It is quite clear. Leonidas will pick you up at three o'clock. The helicopter will leave at four o'clock. Our guests will arrive at seven o'clock. You must be ready to greet them. I do not want you to be late like last time. It was . . . it was unseemly. Are you listening? Fleur?'

'Of course I'm listening!' said Fleur. 'But there's

someone knocking at the door. I'll just go and see who it is . . .' She waited a couple of seconds, then firmly replaced the receiver. A moment later, she picked it up again.

'Hello? Could you send someone up for my luggage, please?'

Downstairs, the hotel lobby was calm and tranquil. The woman from Take Hat! saw Fleur walking past the boutique, and gave a little wave, but Fleur ignored her.

'I'd like to check out,' she said, as soon as she got to the reception desk. 'And to make a withdrawal of money. The account is in the name of Sakis Papandreous.'

'Ah, yes.' The smooth, blond-haired receptionist tapped briefly at her computer, then looked up and smiled at her. 'How much money would you like?' Fleur beamed back at her.

'Ten thousand pounds. And could you order me two taxis?' The woman looked up in surprise.

'Two?'

'One for me, one for my luggage. My luggage is going to Chelsea.' Fleur lowered her eyes beneath her gauzy veil. 'I'm going to a memorial service.'

'Oh dear, I am sorry,' said the woman, handing Fleur several pages of hotel bill. 'Someone close to you?'

'Not yet,' said Fleur, signing the bill without bothering to check it. She watched as the cashier counted thick wads of money into two crested envelopes, then tenderly took them both, placed them in her Osprey bag and snapped it shut. 'But you never know.'

* * *

Richard Favour sat in the front pew of St Anselm's Church with his eyes closed, listening to the sounds of people filling the church – muted whisperings and shufflings, the tapping of heels on the tiled floor, and 'Jesu, Joy of Man's Desiring' being played softly on the organ.

He had always hated 'Jesu, Joy of Man's Desiring'; it had been the suggestion of the organist at their meeting three weeks previously, after it had become apparent that Richard could not name a single piece of organ music of which Emily had been particularly fond. There had been a slightly embarrassed silence as Richard vainly racked his brains, then the organist had tactfully murmured. ' "Jesu, Joy of Man's Desiring" is always very popular . . .' and Richard had agreed in hasty relief.

Now he gave a dissatisfied frown. Surely he could have thought of something more personal than this turgid, over-popular tune? Emily had certainly been a music-lover, always going to concerts and recitals when her health allowed it. Had she never once turned to him, eyes alight, saying, 'I love this piece, don't you?' He screwed up his eyes and tried to remember. But the only vision that came to him was of Emily lying in bed, eyes dulled, wan and frail and uncomplaining. A spasm of guilty regret went through him. Why had he never asked his wife what her favourite piece of music was? In thirty-three years of marriage, he had never asked her. And now it was too late. Now he would never know.

He rubbed his forehead wearily, and looked down at the engraved order of service on his lap. The words stared back up at him. *Service of Memorial and Thanksgiving for the life of Emily Millicent Favour.* Simple black lettering, plain white card. He had resisted all attempts by the printers to introduce such prized features as silver borders or embossed angels. Of that, he thought, Emily would have approved. At least . . . he hoped she would.

It had taken Richard several years of marriage to Emily to realize that he didn't know her very well, and several more for him to realize that he never would. At the beginning, her serene remoteness had been part of her appeal, along with her pale, pretty face and the neat, boyish figure which she kept as resolutely hidden as she did her innermost thoughts. The more she had kept herself hidden, the more tantalized Richard had become; he had approached their wedding day with a longing bordering on desperation. At last, he had thought, he and Emily would be able to reveal their secret selves to each other. He had yearned to explore not only her body but her mind, her person; to discover her most intimate fears and dreams; to become her life-long soulmate.

They'd been married on a bright, blustery day, in a little village in Kent. Emily had looked composed and serene throughout; Richard had supposed she was simply better than him at concealing the nervous anticipation that surely burned as intensely within her as it did in him – an anticipation which had become stronger as the day was swallowed up and the beginning of their life together drew near.

Now he closed his eyes, and remembered those first, tingling seconds, as the door had shut behind the porter and he was alone with his wife for the first time in their Eastbourne hotel suite. He'd gazed at her as she took off her hat with the smooth, precise movements she always made, half-longing for her to throw the silly thing down and rush into his arms, and half-longing for this delicious, uncertain waiting to last for ever. It had seemed that Emily was deliberately delaying the moment of their coming together; teasing him with her cool, oblivious manner, as though she knew exactly what was going through his mind.

And then, finally, she'd turned, and met his eye. And he'd taken a breath, not knowing quite where to start; which of his pent-up thoughts to release first. And she'd looked straight at him with remote blue eyes and said, 'What time is dinner?'

Even then, he'd thought she was still teasing. He'd thought she was purposely prolonging the sense of anticipation, that she was deliberately stoppering up her emotions until they became too overwhelming to control, when they would flood out in a huge gush to meet and mix with his. And so, patiently, awed by her apparent self-control, he'd waited. Waited for the gush; the breaking of the waters; the tears and the surrender.

But it had never happened. Emily's love for him had never manifested itself in anything more than a slow drip-drip of fond affection; she'd responded to his every caress, his every confidence, with the same degree of lukewarm interest. When he tried to spark a more powerful reaction in her, he'd been met first by incomprehension, then, as he grew more strident, by an almost frightened resistance.

Eventually he'd given up trying. And gradually, almost without his realizing, his own love for her had begun to change in character. Over the years, his emotions had stopped pounding at the surface of his soul like a hot, wet tidal wave and had receded and solidified into something firm and dry and sensible. And Richard, too, had become firm and dry and sensible. He'd learned to keep his own counsel, to gather his thoughts dispassionately and say only half of what he was really thinking. He'd learned to smile when he wanted to beam, to click his tongue when he wanted to scream in frustration; to restrain himself and his foolish thoughts as much as possible.

Now, waiting for her memorial service to begin, he blessed Emily for those lessons in self-restraint. Because if it hadn't been for his ability to keep himself in check, the hot, sentimental tears which bubbled at the back of his eyes would now have been coursing uncontrollably down his cheeks, and the hands which calmly held his order of service would have been clasped over his contorted face, and he would have been swept away by a desperate, immoderate grief.

The church was almost full when Fleur arrived. She stood at the back for a few moments, surveying the faces and clothes and voices in front of her; assessing the quality of the flower arrangements; checking the pews for anyone who might look up and recognize her.

But the people in front of her were an anonymous bunch. Men in dull suits; ladies in uninspired hats. A flicker of doubt crossed Fleur's mind. Could Johnny have got this one wrong? Was there really any money lurking in this colourless crowd?

'Would you like an order of service?' She looked up to see a long-legged man striding across the marble floor towards her. 'It's about to start,' he added with a frown.

'Of course,' murmured Fleur. She held out her pale. scented hand. 'Fleur Daxeny. I'm so glad to meet you . . . Sorry, I've forgotten your name . . .'

'Lambert.'

'Lambert. Of course. I remember now.' She paused, and glanced up at his face, still wearing an arrogant frown. 'You're the clever one.'

'I suppose you could say that,' said Lambert, shrugging.

Clever or sexy, thought Fleur. All men want to be one or the other – or both. She looked at Lambert again. His features looked overblown and rubbery, so that even in repose he seemed to be pulling a face. Better just leave it at clever, she thought.

'Well, I'd better sit down,' she said. 'I expect I'll see you later.'

'There's plenty of room at the back,' Lambert called after her. But Fleur appeared not to hear him. Studying her order of service with an absorbed, solemn expression, she made her way quickly to the front of the church.

'I'm sorry,' she said, pausing by the third row from the front. 'Is there any room? It's a bit crowded at the back.'

She stood impassively while the ten people filling the row huffed and shuffled themselves along; then, with one elegant movement, took her place. She bowed her head for a moment, then looked up with a stern, brave expression.

'Poor Emily,' she said. 'Poor sweet Emily.'

'Who was that?' whispered Philippa Chester as her husband returned to his seat beside her.

'I don't know,' said Lambert. 'One of your mother's friends, I suppose. She seemed to know all about me.'

'I don't think I remember her,' said Philippa. 'What's her name?'

'Fleur. Fleur something.'

'Fleur. I've never heard of her.'

'Maybe they were at school together or something.'

'Oh yes,' said Philippa. 'That could be it. Like that other one. Joan. Do you remember? The one who came to visit out of the blue?'

'No,' said Lambert.

'Yes you do. *Joan*. She gave Mummy that hideous glass bowl.' Philippa squinted at Fleur again. 'Except this one looks too young. I like her hat. I wish I could wear little hats like that. But my head's too big. Or my hair isn't right. Or something.'

She tailed off. Lambert was staring down at a piece of paper and muttering. Philippa looked around the church again. So many people. All here for Mummy. It almost made her want to cry.

'Does my hat look all right?' she said suddenly.

'It looks great,' said Lambert without looking up.

'It cost a bomb. I couldn't believe how much it cost. But then, when I put it on this morning, I thought . . .'

'Philippa!' hissed Lambert. 'Can you shut up? I've got my reading to think about!'

'Oh yes. Yes, of course you have.'

Philippa looked down, chastened. And once again she felt a little pinprick of hurt. No-one had asked her to do a reading. Lambert was doing one, and so was her little brother Antony, but all she had to do was sit still in her hat. And she couldn't even do that very well.

'When I die,' she said suddenly, 'I want *everyone* to do a reading at my memorial service. You, and Antony, and Gillian, and all our children . . .'

'If we have any,' said Lambert, not looking up.

'If we have any,' echoed Philippa morosely. She looked around at the sea of black hats. 'I might die before we have any children, mightn't I? I mean, we don't know when we're going to die, do we? I could die tomorrow.' She broke off, overcome by the thought of herself in a coffin, looking pale and waxy and romantic, surrounded by weeping mourners. Her eyes began to prickle. 'I could die tomorrow. And then it would be . . .'

'Shut up,' said Lambert, putting away his piece of

paper. He stretched his hand down out of sight and casually pinched Philippa's fleshy calf. 'You're talking rubbish,' he murmured. 'What are you talking?'

Philippa was silent. Lambert's fingers gradually tightened on her skin, until suddenly they nipped so viciously that she gave a sharp intake of breath.

'I'm talking rubbish,' she said, in a quick, low voice.

'Good girl,' said Lambert. He released his fingers. 'Now, sit up straight and get a grip.'

'I'm sorry,' said Philippa breathlessly. 'It's just a bit . . . overwhelming. There are so many people here. I didn't know Mummy had all these friends.'

'Your mother was a very popular lady,' said Lambert. 'Everyone loved her.'

And no-one loves me, Philippa felt like saying. But instead, she prodded helplessly at her hat and tugged a few locks of wispy hair out from under the severe black brim, so that by the time she stood up for the first hymn, she looked even worse than before.

# TWO

'The day thou gavest, Lord, is ended,' sang Fleur. She forced herself to look down at the hymn-book and pretend that she was reading the words. As though she didn't know them off by heart; as though she hadn't sung them at too many funerals and memorial services to count. Why did people always choose the same dreary hymns for funerals? she thought. Didn't they appreciate how boring it made things for the regular funeral gatecrasher?

The first funeral that Fleur had gatecrashed had been by accident. Wandering down a little Kensington back street one dull morning, wondering if she might be able to get herself a job in an expensive art gallery, she had seen an assembly of smart people milling on the pavement outside a small but distinguished Catholic church. With an aimless curiosity, she had slowed down as she reached them; slowed down, and then stopped. She had stood, not quite in the group but not quite out of it, and listened as hard as she could to as many conversations as possible. And gradually she'd realized, as she heard talk of trusts, of family diamonds. of Scottish islands, that these people had money. Serious money.

Then, suddenly, the spattering rain had turned into a drenching pour, and the people on the pavement had unfurled twenty-five umbrellas in unison, like a flock of blackbirds taking off. And it had seemed entirely natural for Fleur to choose a benevolent looking elderly man, and to meet his eye tentatively, and to creep, with a grateful smile, under the shelter of his Swaine Adeney Brigg dome of black silk. It hadn't been easy to talk, above the rain and the chatter, and the cars swooshing by, so they'd simply smiled at each other, and nodded. And by the time the choir had stopped rehearsing, and the church doors had opened, they'd assumed the companionship of old friends. He'd ushered her into the church, and handed her an order of service, and they'd taken seats together near the back.

'I didn't know Benjy awfully well,' the elderly man had confided as they sat down. 'But he was a dear friend of my late wife's.'

'He was a friend of my father's,' Fleur had replied, glancing down at the order of service, and quickly committing the name 'Benjamin St John Gregory' to memory. 'I didn't know him at all. But it's nice to show respect.'

'I agree,' the elderly man had said, beaming at her and extending his hand. 'Now let me introduce myself. My name's Maurice Snowfield.'

Maurice Snowfield had lasted for three months. He hadn't been quite as rich as Fleur had hoped, and his gentle, absent-minded manner had nearly driven her crazy. But by the time she left his Wiltshire house, she had enough of his money to pay two terms of her daughter Zara's school fees in advance, and a brand new wardrobe of black suits.

'. . . till all thy creatures own thy sway.' There was a rustling sound around the church, as everyone closed their hymn-book, sat down, and consulted the order of service. Fleur took the opportunity to open her bag and look again at the little note which Johnny had sent her, clipped to a cutting from a newspaper announcements column. The announcement was of the memorial service of Emily Favour at St Anselm's Church on 20 April. 'A good bet,' Johnny had scribbled. 'Richard Favour very rich, very quiet.'

Fleur peered at the front pew. She could see the man with the rubbery face, who had given the first reading, and, next to him, a mousy blonde woman in a terrible hat. Then there was a teenaged boy, and an older woman in an even more terrible hat . . . Fleur's eyes passed quickly along and then stopped. Sitting at the other end of the pew was an unobtrusive, greying man. He was leaning forward, with his shoulders hunched. his head resting on the wooden panel in front of him.

She stared critically at him for a few seconds. No, he wasn't pretending – he had loved his wife. He missed her. And, judging by his body language, he didn't talk to his family about it.

Which made things so much easier. The truly grief-stricken were the easiest targets – the men who couldn't imagine ever falling in love again; who vowed to remain faithful to their dead wives. In Fleur's experience, all that meant was that when they did fall for her they were convinced that it must be real love.

They'd asked Richard if he wanted to give the eulogy.

'You must be used to giving speeches,' the vicar had said, 'business speeches. This would be much the same – just a description of your wife's character, maybe an anecdote or two, some mention of the charities she was involved with, anything that reminds the congregation of the real Emily . . .' And then he'd tailed away at Richard's sudden bleak expression, and added gently, 'You don't have to – perhaps you'd find it too upsetting?'

And Richard had nodded.

'I think I would,' he'd muttered.

'Quite understandable,' the vicar had said briskly. 'You're not alone.'

But he *was* alone, Richard had thought. He was alone in his misery; isolated in the knowledge that his wife had died and no-one but him would ever realize just how little he'd known her. The loneliness which he'd felt throughout his marriage now seemed unbearably intensified; distilled into a bitterness not unlike anger. The real Emily! he felt like shouting. What did I ever know of the real Emily?

And so the job of giving the eulogy had fallen to their

old friend, Alec Kershaw. Richard sat up straight as Alec approached the lectern, patted together the little white cards in front of him, and looked up over his rimless half-moon spectacles at the congregation.

'Emily Favour was a brave, charming and generous woman,' he began, in raised, formal tones. 'Her sense of duty was matched only by her sense of compassion and her devotion to helping others.'

Alec paused, and glanced at Richard. And as he saw Alec's expression, Richard felt a jolt of understanding pass through him. Alec hadn't really known Emily, either. These words were hollow; conventional – designed to do the job rather than speak the truth.

Richard began to feel a ridiculous sensation of alarm – panic, almost. Once this eulogy had been heard, once the service was over and the congregation had left the church, then that would be it. That would be the official version of Emily Favour's character. Story finished; file closed; nothing more to learn. Could he bear it? Could he bear to live with the final assessment of his wife as nothing more than a collection of well-meaning clichés?

'Her charity work was unparalleled – in particular her work for the Rainbow Fund and St Bride's Hospice. I think many of us will remember the first Greyworth Golf Club Christmas auction, an event which has become a regular fixture in all our diaries.'

Fleur felt a yawn creeping through her body. Was this man never going to stop?

'And, of course, mention of Greyworth Golf Club brings us to another most important aspect of Emily Favour's life. What some might describe as a hobby . . . a game. Of course, the rest of us know that it's a *far* more serious matter than that.'

Several members of the congregation tittered obligingly, and Fleur looked up. What was he talking about?

'When she married Richard, Emily had the choice of becoming golf widow or golf partner. Golf partner she became. And despite the ill health which dogged her, she developed an enviably steady game, as all of us who witnessed her fine winning performance in the Ladies' Foursome can verify.'

Golf widow or golf partner, thought Fleur idly. Widow or partner. Well, that's easy – widow wins, every time.

After the service, Richard made his way to the west door, as the vicar had suggested, in order to greet friends and family. 'People appreciate an opportunity to show their condolences personally,' the vicar had said. Now Richard wondered whether this was really true. Most of the congregation scuttled past him, throwing hurried, indistinct phrases of sympathy at him like superstitious charms. A few stopped, met his gaze directly, shook his hand; even embraced him. But these were, surprisingly often, the people he barely knew: the representatives from law firms and private banks; the wives of business acquaintances.

'On to the Lanesborough,' Lambert was saying self-importantly on the other side of the door. 'Drinks at the Lanesborough.'

An elegant woman with red hair stopped in front of Richard and held out a pale hand. Weary of shaking hands, Richard took it.

'The thing is,' the woman said, as though carrying on a conversation they'd already begun, 'the loneliness won't last for ever.' Richard gave a little start, and felt the drooping eyelids of his mind jerk open.

'What did you say?' he began. But the woman was gone. Richard turned to his fifteen-year-old son, Antony, who was standing beside him.

'Who was that?' he said. Antony shrugged.

'Dunno. Lambert and Philippa were talking about her. I think she might have known Mum at school.'

'How did she know . . .' began Richard, and stopped. He had been going to say, How did she know I was lonely? But instead, he turned and smiled at Antony, and said, 'You read very well.' Antony shrugged.

'I s'pose.' In the unconscious movement which he repeated every three minutes or so, Antony put a hand up to his face and rubbed his brow – and for a few moments the dark red birthmark which leapt across his eye like a small lizard was masked. Every three minutes of his waking life, without even knowing that he did it, Antony hid his birthmark from view. As far as Richard knew he'd never been teased because of the birthmark; certainly at home, everybody had always behaved as though it wasn't there. Nevertheless, Antony's hand shot up to his face with almost desperate regularity, and occasionally hovered there for longer, for hours at a time, protecting the little red lizard from scrutiny like a watchful guardian angel.

'Well,' said Richard.

'Yeah,' said Antony.

'Perhaps we should be going.'

'Yeah.'

And that was it. Conversation over. When had he stopped talking to Antony? Richard wondered. How had those adoring, unembarrassed soliloquies addressed to his infant son managed to turn, over the years, into such empty, public exchanges?

'Right,' he said. 'Well. Let's go, then.'

The Belgravia Room at the Lanesborough was nicely full when Fleur arrived. She accepted a glass of buck's fizz from a tanned Australian waiter and made her way directly towards Richard Favour. When she got near, she changed path very slightly, as though to walk straight past him.

'Excuse me.' His voice hit the back of her head, and Fleur felt a small dart of triumph. Sometimes she could spend half an hour walking back and forth before the object of her attention spoke to her.

She turned, as quickly as possible without looking rushed, and gave Richard Favour the warmest, widest smile she could muster. Playing hard to get with widowers was, she had come to realize, a complete waste of time. Some lacked the energy for pursuit; some lacked confidence; some began to grow suspicious during the very process of winning her. Better to leap straight into their lives; to become part of the status quo as quickly as possible.

'Hello again,' said Fleur. She took a sip of buck's fizz and waited for him to speak. If any beady-eyed family members were watching, they would see him chatting her up – not the other way round.

'I wanted to say thank you,' said Richard, 'for your kind words. I thought you spoke – as though you knew what this process is like.'

Fleur looked tenderly down at her drink for a few moments, deciding which story to choose. Eventually she looked up, and gave him a brave smile.

'I'm afraid I do. I've been through it myself. A while ago now.'

'And you survived it.'

'I survived it,' echoed Fleur. 'But it wasn't easy. It can be hard just knowing who to talk to. Often one's family is simply too close.'

'Or not close enough,' said Richard, thinking, bleakly, of Antony.

'Exactly,' said Fleur. 'Not close enough to know what you're really going through; not close enough to . . . to share the grief.' She took another sip of buck's fizz. and looked at Richard. He suddenly looked desolate. Drat, she thought. Have I gone too far?

'Richard?' Fleur looked up. The rubbery man was bearing down on them. 'Derek Cowley's just arrived. You remember – software director of Graylows.'

'I saw him in the church,' said Richard. 'Who on earth invited him?'

'I did,' said Lambert. 'He's a useful contact.'

'I see.' Richard's face tightened.

'I've had a chat with him,' Lambert continued obliviously, 'but he wants to talk to you, too. Could you have a word? I haven't mentioned the contract yet . . .' He broke off, as though noticing Fleur for the first time. I get it, thought Fleur, narrowing her eyes. Women don't count.

'Hello there,' he said. 'Sorry, what was your name?'

'Fleur,' said Fleur. 'Fleur Daxeny.'

'That's right. And you're – what? An old school friend of Emily's?'

'Oh no.' Fleur smiled prettily at him.

'I thought you were a bit young for that,' said Lambert. 'So how did you know Emily?'

'Well, it's interesting,' said Fleur, and took another thoughtful sip. It was surprising just how often a tricky question could be stalled by pausing to sip at a drink or eat a cocktail snack. More often than not, during the silence, someone passing by would see that conversation had temporarily come to a standstill and take the opportunity to join the group – and her answer would be conveniently forgotten.

But today no-one interrupted them, and Lambert was still looking at her with blunt curiosity.

'It's interesting,' said Fleur again, directing her gaze at Richard. 'I only met your wife twice. But each time, she had a great effect on me.'

'Where did you meet?' said Lambert.

'At a lunch,' said Fleur. 'A big charity lunch. We were at the same table. I complained about the food, and Emily said she quite agreed but she wasn't the sort to complain. And then we just started talking.'

'What did you talk about?' Richard peered at Fleur.

'Everything,' said Fleur. She looked back at Richard; noticed his yearning eyes. 'I confided in her about all sorts of things,' she said slowly, lowering her voice so that Richard unconsciously leaned forward, 'and she confided in me. We talked about our lives . . . and our families . . . and the choices we'd made . . .'

'What did she say?' Richard's question burst forth from him before he could stop it. Fleur shrugged.

'It was a long time ago now. I'm not sure if I even remember exactly.' She smiled. 'It was nothing, really. I expect Emily forgot all about me long ago. But I . . . I always remembered her. And when I saw the memorial announcement, I couldn't resist coming along.' Fleur lowered her eyes. 'It was rather presumptuous. I hope you don't mind.'

'Of course I don't mind,' said Richard. 'Any friend of Emily's is absolutely welcome.'

'Funny she never mentioned you,' said Lambert, looking at her critically.

'I would have been surprised if she had,' replied Fleur, smiling at him. 'It was really nothing. A couple of long conversations, many years ago.'

'I wish . . . I wish I knew what she'd told you.' Richard

gave an embarrassed little laugh. 'But if you don't remember . . .'

'I remember bits.' Fleur smiled tantalizingly at him. 'Little snippets. Some of it was quite surprising. And some was quite . . . personal.' She paused, and glanced sidelong at Lambert.

'Lambert, you go and talk to Derek Cowley,' said Richard at once. 'I might have a word with him later on. But now I'd like . . . I'd like to talk a little further with Mrs Daxeny.'

Fifteen minutes later, Fleur emerged from the Lanesborough and got into a taxi. In her pocket was Richard Favour's telephone number and in her diary was an appointment for lunch with him the next day.

It had been so easy. The poor man was quite obviously desperate to hear what she had to say about his wife – but too well-mannered to interrupt her as she digressed, apparently unwittingly, on to other subjects. She'd fed him a few innocuous lines, then suddenly glanced at her watch and exclaimed that she must be shooting off. His face had fallen and for a few seconds he'd seemed resigned to the disappointment of ending the conversation there. But then, almost as Fleur was giving up on him, he'd pulled out his diary and, in a slightly shaking voice, asked Fleur if she might like to have lunch with him. Fleur suspected that making lunch appointments with strange women was not something Richard Favour had done very often. Which was fine by her.

By the time the taxi pulled up in front of the Chelsea mansion block where Johnny and Felix lived, she had scribbled down on a piece of paper all the facts she could remember about Emily Favour. 'Ill-health', she underlined. 'Golf', she underlined twice. It was a pity she didn't know what the woman looked like. A photograph would have been useful. But then, she didn't intend to talk about Emily Favour for very long. Dead wives were, in her experience, best avoided.

As she hopped out of her taxi, she saw Johnny on the pavement outside the front door of the mansion block, watching carefully as something was unloaded from a delivery van. He was a dapper man in his late fifties, with nut-brown hair and a permanent suntan. Fleur had known him for twenty years; he was the only person she had never lied to.

'Darling!' she called. 'Johnn-ee! Did you get my luggage all right?' He turned at the sound of his name, frowning petulantly at the interruption. But when he saw it was Fleur, the frown disappeared.

'Sweetheart!' he cried. 'Come and see this.'

'What is it?'

'It's our new epergne. Felix bid for it yesterday. Quite a snip, we thought. Careful!' he suddenly snapped. 'Don't knock it!'

'Is Felix in?'

'Yes he is. Go on up. I said careful, you moron!'

As she mounted the stairs to the first floor, she could hear Wagner coming, loud and insistent, from Johnny's flat; as she stepped inside, the volume seemed to double.

'Felix!' she called. But he couldn't hear her. She went into the drawing room to see him standing in front of the mirror, a portly middle-aged man, singing along with Brünnhilde in a shrieking falsetto.

When Fleur had first heard Felix's high, fluting voice, she had thought there must be something horrendously wrong with him. But she'd soon learned that he made his living from this strange sound, singing services in churches and cathedrals. Sometimes she and Johnny would go to hear Felix singing Evensong at St Paul's Cathedral or Westminster Abbey, and would see him solemnly processing and bowing in his white frills. More rarely, they would see him attired in tails, singing in a performance of Handel's *Messiah* or Bach's *St Matthew Passion*.

Fleur didn't enjoy the sound of Felix's voice, and found the *St Matthew Passion* very boring indeed. But she always sat in the front row and applauded vigorously and joined Johnny in his cries of 'Bravo!' Because Fleur owed Felix a great deal. Memorial services, she could find out about from the papers – but it was Felix who always knew about the funerals. If he wasn't singing at them himself, he knew someone who was. And it was at the smaller, more intimate funerals that Fleur had always done best.

When Felix saw her reflection he gave a little jump, and stopped singing.

'Not really my range,' he shouted over the music.

'A bit low for me. How was the memorial service?'

'Fine!' shouted Fleur. She went over to the CD player and turned the volume down. 'Fine,' she repeated. 'Quite promising. I'm having lunch with Mr Favour tomorrow.'

'Oh well done!' said Felix. 'I was going to tell you about a funeral we're doing tomorrow. Rather nice; they've asked for "Hear My Prayer". But if you're fixed up . . .'

'You'd better tell me anyway,' said Fleur. 'I'm not entirely convinced about this Favour family. I'm not sure there's any money.'

'Oh really?'

'Terrible hats.'

'Hmm. Hats aren't everything.'

'No.'

'What did Johnny say about them?'

'What did Johnny say about what?' Johnny's high voice came through the doorway. 'Careful, you oaf! In there. Yes. On the table.'

A man in overalls entered the room and placed on the table a large object, shrouded in brown paper.

'Let me see!' exclaimed Johnny. He began to tear the paper off in strips.

'A candelabra,' said Fleur. 'How, nice.'

'It's an epergne,' corrected Johnny. 'Isn't it beautiful?'

'Clever little me,' said Felix. 'To find such a gorgeous thing.'

'I bet it cost a fortune,' said Fleur sulkily. 'You could have given that money to a good cause, you know.'

'Like you? I don't think so.' Johnny took out a handkerchief and began to polish the epergne. 'If you want money so badly, why did you leave the lovely Sakis?'

'He wasn't lovely. He was an overbearing bully. He used to order me about, and shout at me . . .'

'. . . and buy you suits from Givenchy.'

'I know,' said Fleur regretfully. 'But I couldn't stand him for one more moment. And besides, he wouldn't give me a Gold Card.' She shrugged. 'So there was no point.'

'Why any of these men ever gives you a credit card is quite beyond me,' said Felix.

'Yes,' said Fleur. 'Well, it would be, wouldn't it?'

'*Touché*,' said Felix cheerfully.

'But you did pretty well out of him, didn't you?' said Johnny.

'Little bits, here and there. Some cash. But not enough.' Fleur sighed, and lit a cigarette. 'What a bloody waste of time.'

'That'll be a pound in the swear box, thank you,' said Felix at once. Fleur rolled her eyes and felt in her bag for her purse. She looked up.

'Can you change a fifty-pound note?'

'Probably,' said Felix. 'Let me look in the box.'

'You know, Fleur,' said Johnny, still polishing, 'your little bits and pieces probably add up to what most people call a fortune.'

'No they don't,' said Fleur.

'How much have you got stashed away now?'

'Not enough.'

'And how much is enough?'

'Oh Johnny, stop quizzing me!' said Fleur irritably. 'It's all your fault. You told me Sakis would be a pushover.'

'I told you nothing of the sort. I merely told you that according to my sources he was a multimillionaire and emotionally vulnerable. Which turned out to be absolutely true.'

'He'll be even more vulnerable tonight when he realizes you've scooted,' said Felix, depositing Fleur's fifty-pound note in a large tin decorated with pink cherubs.

'Don't start feeling sorry for him,' exclaimed Fleur.

'Oh I don't! Any man who allows himself to be duped by you deserves everything he gets.' Fleur sighed.

'I had a good time on his yacht, at any rate.' She blew out a plume of smoke. 'It's a pity, really.'

'A great pity,' said Johnny, standing back to admire the epergne. 'Now I suppose we've got to find you someone else.'

'And you needn't expect another rich Greek,' put in Felix. 'I don't often get asked to sing at Orthodox bashes.'

'Did you go to the Emily Favour memorial service?'

'Yes I did,' said Fleur, stubbing out her cigarette. 'But I wasn't impressed. Is there really any money there?'

'Oh *yes*,' said Johnny, looking up. 'At least, there should be. My chum at de Rouchets told me that Richard Favour has a personal fortune of millions. And then there's the family company. There should be plenty of money.'

'Oh well, I'm having lunch with him tomorrow. I'll try and find out.' Fleur wandered over to the mantelpiece and began to leaf through the stiff, engraved invitations addressed to Johnny and Felix.

'You know, perhaps you should lower your sights a little,' suggested Felix. 'Settle for a plain old millionaire once in a while.'

'Come on. A million goes nowhere these days,' said Fleur. 'Nowhere! You know that as well as I do. And I need security.' Her eye fell on a silver-framed photograph of a little girl with fair, fluffy hair haloed in the sunlight. '*Zara* needs security,' she added.

'Dear Zara,' said Johnny. 'We haven't heard from her for a while. How is she?'

'Fine,' said Fleur vaguely. 'At school.'

'Which reminds me,' said Johnny. He glanced at Felix. 'Have you told her?'

'What? Oh that. No.'

'What is it?' said Fleur suspiciously.

'Someone telephoned us last week.'

'Who?'

'Hal Winters.' There was a short silence.

'What did he want?' said Fleur eventually.

'You. He wanted to get in touch with you.'

'And you told him . . .'

'Nothing. We said we didn't know where you were.'

'Good.' Fleur exhaled slowly. She met Johnny's eye, and quickly looked away.

'Fleur,' said Johnny seriously, 'don't you think you should call him?'

'No,' said Fleur.

'Well I do.'

'Well I don't! Johnny, I've told you before. I don't talk about him.'

'But . . .'

'Do you understand?' exclaimed Fleur angrily. 'I don't talk about him!'

And before he could say anything else, she picked up her bag, tossed back her hair and walked quickly out of the room.

# THREE

Lambert put the phone down and stared at it for a few seconds. Then he turned to Philippa.

'Your father's a fool,' he exclaimed. 'A bloody fool!'

'What's he done?' asked Philippa nervously.

'He's got involved with some bloody woman, that's all. I mean, at his age!'

'And so soon after Mummy's death,' put in Philippa.

'Exactly,' said Lambert. 'Exactly.' He looked at Philippa approvingly, and she felt a glow of pleasure spread over her neck. Lambert didn't often look approvingly at her.

'That was him phoning, to say he's bringing this woman along to lunch today. He sounded . . .' Lambert contorted his face reflectively, and Philippa looked away quickly, before she could find herself articulating the thought that she was married to an extremely ugly man. 'He sounded drunk,' Lambert concluded.

'At this time in the morning?'

'Not *alcohol* drunk,' said Lambert impatiently. 'Drunk

with . . .' He broke off, and for a few moments, he and Philippa looked at each other.

'With happiness,' said Philippa eventually.

'Well, yes,' said Lambert grudgingly. 'I suppose that must be it.'

Philippa leaned forward towards the mirror and began to apply liquid eyeliner shakily to her eyelid.

'Who is she?' she asked. 'What's her name?'

'Fleur.'

'Fleur? The one from the memorial service? The one with the lovely hat?'

'For God's sake, Philippa! Do you think I asked him about her hat? Now, hurry up.' And without waiting for an answer, he left the room.

Philippa gazed silently at her reflection; at her watery blue eyes and pale, mousy hair and slightly flushed cheeks. Through her mind rushed a torrent of imaginary words; words Lambert might have said if he had been a different person. He might have said, 'Yes darling, I expect that's the one' . . . or he might have said, 'Philippa, my love, I only had eyes for you at the memorial service' . . . or he might have said, 'The one with the lovely hat? You had the loveliest hat of all.' And then she would have said, in the confident, teasing tones she could never recreate in real life, 'Come on, sweetheart. Even you must have noticed that hat!' And then he would have said, 'Oh *that* hat!' And then they both would have laughed. And then . . . and then he would have kissed her on the forehead, and then . . .

'Philippa!' Lambert's voice came ringing sharply

through the flat. 'Philippa, are you ready?' Philippa jumped.

'I'll be five minutes!' she called back, hearing the wobble in her voice and despising it.

'Well, get on with it!'

Philippa began to search confusedly through her make-up bag for the right shade of lipstick. If Lambert had been a different person, perhaps he would have called back, 'Take your time', or 'No hurry, dearest', or maybe he would have come back into the room, and smiled at her, and fiddled with her hair, and she would have laughed, and said, 'You're holding me up!' and he would have said, 'I can't help it when you're so gorgeous!' And then he would have kissed her fingertips . . . and then . . .

In the corner of the room, the phone began to ring in a muted electronic burble. Lost in her own private dream-world, Philippa didn't even hear it.

In the study, Lambert picked up the phone.

'Lambert Chester here.'

'Good morning, Mr Chester. It's Erica Fortescue from First Bank here. I wonder if I might have a quick word?'

'I'm about to go out. Is it important?'

'It's about your overdraft, Mr Chester.'

'Oh.' Lambert looked cautiously towards the door of the study – then, to make sure, kicked it shut. 'What's the problem?'

'You seem to have exceeded your limit. Quite substantially.'

'Rubbish.' Lambert leaned back, reached inside his mouth and began to pick his teeth.

'The balance on that account is currently a debit of over three hundred thousand pounds. Whereas the agreed limit was two hundred and fifty.'

'I think you'll find,' said Lambert, 'it was raised again last month. To three hundred and fifty thousand.'

'Was that confirmed in writing?'

'Larry Collins fixed it up for me.'

'Larry Collins has left the bank.' Erica Fortescue's voice came smoothly down the line.

Fuck, thought Lambert. Larry's been sacked. Stupid bugger.

'Well, he confirmed it in writing before he left,' he said quickly. He could easily knock up some letter.

'There's nothing in our files.'

'Well I expect he forgot.' Lambert paused, and his face twisted into a complacent sneer. 'Maybe he also forgot to tell you that in two years' time I'll be coming into more money than either of you has ever seen.' That'll sort you, he thought, you stupid officious bitch.

'Your wife's trust fund? Yes, he did tell me about it. Has that been confirmed?'

'Of course it has. It's all set up.'

'I see.'

'And you're still worried about my pathetic little overdraft?'

'Yes, Mr Chester, I am. We don't generally accept spouses' assets as collateral on sole accounts.' Lambert stared at the phone in anger. Who did this tart think she was? 'Another thing . . .'

'What?' He was beginning to feel rattled.

'I was interested to see that there's no mention of the trust fund in your wife's file here. Only in your own file. Is there a reason for that?'

'Yes there is,' snapped Lambert, his guard down. 'It's not mentioned in my wife's file because she doesn't know about it.'

The files were empty. All empty. Fleur stared at them in disbelief, flicking a few of them open, checking for stray documents, bank statements, anything. Then, hearing a noise, she quickly pushed the drawers of the metal cabinet shut and hurried over to the window. When Richard came into the room, she was leaning out, breathing in the London fumes rapturously.

'Such a wonderful view,' she exclaimed. 'I adore Regent's Park. Do you often visit the Zoo?'

'Never,' said Richard, laughing. 'Not since Antony was little.'

'We must go,' said Fleur. 'While you're still in London.'

'This afternoon, perhaps?'

'This afternoon we're going to Hyde Park,' said Fleur firmly. 'It's all arranged.'

'If you say so.' Richard grinned. 'But now we'd better get going if we're not going to be late for Philippa and Lambert.'

'OK.' Fleur smiled charmingly at Richard and allowed

herself to be led from the room. At the door she glanced fleetingly around, wondering if she'd missed something. But the only businesslike piece of furniture she could see was the filing cabinet. No desk; no bureau. His paperwork must all be somewhere else. At the office. Or at the house in Surrey.

On the way to the restaurant, she allowed her hand to fall easily into Richard's, and as their fingers linked she saw a tiny flush spread across his neck. He was such a buttoned-up English gentleman, she thought, trying not to laugh. After four weeks, he had progressed no further than kissing her, with dry, diffident, out-of-practice lips. Not like brutish Sakis, who had dragged her off to a hotel room after their very first lunch date. Fleur winced at the memory of Sakis's thick, hairy thighs; his barked commands. Much better this way. And to her surprise, she rather liked being treated like a high-school virgin. She walked along beside Richard with a smile on her face, feeling wrapped up and protected and smug, as though she really did have a virtue to protect; as though she were saving herself for that special moment.

Whether she could wait that long was another matter. Four weeks of lunches, dinners, films and art galleries – and she still had no hard evidence that Richard Favour had serious money. So he had a few nice suits; a London flat; a Surrey mansion; a reputation of wealth. That didn't mean anything. The houses might be mortgaged up to the hilt. He might be about to go bust. He might be about to ask *her* for money. It had happened to her once before – and ever since, Fleur had been wary. If she couldn't find hard proof of money she was wasting her time. Really, she should have been off by now. On to the next funeral; the next sucker. But . . .

Fleur paused in her thoughts, and tucked Richard's arm more firmly under her own. If she was honest with herself, she had to admit that her self-confidence had slightly fallen since she'd left Sakis. In the last few weeks she had attended three funerals and five memorial services – but so far Richard Favour was her only promising catch. Meanwhile Johnny and Felix, sweet as they were, had begun to get fidgety at the sight of her luggage littering their spare room. She didn't usually spend so long between men ('resting', as Felix put it); usually it was straight out of one bed and into another.

If only, thought Fleur, she could speed Richard up a bit: secure a place in his bed; work her way into his household. Then she'd be able to assess his finances properly and at the same time solve the problem of a place to stay. Otherwise – if things didn't work out soon – she would be forced to take the sort of steps she'd vowed she'd never stoop to. She would have to find a flat of her own. Maybe even look for a job. Fleur shuddered, and her jaw tightened in determination. She would just have to get Richard into bed. Once that had happened, everything would become easy.

As they turned into Great Portland Street, Richard felt Fleur nudge him.

'Look!' she said in a low voice. 'Look at that!'

Richard turned his head. On the other side of the road were two nuns standing on the pavement, apparently engaged in a bitter dispute.

'I've never seen nuns arguing before,' said Fleur, giggling.

'I don't think I have either.'

'I'm going to talk to them,' said Fleur suddenly. 'Wait here.'

Richard watched in astonishment as Fleur strode across the road. For a few moments she stood on the pavement opposite, a vibrant figure in her scarlet coat, talking to the black-habited nuns. They seemed to be nodding and smiling. Then all of a sudden she was coming back across the road towards him, and the nuns were walking away in apparent harmony.

'What happened?' exclaimed Richard. 'What on earth did you say?'

'I told them the Blessed Virgin Mary was grieved by discord.' Fleur grinned at Richard's incredulous expression. 'Actually, I told them how to get to the tube station.'

Richard gave a sudden laugh.

'You're a remarkable woman!' he said.

'I know,' said Fleur complacently. She tucked her hand under his arm again, and they began to walk.

Richard stared at the pale spring sunlight dappling the pavement, and felt a bubbling exhilaration rise through his body. He had known this woman for a mere four weeks, and already he couldn't imagine life without her. When he was with her, drab everyday events seemed transformed into a series of shiny moments to relish; when he wasn't with her, he was wishing that he was. Fleur seemed to turn life into a game – not the rigid maze of rules and conventions to which Emily had so tirelessly adhered, but a game of chance; of who dares wins. He found himself waiting with a childish excitement to hear what she would say next; what plan she would surprise him with. He had seen more of London over the last four weeks than ever before; laughed more than ever before; spent more money than he had for a long time.

Often his mind would return to Emily, and he would feel a pang of guilt – guilt that he was spending such a lot of time with Fleur, that he was enjoying himself so much, that he had kissed her. And guilt that his original motivation for pursuing Fleur – to discover as much about Emily's hidden character as he could – seemed to have taken second place to that of simply being with her. Sometimes in his dreams he would see Emily's face, pale and reproachful; he would wake in the night, curled up in grief and sweating with shame. But by morning Emily's image had always faded, and all he could think about was Fleur.

'She's stunning!' said Lambert in outraged tones.

'I *told* you,' said Philippa. 'Didn't you notice her at the memorial service?'

Lambert shrugged.

'I suppose I thought she was quite attractive. But . . .

just look at her!' Just look at her next to your father! he wanted to say.

They watched in silence as Fleur took off her scarlet coat. Underneath she was wearing a clinging black dress; she gave a little wriggle and smoothed it down over her hips. Lambert felt a sudden stab of angry desire. What the hell was a woman like that doing with Richard, when he was stuck with Philippa?

'They're coming,' said Philippa. 'Hello, Daddy!'

'Hello darling,' said Richard, kissing her. 'Lambert.'

'Richard.'

'And this is Fleur.' Richard couldn't stop the smirk of pride spreading across his face.

'I'm so glad to meet you,' said Fleur, smiling warmly at Philippa and holding out her hand. After a moment's hesitation, Philippa took it. 'And Lambert, of course, I've already met.'

'Very briefly,' said Lambert, in discouraging tones. Fleur gave him a curious look, then smiled again at Philippa. Slightly unnerved, Philippa smiled back.

'I'm sorry we're a little late,' said Richard, shaking out his napkin. 'We ahm . . . we got into a contretemps with a pair of nuns. Nuns on the run.' He glanced at Fleur and with no warning they both began to laugh.

Philippa looked uneasily at Lambert, who raised his eyebrows.

'I'm sorry,' said Richard, still chuckling. 'It's too long to explain. But it was terribly funny.'

'I expect it was,' said Lambert. 'Have you ordered drinks?'

'I'll have a Manhattan,' said Richard.

'A what?' Philippa slared at him.

'A Manhattan,' repeated Richard. 'Surely you've heard of a Manhattan?'

'Richard was a Manhattan virgin until last week,' said Fleur. 'I just adore cocktails. Don't you?'

'I don't know,' said Philippa. 'I suppose so.' She took a sip of her fizzy water and tried to remember the last time she'd had a cocktail. Then, to her disbelief, she noticed her father's hand creeping under the table to meet Fleur's. She glanced at Lambert; he was gazing, transfixed, at the same thing.

'And I'll have one too,' said Fleur cheerfully.

'I think I'd better have a gin,' said Philippa. She felt slightly faint. Was this really her father? Holding hands with another woman? She couldn't believe it. She'd never even seen him holding hands with her mother. And here he was, grinning away as though Mummy had never existed. He wasn't behaving like her father, she thought. He was behaving as though . . . as though he were a normal man.

Lambert was the tricky one, thought Fleur. It was he who kept giving her suspicious looks; who kept quizzing her on her background and probing her on exactly how well she'd known Emily. She could almost see the phrase 'gold-digger' forming itself in his mind. Which was good if it meant there was some money to be had – but not if it meant he was going to rumble her. She would have to butter him up.

So, as the puddings arrived, she turned to him and adopted a deferential, almost awed expression.

'Richard's told me that you're his company's computer expert.'

'That's right,' said Lambert, sounding bored.

'How marvellous. I know nothing about computers.'

'Most people don't.'

'Lambert designs computer programs for the company,' said Richard, 'and sells them to other firms. It's quite a profitable sideline.'

'So are you going to be another Bill Gates?'

'Actually, my approach is completely different from Gates's,' said Lambert coldly. Fleur looked at him to see if he was joking but his eyes were hard and humourless. Goodness, she thought, trying not to laugh. Never underestimate a man's vanity.

'But you still might make billions?' Lambert shrugged.

'Money doesn't interest me.'

'Lambert doesn't bother about money,' put in Philippa, giving an uncertain little laugh. 'I do all our book-keeping.'

'A task eminently suited to the female mind,' said Lambert.

'Hang on a minute, Lambert,' protested Richard. 'I don't think that's quite fair.'

'It may not be fair,' said Lambert, digging a spoon into his chocolate mousse, 'but it's true. Men create, women administrate.'

'Women create babies,' said Fleur.

'Women *produce* babies,' said Lambert. 'Men create them. The woman is the passive partner. And who determines the sex of a baby? The man or the woman?'

'The clinic,' said Fleur. Lambert looked displeased.

'You don't seem to appreciate the point of what I'm saying,' he began. 'Quite simply . . .' But before he could continue, he was interrupted by a ringing, female voice.

'Well, what a surprise! The Favour family *en masse*!' Fleur looked up. A blonde woman in an emerald green jacket was bearing down on them. Her eyes swivelled from Richard to Fleur, to Lambert, to Philippa, and back to Fleur. Fleur returned her gaze equably. Why did these women have to wear so much make-up? she wondered. The woman's eyelids were smothered in bright blue frosting; her eyelashes stuck straight out from her eyes in black spikes; on one of her teeth there was a tiny smear of lipstick.

'Eleanor!' said Richard. 'How nice to see you. Are you up with Geoffrey?'

'No,' said Eleanor. 'I'm having lunch with a girlfriend; then we're off to the Scotch House.' She shifted the gilt chain strap of her bag from one shoulder to the other. 'Actually, Geoffrey was saying only the other day that he hadn't seen you at the club recently.' Her voice held a note of enquiry; again her eyes slid towards Fleur.

'Let me introduce you,' said Richard. 'This is a friend of mine, Fleur Daxeny. Fleur, this is Eleanor Forrester. Her husband is captain of the golf club down at Greyworth.'

'How nice to meet you,' murmured Fleur, rising from

her seat slightly to shake hands. Eleanor Forrester's hand was firm and rough; almost masculine except for the red-painted nails. Another golfer.

'Are you an old friend of Richard's?' asked Eleanor.

'Not really,' said Fleur. 'I met Richard for the first time four weeks ago.'

'I see,' said Eleanor. Her spiky eyelashes batted up and down a few times. 'I see,' she said again. 'Well, I suppose I'd better be off. Will you be playing in the Spring Meeting, any of you?'

'I certainly will,' said Lambert.

'Oh, I expect I will too,' said Richard. 'But who knows?'

'Who knows,' echoed Eleanor. She looked again at Fleur, and her mouth tightened. 'Very nice to meet you, Fleur. Very interesting indeed.'

They watched in silence as she walked briskly away, her blond hair bouncing stiffiy on the collar of her jacket.

'Well,' exclaimed Lambert when she was out of earshot. 'That'll be all over the club tomorrow.'

'Eleanor was a really good friend of Mummy's,' said Philippa apologetically to Fleur. 'She probably thought . . .' She broke off awkwardly.

'You know, you'll have to watch it,' said Lambert to Richard. 'You'll get back to Greyworth and find everyone's been talking about you.'

'How nice,' said Richard, smiling at Fleur, 'to be the centre of attention.'

'It may seem funny now,' said Lambert. 'But if I were you . . .'

'Yes, Lambert? What would you do?'

A note of steel had crept into Richard's voice, and Philippa shot Lambert a warning look. But Lambert ploughed on.

'I'd be a bit careful, Richard. Frankly, you don't want people getting the wrong idea. You don't want people gossiping behind your back.'

'And why should they gossip behind my back?'

'Well I mean, it's obvious, isn't it? Look, Fleur, I don't want to offend you, but you understand, don't you? A lot of people were very fond of Emily. And when they hear about you . . .'

'Not only will they hear about Fleur,' said Richard loudly, 'but they will meet her, since she will be coming down to stay at Greyworth as soon as possible. And if you have a problem with that, Lambert, then I suggest you keep well away.'

'I only meant . . .' began Lambert.

'I know what you meant,' said Richard. 'I know only too well what you meant. And I'm afraid I think a lot less of you for it. Come on Fleur, let's leave.'

Out on the pavement, Richard took Fleur's ann.

'I'm so sorry about that,' he said. 'Lambert can be most objectionable.'

'It's quite all right,' said Fleur quietly. My God, she thought, I've had it a lot more objectionable than that. There was the daughter who tried to pull my hair out, the neighbour who called me a slut . . .

'And you will come down to Greyworth? I'm sorry, I

should have asked first.' Richard looked at her anxiously. 'But I promise you'll enjoy it down there. We can go for long walks, and you can meet the rest of the family . . .'

'And learn to play golf?'

'If you'd like to.' He smiled. 'It's not compulsory.' He paused awkwardly. 'And of course, you'd . . . you'd have your own room. I wouldn't want you to . . . to . . .'

'Wouldn't you?' said Fleur softly. 'I would.' She raised herself on tiptoe and gently kissed Richard on the lips. After a moment, she softly pushed her tongue inside his mouth. Immediately, his body stiffened. With shock? With desire? She casually ran a hand down the back of his neck and waited to find out.

Richard stood completely still, with Fleur's mouth open against his, her words echoing in his mind, trying to marshal his thoughts and yet completely unable to. He felt suddenly rigid, almost paralysed with excitement. After a few moments Fleur moved her lips softly to the corner of his mouth, and he felt his skin explode with delicious sensation. This was how it should have been with Emily, he thought dizzily, trying not to keel over with headiness. This was how it should have felt with his beloved wife. But Emily had never aroused him like this woman – this bewitching woman whom he'd only known for four weeks. He had never felt anticipation like this before. He'd never felt like . . . like *fucking* a woman before.

'Let's get a cab,' he said, in a blurred voice, pulling himself away from Fleur. 'Let's go back to the flat.' He could hardly bear to speak. Each word seemed to sully the moment; to spoil the conviction inside him that he was on the brink of a perfect experience. But one had to break the silence. One had somehow to get off the street.

'What about Hyde Park?'

Richard felt as though Fleur were torturing him.

'Another day,' he managed. 'Come on. Come on!'

He hailed a taxi, bundled her inside, mumbled an address to the taxi driver and turned back to Fleur. And at the sight of her, his heart nearly stopped. As Fleur had leaned back on the black leather taxi seat, her dress had mysteriously hitched itself up until the top of one of her black stockings was just visible.

'Oh God,' he said indistinctly, staring at the sheer black lace. Emily had never worn black lace stockings.

And suddenly a cold flash of fear went through him. What was he about to do? What had happened to him? Images of Emily came flashing through his mind. Her sweet smile; the feeling of her hair between his fingers. Her slim legs; her neat little buttocks. Cosy, undemanding times; nights of fondness.

'Richard,' said Fleur huskily, running a finger gently along his thigh. Richard flinched in panic. He felt terrified. What had seemed so clear on the pavement now seemed muddied by memories that would not leave his mind alone; by a guilt that rose up, choking his throat till he could hardly breathe. Suddenly he felt close to tears. He could not do this. He would not do it.

And yet desire for Fleur still whirled tormentingly about his body.

'Richard?' said Fleur again.

'I'm still married,' he found himself saying. 'I can't do this. I'm still married to Emily.' He stared at her, waiting for some relief to his agony; some internal acknowledgement that he was doing the right thing. But there was none. He felt awash with conflicting emotions, with physical needs, with mental anguish. No direction seemed the right one.

'You're not really married to Emily any more,' said Fleur, in slow soft tones. 'Are you?' She put up a hand and began to caress his cheek, but he jerked away.

'I can't!' Richard's face was white with despair. He sat forward with taut cheeks and glittering eyes. 'You don't understand. Emily was my wife. Emily's the only one . . .' His voice cracked and he looked away.

Fleur thought for a moment, then quickly adjusted her dress. By the time Richard had gained control of himself and looked back towards her the lacy stockings had disappeared under a sea of decorous black wool. He looked silently at her.

'I must be a great disappointment to you,' he said eventually. 'I'd quite understand if you decided . . .' he shrugged.

'Decided what?'

'That you didn't want to see me any more.'

'Richard, don't be so silly!' Fleur's voice was soft, compassionate, and just a little playful. 'You don't imagine that I'm only after you for one thing?' She gave him a tiny smile, and after a few seconds Richard grinned back. 'We've been having such wonderful times together,' continued Fleur. 'I'd hate either of us to feel pressured . . .'

As she was speaking, she caught a glimpse of the taxi driver's face in the rear-view mirror. He was staring at them both in transparent astonishment, and Fleur suddenly wanted to giggle. But instead she turned to Richard and in a quieter voice, said,

'I'd love to come down and stay at Greyworth and I'd be very happy to have my own bedroom. And if things move on . . . they move on.'

Richard looked at her for a few seconds, then suddenly grasped her hand.

'You're a wonderful woman,' he said huskily. 'I feel . . .' He clasped her hand tighter. 'I feel suddenly very close to you.' Fleur stared back at him silently for a moment, then modestly lowered her eyes.

Bloody Emily, she thought. Always getting in the way. But she said nothing, and allowed Richard's hand to remain clutching hers, all the way back to Regent's Park.

# FOUR

Two weeks later, Antony Favour stood in the kitchen of The Maples, watching as his Aunt Gillian whipped cream. She was whipping it by hand, with a grim expression and a mouth which seemed to grow tighter at each stroke of the whisk. Antony knew for a fact that inside one of the kitchen cupboards lived an electric whisk; he'd used it himself to make pancakes. But Gillian always whipped cream by hand. She did most things by hand. Gillian had been living in the house since before Antony was born, and for as long as he could remember she'd been the one who did all the cooking, and told the cleaner what to do, and walked around after the cleaner had left, frowning, and polishing again over surfaces which looked perfectly clean. His mother had never really done any of that stuff. Some of the time she'd been too ill to cook, and the rest of the time she'd been too busy playing golf.

A vision of his mother came into Antony's mind. Small, and thin, with silvery blond hair and neat tartan trousers. He remembered her blue-grey eyes; her expensive rimless spectacles; her faint flowery scent. His mother had always looked neat and tidy; silver and blue. Antony looked surreptitiously at Gillian. Her dull grey hair had separated into two heavy clumps; her cheeks were bright red; her shoulders were hunched up in their mauve cardigan. Gillian had the same blue-grey eyes as his mother, but apart from that, Antony thought, it was difficult to believe that they'd been sisters.

He looked again at Gillian's tense expression. Ever since Dad had called to tell them he'd be bringing this woman to stay, Gillian had been walking around looking even more grim than usual. She hadn't said anything – but then, Gillian didn't often say very much. She never had an opinion; she never said when she was pissed off. It was up to you to guess. And now, Antony guessed, she was seriously pissed off.

Antony himself wasn't quite sure how he felt about this woman. He'd lain in bed the night before, thinking about his mother and his father and this new woman, waiting for a sudden gut reaction; a stab of emotion to point him in the right direction. But nothing. He'd had no particularly negative emotions, nor any positive ones, just a kind of astonished acknowledgement that this thing was happening; that his father was seeing another woman. Occasionally the thought would hit him as he was in the middle of something else, and he'd feel so shocked that he would have to stare ahead and breathe deeply and blink several times, to stop his eyes filling with tears, for Christ's sake. But other times it seemed completely natural; almost something he'd been expecting.

He'd got used to telling people that his mother was dead; perhaps telling them that his father had a girlfriend was just the next step along. Sometimes it even made him want to laugh.

Gillian had finished whipping the cream. She shook the whisk and dumped it in the sink without even licking it. Then she sighed heavily and rubbed her forehead with her hand.

'Are we having pavlova?' said Antony.

'Yes,' said Gillian. 'With kiwi fruit.' She shrugged. 'I don't know if it's what your father wants. But it'll just have to do.'

'I'm sure it'll be great,' said Antony. 'Everyone loves pavlova.'

'Well, it'll just have to do,' repeated Gillian. She looked wearily about the kitchen and Antony followed her gaze. He loved the kitchen; it was his favourite room. About five years ago his parents had had it done up like a huge farmhouse kitchen, with terracotta tiles everywhere, and an open fire, and a huge wooden table with really comfortable chairs. They'd bought five million pots and pans and stuff, all out of expensive catalogues, and hung garlic on the walls and got a woman to come in and arrange dried flowers all over the place.

Antony could have spent all day in the kitchen in fact, now they'd installed a telly on the wall, he often did. But Gillian seemed to hate it. She'd hated it as it was before – 'all white and clinical', she'd called it – and she still hated it, even though she'd been the one to choose the tiles and tell the designer where everything should go. Antony didn't understand it.

'Can I help?' he said. 'Can I peel the potatoes or something?'

'We're not having potatoes,' said Gillian irritably, as if he should have known. 'We're having wild rice.' She frowned. 'I hope it's not too difficult to cook.'

'I'm sure it'll be delicious,' said Antony. 'Why don't you use the rice cooker?'

His parents had given Gillian a rice cooker three Christmases ago. The year before that they'd given her an electrical juicer; since then there had been an automatic herb shredder, a bread slicer and an ice-cream maker. As far as Antony knew, she'd never used any of them.

'I'll manage,' said Gillian. 'Why don't you go outside? Or do some revision?'

'Honestly, I don't mind helping,' said Antony.

'It's quicker if I do it myself.' Gillian gave another heavy sigh and reached for a cookery book. Antony looked at her silently for a few moments, then shrugged and walked out.

It was a nice day, and he was, he thought, quite glad to get out into the sunshine. He wandered out of the drive of The Maples and along the road towards the clubhouse. All the roads on the Greyworth estate were private and you had to have a security pass to get in, so most of the time there were hardly any cars; just people who had houses on the estate or who were members of the golf club.

Maybe, Antony thought as he walked, there was time for a quick nine holes before Dad arrived. He was supposed to be revising for his exams this week; that was the reason he was at home. Ahead of him stretched a week-long home study period. But Antony didn't need to study – he knew all the stuff they were going to ask. Instead he was planning to spend his days lazing around, playing golf, a bit of tennis maybe. It depended on who was around. His best friend, Will, was away at school like him, and Will's school didn't have home study periods. 'You jammy bastard,' Will had written. 'Just don't blame me if you fail everything.' Antony had to agree. It was bloody jammy. His dad hadn't been at all impressed. 'What are we paying your fees for,' he'd exclaimed, 'if all they do is send you back home?' Antony didn't know. He didn't care. It wasn't his problem.

The road to the clubhouse was downhill, lined with grass and trees and the gates to other people's houses. Antony glanced at each driveway as he passed, assessing from the presence of cars who was at home and who wasn't. The Forresters had a new white Jeep, he noticed, pausing by their gate. Very nice.

'Hey Antony! Like my Jeep?' Antony started, and looked up. Sitting on the grass about fifty yards down the road were Xanthe Forrester and Mex Taylor. Their legs were entwined in a tangle of 501s and they were both smoking. Antony fought with a desire to turn round and pretend he hadn't heard. Xanthe was about his own age; he'd known her for ever. She'd always been a bitchy little girl; now she was just a bitch. She always managed to make him feel stupid and awkward and ugly. Mex Taylor was new to Greyworth. All Antony knew was that he was in the upper sixth at Eton and played off seven and all the girls thought he was great. Which was enough.

He walked slowly down the hill towards them, trying not to rush, trying to keep his breath steady, trying to think of something clever to say. Then, as he neared them, Xanthe suddenly put out her cigarette and began kissing Mex, clutching his head and writhing about as though she were in some stupid movie. Antony told himself furiously that she was just showing off. She probably thought he was jealous. She probably thought he'd never snogged anyone in his life before. If only she knew. At school, they were bussed off to dances nearly every weekend, and Antony always came away with a couple of love bites and a phone number, no problem. But that was at school, where there was no childhood history; where people took him for what he was. Whereas Xanthe Forrester, Fifi Tilling – all that little clique – still thought of him as square old Antony Favour, good for a round of golf but not much else.

Suddenly Xanthe pulled herself away from Mex.

'My phone! It's vibrating!' She darted a wicked look at Mex, glanced at Antony, then pulled her mobile phone from the bright red leather holster on her hip.

Antony looked awkwardly at Mex and, in spite of himself, felt his hand shoot up protectively to his eye, covering his birthmark.

'Hi? Fifi! Yeah, I'm with Mex!' Xanthe's voice was triumphant.

'Want a smoke?' said Mex casually to Antony. Antony considered. If he said yes, he would have to stay and talk to them. And someone might see him and tell his dad, which would be a real hassle. But if he said no, they'd think he was square.

'OK.'

Xanthe was still babbling away into her phone, but as Antony lit up, she paused and said with a giggle, 'Antony! Smoking! That's a bit daring for you, isn't it?' Mex gave Antony an amused look and Antony felt himself flushing.

'It's so cool!' said Xanthe, putting her phone away. 'Fifi's parents are away until Friday. We're all meeting at hers tonight,' she added to Mex. 'You, me, Fifi and Tania. Tania's got some stuff.'

'Sounds good,' said Mex. 'What about . . .' He jerked his head towards Antony. Xanthe pulled the briefest of faces at Mex, then turned to Antony.

'D'you want to meet up, Antony? We're watching *Betty Blue* on Fifi's laser disc.'

'I can't, I'm afraid,' said Antony. 'My dad's . . .' He paused. He wasn't about to tell Xanthe that his dad had a girlfriend. 'My dad's coming home,' he said weakly.

'Your dad's coming home?' said Xanthe incredulously. 'You can't come out because your dad's coming home?'

'I think that's really nice,' said Mex kindly. 'I wish I was that close to my dad.' He smirked at Xanthe. 'It would help if I didn't hate his guts.'

Xanthe burst into peals of laughter.

'I wish I was closer to my dad,' she said. 'Maybe then he would have given me a Jag instead of a Jeep.' She lit up another cigarette.

'How come you've got a Jeep?' said Antony. 'You can't drive yet. You're only fifteen.'

'I can drive on private roads,' retorted Xanthe. 'Mex is teaching me. Aren't you, Mex?' She lay back on the grass and ran her fingers through her blond curls. 'And that's not all he's teaching me. Know what I mean?' She blew a circle of smoke into the air. 'Actually, you probably don't.' She winked at Mex. 'I don't want to shock Antony. He still kisses with his mouth closed.'

Antony stared at Xanthe in furious embarrassment, searching in his mind for some witty put-down. But the co-ordination between his brain and his mouth seemed to have disappeared.

'Your dad,' said Xanthe musingly. 'Your dad. What did I hear about him the other day?' Suddenly she sat up. 'Oh yes! He's got a floosie, hasn't he?'

'No he hasn't!'

'Yes he has! Mum and Dad were talking about it. Some woman in London. Really pretty, apparently. Mum caught them having lunch.'

'She's just a friend,' said Antony desperately. All his nonchalance had disappeared. Suddenly he hated his father; even hated his mother for dying. Why couldn't everything have stayed as it was?

'I heard about your mum,' said Mex. 'Rough.'

You don't know anything about it! Antony wanted to shout. But instead he stubbed out his cigarette awkwardly with his foot, and said,

'I've got to go.'

'Too bad,' said Xanthe. 'You were really turning me on, standing there in those sexy trousers. Where'd you get them? A jumble sale?'

'Catch you later,' said Mex. 'Have a nice time with your dad.'

As Antony began to walk off, he heard a suppressed snigger, but he didn't look back until he reached the corner. Then he allowed himself a quick glance behind him. Xanthe and Mex were kissing again.

Quickly he rounded the corner and sat down on a low stone wall. Through his mind ran all the phrases he'd heard from grown-ups over the years. *People who tease you are just immature . . . Don't take any notice – then they'll get bored . . . If they attach more importance to your looks than your personality, then they're not worth having as friends.*

So what was he supposed to do? Ignore everyone except Will? End up with no friends at all? The way he saw it, he had two choices. Either he could be lonely, or he could get on with the crowd. Antony sighed. It was all very well for grown-ups. They didn't know what it was like. When was the last time someone had been bitchy to his dad? Probably never. Grown-ups weren't bitchy to each other. They just weren't. In fact, grown-ups, thought Antony morosely, should stop complaining. They had it bloody easy.

Gillian sat at the huge wooden table in her dead sister's kitchen, looking blankly at a heap of French beans. She felt weary, almost too weary to raise the knife. Since Emily's death an apathy had been creeping up on her which alarmed and confused her. She knew no other way of dealing with it than by throwing herself wholeheartedly into the household tasks which filled her day. But the harder she worked, the less energy she seemed to have. When she sat down for a break she felt like stopping for ever.

She leaned forward on her elbows, feeling lethargic and heavy. She could feel her own weight sinking into the farmhouse chair, the mass of her solid, unbeautiful body. Ample breasts encased in a sensible bra, bulky legs hidden under a skirt. Her cardigan was thick and weighty; even her hair felt heavy today.

For a few minutes, she stared down at the table, tracing the grain of the wood with her finger, trying to lose herself in the whorls and loops, trying to pretend she felt normal. But as her finger reached a dark woody knot, she stopped. There was no point pretending to herself. She didn't just feel heavy. She didn't just feel apathetic. She felt scared.

The phone call from Richard had been brief. No explanation beyond the fact that he was bringing a woman down to stay and she was called Fleur. Gillian stared at her stubby, roughened fingertip and bit her lip. She should have realized that this would happen; that sooner or later Richard would find a . . . a female companion. But somehow she had imagined everything carrying on as normal: Richard, Antony and herself. Not so very different from when Emily had been alive – from all the times that the three of them had sat eating supper together, with Emily upstairs in bed.

She was a fool. Of course everything couldn't have continued like that for ever. For one thing, Antony was nearly grown up. Before long he'd be leaving school and going off to university. And did she expect to carry on living at The Maples then? Just her and Richard? She had no idea what Richard thought of her. Did he see her as any more than Emily's sister? Did he consider her a friend? Part of the family? Or did he expect her to leave, now that Emily was dead? She had no idea. In all the years she'd lived in his house, she'd rarely spoken to Richard directly. Their communications, such as they were, had always been through Emily. And now that Emily had gone, they didn't communicate at all. In the months since her death they had discussed nothing more significant than arrangements for meals. Gillian had not questioned her position; neither had Richard.

But now everything was different. Now there was a woman called Fleur. A woman she knew nothing about.

'You'll *love* her,' Richard had added just before putting the phone down. This Gillian doubted. Of course, he'd meant 'love' in the casual, modern use of the word. She'd heard it bandied about by the women in the clubhouse bar – I *love* your dress . . . Don't you just *love* this scent. Love, love love. As though it meant nothing; as though it weren't a sacrosanct word, a precious syllable, to be used sparingly. Gillian loved human beings, not handbags. She knew with a fierce certainty whom she loved, whom she had loved, whom she would always love. But in her adult life she had never uttered the word aloud.

Outside, a cloud moved, and a shaft of sunlight landed on the table.

'It's a nice day,' said Gillian, listening to her voice fall into the dead silence of the kitchen. She'd been talking to herself more and more, recently. Sometimes, with Richard up in London and Antony away at school, she was alone in the house for days at a time. Empty, lonely days. She didn't have any friends at Greyworth; when the rest of the family were away, the phone soon stopped trilling. Many of Emily's friends had gained the impression over the years that Gillian was more a paid housekeeper than a member of the family – an impression which Emily had never bothered to correct.

Emily. Gillian's thoughts paused. Her little sister Emily, dead. She closed her eyes and rested her head in her hands. What kind of world was it where a younger sibling died before the elder? Where a married sister's frail body might be almost destroyed by repeated miscarriages, while her spinster sister's sturdy frame was never put to the test? Gillian had nursed Emily through each miscarriage, nursed her through the birth of Philippa and – much later Antony. She'd watched as

Emily's body gradually gave up; watched as everything faded away. And now she was left alone, living in a family that wasn't really hers, waiting for the arrival of her sister's replacement.

Maybe it was time to leave and start on a new life. After Emily's generous bequest she was now financially independent. She could go anywhere, do anything. A series of visions flipped through her mind like the pictures in a retirement plan brochure. She could buy a cottage by the sea. She could take up gardening. She could travel.

Into Gillian's thoughts crept the memory of an offer made many years ago, an offer which had thrilled her so much that she'd run and told Emily straight away. A trip round the world, with Verity Standish.

'You remember Verity,' she'd said excitedly to Emily, who stood by the fireplace, fiddling with a piece of porcelain. 'She's just taking off! Flying to Cairo in October and going on from there. She wants me to come too! Isn't it exciting?'

And she'd waited for Emily to smile, to ask questions, to welcome Gillian's delight as wholeheartedly as Gillian had welcomed Emily's own many happinesses over the years. But Emily had turned, and without waiting for Gillian's breath to subside, had said, 'I'm pregnant. Four months.'

Gillian had caught her breath and stared at Emily, startled tears of delight springing into her eyes. She had thought – everyone had thought – that Emily would never have another child. Every one of her pregnancies since Philippa had ended in miscarriage before twelve weeks; it had seemed unlikely that she would ever carry another baby to term.

She'd hurried over and clasped Emily's hands in joy.

'Four months! Oh, Emily!' But Emily's blue eyes had bored into Gillian's reproachfully.

'Which means the baby's due in December.'

Suddenly Gillian had realized what she meant. And for once in her life she'd tried to resist Emily's dominance.

'You won't mind if I still go on the trip?' She'd adopted a cheery, matter-of-fact voice. 'Richard will be very supportive, I'm sure. And I'll be back in January, I can take over then.' She had begun to falter. 'It's just that this is such a wonderful . . .'

'Oh you go!' Emily had exclaimed in a brittle voice. 'I can easily hire a maternity nurse. And a nanny for Philippa. It'll be fine.' She'd flashed Gillian a little smile, and Gillian had stared back at her with a miserable wariness. She knew this game of Emily's; knew that she was always too slow to anticipate the next move.

'And I'll probably keep the nanny on after you come back.' Emily's silvery voice had travelled across the room and lodged itself like a painful splinter in Gillian's chest. 'She can have your room. You won't mind, will you? You'll probably be living elsewhere by then.'

She should have gone anyway. She should have called Eniily's bluff and gone with Verity. She could have travelled for a few months, come back and joined the family again. Emily wouldn't have rejected her help.

She felt sure of that now. *She should have gone.* The words echoed bitterly in her mind and she felt her entire body tense up as the regrets of fifteen years circled around her like poisoned blood.

But she had not gone. She had caved in, as she'd always caved in to Emily, and she had stayed for the birth of Antony. And it was after his birth that she'd realized that she could never go; that she could never leave the house by her own choice. Because Emily didn't love little Antony. But Gillian loved him more than anything else in the world.

'So, tell me about Gillian,' said Fleur, leaning comfortably back in her seat.

'Gillian?' said Richard absently. He put on his indicator. 'Go on, let me in, you idiot.'

'Yes, Gillian,' said Fleur, as the car changed lanes. 'How long has she been living with you?'

'Oh, years. Since . . . I don't know, since Philippa was born, maybe.'

'And do you get on well with her?'

'Oh yes.'

Fleur glanced at Richard. His face was blank and uninterested. So much for Gillian.

'And Antony,' she said. 'I haven't met him yet either.'

'Oh, you'll like Antony,' said Richard. A sudden enthusiasm came into his face. 'He's a good lad. Plays off twelve, which is pretty good for his age.'

'Marvellous,' said Fleur politely. The more time she spent with Richard, the more clear it was becoming that she was going to have to take up this appalling game. She tried to imagine herself in a pair of golfing shoes, with tassles and spikes, and gave a little shudder.

'It's lovely country round here,' she said, looking out of the window. 'I didn't realize Surrey had sheep.'

'The odd sheep,' said Richard. 'The odd cow, too.' He paused, and his mouth began to twitch humorously. Fleur waited. The twitching mouth meant he was going to make a joke. 'You'll meet some of Surrey's finest cows down at the golf club,' said Richard eventually, and gave a snort of laughter. Fleur giggled along, amused at him rather than the joke. Was this really the same stiff, dull man she'd met six weeks ago? She could hardly believe it. Richard seemed to have plunged into a life of merriment with an almost zealous determination. Now it was he who phoned her up with outlandish suggestions, who cracked jokes, who planned outings and amusements.

In part he was trying to compensate, she guessed, for the lack of physical intimacy in their relationship; a lack which he clearly believed troubled her as much as it troubled him. She had told him once or twice that it didn't matter – but not too convincingly; not too unflatteringly. And so, to allay both their frustrations, he'd begun to fill their nights with substitutes. If he could not entertain her in bed, he could entertain her in theatres and cocktail bars and night clubs. Every morning he called her at ten o'clock with a plan for the evening. To her surprise, Fleur had started to look forward to his calls.

'Sheringham St Martin!' she suddenly exclaimed, noticing a sign out of the window.

'Yes, it's a pretty village,' said Richard.

'That's where Xavier Formby's opened his new restaurant. I was reading about it. The Pumpkin House. Apparently it's wonderful. We must go some time.'

'Let's go right now,' said Richard at once. 'Have supper there. Perfect! I'll give them a call, see if there's a table.'

Without pausing, he reached down to his phone and punched in the number for Directory Enquiries. Fleur looked at him carefully. Was there any reason for her to point out that this Gillian character had probably organized dinner for them already? Richard didn't seem to care – in fact he seemed almost oblivious of Gillian. In some families it was well worth winning round the womenfolk – but what was the point here? She might as well play along with Richard. After all, he was the one with the money. And if he wanted to go out to dinner, who was she to persuade him otherwise?

'You have?' Richard was saying. 'Well, we'll be right along.' Fleur beamed at him.

'You're so clever.'

'*Carpe diem*,' said Richard. 'Seize the day.' He smiled at her. 'You know, when I was a boy I never understood that saying. I thought it was "sees" as in "to see". Sees the day. It never seemed to make sense.'

'But it makes sense now?' said Fleur.

'Oh yes,' said Richard. 'It makes more and more sense.'

* * *

The phone rang at seven o'clock, just as Antony had finished laying the table. As Gillian answered, he stood back to admire it. There were lilies in vases, and lacy white napkins and candles waiting to be lit, and from the kitchen was coming a wonderful smell of roast lamb. Time for a gin, thought Antony. He looked at his watch. Surely his father would be here soon?

Suddenly Gillian appeared at the door of the dining room, wearing the blue dress she always put on for special occasions. Her face was grim, but that didn't necessarily mean anything.

'That was your father,' she said. 'He won't be here till later.'

'Oh. How much later?' Antony straightened a knife.

'About ten, he said. He and this woman are eating out.' Antony's head shot up.

'Eating out? But they can't!'

'They're at the restaurant now.'

'But you've made supper! Did you tell him? Did you say there was roast lamb waiting in the oven?' Gillian shrugged. She had the resigned, weary expression on her face that Antony hated.

'Your father can eat out if he likes,' she said.

'You should have said something!' cried Antony.

'It's not for me to tell your father what to do.'

'But if he'd realized, I'm sure . . .' Antony broke off and looked at Gillian in frustration. Why the hell hadn't she said something to Dad? When he got back and saw what he'd done, he'd feel terrible.

'Well, it's too late now. He didn't say which restaurant he was at.'

She looked almost pleased, thought Antony, as though she got some satisfaction from having all her efforts wasted.

'So we'll just eat it all ourselves?' He sounded aggressive, he knew, but he didn't care.

'I suppose so.' Gillian looked down at herself. 'I'll go and get out of this dress,' she said.

'Why don't you keep it on?' said Antony, desperate somehow to salvage the occasion. 'You look nice.'

'It'll get all creased. There's no point messing it up.' She turned, and made her way towards the stairs.

Well fuck it, thought Antony. If you don't want to make an effort, then neither do I. He remembered Xanthe Forrester and Mex Taylor that morning. They had actually invited him out, hadn't they? Maybe they weren't so bad, after all.

'I might go out then,' he said. 'If we're not having a big dinner or anything.'

'All right,' said Gillian, without looking back.

Antony went over to the phone and dialled Fifi Tilling's number.

'Hello?' Fifi's voice was bubbling over with fun; there was music in the background.

'Hi, it's Antony. Antony Favour.'

'Oh right. Hi, Antony. Hey, everyone,' she called, 'Antony's on the phone.' In the background, he thought he could hear sniggers.

'I wasn't going to be free this evening,' he said

awkwardly, 'but now I am. So I could come round or something. Xanthe said everyone was getting together.'

'Oh. Yeah.' There was a pause. 'Actually we're all about to go out to a club.'

'Great. Well, I'm on for that.' Did he sound friendly and laid-back, or anxious and desperate? He couldn't tell.

'The thing is, actually, the car's full.'

'Oh, right.' Antony looked at the receiver; not sure. Was she trying to say . . .

'Sorry about that.' Yes, she was.

'No problem.' He tried to sound casual. Amused, even. 'Maybe another time.'

'Oh. Yeah. Sure.' Fifi sounded vague. She wasn't even listening to him.

'Well, bye then,' said Antony.

'Bye Antony. See you around.'

Antony put the phone down and felt a wave of humiliation rise through him. They would have found room for him if they'd wanted to. He looked down at his hands and saw that they were shaking. He felt hot with embarrassment, even though he was alone in the room.

It was all his bloody dad's fault – if he'd arrived on time, that phone call wouldn't have happened. Antony leaned back in his chair. He found that thought gratifying. Yeah, it was his dad's fault. An invigorating resentment began to wash through him. And it was Gillian's fault too. What was her bloody problem? Why hadn't she just given his dad some grief and told him to come right home?

For a few minutes he sat, fiddling with a napkin, thinking how pissed off he was with them both, and looking at the table which he'd laid. What an effort for nothing. Well, it could all just stay there. He wasn't about to put everything away again.

Then it occurred to him that Gillian might call down and suggest that he did exactly that, so before she could he got up and wandered into the kitchen. The lamb was still roasting away in the oven, and sitting majestically on the table was the pavlova, smothered in whipped cream and decorated with kiwi fruit. Antony looked at it. If they weren't going to do supper properly, then there was no harm in him having a bit, was there? He pulled out a chair, picked up the remote control and zapped it several times at the screen of the television. Then, as the kitchen filled with the glitzy sound of a game show, he picked up a spoon, dug it into the shiny meringue, and began to munch.

# FIVE

Breakfast had been laid in the conservatory.

'What a lovely room,' said Fleur politely, looking at Gillian's face, searching for eye contact. But Gillian was looking down at her plate. She had not once met Fleur's eye since she and Richard had arrived the night before.

'We like it,' said Richard cheerfully. 'Especially in the spring. In the summer, it sometimes gets too hot.'

There was another silence. Antony put down his teacup and everyone seemed to listen intently to the little tinkle.

'We built the conservatory about . . . ten years ago,' continued Richard. 'Is that right, Gillian?'

'I expect so,' said Gillian. 'More tea, anyone?'

'Yes please,' said Fleur.

'Right. Well I'll make another pot, then,' said Gillian, and she disappeared into the kitchen.

Fleur took a bite of toast. Things were going rather well, she thought, despite the uneaten roast lamb and pavlova. It had been the boy, Antony, who had confronted them the night before, almost as soon as they had got inside the door, and informed them that Gillian had spent all day cooking. Richard had looked horror-struck, and Fleur had put on a most convincing show of dismay. Fortunately, no-one seemed to blame her. Equally fortunately, it was obvious this morning that no-one was going to mention the matter again.

'Here you are.' Gillian had returned with the teapot.

'Wonderful,' said Fleur, smiling into Gillian's unreceptive face. It was going to be easy, she thought, if all she would have to deal with were awkward silences and a few resentful glares. Glares didn't bother her at all; neither did raised eyebrows; neither did sidelong comments. That was the blessedness of preying on the reserved British middle classes, she thought, sipping at her tea. They never seemed to talk to each other; they never wanted to rock the boat; they seemed almost more willing to lose all their money than to undergo the embarrassment of a direct confrontation. Which meant that for someone like her, the way was clear.

She looked curiously at Gillian. For someone who presumably had access to funds, Gillian was wearing particularly hideous clothes. Dark green trousers – slacks, Fleur supposed they would be called – and a blue embroidered cotton shirt with short, workmanlike sleeves. As she leaned over with the teapot, Fleur glimpsed Gillian's upper arms – solid slabs of white, opaque, almost dead-looking skin.

Antony's clothes were a bit better. Fairly standard jeans and a rather nice red shirt. It was a shame about his birthmark. Had they not been able to treat it? Possibly not, because it stretched right across his eye. If he'd been a girl, of course, he'd have been able to wear make-up . . . Other than that, thought Fleur, he was a handsome boy. He took after his father.

Fleur's gaze flitted idly over to Richard. He was leaning back in his chair, looking out of the conservatory into the garden, with an apparent look of contentment on his face, as though he were beginning a holiday. As he felt her eyes on him, he glanced up and smiled. Fleur smiled back. It was easy to smile at Richard, she thought. He was good man, kind and considerate, and not nearly as dull as she had first feared. These last few weeks had been fun.

But it was money she needed, not fun. She hadn't persevered so hard in order to end up with a limited income and holidays in Majorca. Fleur gave an inward sigh, and took another sip of tea. Sometimes the effort of pursuing money quite exhausted her; sometimes she began to think that Majorca would not be so bad after all. But that was weakness. She hadn't come so far simply to give up. She would achieve her goal. She *had* to achieve it. Apart from anything else, it was the only goal she had.

She looked up at Richard and smiled.

'Is this the largest house on the Greyworth estate?'

'I don't think so,' said Richard. 'One of the largest, I suppose.'

'The Tillings have got eight bedrooms,' volunteered Antony. 'And a snooker room.'

'There you are.' Richard grinned. 'Trust Antony to be on the ball.'

Antony said nothing. He found the sight of Fleur across the table from him unsettling. Was this woman really going out with his dad? She was gorgeous. Gorgeous! And she made his dad look different. When the two of them had arrived the night before, all smart and glamorous looking, they'd looked as if they came from someone else's family. His dad didn't look like his dad. And Fleur certainly didn't look like anyone's mum. But she wasn't a floosie, either, thought Antony. She wasn't a dolly-bird. She was just . . . beautiful.

Reaching for his cup, Richard saw Antony staring at Fleur with undisguised admiration. And in spite of himself, he felt a little dart of pride. That's right, my boy, he felt like saying. Life's not over for me yet. At the back of his mind ran guilty thoughts like a train: remembered images of Emily sitting just where Fleur now sat; memories of family breakfasts with Emily's tinkling laugh rising above the conversation. But he stamped on them every time they surfaced; refused to allow his sentimentality to get the better of him. Life was for living; happiness was for taking; Fleur was a wonderful woman. Sitting in the bright sunshine, there seemed nothing more to it than that.

After breakfast, Richard disappeared to get ready for golf. As he had explained to Fleur, today was the Banting Cup. Any other Saturday, he would have forgone golf to show her around the place. But the Banting Cup . . .

'Don't worry,' Fleur had said at once. 'I'll be fine.'

'We can meet up for a drink afterwards,' Richard had added. 'Gillian will bring you down to the clubhouse.' He'd paused, and his brow had wrinkled. 'Do you mind?'

'Of course not,' Fleur had said, laughing. 'I'll have a lovely morning on my own.'

'You won't be on your own!' Richard had said. 'Gillian will look after you.'

Now Fleur eyed Gillian thoughtfully. She was taking clean plates from the dishwasher and stacking them in a pile. Every time she bent down she gave a little sigh; every time she stood up she looked as though the effort might kill her.

'Lovely plates,' said Fleur, getting up. 'Simply beautiful. Did you choose them?'

'What, these?' said Gillian. She looked at the plate in her hand as though she hated it. 'Oh no. Emily chose them. Richard's wife.' She paused, and her voice became harsher. 'She was my sister.'

'I see,' said Fleur.

Well, it hadn't taken long to get on to that subject, she thought. The dead, blameless wife. Perhaps she had underestimated this Gillian. Perhaps the attack would begin now. The pursed lips, the hissed threats. *You're not welcome in my kitchen*. She stood, watching Gillian and waiting. But Gillian's face remained impassive; pale and pouchy like an undercooked scone.

'Do you play golf?' said Fleur eventually.

'A little.'

'I don't play at all, I'm afraid. I must try to learn.'

Gillian didn't reply. She had begun to put the plates back on the dresser. They were hand-painted pottery plates, each decorated with a different farmyard animal. If they were going to be displayed, thought Fleur, they should at least go the right way up. But Gillian didn't seem to notice. Each plate went back on the dresser with a crash, until the top shelf and half the second shelf were filled with animals at assorted angles. Then all of a sudden the animals came to an end and she began to fill the rest of the shelves with blue and white patterned china. No! Fleur wanted to exclaim. Can't you see how ugly that looks? It would take two minutes to make it look nice.

'Lovely,' she said, as Gillian finished. 'I adore farmhouse kitchens.'

'It's difficult to keep clean,' said Gillian glumly. 'All these tiles. You chop vegetables and all the bits go in between.'

Fleur looked around vaguely, wondering what she could find to say on the subject of chopped vegetables. The room reminded her uncomfortably of a kitchen in Scotland in which she'd shivered for an entire shooting season, only to discover at the end that her titled host was not only heavily in debt, but had been two-timing her all along. Bloody upper classes, she thought savagely. Waste-of-time losers.

'Excuse me,' said Gillian. 'I've got to get to that

cupboard.' She reached down, past Fleur, and emerged with a grater.

'Let me help,' said Fleur. 'I'm sure there's something I can do.'

'It's easier if I do it myself.' Gillian's shoulders were hunched and her eyes refused to meet Fleur's. Fleur gave an inward shrug.

'OK,' she said. 'Well, I might pop upstairs and do some bits and pieces. What time are we going to the clubhouse?'

'Twelve,' said Gillian, without looking up.

'Plenty of time, thought Fleur, as she made her way up the stairs. With Richard and Antony both out and Gillian grating away in the kitchen, now was the perfect opportunity to find out what she needed. She walked slowly down the corridor, mentally valuing as she went. The wallpaper was dull but expensive; the pictures were dull and cheap. All the good paintings had obviously been crammed into the drawing room downstairs, where visitors could see them. Emily Favour, she thought, had probably been the sort of woman to wear expensive dresses and cheap underclothes.

She walked straight past the door to her bedroom and turned down a tiny flight of stairs. The beauty of being new to a house was that one could always claim to be lost. Especially since the guided tour the night before had been so vague. 'Down there's my office,' Richard had said, gesturing towards the stairs. And Fleur had not so much as flickered, but had given a tiny yawn and said, 'All that wine's making me feel snoozy!'

Now she descended the flight of stairs with determination. At last she was starting on the real business in hand. Behind that door she would discover the true extent of Richard's potential – whether he was worth bothering with, and how much she could take him for. She would quickly work out whether it was worth waiting for a particular time in the year; if there were any unusual factors she should take into account. She suspected not. Most men's financial affairs were remarkably similar. It was the men themselves who differed.

The thought of a new project filled her with a slight exhilaration, and she felt her heart beat more quickly as she reached for the door handle and pushed. But the door didn't budge. She tried again – but it was no good. The door to the office was locked.

For a few seconds she stared at the glossy white panels in outrage. What kind of man locked the door to the office in his own house? She tried the handle one more time. Definitely locked. She felt like giving it a little kick. Then self-discipline took over. There was no point lingering there and risking being seen. Quickly she turned and retreated up the steps, down the corridor and into her room. She sat down on her bed and gazed crossly at her reflection in the mirror. What was she going to do now? That door stood between her and all the details she needed. How could she proceed without the right information?

'Damn and blast,' she said aloud. 'Blast and damn. Damn and blast.' Eventually the sound of her own voice cheered her. It wasn't so bad. She would work something out. Richard couldn't keep the office locked all the time – and if he did, she would just have to find the key. Meanwhile . . . Fleur ran an idle hand through her hair. Meanwhile, she could always have a nice long bath and wash her hair.

At half-past eleven Gillian came trudging up the stairs. Fleur thought for a moment then, still wearing her dressing gown, she came out onto the landing. Gillian would prove a distraction, if nothing else.

'Gillian, what shall I wear to the clubhouse?' she asked. She tried to meet Gillian's eye. 'Tell me what to wear.' Gillian gave a little shrug.

'There aren't really any rules. Fairly smart, I suppose.'

'Too vague! You'll have to come and help me decide. Come on!' Fleur went back into her room and after a moment's hesitation, Gillian followed.

'My smartest clothes are all black.' said Fleur. 'Does anyone at the golf club wear black?'

'Not really,' said Gillian.

'I didn't think so.' Fleur gave a dramatic little sigh. 'And I so wanted to blend in. Can I see what you're wearing?'

'I'm not wearing anything special,' said Gillian in a rough, almost angry voice. 'Just a blue dress.'

'Blue! I tell you what . . .' Fleur rummaged around in one of her bags. 'Do you want to borrow this?' She produced a long blue silk scarf and draped it over Gillian's shoulder. 'Some fool gave it to me. Do I look the sort of woman who can wear blue?' She rolled her eyes at Gillian and lowered her voice. 'He also seemed to think I was size eight and liked wearing red underwear.' She shrugged. 'What can you do?'

Gillian stared back at Fleur feeling her colour rise. Something unfamiliar was happening at the back of her throat. It felt a bit like laughter.

'But it should suit you perfectly,' said Fleur. 'It's exactly the same colour as your eyes. I wish I had blue eyes!' She scrutinized Gillian's eyes and Gillian began to feel hot.

'Thank you,' she said abruptly. She looked down at the blue silk. 'I'll try it. But I'm not sure it'll suit the dress.'

'Shall I come and help you? I know how to tie these things.'

'No!' Gillian almost shouted. Fleur was overwhelming her. She had to get away. 'I'll just go now and change. And I'll see.' She hurried out of the room.

In the safety of her own bedroom Gillian stopped. She picked up the end of the scarf and rubbed the smooth fabric across her face. It smelt sweet. Like Fleur. Sweet and soft and bright.

Gillian sat down at her dressing table. Fleur's voice rang in her ears. A bubble of laughter was still at the back of her throat. She felt enlivened; out of breath; almost overcome. That's charm, she suddenly thought. Real charm wasn't the gushing and kisses of the frosted women at the golf club. Emily had been called a charming woman, but her eyes had held splinters of ice and her tinkling laugh had been saccharine and humourless. Fleur's eyes were warm and all-inclusive and when she laughed she made everyone else want to laugh too. That was real charm. Of course Fleur didn't really mean any of it. She didn't really want blue eyes; she didn't really need Gillian's advice. Nor – Gillian was sure – did she want to blend in with the others at the golf club. But, just for a few seconds, she'd made Gillian feel warm and wanted and in on the joke. Never before had Gillian been in on the joke.

The clubhouse at Greyworth had been built in an American colonial style, with a large wooden veranda overlooking the eighteenth green.

'Is this the bar?' asked Fleur as they arrived. She looked around at the tables and chairs; the gins: the flushed, jolly faces.

'The bar's in there. But in the summer everyone sits outside. It's terribly hard to get a table.' Gillian looked around, eyes screwed up. 'I think they're all taken.' She sighed. 'What would you like to drink?'

'A Manhattan,' said Fleur. Gillian looked at her dubiously.

'What's that?'

'They'll know.'

'Well . . . all right then.'

'Wait a moment,' said Fleur. She reached towards Gillian and tugged at the ends of the blue scarf. 'You need to drape it more. Like this. Don't let it get wrinkled up. OK?' Gillian gave a tiny shrug.

'It's all such a fuss.'

'The fuss is what makes it fun,' said Fleur. 'Like having seams on your stockings. You have to check them every five minutes.'

Gillian's expression became gloomier still.

'Well, I'll get the drinks,' she said. 'I expect there'll be an awful queue.'

'Do you want some help?' Fleur asked.

'No, you'd better stay out here and wait for a table.'

She began to walk towards the glass doors leading to the bar. As she reached them she slowed very slightly, almost imperceptibly reached for the ends of the scarf, and pulled them into place. Fleur gave a tiny smile. Then, moving unhurriedly, she turned and looked around the veranda. She was aware that she had begun to attract a few interested glances. Red-faced golfing men were leaning across to their chums; sharp-eyed golfing women were nudging each other.

Quickly Fleur assessed the tables on the veranda. Some overlooked the golf course, some didn't. Some had parasols, others didn't. The best one was in the corner, she decided. It was large and round, and there were only two men sitting at it. Without hesitating, Fleur walked over and smiled at the plumper of the two men. He was dressed in a bright yellow jersey and halfway down a silver tankard of beer.

'Hello,' she said. 'Are you two alone?' The plump man became a degree pinker and cleared his throat.

'Our wives will be joining us.'

'Oh dear.' Fleur began to count the chairs. 'Might

there still be room for my friend and me? She's just getting our drinks.'

The men glanced at each other.

'The thing is,' continued Fleur, 'I'd so like to look at the golf course.' She began to edge towards the table. 'It's very beautiful, isn't it?'

'One of the best in Surrey,' said the thinner man gruffly.

'Just look at those trees!' said Fleur, gesturing. Both men followed her gaze. By the time they turned back, she was sitting down on one of the spare chairs. 'Have you been playing today?' she said.

'Now look here,' said one of the men awkwardly. 'I don't mean to . . .'

'Did you play in the Banting Cup? What exactly *is* the Banting Cup?'

'Are you a new member? Because if you are . . .'

'I'm not a member at all,' said Fleur.

'You're not a member? Do you have a guest pass?'

'I'm not sure,' said Fleur vaguely.

'This is bloody typical,' said the thinner man to the yellow-jerseyed man. 'Absolutely no bloody security.' He turned to Fleur. 'Now look, young woman, I'm afraid I'm going to have to ask you . . .'

'Young woman?' said Fleur, sparkling at him. 'You are kind.'

He stood up angrily.

'Are you aware that this is a private club and that trespassers will be prosecuted? Now I think the best thing is for you and your friend . . .'

'Oh, here comes Gillian,' interrupted Fleur. 'Hello, Gillian. These nice men are letting us sit at their table.'

'Hello, George,' said Gillian. 'Is anything wrong?'

There was a tiny silence, during which Fleur turned unconcernedly away. A confused, embarrassed conversation broke out behind her. The men hadn't realized that Fleur's friend was Gillian! They'd had no idea. They'd thought . . . No, of course they hadn't thought. Well, anyway . . . a small world, wasn't it? What a small world. And there were the drinks.

'Mine's the Manhattan,' said Fleur, turning round. 'How do you do? My name is Fleur Daxeny.'

'Alistair Lennox.'

'George Tilling.'

'I've found my guest pass,' said Fleur. 'Do you want to see it?' Both the men began to harrumph awkwardly.

'Any friend of Gillian's . . .' began one.

'Actually, I'm more a friend of Richard's,' said Fleur.

'An old friend?'

'No, a new friend.'

There was a pause, during which a flash of comprehension passed through George Tilling's eyes. Now you remember, thought Fleur. I'm that piece of gossip your wife was trying to tell you while you were reading the newspaper. Now you wish you'd listened a bit harder, don't you? And she gave him a tiny smile.

'You realize you're the subject of a lot of gossip?' said Alec, as they reached the seventeenth green. Richard gave a little smile, and took out his putter.

'So I gather.' He looked up at his old friend; kindly and concerned. 'What you don't realize is that being the subject of gossip is actually quite fun.'

'It's no joke,' said Alec. His Scottish accent was becoming more pronounced, as it always did when he was anxious. 'They're saying . . .' He broke off.

'What are they saying?' Richard held up a hand. 'Let me putt first.'

With no hesitation he sank the ball from ten feet.

'Good shot,' said Alec automatically. 'You're playing well today.'

'What are they saying? Come on, Alec. You might as well get it off your chest.' Alec paused. A look of pain passed across his face.

'They're saying that if you persist with this woman, you might not be nominated for captain after all.' Richard's mouth tightened.

'I see,' he said. 'And have any of them actually met "this woman", as you so charmingly put it?'

'I think Eleanor's been saying . . .'

'Eleanor met Fleur once, briefly, in a London restaurant. She has absolutely no right . . .'

'Rights and wrongs don't come into it. You know that. If the club takes against Fleur . . .'

'Why should they?'

'Well . . . She's quite different from Emily, isn't she?'

Richard had known Alec since the age of seven and had never before in his life felt like hitting him. But now he felt a surge of violent anger against Alec; against them all. He watched in silence as Alec muffed his putt, feeling his fists clench and his jaw tighten. As the ball eventually plopped into the hole, Alec looked up and met his tense stare.

'Look,' he said apologetically. 'You may not care what the club thinks. But . . . well, it's not just the club. I'm worried for you. You have to admit that Fleur seems to have taken over your entire life.' He replaced the flag and they began to walk slowly towards the eighteenth tee.

'You're worried for me,' repeated Richard. 'And what exactly are you worried about? That I might be enjoying myself too much? That I might be happier now than I've ever been in my life before?'

'Richard . . .'

'Well what, then?'

'I'm just worried you'll be hurt, I suppose.' Alec looked away awkwardly.

'My word,' said Richard. 'We are becoming frank with one another.'

'You know what I mean.'

'All I know is that I'm happy, Fleur's happy, and the rest of you should mind your own business.'

'But you've just plunged in . . .'

'Yes, I've plunged in. And do you know what? I've discovered that plunging in is the best way to live.'

They had reached the tee. Richard took out his ball and looked straight at Alec.

'Have you ever plunged into anything in your life?' Alec was silent. 'I didn't think so. Well, you know, maybe you should try it.'

Richard placed his ball on the tee and, with a set jaw, took a few practice swings. The eighteenth was long and tricky, looping round a little lake to the right. Richard and Alec had always agreed that it was safer to play round the lake than to risk losing a ball in the water. But today, without looking at Alec, Richard hit the ball boldly to the right, directly towards the lake. They both watched in silence as the little ball soared over the surface of the water and landed safely on the fairway.

'I think . . . you made it,' said Alec faintly.

'Yes,' said Richard. He didn't sound surprised. 'I made it. You probably would too.'

'I don't think I'd try.'

'Yes well,' said Richard. 'Maybe that's the difference between us.'

# SIX

To Fleur's astonishment, it was four weeks later. The July sun streamed into the conservatory every morning, Antony was home from school for the holidays, Richard's lower arms were turning brown. Talk at the clubhouse was of nothing but flights, villas and housesitters.

Fleur was now a familiar figure at the clubhouse. Most mornings, when Richard had gone off to the office, she and Gillian had taken to strolling down to the Greyworth health club – for which Richard had bought Fleur a season's membership. They would swim a little, sit in the Jacuzzi a little, drink a glass of fresh passion fruit juice and stroll back again. It was a pleasant, gentle routine, which even Gillian now appeared to enjoy – despite her initial resistance. Persuading her to come along the first time had been almost impossible and Fleur had only succeeded by appealing to Gillian's sense of duty as a hostess. Most of Gillian's life, it seemed, was governed by a sense of duty – a concept completely alien to Fleur.

She took a sip of coffee and shut her eyes, feeling the sun on her face. Breakfast was over; the conservatory was now empty apart from her. Richard had gone off for a meeting with his lawyer; he'd be coming back later for a round of golf with Lambert and some business contact or other. Antony was off somewhere doing, she supposed, teenage things. Gillian was upstairs, supervising the cleaner. Supervision – another concept completely alien to Fleur. One either did a task oneself, she thought, or one left it to other people and didn't bother about it. But then, she'd always been lazy. And she was becoming lazier. Too lazy.

A pang of self-reproach darted through her. She'd been living in Richard Favour's house for four weeks. Four weeks! And what had she accomplished in that time? Nothing. After the initial attempt on his office she'd let the subject of money slip comfortably from her mind; let herself slide into an easy sunlit existence in which one day melted into another and suddenly she was four weeks older. Four weeks older and not a penny richer. She hadn't even gone near his office again. For all she knew, it was unlocked and stashed full of gold bullion.

'A penny for your thoughts,' said Gillian, appearing at the door of the conservatory.

'They're worth more than a penny,' retorted Fleur cheerfully. 'A lot more.'

She looked quizzically at Gillian's attire. She was wearing a tangerine-coloured dress with a nasty, fussy neckline and, draped straight across it, Fleur's blue scarf. Not a day went by now without Gillian wearing that scarf, always in exactly the way Fleur had shown her – no matter what the outfit. Fleur supposed she should be flattered, but instead she was beginning to feel irritated. Was the only answer to supply the woman with a scarf in every colour?

'We'd better be off in a moment,' said Gillian. 'I don't know what the form is. Maybe everybody arrives late. Fashionably late.' She attempted a little laugh.

'Fashionably late is out,' said Fleur idly. 'Although I suppose it might still be fashionable in Surrey.'

This afternoon, she thought to herself. This afternoon she'd have another shot. Perhaps while Richard was out on the golf course. She could keep Gillian in the kitchen by suggesting that she make a cake. And maybe she could find some reason to borrow Richard's keys. She would be in and out before anyone even wondered where she was.

'I don't know who'll be there,' Gillian was saying. 'I've never been to this kind of thing before.'

Gillian seemed unusually loquacious, thought Fleur. She raised her eyes and Gillian met them imploringly. My God, she's nervous, thought Fleur. I'm the impostor and she's the one who's nervous.

They were about to walk down to Eleanor Forrester's house, to have brunch and look at the range of jewellery which Eleanor energetically sold whenever she had the chance. Gillian had apparently never been to one of Eleanor's brunch mornings before. Reading between the lines, thought Fleur, Gillian had never been asked before.

Fleur's own instinct, when Eleanor had asked her, had been to turn the invitation down. But then she'd seen Richard's delighted smile, and she'd remembered her own guiding principle. If a man smiles, do it again; if he smiles again, don't stop.

'Of course,' she'd said, darting a glance at Gillian's stiff, averted cheek. 'We'd love to come, wouldn't we Gillian?' After that, she hadn't known which to enjoy most, the embarrassed expression on Gillian's face or the discomfited one on Eleanor Forrester's.

Gillian was shifting from one foot to another and mangling the end of the scarf in her anxious fingers. For the sake of the scarf if nothing else, Fleur got to her feet.

'OK,' she said. 'Let's go and look at this woman's baubles.'

Eleanor's garden was large and sloping with many arbours and wrought-iron benches. Two trestle tables had been erected on the lawn; one covered with food, the other with jewellery.

'Have some buck's fizz!' exclaimed Eleanor as they arrived. 'I don't have to ask if you're driving, do I? Did you hear about poor James Morrell?' she added in an undertone. 'Banned for a year. His wife's *furious*. Now, go and sit down. A lot of the girls are here already.'

The 'girls' were aged between thirty-five and sixty-five. They were all tanned, fit and vivacious. Many wore brightly coloured clothes with what looked like expensive appliqué work. Little tennis players careered across bosoms; little golfers danced up and down arms, endlessly striking tiny beaded golf balls.

'Aren't these fun?' said one woman, noticing Fleur's gaze. 'Foxy sells them! Polo shirts, trousers, everything, really. Foxy Harris. I'm sure she'll tell you about them when she arrives.'

'I'm sure she will,' murmured Fleur.

'Emily had quite a collection of Foxy's clothes,' chimed in another woman, dressed entirely in pink. 'She always looked absolutely lovely in them!'

Fleur said nothing.

'Were you a close friend of Emily's, Fleur?' asked the pink woman.

'Not really,' said Fleur.

'No, I thought you couldn't have been,' said the woman. 'I suppose I knew her the best out of all of us. I expect she mentioned me. Tricia Tilling.'

Fleur gestured vaguely with her hand.

'We all miss her,' said Tricia. She paused as though lost in memories. 'And of course, Richard was devoted to her. I used to think, I'll never see a couple as much in love as Richard and Emily Favour.' Fleur was aware of Gillian shifting awkwardly beside her. 'They were *made* for each other,' continued Tricia. 'Like . . . gin and tonic.'

'What a beautiful thought,' said Fleur.

Tricia's eyes met hers appraisingly.

'That's a lovely watch, Fleur,' she said. 'Did Richard

buy that for you?' She gave a little laugh. 'George is always buying me little things here and there.'

'Is he?' said Fleur. She idly fingered the watch and said nothing more. From the corner of her eye she was aware of Tricia's satisfied face.

'You know,' said Tricia, as though beginning on a new subject, 'poor Graham Loosemore has got into an awful pickle. You remember Graham?' There was, a murmur of assent.

'Well, he went to the Philippines on holiday – and married a local girl! All of eighteen. They're living together in Dorking!' There was a general gasp. 'She's after his money, of course.' Tricia drew up her face as though gathering the neck of a shoe-bag. 'She'll have a baby so she can claim support, and then she'll be off. She'll probably get . . . half the house? That's two hundred thousand pounds! And all for a silly mistake. The fool!'

'Maybe he's not a fool,' said Fleur idly, and winked at Gillian.

'What?' snapped Tricia.

'How much would you pay a strapping young Filipino to make love to you every night?' Fleur grinned at Tricia. 'I'd pay quite a lot.' Tricia goggled at Fleur.

'Just exactly what are you saying?' she whispered, in tones prepared to be astounded.

'I'm saying . . . maybe this girl is worth it.'

'Worth it?'

'Maybe she's worth two hundred thousand pounds. To him, at any rate.'

Tricia stared at Fleur as though suspecting trickery.

'These wealthy widowers have to be very careful,' she said eventually. 'They're terribly vulnerable.'

'So are wealthy widows,' said Fleur casually. 'I find I have to be on my guard constantly.' Tricia stiffened. But before she could speak, Eleanor Forrester's voice interrupted the group.

'More buck's fizz? And then I'll start the presentation. Did I tell you all about poor James Morrell?' she added, handing round glasses. 'Banned for a year! And he was only a tiny bit over the limit! I mean, which of us hasn't been a tiny bit over?'

'Me,' said Fleur, putting her glass down on the grass without drinking from it. 'I don't drive.'

A babble broke out around her. How could Fleur not drive? How did she manage? What about the school run? The shopping?

Tricia Tilling's voice rose truculently above the rest.

'I suppose you have a chauffeur, do you, Fleur?'

'Sometimes,' said Fleur.

Suddenly, without meaning to, she remembered sitting behind her father's driver in Dubai, leaning out of the window into the hot dusty street and being told in Arabic to sit still. They'd been driving past the gold souk. Where had they been going? Fleur couldn't remember.

'Now, are we ready?' Eleanor's voice pierced Fleur's consciousness. 'I'll start with brooches. Aren't these fun?'

She held up a gold tortoise and a diamanté spider

and began to talk. Fleur stared ahead politely. But the words washed over her. Memories, unbidden, were flooding into her mind. She was sitting with Nura el Hassan and they were giggling. Nura was dressed in pale silk; her small brown hands were holding a string of beads. They were a present; a ninth birthday present. She'd put them round Fleur's neck and they'd both giggled. Fleur hadn't admired the beads aloud. If she had done so, Nura would have been obliged, under custom, to give the beads to Fleur. So Fleur had simply smiled at Nura, and smiled at the beads, to let Nura know that she thought they were very pretty. Fleur knew Nura's customs better than her own. She had never known anything else.

Fleur had been born in Dubai, to a mother who ran off to South Africa with her lover six months later and a rather older father who equated bringing up a child with throwing money at it. In the shifting, rootless world of Dubai expatriates, Fleur learned to lose friends as easily as she made them, to greet a new intake at the British School at the beginning of every year and say goodbye to them at the end; to use people for the brief period that she had them – and then discard them before she herself was discarded. Throughout, only Nura bad remained constant. Many Islamic families would not allow the Christian – in truth, heathen – Fleur to play with their children. But Nura's mother admired the pretty, insolent little redhead; pitied the businessman who was having to raise a daughter as well as hold down a demanding job.

And then, when Fleur was only sixteen, her father had suddenly suffered massive liver failure. He had died leaving Fleur a surprisingly small amount of money: not enough for her to continue living in the luxury apartment; not enough for her to stay on at the British School. The el Hassan family had kindly taken Fleur in to live with them while her future was decided. For a few months, she and Nura had slept in next-door bedrooms. They had become closer than ever; had discussed and compared themselves endlessly. At the age of sixteen, Nura was considered ready to marry; her parents were in the process of arranging a match. Fleur was alternately aghast and fascinated at the thought.

'How can you stand it?' she would exclaim. 'Marrying some man who'll just boss you about?' Nura always simply shrugged and smiled. She was a remarkably pretty girl, with smooth skin, dancing eyes and rounded features verging already on plumpness.

'If he is too bossy, I will not marry him,' she said once.

'Won't your parents make you?'

'Of course not. They will let me meet him and then we will talk about it.'

Fleur stared her. Suddenly she felt jealous. Nura's life was being comfortably mapped out for her, while her own wavered uncertainly in front of her like a broken spider's web.

'Perhaps I could marry, like Nura,' she said the next day to Nura's mother, Fatima. She gave a little laugh, as though she were joking, but her eyes scanned Fatima's face sharply.

'I'm sure you will marry,' said Fatima. 'You will find a handsome Englishman.'

'Maybe I could marry an Arab,' said Fleur. Fatima laughed.

'Would you convert to Islam?'

'I might,' said Fleur desperately, 'if I had to.'

Fatima looked up. 'Are you serious?'

Fleur gave a tiny shrug. 'You could . . . find me someone.'

'Fleur.' Fatima rose and took Fleur's hands. 'You know you would not make a suitable bride for an Arab. It is not just that you are not Islamic. You would find the life too difficult. Your husband would not allow you to answer back in the way that we do. You would not be allowed to go out without his permission. My husband is very liberal. Most are not.'

'Are you going to find a liberal man for Nura?'

'We hope so, yes. And you will find a man too, Fleur. But not here.'

Two days later the betrothal was announced. Nura was to marry Mohammed Abduraman, a young man from one of the wealthiest families in the Emirates. It was generally acknowledged that she had done very well indeed.

'But do you love him?' asked Fleur that night.

'Of course I love him,' said Nura. But her eyes were distant, and she wouldn't discuss it further.

Immediately the family was plunged into

preparation. Fleur wandered about, unnoticed, watching with disbelief the amount of money being spent on the wedding. The bolts of silk, the food, the gifts for all the guests. Nura was whisked away into a whirl of veils and scented oils. Soon she would be whisked away for ever. Fleur would be on her own. What was she to do? The el Hassan family didn't want her any more. Nobody wanted her any more.

At nights she lay quite still, smelling the sweet musky scent of the house, allowing the tears to trickle down the sides of her face, trying to plot her future. Nura's parents thought she should go back to England, to the aunt in Maidenhead whom she'd never met.

'Your family is the most important,' Fatima had said, with the confidence of one surrounded by an extended web of loyal family members. 'Your own family will care for you.'

Fleur knew she was wrong. It was different in England. Her father's sister had never shown any interest in her. She was going to have to rely on herself.

And then Nura's betrothal party had been held. It was an all-female affair, with sweetmeats and games and much giggling. Halfway through, Nura took out a little box.

'Look,' she said. 'My betrothal ring.'

On her hand it looked almost incongruous, a huge diamond set in an intricate web of gold. The room was filled with satisfactory gasps; even by Arabic standards it was enormous.

That's got to be worth a hundred thousand dollars,

thought Fleur. At least. A hundred thousand dollars, sitting on Nura's finger. It's not even as though she's ever going to be able to show it off properly. She'll probably hardly ever wear it. A hundred thousand dollars. What could you do with a hundred thousand dollars?

And then, before she could stop herself, it happened. Fleur put her cup down, stared straight at Nura and said,

'I do so admire your diamond ring, Nura. I admire it greatly. I wish I had one like it.'

The room fell silent. Nura turned pale; her lips began to quiver. Her eyes met Fleur's, shocked and hurt. There was an infinitesimal pause, during which no-one seemed to breathe. Everyone in the room leaned forward. Then, slowly and carefully, Nura loosened the diamond ring from her finger, reached out and dropped it into Fleur's lap. She looked at it for a moment, then rose and left the room. Fleur's last image of Nura was two dark, betrayed eyes.

That night, Fleur had sold the diamond for a hundred and twenty thousand dollars. She'd caught a flight to New York the next morning and she'd never seen Nura again.

Now, nearly twenty-five years later, sitting in Eleanor Forrester's garden, Fleur felt a wrenching in her chest, a hotness in her eyes. If I end up mediocre, she thought furiously – if I end up the English housewife I could have been all along – then the diamond was for nothing. I lost Nura for nothing. And I can't stand that. I can't *stand* it.

She blinked hard, and looked up, and focused anew on the gilt chain which Eleanor Forrester was holding aloft. I'll buy a necklace, she thought, and I'll have brunch, and then I'll take Richard Favour for everything I can.

Oliver Sterndale leaned back in his chair and looked at Richard with mild exasperation.

'You do realize,' he said for the third time, 'that once this money goes into trust, it's not your money anymore?'

'I know,' said Richard. 'That's the whole point. It'll be the children's.'

'It's a lot of money.'

'I know it's a lot of money.'

They both looked down at the numbers in front of them. The figure in question was underlined at the bottom of the page – a single one followed by a trail of noughts like a little caterpillar.

'It's not that much,' said Richard. 'Not really. And I do want the children to have it. Emily and I agreed.'

Oliver sighed, and began to tap his pen against his hand.

'Death duties . . .' he began.

'This isn't about death duties. This is about . . . security.'

'You can give your children security without signing over vast amounts of money to them. Why not buy Philippa a house?'

'Why not give her a vast amount of money?' There

was the glimmer of a smile on Richard's face. 'In the end it doesn't make much difference.'

'It makes a huge difference! All sorts of things could happen to make you regret handing over your entire fortune prematurely.'

'Hardly my entire fortune!'

'A subtantial part of it.'

'Emily and I discussed it. We agreed that it would be perfectly possible to live comfortably on the remainder. And there's always the company.'

The lawyer leaned back in his chair, thoughts battling against each other in his face.

'When did you decide all this?' he asked at last. 'Remind me.'

'Around two years ago.'

'And did Emily know then that . . .'

'That she was going to die? Yes, she did. But I don't see what relevance that has.' Oliver stared at Richard. For a moment he seemed about to say something, then he sighed and looked away.

'Oh, I don't know,' he muttered. 'What I *do* know,' he stated more firmly, 'is that by giving away such a large quantity of money you may be hampering your own future.'

'Oliver, don't be melodramatic!'

'What you and Emily may not have considered is the possibility that your life might change to some degree after she died. I understand you have a . . . friend staying at the moment.'

'A woman, yes.' Richard smiled. 'Her name's Fleur.'

'Well then.' Oliver paused. 'It may seem a ridiculous idea now. But what would happen if you were, say, to remarry?'

'It doesn't seem a ridiculous idea,' said Richard slowly. 'But I can't see what it has to do with giving this money to Philippa and Antony. What does money have to do with marriage?' The lawyer looked aghast.

'You're not serious?'

'Half-serious.' Richard relented. 'Look, Oliver, I'll think about it. I won't rush into anything. But you know, I'm going to have to do something with the money sooner or later. I've been gradually liquidizing it over the last few months.'

'It won't do any harm in a deposit account for a while. Better to lose a bit of income than rush into the wrong decision.' Oliver Suddenly looked up. 'You haven't told either of the children about this plan? They aren't expecting it?'

'Oh no. Emily and I agreed it would be better for them not to know. And also that they should wait till the age of thirty before coming into control of the money. We didn't want them thinking they didn't have to make an effort in life.'

'Very wise. And no-one else knows?'

'No. No-one else.'

Oliver sighed and pressed the buzzer on his desk for more coffee.

'Well, I suppose that's something.'

* * *

The money was his. Practically his. As soon as Philippa turned thirty . . . Lambert's grip tightened irritably on the steering wheel. What was so magic about the age of thirty? What would she have at the age of thirty that she didn't have at the age of twenty-eight?

When Emily had first told him about Philippa's money, he'd thought she meant straight away. Next week. He'd felt an exploding exhilaration rush through his body, which must have shown in his face, because she'd smiled – a satisfied smile – and said, 'She won't come into it till she's thirty, of course.' And he'd smiled back knowingly, and said 'Of course,' when really he'd been thinking, Why not? Why the fuck not!

Bloody Emily. Of course she'd done it deliberately. Told him early so she could watch him waiting. It was just another of her power games. Lambert smiled unwillingly to himself. He missed Emily. She'd been the only one in this whole blasted family that he'd really clicked with, from the moment they'd first met. It had been at a company reception, soon after he'd been taken on as technical director. She'd been standing quietly next to Richard, listening to the jovial anecdotes of the marketing director – a man whom, it later transpired, she despised. Lambert's eyes had caught hers off-guard – and in an instant he'd seen through that gentle, docile manner to the steely contempt behind. He'd seen the real Emily. As she'd met his gaze she'd clearly realized how much she'd given away. 'Introduce me to this nice young man,' she'd immediately said to Richard. And as Lambert's hand had met hers, her mouth had twisted up in a faint acknowledgement.

Two weeks later he'd been invited to The Maples for the weekend. He'd bought a new blazer, played golf with Richard and taken walks round the garden with Emily. She had done most of the talking. She'd spoken on a series of vague, apparently unconnected topics. Her dislike of the marketing director; her admiration for those who understood computers; her desire for Lambert to become acquainted with the rest of her family. Some weeks after that, the marketing director had been fired for sending out a computer mailshot full of embarrassing mistakes. It was about the same time, remembered Lambert, that Richard had upgraded Lambert's company car. 'Emily's been chiding me,' he'd said with a smile. 'She thinks we'll lose you if we don't treat you properly!'

And then he'd been invited down to The Maples again, and introduced to Philippa. Philippa's boyfriend Jim had been there too, a long-limbed lad of twenty-two who had just left university and wasn't quite sure what he wanted to do next. But as Enilly had later explained to everyone in the clubhouse bar, Lambert had quite literally swept Philippa off her feet. 'On the sixteenth hole!' she'd added, with a little laugh. 'Philippa lost her ball in that boggy patch. She got stuck, and Lambert just lifted her up and carried her back to the fairway!' Now Lambert frowned at the memory. Philippa had been heavier than he expected; he'd nearly pulled a muscle heaving her up out of that mud. On the other hand, she'd also been richer than he'd expected. He'd married Philippa thinking he was buying himself financial security. The news that he was in fact going to be extremely rich had come as an unexpected prize.

He glanced out of the car window. The dreary suburbs of outer London were beginning to turn into Surrey; they'd be at Greyworth in half an hour. Philippa was silent in the seat next to him, engrossed in one of her romantic novels. His wife, the millionairess. The multimillionairess, if Emily had been speaking the truth. Except she wasn't a millionairess, not yet. A familiar resentment ran through Lambert and he felt his teeth begin to grind together. It was unreasonable, treating Philippa like a child who couldn't be trusted. If she was to have the money anyway, then why not give it to her straight away? And why keep it a secret from her? Neither she nor Antony seemed to have any inkling that they were potentially very rich people: that they would never have to work if they didn't want to; that life was going to be easy for them. When Philippa sighed and fretted over the price of a new pair of shoes, Lambert felt like shouting, For God's sake, you could afford twenty pairs if you wanted them! But he never did. He didn't want his wife planning how to spend her money. He had plans enough of his own.

He glanced in his rear-view mirror at a Lagonda roaring up the fast lane and his grip tightened covetously on the wheel. Two years, he thought. Only two years to go. His only problem at the moment was the bank. Lambert frowned. He had to think of a solution to the bank problem. Fucking morons. Did they want the business of a potentially very rich person, or what? In the last few weeks, one idiot after another had been calling him, asking to arrange a meeting, querying his overdraft again and again. He was going to have to do something, before they got it into their little heads to call Philippa. She didn't know anything about it. She didn't even know he had that third account.

Again, Lambert went over the possibilities in his mind. The first was to ignore the bank completely. The second was to go along and see them, admit he didn't have the funds to pay off the overdraft and get an extension on it until Philippa came into her money. A two-year extension? It wasn't inconceivable. But neither was it very likely. They might decide they needed more assurance than that. They might decide to call his employer for a guarantee. Lambert scowled. They'd call Richard. He could just imagine Richard's sanctimonious attitude. Perfect, organized Richard, who never even had a gas bill outstanding. He would call Lambert into his office. He would talk about living within one's means. He'd quote fucking Dickens at him.

No. That wouldn't do. Lambert paused, and took a deep breath. The third option was somehow to keep the piranhas at the bank happy. Lob a healthy chunk of money at them. Fifty thousand pounds or so. At the same time, he could imply that he considered their lack of trust in him most surprising, bearing in mind his future prospects. He could talk about taking his money elsewhere. Put the wind up them properly. Lambert smiled grimly to himself. That was the best option of the three. By far the best. It had almost no disadvantages – just one. Which was that he didn't have fifty thousand pounds. Not yet.

# SEVEN

As they pulled into the drive of The Maples, Philippa looked up from her romantic novel with bleary eyes.

'Are we here already?'

'No, we're on fucking Mars.'

'I haven't finished! Give me two minutes. I must just see what happens. I mean, I know what's going to happen, but I must just see . . .' She tailed off. Already her eyes were back down on the page, greedily devouring the text like a box of Milk Tray.

'For God's sake,' said Lambert. 'Well, I'm not sitting around here.' He got out of the car and banged the door shut. Philippa didn't flicker.

The front door was open but the house felt empty. Lambert stood in the hall and cautiously looked around. No sign of Gillian. Richard's car wasn't there; maybe he and, his redhead had gone out together. Maybe no-one was about. Maybe he had the house to himself.

Lambert felt a thrill of satisfaction. He hadn't

expected this. He'd thought he would have to creep about at night, or maybe even wait until another time. But this was perfect. He could put his plan into action at once.

Swiftly he mounted the broad staircase. The corridor upstairs was quiet and motionless. He stopped at the top of the stairs, listening for sounds of life. But there were none. Looking behind him to check once more that he wasn't being observed, Lambert moved cautiously towards Richard's office. It was a tucked-away room, completely separate from the bedrooms and usually kept locked. If anyone saw him there it would be impossible to pretend that he'd strayed there on the way somewhere else.

Not that it should matter, thought Lambert, fingering the key in his pocket. Richard trusted him. After all, he'd given him a key to the office – just in case of emergency, he'd said. If questioned, Lambert could always say that he'd been after some piece of information to do with the company. In fact Richard kept very little company information at home. But he would give Lambert the benefit of the doubt. People generally did.

The office door was closed. But as he tried to turn the key he realized that it was unlocked. Quickly he put the key away in his pocket. This way, if anyone saw him, he would be on safe ground. ('I saw the door was open, Richard, so I thought I'd better just check . . .') He went inside, and quickly headed for the filing cabinet. Bank statements, he muttered under his breath. Bank statements. He opened a drawer and began to flip through the files.

Fifty thousand pounds wasn't a lot of money. Not for someone like Richard, it wasn't. Richard had so much money, he could easily spare that much. He would never even notice it was missing. Lambert would borrow fifty grand, use it to solve his problems with the bank and then put it back. Five thousand pounds here, ten thousand pounds there – he'd take it out in bits and pieces, then put it back again when he had the chance. As long as the bottom lines added up at the end of the year, no-one would be the wiser.

Forging Richard's signature wasn't a problem. Setting up the transfers wasn't a problem. Deciding which accounts to go into was more tricky. He didn't want to find he'd wiped out the housekeeping account, or this year's holiday fund. Knowing Richard, every bit of money, large or small, was probably allocated to something or other. He would have to be careful.

Lambert closed the top drawer and opened the second one down. He began to flip through the files. Suddenly a sound made him stop, fingers still poised. Something was behind him. Something – or someone . . .

He spun round, and felt his face freeze in disbelief. Sitting at Richard's desk, legs calmly crossed, was Fleur. His mind began to race. Had she been there all the time? Had she seen him . . .

'Hello Lambert,' said Fleur pleasantly. 'What are you doing in here?'

* * *

Philippa finished the last page of her book and leaned back, feeling both satisfied and slightly sick. Words and images jangled in her mind; in her nostrils the aroma of car upholstery mingled uneasily with the lingering smell of Lambert's driving peppermints. She opened the door and breathed in dazedly, trying to wrench herself away from fiction, into reality. But in her mind she was still on the Swiss Alps with Pierre, the dashing ski instructor. Pierre's manly mouth was on hers; his hands were in her hair; music was playing in the background . . . When Gillian suddenly banged on the car she gave a little shriek and jumped, bashing her head against the window frame.

'I've been picking strawberries,' said Gillian. 'Do you want a drink?'

'Oh,' said Philippa. 'Yes. I could do with a cup of coffee.'

She got out of the car with stiff, stumbling legs, shook herself down and followed Gillian into the house. Pierre and the Alps began to recede from her mind like an ill-remembered dream.

'Is Daddy out?' she said, sitting feebly down on a kitchen chair.

'He's at a meeting with Oliver Sterndale,' said Gillian. 'Antony's out, too.' She began to run water into the kettle.

'I suppose we are a bit early. What about . . .' Philippa pulled a tiny face.

'What about what?'

'You know. Fleur!'

'What about her?' said Gillian shortly.

'Well . . . where is she?'

'I don't know,' said Gillian. She paused. 'We only got back from Eleanors brunch a short while ago.'

'Eleanor's brunch?'

'Yes.'

'You went to Eleanor Forrester's brunch?'

'Yes.' Gillian's face seemed to close up under Philippa's astonished gaze. 'A lot of nonsense, really,' she added roughly.

'Did you buy anything?'

'I did in the end. This.' Gillian pulled aside her blue scarf to reveal a little gold tortoise sitting on her lapel. She frowned. 'I don't know if I'm wearing it right. It'll probably pull at the fabric and spoil the dress.'

Philippa stared at the little tortoise. Gillian never bought brooches. Neither did she usually go to Eleanor's brunches. It had always been Philippa and her mother who went, while Gillian stayed behind. Gillian had always stayed behind. And now, thought Philippa with a sudden jealousy, it was Gillian and Fleur who had gone, and she who had been left behind.

Fleur did so enjoy shocking men. It was almost worth the inconvenience of being interrupted to see Lambert's face staring speechlessly at her. Almost, but not quite. For things had been going so well until he'd arrived. She'd found the office door unlocked, had quickly slipped in and begun to look for what she wanted. And she would have found it, too, if she hadn't been interrupted. Richard was obviously a highly organized person. Everything in his office was filed and listed and paperclipped. She'd headed first of all to his desk, in search of recent correspondence – and had been rootling through his desk drawer when the door opened and Lambert came in.

Immediately, she had sunk underneath the desk, with an ease borne of practice. For a few minutes she'd wondered whether or not to get up. Should she keep still and wait until he'd gone? Or might Lambert glance over and spot her? Certainly it would be better to surprise him than to be discovered cowering under the furniture.

Then she'd noticed that Lambert didn't look quite at ease himself. His demeanour was almost . . . shifty. What was he doing, leafing through the filing cabinet? Did Richard know? Was something going on that she should know about? If so, it might be in her interests to let him know that she'd seen him. She'd thought for a moment, then before Lambert could slip away, she'd stood up, sat down casually on Richard's chair, and waited for him to turn round. Now she looked with relish at his bulging eyes; his rising colour. Something was going on. But what?

'Is this your office, too?' she asked, in tones almost innocent enough to fool. 'I didn't realize.'

'Not exactly,' said Lambert, regaining his composure slightly. 'I was just checking something for the company. For the company,' he repeated, more belligerently. 'There's a lot of highly confidential stuff in here. In fact, I'm wondering what you're doing in here at all.'

'Oh, me!' said Fleur. 'Well, I was just looking for something that I left here last night.'

'Something you left here?' He sounded disbelieving. 'What was it? Shall I help you look?'

'Don't worry,' said Fleur, getting up and coming towards him. 'I found it.'

'You found it,' said Lambert, folding his arms. 'Might I ask what it was?'

Fleur paused, then opened her hand. Inside was a pair of black silky, knickers.

'They were undemeath the desk,' she said confidentially. 'So easy to mislay. But I didn't want the cleaner to be shocked.' She glanced at his scarlet face, 'You're not shocked, are you, Lambert? You did ask.'

Lambert didn't reply. He seemed to be having trouble breathing.

'It might be better not to mention this to Richard,' said Fleur, moving close to Lambert and looking him straight in the eye. 'He might be a little . . . coy.' She paused for a moment, breathing a little more quickly than usual and leaning very slightly towards Lambert's face. He looked transfixed.

And suddenly she was gone. Lambert remained exactly where he was, still feeling her breath on his skin, still hearing her voice in his ear, replaying the scene in his mind. Fleur's underwear – her black silky underwear – had been under the desk. Which must mean that she and Richard . . . Lambert swallowed. She and Richard . . .

With a bang, he closed the filing cabinet drawer and turned away He couldn't concentrate any more; he couldn't focus. He couldn't think about statements and balances. All he could think about was . . .

'Philippa!' he barked down the stairs. 'Come up here!' There was silence. 'Come up here!' he repeated. Eventually Philippa appeared.

'I was talking to Fleur,' she complained, hurrying up the stairs.

'I don't care. Come in here.' He took Philippa's hand and led her quickly to the end bedroom in which they always stayed. It had been Philippa's as a child, a fantasy land of roses and rabbits, but as soon as she left home, Emily had torn down the wallpaper and replaced it with dark green tartan.

'What do you want?' Philippa wrenched her arm out of Lambert's grasp.

'You. Now.'

'Lambert!' She looked uneasily at him. He was staring at her with a glassy, unfocused gaze. 'Get that dress off.'

'But Fleur . . .'

'Fuck Fleur.' He watched as Philippa hurriedly pulled her dress over her head, then closed his eyes and pulled her close, squeezing her flesh painfully between his fingers. 'Fuck Fleur,' he repeated in a blurry voice. 'Fuck Fleur.'

* * *

Richard arrived back from his meeting to find Fleur reclining in her usual spot in the conservatory.

'Where are Philippa and Lambert?' he asked. 'Their car's in the drive.' He looked at his watch. 'We tee off in half an hour.'

'Oh, I expect they're around somewhere,' murmured Fleur. 'I did catch a glimpse of Lambert earlier.' She stood up. 'Let's have a quick walk around the garden.'

As they walked, she took Richard's arm and said casually,

'I suppose you and Lambert know each other pretty well. Now that you're family.' She looked carefully at his face as she spoke, and saw a fleeting expression of distaste appear on it, which was quickly supplanted by one of reasonable, civilized tolerance.

'I've certainly got to know him better as a person,' said Richard. 'But I wouldn't say—'

'You wouldn't call yourself his friend? I gathered that. So you don't have long talks with him? Confide in him?'

'There's a generation gap,' said Richard defensively. 'It's understandable.'

'Completely understandable,' said Fleur, and rewarded herself with a little smile. What she had suspected was indeed the case. The two never spoke. Which meant Lambert was not going to accost Richard with tales of sex on the floor of his office. He wasn't going to check out her story; she was safe.

What Lambert's own story was, she had no idea. Once upon a time she might have felt compelled to find out. But experience had taught her that in every family there was someone with a secret. There was always one family member with a hidden agenda; sometimes there were several. Trying to use internal arguments for her own gain never worked. Family disputes were always irrational, always long-standing and the warriors always flipped over to the other side as soon as anyone else touched them. The best thing was to ignore everyone else and pursue her own goal as quickly as she could.

They walked on for a few minutes silently, then Fleur said,

'Did you have a good meeting?' Richard shrugged, and gave her a tense little smile.

'It made me think. You know, I still feel that there were parts of Emily which I knew nothing about.'

'Was the meeting about Emily?'

'No . . . but it concerned some affairs we discussed before she died.' Richard frowned. 'I was trying to remember her reasoning; her motivation for doing things,' he said slowly. 'And I realized that I don't *know* why she wanted certain things done. I suppose she didn't tell me – or I've forgotten what she said. And I never knew her character well enough to work it out now.'

'Perhaps I could help,' said Fleur. 'If you told me what it was all about.' Richard looked at her.

'Maybe you could. But I feel . . . this is something I've got to puzzle out for myself. Can you understand that?'

'Of course,' said Fleur lightly and squeezed his arm affectionately. Richard gave a little laugh.

'It's not really important. It won't affect anything I do. But—' he broke off and met Fleur's eyes. 'Well, you know how I feel about Emily.'

'She was full of secrets,' said Fleur, trying not to yawn. Hadn't they talked enough about this blessed woman already?

'Not secrets,' said Richard. 'I hope not secrets. Simply . . . hidden qualities.'

As soon as he had come, Lambert's proxy affection for Philippa vanished. He unfastened his lips from her neck and sat up.

'I've got to get going,' he said.

'Couldn't we just lie here for a bit?' said Philippa wistfully.

'No we couldn't. Everyone'll be wondering where we are.' He tucked his shirt in and smoothed his hair down and suddenly he was gone.

Philippa heaved herself onto her elbows and looked around the silent room. In her mind, she had begun to organize Lambert's quick fuck into an example of his passion for her; an anecdote to be confided to the bubbly friends that she would one day have. 'Honestly, he was *so* desperate for me . . . We just disappeared off together . . .' Giggles. 'It was so romantic . . . Lambert's always like that, a real man of the moment . . .' More giggles. Admiring looks. 'Oh Phil, you're so lucky! . . . I can't *remember* the last time we had sex . . .'

But now, slicing through the laughing voices, there was another voice in her head. Her mother's voice. 'You disgusting girl.' An icy blue stare. Philippa's diary being waved incriminatingly in the air. Her secret adolescent fantasies, opened up and exposed.

As though the last fifteen years had never happened, Philippa began to feel a teenager's panic and humiliation begin to rise through her. Her mother's voice, cutting through her thoughts again. 'Your father would be shocked if he saw this. A girl of your age, thinking about sex!'

Sex! The word had rung shockingly through the air, edged with sordid, unspeakable images. Philippa's embarrassment had suffused her face; her lungs. She had wanted to scream; she'd been unable to look her mother in the eye. The next term she'd allowed several of the sixth-formers from the neighbouring boys' boarding school to screw her behind the hedges on the hockey pitches. Each time the experience had been painful and embarrassing and she'd silently wept as it was happening. But then, she'd thought miserably, as one sixteen-year-old after another panted beer-breath into her face, that was all she deserved.

Lambert came downstairs to find Fleur and Richard arm in arm in the hall.

'Fleur's decided to come with us round the golf course,' said Richard. 'Isn't that a splendid idea?' Lambert looked at him, aghast.

'What do you mean?' he exclaimed. 'She can't come with us! This is a business game.'

'I won't get in your way,' said Fleur.

'We'll be having confidential business discussions.'

'On a golf course?' said Fleur. 'They can't be that confidential. Anyway, I won't be listening.'

'Fleur very much wants to see the course,' said Richard. 'I don't think there's any harm.'

'You don't mind, do you Lambert?' said Fleur. 'I've been here four weeks. and all I've seen is the eighteenth green.' She smiled at him from under her lashes. 'I'll be as quiet as a little mouse.'

'Perhaps Philippa could come along too,' suggested Richard.

'She's already fixed up to have tea with Tricia Tilling,' said Lambert at once. God help us, he thought, they didn't want a gaggle of women trailing around after them.

'Dear Tricia Tilling,' said Fleur. 'We had a lovely chat this morning.'

'Fleur's becoming quite a regular fixture at the club!' said Richard, beaming fondly at her.

'I bet she is,' said Lambert.

There was a sound on the stairs and they all looked up. Philippa was descending, looking rather flushed.

'Hello Fleur,' she said breathlessly. 'I was going to say, how about coming with me to Tricia's this afternoon? I'm sure she wouldn't mind.'

'I'm otherwise engaged,' said Fleur. 'Unfortunately.'

'Fleur's accompanying us around the golf course,'

said Richard with a smile. 'A most unexpected treat.'

Philippa looked at Lambert. Why didn't he ask her to come round the golf course, too? If he'd asked her, she would have cancelled tea with Tricia Tilling. She began to imagine the phone call she'd make. 'Sorry, Tricia, Lambert says I've simply got to go along . . . something about bringing him good luck!' An easy laugh. 'I know . . . these men of ours – aren't they something else?'

'Philippa!' She jumped, and the relaxed, laughing voices in her head vanished. Lambert was looking impatiently at her. 'I said would you look in at the pro shop and ask if they've mended that club yet.'

'Oh, all right,' said Philippa. She watched as the three of them left – Richard laughing at something Fleur had said; Lambert swinging his cashmere sweater over his shoulders. They were off to have a good time, and she was consigned to an afternoon with Tricia Tilling. She gave a gusty sigh of resentment. Even Gillian had more fun than her.

Gillian sat in the conservatory shelling peas and watching as Antony mended a cricket bat. He'd always been good with his hands, she thought. Careful, methodical, reliable. At the age of three, his nursery school teachers had been bemused at his paintings – always a single colour, completely covering the sheet of paper. Never more than one colour; never a single missed spot. Bordering on the obsessive. Perhaps these days, she thought, they would worry that he was too tidy for a three-year-old; take him off for counselling or workshops. Even back then, she'd sometimes detected a note of concern in the teachers' eyes. But no-one had said anything. For it had been obvious that Antony was a well-loved, well-cared-for child.

Well loved. Gillian stared fiercely out of the window. Well loved by everyone except his own mother. His own shallow selfish mother. A woman who'd recoiled with dismay at the sight of her own baby. Who had peered at the tiny disfigurement as though she could see nothing else, as though she weren't holding a perfect, healthy baby for whom she and everyone else ought to have been eternally grateful.

Of course, Emily had never said anything to the outside world. But Gillian had known. She'd watched as Antony had grown into a chuckling, beaming toddler, running around the house, arms outstretched, ready to embrace the world – confident that it must love him as much as he loved all of it. And then she'd watched as the little boy had gradually become aware that his mother's face perpetually held an expression of slight disapproval towards him; that she occasionally shrank from him when no-one else was watching; that she only fully relaxed when his face was averted and she couldn't see the tiny lizard leaping across his eye. The first day Antony had raised his little hand to his eye, concealing his birthmark from the world, Gillian had waited until the evening and confronted Emily. All her frustrations and anger had erupted in a tearful tirade, while Emily sat at her dressing table, brushing her hair; waiting. Then, when Gillian had finished, she'd looked round with a cold, contemptuous stare. 'You're just jealous,' she'd said. 'It's unhealthy! You wish Antony were your baby. Well, he's not yours, he's mine.'

Gillian had stared at Emily in shock, suddenly less sure of herself. Did she really wish Antony were hers? Was she unhealthy?

'You know I love Antony,' Emily had continued. 'Everyone knows I love him.' She'd paused. 'Richard's always saying how wonderful I am with him. And who cares about a birthmark? We never even notice it.' Her eyes had narrowed. 'In fact I'm surprised at you, Gillian, mentioning it all the time. We think the best thing is to ignore it.'

Somehow she'd twisted and reversed Gillian's words until Gillian had felt confused and unsure of her own motives. Was she becoming a frustrated, jealous spinster? Did her love for Antony border on possessiveness? It was Emily, after all, who was his natural mother. And so she'd backed down and said nothing more. And, after all, Antony had grown up a pleasant, problem-free child.

'There!' Antony held out the cricket bat.

'Well done,' said Gillian. She watched as he stood up and tried the bat out. He was tall now; an adult, practically. But sometimes as she caught a glimpse of his sturdy arms or smooth neck, she saw again in him that happy, chunky baby who had laughed up at her from his cot; whose hands she'd held as he took his first few steps; whom she'd loved from the moment he was born.

'Careful,' she said gruffly, as he swung the bat towards a large, painted plant pot.

'I *am* being careful,' he said irritably. 'You always fuss.'

He took a few imaginary swings. Gillian silently shelled a few more peas.

'What are you going to do this afternoon?' she asked at last.

'Dunno,' said Antony. 'I might get a video out. Or even a couple. It's so *boring*, with Will away.'

'What about the others? Xanthe. And that new boy, Mex. You could organize something with them?'

'Yeah, maybe.' His face closed up and he turned away, swinging the bat viciously through the air.

'Careful!' exclaimed Gillian. But it was too late. As he swung back, there was, a crack and then a crash as he hit a terracotta pot off its stand and onto the tiled floor.

'Look what you've done!' Her voice snapped roughly through the air. 'I told you to be careful!'

'I'm sorry, OK?'

'It's all over the floor!' Gillian stood up and gazed despairingly at the pieces of terracotta, the clumps of earth, the fleshy leaves.

'Honestly. It's not such a disaster.' He bent down and picked up a piece of terracotta. A clod of earth fell onto his shoe.

'I'd better get a brush.' Gillian sighed heavily and put down the peas.

'I'll do it,' said Antony. 'It's no big deal.'

'You won't do it properly.'

'I will! Isn't there a broom around here somewhere?'

Antony's eyes swept the conservatory and suddenly stopped as his gaze reached the door. 'Jesus Christ!' he exclaimed. The piece of terracotta fell out of his band, smashing on the floor.

'Antony! I've told you before—'

'Look!' he interrupted. 'Who's that?'

Gillian turned and followed his gaze. Standing on the other side of the door was a girl with long, white-blond hair, dark eyebrows and a suspicious expression.

'Hi,' she said through the glass. Her voice was high-pitched and had an American accent. 'I guess you weren't expecting me. I've come to stay. I'm Zara. I'm Fleur's daughter.'

# EIGHT

By the time they came off the eighteenth green, Lambert was bright red, sweating and grimacing with frustration. Fleur had dominated the attention all the way round the course, sashaying along beside Richard as though she were at a tea party, interrupting the discussion to ask endless questions, behaving as though she had as much right to be there as Lambert did himself. Bloody impertinent bitch.

A remark made by his old housemaster suddenly came into Lambert's mind. *I'm all for equality in women . . . they're all equally inferior to men!* A little chuckle had gone around the select group of sixth-formers whom Old Smithers had been entertaining with sherry. Lambert had chortled, particularly loudly, acknowledging the fact that he and Old Smithers had always shared the same sense of humour. Now his frown softened slightly; a reminiscent look passed over his features. For a few moments he found himself wishing he was a sixth-former once again.

It was a fact which Lambert rarely admitted to himself that the happiest and most successful years of his life had, so far, been those spent at school. He had attended Creighton – a minor public school in the Midlands – and had soon found himself one of the brightest, strongest and most powerful boys in the school. A natural bully, he had soon established around himself a sycophantic entourage, mildly terrorizing younger boys and sneering in packs at the local lads in the town. The boys at Creighton were for the most part third-rate plodders who would never again in their lives achieve the superior status which was accorded to them in this little town; therefore they made the most of it, striding around the streets in their distinctive greatcoats and flamboyant ties, braying loudly and picking fights with what were known as the townies. Lambert had rarely actually fought himself but had become known as the author of a great number of disparaging remarks about the 'plebs' which had eventually given him the reputation of a wit. The masters – themselves insular, bored and discouraged with life – had not reprimanded him but tacitly encouraged him in this role; had fed his pompous, superior manner with winks and chortles and snobbish asides. Lambert's timid mother had delighted in her tall, confident son with his loud voice and forthright views, which by the time he reached the sixth form, were dismissive of almost everyone at Creighton and almost everyone outside of Creighton, too.

The exception was his father. Lambert had always

idolized his father – a tall, swaggering man with an overbearing manner which Lambert still unconsciously emulated. His father's moods had been violent and unpredictable, and Lambert had grown up desperate for his approval. When his father made fun of the young Lambert's rubbery-looking face or clipped him too vigorously round the head, Lambert would force himself to grin back and laugh; when he spent whole evenings bellowing at Lambert's mother, Lambert would creep upstairs to his bedroom, telling himself furiously that his father was right; his father was always right.

It had been Lambert's father who insisted he attend Creighton School, as he had done. Who taught him to mock the other boys in the village; who took him to Cambridge for the day and proudly pointed out his old college. It was his father, Lambert believed, who knew about the world; who cared about his future; who would guide him in life.

And then, when Lambert was fifteen, his father announced that he had a mistress, that he loved her and that he was leaving. He said he'd come back and visit Lambert; he never did. Later they heard that he'd only lasted six months with the mistress; that he'd gone abroad; that no-one knew where he was.

Filled with a desperate, adolescent grief, Lambert had taken his anger out on his mother. It was her fault his father had left. It was her fault that there was now no money for holidays; that letters had to be written to the headmaster of Creighton, pleading for a reduction in the fees. As their situation grew more and more wretched, Lambert's swagger grew more pronounced; his contempt for the town plebs grew fiercer – and his idolatry for his absent father grew even stronger.

Against the advice of his masters, he tried for Cambridge – for his father's old college. He was granted an interview but on the strength of his interview he was turned down. The sense of failure was almost more than he could bear. Abruptly he announced that he was not going to waste his time with university. The masters remonstrated with him, but only mildly; he was on the way out of their lives and therefore of waning interest. Their attention was now focusing on the boys lower down the school; the boys Lambert had used to beat for burning his toast. What Lambert did with his life, they didn't really care. His mother, who did care, was roundly ignored.

And so Lambert had gone straight to London, straight into a job in computing. The pompous manner which might have been rubbed off by Cambridge remained, as did his feeling of innate superiority. When others of inferior schooling were promoted above him, he retaliated by wearing his OC tie to work. When his flat mates organized weekend gatherings without him, he retaliated by driving back up to Creighton and displaying his latest car to anyone who would look. It was unthinkable to Lambert that those around him should not admire him and defer to him. Those who didn't, he dismissed as being too ignorant to bother with. Those who did, he secretly despised. He was unable to make friends; unable even to understand any relationship based on equality. Those who would tolerate his company for even a couple of hours had been few and were becoming fewer when he moved to Richard's company. And at that point his life had been transformed. He had married the boss's daughter and moved on to a new level and his status had become, in his own mind, assured for good.

Richard, he was certain, appreciated his superior attributes – his intellect, his breeding, his ability to make decisions – although not as fully as Emily had appreciated them. Philippa was a little fool who thought flowers looked nicer on a tie than Old Creightonian stripes. But Fleur . . . Lambert scowled, and wiped a drip of sweat from his brow. Fleur didn't obey the rules. She seemed heedless of his rank as Richard's son-in-law and almost oblivious of social convention. She was too slippery; he couldn't place her. What was her age exactly? What was her accent exactly? Where did she fit into his scheme of things?

'Lambert!' Philippa's voice interrupted his thoughts. She was coming towards the eighteenth green, merrily waving her bag at him.

'Philippa!' His head jerked up; in his state of frustration he felt almost glad to see his wife's familiar face, slightly flushed. Tea with Tricia had clearly metamorphosed into G and T with Tricia.

'I thought I'd catch you playing the eighteenth! But you've finished already! That was pretty quick!'

Lambert said nothing. When Philippa was in full

voluble flight she would scoop everything up from a subject that could possibly be mentioned, leaving no crumbs for an answer.

'Good game?' Lambert shot a glance behind him. Richard and the two men from Briggs & Co. were some way behind, walking slowly, all listening to something Fleur was saying.

'Bloody awful game.' He stepped off the course and without waiting for the others began to stride towards the trolley shed, his spikes. clattering noisily on the path.

'What happened?'

'That bloody woman. All she did was ask questions. Every fucking five minutes. "Richard, could you explain that again to a very stupid lay-woman?" "Richard, when you say cashflow, what exactly do you mean?" And I'm trying to impress these guys. Christ, what an afternoon.'

'Maybe she's just interested,' said Philippa.

'Of course she isn't interested. Why would she be interested? She's just a stupid tart who likes having all the attention.'

'Well, she certainly looks very good,' said Philippa wistfully, turning to survey Fleur.

'She looks terrible,' said Lambert. 'Far too sexy for a golf course.' Philippa giggled.

'Lambert! You're awful!' She paused, then added in needlessly hushed tones, 'We were talking about her this afternoon, actually. Tricia and I.' She lowered her voice further. 'Apparently she's really rich! Tricia told me. She's got a chauffeur and everything! Tricia said she thought Fleur was super.' Philippa darted a bright-eyed glance at Lambert. Tricia thinks . . .'

'Tricia is a moron.' Lambert wiped the sweat off his brow again and wondered why the hell he was talking about Fleur to his wife. He turned and looked at Fleur sauntering along in her white dress, looking at him with her mocking green eyes. The arousal which he had fought all afternoon began to stir in him again.

'Christ what a fiasco,' he said coarsely, turning back, running a frustrated hand over Philippa's inferior buttocks. 'I need a bloody drink.'

Unfortunately the chaps from Briggs & Co. didn't have time for a drink. Regretfully they shook hands and, with one last admiring glance at Fleur, got back into their Saab and drove off. The others stood politely in the car park, watching them manoeuvre the car past rows of glossy BMWs, the occasional Rolls-Royce, a sprinkling of pristine Range Rovers.

Philippa felt a twinge of disappointment as their car disappeared through the gates. She had looked forward to meeting them, chatting to them, perhaps flirting a little, perhaps even organizing a dinner party for them and their wives. Since marrying Lambert two years before, she had only given one dinner party, for her parents and Antony. And yet at home she had an elegant dining room with a table big enough for ten, and a kitchen full of expensive saucepans, and a 'Dinner Party' book full of recipes and time-saving tips, laboriously copied out of magazines.

She had always thought that being married to Lambert would mean she spent the evenings entertaining Lambert's friends: cooking elaborate dishes for them, perhaps striking up jolly acquaintanceships with their wives. But now it appeared that Lambert didn't have any friends. And neither, if she was honest, did she – only people at Greyworth who had been her mother's friends, and people from work, who were always leaving to go to other jobs and never seemed to be free in the evenings anyway. Her contemporaries from university had long since dispersed about the country; none of them lived in London.

Suddenly Fleur laughed at something Richard had said, and Philippa's head jerked up. If only Fleur could be her friend, she thought wistfully. Her best friend. They could go out to lunch, and have little private jokes which only they understood, and Fleur would introduce her to all *her* friends, and then Philippa would offer to host a dinner party for her in London . . . In her mind, Philippa's dining room became filled with amusing, delightful people. Candles burning, flowers everywhere, all her wedding china out of its wrappers. She would pop into the kitchen to check on the seafood brochettes with civilized laughter in her ears. Lambert would come in after her ostensibly to replenish glasses, but really to tell her how proud he was of her. He would put the glasses down, then draw her towards him in a slow embrace . . .

'Is that Gillian?' Fleur's voice, raised in astonishment, woke Philippa from her reverie. 'What's she doing here?'

Everyone looked up, and Philippa tried to catch Fleur's eye; to start the seeds of friendship between them. But Fleur didn't see her. Fleur was looking up at Richard as though no one else in the world existed.

Watching Gillian approach across the car park, Richard gradually pulled Fleur closer and closer to him until they were practically hip to hip.

'I'm so glad you came along,' he murmured in her ear. 'I'd forgotten how interminable these games can be. Especially when Lambert's involved.'

'I enjoyed it,' said Fleur, smiling demurely at him. 'And I certainly learned a lot.'

'Would you like some golf lessons?' said Richard immediately. 'I should have suggested it before. We can easily fix some up for you.'

'Maybe,' said Fleur. 'Or maybe you could teach me yourself.' She glanced up at Richard's face, still flushed from the sun, still exhilarated from his victory. He looked as relaxed and happy as she'd ever seen him.

'Hello Gillian,' said Richard, as she came within earshot. 'What good timing. We're just about to have a drink.'

'I see,' said Gillian distractedly. 'Are the people from Briggs and Co. still around?'

'No, they had to shoot off,' said Richard. 'But we're going to have a celebratory drink on our own.'

'Celebrate?' said Lambert. 'What's there to celebrate?'

'The preferential rate which Briggs and Co. have offered us,' said Richard, his mouth twisting into a smile. 'Which Fleur charmed them into offering us.'

'A preferential rate?' said Philippa, ignoring Lambert's disbelieving scowl. 'That's marvellous!' She smiled warmly at Fleur.

'It would be marvellous,' said Fleur, 'if they weren't a pair of utter crooks.'

'What?' They all stared at her.

'Didn't you think so?' she said.

'Well . . .' said Richard doubtfully.

'Of course I didn't think so!' said Lambert. 'These chaps are chums of mine.'

'Oh,' said Fleur. She shrugged. 'Well I don't want to offend anyone. But I thought they were crooks, and if I were you I wouldn't do business with them.'

Philippa glanced at Lambert. He was breathing heavily and his face was an even brighter scarlet than before.

'They cheat a little on the golf course, maybe,' said Richard uncomfortably. 'But . . .'

'Not just on the golf course,' said Fleur. 'Trust me.'

'Trust you?' exclaimed Lambert, as though unable to keep quiet any more. 'What the hell do you know about anything?'

'Lambert!' said Richard sharply. He looked fondly down at Fleur. 'Tell you what, darling, I'll think about it. Nothing's signed yet.'

'Good,' said Fleur.

'Fleur,' said Gillian quietly. 'You've got—'

'What do you mean, you'll think about it?' Lambert's scandalized voice exploded across hers. 'Richard, you're not taking this rubbish of Fleur's seriously?'

'All I've said, Lambert,' said Richard tightly, 'is that I'll think about it.'

'For Christ's sake, Richard! The deal's all set up!'

'It can be un-set up.'

'I don't believe I'm hearing this!'

'Fleur,' said Gillian more urgently. 'You've got a visitor back at the house.'

'Since when was Fleur consulted on company decisions?' Lambert's face was almost purple. 'Whose advice are you going to ask next? The milkman's?'

'I'm just giving an opinion,' said Fleur, shrugging. 'You can ignore it if you like.'

'Fleur!' Gillian's voice rose harshly into the air. Everyone turned to look at her. 'Your daughter's here.'

There was silence.

'Oh, is she?' said Fleur casually. 'Yes, I suppose it must be the end of term. How did she get here?'

'Your daughter?' said Richard, giving a little, uncertain laugh.

'I told you about my daughter,' said Fleur. 'Didn't I?'

'Did you?'

'Perhaps I didn't.' Fleur sounded unconcerned.

'The woman is a nutter!' muttered Lambert to Philippa.

'She just arrived out of the blue,' said Gillian, in tones of stupefaction. 'Is her name Sarah? I couldn't quite make it out.'

'Zara,' said Fleur. 'Zara Rose. Where is she now?' she added, almost as an afterthought.

'She's gone out for a walk,' said Gillian, as though this surprised her the most of all, 'with Antony.'

Antony looked again at Zara and tried to think of something to say. They'd been walking for ten minutes now in complete silence. Zara's hands were in her pockets and her shoulders were hunched up, and she was staring straight ahead as though she didn't want to catch anyone's eye. They were very thin shoulders, thought Antony, glancing at her again. In fact Zara was one of the thinnest people he'd ever seen. Her arms were long and bony; her ribs were practically visible through her T-shirt. No tits to speak of, even though she was . . . how old was she?

'How old are you?' he asked.

'Thirteen.' Her voice was American and raspy and not very friendly. She shook back her long white-blond hair and hunched her shoulders again. Her hair was bleached, thought Antony knowledgeably, pleased with himself for having noticed.

'And . . . where do you go to school?' This was more like it. Small talk.

'Heathland School for Girls.'

'Is it nice?'

'It's a boarding school.' She spoke as though that were answer enough.

'Did you . . . When did you move here from the States?'

'I didn't.' Oh ha-ha, thought Antony.

'Canada, then,' he said.

'I've lived in Britain all my life,' she said. She sounded bored. Antony stared at her, perplexed.

'But your accent . . .'

'I have an American accent. So what? It's my choice.' For the first time she turned towards him. Her eyes were extraordinary, he thought – green like Fleur's but deep-set and fierce-looking.

'You just decided to speak with an American accent?'

'Yup.'

'Why?'

'Just did.'

'How old were you?'

'Seven.'

They walked for a while in silence. Antony tried to remember himself at seven. Could he have made a decision like that? And stuck with it? He thought not.

'I guess your dad's rich, right?' Her voice rasped through the air and Antony felt himself blushing.

'Quite rich, I suppose,' he said. 'I mean, not that rich. But you know. Well off. Relatively speaking.' He knew he was sounding awkward and pompous, but there was nothing he could do about it. 'Why do you want to know?' he said, retaliating.

'No reason.' She took her hands out of her pockets and began to examine them. Antony followed her gaze. They were thin hands, tanned pale brown, with a single, huge silver ring on each. Why? thought Antony in sudden fascination. Why are you staring at your hands? Why are you frowning? What are you looking for?

Abruptly she seemed to get bored with her hands

and thrust them back into her pockets. She turned to Antony.

'You mind if I smoke a joint?'

Antony's heart missed a beat. This girl was only thirteen. How could she be smoking joints?

'No . . . I don't mind.' He could hear his voice slipping higher and higher, into a register of slight panic.

'Where do you go to smoke? Or don't you?'

'Yes,' said Antony, too quickly. 'But mostly at school.'

'OK.' She shrugged. 'Well, there must be somewhere, in all this forest.'

'There's a place down here.' He led the way off the road and into the wood. 'People come here to—' How could this girl be only thirteen? She was two years younger than him. It was incredible. 'You know,' he finished feebly.

'Have sex.'

'Well.' His face felt hot; his birthmark seemed to throb with embarrassment. 'Yeah.' They had arrived at a little clearing. 'Here we are.'

'OK.' She crouched down on her haunches, took a little box from her pocket and efficiently began to roll a joint.

As she lit it and inhaled, Antony waited for her to look up and say Wow this is great stuff, like Fifi Tilling always did. But Zara said nothing. She had none of the excited self-consciousness that surrounded the drug-takers of his experience, in fact she seemed barely aware that he was there. She inhaled silently again, then passed the joint to him.

This afternoon, thought Antony, I was going to sit at home and watch a couple of crummy videos. And instead, here I am smoking dope with the most extraordinary thirteen-year-old girl I've ever met.

'Is your family friendly?' she asked suddenly.

'Well,' said Antony, feeling thrown again. Into his mind came the parties his parents had always held at Christmas. Decorations and mulled wine; everyone dressed up and having a jolly time. 'Well, yes,' he said, 'I think we're pretty friendly. You know. We've got loads of friends and stuff.'

His words rose into the silent forest air; Zara gave no indication that she'd heard him. Her face was covered in dappled shadows from the trees and it was difficult to make out an expression. After another pause she spoke again.

'What do you all think of Fleur?'

'She's great!' said Antony with genuine enthusiasm. 'She's such a laugh. I never thought—'

'Don't tell me. You never thought your dad would date again,' said Zara, and inhaled again on the joint. Antony looked curiously at her.

'No,' he said, 'I didn't. Well, you don't, do you? Think of your parents dating.' Zara was silent.

Suddenly there was a sound. Footsteps were coming towards them; indistinct voices were rising above the trees. In one swift movement Zara put out the joint and buried it in the earth. Antony leaned casually back on one elbow. A moment later, Xanthe Forrester and Mex Taylor arrived in the clearing. Xanthe was holding a bottle of vodka, her cheeks were flushed and her shirt was unbuttoned, revealing a pink gingham bra. When she saw Antony and Zara she stopped short.

'Antony!' she said in nonplussed tones. 'I didn't know you—'

'Hi Xanthe. This is Zara,' said Antony. He looked at Zara. 'This is Xanthe and Mex.'

'Hello there,' said Mex, and winked at Antony.

'Hi,' said Zara.

'Actually, we'd better be going,' said Antony. He stood up and held out a hand to help Zara, but she ignored it, rising to her feet from her cross-legged position in one seamless action. Xanthe giggled and he felt his hand shoot defensively up to his birthmark.

'Antony's always such a gentleman, isn't he?' said Xanthe, looking with bright, colluding eyes at Zara.

'Is he?' Zara spoke politely, defusing the joke. Xanthe flushed slightly, then decided to giggle again.

'I'm so pissed!' she said. She held out the bottle to Zara. 'Have some.'

'I don't drink,' said Zara. 'But thanks anyway.' She put her hands into her pockets and hunched her shoulders up again.

'We'd better go,' said Antony. 'Your mother might be back.'

'Your mother?' said Xanthe at once. 'Who's your mother?' Zara looked away.

'Fleur,' she said. She sounded suddenly weary. 'My mother's Fleur.'

* * *

As they walked back to The Maples, the sun disappeared behind a cloud, casting the road into shadow. Zara stared stonily ahead, quelling the feeling of tearfulness inside her with a frown which grew more severe with every step. It was always like this at first; she'd be OK in a day or two. Homesickness, the people at school called it. But she couldn't really be feeling homesick, because she didn't have a home to be sick for. There was school, with its smell of polish and its hockey pitches and its lumpish, stupid girls, and there was Johnny and Felix's flat, where there wasn't really room for her, and then there was wherever Fleur was staying. And that was how it had always been, ever since she could remember.

She'd been at boarding school since she was five. Before that, they must have had some kind of home, she guessed, but she couldn't really remember, and Fleur claimed she couldn't remember either. So her first home had really been the Court School in Bayswater, a cosy house full of diplomats' children tucked into bed with expensive teddies. She'd loved it there, had loved all the teachers passionately, especially Mrs Burton, the headmistress.

And she'd loved Nat, her best friend, whom she'd met on her first day there. Nat's parents were working in Moscow and, he'd confided to her over bedtime hot chocolate, didn't love him at all, not one tiny bit.

'My mother doesn't love me either,' she'd said at once.

'I think my *mother* loves me,' Nat had said, eyes huge

over the rim of his white china mug, 'but my father hates me.' Zara had thought for a moment.

'I don't know my father,' she'd confessed eventually, 'but he's American.' Nat had looked at her with respect.

'Is he a cowboy?'

'I think so,' Zara had replied. 'He wears a great big hat.'

The next day, Nat had drawn a picture of Zara's father wearing his hat, and their friendship had been sealed. They had sat next to each other in all their lessons and played together at breaktime and been each other's partners in the school crocodile and sometimes – which was strictly forbidden – even crept into each other's bed at night and told each other stories.

And then, when she was seven, Zara had arrived back at school after a half-term of sipping strawberry milk shakes in a Kensington hotel suite, to find Nat's bed stripped and all his things gone from his cupboard. Mrs Burton had begun to explain kindly to her that Nat's parents had with no warning moved from Moscow to Washington and plucked him from the Court School to go and live with them – but before she could finish, Zara's screeches of grief were echoing all over the school. Nat had left her. His parents did love him after all. And he had gone to America, where her father was a cowboy, and he hadn't taken her.

For a week she wept every day, refusing to eat, refusing to write to Nat, refusing at first to speak at all, then only in her notion of an American accent. Eventually Fleur had been summoned to the school and Zara had begged her, hysterically, to please take her to live in America.

But instead, Fleur whipped her straight out of the Court School and sent her off to a nice healthy girls' preparatory school in Dorset, where farmers' daughters rode their own ponies and kept dogs and didn't form unnatural attachments to each other. Zara had arrived, the oddity from London, prone to tears and still clinging to her American accent. She had been the oddity ever since.

She was incredible, just like Fleur was incredible – but completely different. Antony walked silently beside Zara, his head buzzing with thoughts, his body filled with a faint excitement. The implications of Zara's arrival were only now beginning to take shape in his mind. If she stayed at The Maples for a bit then he'd have someone to hang out with. Someone to impress the others with. Xanthe's face had been something else when she saw Zara. Even Mex had looked impressed.

He suddenly found himself fervently hoping that his dad didn't do anything idiotic, like break up with Fleur. It was nice, having Fleur around. And it would be even nicer having Zara around the place. She wasn't exactly the friendliest person in the world but that didn't matter. And maybe she'd loosen up after a while. Surreptitiously, he glanced at Zara's face. Her forehead was furrowed and her jaw was tense and her eyes were glittering. Bolshy, thought Antony. She's probably pissed off that we got interrupted before she'd finished smoking her joint. Druggy people were always a bit funny.

Just then they turned a corner, and the evening sun fell on Zara's face. Antony's heart gave a little jolt. For in that brief glint of light her thin cheeks looked less harsh than wistful, and her eyes seemed to be glittering not with anger but with tears. And she suddenly seemed less like a druggy person and more like a lonely little girl.

By the time they arrived back at The Maples, Zara had been allocated a bedroom, and everyone was waiting for her.

'Darling!' said Fleur, as soon as she and Antony came in through the front door; before anyone else could speak. 'Let's go straight upstairs to your room, shall we?' She smiled at Richard. 'You don't mind if I have a few moments alone with my daughter?'

'Absolutely not! Take your time!' Richard smiled encouragingly at Zara. 'Just let me say how glad I am to welcome you, Zara. How glad we all are.'

Zara was silent as they walked up the stairs and along the corridor to her room. Then, as the door shut, she turned on Fleur.

'You didn't tell me where you were.'

'Didn't I? I meant to, poppet.' Fleur went over to the window and pushed it open. 'That's better.' She turned round. 'Don't look so cross, sweetheart. I knew Johnny would tell you where I was.'

'Johnny was away.' She spat each word out with a

separate emphasis. 'Term broke up a week ago. I had to check into a hotel.'

'Oh yes?' said Fleur interestedly. 'Which one?' Zara's neck became rigid.

'It doesn't matter which one. You should have let me know where you were. You said you would.'

'I really did mean to, poppet. Anyway, you got here. That's the main thing.'

Zara sat down on a green upholstered dressing-table stool and looked at Fleur's reflection in the mirror.

'What happened to Sakis?' she said. Fleur shrugged.

'I moved on. These things happen.' She waved her hands vaguely in the air.

'No money, huh?' said Zara. 'He seemed loaded to me.' Fleur flushed in irritation.

'Be quiet!' she said. 'Someone might hear.' Zara shrugged. She pulled a piece of gum from her pocket and began to chew.

'So, who's this guy?' she said, gesturing around. 'Is he rich?'

'He's very nice,' said Fleur.

'Where d'you meet him? A funeral?'

'A memorial service.'

'Uh-huh.' Zara opened a drawer of the dressing table, looked at the lining paper for a moment, then closed it again. 'How long are you planning to stay here?'

'That all depends.'

'Uh-huh.' Zara chewed some more. 'Aren't you going to tell me any more?'

'You're a child,' said Fleur. 'You don't need to know everything.'

'I do!' retorted Zara. 'Of course I do!' Fleur flinched.

'Zara, keep your voice down!'

'Listen, Fleur,' hissed Zara angrily. 'I do need to know. I need to know what's going on. You used to tell me. Remember? You used to tell me where we were going and who the people were and what to say. Now you just expect me to . . . to just *find* you. Like, you could be staying anywhere, but I have to *find* you, and then I have to say all the right stuff, and not make any mistakes . . .'

'You don't have to say anything.'

'I'm not ten years old any more. People talk to me. They ask me questions. I can't just keep saying I don't know or I can't remember.'

'You're an intelligent girl. You can think on your feet.'

'Aren't you afraid I'll make a mistake?' Zara looked at Fleur with hostile, challenging eyes. 'Aren't you afraid I'll ruin everything for you?'

'No,' said Fleur, at once, 'I'm not. Because you know that if you do, you're in trouble as much as I am. School fees don't come out of thin air, you know, and neither does that dreadful stuff you smoke.' Zara's head jerked up. 'Johnny told me,' Fleur said. 'He was shocked.'

'Johnny can go screw himself.' A corner of Fleur's mouth twisted into a smile.

'That'll be a pound in Felix's swear box,' she said. In spite of herself, Zara grinned down at her hands. She chewed some more and looked at the huge silver ring on her left hand, the one Johnny had given her during that awful week in between leaving the Court School and going to Heathland School for Girls. Whenever you're feeling low, he'd told her, just polish your ring and you'll see my reflection smiling back at you. And she'd believed him. She still half did.

'Johnny wants you to call him, by the way,' she said. 'It's very urgent.' Fleur sighed.

'What is it this time?' Zara shrugged.

'I don't know. He wouldn't tell me. Something important, I guess.'

'A funeral?'

'I don't know.' Zara's voice was patient. 'He wouldn't tell me. I already said that.'

Fleur sighed again, and examined her nails.

'Urgent. What does that mean? I expect he's choosing new wallpaper.'

'Or he's having a party and he doesn't know what to wear.'

'Maybe he's lost his dry-cleaning ticket again. Do you remember?' Fleur met Zara's eyes and for the first time since meeting they smiled at each other. This always happens, thought Zara. We get on best when we're talking about Johnny. The rest of the time, forget it.

'Well, I'll see you later,' said Fleur abruptly, standing up. 'And since you're so interested in fine details, perhaps I should tell you that Richard Favour's late wife was called Emily and she was a friend of mine long ago. But we don't talk about her very much.'

'No,' said Zara, spitting her gum into the bin. 'I'll bet you don't.'

At eight o'clock, Gillian brought a jug of Pimm's into the drawing room.

'Where's Daddy?' said Philippa, coming into the room and looking around. 'I've hardly seen him today and we can't stay too late.'

'He's still working,' said Lambert. 'In his office.' He took the glass that Gillian offered and took several large swigs, feeling as though if he didn't get some alcohol inside him, he would simmer over with frustration. Since arriving back, he'd sidled along to the office as often as he could, but each time the door had been slightly open and the desk lamp had been on and the back of Richard's head had been just visible through the chink. The bastard hadn't budged. So it looked as though he'd missed his chance. He was going to have to go back to London no closer to sorting out his overdraft problem. Not to mention the deal with Briggs & Co., a deal which should have been signed and sealed by six o'clock. A feeling of suppressed fury burned in Lambert's chest. What a bloody disaster the day had turned out to be. And it was all the fault of that fucking woman, Fleur.

'Lambert, have you met Zara?' And there she was again, wearing a tight red dress that made her look like a whore, smiling as if she owned the place, shepherding her bloody daughter into the room.

'Hello Zara,' he said, staring at the curve of Fleur's

breasts under her dress. Zara. What kind of bloody stupid name was that?

'Hello!' Philippa came rushing over to Zara with bright-eyed enthusiasm. Whilst walking back to the house, another idea had occurred to her. She could become friendly with Fleur's daughter. She would be an older sister figure. The two of them would talk about clothes and make-up and boyfriend troubles, and the younger girl would confide in her, and Philippa would issue kindly advice . . . 'I'm Philippa,' she said, smiling warmly at Zara. 'Antony's older sister.'

'Hi Philippa.' Zara's voice was flat and uninterested. There was a little silence.

'Would you like some lemonade, dear?' said Gillian.

'Water, thank you,' said Zara.

'We can eat soon,' said Gillian, looking at Philippa, 'if you have to get off. As soon as your father comes downstairs. Why don't you call him, and we'll all sit down.'

'OK,' said Philippa, loitering slightly. She looked again at Zara. She had never seen anyone, she thought, quite so thin. She could have been a model. Was she really only thirteen? She looked more like—

'Philippa!' Gillian's voice interrupted her thoughts.

'Oh, sorry,' said Philippa. 'Daydreaming again!' She tried to catch Zara's eye in a giggle, but Zara gazed stonily past her. Immediately Philippa felt slighted. Just who did this girl think she was?

Richard appeared at the door.

'Sorry to have kept you,' he said. 'There were a few things I had to think about.'

Philippa was aware of Lambert glancing up sharply, then looking away again. She nudged him gently, meaning to catch his eye and roll her eyes expressively in the direction of Zara. But Lambert ignored her. She gave a hurt little sniff. Everyone was ignoring her tonight, even her own husband.

'But now let's have a toast,' continued Richard. He took the glass which Gillian was holding out to him, and held it up. 'Welcome to Zara.'

'Welcome to Zara,' chorused the others obediently.

Philippa looked down into her drink. When was the last time anyone had toasted her? When was the last time anyone had welcomed her anywhere? Everyone ignored her, even her own family. She didn't have any friends. Gillian didn't care about her any more. No-one cared about her any more. Philippa blinked a few times, and squeezed hard on the few real emotions in her mind, until slowly a tear oozed out of her eye and onto her cheek. Now they've made me cry, she thought. I'm crying, and no-one's even noticing. Another tear oozed onto her cheek, and she sniffed again.

'Philippa!' Richard's alarmed voice interrupted the conversation. 'Are you all right, darling?'

Philippa looked up, with a trembling face.

'I'm OK,' she said. 'I was just thinking . . . about Mummy. I-I don't know why.'

'Oh, my darling.' Richard hurried over.

'Don't worry,' said Philippa. 'I'm fine, really.' She gave another sniff, and smiled at her father, and allowed him to put an arm round her shoulder and lead her out of the room. Everyone was silent; everyone was looking at her tear-stained face with concern. As she neared Zara, Philippa glanced up, ready to meet another sympathetic face, stare bravely ahead and then lower her eyes. But as soon as Zara's dispassionate gaze met hers, Philippa felt a shiver go through her and her expression begin to slip. In front of this girl she felt foolish and transparent, as though Zara somehow knew exactly what she was thinking.

'I'm sorry for you,' said Zara quietly.

'What do you mean?' said Philippa, feeling rattled.

Zara's expression didn't flicker.

'Losing your mother.'

'Oh. Thank you.' Philippa exhaled sharply, and tried to reform her features into the brave stare. But she didn't feel brave any more. Her tears had dried; no-one was looking at her; Lambert had started discussing the cricket with Antony. The moment was gone and it was Zara who had spoiled it all for her.

# NINE

Two weeks later, Richard looked up from his copy of *The TImes* and chortled.

'Look at that!' he said, pointing to a tiny item on the business pages entitled 'Accountant Suspended'. Fleur's eyes ran down the few lines of text and a smile appeared on her face.

'I told you!' she said. 'I knew those people were crooks.'

'What's happened?' said Gillian, coming into the room. Richard looked up delightedly.

'The people we played golf with the other week. Briggs & Co. One of them's been caught fiddling the books of another company. It's in the paper.'

'Gracious,' said Gillian confusedly. 'Is that a good thing?'

'No. The good thing is that we decided not to hire them. The good thing is that Fleur cottoned onto them.' Richard reached for Fleur's hand and squeezed it affectionately. 'Fleur's the good thing around here,' he said. 'As I think we all agree.' He glanced up at Gillian. 'You look nice.'

'I'm off to my bridge lesson,' said Gillian. She looked at Fleur. 'Are you sure you won't come?'

'Darling, I got quite lost last week. I still can't remember how many tricks in a suit. Or is it the other way round?' Fleur wrinkled her nose at Gillian, who laughed. 'And Tricia was very keen to find a partner. So off you go. Have a lovely time.'

'Well . . .' Gillian paused, smoothing her jacket down over her hips. It was a new, pale-blue linen jacket, bought during a shopping trip with Fleur the week before. She was wearing with it a long, cream-coloured skirt, also new, and the blue scarf which Fleur had given her. 'If you're really sure.'

'I'm positive,' said Fleur. 'And remember I'm doing the supper tonight. So no hurrying back.'

'All right, then.' A little smile came to Gillian's face. 'I am enjoying these lessons, you know. I never thought a card game could be so invigorating!'

'I always used to enjoy a game of bridge,' said Richard, 'but Emily was never keen.'

'You have to concentrate quite hard,' said Gillian, 'but that's what I enjoy about it.'

'I'm glad,' said Richard, smiling at her. 'It's nice to see you taking up a hobby.' Gillian flushed slightly.

'It's just a bit of fun,' she said. She looked at Fleur. 'I'll probably be back in time to get supper. There's no need for you to do it.'

'I want to do it!' said Fleur. 'Now go, or you'll be late!'

'All right,' said Gillian. She hovered for a moment more, then hitched up her bag and walked as far as the door. There she stopped, and looked back.

'Everything should be in the fridge, I think,' she began. Richard started to laugh.

'Gillian, just go!'

When she had finally managed to leave, they relapsed into a companionable silence.

'I'm surprised Lambert hasn't telephoned,' said Richard suddenly. 'He must have seen the papers this morning.'

'He's probably embarrassed,' said Fleur.

'He may well be,' said Richard, 'but he also owes you an apology.' He sighed and put down his paper. 'I'm afraid to confess that the better I know Lambert, the less I like him. I suppose Philippa must love him, but . . .' He tailed away and shrugged.

'Were you surprised when they got married?' said Fleur.

'Yes, I was,' said Richard. 'I thought possibly they were hurrying into it. But they seemed very keen on the idea. And Emily was terribly pleased. She didn't seem surprised at all.' He paused. 'A mother's intuition, I suppose.'

'What about a father's intuition?'

'Temporarily out of order, I should think.' He grinned. 'I mean, they seem very happy now. Don't you think?'

'Oh yes,' said Fleur. 'Very happy.' She paused, then added, 'But I agree with you about Lambert. I was quite taken aback at the way he seemed so hostile towards me. Almost . . . distrustful.' She looked at Richard with a hurt expression. 'I was only giving my opinion.'

'Of course you were!' said Richard hotly. 'And your opinion was absolutely spot on! That Lambert's got a lot to answer for. If it weren't for you—' He broke off and gazed across the table at Fleur with more love in his face than she'd ever seen there before.

Fleur stared at him for an instant, thinking quickly. Then suddenly she exclaimed, 'Oh no!' and clasped her hand to her mouth.

'What?'

'Nothing,' said Fleur. 'It doesn't matter.' She sighed. 'It's just my purse. You remember I lost it last week?'

'Did you?'

'Didn't I tell you? Yes, I lost it out shopping. I reported it to some policeman or other but you know what they're like . . .'

'I had no idea!' said Richard. 'Did you cancel your cards?'

'Oh yes,' said Fleur. 'In fact, that's the problem. I haven't got any replacements.'

'Do you need some money?' Richard began to feel in his pocket. 'Darling, you should have said!'

'The trouble is, the replacements will take a while,' said Fleur. She frowned. 'It's all a bit complicated. You know I bank in the Cayman Islands. And Switzerland, of course.'

'I didn't,' said Richard, 'but nothing surprises me about you any more.'

'They're very good generally,' said Fleur, 'but they're hopeless about issuing new cards.'

'You should try a normal bank, like the rest of us,' said Richard.

'I know,' said Fleur, 'but my accountants recommended I go offshore for some reason . . .' She spread her hands vaguely.

'Here's a hundred pounds,' said Richard, holding out some notes.

'I've got cash,' said Fleur distractedly. 'It's just that . . . I've only just remembered it's Zara's birthday next week. I'd completely forgotten!'

'Zara's birthday!' said Richard. 'I had no idea.'

'I really want to buy her something nice.' She tapped her nails urgently on the arm of her chair. 'What I really need is my replacement Gold Card. But quickly.'

'Let me give them a ring,' said Richard.

'I'm telling you,' said Fleur, 'they're hopeless.'

She tapped her nails on the chair a few more times. Then suddenly she looked up.

'Richard, you've got a Gold Card, haven't you? Could you get me on it quickly? In the next couple of days? Then I could whiz over to Guildford and get Zara something nice – and by then my replacements might just have come through. If I'm lucky.' She looked seriously at him. 'I know it's a lot to ask you . . .'

'Well,' said Richard, 'no, it's not. I'm only too happy to help. But I don't think we need to go to all the trouble of another Gold Card. Why don't I just lend you some money?'

'Cash?' Fleur shuddered. '1 never carry cash when I'm shopping. Never! It makes me feel as though I'm asking to be attacked.'

'Well, then, why don't I come shopping with you for Zara's presents? I'd enjoy doing that. You know,' Richard's face softened, 'I've become very fond of Zara. Although I do wish she'd eat more.'

'What?' Fleur stared at him, temporarily diverted.

'All these salads and glasses of water! Each time I watch her picking at her food like a little bird, I have an overwhelming urge to cook her a plate of bacon and eggs and force her to eat them!' Richard shrugged. 'I'm sure you're doing the right thing, not drawing attention to her eating habits. And I'm sure there isn't really a problem there. But she is so terribly thin.' He smiled. 'Knowing Zara, I don't suppose she'd take kindly to being told what to eat!'

'No,' said Fleur. 'I don't suppose she would.'

'But she'll have a birthday cake, at any rate!' Richard's eyes began to shine. 'We'll plan a party for her. Perhaps we could make it a surprise!'

'When can you get me on your Gold Card? By Saturday?'

'Fleur, I'm not sure about this Gold Card scheme.'

'Oh.' Fleur stared at him. 'Why not?'

'It's just . . . something I've never done. Put someone else on my card. It doesn't seem necessary.'

'Oh. I see.' Fleur thought for a moment. 'Wasn't Emily on your card?'

'No, she · had her own. We always kept money affairs separate. It seemed sensible.'

'Separate?' Fleur stared at Richard with features which she hoped displayed surprise, rather than the irritation which had begun to spark inside her. How dared he balk at putting her on his Gold Card? she thought furiously. What was happening to her? Was she losing her touch? 'But that's not natural!' she said out loud. 'You were married! Didn't you want to . . . to share everything?' Richard rubbed his nose.

'I wanted to,' he said, 'at first. I liked the idea of a joint bank account. I wanted to pool everything. But Emily didn't. She wanted everything more cut and dried. So she had her own account and her own credit cards and—' He broke off and smiled sheepishly. 'I'm not sure how we got on to this subject. It's very boring.'

'Zara's birthday,' said Fleur.

'Oh yes,' said Richard. 'Don't worry – we'll give Zara a wonderful birthday.'

'And you don't think it would be more sensible for me to put my name on your card? Just to whiz round the shops with.'

'Not really,' said Richard. 'But, if you like, we can apply for one for you in your own name.'

'OK,' said Fleur lightly. Her jaw tightened imperceptibly and she stared at her nails. Richard turned to the sports section of *The Times*. For a few minutes there was silence. Then suddenly without looking up, Fleur said, 'I might be going to a funeral soon.'

'Oh dear!' Richard looked up.

'A friend in London has asked me to call him. We've been expecting bad news for a while. I've got a feeling this might be it.'

'I know what it's like,' said Richard soberly. 'These things can drag on and on. You know, I sometimes think it's better—'

'Yes,' said Fleur, reaching for *The Times* and turning to the announcements column. 'Yes, so do I.'

'How long are you going to stay with us?' asked Antony. He was sitting with Zara in a secluded corner of the garden, idly plucking strawberries from the patch and eating them, while she pored intently over a thick, glossy magazine. Zara looked up at him. She was wearing opaque black sunglasses and he couldn't read her expression.

'I don't know,' she said, and looked down at her magazine again.

'It would be great if you were still here when Will gets back,' said Antony. He waited for Zara to ask who Will was or where he was. But all she did was chew a few times on her gum, and turn the page. Antony ate another strawberry and wondered why he didn't just go off and play golf or something. Zara didn't need looking after; she hardly ever said anything; she never smiled or laughed. It wasn't as if they were having a riotous time together. And yet something about her fascinated him. He would actually be quite happy, he admitted to himself, to sit staring at Zara all day and do nothing else. But at the same time it felt wrong, to sit alone with someone and not at least try to talk to them.

'Where do you normally live?' he said.

'We move around,' said Zara.

'But you must have a home.' Zara shrugged. Antony thought for a moment.

'Like . . . where were you last holidays?'

'Staying with a friend,' said Zara. 'On his yacht.'

'Oh right.' Antony shifted on the grass. Yachts were outside his experience. All he knew, from people at school, was that you had to be bloody rich to have one. He looked at Zara with new respect, wondering if she would elaborate. But her attention was still fixed on her magazine. Antony looked over her shoulder at the pictures. They were all of girls like Zara, thin and young, with bony shoulders and hollow chests, staring with huge sad eyes at the camera. None of them looked any older than Zara. He wondered if she recognized herself in the pictures or whether she was just looking at the clothes. Personally he thought every outfit more frightful than the one before.

'Do you like designer clothes?' he tried. He looked at the T-shirt she was wearing. Might that be by some famous designer? He couldn't tell. 'Your mother wears lovely clothes,' he added politely. An image popped into his mind of Fleur in her red dress, all curves and shiny hair and bubbling laughter. Zara couldn't have been more different from her mother if she'd tried. Then it occurred to him that perhaps she did try.

'What's your star sign?' Her raspy voice interrupted his thoughts.

'Oh. Aries.' Without looking up, she began to read aloud.

' "Planetary activity in Pluto is transforming your direction in life. After the 18th, you will enter a more purposeful phase".' She turned the page.

'Do you really believe in all that stuff?' said Antony, before she could continue.

'It depends what it says. When it's good, I believe it.' She glanced up at him and a little grin appeared at the comer of her mouth.

'So what does yours say? What are you?'

'Sagittarius.' She threw the magazine down. 'Mine says get a life and stop reading crappy horoscopes.' She threw her head back and breathed in deeply. Antony thought fast. Now was the moment to get a conversation going.

'Do you ever go out clubbing?' he said.

'Sure,' said Zara. 'When we're in London. When I have someone to go with.'

'Oh, right.' Antony thought again. 'Is London where your dad lives?'

'No. He lives in the States.'

'Oh right! Is he American?'

'Yes,'

'Cool! Whereabouts does he live?' This was great, thought Antony. They could start talking about where they'd been in the States. He could tell her about his school trip to California. Maybe he could even get out his photos.

'I don't know.' Zara looked away. 'I've never seen him. I don't even know his name.'

'What?' Antony, who had been poised to display his knowledge of San Francisco, found himself exhaling sharply instead. Had he heard her right? 'You don't know your dad's name?' he said, trying to sound interested rather than shaken.

'No.'

'Hasn't your . . .' Whatever he said, it was going to sound stupid. 'Hasn't your mother told you?'

'She says it doesn't matter what he's called.'

'Do you know anything about him?'

'Nope.'

'So how do you know he lives in the States?'

'That's the only thing she's ever told me. Ages ago, when I was a little kid.' She hunched her knees to her chest. 'I always used to think . . .' She raised her head and sunlight flashed off her shades. 'I always used to think he was a cowboy.'

'Maybe he is,' said Antony. He stared at Zara, all scrunched up and bony, and imagined her relaxed and laughing, sitting on a horse, in front of a tanned, heroic cowboy. It seemed as likely as anything else.

'Why won't your mother tell you?' he said bluntly. 'Isn't that against the law or something?'

'Maybe,' said Zara. 'That wouldn't worry Fleur.' She sighed. 'She won't tell me because she doesn't want me trying to find him. It's like . . . he's her past, not mine.'

'But he's your father!'

'I know,' said Zara. 'He's my father.' She pushed her shades up, off her face and looked straight at Antony. 'Don't worry. I am going to find him,' she said.

'How?'

'When I'm sixteen,' said Zara. 'Then she's going to tell me who he is. She's promised.' Antony stared at her. Her eyes were faintly gleaming. 'Two and a half years to go. Then I'll be off to the States. She can't stop me.'

'I'll have left school by then,' said Antony eagerly. 'I could come with you!'

'OK,' said Zara. She met his eyes and, for the first time, she smiled properly at him. 'We'll both go.'

Later on, they both wandered in, hot and sunburned, to find Richard sitting alone in the kitchen, a glass of beer in front of him. It was quiet and still and the light of early evening streamed in through the window and across his face. Antony opened the fridge and got out a couple of cans.

'Did you play golf today?' he asked his father.

'No. Did you?'

'No.'

'I thought you guys were golf addicts,' said Zara. Richard smiled.

'Is that what your mother told you?'

'It's obvious,' said Zara. 'You live on a golf course, for Christ's sake.'

'Well, I do enjoy a game of golf,' said Richard. 'But it's not the only thing in the world.'

'Where's Fleur?' said Zara.

'I don't know,' said Richard. 'She must have popped out somewhere.'

Richard no longer winced when he heard Zara refer

to her mother as 'Fleur'. Sometimes he even found it faintly endearing. He watched as Antony and Zara settled themselves on the windowseat with drinks; comfortably, like a pair of cats. Zara's was a low-calorie drink, he noticed – and he wondered again how much she weighed. Then he chided himself. She wasn't his daughter; he mustn't start behaving as though she were.

But still. Oliver Sterndale's words rang again through his mind. What would happen if you were, say, to remarry?

'What indeed?' said Richard aloud. Antony and Zara looked up. 'Don't mind me,' he added.

'Oh right,' said Antony politely. 'Do you mind if we have the telly on?'

'Not at all,' said Richard. 'Go ahead.'

As the kitchen filled with chattering sound, he took a sip of beer. The money was all still on deposit, waiting for him to make up his mind. A small fortune, to be split between his two children. It had seemed such an obvious step when he'd discussed it with Emily. The picture had seemed complete; the cast of players had seemed finite.

But now there were two more players in the scene. There was Fleur. And there was little Zara. Richard leaned back and closed his eyes. Had Emily ever thought that he might marry after her death? Or had she, like him, believed that their love could never be supplanted? The possibility of remarriage had never, not once, crossed his mind. His grief had seemed too huge; his love too strong. And then he'd met Fleur, and everything had started to change.

Did he want to marry Fleur? He didn't know. At the moment he was still enjoying the fluid, day-to-day nature of their existence together. Nothing was defined, there were no outside pressures, the days were floating by agreeably.

But it was not in Richard's nature to float indefinitely; it was not in his nature to ignore problems in the hope that they would go away. Problems must be addressed. In particular, the problem of . . . the problem of . . . Richard squirmed awkwardly in his seat. As usual, his thoughts wanted to shy away from the subject. But this time he forced them back; this time he confronted the very word in his thoughts. Of sex. The problem of sex.

Fleur was an understanding woman, but she would not understand for ever. Why should she, when Richard didn't understand himself? He adored Fleur. She was beautiful and desirable and every other man envied him. Yet whenever he came to her bedroom and saw her lying in bed, staring at him with those mesmerizing eyes, inviting him in, a guilty fear came over him, subsuming his desire and leaving him pale and shaking with frustration.

He had thought until now that this factor alone would prove the obstacle to his marrying Fleur; had resigned himself to the fact that before long she would make her excuses and move off, like an exotic insect, to another, more fruitful flower. But she seemed in no hurry to leave. She almost seemed to know something he didn't. And so Richard had begun to wonder whether he weren't looking at the problem in the wrong way. He had been telling himself that the lack of sex came in the way of a marriage. But might it not be that the lack of a marriage was coming in the way of sex? Might it not be that until he fully committed himself to Fleur, he would feel unable to cast off the shadow of Emily? And had Fleur – perceptive Fleur – already realized this? Did she understand him better than he understood himself?

Taking another sip of his beer, Richard resolved to talk to Fleur about it that very night. He wouldn't make the mistake he had made with Emily, of leaving things unsaid until it was too late. With Fleur it would be different. With Fleur there would be no hidden thoughts. With Fleur, thought Richard, nothing was secret.

# TEN

Fleur rarely dwelled on mistakes or misfortune. Striding swiftly along the paths of the Greyworth estate, blinking as the dazzling evening sunlight caught her in the eye, she did not allow herself to consider that the past few months with Richard Favour might all have been for no financial gain whatsoever. Instead, she focused her mind fully ahead. The next funeral, the next memorial service, the next conquest. Thinking positive was Fleur's speciality. She would call Johnny and fix herself up some more funerals and Richard Favour would become just another name from the past.

In fact, she rationalized, leaning against a tree to catch her breath, it had been no bad thing for her to stay at The Maples for a while, money or no money. After all, few of the men whose hospitality she had enjoyed in the past had allowed her to get away with doing so very little as Richard Favour did. The demands he made on her were practically zero. She wasn't required to exert herself in the bedroom. She wasn't required to exert herself in the kitchen. She wasn't expected to host elaborate functions, nor to remember people's names, nor to profess fondness for any small children or animals.

This time with Richard had been a recharging time. A rest-cure, practically. She would emerge refreshed and regenerated, ready for the next challenge. And it was unrealistic to suppose that she would leave The Maples with no money whatsoever. She would manage to mop up a couple of thousand before she left, maybe more. She wouldn't exactly steal it – breaking the law directly wasn't Fleur's style. But twisting the law to suit her own ends was exactly her style, as was judging exactly how much she could risk taking from a man without provoking a chase.

She had reached The Meadows – a remote corner of the Greyworth estate laid over to natural beauty which was rarely visited. Glancing around to check no-one was around to overhear, she took her mobile phone from her bag, switched it on, and dialled Johnny's number.

'Johnny.'

'Fleur! At last!'

'What do you mean, at last?' said Fleur, frowning slightly.

'Didn't Zara tell you to ring me?'

'Oh,' said Fleur, remembering. 'Yes, she did. She said you were in a tizz.'

'Yes, I am. And it's all your fault.'

'My fault? Johnny, what are you talking about?'

'It's not *what* I'm talking about,' said Johnny, in a

voice laden with drama. 'It's *who* I'm talking about.' Fleur had a sudden mental picture of him standing by the mantelpiece in his Chelsea drawing room, sipping sherry, enjoying every moment of their conversation.

'All right, Johnny,' she said patiently. 'Who are you talking about?' There was a perfectly timed pause, then Johnny said,

'Hal Winters. That's who.'

'Oh, for God's sake.' Rattled, Fleur found herself snapping more loudly than she had meant to. 'Not that old story again. I've told you, Johnny . . .'

'He's in London.'

'What?' Fleur felt the colour drain from her cheeks. 'What's he doing in London?'

'Looking for you.'

'How can he be looking for me? He wouldn't know where to start.'

'He started with us.'

'I see.' Fleur stared ahead for a few seconds, as thoughts whirled round her mind. An evening breeze rustled the trees and blew through her hair, warm and soft. Here at Greyworth, London seemed another country. And yet it was under an hour away. Hal Winters was under an hour away.

'So what did you tell him?' she said at last. 'I hope you sent him away.'

'We stalled him,' said Johnny.

'Meaning?'

'Meaning in a few days' time, he's going to be back on our doorstep, wanting to know if we've got anywhere.'

'And you'll just tell him that you haven't,' said Fleur briskly.

'No we won't.'

'What?' Fleur stared at the receiver.

'Felix and I have discussed it. We think you should agree to see him.'

'Well you can both bugger off!'

'Fleur . . .'

'I know. A pound in the bloody swear box.'

'Fleur, listen to me.' Suddenly the drama was gone from Johnny's voice. 'You can't keep running away for ever.'

'I'm not running away!'

'What do you call your life, then?'

'I . . . What do you mean? Johnny, what is all this?'

'You can't treat Hal Winters like you treat all the others. You can't run away from him. It's not fair.'

'Who are you to tell me what's fair and what isn't?' said Fleur furiously. 'You've got nothing to do with it. And if you tell Hal Winters where I am . . .'

'I wouldn't do that without your permission,' said Johnny. 'But I'm asking you to change your mind. If you could have seen his face you'd understand. He's desperate.'

'Why should he be desperate to see me?' said Fleur sharply. 'It's not as though he knows.'

'But he does know!' said Johnny. 'That's the whole point! He does know!' Fleur felt her legs weaken beneath her.

'He knows?'

'He doesn't exactly know,' amended Johnny. 'But he's obviously found something out. And now he wants the whole story.'

'Well, he can bugger off too.'

'Fleur, grow up! He deserves to know the truth. You know he does. And Zara deserves to meet her father.'

Gillian arrived back from her bridge lesson to find Richard on his third glass of beer, Antony and Zara engrossed in the television, no sign of Fleur and no sign of supper.

'What's everyone been doing?' she said shortly, dumping her bag on the kitchen table and opening the fridge. All the dishes and packets that she had set aside for Fleur were still there, untouched.

'Nothing,' said Richard idly. 'Just sitting.' He glanced up and smiled at Gillian. She half-smiled back, but on her face was the beginnings of a frown. Richard looked past her at the fridge, and suddenly realized what had happened.

'Gillian! The supper! I'm so sorry. Quick, Antony, let's help Gillian.' He leapt to his feet, and Antony slowly followed suit.

'What's wrong?' he said, eyes still glued to the television, moving like a zombie across the kitchen.

'Well, Fleur . . .' Richard tailed away in discomfiture. 'Oh dear. Oh Gillian, I'm terribly sorry.'

'It doesn't matter,' said Gillian, staring gloomily down at the unassembled ingredients before her.

'Fleur promised to make supper, right?' Zara's voice cut harshly across the kitchen.

'Well, she did make some mention of it,' said Richard feebly. 'I've no idea where she's got to.' Zara rolled her eyes.

'What I would do,' she said, 'is order take-out and make her pay for it. Forget all this stuff.' She gestured at the table. 'Get something easy and expensive. You got a phone book?'

'It'll be just as quick for me to do it,' said Gillian, taking off her jacket with a sigh. 'And we've got everything out now.'

'Yeah, so we put it away again. And we make a phone call. And they deliver the food. How quick is that? Quicker than peeling a pile of carrots.' Zara shrugged. 'It's up to you. But I'd go for take-out. This stuff'll keep, right?'

'Well, yes,' said Gillian grudgingly. 'Most of it.'

'Which things won't? Tell us exactly, then we can keep those bits out and eat them. Is it like . . . salad type stuff?' Zara grinned at Antony. 'You can tell I failed Home Ec.' She turned back to Gillian. 'What won't keep?'

'I'll . . . I'll have to have a look.'

Gillian moved away from Zara and prodded a packet of lettuce. It was ridiculous; the girl was only a child. But Zara's easy analysis of the situation left her feeling suddenly unsure of herself. Inside, a familiar mass of resentment had already built up; grumbling phrases were on her lips; her face was poised to frown in martyred gloom. That was the role she knew; that was the role which everyone expected. Everyone but Zara.

'I should add that I can't stand Indian,' added Zara, taking a swig from her can. 'And we don't want some crummy pizza. Do you have a good Thai take-out place round here?'

'I have no idea,' said Richard, starting to laugh. 'We're not really "take-out" sort of people. Are we Gillian?'

'I don't know,' said Gillian. Weakly, she sat down. Antony was already putting her dishes and labelled plastic boxes back into the fridge. Zara was scanning the Yellow Pages. The moment for righteous indignation had gone; had dissipated. She felt strangely robbed, and at the same time, uplifted.

'I don't think I've ever had Thai food,' she said cautiously.

'Oh, then we absolutely have to have Thai,' said Zara at once. 'Thai food is just the best.' She looked up with an animated face. 'These friends of ours in London, they live right above a Thai food place. I practically live off the stuff when I'm staying with them. Antony, how does this stupid book work? Find me the Thai take-out page.'

'Oh, right.' Obediently, Antony trotted over to Zara's side and began to leaf through the pages. Richard caught Gillian's eye and she felt a sudden urge to giggle.

'OK,' said Zara. 'Let's try these.' She picked up the phone and dialled briskly. 'Hello? Could you please fax me your menu? I'll give you the number,'

'Gillian, why don't you have a drink,' said Richard in

an undertone. His eyes were twinkling. 'Dinner seems to be well under control.'

'Cool,' said Zara, putting down the phone. 'The menu'll be here any minute. Shall I choose?'

'I'll help,' said Antony. 'Dad, can we have the key to your office? We need to get at the fax.'

'You don't mind if I order for everyone?' said Zara.

'You go ahead,' said Richard. He handed the office key to Antony and watched as he and Zara hurried out of the kitchen.

'I was beginning to worry about Zara's eating habits,' he remarked to Gillian when the two of them were out of earshot. 'I think I was worrying about nothing. I've never seen her look so sparky.'

He stood up, stretched, and went into the larder.

'But I am sorry, Gillian,' he said, returning with a bottle of wine. 'About Fleur, I mean. It's not like her to let people down.'

'I know it isn't,' said Gillian. 'I imagine something must have happened to hold her up.'

'I hope she's all right.' Richard frowned, and handed Gillian a glass of wine. 'Perhaps I'll ring the clubhouse in a minute. See if she went for a swim.'

'Good idea,' said Gillian. She took a deep breath. 'And there's no need to apologize. What does a meal matter? It's only food.'

'Well,' said Richard awkwardly. 'Even so.'

'I know I have a tendency to take these things too seriously.' Gillian bit her lip. 'I get . . . what would Antony say? Stressed out. By silly little things.'

She sighed. 'I'm the one who should be sorry.'

'Nonsense!' said Richard. 'Goodness me, Gillian . . .' She ignored him.

'But I think I'm changing.' She sat back, took a sip of wine and looked at Richard over the rim of her glass. 'Fleur's changing me.'

Richard gave a gallant little laugh.

'Changing our charming Gillian? I hope not!'

'Richard!' There was a blade of anger in Gillian's voice. 'Don't be polite to me, please. Tell me I'm changing for the better.' She took a deep sip of wine. 'I know you and I don't usually speak to each other on this . . .'

'This level.' Richard's expression was suddenly serious.

'Exactly. This level.' She swallowed. 'But you must realize as well as I that since Fleur has been here things have been different. There's something about Fleur . . .' She tailed away and blinked a few times.

'I know,' agreed Richard. 'There is.'

'Fleur is kind to me in a way that my own sister never was,' said Gillian in a voice which trembled slightly.

'Emily?' Richard stared at her.

'Emily was a dear sister to me. But she had her faults. She did things that were thoughtless and unkind.' Gillian raised her head and looked straight at Richard. Her blue eyes were glistening. 'Perhaps I shouldn't be telling you this now,' she said. 'But it's the truth. Emily was unkind to me. And Fleur is kind. That's all.'

Fleur had arrived back at The Maples, gone straight

upstairs and into her bedroom. Now she was seated in front of the mirror in her bedroom, wearing her black veiled hat, staring at her reflection. She had been sitting there for half an hour without moving, waiting for the unfamiliar feeling of disquiet to subside. But still her insides felt clenched and her brow was screwed up in wrinkles, and Johnny's voice rang in her ear, cross and pestering like a woodpecker. 'Why won't you see him? Why won't you face up to your past? When are you going to stop running?'

Never before had she heard Johnny so stern; so unbiddable.

'What do you expect me to do? Invite him to stay?' she'd said, trying to sound flippant. 'Introduce him to Richard? Come on, Johnny. Be serious.'

'I expect you to acknowledge his existence,' said Johnny. 'You could meet him in London.'

'I couldn't. I haven't got time.'

'You haven't got time.' Johnny's voice was scathing. 'Well, perhaps Zara has got time.'

'She can't meet her father yet! She . . . she isn't ready! She needs to be prepared!'

'And you're going to do that, are you?'

There was silence.

'OK, Fleur, have it your own way,' said Johnny at last. 'You let me know when Zara's ready to meet her father, and I'll keep putting him off for the moment. But that's all I'm doing.'

'Johnny, you're a doll . . .'

'No more funerals,' said Johnny. 'No more

invitations. No more arriving out of the blue and expecting to use our spare room.'

'Johnny!'

'I'm not pleased with you, Fleur.'

And as she stared disbelievingly at the phone, he'd rung off, and a cold chunk of dismay had descended into her stomach. Everything was suddenly going wrong. Richard wouldn't give her a Gold Card; Johnny was cross with her; Hal Winters was in the country.

Hal Winters. The very name irritated her. He'd already caused enough trouble in her life; now here he was again, turning up out of the blue, threatening to ruin everything, turning her friends against her. Turning Johnny against her. A pang of alarm ran through Fleur. If she lost Johnny, who did she have? Who else was there for her?

Never before had Fleur realized quite how much she depended on Johnny and Felix. For twenty years, Johnny's flat had been at her disposal. For twenty years she had confided in him, gossiped with him, shopped with him. She had thought nothing of it. If asked, she would have described their friendship as casual. Now that it was under threat, it seemed suddenly far more than that. Fleur closed her eyes. She and Johnny had never disagreed before over anything more significant than the colour of a sofa. He had scolded her often enough in the past, but always with a twinkle in his eye. Never seriously, never like this. This, he was taking seriously. This time he meant business. And all because of a man named Hal Winters.

Fleur stared angrily at her reflection. She looked a sophisticated, elegant woman. She could be the consort of an ambassador. A prince. And Hal Winters was . . . what? A drugs salesman from Scottsdale, Arizona. A cheap drugs salesman who fourteen years ago had coupled nervously with her in the back of his Chevy and then brushed his hair carefully back into place so that his mother wouldn't notice anything awry. Who had asked her to keep her distance in public and please not blaspheme in front of his family.

Bitterly, Fleur wondered again how she could have been so stupid. How she could have mistaken that sulky diffidence for gauche charm. How she could have allowed him to invade her body; plant a piece of his second-rate self in her own. She had let him into her life once; never again. A man like Hal Winters could not be recognized as part of her existence. Could never be permitted to claim a piece of her life. And if that meant losing Johnny, then so it would have to be.

Fleur lifted her chin determinedly. Quickly she took off the veiled hat and replaced it with another. A black cloche; a smart, serious hat. She would find a memorial service to wear it to next week. So Johnny refused to feed her any suitable funerals. Well, what of it? She didn't need Johnny. She could survive very well on her own. On the dressing table in front of her were three newspaper clippings. Three London memorial services. Three chances for a fresh start. And this time, she wouldn't sit around for weeks, letting her life slip away. She would pounce at once. If Richard Favour wasn't going to make her a rich woman, then somebody was.

She bit her lip, and quickly reached for another hat; another distraction. This was made from black silk and sprinkled with tiny violets. A very pretty hat, thought Fleur, admiring the picture she made in the mirror. Almost too pretty for a funeral; almost a hat for a wedding.

As she turned her head from side to side, she heard a knock at the door.

'Hello?'

'Fleur! Can I come in?' It was Richard. He sounded flustered.

'Of course!' she called back. 'Come on in!'

The door burst open and in came Richard.

'I don't know what I was thinking of this morning,' he said in a flurry. 'Of course you can have a Gold Card. You have whatever you damn well like! My darling Fleur . . .' Suddenly he seemed to see her for the first time, and broke off. 'That . . . that hat,' be faltered.

'Forget the hat!' Fleur tore it off her head and threw it on the floor. 'Richard, you're a poppet!' She looked up, a dazzling smile on her face. He was standing completely still, staring at her as though he'd never seen her before in his life.

'Richard?' she said. 'Is something wrong?'

He really hadn't expected her to be in her bedroom. He had planned to go and see how the two young people were getting on with the food ordering, then ring the health club and ask whether Fleur was there. But as he'd passed her door, it had occurred to him, at the back of his troubled mind, that he might as well knock on the door, just to be sure. He'd done so perfunctorily, his thoughts elsewhere, swirling uneasily around this new, undigested fact about Emily.

Emily had been unkind to Gillian. He found it painful to frame the thought in his mind. His own, sweet timid Emily, unkind to her own sister. It was an astonishing accusation; one which he found it difficult to believe. But not – and it was this that troubled him the most – not impossible. For even as Gillian had told him there had been, amongst the immediate protestations and shouts of denial around his brain, a small, sober part of him that was not surprised; that perhaps had always known.

As he'd left the kitchen, a pain had begun to jab at his chest and he had felt a renewed grief for Emily the Emily he had loved. A sweet, remote creature with hidden qualities. Qualities he had been desperate to unmask. Was unkindness one of those qualities? You wanted to find out, he told himself bitterly, as he walked up the stairs. And now you have found out. All the time, underneath that mild exterior had been a secret unkindness, from which Gillian had suffered in uncomplaining silence. He could hardly bear to think about it.

And suddenly he'd wanted, above anything else, to see Fleur. Warm, loving Fleur, with not an unkind bone in her body. Fleur, who made Gillian happy and him happy and everybody happy. When he'd heard her voice unexpectedly answer his knock he'd felt an almost tearful love rising through him; an enveloping emotion which propelled him through the door, forced speech from his lips.

And then he'd seen her, sitting in front of the dressing table in a hat. A hat just like Emily had worn on the day of their wedding; a hat just like the one she'd been unpinning as he discovered the first of the cold, steely gates that would forever lie between them. Part of him had expected Fleur to do the same as Emily had then. To unpin her hat, and lay it aside carefully, and look straight through him, and ask, 'What time's dinner?'

But instead, she'd thrown it aside in a whirl, as though contemptuous of anything which got in the way of them. The two of them. Him and Fleur. Now she was holding out her arms to him. Warm and open and loving.

'Fleur, I love you,' he found himself saying. 'I love you.' A tear fell from his eye. 'I love you.'

'And I love you.' She caught him up in an exuberant hug. 'You sweet man.'

Richard buried his head in Fleur's pale neck, feeling tears suddenly stream from his eyes. Tears that mourned the loss of his perfect Emily, the discovery of her fallibility; which marked the passing of his innocence. His mouth was wet and salty when he eventually raised it to Fleur's; began to pull her closer to him, suddenly wanting to feel her warm skin against his own, wanting to break down all barriers between them.

'Why did I wait?' he murmured as his hands feverishly roamed the body she had been offering him for weeks. 'Why on earth did I wait?'

Struggling out of his clothes, feeling her bare skin in patches against his, was an agony of frustration. As her hands ran lightly down his back, he began to shiver with a desperate anticipation, almost frightened that having pitched over the edge he would never make the other side.

'Come here.' Her voice was low and melodious in his ear; her fingers were warm and confident on his body. He felt unable to reciprocate, unable to do anything but shudder in a paralysis of delight. And then, slowly, she took him into her mouth, and he felt a disbelieving ecstasy which he couldn't begin to control; which he couldn't begin to measure; which made him whimper and cry out until he suddenly fell, spent and exhausted, into her arms.

'I . . .'

'Sssh.' She put a finger against his lips and he fell silent. He lay against her, listening to her heartbeat, and felt like a child, naked and vulnerable and accepting.

'I will give you anything,' he whispered at last. 'Anything you want.'

'All I want is you,' said Fleur softly. He felt her fingers twining in his hair. 'And I've got you, haven't I?'

# ELEVEN

A few days later a package arrived for Fleur through the post. Inside was a shiny golden American Express card.

'Cool!' said Antony, as she opened it at breakfast. 'A Gold Card. Dad, why can't I have one of those? Some of the blokes at school have got them.'

'Then their parents are very stupid as well as very rich,' said Richard, grinning. 'Now, where's a pen? You should sign it straight away, Fleur. It wouldn't do if it fell into the wrong hands.'

'I'll be very careful,' said Fleur, smiling at him. She squeezed his hand. 'It's very good of you, Richard. Now'll be able to get something really super for Zara.'

'Zara?' Antony looked up.

'It's Zara's birthday this week,' said Richard.

'Her birthday?' echoed Antony.

'On Wednesday. Is that right, Fleur?'

'Yes,' said Fleur, signing the Gold Card with a flourish. 'I'll go into Guildford this morning.'

'Would she like it if I made a cake, do you think?' enquired Gillian.

'I'm sure she would,' said Fleur, smiling warmly at Gillian.

'How old is she going to be?' said Antony.

'Fourteen,' said Fleur, after a moment's hesitation.

'Oh right.' Antony frowned slightly. 'Because I thought she wasn't fourteen for a while yet.'

'Lying about her age already!' said Fleur, and gave a peal of laughter. 'Antony, you should be flattered!' Antony coloured slightly, and looked down at his plate.

'What about . . .' Gillian hesitated, glanced at Richard, then continued. 'What about Zara's father? Will he want to . . . visit her?' She flushed. 'Perhaps I shouldn't have mentioned it. I just thought, if it's her birthday . . .'

'Gillian, you're very kind,' said Fleur. She took a sip of coffee. 'Unfortunately, Zara's father is dead.'

'Dead?' Antony's head jerked up. 'But I thought . . . I thought Zara's dad lived in America. She told me . . .'

Fleur shook her head sadly.

'Zara found it very difficult to come to terms with her father's death,' she said, and sipped again at her coffee. 'In her mind, he's still alive. She has many different fantasies about him. The current one is that he's living somewhere in America.' She sighed. 'I've been told that the best thing is just to play along with her.'

'But . . .'

'I blame myself,' said Fleur. 'I should have talked to her more about it. But it was a painful time for me, too.'

She broke off, and looked at Antony with wide, sympathetic eyes. Richard took her hand and squeezed it.

'I didn't realize,' said Antony feebly. 'I thought . . .'

'She's coming,' interrupted Gillian quickly. 'Hello Zara,' she exclaimed brightly as Zara entered the conservatory. 'We were just talking about your birthday.'

'My birthday,' echoed Zara, stopping still in the doorway. Her cautious gaze swept the scene and landed on the Gold Card, glinting among the paper packaging on the table. She looked up at Fleur, then back at the Gold Card. 'Sure,' she said. 'My birthday.'

'We want Wednesday to be a really special day for you, darling,' said Fleur. 'With a cake, and candles, and . . .' she spread her hands vaguely.

'Party-poppers,' said Zara tonelessly.

'Party-poppers! What a good idea!'

'Yup,' said Zara.

'Well, that's settled,' said Richard. 'Now, I have some calls to make.' He got up.

'If you'd like a lift into Guildford,' said Gillian to Fleur, 'I could do with popping in myself.'

'Lovely,' said Fleur.

'And what will you two young things do?' said Richard to Antony.

'Dunno,' said Antony. Zara shrugged, and looked away.

'Well,' said Richard comfortably, 'I'm sure you'll think of something jolly.'

* * *

As Zara ate her breakfast, she stared straight downwards and avoided Antony's eyes. An angry disappointment was burning in her chest; she didn't trust herself not to burst into tears. Fleur had got hold of a Gold Card. Which meant they were going to move on. As soon as Fleur had cleaned up, they would be off.

It was just like bouncing a ball, Fleur had explained to her a couple of years before, as they sat in some airport restaurant, waiting for a plane.

'You take the Gold Card, and you cash some money, and the next day you put it back again. Then you cash some more, and put that back again. And you keep going, bouncing higher and higher until you're as high as you can go – then you scoop up all the money and disappear!' She'd laughed, and Zara had laughed too.

'Why don't you just scoop it all up at the beginning?' she'd asked.

'Too suspicious, darling,' Fleur had said. 'You have to work up gradually, so no-one notices.'

'And how do you know when you're as high as you can go?'

'You don't. You try to find out as much as you can before you start. Is he rich? Is he poor? How much can he afford to lose? But then you've just got to guess. And that's part of the game. Two thousand? Ten thousand? Fifty thousand? Who knows what the limit is?'

Fleur had laughed again, and so had Zara. Back then, it had seemed fun. A good game. Now the whole idea made Zara feel sick.

'Do you want to go swimming?' Antony's voice interrupted her thoughts.

'Oh.' With a huge effort, Zara raised her head to meet Antony's gaze. He was staring at her with a peculiar expression on his face, almost as though he could read her thoughts. Almost as though he knew what was going on.

A dart of panic raced through Zara; her face became guarded. In all these years of pretending, she had never yet slipped up. She couldn't allow herself to become careless. If she gave away the truth to Antony, Fleur would never forgive her. Fleur would never forgive her, and she would never get to meet her father.

'Sure,' she said, forcing a casual tone into her voice, shrugging her shoulders. 'Why not.'

'OK.' He was still staring at her weirdly. 'I'll get my stuff.'

'OK,' she said. And she looked down at her bowl of Honey Nut Loops and didn't look up again until he had gone.

Oliver Sterndale was in the office, his secretary informed Richard over the telephone, but he was about to leave on holiday.

'This won't take long,' said Richard cheerfully. As he waited for Oliver's voice, he looked around his dull, ordered office and wondered why he had never thought to have it redecorated. The walls were plain white, unrelieved by pictures, the carpet a functional slate grey.

There was not one object in the room that could be described as beautiful.

Things like the colour of walls had never seemed to matter to him before. But now he looked at the world through Fleur's eyes. Now he saw possibility where before he had only seen fact. He wouldn't sit in this dull little box any longer. He would ask Fleur to redesign the office for him.

'Richard!' Oliver's voice made him jump. 'I'm just on my way.'

'I know. Off on holiday. This won't take long. I just wanted to tell you that I've made up my mind about the trust.'

'Oh yes?'

'I'm going to go ahead with it.'

'I see. And might I ask why?'

'I've realized that what I really want is to make Philippa and Antony financially independent,' said Richard. 'Beholden to no-one, not even . . .' He paused, and bit his lip. 'Not even a member of their own family. Above all, I want them to feel they have control of their own lives.' He frowned. 'I also want to . . . to close a chapter in my life. Start afresh.'

'Starting afresh usually means spending money,' said Oliver.

'I've got money,' said Richard impatiently. 'Plenty of money. Oliver, we've been over this.'

'All right. Well, it's your decision. But I can't do anything about it for a week.'

'There's no hurry. I just thought I'd let you know. I

won't keep you. Have a good holiday. Where are you going?'

'Provence. Some friends have a house there.'

'Lovely,' said Richard automatically. 'Beautiful countryside in that part of the—'

'Yes, yes,' interrupted Oliver impatiently. 'Look, Richard.'

'Yes?'

'Listen. This starting afresh of yours. Does it involve marrying your friend Fleur?'

'I very much hope so,' said Richard, smiling at the receiver. Oliver sighed.

'Richard, please be cautious.'

'Oliver, not again . . .'

'Just think about the implications of marriage for a moment. I gather, for instance, that Fleur has a daughter of school age.'

'Zara.'

'Zara. Indeed. Now, does her mother have the money to support Zara? Or will that be a role which you're expected to take on?'

'Fleur has the money to send her to Heathland School for Girls,' said Richard drily. 'Is that support enough for you?'

'Well, all right – but you're sure that she pays the fees herself? You're sure that they don't come from some sort of income which will stop if she remarries?'

'No, I'm not sure,' replied Richard testily. 'I haven't had the impertinence to ask.'

'Well, if I were you, I should ask. Just to get an idea.'

'Oliver, you're being ridiculous! What does it matter? You know perfectly well I could afford to send a whole orphanage to public school if I wanted to. Trust or no trust.'

'It's the principle of the thing,' said Oliver testily. 'First it's school fees, then it's failing business ventures, and before you know it . . .'

'Oliver!'

'I'm only trying to safeguard your interests, Richard. Marriage is a very serious matter.'

'Did you ask Helen all these questions before you asked her to marry you?' retorted Richard. 'Lucky girl.' Oliver laughed.

'*Touché*. Look, Richard, I really must go. But we'll talk again when I get back.'

'Have a good time.'

'*Au revoir, mon ami*. And do think about what I've said.'

Zara and Antony walked along in silence, swimming things thrown over their shoulders. Zara stared stonily ahead; Antony was frowning perplexedly. Eventually he said, in a burst,

'Why didn't you tell me it was your birthday this week?'

'I don't have to tell you everything.'

'Didn't you want me to know how old you were?' He risked a little smile.

'I'm thirteen,' said Zara flatly. 'Next birthday, I'll be fourteen.'

'This Wednesday, you'll be fourteen,' corrected Antony.

'Whatever.'

'So, what do you want as a present?'

'Nothing.'

'Come on. There must be something.'

'Nope.' Antony sighed.

'Zara, most people look forward to their birthday.'

'Well I don't.' There was a short silence. Antony peered at Zara's face, trying to elicit some response. There was none. He felt as though he had been catapulted back to the beginning again: that he didn't really know Zara at all.

Then it occurred to him that this silent treatment might all be tied up with her dad and . . . and all that business. He swallowed, feeling suddenly mature and understanding.

'If you ever want to talk,' he said, 'about your dad. I'm here.' He stopped, and felt foolish. Of course he was here – where else could he be? 'I'm here for you,' he amended.

'What's there to talk about?'

'Well, you know . . .'

'I don't. That's the problem. I don't know anything about him.'

Antony sighed.

'Zara, you have to face up to the truth.'

'What truth? You think I won't find him?'

'Zara . . .' She turned her head, finally, and looked at him.

'What? Why are you looking at me like that?'

'Your mother told us.'

'Told you what?'

'That your father's dead.'

'What!' Her screech rose high into the wood; a crow flapped noisily out of the treetops. Antony stared at her in alarm. Her face was white, her nostrils flared, her chin taut and disbelieving. 'Fleur said what?'

'She just told us about your father. Zara, I'm really sorry. I know what it's like when—'

'He isn't dead!'

'Oh God. Look, I shouldn't have said anything.'

'He's not dead, all right?' To Antony's dismay, a tear sprang from Zara's eye.

'Zara! I didn't mean . . .'

'I know you didn't.' She stared down at the ground. 'Look, it's not your fault. This is just something that . . . I have to deal with.'

'Right,' said Antony uncertainly. He didn't feel mature and understanding any more. On the contrary, he felt as though he'd cocked things up completely.

Fleur arrived back from Guildford laden with presents not only for Zara, but also for Richard, Antony and Gillian.

'Zara has to wait until Wednesday,' she said gaily to Richard, pulling out a flamboyant silk tie. 'But you don't. Put it on! See how it looks. I spent quite a lot,' she added, as Richard put the tie around his neck. 'I hope your card can take it. Some credit companies get jumpy whenever you spend more than fifty pounds.'

'I wouldn't worry,' said Richard, knotting the tie. 'That's beautiful, Fleur! Thank you.' He glanced at the plastic bags littering the hall. 'So, a successful trip, I take it?'

'Wonderful,' beamed Fleur. 'I got a present for the whole family, too.' She pointed to a box which had been carried in by the taxi driver. 'It's a video camera.'

'Fleur! How extraordinarily generous of you!'

'That's why I asked about the credit card,' said Fleur, grinning at him. 'It cost quite a lot.'

'I bet it did,' said Richard. 'Goodness me . . .'

'But don't worry. I've already asked my bank in the Cayman Islands to transfer some funds to your account. They can do that overnight, apparently, even though sending me a chequebook seems beyond their capabilities.' Fleur rolled her eyes, then grinned. 'Won't we have fun with this? I've never used a video camera before.' She began to rip at the packaging.

'Neither have I,' replied Richard, watching her. 'I haven't the first idea how to use one.'

'Antony will know. Or Zara.'

'I expect you're right.' Richard frowned slightly. 'Fleur, we've never talked about money, have we?'

'No,' said Fleur. 'We haven't. Which reminds me.' She glanced up at him. 'Would you mind terribly if I made a credit payment to your Gold Card account? I've got some money coming through, and believe it or not, for me at the moment, that would be the most convenient place to deposit it.' She rolled her eyes, then tugged some more at the wrapping of the video camera.

'Oh,' said Richard. 'No. Of course I wouldn't mind. How much?'

'Not very much,' said Fleur carelessly. 'About twenty thousand pounds. I don't know if your card is used to transactions like that.'

'Well, not every day of the week,' said Richard, starting to laugh. 'But I think it could probably cope. Are you sure you don't have somewhere else more orthodox?'

'It would just be for a bit,' said Fleur. 'While I sort out my banking arrangements generally. You don't mind, do you?' She gave a final tug, and lifted the video camera out of its box. 'Oh my God, look at all these buttons! They told me it was easy to use!'

'Perhaps it's easier than it looks. Where are the instructions?'

'They must be in here somewhere. The thing is,' she added, starting to root through the packaging, 'this money's come through rather unexpectedly. From a trust. You know what these family trusts are like.'

'I'm learning,' said Richard.

'And I haven't decided what to use it for yet. I could pay a load of Zara's school fees in advance, in which case I want to keep it ready. Or I could do something else. Invest it, maybe. Here we are! User's Manual.' They both stared at the thick, glossy paperback. 'And this is the Upgrade Supplement,' added Fleur, picking up a further volume. She began to giggle.

'I think I was imagining more of a leaflet,' said

Richard. 'A slim pamphlet.' He reached for the manual and flipped through it a couple of times. 'So you pay Zara's school fees yourself?'

'But of course,' said Fleur. 'Who else did you think might pay them?'

'I thought perhaps Zara's father's family might have offered . . .'

'No,' said Fleur. 'We don't really speak.'

'Oh dear. I didn't realize.'

'But I have some money of my own. Enough for Zara and me.'

She looked at him with luminous eyes, and suddenly Richard felt as though he were trespassing on very private ground. What right did he have to quiz her on matters of money, when he hadn't yet proposed marriage to her? What could she think of him?

'Forgive my curiosity,' he said hastily. 'It's none of my business.'

'Look!' Fleur beamed back at him. 'I think I've found the zoom!'

Antony and Zara arrived back from swimming to find Fleur and Richard still sitting in the hall, poring over the instructions.

'Excellent,' Antony said immediately. 'We've got one of these at school. Shall I have a go?' He picked the video up, took a few steps back and pointed it at the others. 'Now smile. Smile, Dad! Smile, Zara!'

'I don't feel like smiling,' she said, and stumped up the stairs.

'I think she's a bit upset,' Antony said apologetically to Fleur, 'about her dad.'

'I see,' said Fleur. 'Maybe I'd better go up and have a little talk with her.'

'OK,' said Antony, already peering through the viewfinder again. 'Dad, you've got to look *natural*.'

Zara was in her room, sitting on the bed, with her arms clasped round her knees.

'So my father's dead, is he?' she said as Fleur entered the room. 'Fleur, you're a bitch.'

'Don't talk to me like that!'

'Or what?'

Fleur stared at her for a moment. Then, unexpectedly, she gave Zara a sympathetic smile.

'I know things are difficult for you at the moment, darling. It's perfectly normal to be a little moody at your age.'

'I'm not moody! And it's not my fucking birthday on Wednesday, either.'

'Surely you're not going to complain about that! Extra presents, a party . . . It's not even as if it's the first time.' Fleur peered at her reflection in the mirror and smoothed an eyebrow with her thumb. 'You didn't complain when you were ten twice.'

'That's because I was ten,' said Zara. 'I was young. I was dumb. I didn't think it mattered.'

'It doesn't.'

'It does! I just want a regular birthday like everyone else.'

'Yes, well, we all want things we can't have, I'm afraid.'

'And what do you want?' Zara's voice was dry and hostile. She met Fleur's eyes in the mirror. 'What do you want, Fleur? A big house? A big car?'

'Darling . . .'

'Because what I want is for us to stay here. With Richard and Gillian and Antony. I want to stay.' Her voice cracked slightly. 'Why can't we stay?'

'It's all very complex, poppet.' Fleur took out a lipstick and began to apply it carefully.

'No it's not! We could stay here if you wanted to! Richard loves you. I know he does. You two could get married.'

'You're such a child still.' Fleur put down the lipstick and smiled at Zara affectionately, 'I know you've always wanted to be a bridesmaid. When was it that we bought that sweet pink dress for you?'

'It was when I was nine! Jesus!' Zara sprang to her feet in frustration.

'Darling, keep your voice down.'

'Don't you understand?' Suddenly two fat tears sprang onto Zara's cheeks, and she brushed them away impatiently. 'Now I just want . . . I just want a house where I live. You know, like when people say "Where do you live?" And I always have to say "Sometimes in London and sometimes in other places." '

'What's wrong with that? It sounds very glamorous!'

'No-one else lives in "other places". They all have a home!'

'Poppet, I know it's hard for you.'

'It's hard for me because you make it hard!' cried

Zara. 'If you wanted to, we could just stay somewhere. We could have a home.'

'One day we will, darling. I promise. When we're really comfortably off, we'll set up home somewhere, just the two of us.'

'No we won't,' said Zara bitterly. 'You told me we'd be settled by the time I was ten. And look, now I'm thirteen – oops, sorry, fourteen. And we still live with whoever you happen to be fucking.'

'That's enough!' hissed Fleur angrily. 'Now you just listen to me! Quite apart from your atrocious language, which we'll ignore for now, might I point out that you are still a very young girl who doesn't know what's best for her? That I am your mother? That life hasn't been easy for me, either? And that as far as I'm concerned, you've had a wonderful life, full of opportunities and excitements which most girls your age would kill for?'

'Fuck your opportunities!' cried Zara. More tears began to stream down her face. 'I want to stay here. And I don't want you telling people my father's dead!'

'That was unfortunate,' said Fleur, frowning slightly. 'I am sorry about that.'

'But not about the rest,' shuddered Zara. 'You're not sorry about the rest.'

'Darling.' Fleur came over and tenderly wiped away Zara's tears. 'Come on, little one! How about you and I have lunch tomorrow? And have manicures? Just the two of us. We'll have fun.'

Zara gave a silent, shaking shrug. Tears were now

coursing down her face onto her neck, dripping in spots onto her T-shirt.

'I can't believe you're really a teenager,' said Fleur fondly. 'Sometimes you only look about ten years old.' She pulled Zara close and kissed the top of her head. 'Don't you worry, poppet. It'll all come right in the end. We'll sort our lives out.' A fresh stream of tears ran down Zara's face; she was struggling to speak.

'You're tired,' said Fleur. 'You've probably been overdoing it. I think the best thing is if I leave you to get some rest. Have a nice hot bath, and I'll see you downstairs later.' Affectionately she took one of Zara's long blond tresses in her fingers, held it up to the light and let it drop again. Then, without giving Zara another glance, she picked up her lipstick, glanced at her reflection, and left the room.

# TWELVE

Philippa was becoming worried about Lambert. Over the last few weeks he had seemed permanently in a sullen mood; permanently irritated with her. And now his mood was descending from surliness to a snappish anger. Nothing she said was right; nothing she did could please him.

It had all begun with the Briggs & Co. fiasco. The day of the golf game had been bad enough. Then his friend had been exposed in the press as a crook, and Lambert had exploded with a savage anger which seemed primarily directed at Fleur. Philippa suspected that her father had probably had a few words with Lambert at work, which couldn't have helped matters. And now he greeted every morning with a miserable gloom, arrived home from work each evening frowning, and snarled at her if she tried to cheer him up.

To begin with, she hadn't minded. She'd almost welcomed the challenge of Helping her Husband through a Difficult Time. 'For better for worse, for richer for poorer', she'd muttered to herself several times a day. 'To love and to cherish.' Except that Lambert didn't particularly seem to want her love or her cherishing. He didn't seem to want her around at all.

She'd consulted magazine articles on the subject of relationships, and leafed through books at the library, then tried to implement some of the suggestions. She'd tried new recipes for dinner, she'd tried suggesting that the two of them took up a new hobby together, she'd tried asking him seriously if he'd like to discuss things, she'd tried instigating sex. And to each of her attempts she'd received the same frown of displeasure.

There was no-one she could talk to about it. The girls at work talked freely enough about their husbands and boyfriends, but Philippa had always refrained from joining in. For one thing, she had a natural modesty which stopped her from confiding bedroom secrets over the coffee machine. For another – and if she were honest, this was the real reason – Lambert seemed so different from everyone else's husband that she felt embarrassed to tell the others the truth. They all seemed to be married to cheery chaps who liked football, the pub and sex; who appeared at office parties and, even if complete strangers to each other, immediately found a common, joky blokes' footing. But Lambert wasn't like that. He didn't follow the football, nor did he go to the pub. Sometimes he liked sex; sometimes it almost seemed to disgust him. And at office functions he always sat apart from everyone else, smoking a cigar, looking bored. Afterwards, in the car, he would mock the accents of everyone she worked with, and Philippa would find herself sadly abandoning her scheme of inviting a few nice couples home for dinner.

They hadn't been back to The Maples since the day of the golf débâcle. Every time she suggested it, Lambert scowled and said he hadn't got time. And although she could have gone home on her own, she didn't want to. She didn't want anyone guessing anything was wrong. And so she sat in with Lambert, night after night, watching the television and reading novels. At the weekends, when every other couple seemed to have plans, she and Lambert had none. They got up, and Lambert went to his study and read the paper, and then it was lunchtime, and then sometimes Philippa went out and wandered round the shops. And every day she felt more lonely.

Then, with no warning whatsoever, Fleur rang Philippa up.

'Philippa, it's Fleur. I'm up in London on Friday for a memorial service. How about a spot of lunch?'

'Lunch? Gosh!' Philippa felt herself blushing and her heart beginning to thud, as though she were being asked on a date. 'I'd love to!'

'I know you'll be at work,' Fleur said, 'otherwise I'd suggest meeting earlier and doing some shopping.'

'I'll take the day off,' Philippa found herself saying. 'I've loads of spare holiday.'

'Lucky you! Well, why don't you meet my train? I'll let you know which one. And we can take it from there.'

As Philippa rang off, she was filled with elated lightness. Fleur wanted to be her friend. Immediately a picture came into her mind of the two of them, giggling together as they ordered a meal in an expensive restaurant; daring one another to try on outlandish outfits. Arranging another meeting. Philippa hugged herself with excitement. Fleur was her friend!

'I'm having lunch with Fleur on Friday,' she called to Lambert, trying to sound casual. 'She's up in London.'

'Bully for her.'

'She's going to a memorial service,' said Philippa, unable to stop a flow of happy words from spilling out of her. 'I wonder whose? Someone from her family, I expect. Or a friend maybe. She'll probably look quite smart. I wonder what I should wear? Shall I buy something new?'

As Philippa's voice babbled on, Lambert's mind was elsewhere. In front of him was another tightly worded letter from the bank, requiring solid assurance that he was going to be able to pay off his substantial, unapproved overdraft. He had to lay his hands on some money and soon. Which meant going down to The Maples again and getting into Richard's office. But it was risky. Particularly since he wasn't in Richard's good books at the moment. Lambert scowled. The old fool had called him into his office at work and ticked him off for insulting Fleur. Ticked him off! Never mind that Fleur had completely fucked up their game; that she had no idea how to behave on a golf course. But of course there was no point talking sense to Richard at the moment. He'd fallen under the spell of Fleur and there was nothing to be done about it except wait for it to pass and, preferably, avoid The Maples until Richard had snapped out of it.

'What I really need is some shorts,' Philippa was saying, next door, as though she thought he was still listening. 'For the weekends. Kind of tailored, but not too smart . . .'

The problem was that he couldn't wait until Richard had snapped out of it. He needed money quickly. Lambert took a sip of beer from the heavy silver tankard on his desk and stared at the letter again. Fifty thousand would keep the bank quiet. He was sure it would. And it was waiting for him at The Maples. If he could be certain that he wouldn't cock things up; that he wouldn't be discovered . . . A sudden unwanted memory came to him of Fleur's voice behind him, startling him as he leafed through Richard's files, and he felt again a prickling of cold sweat on the back of his neck. Of course she hadn't suspected anything, why should she? But if that had been Richard . . .

Suddenly Philippa's voice pierced his consciousness.

'Apparently Daddy'll be away at a meeting that day,' she was saying, 'and Gillian's got her bridge lesson.' Lambert's head twitched up. 'Otherwise Fleur would have suggested they came along too. But I think it's quite nice, don't you? Just the two of us? Like a kind of, you know, bonding thing?'

Lambert stood up and stalked into the next room.

'What did you say? Your father's got a meeting on Friday?'

'Yes. He's got to go to Newcastle, apparently.'

'First I've heard of it.'

'Oh dear. Hasn't he asked you to go, too?' Philippa bit her lip. 'You could come to lunch with Fleur and me,' she said doubtfully. 'If you want to.'

'Don't be stupid. Me have lunch with a pair of gigglers like you?'

Philippa tittered, pleased by the notion of herself and Fleur as a pair of gigglers. Feeling suddenly generous, Lambert grinned back at her.

'You two ladies have your lunch together,' he said. 'I've more important things to do that day.'

Wednesday dawned bright and hot and blue. By the time Zara arrived downstairs, the breakfast table had been laid in the garden. A huge posy of flowers was arranged beside her place, a silver helium balloon rose shimmering from the back of her chair, and her plate was covered in cards and packages.

'Happy birthday!' cried Antony as soon as he saw her stepping out of the conservatory. 'Gillian, Zara's here! Get the buck's fizz! That was my idea,' he said to Zara. 'Buck's fizz for breakfast. And pancakes.'

Zara said nothing. She was staring at the decorated table as though she'd never seen anything like it before.

'Is this all for me?' she said at last, in a husky voice.

'Well, of course it is! It's your birthday! Sit yourself

down,' he added, in a host-like voice. 'Have some strawberries.'

Fleur appeared on the lawn holding a cafetière, and smiled prettily at Zara.

'Happy birthday, darling. Would you like some coffee?'

'No,' said Zara.

'Suit yourself.' Fleur shrugged.

'You must have a strawberry, though,' insisted Antony. 'They're delicious.'

Zara sat down and looked at the cards piled on her plate. She seemed slightly dazed.

'Cool balloon, huh?' said Antony happily. 'It's from Xanthe and Mex.'

'What?' She looked up to see if he was joking.

'They heard it was your birthday. I think there's a card from them, too. And I said we might meet them for a drink later. But it depends what you want to do.'

'They sent me a balloon,' said Zara in stupefaction. She tugged at the string and watched it float back up. 'But I hardly know them.' She looked up at him. 'And I thought you hated them.'

'Xanthe's not so bad.' Antony grinned sheepishly at her. 'Now, go on, open some of your presents.'

'Wait!' called Richard from the conservatory. 'I want to get this on video!'

'Oh for God's sake,' said Antony. 'We'll be here all day.'

Gillian arrived in the garden, bearing a tray of glasses filled with orange juice and champagne bubbles.

'Happy birthday, Zara!' she exclaimed. 'What a lovely day!'

'Thank you,' muttered Zara.

'OK?' called Richard. 'I'm filming. You can start opening your presents.'

'Open mine first,' said Antony excitedly. 'That red stripy one.'

Zara picked up the parcel and looked at it for a few moments without saying anything.

'That looks lovely,' said Fleur gaily. Zara's gaze shot towards Fleur and away again. Then, biting her lip, she began to tug at the wrapping. Onto her lap fell a small framed print.

'It's America,' said Antony. 'It's a map of America. For when you . . . when you go there.' Zara looked up at him. Her chin was shaking.

'Thank you Antony,' she said, and burst into tears.

'Zara!'

'What's wrong, poppet?'

'Don't you like it?' asked Antony anxiously.

'I love it,' whispered Zara. 'I'm sorry. It's just . . .'

'It's just that you need a good sip of buck's fizz and some pancakes inside you,' said Gillian briskly. 'You know, it's not easy, turning fourteen. I remember it well. Come on Zara.' She patted Zara's bare, thin shoulder. 'You come and help me bring out the breakfast, and we'll have the rest of the presents in a little while.'

'Aren't you enjoying your birthday, then?' asked Antony later on. They were sitting at the bottom of the garden in a hidden sun-trap, listening to the pounding of Zara's new portable ghetto blaster.

'Sure.'

'You don't look very happy.'

'I'm fine, all right?' she snapped.

Antony waited for a few minutes. Then he said, casually, 'Zara, what's your star sign?'

'Sagi—' she began, then stopped. 'I don't believe in all that phooey.'

'Yes you do. You were reading your horoscope the other day.'

'That doesn't mean I believe it. Jesus, if every time you read a horoscope—'

'You still know what your sign is though, don't you?' he interrupted. 'It isn't Sagittarius. It can't be. So what is it?'

'Why do you want to know?' She sat up, knocking her diet lemonade onto her jacket. 'Fuck,' she said. 'I'll go and get a cloth.'

'No you won't! Don't change the subject! Zara, what's your star sign?'

'Look, you asshole, my jacket's drenched.'

'So what? You drenched it on purpose. God, you must think I'm really stupid.' She began to move, and he shot out a strong hand, pinning her wrist to the ground. 'Zara, what's your star sign? Tell me!'

'For Christ's sake!' She gave him a scornful look and tossed back her hair. 'OK,' she said. 'It's Scorpio.'

'Wrong.' He leaned back. 'It's Leo.'

'So what?' snapped Zara. 'Scorpio, Leo. Who gives a shit?'

'Zara, what's going on?'

'Don't ask me. You're the one behaving like an asshole.'

'It's not really your birthday today is it?'

'Of course it is.' She looked away and took a piece of gum from her pocket.

'It's not! Your birthday is between the 22nd of November and the 21st of December. I looked up Sagittarius.' He shuffled round on the grass until he could see her face, and gazed pleadingly at her. 'Zara, what's going on? Whatever it is, I won't tell anyone, I promise. Zara, I'm your friend, aren't I?'

She shrugged silently and put the gum in her mouth.

Antony looked at her for a while. Then he said, 'I don't think your father's dead, either.' He spoke slowly, not taking his eyes from her face. 'I think he's still alive. I think your mother was lying about that, too.'

Zara was chewing quickly, almost desperately, staring away from him at the trees.

'Tell me,' begged Antony. 'I won't tell anyone. Who would I tell, anyway? I don't know anyone to tell.'

Zara gave a short laugh.

'You know plenty of people to tell,' she said. 'Your father . . . Gillian . . .'

'But I wouldn't!' exclaimed Antony. He lowered his voice. 'Whatever it is, I won't tell them. But I want to know the truth. I want to know when your real birthday is. And why you're pretending it's today. And . . . and everything.'

There was a long pause. Then Zara turned to him.

'OK, listen,' she said in a low voice. 'If you tell anyone else what I'm about to tell you, I'll say that you tried to rape me.'

'What?' Antony stared at her in horror.

'I'll say you asked me to come down to the bottom of the garden and you held me to the ground. By the wrists.' She stopped and looked at Antony's hand the hand which, a few minutes before, had pinned her down on the grass. A fiery red colour came to his cheeks. 'And then I'll say you tried to rape me.'

'You little . . .'

'They probably won't press charges. But they'll interview you. That won't be nice. And some people will think you did it. Some people always do.'

'I just don't believe . . .' He was staring at her, panting slightly.

'You see, I mean it,' said Zara deliberately. 'You're not allowed to tell. If you say anything to your father or Gillian, or anyone – I'll go to the police. And you'll be in shit.' She spat her gum out. 'Now, do you want to know or don't you?'

Richard felt as though his life was finally falling into place. He sat in his chair watching Fleur leaf through a book of wallpaper patterns, and wondered how he could have mistaken what he had with Emily for true love. He could hardly bear to think of all the wasted years; years spent living in sombre shades of charcoal. Now he was living in bright, solid colour; in splashes of vibrant hues that jumped off the page and took the eye by surprise.

'You'll have to decide if you want painted walls or wallpaper in your office,' said Fleur. She looked at him over her sunglasses. 'And give me a budget.'

'I'll give you whatever you like,' said Richard. He met her eye and she gave him a delicious, secretive smile. In response, he felt his skin tingle slightly under his shirt, as though in anticipation of another night of pleasure.

Fleur no longer occupied her own bedroom. She now slept with him every night, her body curving up against his, her hair falling across his pillow. Every morning her smile was waiting for him; every morning his heart gave a leap as he saw her again. And they talked more now than they had ever done, and Richard felt happier than he had ever done, and Fleur's eyes sparkled even more than they had before. She seemed to glow with happiness and excitement at the moment, thought Richard, and there was a spring in her step which hadn't been there before. A spring – his mouth twisted into a small, embarrassed smile – which he had put there.

And when he asked her to marry him, everything would be complete. When Oliver had returned from holiday, when he had sorted out the trust, when he had finally closed the chapter on Emily. He would choose a suitable moment, a suitable place, a suitable ring . . . A quiet, suitable wedding. And then an exuberant, noisy, joyful honeymoon. The honeymoon he'd been waiting for all his life.

* * *

When Zara had finished telling him, Antony flopped down onto the grass and stared up at the blue sky.

'I don't believe it,' he said. 'She goes to all that trouble just to get hold of a Gold Card?'

'You can do a lot of damage with a Gold Card,' said Zara.

'But I mean . . .' He broke off, and frowned. 'I don't understand. How does your dad being dead fit into it?'

'She told your father she was a widow. I guess she thought it made her seem more appealing.'

For a few moments Antony was silent. Then he said slowly, 'So all the time, she's just been after him for his money.' He sat up. 'It's crazy! I mean, we're not that rich.'

'Maybe she made a mistake. Or maybe you're richer than you think.'

'God, poor Dad. And he hasn't got a clue! Zara, I've got to tell him.'

'Then he pinned me down on the grass, Your Honour,' Zara started to recite tonelessly. 'I tried to struggle, but he was stronger than me.'

'All right!' said Antony irritably. 'I won't say anything. But I mean, bloody hell! My dad can't afford to lose loads of money!'

'Think of it as payment,' said Zara. 'Fleur always does.'

'What, so she's done this before?' Antony stared at Zara. 'Gone out with men just for their money?'

Zara shrugged, and looked away. It had been easy to feed Antony a limited, edited version of the truth, a truth which, even if he did blab, wouldn't ruin everything for Fleur. She'd painted Fleur as a silly spendthrift, who was desperate for a Gold Card, who would fritter Richard's money on high heels and haircuts. And he was shocked by that. What would happen if she told him the real facts? Told him that her mother was a cynical, heartless confidence trickster? Who entered people's lives because of their vulnerability and desperation; who escaped freely because of their embarrassment and wounded pride?

The truth was there, inside her; she felt as though there was only a thin curtain hiding it from the rest of the world. If he stretched out a hand and tugged, the thin material would come tumbling down and he would see all the deceits, the ugly lies and stories, curled up in her brain like snakes. But he wouldn't stretch out his hand. He thought he'd prised the truth out of her already. It would never occur to him that there was more.

'So basically, she's just a prostitute!' he was saying.

'She takes what she's worth,' snapped back Zara. 'Hasn't your dad had a good time over the last few months?' Antony stared at her.

'But he really thinks she loves him. I did too. I thought she loved him!'

'Well, maybe she does.'

'People who love each other aren't interested in money!'

'Of course they are,' said Zara scornfully. 'Wouldn't you rather have a girlfriend who could buy you a Porsche? And if you say no, you're lying.'

'Yeah, but real love is different!' protested Antony. 'It's about the person inside.'

'It's about everything,' retorted Zara. 'It's about money first, looks second, and personality if you're desperate.'

'God you're twisted! Money doesn't come into it! I mean . . . suppose you marry someone really rich and there's a stockmarket crash and they lose all their money?'

'Suppose you marry someone really nice and there's a car crash and they lose all their personality? What's the difference?'

'It isn't the same! You know it's not the same.' He peered at her. 'Why are you defending your mother?'

'I don't know!' cried Zara jerkily. 'Because she's my mother, I guess! I've never talked to anyone about her before. I never realized—' She broke off. 'Oh, for God's sake! I wish I'd never told you!'

'So do I! What a bloody mess.'

They stared at each other in fury .

'Look,' said Zara eventually. 'Your dad's not stupid. He's not going to let her rip him off completely, is he?' She forced herself to meet his eye unwaveringly.

'No,' said Antony. He exhaled slowly. 'I suppose not.'

'And you like having her around, don't you?'

'Of course I do! I love having her around. And I like . . . I like having you around.'

'Good,' said Zara. She slowly smiled at him. ''Cause I like being around.'

* * *

Later on they wandered back up to the house to find Fleur and Richard arguing good-humouredly about wallpaper.

'Antony!' exclaimed Fleur. 'Talk some sense into your father. First he gives me *carte blanche* to redecorate his office, then he says he won't have anything but stripes or fleur-de-lis.'

'I don't know what fleur-de-lis is,' said Antony. He stared at Fleur. His image of her in his mind had changed now that he knew the truth; as they'd walked towards her he'd honestly expected that she would look different. More . . . monster-like. He'd found himself dreading the moment of meeting her eye. But there she was, just the same, warm and pretty and friendly. And now she was smiling at him, and he was grinning back, and suddenly he found himself wondering if everything Zara had said about her could really be true.

'Tell you what,' said Richard to Fleur. 'Why not get some more wallpaper books when you're in London? I'm sure we can reach a compromise. Just remember, I'm the one who has to sit in the room and try to work.' He grinned at Antony and Zara. 'Fleur is very keen on orange walls.'

'Not orange. Terracotta.'

'When are you going to London?' asked Zara.

'On Friday,' said Fleur. 'The day after tomorrow.'

'Your mother has to go to a memorial service,' said Richard.

Zara froze; her face turned pale.

'You're going to a memorial service?' she said.

'That's right,' said Fleur.

'A memorial service?' repeated Zara disbelievingly. 'You're going to a *memorial* service?'

'Yes darling,' said Fleur impatiently. 'And please stop making such a fuss.' Her eyes bored into Zara's. 'I'll only be gone a day. It's for poor Hattie Fairbrother,' she added casually. 'You remember Hattie, don't you darling?' Zara flinched, and turned away.

'Zara!' They were interrupted by Gillian. 'You've got a phone call. Someone called Johnny.'

'Johnny?' Zara's head shot up. 'Johnny's on the phone? OK, I'm coming! I'm coming! Don't let him hang up!' And without looking back, she bounded into the house.

'Do you want a Diet Coke?' Antony called, but she wasn't listening. 'I'll just . . . see if she wants a Diet Coke,' he said to the others, and disappeared after her.

Richard looked at Fleur.

'Zara seemed very upset at the idea of you going to a memorial service,' he said.

'I know,' said Fleur. 'Ever since her father passed away, anything to do with death upsets her.' She looked sad. 'I try not to press the point.'

'Of course,' said Gillian. 'It's perfectly understandable.'

'Poor little thing,' said Richard. His eyes twinkled slightly. 'And who's Johnny? A special friend of Zara's?'

'A friend of us both,' said Fleur. Her face closed up slightly. 'I've known him for years.'

'You should ask him to stay,' suggested Richard. 'I'd like to meet some of your friends.'

'Maybe,' said Fleur, and changed the subject.

* * *

Zara had disappeared into the tiny room off the hall that contained nothing but a telephone, a chair and a little table for messages. As she came out, Antony was waiting for her. He stared at her: her eyes were sparkling; she looked suddenly cheerful again.

'So, who's Johnny?' he said, before he could stop himself. 'Your boyfriend?'

'Don't be dumb!' said Zara. 'I haven't got a boyfriend. Johnny's just a friend. A really good friend.'

'Oh yeah?' said Antony, trying to sound lighthearted and teasing. 'I've heard that one before.'

'Antony, Johnny's fifty-six!'

'Oh,' said Antony, feeling foolish.

'And he's gay!' added Zara.

'Gay?' He stared at her.

'Yes, gay!' She giggled. 'Satisfied now?' She started to head into the garden.

'Where are you going?' called Antony, running after her.

'I have a message for Fleur from Johnny.'

They arrived on the lawn together, panting.

'OK, Johnny says he hopes you've changed your mind and will you give him a call if you have,' announced Zara.

'About what?' said Fleur.

'He said you knew what he was talking about. And . . . he also said he might take me to New York! As a special fourteenth birthday treat!' She darted a triumphant glance at Fleur.

'New York!' exclaimed Antony. 'Fantastic!'

'How nice,' said Fleur acidly.

'Anyway, that's the message.' Zara took a piece of gum from her pocket and happily began to chew. 'So, are you gonna call him?'

'No,' said Fleur, snapping the wallpaper book shut. 'I'm not.'

# THIRTEEN

On Friday morning, Richard left early for his meeting, and Fleur breathed a sigh of relief. She was finding his continual presence a little oppressive. As the weather reached summer perfection, he was taking great swaths of time off work – days of long-owed holiday, he'd explained – and spending them all at home. The first time he'd used the word 'holiday', Fleur had smiled prettily, and wondered whether she could persuade him to take her to Barbados. But Richard didn't want to go away. Like a love-struck adolescent, all he wanted was to be with her. He was in her bed all night; he was at her side all day; she couldn't escape him. The day before, she'd actually found herself suggesting that the two of them play golf together. Anything, to break up the monotony. We'll have to be careful, she found herself thinking as she drank the last of her breakfast coffee, or we'll fall into a rut.

Then, abruptly, she pulled herself up. She wasn't going to fall into a rut with Richard because she wasn't going to stay with Richard. By three o'clock that afternoon, she would be at the memorial service of Hattie Fairbrother, wife of the retired business magnate Edward Fairbrother; by the time the reception was over she might have new plans entirely.

She stood up, checking her black suit for creases, and went upstairs. As she passed the office door, she lingered. She still hadn't had a chance to explore Richard's affairs. Now that she was officially decorating the office, it should have been easy. She could wander in whenever she chose, poke around, open drawers and close them again, find out everything she wanted to about Richard's business affairs, and no-one would suspect anything. And yet with Richard in constant adoration at her side, it was harder than she had imagined to find a moment when she could be alone in there. Besides which, she was almost sure that he was not quite in the league she had hoped. Johnny had got it wrong. Richard Favour was no more than a moderately well-off man, whose Gold Card would net her perhaps fifteen, perhaps twenty thousand pounds. It was almost not worth bothering to look through his dull little books.

But force of habit drew her towards the office door. Her taxi would be arriving in a few minutes, to take her to the station, but there was time to have a quick glance through his most recent correspondence. And she was, after all, supposed to be decorating the place. She let herself into the office with the duplicate key he'd given her, looked around at the bleak walls and shuddered.

Her eye fell on the large window behind the desk; in her mind she saw it curtained in a large, dramatic swag of deep green. She would match the curtains with a dark green carpet. And on the walls, a set of antique golfing prints. She would pick some up for him at auction, perhaps.

Except of course she wouldn't do anything of the sort. Biting her lip, Fleur sat down on Richard's chair and swivelled round idly. Out of the window she could just see the garden: the lawn, the pear tree, the badminton net which Antony and Zara had left up the night before. They were familiar sights. Too familiar. It would be surprisingly difficult to leave them. And, if she were honest with herself, it would be surprisingly difficult to leave Richard.

But then, life was surprisingly difficult. Fleur's chin tightened and she tapped her fingernails and the polished wood of the desk, impatient with herself. She hadn't yet achieved her goal. She wasn't yet a rich woman. Therefore she would have to move on; she had no choice. And there was no point hanging around here endlessly for the last dribs and drabs. Richard wasn't the sort who would suddenly splash out on a last-minute couture dress or diamond bracelet. As soon as she had worked out how much he could afford to lose, she would bounce his Gold Card up to the limit, take the cash and go. If she got the amount just right – as she would – then he would quietly pay it off, say nothing, lick his wounds in private and put the whole affair down to experience. They always did. And by that time, she would be in another family, another home, perhaps even another country.

Sighing, she pulled Richard's in-tray towards her and began to flip through his most recent correspondence. Her fingers felt slow and reluctant; her mind was only half-concentrating. What she was looking for she hardly knew. The thrill of pursuit seemed to have evaporated inside her; her drive had lost its edge. Once she would have scanned each letter urgently, searching for clues; seeking opportunities for financial gain. Now her eyes fell dully on each page, taking in a few words here, a few words there, then moving on. There was a short letter about the lease on Richard's London flat. There was a request for donations from a children's charity. There was a bank statement.

As she pulled it from its envelope, Fleur felt a small quickening inside her. At least this should prove interesting. She unfolded the single sheet and her gaze flicked automatically to the final balance, already estimating in her mind what sort of figure she might expect to see. And then, as, her eyes focused, and she realized what she was looking at, she felt a shock jolt round her body. Her fingers felt suddenly clammy; her throat was dry; she couldn't breathe.

No, she thought, trying to keep control of herself. That couldn't be right. It simply couldn't be right. Could it? She felt dizzy with astonishment. Was she reading the figures correctly? She closed her eyes, swallowed, took a deep breath and opened them again. The same number sat, ludicrously, in the credit column.

She gazed at it, devouring it with her mind. Could it possibly be correct? Was she really looking at—

'Fleur!' called Gillian from downstairs. Fleur jumped; her eyes darted towards the door. 'Your taxi's here!'

'Thank you!' called back Fleur. Her voice felt high and unnatural; suddenly she realized that her hand was, shaking. She looked at the figure again, feeling slightly faint. What the hell was going on? No-one, but *no-one* kept a sum like that just sitting in a bank account. Not unless they were very stupid – which Richard wasn't – or unless they were, very, very rich indeed . . .

'Fleur! You'll miss your train!'

'I'm coming!' Quickly, before Gillian decided to come and fetch her, Fleur put the bank statement back where she had found it. She had to think about this. She had to think very carefully indeed.

Philippa had bought an entirely new outfit for her day out with Fleur. She stood by the ticket barrier at Waterloo station, feeling conspicuous in her pale pink suit, and wondering whether she should have gone for something more casual. But as soon as she saw Fleur her heart gave a relieved bounce. Fleur looked even more dressed up than she did. She was wearing the same black suit she'd been wearing when Philippa had first seen her at the memorial service, topped with a glorious black hat, covered in tiny purple flowers. People were staring as she made her way along the concourse, and Philippa felt a glow of pride. This groomed, elegant beauty was her friend. Her friend!

'Darling!' Fleur's kiss was more showy than warm, but Philippa didn't mind. She imagined, with a rush of exhilaration, the picture the two of them made standing in their suits – one pink, one black. Two glamorous women, meeting for lunch. If, yesterday, she'd seen such a sight, she would have been filled with wistful envy; today she *was* the sight. She *was* one of those glamorous women.

'Where shall we go first?' asked Fleur. 'I've booked a table at Harvey Nichols for twelve-thirty, but we could begin somewhere else. Where would you like to shop?'

'I don't know!' exclaimed Philippa excitedly. 'Let's look on the map. I've got a tube pass . . .'

'I was thinking more of a taxi,' interrupted Fleur kindly. 'I never travel by tube if I can help it.' Philippa looked up, and felt an embarrassed crimson staining her cheeks. For a horrible moment she felt as though the day might have been spoiled already. But suddenly Fleur laughed, and put her arm through Philippa's.

'I shouldn't be so fussy,' she said. 'I expect you travel on the tube all the time, don't you, Philippa?'

'Every day,' said Philippa. She forced herself to flash a smile at Fleur. 'But I'm willing to break the habit.'

Fleur laughed. 'That's my girl.' They began to walk towards the taxi rank, and Philippa allowed her arm to stay in Fleur's. She felt almost dizzy with excitement, as though she were embarking on some sort of love affair.

In the taxi, Philippa turned to Fleur expectantly, waiting for the start of some hilarious, intimate gossip. She could feel a laugh bubbling up at the back of her throat; even had an affectionate gesture prepared. 'Oh Fleur!' she would exclaim, at an appropriate moment, 'You're just too much!' And she would squeeze Fleur's arm, just like an old established friend. The taxi driver would look at them in the mirror and think they were lifelong chums. Or maybe even sisters.

But Fleur was gazing silently out of the window at the traffic. Her forehead was creased in a slight frown and she was biting her lip and she looked, thought Philippa uneasily, as though she didn't want to be disturbed. As if she were thinking about something; as if she didn't really want to be there at all.

Then, suddenly, she turned towards Philippa.

'Tell me, are you and Lambert happy together?' she said. Philippa gave a startled jump. She didn't want to think about Lambert today. But Fleur was waiting for an answer.

'Oh yes,' she said, and gave Fleur a bright smile. 'We have a very happy marriage.'

'A happy marriage,' echoed Fleur. 'What exactly makes a happy marriage?'

'Well,' said Philippa doubtfully. 'You know.'

'Do I?' said Fleur. 'I'm not sure I do.'

'But you were married, weren't you?' said Philippa. 'To Zara's father.'

'Oh yes,' said Fleur vaguely. 'Of course I was. But not happily.'

'Really? I didn't know that,' said Philippa. She looked at Fleur uneasily, wondering if she wanted to talk about her unhappy marriage. But Fleur gave an impatient wave of the hand.

'What I really mean is, why does one get married in the first place?' She gazed at Philippa. 'What made you decide to get married to Lambert?'

A tremor of alarm went through Philippa, as though she were being questioned on the wrong special subject. Swift, positive images of herself and Lambert passed through her mind: the two of them on their wedding day; their honeymoon in the Maldives; Lambert tanned and affectionate; afternoons of sex underneath a mosquito net.

'Well, I love Lambert,' she found herself saying. 'He's strong, and he looks after me . . .' She glanced at Fleur.

'And?' said Fleur.

'And we have fun together,' said Philippa hesitantly.

'But how did you know he was the right man for you?' persisted Fleur. 'How did you know it was the right time to stop looking and . . . and settle down for good?'

Philippa felt a flush come to her cheeks.

'I just knew,' she said, in a voice which was too high and defensive.

And suddenly into her mind flashed a memory of her mother; a memory she thought she'd quashed for ever. Her mother, sitting up in bed, fixing Philippa with her ice-blue stare, saying, 'You say yes to Lambert, Philippa, and be grateful. What other man is going to want a girl like you?'

'Jim wanted me,' Philippa had quavered.

'Jim?' her mother had snapped. 'Your father despises Jim! He'd never let you marry Jim. You'd better accept Lambert.'

'But . . .'

'But nothing. This is your only chance. Look at you! You're not pretty, you're not charming, you're not even a virgin. What other man will want you?'

As she'd listened, Philippa had felt sick, as though she were physically being torn apart. Now suddenly, she felt sick again.

' "You just knew".' Fleur sounded dissatisfied. 'But I just knew this was the hat for me.' She gestured at her head. 'And then, when I'd bought it, I saw an even better one.'

'It's a lovely hat,' said Philippa feebly.

'The thing is,' said Fleur, 'you can have more than one hat. You can have twenty hats. But you can't have twenty husbands. Don't you ever worry that you chose too soon?'

'No!' said Philippa at once. 'I don't. Lambert's perfect for me.'

'Well, good,' said Fleur. She smiled at Philippa. 'I'm glad for you.'

Philippa stared at Fleur, and felt her bright happy smile start to fade away, and suddenly wished, for the first time in her life, that she'd been more honest. She could have confided in Fleur; she could have shared her worries and asked for advice. But her foremost instinct had been to paint a rosy, romantic picture of herself; a picture that Fleur would appreciate and, quite possibly, envy. And now her chance to tell the truth was gone.

Lambert arrived at The Maples shortly after Gillian had left for her bridge class. He parked the car, let himself into the house and stood in the hall, listening for voices. But the house was silent, as he'd expected it to be. The night before he'd rung up and casually mentioned to Gillian that he might drop by between meetings.

'But no-one will be here,' she'd said. 'Richard's going to Newcastle, I'll be playing bridge, and Antony will probably be out with Zara, practising for the Club Cup.'

'I'll pop in anyway,' Lambert had replied casually, 'since I'm passing.'

Now, without hesitating, he headed for Richard's office. It would be a simple matter to find the information he needed, then, when he got back home, transfer an appropriate sum of money into his own account. He would be able to have a cheque ready for the bank within a week, which would buy him a few months. And then, by Christmas, Philippa would be twenty-nine and the trust money would be even nearer and his inconvenient financial problems would be over for ever.

As he entered the office he found himself, ludicrously, bending down to check under the desk. As if he didn't know that Fleur was in London, with his own wife. Attending another memorial service. Didn't the woman have anything better to do with her time than go to bloody memorial services? He frowned at the dusty carpet, then stood up and strode over to the filing cabinet and pulled open the third drawer; the drawer which he hadn't reached last time. And there, like a reward, were files and files of Richard's bank statements.

'Bingo,' he muttered softly under his breath. He knelt down and, at random, pulled out a file marked 'Household'. The statements were neatly clipped together; as he fanned through them, he began to feel a sense of anticipation. Here was Richard's financial life, laid out for him to see. The wealth that, one day, would be his and Philippa's. Except that in this account, there was little evidence of wealth. The balance never seemed to rise above three thousand pounds. What bloody good was that?

Impatiently he replaced it, and pulled out another, rather tattered, marked 'Children'. Pocket money, thought Lambert contemptuously, and threw it down on the floor, where it fell open. His hand was outstretched towards another file as he glanced casually down at it. What he saw made him freeze in shock. The top statement was dated the previous month, and the balance was approaching ten million pounds.

'How many courses shall we have?' said Philippa, squinting at the menu. 'Three?'

'Ten million,' said Fleur absently.

'What?' Philippa looked up.

'Oh, nothing.' Fleur smiled. 'Sorry, I was miles away.' She began to take off her hat and shake back her red-gold hair. In the corner of the restaurant, a young waiter watched admiringly.

'Ten million miles away,' said Philippa, and laughed heartily. The day had, so far, more than lived up to her expectations. She and Fleur had sauntered from shop to shop, trying on clothes, squirting scent on one another and laughing merrily, attracting attention like two birds of paradise. The magazines were wrong, thought Philippa. They all said that the Way to Get your Man was to go around with someone uglier than yourself. But it wasn't true. Fleur was much prettier than her, even if she was much older – but today, instead of feeling inadequate, Philippa had felt elevated to Fleur's status. And people had treated her differently. They had smiled at her, and men had opened the door for her, and young office girls rushing past had looked at her with envy in their eyes. And Philippa had relished every moment.

'Oh, I don't know,' said Fleur suddenly. 'It's all so difficult. Why can't life be straightforward?' She sighed. 'Let's have a cocktail.' She beckoned to the young waiter, who came striding over.

'A Manhattan,' said Fleur, smiling at him.

'Two,' said, Philippa. The waiter grinned back at her. He was, thought Philippa, extraordinarily good-looking. In fact, everybody who worked in expensive shops seemed to be good-looking.

'Excuse, me, ladies.' Another waiter was approaching their table. He was holding a silver tray, on which reposed a bottle of champagne. 'This has been ordered and pre-paid for you.'

'No!' Fleur burst into peals of laughter. 'Champagne!' She looked at the bottle. 'Very good champagne, in fact. Who ordered it for us?' She looked around. 'Are we allowed to know?'

'It's just like a film,' said Philippa excitedly.

'I have a message card for a Mrs Daxeny,' said the head waiter.

'Aha!' said Fleur. 'So they know our names!'

'Read it!' said Philippa.

Fleur ripped open the little card.

' "Have a lovely lunch, my sweethearts," ' she read, ' "and I wish I could be there with you. Richard" '. Fleur looked up. 'It's from your father,' she said. She sounded astonished. 'Your father sent us champagne.'

'I thought it was from an anonymous prince,' said Philippa disappointedly. 'How did Daddy know where we'd be?'

'I must have told him,' said Fleur slowly. 'And he must have remembered, and ordered this for us over the phone, and hoped that we wouldn't change our lunch plans. And all the time he said nothing about it.'

'Shall I open it?' said the head waiter.

'Ooh yes!' said Philippa.

'Yes please,' said Fleur. She picked up the little card and gazed at it for a few seconds. 'What an extraordinarily thoughtful man your father is.'

'Actually, I think I'll still have my Manhattan,' said Philippa. 'And then go on to champagne. After all, I'm not driving anywhere!' She glanced up brightly at Fleur. 'Are you OK?'

'I'm fine,' said Fleur, frowning slightly. 'I was just . . . thinking.'

They both watched as, with the tiniest of whispered pops, the head waiter opened the champagne and poured out a single glass. He handed it ceremonially to Fleur.

'You know, men don't usually manage to take me by surprise,' she said, as though to herself. 'But today . . .' she took a sip. 'This is delicious.'

'Today you've been taken by surprise,' said Philippa triumphantly.

'Today I've been taken by surprise,' agreed Fleur. She took another sip and looked thoughtfully at her glass. 'Twice.'

The sound of the cleaner's key in the front door made Lambert give a startled jump. With fumbling hands he replaced all the bank statements in the filing cabinet, hurried out of the office, and sauntered down the stairs. He gave the cleaner a cheery smile as he passed her in the hall, but his heart was beating hard and shock was still needling down his back.

Ten million liquid assets. That had to be the money for the trust. But it wasn't in trust, it was still in Richard's account. What was going on? He reached his car and paused, panting slightly, trying not to let panic overwhelm him. The money wasn't in trust. Which meant Philippa wasn't the millionairess he'd thought she was. And he had an enormous overdraft and no means of paying it off except her.

He opened the car door, got in, and rested his clammy head on the steering wheel. It didn't make sense. Had Emily been *lying* to him? She'd promised him that Philippa was going to be rich. She'd told him they were going to sort it out straight away. She'd said the money would be put in Philippa's name; that as soon as she turned thirty it would be hers. And instead, where was it? It was still in Richard's name. From the look of things, Richard had been liquidizing his assets for months. He was obviously planning to do something with the money. But what? Give it to Philippa? Or throw it to the fucking birds? Nothing would have surprised Lambert any more. And the worst thing was, there was absolutely nothing he could do about it.

As the puddings arrived, Philippa leaned across the table and looked Fleur in the eye. Fleur looked back at her. Philippa had drunk two Manhattans and at least her share of the champagne and had become more and more garrulous and less and less distinct. Her cheeks were flushed and her hair was dishevelled and she seemed to have something important to say.

'I lied to you.' Her words came tumbling out, and Fleur peered at her in surprise.

'I'm sorry?'

'No, *I'm* sorry. I mean, you're my best friend, and I lied to you. You're my best friend,' repeated Philippa with a swaying emphasis. 'And I lied to you.' She reached for Fleur's hand and blinked back a couple of tears. 'About Lambert.'

'Really? What did you tell me about Lambert?' Fleur disentangled her hand and reached for her spoon. 'Eat your pudding.'

Obediently, Philippa picked up her spoon and cracked the surface of her *crème brûlée*. Then she looked up.

'I told you I loved him.'

Fleur unhurriedly finished her mouthful of chocolate mousse.

'You don't love Lambert?'

'Sometimes I think I do – but,' Philippa shuddered. 'I don't really.'

'I don't blame you.'

'I'm trapped in a loveless marriage.' Philippa gazed at Fleur with bloodshot eyes.

'Well then leave it.' Fleur took another spoonful of chocolate mousse.

'You think I should leave Lambert?'

'If he doesn't make you happy, then leave him.'

'You don't think maybe I should have an affair?' said Philippa hopefully.

'No,' replied Fleur firmly. 'Definitely not.' Philippa took a spoonful of *crème brûlée*, munched half-heartedly, then took another one. A tear rolled down her cheek.

'But what if I leave Lambert and then . . . and then I realize I do love him really?'

'Well, then, you'll know.'

'But what if he won't have me back? I'll be on my own!'

Fleur shrugged.

'So what?'

'So what? I couldn't stand to be on my own!' Philippa's voice rose above the clamour of the restaurant. 'Do you know how difficult it is to meet people these days?'

'I do,' said Fleur. She allowed herself a tiny smile. 'You have to look in the right places.'

'I couldn't stand to be on my own,' repeated Philippa doggedly. Fleur sighed impatiently.

'Well then, stay with him. Philippa, you've had a lot to drink . . .'

'No, you're right,' interrupted Philippa. 'I'm going to leave him.' She shuddered. 'He's disgusting.'

'I have to agree with you there,' said Fleur.

'I didn't want to marry him,' said Philippa. A fresh flurry of tears fell onto the table.

'And now you're going to leave him,' said Fleur, stifling a yawn. 'So that's all right. Shall we get the bill?'

'And you'll help me through it?'

'Of course.' Fleur raised her hand and two waiters with identical blond haircuts immediately descended.

'Our bill, please,' she said. Philippa looked at her watch.

'You've got to go to your service, haven't you?' she said blearily. 'Your memorial service.'

'Well, you know, I may not go to the memorial service, after all,' said Fleur slowly. 'I'm not sure . . .' She paused. 'Hattie wasn't such a great friend to me. And

I'm not really in the mood for it. It's . . . a bit of a difficult situation.'

Philippa wasn't listening.

'Fleur?' she said, wiping her eyes, 'I really like you.'

'Do you, darling?' Fleur smiled kindly at her. How on earth, she wondered, could someone like Richard have produced such a characterless lump of self-pity?

'Are you going to marry Daddy?' sniffed Philippa.

'He hasn't asked me,' replied Fleur swiftly, giving Philippa a dazzling smile.

The bill arrived in a leather folder; without looking at it, Fleur placed Richard's Gold Card inside it. They both watched silently as it was borne away by one of the identical waiters.

'But if he does ask you,' said Philippa. 'If he does. Will you?'

'Well,' said Fleur slowly. She leaned back in her chair. Ten million, she thought. The idea ran round her mind like a big shiny ball-bearing. Ten million pounds. A fortune by any standards. 'Who knows?' she said at last, and drained her glass.

'So, do you reckon your mother will marry my father?' asked Antony, flopping down on the immaculate green turf of the putting green.

'I don't know,' said Zara irritably. 'Stop asking me that. I can't concentrate.' She screwed up her nose, took a deep breath, and jabbed at the golf ball with her putter. It trickled a few inches towards the hole, then stopped. 'There. Look what you made me do. That was crap.'

'No it wasn't,' said Antony. 'You're picking it up really well.'

'I'm not. It's a stupid game.' She banged her putter crossly on the ground, and Antony looked around nervously to check no-one had seen her. But few people were about. They were on the junior putting green, an out of the way practice area shielded by pine trees and usually empty. Antony had spent half the morning practising his putting in preparation for the Club Cup, the major golfing event of the summer. The other half he'd spent retrieving the golf balls which Zara seemed unable to prevent flying over the hedge every few minutes.

'Putting's supposed to be, like, really controlled,' he said. 'You should just imagine . . .'

'There's nothing to imagine,' snapped Zara. 'I know what I've got to do. Get the fucking ball into the hole. It's just I can't do it.' She threw her putter down on the ground, and sat down beside Antony. 'I don't know how you can play this dumb game. You don't even burn off any calories.'

'You kind of get hooked on it,' said Antony. 'Anyway, you don't need to lose weight.' Zara ignored him and hunched her shoulders up. For a few moments neither of them said anything.

'So, come on,' said Antony at last. 'How come you're in such a bad mood?'

'I'm not.'

'Yes you are. You've been in a terrible mood all day. Ever since your mum left this morning.' He paused. 'Is it because . . .' He broke off awkwardly.

'What?'

'Well. I just wondered if maybe you knew the person whose memorial service she's going to. And maybe that was why you were a bit—'

'No,' interrupted Zara. 'No, that's not it.' She turned away from him slightly; her face looked fiercer than ever.

'It'll be great when you go to New York,' said Antony brightly.

'If I go.'

'Of course you'll go! Your friend Johnny's going to take you!'

Zara shrugged.

'I don't see it happening somehow.'

'Why not?' She shrugged again.

'I just don't.'

'You're just feeling a bit miserable,' said Antony understandingly.

'I'm not *miserable*. I'd just like . . .'

'What?' said Antony eagerly. 'What would you like?'

'I'd like to know what's going to happen. OK? I'd just like to know.'

'Between your mum and my dad?'

'Yeah.' Her mutter was almost imperceptible.

'I think they're going to get married.' Antony's voice bubbled over with enthusiasm. 'I bet Dad asks her really soon. And then all that stuff with the Gold Card . . .' He lowered his voice slightly. 'Well, it won't matter any more, will it? I mean, she'll be his wife!

They'll share all their worldly goods anyway!' Zara looked at him.

'You've got it all neatly sorted out in your mind, haven't you?'

'Well.' He coloured slightly and plucked at the close-shorn grass.

'Antony, you're so fucking *decent*.'

'I'm not!' he retorted angrily. Zara gave a sudden laugh.

'It's not a *bad* thing to be.'

'You make me sound really square,' he protested. 'But I'm not. I've done loads of . . . stuff.'

'What have you done?' said Zara teasingly. 'Shoplifting?'

'No. Of course not!'

'Gambling, then?' said Zara. 'What about sex?' Antony flushed and Zara moved closer to him. 'Have you ever had sex, Antony?'

'Have you?' he parried.

'Don't be dumb. I'm only thirteen years old.'

Antony felt a sudden swoosh of relief.

'Well, how am I supposed to know?' he said truculently. 'You might have done. I mean, you smoke dope, don't you?'

'That's different,' said Zara. 'Anyway,' she added, 'if you have sex too young you get cervical cancer.'

'So-vital cancer?' said Antony, mishearing. 'What's that?'

'Cer-vi-cal, dummy! Cancer of the cervix. You know what the cervix is? It's right here.' She pointed to a spot at the top of her jeans fly-buttons. 'Right up inside.' Antony followed her finger with his gaze; as he did so he felt blood start to rush to his head. His hand shot up confusedly to his birthmark.

'Don't cover it up,' said Zara.

'What?' His voice felt strangled.

'Your birthmark. I like it. Don't cover it up.'

'You like it?'

'Sure. Don't you?' Antony looked away, not knowing quite what to say. No-one ever mentioned his birthmark; he'd got used to pretending he thought it wasn't there.

'It's sexy.' Her voice fell, soft and raspy on his ears. Antony felt his breathing quicken. No-one had ever called him sexy before.

'My mother hated it,' he said, without meaning to.

'I bet she didn't,' said Zara encouragingly.

'She did! She . . .' He broke off. 'It doesn't matter.'

'Sure it matters.'

For a few silent moments Antony stared downwards. Years of loyalty to his mother battled with a sudden, desperate yearning to unburden himself.

'She wanted me to wear an eyepatch, to hide it,' he said, suddenly.

'An eyepatch?'

Antony swivelled round to meet Zara's incredulous gaze.

'When I was about seven. She asked me if I didn't think it would be fun to wear an eyepatch. Like a pirate, she said. And she pulled out this . . . this horrible black plastic thing, on elastic.'

'What did you do?'

Antony closed his eyes and remembered his mother, staring at him with that look of distaste, half masked by a bright, fake smile. A pain grabbed him in the chest and he took a deep, shuddering breath.

'I just sort of stared at it, and said, But I won't be able to see if I wear an eyepatch. And then she laughed, and pretended she was just joking. But . . .' He swallowed. 'I knew she wasn't. Even then, I knew. She wanted me to cover my eye up so no-one could see my birthmark.'

'Jesus. What a bitch.'

'She wasn't a bitch!' Antony's voice cracked. 'She was just . . .' He bit his lip.

'Well, you know what? I think it's sexy.' Zara moved closer still. 'Very sexy.' There was an infinitesimal pause. Zara met his eyes.

'Does . . . does kissing give you cervical cancer?' asked Antony eventually. His voice sounded husky to his own ears; his heart was pulsing loudly in his chest.

'I don't think so,' said Zara.

'Good,' said Antony.

Slowly, self-consciously, he put an arm round her skinny shoulders and pulled her towards him. Her lips tasted of mint and Diet Coke; her tongue found his immediately. She's been kissed before, he thought hazily. She's been kissed lots. More than me, probably. And as they drew apart he looked at her cautiously, half expecting her to be giggling at him; half expecting her to humiliate him with some barbed, experienced comment.

But to his horrified surprise, she was gazing into the distance and a tear was running down her cheek. Visions of accusations and useless denials raced terrifyingly through his mind.

'Zara, I'm sorry!' he gasped. 'I didn't mean . . .'

'Don't worry,' she said in a low voice. 'It's not you. It's nothing to do with you.'

'So you didn't mind . . .' He stared at her, panting slightly.

'Of course I didn't mind,' she said. 'I wanted you to kiss me. You knew that.' She wiped away the tear, looked up at him and smiled. 'And you know what? Now I want you to kiss me again.'

By the time she arrived home, Philippa had a throbbing headache. After Fleur had left in a taxi for Waterloo, she had continued shopping by herself, wandering into the cheaper shops which Fleur had ignored but which she secretly preferred. Now her shoes felt too tight, and her hair was falling out of shape, and she felt raw and grimy from the London streets. But as she let herself in, she heard an unfamiliar voice in the study, and her heart quickened. Perhaps Lambert had invited guests over. Perhaps they would have an impromptu supper party. What a good thing she was wearing her pink suit; they'd think she wore clothes like this every day. She hurried down the hall, checking her reflection in the mirror, adopting a sophisticated yet welcoming expression, and threw open the door of the study.

But Lambert was alone. He was slumped in the armchair by the fire, listening to a message on the answer machine. A woman's voice which Philippa didn't recognize was saying, 'It is absolutely *imperative* that we meet without delay to discuss your situation.'

'What situation?' said Philippa.

'Nothing,' snapped Lambert. Philippa looked at the machine's red light.

'Is she on the line now? Why don't you just pick up and speak to her?'

'Why don't you just shut up?' snarled Lambert.

Philippa looked at him. As the afternoon had worn on, she'd begun to think that perhaps her marriage was not the loveless shell she had described; that perhaps there was hope in it. Her determination to leave Lambert had melted away, leaving behind only a familiar, faded disappointment that life had not turned out quite the way she had imagined.

But now, suddenly she felt her resolve return. She took a deep breath, and clenched her fists.

'You're always so bloody rude to me!' she exclaimed.

'What?' Lambert's head moved round slowly until he was looking at her in what seemed genuine astonishment.

'I'm sick of it!' Philippa advanced into the room, realized she was still holding two carrier bags, and put them down. 'I'm sick of the way you treat me. Like a skivvy! Like an imbecile! I want some respect!' She stamped her foot triumphantly and wished she had a bit more of an audience. Phrases were springing plentifully to her lips; scenes of confrontation from a thousand novels were filling her mind. She felt like a romantic, feisty heroine. 'I married you for love, Lambert,' she continued, lowering her voice to a tremble. 'I wanted to share your life. Your hopes, your dreams. And yet you cut me out; you ignore me . . .'

'I don't ignore you!' said Lambert. 'What are you talking about?'

'You treat me like shit,' said Philippa, tossing her hair back. 'Well, I've just about had enough. I want out.'

'You what?' Lambert's voice rose in an astonished squawk. 'Philippa, what the fuck's wrong with you?'

'Ask yourself the same question,' said Philippa. 'I'm going to leave you, Lambert.' She lifted her chin high, picked up her carrier bags and headed for the door. 'I'm going to leave you, and there's nothing you can do about it.'

# FOURTEEN

Fleur arrived back from London to find Geoffrey Forrester, captain of Greyworth Golf Club, shaking hands with Richard in the hall.

'Aha!' said Geoffrey, as he saw Fleur. 'You're just in time to hear the good news. Shall I tell Fleur, Richard, or do you want to?'

'What is it?' said Fleur.

'Geoffrey's just informed me that, if I'm willing, I'm to be nominated as captain of the club,' said Richard. Fleur looked at him. He was obviously trying to keep his face sober but his mouth had twisted into a smile, and his eyes were shining with delight.

'As I told Richard, the committee voted unanimously in favour of him,' said Geoffrey. 'Which doesn't always happen, I can tell you.'

'Well done, darling!' said Fleur. 'I'm so pleased.'

'Anyway, I'd better shoot off,' said Geoffrey, looking at his watch. 'So, Richard, you'll let me know your decision in the morning?'

'Absolutely,' said Richard. 'Good night, Geoffrey.'

'And I hope we'll be seeing the two of you up at the Club Cup?' said Geoffrey. 'No excuses now, Richard!' He gave Fleur a jovial grin. 'Tell you what, Fleur, isn't it about time you took up the game yourself?'

'I'm not sure I'm really a golfer,' said Fleur, smiling back at him.

'It's never too late to start!' Geoffrey chuckled. 'We'll get you yet, Fleur! Won't we Richard?'

'I hope so,' said Richard. He reached for Fleur's hand and gave it a squeeze. 'I certainly hope so.'

They watched as his car roared out of the drive, then walked back inside the house.

'What decision was he talking about?' said Fleur.

'I told Geoffrey that I couldn't agree to being nominated until I'd consulted you first,' said Richard.

'What?' Fleur stared at him. 'But why? You want to be captain, don't you?' Richard sighed.

'Of course I want to – on one level. But it's not as simple as that. Being captain is, as well as being a huge honour, a huge commitment.' He lifted a strand of Fleur's hair and brushed it against his lips. 'If I take it on, I'll have to spend far more time at the club than I have been doing recently. I'll have to play more, get my game up to form again, attend meetings . . .' He spread his hands. 'There's a lot to it. And all of that will mean I have less time to spend with you.'

'But you'll be captain! Isn't that worth it?' Fleur narrowed her eyes. 'Isn't being captain of Greyworth what you've always wanted?'

'It's funny,' said Richard. 'I've thought for years that it was exactly what I wanted. Being captain of Greyworth was – well, it was my goal. And now I've got my goal within my grasp, I can't quite remember what I wanted it for. The goal posts have shifted.' His nose began to twitch. 'Or should I perhaps say, the eighteenth flag has shifted.' He gave a little snuffle of laughter, but Fleur was frowning distractedly.

'You can't just abandon your goal,' she said suddenly. 'If it's something you've been aiming for all your life.'

'I don't see why not. The question is, why was I aiming for it?' said Richard. 'And what happens if I don't particularly value what it has to offer any more?' He shrugged. 'What if I'd prefer to spend my time with you, rather than going round the course with some bore from a neighbouring golf club?'

'Richard, you can't just cop out!' exclaimed Fleur. 'You can't just settle for . . . a nice quiet life! You've always wanted to be captain of Greyworth and now here's your chance. People should grasp the opportunities they're given in life. Even if it means—' She broke off, breathing hard.

'Even if it means they're unhappy?' Richard laughed.

'Maybe, yes! Better to take the opportunity and be unhappy than pass it up and always regret it.'

'Fleur.' He took both her hands and kissed them. 'You're extraordinary; absolutely extraordinary! I can't imagine a more encouraging, supportive wife . . .'

There was a sharp silence.

'Except I'm not your wife,' said Fleur slowly. Richard

looked down. He took a deep breath, then looked up, straight at her.

'Fleur,' he began.

'Richard, I have to go and shower,' said Fleur, before he could continue. 'I'm absolutely filthy from London.' She disentangled herself from his grasp and headed quickly for the stairs.

'Of course,' said Richard quietly. Then he smiled up at her. 'You must be exhausted. And I haven't even asked you how the memorial service went.'

'I didn't go in the end,' said Fleur. 'I was too busy having fun with Philippa.'

'Oh good! I'm very glad you two are making friends.'

'And thank you for the champagne!' added Fleur, from halfway up the stairs. 'We were so surprised.'

'Yes,' said Richard. 'I hoped you would be.'

Fleur headed straight for the bathroom, turned both bath taps on and locked the door. Her mind felt fuddled; she needed to think. Sighing, she sat down on the bathroom seat – a hideous upholstered affair – and stared at her reflection in the mirror.

What was her own goal in life? The answer came immediately, without her even thinking. Her goal was to acquire a large amount of money. What was a large amount of money? Ten million pounds was a large amount of money. If she married Richard, she would have a large amount of money.

'But not on my own terms,' said Fleur aloud to her reflection. She sighed, and pushed her shoes off. Her feet were aching very slightly from the London streets, despite the soft, expensive leather of her shoes; despite the many taxis.

Could she stand to become Richard's wife? Mrs Richard Favour, of Greyworth. Fleur shuddered slightly; the very thought stifled her. Men changed after marriage. Richard would buy her tartan trousers and expect her to take up golf. He would give her an allowance. He would be there every morning when she woke up, smiling at her with that eager, innocent smile. If she planned a trip abroad, he would come too.

But at the same time . . . Fleur bit her lip. At the same time, he had a lot of money. He was an opportunity that might not come her way again. She tore off her jacket and tossed it over the towel rail. The sight of the black silk suddenly reminded her of the memorial service she'd missed that afternoon. A chance passed up. Who might have been at that service? What fortunate meeting might have occurred if she'd gone?

'Make up your mind,' said Fleur to her reflection, stepping out of her skirt, undoing her bra. 'Either you take what's going, or you leave.'

She ripped her stockings off, padded over to the bath and swung her feet over the side. As she lowered them into the hot, foamy water she felt her whole body start to relax and her mind blank out.

A knock at the door made her jump.

'It's me!' came Richard's voice. 'I've brought you up a glass of wine.'

'Thanks, darling!' called back Fleur. 'I'll get it in a second.'

'And Philippa's on the phone. She wants to speak to you.' Fleur rolled her eyes. She'd had enough of Philippa for one day.

'Tell her I'll call her back.'

'Right you are. I'm leaving the glass here,' came Richard's voice again. 'Just outside the door.'

She imagined him stooping down; carefully placing the glass on the carpet outside the bathroom door; looking at it, wondering whether she might not knock it over by mistake, then bending down again and moving it a few inches further back before tiptoeing away. A careful prudent man. Would he let her spend all his money? Quite possibly not. And then she would have married him for nothing.

Philippa put the telephone receiver down and bit her lip. A fresh flood of tears poured down her red, raw face; she felt as though her insides were being wrenched apart. There was no-one else she could phone. No-one else she could confide in. She had to talk to Fleur, and Fleur was in the bath.

'Oh God,' she said aloud. 'Oh God help me.'

She sank off the sofa onto the floor and began to weep frenziedly, clutching her stomach, rocking back and forwards. Her pink suit was crumpled and tear-stained but she didn't care what she looked like; there was no-one to see her. No-one to hear her.

Lambert had slammed the door half an hour before,

leaving her sitting in numb, silent mortification. For a while she'd crouched on the sofa, unable to move without a pain hitting her in the stomach and tears springing to her eyes. Then, as her breathing calmed, she'd somehow managed to get to the phone and dial the number of The Maples and ask for Fleur in a voice that sounded normal. Fleur, she'd thought desperately. Fleur. If only I can talk to Fleur.

But Fleur was in the bath and couldn't talk to her. And as she'd said goodbye to her father, the tears had once more started to pour down her face, and she'd sunk to the floor, and wondered why a day that had started off so perfectly should have ended up in a mess of humiliation.

He'd laughed at her. To begin with, Lambert had laughed at her. A nasty, mocking laugh which had made her throw her shoulders back and look him in the eyes and say, in an even more feisty voice than before, 'I'm leaving you!' A zingy adrenalin had begun to pump round her body, a smile had come to her lips, and it had occurred to her that she should have done this ages ago. 'I expect I'll go to my father's house,' she'd added in a businesslike way. Until I get settled in my own place.' And Lambert had looked up and said,

'Philippa, shut up, will you?'

'Lambert, don't you understand? I'm leaving you!'

'No you're not.'

'Yes I am!'

'No you're bloody not.'

'I am! You don't love me, so what's the point in carrying on together?'

'The point is, we're fucking married. All right?'

'Well maybe I don't want to be fucking married any more!' she'd cried.

'Well maybe I do!'

And Lambert had got to his feet, come over and taken her wrist. 'You're not leaving me, Philippa,' he'd said, in a voice she hardly recognized; a voice which almost frightened her. He was bright red and trembling; he looked as though he was possessed. 'You're not fucking leaving me, all right?'

And she'd felt flattered. She'd gazed up at his desperate face and thought, that's love. He really does love me. She was about to succumb, to caress his chin and call him darling. When he moved towards her, she'd felt a smile creep across her face and prepared herself for a passionate, reuniting embrace. But suddenly his hands were grasping her roughly about the throat.

'You won't leave me!' he hissed. 'You won't ever leave me!' And his hands had tightened around her neck until she was hardly able to breathe, until she felt she would retch against the pressure on her throat.

'Tell me you won't leave me! Say it!'

'I won't leave you,' Philippa had managed in a hoarse voice.

'That's more like it.'

Suddenly he'd let her go, dropping her down onto the sofa like a child dropping an unwanted toy. She hadn't looked up as he'd left; hadn't asked him where he was going. Her entire body was riveted to the spot in misery. When she'd heard the door slamming, she'd felt tears of relief pouring down her face. Eventually she'd made her way shakily to the phone, jabbed in the number of The Maples and asked for the only person she could possibly tell about this. Somehow she'd managed to talk to her father in the semblance of a normal voice, giving away nothing. Somehow she'd managed to say that of course it didn't matter, cheerio Daddy, see you soon. But as soon as she'd put the phone down, she'd collapsed onto the carpet, a soggy mess of misery. Because Fleur was unavailable, and there was no-one else she could turn to.

Richard put down the receiver and gazed affectionately at it. He found it rather pleasing that Philippa had phoned wanting to speak to Fleur rather than him. It just showed, he thought, that Fleur was becoming more and more a member of the family: attached not simply to himself, but to all of them. Gillian was certainly very fond of Fleur. Antony seemed to enjoy her company well enough, and Richard grinned to himself – he certainly liked young Zara.

In the space of a summer, Fleur had become so much part of all their lives that he found it difficult to remember how they'd existed before her. At the beginning she'd seemed a foreign, exotic creature, full of strange ideas, completely at odds with the life he led; with the life they all led. But now . . . Richard frowned. Now she seemed entirely normal. She was just Fleur. Whether she'd changed, or whether they'd changed, he wasn't entirely sure.

And it wasn't just within the family that the transformation had taken place, thought Richard, pouring himself a glass of wine. All those looks of disapproval in the clubhouse had, somewhere along the line, vanished. All the gossip had melted away. Now Fleur was as well respected at Greyworth as he was himself. His nomination as captain honoured her as much as it did him.

Richard bit his lip. It was time for him to honour her too. It was time for him to get his affairs in order; time for him to buy an engagement ring; time for him to ask Fleur – properly – to be his wife.

By lunchtime the next day, Fleur had not yet found a moment to call Philippa back.

'She phoned again,' said Gillian, slicing tomatoes for lunch in the kitchen. 'While you were out having your fitness assessment. She sounded very upset that she'd missed you for the third time.'

'I've got very good stamina,' said Fleur, staring at the sheet of paper in her hand. 'But my lung capacity is terrible.' She looked up. 'Why should that be, I wonder?'

'Too much smoking,' said Zara.

'I don't smoke!'

'No, but you used to.'

'Only very briefly,' retorted Fleur. 'And I lived in the Swiss Alps for six months. That should have repaired any lung damage, shouldn't it?'

'You also had another phone call from your friend Johnny,' said Gillian, glancing at the pad of paper by the kitchen phone. 'You know, that's the fourth time he's phoned this week.'

'Jesus!' said Zara. 'Haven't you two made it up yet?'

'He was quite adamant that he needed to speak to you,' added Gillian. 'I did promise I'd try to persuade you to phone him.'

'I'm not in the mood for Johnny,' said Fleur, frowning. 'I'll call him later.'

'Call him now!' exclaimed Zara. 'If he wants you to call, he must have a good reason. What if its urgent?'

'Nothing in Johnny's life is urgent,' said Fleur scathingly. 'He hasn't a care in the world.'

'And I suppose you have?' shot back Zara.

'Zara,' interrupted Gillian diplomatically, 'why don't you go and pick me some strawberries from the garden?' There was a short silence. Zara glared at Fleur.

'OK,' she said at last, and got to her feet.

'And maybe I'll find time to phone Johnny later,' said Fleur, examining her nails. 'But only maybe.'

Lambert was nearing crisis point. He sat in his office, shredding paper between his fingers, staring out of the window, unable to concentrate. Over the last few days he had received no fewer than three messages from Erica Fortescue at First Bank, exhorting him to contact her urgently. So far he'd managed to avoid speaking to her. But he couldn't run away for ever. What if she came into his office? What if she called Richard?

His overdraft now stood at three hundred and thirty thousand pounds. Lambert felt a cold sweat steal over his forehead. How had it become so large? How had he spent so much? What did he have to show for it? He had a car, some clothes, some watches. He had some friends; chaps and their wives whom he'd bought with bottles of brandy at his club, tickets to the opera, boxes at the cricket. He'd always pretended he was doling out freebies; his friends had always believed him. If they'd ever thought he was paying for everything out of his own pocket they would have been embarrassed; would probably have laughed at him. Now Lambert's cheeks flushed with an angry humiliation. Who were these friends? Mindless idiots whose names he could barely remember. And it was to show them a good time that he'd got himself into this trouble.

What had Emily been playing at, telling him he was going to be a rich man? What the fuck had she been playing at? A cold fury rose through Lambert and he cursed her for being dead, cursed her for having flitted out of the world leaving loose ends floating in the wind. What was the truth? Was Philippa going to be rich? Was that money going to be hers? Or had Richard changed his mind? Had the whole trust story been an invention of Emily's? He wouldn't have put it past her, the manipulative bitch. She'd encouraged him to think he was rich; encouraged him to start spending more than he had done before. And now he was in debt and all her hints and promises had come to nothing.

Except – Lambert bit his lip – he couldn't be sure that

they would come to nothing. It was still tantalizingly possible that Richard would deliver. Maybe he was still going to put some of that money into trust for Philippa. Maybe when she turned thirty she would become a millionairess, just as Emily had promised. Or maybe Richard had now decided to wait a bit longer until she was thirty-five, perhaps, or forty.

It was torturous, not knowing. And he had no way of finding out. Richard was a secretive bastard – he would never tell Lambert anything – and of course Philippa knew nothing. Philippa knew nothing about anything. A sudden memory came into Lambert's mind of Philippa's red, contorted face the night before. She'd been sobbing on the sofa when he'd stormed out of the house; he hadn't seen her since then.

He'd over-reacted to her feeble threat of leaving him; he realized that now. Of course, she hadn't meant it; Philippa would never leave him. But at the time, she'd rattled him. He'd felt white-hot panic flashing through his body and a conviction that he must, at all costs, stop her. He had to remain married to Philippa; he had to keep things ticking over, at least until he knew where he stood. And so he'd lashed out. Maybe he'd overdone it a bit, maybe he'd upset her a bit too much. But at least that would keep her quiet for a while; give him time to sort himself out.

The phone rang, and he felt a spasm of fear zip through him. Perhaps this was Erica Fortescue from First Bank, he thought, ridiculously. She was down in reception; she was on the way up . . .

It rang again, and he snatched it up.

'Yes?' he barked, trying to conceal his nerves.

'Lambert?' It was his secretary, Lucy. 'Just to say, I've rearranged that meeting for you.'

'Good,' said Lambert, and put the phone down. He couldn't face any meetings at the moment; couldn't face anyone. He had to have some time to think what to do.

Should he just go to Richard, explain the situation and ask for a bail-out? Would Richard willingly hand over that kind of money? The total sum sprang into his mind again, and he shuddered. The figure which had seemed so reasonable when viewed against the mountain of Philippa's future fortune now seemed outlandish. He closed his eyes and imagined telling Richard; asking humbly for assistance; sitting silently while Richard lectured him. His life would be a misery. What a fucking nightmare.

This was all Larry Collins's fault, Lambert thought suddenly. Larry, his chum at the bank. Larry, who had *invited* Lambert to take out an overdraft. He'd been impressed by Lambert's assurances that soon Philippa would be coming into millions. He'd told Lambert he was a valued customer. He'd said the paperwork didn't matter; he'd upped the limit without question. If he hadn't been such an irresponsible moron; if his bosses hadn't been so fucking *blind* – then Lambert would never have had such a big overdraft limit in the first place and the whole problem would never have arisen. But no-one had thought to check up, Lambert's overdraft had risen like the sun – and only then had Larry been fired. Larry was safely out of the picture, thanks very much, and it was Lambert who'd been left to pick up the pieces.

What was he to do? If he kept to his original plan – took fifty thousand from the ten million account and threw it at the bank to keep them happy – then he'd have to find a way of paying Richard back before the end of the year. He couldn't just leave it; Richard would notice a deficit of fifty thousand. So he'd need another overdraft. But who would authorize another overdraft now that Larry was gone? Who would authorize another overdraft for him without any proof that Philippa's trust fund was established? Lambert clenched his fists in frustration. If only he had proof. Some little corroborating piece of evidence. Something that would convince some fool somewhere to let him keep his overdraft. A document, or a letter. Something signed by Richard. Anything would do.

# FIFTEEN

Two weeks later Richard sat in Oliver Sterndale's office, signing his name repeatedly on different pieces of paper. After the last signature he replaced the cap on Oliver's fountain pen, looked at his old friend and smiled.

'There,' he said. 'All done.'

'All gone, more like,' said Oliver tetchily. 'You do realize that you're now practically a pauper?'

Richard laughed.

'Oliver, for someone who has just signed away ten million pounds, I have an indecently large amount of money left to call my own. As well you know.'

'I know nothing of the sort,' said Oliver. His eyes met Richard's and suddenly twinkled. 'However, since you have been so consistently wedded to this little scheme, may I offer my congratulations on its successful completion?'

'You may.'

'Well then, congratulations.'

They both looked at the contracts, lying in thick piles on the desk.

'They're going to be two very rich young people,' said Oliver. 'Have you decided when to tell them?'

'Not yet,' said Richard. 'There's still plenty of time.'

'There's a fair amount of time,' said Oliver. 'But you do need to give them some warning. Especially Philippa. You don't want to find it's the eve of her thirtieth birthday, and you're suddenly trying to find the words to tell her she's about to become a multi-millionairess. These announcements have a nasty habit of backfiring.'

'Oh, I'm aware of that,' said Richard. 'In fact, I thought I might bring both Philippa and Antony in here, say in a few weeks' time, and we could both explain it to them. Since you're the trustee of the fund.'

'Good idea,' said Oliver. 'Splendid idea.'

'You know, I feel liberated,' said Richard suddenly. 'This has been hanging over me more than I'd realized. Now I feel able to—' He broke off, and coloured slightly.

'To pursue your fresh start?'

'Exactly.'

Oliver cleared his throat delicately.

'Richard, is there anything which – as your lawyer – I should know?'

'I don't believe so.'

'But you would let me know if there were . . . anything.'

'Naturally I would.' A small smile played about

Richard's lips, and Oliver gazed at him severely.

'And by that I don't mean a fax from Las Vegas saying "Guess what, I'm hitched".' Richard burst into laughter.

'Oliver, who do you think I am?'

'I think you're a decent man and a good friend.' Oliver's eyes bored into Richard's. 'And I think you may need protection.'

'From whom, may I ask?'

'From yourself. From your own generosity.'

'Oliver, just what are you saying?'

'I'm saying nothing. Just promise me you won't get married without telling me first. Please.'

'Honestly, Oliver, I wouldn't dream of it. And anyway, who says I'm getting married?'

Oliver gave him a wry smile.

'Do you really want me to answer that? I can give you a list of names, if you like. Beginning with my own wife.'

'Perhaps you'd better not.' Richard chuckled. 'You know, I really don't care who says what about me any more. Let them gossip all they like.'

'Did you use to care?'

Richard thought for a minute.

'I'm not sure I did. But Emily used to worry terribly. And so of course I always used to worry too, on her behalf.'

'Yes,' said Oliver. 'I can imagine.' He grinned at Richard. 'You've certainly changed, haven't you?'

'Have I?' said Richard innocently.

'You know you have.' Oliver paused. 'And quite

seriously, I'm glad things are working out so well for you. You deserve it.'

'I'm not sure I do,' said Richard. 'But thank you anyway, Oliver.' For a moment the two men's eyes met; then Richard looked away. 'And thanks for coming in on a Saturday morning,' he said lightly. 'On Club Cup morning, too!'

'It was no trouble.' Oliver leaned back comfortably in his chair. 'I'm not teeing off until twelve. What about you?'

'Half-past. Just enough time to get in some putting practice. I certainly need it. You know, I've barely played this summer.'

'I know,' said Oliver. 'That's what I said. You've changed.'

By eleven o'clock, Philippa was finally ready to leave the flat. She peered at herself in the mirror and gave her hair one last tug.

'Come on,' said Lambert. 'I tee off at one, remember.'

'There's plenty of time,' said Philippa tonelessly. Without meeting his eye, she followed him down the stairs.

How had it happened? she wondered for the hundredth time, as they both got into the car. How had she let Lambert back into her life without a protest; without so much as a question mark? He had arrived back at the flat, three days after the row, holding a bottle of wine and some flowers.

'These are for you,' he'd said gracelessly at the door of

the sitting room, and her head had jerked round from the television in shock. She'd thought she would never see Lambert again. At one point, she'd considered changing the locks of the flat; then she'd discovered how much it cost and decided to spend the money on a crate of Baileys instead. By the time Lambert arrived back, she was on the fourth bottle.

The alcohol must have dimmed her faculties, she thought. Because as she'd looked at him, standing in the doorway, not sneering or swaggering but not looking particularly penitent either, she'd found herself entirely devoid of emotion. She'd tried as hard as she could to conjure up the anger and hatred which she knew should be burning inside her; tried to think of some appropriate insult to hiss at him. But nothing came to mind except 'You bastard.' And when she said it, it was in such lacklustre tones that she might as well not have bothered.

He'd given her the flowers, and she'd found herself looking at them and thinking they were rather nice. Then he'd opened the wine and poured it into a glass for her, and although she was feeling slightly sick, she'd drunk it. And once she'd taken his flowers and drunk his wine, it had seemed to be tacitly agreed between them that he was back, that he was forgiven, that the rift between them was healed.

It was as though the whole thing had never happened. As though she'd never threatened to leave him; he'd never touched her. As though none of the shouting and sobbing had occurred. He never referred to it and neither did she. Whenever she opened her mouth to speak about it, she began to feel sick and her heart began to pound, and it seemed so much easier to say nothing. And the more days that passed, the more remote and shadowy the whole thing seemed, and the less convinced she felt of her ability to tackle him on the subject.

Yet she wanted to. Part of her wanted to shout at him again; to work herself up into a frenzy and scream at him until he crumpled in guilt. Part of her wanted to relive the entire confrontation, this time as the heroine, the victor. And part of her wanted to find the energy to let the world know what had happened.

Because no-one knew. Fleur didn't know; her father didn't know; none of her friends knew. She had been through the worst crisis of her life, had come through it somehow, and no-one knew. Fleur still had not phoned her back. It had been over two weeks and she still hadn't phoned back.

Philippa felt angry tears spring to her eyes, and she looked out of the car window. At first, she'd kept ringing The Maples, frantic to talk to Fleur; desperate for some help and advice. Then Lambert had arrived back, and the two of them had seemed to patch things up – and Philippa had found herself wanting to relay her story to Fleur not so much for help as for the shocked admiration that it would surely provoke. Every time the phone had rung, she'd jumped to answer, thinking it was Fleur, ready to tell in low tones what had been happening to her; ready to savour the reaction at the other end. But Fleur hadn't called back and hadn't called back, and eventually Philippa had given up expecting her to. Perhaps Fleur was just hopeless with phones, she'd rationalized to herself. Perhaps she hadn't received any of Philippa's messages. Perhaps she'd always tried ringing just when Philippa was on the line to someone else.

But today was different; today they didn't need phones. She would have Fleur all to herself, and she would tell her the whole story. At the thought, Philippa felt an exhilarating anticipation begin to fizz inside her. She would tell Fleur every detail of what had happened. And Fleur would be astounded that Philippa had got through such a trauma on her own; astounded, and consumed with guilt.

'I had no-one,' Philippa heard herself saying to Fleur, in matter-of-fact tones. 'When you didn't call back . . .' She would give a little shrug. 'I was desperate. Of course, I turned to the bottle.'

'Oh darling. You didn't. I feel terrible!' Fleur would grasp her hands pleadingly; Philippa would simply give another little shrug.

'I got through it,' she would say carelessly. 'Somehow I got through it. Jesus, it was hard, though.'

'What?' said Lambert suddenly. 'Are you talking to me?'

'Oh!' said Philippa, and felt her cheeks turn red. 'No, I'm not.'

'Muttering away to yourself,' said Lambert. 'No wonder everyone thinks you're mad.'

'They don't think I'm mad,' said Philippa.

'Whatever,' said Lambert. Philippa looked crossly at him and tried to think of a clever retort. But her mind felt stultified in the real world; her words mismatched and fell apart in her mouth. Already she was flying happily back to Fleur, who would listen to her story, and gasp, and take Philippa's hand, and vow never to let her down again.

'Cool,' said Zara, as she and Antony approached the clubhouse. 'Look at all those flaggy things.'

'Bunting.'

'What?'

'Bunting. It's what they're called.' Zara gazed at him sceptically for a moment. 'Well anyway, they always decorate the clubhouse on Club Cup day,' continued Antony. 'And there's a band in the garden. It's quite fun. We'll get a cream tea later on.'

'But we have to go round the golf course first?'

'That's kind of the point.'

Zara gave a melodramatic sigh and collapsed onto the clubhouse steps.

'Look,' said Antony anxiously, sitting down beside her. 'I'll understand if you don't want to caddy for me after all. I mean it's a hot day, and everything.'

'Are you trying to fire me?'

'No! Of course not!'

'Well, OK then.' Zara squinted at Antony. 'You nervous?'

'Not really.'

'Who's going to do better? You, or your father?'

'Dad, I expect. He always does.'

'But he hasn't been practising all week like you have.' Antony shrugged awkwardly.

'Still. He's a bloody good golfer.' They sat in silence for a while.

'And you're a bloody good kisser,' said Zara suddenly. Antony's head jerked up in astonishment.

'What?'

'You heard.' She grinned. 'Should I say it again?'

'No! Someone might hear!'

'So what? It's the truth.' Antony flushed scarlet. A group of chattering women was coming up the club-house steps, and he turned his face away from them.

'And you're . . .' he began. 'I mean . . .'

'Don't feel you have to compliment me in return,' said Zara. 'I know I'm good. I was taught by an expert.'

'Who?' said Antony, feeling jealous.

'Cara.'

'Who the hell's Cara?'

'This Italian girl. Didn't I tell you about her? We were living in her house last summer. She had a rich daddy too. In the Mafia, I think.'

'A girl?' Antony goggled at her.

'Sure. But much older. She was seventeen. She'd kissed, like, loads of people.'

'How did she teach you?'

'How do you think?' Zara grinned at him.

'Jesus.' Antony's face grew even redder.

'She had a younger brother,' said Zara. 'But he was

only interested in his dumb computer. Want some gum?' She looked up at Antony's face and laughed. 'You're shocked, aren't you?'

'Well, I mean . . . You were only twelve!' Zara shrugged.

'I guess they start early over there.' She unwrapped her gum and began to chew. Antony watched her silently for a few minutes.

'So what happened?' he asked eventually.

'What do you mean, what happened?'

'Why didn't you stay living with them?'

Zara looked away.

'We just didn't.'

'Did your mother and the Italian guy have a fight?'

'Not exactly,' said Zara. She looked around, and lowered her voice. 'Fleur got tired of living in Italy. So one night we just scooted.'

'What, just left?'

'Yup. Packed our bags and left.'

Antony stared at her for a moment, thinking.

'You're not . . .' He swallowed, and rubbed his shoe along the step. 'You're not going to scoot this time, are you?'

There was a long silence.

'I hope not,' said Zara eventually. 'I really hope not.' She hunched her shoulders and looked away. 'But with Fleur, you never know.'

Fleur was sitting in the clubhouse bar, watching as the competitors and their wives milled about, greeting one another; joshing each other on their form, breaking off mid-conversation to shriek to new arrivals. She felt at home here, she thought comfortably, leaning back and sipping her drink. The ambience here reminded her of her childhood; of the expatriate club in Dubai. These shrieking Surrey women could equally well have been the expat wives who had sat in clusters at the bar, drinking gin and admiring one another's shoes and complaining in low voices about their husbands' bosses. Those jovial chaps with their pints of beer could equally well have been the business acquaintances of her father: successful, tanned, obsessively competitive. In Dubai the golf courses had been sand-coloured, not green, but that was the only difference. That was the atmosphere in which she'd grown up; that was the atmosphere which felt, to her, most like home.

'Fleur!' A voice interrupted her thoughts, and she looked up to see Philippa. She was dressed in a white trouser suit and was gazing at Fleur with an intense, almost frightening expression.

'Philippa,' said Fleur lightly. 'How nice to see you again. Is Lambert playing in the Club Cup?'

'Yes, he is.' Philippa began to fiddle with her bag, tugging awkwardly at the zip until it stuck. 'And I wanted to talk to you.'

'Good,' said Fleur. 'That will be nice. But first let me get you a drink.'

'Drink!' said Philippa obscurely. 'My God, if you knew.' She sat down with a huge sigh. 'If you only knew.'

'Yes,' said Fleur doubtfully. 'Well, you just sit there, and I'll be back in a second.'

At the bar she found Lambert pushing his way to the head of the queue.

'Oh, hello,' he said unenthusiastically.

'I've come to buy your wife a drink,' said Fleur. 'Or perhaps you were planning to buy her one yourself?' Lambert sighed.

'What does she want?'

'I've no idea. A glass of white wine, I should think. Or a Manhattan.'

'She can have wine.'

'Good.' Fleur glanced back at Philippa, who was frantically searching through her handbag for something; a tissue, judging by the redness of her nose. Could the girl not invest in some decent face-powder? Fleur gave a little shudder and turned back to the bar. Suddenly it occurred to her that if she returned to Philippa's table she would probably be stuck with her all afternoon.

'Right,' she said slowly. 'Well, I think I'll go and find Richard, to wish him good luck. Philippa's over there by the window.'

She waited for Lambert to grunt in response, then swiftly moved off, threading her way through the throng, keeping her head firmly averted from Philippa's until she was safely out of the bar.

On the steps of the clubhouse she found Richard, Antony and Zara.

'All set?' she said cheerfully. 'Who tees off first?'

'Dad,' said Antony. 'And I'm soon after.'

'*We're* soon after,' corrected Zara. 'I'm Antony's caddy,'

she informed Richard. 'I tell him which club to use. The big one or the little one.'

'Yeah, right,' said Antony. 'You don't even know what the clubs are called.'

'Sure I do!'

Richard met Fleur's eye and smiled.

'And tonight we have a nice celebration supper,' he said.

'There may not be anything to celebrate,' said Antony.

'Oh, I hope there will,' said Richard.

'So do I,' said Zara, looking at Antony. 'I don't want to hang around with a loser.' Fleur laughed.

'That's my girl.'

'Right,' said Richard. 'Well, I'd better start getting ready.'

'Who's that?' said Antony, interrupting him. 'That man. He's waving at us!'

'Where?' said Fleur.

'He's just come in through the gate. I've no idea who he is.'

'Is he a member?' said Richard, and they all turned to look, squinting in the sunshine.

The man was dapper and tanned and had nut-brown hair. He was dressed in immaculate pale linen and gazing with slight dismay at the pink culottes of the woman who was striding along in front of him. As they stared at him, he looked up and waved again. Fleur and Zara gasped in unison. Then Zara gave a huge whoop and began running towards him.

'Who on earth is it?' exclaimed Richard, watching as

the strange man caught Zara in a huge hug. 'Is it a friend of yours?'

'I don't believe it,' said Fleur in a faint voice. 'It's Johnny.'

# SIXTEEN

'I should have called,' said Fleur. She stretched her legs down the grassy bank on which she and Johnny were sitting. In the distance was the fourteenth hole; a man in a red shirt was lining up to putt. 'I'm sorry. I thought you were still cross with me.'

'I was. And I'm even crosser with you now!' exclaimed Johnny. 'Do you know what an effort it's been for me to come down here? You know I never leave London if I can help it.'

'I know,' said Fleur. 'But you're here now. I'm so glad we're still friends . . .'

'I had to *battle* to find out what time the train left. Then I realized I didn't know which station I should catch it from and I had to ring up again and the person I'd spoken to before had gone on a tea-break!' Johnny shook his head. 'The inefficiency of the system! And as for the train itself . . .'

'Well, it's lovely to see you,' said Fleur soothingly. 'How long are you staying?'

'I'm not staying! Good God, there are limits!'

'That'll be a pound in the swear box,' said Fleur idly. She lay back and felt the sun beat down on her face. It would be nice to be back in London with Johnny and Felix, she thought. Shopping, gossiping, the odd funeral . . .

'You seem very at home here,' said Johnny, looking around. 'Quite the little Surrey wife. Have you taken up golf?'

'Of course not.'

'I'm glad to hear it. Such a deeply suburban game.'

'It's not so bad,' said Fleur defensively. 'Zara's been learning to play, you know.'

'Ah well,' said Johnny fondly. 'Zara never did have any taste.'

'It's a shame she had to go off and caddy.'

'Well, it's you I wanted to speak to,' said Johnny. 'That's why I've come down here. Since you wouldn't return my calls, you left me no other choice.'

'What do you want to speak to me about?' asked Fleur. Johnny was silent. Fleur abruptly sat up. 'Johnny, this isn't going to be about Hal Winters, is it?'

'Yes it is.'

'But you were going to get rid of him for me!'

'No I wasn't! Fleur, he's not some sort of household pest. He's your daughter's father. You told me you would prepare her for meeting him. Which you clearly haven't.'

'Zara doesn't need a father,' said Fleur sulkily.

'Of course she does.'

'She's got you.'

'Darling, it's hardly the same,' said Johnny, 'is it?' Fleur gave a little shrug, feeling her mouth twitching into a smile, in spite of herself.

'Perhaps not,' she said.

'Zara deserves the real thing,' said Johnny. 'And I can tell you, she's going to get it.'

'What do you mean?'

'Hal Winters is coming down here next Saturday. To meet Zara, ready or not.'

'What?' Fleur felt her face pale in shock. 'He's what?'

'It's all fixed up.'

'How dare you fix it up! It's got nothing to do with you!'

'It's got everything to do with us! If you abdicate responsibility, someone has to take over. I'll tell you, Felix was all for bringing him straight down in a taxi! But I said no, it's only fair to warn Fleur.' Johnny took a handkerchief from his pocket and mopped his brow. 'Believe it or not, I'm on your side, Fleur.'

'Well thanks very much!' spat Fleur. She felt slightly panicky and out of control. 'I don't want to see him!' she found herself saying. 'I don't want to see him.'

'You needn't see him. This is between him and Zara.'

'What, and I have nothing to do with it?'

'Of course you do. But you don't need him. Zara does.'

'She's fine!'

'She's not fine. She's on the telephone to me

constantly about America; about her father. Fleur, she's obsessed!'

For a moment, Fleur stared at him, her face taut; her mouth thin. Then suddenly she relaxed.

'OK,' she said. 'Fine. You're absolutely right. Bring Mr Winters down next Saturday. But don't tell Zara yet. I'll prepare her myself.'

'Fleur . . .'

'I promise! This time I really will.' Johnny looked at her suspiciously.

'And you'll make sure she's here to meet him?'

'Of course I will darling,' said Fleur lightly, and, closing her eyes, she leaned back again in the sun.

Philippa was sitting alone at a table in the garden. In front of her was a pot of tea, several huge scones and a bottle of wine which she'd won on the tombola. In the corner of the garden, the band was playing 'Strangers in the Night', and several children were attempting to dance with each other in front of the bandstand. A tear fell from Philippa's eye into her tea. She was all alone. Fleur had completely deserted her; Gillian was on the other side of the garden, chatting merrily to some woman Philippa had never met before. No-one had even asked her how she was, or why she looked so pale; no-one was interested in her. She took a sip of tea and looked wanly around. But everybody was laughing or talking or enjoying the music.

Suddenly she saw Zara and Antony coming towards her table. She gazed into the middle distance and pushed the plate of scones very slightly away from her to indicate her loss of appetite.

'Hi Philippa!' Antony's voice was exuberant. 'Is there enough tea for us?'

'Plenty,' whispered Philippa.

'Cool,' said Zara. She beamed at Philippa. 'You won't guess how well Antony played. Tell her, Antony.'

'I went round in sixty-eight,' said Antony, blushing red. A huge smile spread across his face.

'Sixty-eight!' echoed Zara.

'Is that good?' said Philippa dully.

'Of course it's good! It's the best!'

'Because of my handicap,' put in Antony quickly. 'My handicap's still pretty high, so I should do quite well.'

'You should win, you mean,' said Zara. 'Antony's the champion!'

'Sssh!' said Antony awkwardly. 'I'm not! Not yet.'

'Wait till we see your dad! You did better than him, you know!'

'I know,' said Antony. 'I feel a bit bad about that.'

Zara rolled her eyes.

'That's so typical. If I could ever beat Fleur at anything, I'd never let her forget it.'

'Where is Fleur?' said Philippa in a high-pitched voice.

'With Johnny, I guess.'

'Johnny?'

'This friend of ours,' said Zara casually. 'He came down on a surprise visit. He's, like, her closest friend.'

'I see,' said Philippa.

'Oh, and guess what,' said Antony. 'Xanthe Forrester's asked us to her parents' cottage in Cornwall. Just for a few days. D'you think Dad'll let us go?'

'I've no idea,' said Philippa dully. Jealousy was rising sickeningly inside her. Fleur's closest friend was a man named Johnny; a man Philippa had never heard of. She had rushed off to be with him and she hadn't given Philippa another thought.

'I bloody well hope he does,' said Antony. He looked at Zara. 'Shall we have a quick look at the scoreboard?'

'Absolutely,' said Zara, grinning at him. 'Let's look at all those other losers' scores and gloat.'

'No!' protested Antony. 'Just look.'

'You can just look if you like,' said Zara. 'I'm going to gloat.'

By six o'clock the final scores were in, and Antony was officially declared the winner of the Club Cup. As the result was announced, a cheer went up and Antony blushed bright scarlet.

'Well done!' exclaimed Richard. 'Antony, I'm so proud of you!' He patted Antony on the shoulder, and Antony blushed even deeper.

'I knew he was going to win!' said Zara to Richard. 'I just knew it!'

'So did I,' said Gillian, beaming. 'I made pavlova especially.'

'Cool,' said Antony.

'How lovely this all is,' said Fleur. 'Have I said well done yet? Say well done, Johnny.'

'Congratulations, young man,' said Johnny. 'I despise the game of golf and everything associated with it, but congratulations nevertheless.'

'Are you staying for supper?' said Gillian.

'Alas, no,' said Johnny. 'London calls. But I do hope to visit again in a week's time. You'll be back from Cornwall by then?' he said to Zara.

'Sure.'

'Good,' said Johnny. 'Because I'm going to bring you a present.'

Philippa and Lambert joined the group, and a slight pall fell over the atmosphere.

'You're starting early, Lambert,' said Fleur brightly, looking at the brandy glass in Lambert's hand.

'Well played, Antony,' said Lambert, ignoring Fleur and shaking Antony's hand a little too firmly. 'I played like shit.' He took a swig from his glass. 'Like complete shit.'

'I had no idea you were any good at golf, Antony,' said Philippa feebly. She tried to move closer to Fleur. 'Did you know, Fleur?'

'Of course I knew,' said Fleur warmly.

'Well, of course, I've been a bit distracted lately,' began Philippa, in a low voice. But she was interrupted by Johnny.

'My train! It leaves in fifteen minutes! I must call a taxi.'

'Someone will drive you,' said Fleur. 'Who's got a car? Lambert. Would you mind driving Johnny to the station?'

'I don't suppose so,' said Lambert grudgingly.

'Yes, you drive him, Lambert,' said Philippa at once. 'We'll see you back at the house.'

'Excellent,' said Fleur. 'And there'll be room for me too, in your nice big car.' Before Philippa could say anything the three of them rushed off. She stared after them in dismay, and felt a hurt anger growing in her chest. Fleur was behaving as though she wasn't there. As though she just didn't exist; as though she didn't matter.

'Are you all right, Philippa?' said Gillian.

'I'm fine,' snapped Philippa, and turned away. She didn't want Gillian's attention; Gillian was no good. She had to have Fleur.

As the others walked back to The Maples, Zara fell into step with Richard.

'Antony played so well today,' she said. 'You should be really proud of him.'

'I am,' said Richard, smiling at her.

'He was really . . .' Zara screwed up her face to think of the word. 'He was really confident,' she said eventually. 'Really masterful. You should have seen him.'

'He's come on a lot this summer,' said Richard.

'And it's like, he forgot all that birthmark stuff. He just played.'

'What did you say?' Richard frowned at her.

'You know. All that grief with the birthmark.'

'What exactly do you mean?' said Richard carefully. Zara lowered her voice.

'He told me how his mother hated it.' She shrugged. 'You know, the thing with the eyepatch and everything. But I guess he's put it behind him. And I think it really made a difference.'

'Zara, what—' Richard could barely speak. He swallowed, and took a deep breath. 'What thing with the eyepatch?'

'Oh.' Zara looked up at him and bit her lip. 'You don't know? I guess neither of them ever told you.'

In the car, on the way back from the station, Fleur took out a compact. Ignoring Lambert, she began to paint her lips with a long golden brush. Out of the corner of his eye Lambert watched, mesmerized, as she smoothed on the deep glossy colour. With his eyes off the road, he swerved erratically a couple of times into the next lane, and the car behind hooted angrily.

'Lambert!' exclaimed Fleur. 'Are you all right to drive?' She leaned towards him, and sniffed. 'How many brandies did you have at the club?'

'I'm fine,' said Lambert shortly. He pulled up at a set of traffic lights and the car began to throb gently. He could smell Fleur's scent; could see her legs, stretched out in front of him. Long, pale, expensive legs.

'So, Fleur,' he said. 'You're enjoying living with Richard, are you?'

'Of course,' said Fleur. 'Richard's such a wonderful man.'

'A wealthy man, too,' said Lambert.

'Really?' said Fleur innocently.

'He's a fucking wealthy man,' said Lambert. He turned to look at Fleur, and she gave a slight shrug. 'Don't tell me you didn't know he was wealthy,' he said, scowling.

'I hadn't really thought about it.'

'Oh come on!'

'Lambert, let's just get home, shall we?'

'Home,' said Lambert mockingly. 'Yes, I suppose it is your home now, isn't it. Lady consort of Mr Filthy Fucking Rich.'

'Lambert,' said Fleur, in steely tones, 'you're drunk. You shouldn't be driving.'

'Crap.'

The lights turned to amber and Lambert thrust his foot down on the accelerator.

'So you're not interested in money, is that it?' he said, above the noise of the engine. 'You must be the only person in the whole fucking world who isn't.'

'You are a sordid man, aren't you?' said Fleur quietly.

'What's that?'

'You're sordid! A nasty, sordid man!'

'I live in the real world, all right?' Lambert was breathing heavily; his face was growing pink.

'We all live in the real world.'

'What, you? Don't make me laugh! What kind of real world do you live in? No job, no worries, just lie back and take the money.'

Fleur's jaw tightened; she said nothing.

'I suppose you thought Richard was a good bet, did you?' continued Lambert, in slurred tones. 'Spotted him from a mile off. Probably came to his wife's memorial service on purpose to catch him.'

'We're nearly home,' said Fleur. 'Thank God.' She looked at Lambert. 'You could have killed us both. And Johnny.'

'I wish I had. One less poofter on the face of the earth.' There was a short silence.

'I won't hit you,' said Fleur in a trembling voice, 'because you're driving and I don't want to cause an accident. But if you ever say anything like that again . . .'

'You'll beat me up? Well I'm terrified.'

'I won't beat you up,' said Fleur. 'Some of Johnny's friends might.' They pulled into the drive of The Maples, and immediately Fleur opened the door. She looked at Lambert witheringly.

'You make me sick,' she said, and slammed it.

Lambert stared after her, feeling the blood pounding round his head and a slight confusion in his brain. Did he despise her or did he fancy her? She was bloody pissed off with him, at any rate.

He took out his hip flask and swigged some brandy. Sordid, was he? She should try having an overdraft of fucking three hundred thousand pounds. A familiar feeling of panic stole over him, and he took another swig of brandy. He had to do something about that overdraft. He had to get going now, before everyone started assembling for supper and wondering where he was. He looked at the front door, slightly ajar. Fleur had probably run straight off to Richard, to complain about him. Just like a woman. Lambert grinned to himself. Let her complain; let her say what she liked. At least it would keep Richard out of the way for a while.

When they got back to the house, Richard paused.

'I think,' he said to Zara, 'I'd like to have a moment alone with Antony. If you don't mind.'

'Of course not,' said Zara. 'I think he'll be in the garden. We were going to play badminton.' She looked up at Richard, face screwed up uncertainly. 'You don't mind that I told you about the eyepatch, do you?'

'No!' Richard swallowed. 'Of course I don't mind. You did just the right thing.'

He found Antony standing by the badminton post, patiently unwinding the net. For a moment he just stared at his son; his tall, kind, talented son. His perfect son.

'Come here,' he said, as Antony looked up. 'Let me congratulate you properly.'

He pulled Antony towards him and hugged him tightly. 'My boy,' he murmured against Antony's hair, and suddenly found himself trying to fight back tears. 'My boy.' He blinked a few times, then released Antony.

'I'm desperately proud of you,' he said.

'It's quite cool,' said Antony, giving an unwilling grin. He looked down at the badminton net. 'So you don't . . . you don't mind that I beat you, do you?'

'Mind?' Richard gazed at him. 'Of course I don't mind! It's time for you to start beating me. You're a man now!' A pink, embarrassed tinge spread slowly up Antony's neck, and Richard smiled to himself.

'But, Antony, it's not just your talent at golf that I'm

proud of,' he continued. 'I'm proud of all of you. Every single little bit of you.' He paused. 'And I know that Mummy was proud of you too.'

Antony said nothing. His hands clenched tightly around the tangled strings of the badminton net.

'She may not always have shown it,' said Richard slowly. 'It was . . . difficult for her sometimes. But she was very proud of you. And she loved you more than anything in the world.'

'Really?' said Antony in a shaky voice, without looking up.

'She loved you more than anything in the world,' repeated Richard. For a few minutes there was silence. Richard watched as Antony's face slowly relaxed; as his hands loosened around the net. A small smile appeared on the boy's face and suddenly he took a huge breath, almost as though to begin life again.

You believe me, thought Richard; you believe me without question. Thank God for your trusting soul.

Zara had elected to join Gillian in the kitchen, unstacking the dishwasher while Gillian tipped salad leaves out of their plastic packets into a huge wooden bowl. She listened patiently while Gillian chattered away about some trip she was planning, all the time wondering what Antony's dad was saying to him.

'Such a coincidence!' Gillian was saying happily. 'Eleanor's always wanted to go to Egypt too. Apparently Geoffrey refuses to go on holiday anywhere that doesn't have a golf course.'

'So, will you see the Pyramids?'

'Of course! And we'll take a cruise up the Nile.'

'Then you'll get murdered,' said Zara. 'Like in Agatha Christie.' Gillian laughed.

'Do you know, that's just what Eleanor said.'

'I guess it's what everyone says.' Zara picked up a pan and looked at it. 'What the hell's this?'

'It's an asparagus steamer,' said Gillian tartly. 'And don't swear.' Zara rolled her eyes.

'You're as bad as Felix. He makes you put a pound in the swear box.'

'A jolly good idea. We had the same thing at school.'

'Yes well,' said Zara. 'This is the nineties, or hadn't you noticed?'

'I had noticed,' said Gillian. 'But thank you for pointing it out.' She picked up two bottles of salad dressing. 'Shall we have basil or garlic?'

'Both,' suggested Zara. 'Just kind of mix them together.'

'All right,' said Gillian. 'But if it goes wrong, I'm blaming you.'

They both looked up as Fleur came into the kitchen.

'Oh hi,' said Zara. 'Did Johnny make his train all right?'

'Just about,' said Fleur. 'Thank God we weren't both killed. Lambert was drunk! He was swerving about all over the place!'

'Jesus!' said Zara. She glanced at Gillian. 'I mean, goodness me!'

'Sit down,' said Gillian, hurrying over to Fleur. 'You

poor thing!' She frowned. 'You know, it's not the first time this has happened. That Lambert should be prosecuted!'

'Let's call the cops,' said Zara eagerly.

'Put the kettle on, Zara,' said Gillian, 'and make your mother a nice cup of tea.'

'No thanks,' said Fleur. 'I think I'll go upstairs and have a bath.'

'Try on a few hats,' said Zara. 'That should cheer you up.'

'That's enough, Zara,' said Gillian. She looked at Fleur. 'Has Richard heard about this?'

'Not yet.'

'Well, he should.'

'Yes,' said Fleur. 'He will.'

She went out into the hall and began to climb the stairs. As she did so, a voice rang out from below.

'Fleur! There you are! I've been trying to find you all day!'

Fleur looked round. Philippa was hurrying towards her, red-faced, panting slightly.

'Fleur, we need to have a talk,' she was saying. 'I've got so much to tell you. About—' She swallowed, and wiped a tear from her eye. 'About me and Lambert. You just won't believe—'

'Philippa,' interrupted Fleur sharply, 'not now, darling. I'm really not in the mood. And if you want to know why, you can ask your husband.' And before Philippa could reply, she hurried upstairs.

Philippa gazed after Fleur, feeling hurt, disbelieving

tears coming to her eyes. Fleur didn't want to talk to her. Fleur had abandoned her. She felt sick with misery and anger. Now she had no friends; no audience; no-one to tell her story to. And it was all because of Lambert. Lambert had somehow made Fleur angry. He spoiled everything. Philippa clenched her fists and felt her heart begin to beat more quickly. Lambert had ruined her life, she thought furiously. He'd ruined her entire life, and no-one even knew about it. He deserved punishment. He deserved for everyone to know what he was really like. He deserved revenge.

# SEVENTEEN

Half an hour later, supper was ready.

'Where on earth is everybody?' said Gillian, looking up from the oven. 'Where's Philippa?'

'Haven't seen her,' said Antony, opening a bottle of wine.

'And Lambert?'

'Who cares about him?' said Zara. 'Let's just start eating anyway.'

'Actually, I think I saw Philippa in the garden,' said Antony. 'When we were playing badminton.'

'I'll go and fetch her,' said Gillian. 'And can you please tell everybody else that supper's ready?'

'OK,' said Antony.

When Gillian had gone, he went to the door of the kitchen and called, 'Supper's ready!' Then he looked back at Zara and shrugged. 'It's not my fault if they can't hear.' He poured himself a glass of wine and took a sip.

'Hey,' said Zara. 'What about me? Don't I get some?' Antony looked up in surprise.

'You never drink wine!'

'There's always a first time,' said Zara, reaching for his glass. She took a cautious sip and wrinkled her nose. 'I guess it's an acquired taste. I think I'll stick to Diet Coke.'

'There's some in the larder,' said Antony. He looked at Zara and got to his feet.

'There's some in the fridge, too,' said Zara, giggling. But she got up and followed him into the larder. Antony closed the door behind them and put his arms around Zara. Their mouths met with accustomed ease; the door creaked slightly as they leaned against it.

'You're bloody sexy,' said Antony in blurred tones as they separated.

'So are you,' murmured Zara. Encouraged, his hand began to trace a cautious route down her spine.

'I don't suppose there's any chance . . .'

'No,' said Zara cheerfully. 'Absolutely none.'

Lambert heard Antony's voice calling out downstairs and felt a spasm of panic rush through him. He had to hurry; had to get out of Richard's office before everyone started to wonder where he was. Frowning, he started typing again, glancing every few seconds towards the door, trying frantically to formulate the right words in his mind.

He'd found a sheaf of Richard's personal writing paper and an old typewriter. He had the details of Richard's bank account in front of him, and the name of his lawyer and a copy of his signature. It should have been easy to knock off a quick all-purpose letter, proving that Richard was in the process of making his daughter – and therefore Lambert – seriously wealthy.

It should have been easy. But Lambert's eyes kept blurring over; his mind felt slow and ponderous; his thoughts were distracted every so often by a sudden memory of Fleur's legs. He jabbed at the typewriter viciously, trying to hurry, cursing every time he made a mistake. He'd already ruined five sheets of paper; torn them out and thrown them on the floor. The whole thing was a nightmare.

He took a swig of brandy and tried to focus his mind. He just needed to concentrate; to hurry up and finish the bloody thing, then get downstairs; behave normally. And then he'd wait for First Bank to phone. 'Oh, you want a guarantee, do you?' he'd say, in tones of surprise. 'You should have said. How's a letter of instruction to Mr Favour's lawyer?' That would stop them in their tracks. They weren't going to question Richard fucking Favour, were they?

'Sum,' he said aloud, hitting each key very carefully, 'of f-i-v-e million. Full stop.'

Five million. God, if it were true, thought Lambert hazily, if it were only true . . .

'Lambert?' A voice interrupted his thoughts, and Lambert's heart stopped beating. Slowly he raised his head. Richard was standing at the door, gazing at him incredulously. 'Just what do you think you're doing?'

Gillian's mind was happily drifting through imagined pictures of Egypt as she wandered out into the garden.

There was a lightness inside her; a lightness which gave energy to her feet, which caused her to smile to herself and hum ill-remembered snatches of popular songs. A holiday with Eleanor Forrester. With Eleanor Forrester of all people! Once upon a time she would have said 'No' automatically; would have thought the scheme quite out of the question. But now she thought, why not? Why should she not at last travel to an exotic, far-away land? Why should she not give Eleanor a chance as a travelling companion? She pictured herself wandering along dusty, sandy paths, gazing up with awe at the remains of a distant, fascinating civilization. Feeling the sun of a different continent beating down on her shoulders; listening to the babbling sounds of an unfamiliar language. Bartering for presents at a colourful street market.

Suddenly, a cracking sound underfoot brought her back to the real world. She looked down at the grass. A glass jar had been left out on the lawn.

'Dangerous!' said Gillian aloud, picking it up. She peered at it. It was an aspirin bottle and it was empty. Somebody must have left it outside without meaning to. There would be some commonsense explanation for its presence in the grass. Nevertheless, a twinge of alarm went through her and without meaning to, she increased her pace.

'Philippa!' she called. 'Supper's ready. Are you in the garden?'

There was a silence. Then suddenly Gillian heard a little groan.

'Philippa!' she called again, sharply. 'Is that you?' She began to walk towards the sound; she found herself running.

Behind the rose bushes at the bottom of the garden, Philippa was lying on the grass, her arms thrown out and her chin stained with vomit. Pinned to her chest was a neatly written letter beginning 'To Everyone I Know'. And beside her on the ground was a second empty aspirin bottle.

'You'd better explain yourself,' said Richard quietly. He looked at the sheet of paper in his hand. 'If this is what I think it is, then you have a lot of explaining to do.'

'It . . . it was a prank,' said Lambert. He stared desperately at Richard, trying to breathe calmly; trying to quell the terrified pounding in his head. He swallowed; his throat felt like sandpaper. 'A jape.'

'No, Lambert,' said Richard. 'This isn't a jape. This is fraud.'

Lambert licked his lips.

'Look, Richard,' he said. 'All it is is a letter. I mean . . . I wasn't going to use it.'

'Oh really,' said Richard at once. 'And for what purpose were you not going to use it?'

'You don't understand!' Lambert tried a little laugh.

'No, I don't understand!' Richard's voice snapped through the air. 'I don't understand how you could possibly think it permissible to enter this office without my consent, to look through my private affairs and to write a letter purporting to be from myself to my solicitor. As for the content of the letter . . .' He flicked it with his hand. 'I find that the most perplexing of all.'

'You mean . . .' Lambert stared at Richard and felt sick. So Emily had lied to him. She'd been playing games with him. That money wasn't coming to Philippa after all. A white-hot fury swept through his body, obliterating caution; wiping out fear.

'It's all right for you!' he suddenly found himself shouting. 'You've got millions!'

'Lambert, you're forgetting yourself.'

'Emily told me I'd be a rich man! Emily said Philippa was coming into a trust. She said I'd be able to afford anything I wanted! But she was bloody lying, wasn't she?'

Richard stared at him, unable to speak.

'Emily said that?' he said at last, in a voice which shook slightly.

'She said I'd married a millionairess. And I believed her!'

Richard stared at him in sudden comprehension.

'You owe money, is that it?'

'Of course that's it. I owe money. Just like everyone else in the world. Everyone except you, of course.' Lambert scowled. 'I've got an overdraft of three hundred thousand pounds.' He looked up and met Richard's incredulous eyes. 'Nothing compared to ten million, is it? You could pay it off tomorrow.'

Richard gazed at Lambert, trying to control his revulsion; reminding himself that Lambert was still his son-in-law.

'Does Philippa know about this?' he asked eventually.

'Of course not.'

'Thank God,' muttered Richard. He looked again at the paper in his hand. 'And what precisely were you planning to do with this?'

'Show it to the bank,' Lambert said. 'I thought it would keep them quiet for a while.'

'So you're brainless as well as dishonest!'

Lambert shrugged. For a few minutes they stared at each other in mutual dislike.

'I'm . . . I'm going to have to think about this,' said Richard at last. 'In the meantime, can I ask you not to mention it to Philippa. Or . . . anyone else.'

'Fine by me,' said Lambert, and he grinned cockily at Richard. Something inside Richard snapped.

'Don't you dare smile at me!' he shouted. 'You've got nothing to smile about! You're a dishonest, unprincipled . . . fraudster! My God, how did Philippa manage to fall in love with you?'

'My natural charm, I suppose,' said Lambert, running a hand through his hair.

'Just get out!' said Richard, shaking with rage. 'Get out of my office, before I . . . before I . . .' He stopped, struggling for words, and Lambert's mouth twisted into a sneer.

But before either of them could say anything else, they were interrupted by Gillian's voice, shrieking from the hall downstairs.

'Richard! Come quickly please! It's Philippa!'

* * *

Gillian had dragged Philippa into the house and dialled for an ambulance. By the time the two men arrived downstairs, Philippa was sitting up and moaning faintly.

'I think she's brought most of the pills back up again,' said Gillian. She frowned, and wiped a tear brusquely away from her eye. 'The silly, silly girl!'

Richard stared in speechless shock at his daughter; at her ungainly, unhappy form.

'Surely she didn't really want to . . .' he began, then stopped, unable to form the words in his mouth.

'Of course not,' said Gillian. 'It was a . . .' her voice faltered, 'a cry for help.'

'But she always seemed—' said Richard, and halted. He'd been about to say Philippa had always seemed happy. But suddenly he realized it wasn't true. It came to him that since she'd grown up, he'd rarely seen Philippa looking positively happy. She'd always seemed anxious, or sulky; when she was in high spirits there was always a slightly hysterical edge to her mood.

But he'd assumed she was more or less all right. Now a miserable guilt plunged through his body. I should have brought happiness to her life, he found himself thinking. I should have made sure she was happy and stable and content. But I left it to her mother and then I left it to her husband. And they failed her. We all failed her.

'Philippa,' said Lambert, bending down. 'Can you hear me?'

Philippa's eyes opened and she gave a louder moan.

'Lambert,' said Gillian. 'I think you should keep away from her.'

'Why?' said Lambert truculently. 'I'm her husband.'

'There was a note,' said Gillian. She passed it to Richard; as he skimmed it with his eyes his face darkened. A vein began to beat in his forehead.

'Give it to me,' said Lambert. 'I've got every right . . .'

'You have no rights!' spat Richard. 'No rights at all!'

'The ambulance is here,' said Gillian suddenly, looking out of the window. 'Who's going to go with her?'

'I will,' said Lambert.

'No,' said Richard at once, 'you won't. I will.'

On the way to the hospital, Richard gazed down at his daughter's face; held her head as she retched into a cardboard dish and smoothed her hair back.

'I didn't want to marry him,' she muttered, and tears coursed down her swollen face. 'He makes me sick!'

'All right, sweetheart,' said Richard gently. 'We'll be there soon. You'll be all right.'

'It was Mummy,' cried Philippa. 'She made me marry Lambert! She said I was ugly and I wasn't a . . .' She broke off and gazed at him with red-rimmed eyes. 'Did you really hate Jim?'

'Who's Jim?' asked Richard helplessly. But Philippa was vomiting again. Richard stared at her in silence. A heavy, bleak depression was creeping through him; he felt as though his happy family of shining jewels was being turned over one by one to reveal a swarm of ugly maggots. What else didn't he know? What else wasn't he being told?

'Where's Fleur?' said Philippa, as soon as she was able to sit up again. 'Does she know?'

'I'm not sure,' said Richard soothingly. 'We needn't tell her if you don't want us to.'

'But I do want her to know!' cried Philippa hysterically. 'I want her to be with me!'

'Yes, darling,' said Richard, feeling suddenly close to tears. 'Yes, so do I.'

Much later Richard arrived home, weary and depressed, to find everyone waiting in the hall for him.

'What happened?' asked Fleur. She hurried over and took his hand. 'Darling, I was so shocked when I heard about it.'

'They're keeping her in overnight,' said Richard. 'They don't think any damage has been done. They're going to . . .' He swallowed. 'They're going to set up some counselling for her.'

'Can we, like, go and visit her?' said Antony uncertainly. Richard looked at him, sitting on the stairs with Zara, and smiled. 'She'll be home tomorrow. Honestly, there's nothing to worry about. It was just a silly scare.'

'But why did she do it?' said Antony. 'I mean, didn't she realize? Didn't she think how frightened we'd all be?'

'I don't think she thought very hard about it at all,' said Richard gently. 'She's a bit confused at the moment.' Suddenly he looked around sharply. 'Where's Lambert?'

'Gone,' said Gillian. 'I packed him off to a hotel for the night.' Her mouth tightened. 'He was too drunk to drive.'

'Well done, Gillian.' Richard's eyes met hers. 'And thank you. If you hadn't gone looking for Philippa . . .'

'Yes, well.' Gillian looked away. 'Let's not think about that.' She glanced at her watch. 'It's late. Time for bed. Antony, Zara, off you go.'

'OK,' said Antony in a subdued voice. 'Well, good night everyone.'

'Good night,' said Zara.

'Antony, I'm sorry we didn't get to celebrate your win properly,' said Richard, suddenly remembering. 'But we will. Another time.'

'Sure, Dad. G'night.'

'I think I'll turn in, too,' said Gillian. She looked at Richard. 'Are you hungry?'

'No,' said Richard. 'Not hungry.' He looked at Fleur. 'But I think I could do with a glass of whisky.' She smiled.

'I'll pour you one,' she said, and disappeared into the drawing room. Richard looked at Gillian.

'Gillian,' he said quietly. 'Did you have any idea that this was on the cards? Did you realize Philippa was so unhappy?'

'No,' said Gillian. 'I had no idea.' She bit her lip. 'And yet when I look back, I wonder whether it wasn't obvious all along. Whether I should have noticed something.'

'Exactly,' said Richard. 'That's exactly how I feel.'

'I feel I let her down,' said Gillian.

'You didn't,' said Richard in suddenly fierce tones. 'You didn't let her down! If anyone let her down, it was her mother.'

'What?' Gillian stared at him.

'Emily let her down! Emily was a . . .' He broke off, breathing hard, and Gillian stared at him in dismay. For a few moments neither said anything.

'I was always convinced that there was a hidden side to Emily,' said Richard. 'I was desperate to find out more about her character.' He looked up bleakly. 'And now it seems that the sweet, innocent Emily I knew was only a . . . a façade! I didn't know the true Emily! I wouldn't have *wanted* to know the true Emily!'

'Oh Richard.' Tears glittered in Gillian's eyes. 'Emily wasn't all bad, you know.'

'I know she wasn't.' Richard rubbed his face. 'But I'd always thought she was perfect.'

'No-one's perfect,' said Gillian quietly. 'No-one in the world is perfect.'

'I know,' said Richard. 'I was a fool. A gullible fool.'

'You're no fool,' said Gillian. She got to her feet. 'Go and drink your whisky. And forget about Emily.' She met his eyes. 'It's time to move on.'

'Yes,' said Richard slowly. 'It is, isn't it?'

Fleur was sitting on the sofa in the drawing room, two tumblers of whisky at her side.

'You poor thing,' she murmured as Richard entered the room. 'What a horrendous evening.'

'You don't know the half of it,' said Richard. He picked up his glass of whisky and drained it. 'Sometimes, Fleur, I wonder if there are any decent people left in the world.'

'What do you mean?' said Fleur, getting up and replenishing his glass. 'Did something else happen tonight?'

'It's almost too sordid to recount,' said Richard. 'You'll be disgusted when you hear.'

'What?' She sat back down on the sofa and looked expectantly at Richard. He sighed and kicked off his shoes.

'Earlier this evening, I found Lambert in my office, attempting to forge a letter from me to my solicitors. He's in money trouble, and he hoped that my name would help to keep his creditors off his back.' Richard took another slug of whisky and shook his head. 'The whole thing is despicable.'

'Is he in serious money trouble?'

'Yes, I'm afraid so.' Richard frowned.

'Don't tell me any more if you don't want to,' said Fleur quickly. Richard took her hand and gave her a wan smile.

'Thank you, darling, for being so sensitive. But I don't have any secrets from you. And it's actually a relief to talk to someone about it.' He sighed. 'Lambert had been given the impression by . . . by someone . . . that Philippa was soon to come into a lot of money. And on the strength of that he began to spend well beyond his means.'

'Oh dear,' said Fleur. She wrinkled her brow. 'Is that why Philippa . . .'

'No. Philippa doesn't know about the money. But they had had a row. Philippa threatened to leave Lambert and things became rather nasty.' Richard looked at Fleur. 'Apparently you and she had a long talk about it in London.'

'Hardly a long talk,' said Fleur, frowning slightly.

'Nevertheless, she found your advice very helpful. She's desperate to see you.' Richard stroked Fleur's hair. 'I think she's beginning to see you as a mother-figure.'

'I'm not sure about that,' said Fleur, giving a little laugh.

'As for Lambert . . .' Richard shrugged. 'I've no idea whether he and Philippa will manage to patch things up, or whether he should be sent packing.'

'Sent packing,' said Fleur, with a shudder. 'He's odious.'

'And dishonest,' said Richard. 'I find it hard to believe now that he didn't marry Philippa for her money in the first place!'

'Is she rich, then?' said Fleur casually.

'She will be,' said Richard. 'When she turns thirty.' He took another swig of whisky. 'The irony is, I only signed the papers this morning.'

For a moment, Fleur was very still, then she looked up and said lightly, 'What papers?'

'This morning I signed a very large amount of money

over into trust for Antony and Philippa.' He smiled at her. 'Five million each, as a matter of fact.'

Fleur stared at Richard for a few seconds.

'Five million each,' she said slowly. 'That makes ten million.' She paused, seeming to listen to the words.

'I know it seems like a lot of money,' said Richard. 'But I wanted to give them financial independence. And I'll still be more than comfortable.'

'You've just given all that money away,' said Fleur faintly. 'To your children.'

'They don't know about it yet,' said Richard. 'But I know I can trust you to keep this to yourself.'

'Of course,' murmured Fleur. She drained her glass and looked up. 'Could you . . . do you think you could pour me another whisky, please?'

Richard rose, poured another measure of the amber liquid into Fleur's glass and walked back over towards her. Suddenly he stopped.

'Fleur, what am I waiting for?' he exclaimed. 'There's something I've been meaning to ask you for a long time. I know that tonight's been very upsetting, but maybe . . . maybe that gives me even more reason to do what I'm about to do.'

Kneeling down on the carpet, still clutching her whisky glass, Richard looked up at Fleur.

'Fleur,' he said, in a trembling voice. 'Fleur, my darling, will you marry me?'

# EIGHTEEN

Early the next morning, a white Jeep pulled up outside The Maples and hooted loudly, waking Richard. Rubbing his eyes, he padded over to the bedroom window and looked out.

'It's Antony's friends,' he said to Fleur. 'They must be leaving early for Cornwall.'

Suddenly there was a knock at the door and Antony's voice said, 'Dad? We're going!'

Richard opened the door and looked at Antony and Zara, standing on the landing. They were dressed identically, in jeans and baseball caps, and each was loaded down with a huge squashy bag.

'So,' he said. 'Off to Cornwall. You will behave yourselves, won't you?'

'Of course we will,' said Antony impatiently. 'Anyway, Xanthe's mum's going to be there.'

'I know,' said Richard. 'I spoke to her yesterday. And mentioned a few ground rules.'

'Dad! What did you say?'

'Nothing very much,' said Richard grinning. 'Just that you were to have a cold bath every morning, followed by an hour of Shakespeare . . .'

'Dad!'

'I'm sure you'll have a lovely time,' said Richard, relenting. 'And we'll see you back here on Friday.'

From outside, the Jeep hooted again.

'Right,' said Antony. He looked at Zara. 'Well, we'd better go.'

'I hope Philippa's OK,' said Zara.

'Yeah.' Antony looked up at Richard and bit his lip. 'I hope she's . . .'

'She'll be fine,' said Richard reassuringly. 'Don't worry. Now, off you go, before Xanthe starts that infernal noise again.'

He watched as they shuffled down the stairs. Zara was almost bent double under the weight of her bag, and he wondered briefly what on earth she was carrying. Then, as he heard the front door slam, he turned back to Fleur.

'That was Antony and Zara,' he said unnecessarily. 'Off to Cornwall.'

'Mmm.' Fleur turned over sleepily, rumpling the duvet around her body. Richard stared at her for a moment, then took a deep breath.

'I don't know what time you want to leave,' he said. 'I'll take you to the station. Just tell me when.'

'All right,' said Fleur. She opened her eyes. 'You don't mind, do you Richard? I just need to have some time to think.'

'Of course you do,' said Richard, forcing a cheerful note into his voice. 'I completely understand. I wouldn't expect you to rush your decision.'

He sat down on the bed and looked at her. Her arms were lying on the pillow above her head; graceful arms, like a ballerina's. Her eyes had drifted shut again, re-capturing the sweet sleep of morning. Through his mind passed the possibility that she might refuse him. And with it came a stab of pain, so strong and sharp it almost frightened him.

Downstairs, Gillian was making a pot of tea. She looked up as Richard entered the kitchen.

'I saw them go,' she said. 'That young man, Mex, was driving. I hope he's responsible.'

'I'm sure he is,' said Richard. He sat down at the kitchen table and looked around.

'The house seems awfully quiet,' he said. 'I miss the thumping music already.' Gillian smiled, and put a mug of tea in front of him.

'What's going to happen about Philippa?' she said. 'Will she come out of hospital today?'

'Yes,' said Richard. 'Unless anything's happened overnight. I'll go and pick her up this morning.'

'I'll come with you,' said Gillian. 'If that's all right.'

'Of course it's all right,' said Richard. 'I'm sure she'd love to see you.' He took a sip of tea, marshalling his thoughts, then looked up. 'There's something else I should tell you,' he said. 'Fleur's going to London for a few days.'

'I see,' said Gillian. She looked at Richard's taut,

pale face. 'You're not going too?' she said hesitantly.

'No,' said Richard. 'Not this time. Fleur . . .' He rubbed his face. 'Fleur needs a little time on her own. To . . . think about things.'

'I see,' said Gillian again.

'She'll be back by Saturday,' said Richard.

'Oh well,' said Gillian cheerfully. 'That's hardly any time at all.' Richard smiled wanly and drained his mug. Gillian looked anxiously at him. 'Would Fleur like some tea, do you think?' she asked. 'I'm about to go upstairs.'

'She doesn't want tea,' said Richard, suddenly remembering. 'But she asked if I could bring her up *The Times*.'

'*The Times*,' said Gillian, looking about the kitchen. 'Here it is. I'll take it up to her if you like.' She picked up the crisp, folded newspaper and looked at it curiously. 'Fleur doesn't usually read the paper,' she said. 'I wonder what she wants it for.'

'I don't know,' said Richard, pouring himself another cup of tea. 'I didn't ask.'

By ten o'clock, Fleur was ready to leave.

'We'll drop you at the station,' said Richard, carrying her suitcase down the stairs, 'and then go on to the hospital.' He paused. 'Philippa will be upset not to see you,' he added lightly.

'It's a shame,' said Fleur. Her eyes met Richard's. 'But I really don't feel I can . . .'

'No,' said Richard hastily. 'Of course not. I shouldn't have said anything.'

'You're a sweet man,' said Fleur, and ran her hand

down Richard's arm. 'And I do hope Philippa comes through this.'

'She'll be all right,' said Gillian, coming into the hall. 'We'll keep her at home for a bit; look after her properly. By the time you come back, she'll probably be right as rain.' She looked at Fleur. 'You look very smart,' she said, 'all in black.'

'Such a useful colour to wear in London,' murmured Fleur. 'It doesn't show the dirt.'

'Will you be staying with your friend Johnny?' asked Gillian. 'Could we reach you there if there was an emergency with Zara?'

'I probably won't stay there, no,' said Fleur. 'I'll probably check into a hotel.' She frowned slightly. 'I'll call you when I've arrived and leave a number.'

'Good,' said Richard. He looked uncertainly at Gillian. 'Well. I suppose we ought to get going.'

As they walked out into the drive, Fleur looked back at the house appraisingly.

'It's a welcoming house, this, isn't it?' she said suddenly. 'A friendly house.'

'Yes,' said Richard eagerly. 'Very friendly. It's . . . well, I think it's a lovely house to have as a home.' Fleur met his eye.

'Yes,' she said kindly, and opened the car door. 'Yes, Richard, I'm sure it is.'

Philippa was sitting up in bed when Richard and Gillian arrived. She watched them walking through the ward, and automatically tried to give them a bright smile. But her mouth felt awkward and her cheeks stiff. She felt as though she might never smile again; as though the freezing shame sinking through her body had caused all her natural reactions to seize up.

She hadn't thought it would be like this. She'd thought she was committing the ultimate romantic gesture; that she'd wake up to find everyone gathered round her bed, blinking back their tears and stroking her hand and promising to make her life better. Instead of which she'd woken to a series of humiliating assaults on her body, administered by nurses with civil phrases on their lips and contempt in their eyes. When she'd glimpsed her father's devastated face, something inside her had crumpled, and she'd felt like crying. Except that suddenly she couldn't cry any more. The ready fountain of tears inside her had dried up; the backdrop of romantic fantasy had fallen, and what was left was cold and dry, like a stone.

She licked her lips as her father and Gillian drew near, took a breath and carefully said, 'Hello.' Her voice sounded strange and tinny to her own ears.

'Hello darling!'

'Hello, Philippa.' Gillian smiled cheerfully at her. 'How are you doing?'

'Much better,' said Philippa carefully. She felt as though she were speaking a foreign language.

'You can come home today,' said her father. 'The discharge papers are ready.'

'That's good,' said Philippa. From a long way away, a thought occurred to her. 'Is Fleur at home?'

'No,' said her father. 'Fleur's gone to London for a few days.'

'I see,' said Philippa. A dulled flicker of disappointment ran through her and died almost immediately. 'Is she coming back?' she asked politely.

'Yes,' said Gillian at once, before Richard could answer. 'Yes, of course she's coming back.'

In the car, very little was said. When they got home, Gillian brought bowls of chicken soup into the conservatory, and Richard sat down opposite Philippa.

'We need to talk about Lambert,' he said cautiously.

'Yes.' Philippa's voice was toneless.

'Do you . . .'

'I never want to see him again.'

Richard looked at Philippa for a long time, then glanced at Gillian.

'Right,' he said. 'Well, as long as you're sure about that.'

'I want a divorce,' said Philippa. 'Everything between Lambert and me is over.' She spooned chicken soup into her mouth. 'This is good.'

'Real chicken stock,' said Gillian. 'Don't tell me they use that in those handy cardboard cartons.'

'And you're sure you won't change your mind?' persisted Richard.

'Yes,' said Philippa calmly. 'I'm quite sure.' She felt liberated; as though she were shedding a pile of unwanted clutter. Her mind felt clean and fresh; her life was free; she could begin again.

* * *

Later that day Lambert arrived by taxi at The Maples, holding a bunch of pink carnations. Richard met him at the front door and led him into the drawing room.

'Philippa's resting upstairs,' he said. 'She doesn't want to see you.'

'That's a shame,' said Lambert. 'I brought these for her.' He put the flowers on a side table, sat down on the sofa and began to polish the face of his watch with his sleeve. 'I expect she's still a bit upset,' he added.

'She is more than a bit upset,' said Richard, trying to keep his voice steady. 'I should tell you straight away that she will be filing for divorce.'

'Divorce?' Without looking up, Lambert ran an unsteady hand through his hair. 'You're joking, aren't you?'

'I'm not joking,' said Richard. 'This is not a subject for jokes.'

Lambert raised his eyes and was taken aback at Richard's tight mouth, the hostility in his gaze. Well Lambert, he thought, you've fucked this one up, haven't you? What are you going to do now? He thought for a moment, then abruptly stood up.

'Richard, I'd like to apologize,' he said, looking at Richard as sincerely as he could. 'I don't know what came over me yesterday. Too much to drink, probably.' He risked a little smile. 'I never meant to abuse your trust, sir.'

'Lambert,' began Richard wearily.

'Philippa's a very highly strung girl,' continued Lambert. 'We've had rows before, but they've always blown over. And I'm sure this will too, if you give us a chance . . .'

'You had your chance!' spat Richard. 'You had your chance, when you stood up in church and vowed to love and cherish my daughter!' His voice increased in volume. 'Did you love her? Did you cherish her? Or did you always see her simply as a source of wealth?'

He broke off, breathing hard, and Lambert stared at him in slight panic, weighing up responses in his mind. Would Richard believe him if he declared undying love for Philippa?

'I'll be honest with you, Richard,' he said at last. 'I'm only human. And man cannot live on bread alone.'

'How dare you quote the Bible at me!' shouted Richard. 'How dare you use my daughter!'

'I didn't use her!' exclaimed Lambert. 'We've had a very happy marriage!'

'You've degraded her, you've exploited her, you've turned her from a happy girl into an emotional wreck.'

'For Christ's sake, she was always an emotional wreck!' snapped Lambert, feeling a sudden sense of injustice. 'Philippa was fucked up well before I knew her! So don't lay that on me, too.'

For a moment, Richard gazed speechlessly at him, then suddenly he turned away.

'I never want to see you again,' he said quietly. 'Your employment is hereby terminated under the terms of your contract.'

'What terms?'

'Gross misconduct,' said Richard coolly. 'Abuse of trust and forgery.'

'I'll fight it!'

'If you fight, you will certainly lose; however, it's your choice. As regards the divorce,' continued Richard, 'you will be hearing from Philippa's lawyer in due course.' He paused. 'And as for the money . . .'

There was a moment of stillness; Lambert found himself leaning forward slightly, filled with sudden hope.

'I will reimburse your debt by a total of two hundred and fifty thousand pounds. No more than that. In return, you will give me a signed guarantee that you will not attempt to make contact with Philippa except through your lawyer, and you will consider the sum to be a full and final divorce settlement.'

'Two hundred and fifty?' said Lambert. 'What about the rest of my overdraft?'

'The rest of your overdraft, Lambert,' said Richard, in a voice that shook slightly, 'is your problem.'

'Two-seventy-five,' said Lambert.

'Two hundred and fifty. Absolutely no more.'

There was a long pause.

'All right,' said Lambert eventually. 'All right, I'll take it. It's a deal.' He held out his hand, then, as Richard made no attempt to take it, dropped it again. He looked with unwilling admiration at Richard. 'You're a tough man, aren't you?'

'I asked your taxi to wait in the drive,' replied Richard. He looked at his watch. 'There's a train at three.' He felt in his pocket. 'Here's the money for your ticket.' He handed an envelope to Lambert, who hesitated, shrugged, then took it.

They walked in silence to the front door.

'I also suggest,' said Richard, opening the door, 'that you resign your membership of Greyworth. Before you find yourself asked to leave.'

'You're setting out to ruin my life!' said Lambert angrily. 'I'll be a broken man!'

'I doubt it,' said Richard. 'People like you are never broken. It's others who are broken. Those who have the misfortune to come in contact with you; those who take you into their lives; who are foolish enough to trust you.'

Lambert looked at him silently for a minute, then got into the taxi and leaned back. The taxi driver started the engine.

'Tell me,' said Richard suddenly. 'Did you ever really care for Philippa? Or was it all a sham?' Lambert screwed up his face thoughtfully.

'Sometimes I quite fancied her,' he said. 'If she dolled herself up a bit.'

'I see,' said Richard. He took a deep breath. 'Please leave. Immediately.'

He watched as the taxi swung round to the entrance of the drive and disappeared.

'Has he gone, then?' Richard turned, to see Gillian standing at the front door. 'I heard you talking to him,' she continued. 'For what it's worth, I thought you were marvellous.'

'Hardly marvellous,' said Richard. He rubbed his face. wearily. 'You know, he wasn't even sorry for the way he'd behaved.'

'There's no point expecting people like that to be sorry,' said Gillian surprisingly. 'You just have to get them out of your life as quickly as you can and forget about them. You mustn't brood.'

'I'm sure you're right,' said Richard. 'But at the moment I can't help brooding. I feel very bitter.' He shook his head soberly, and walked slowly back towards the house. 'How is Philippa?'

'Oh, fine,' said Gillian, taking a few steps forward to meet him. 'She's going to be fine.' She put a hand on his arm and for a few moments they were both silent.

'I miss Fleur,' said Richard. 'I miss Fleur.' He sighed. 'She only left this morning, and already I miss her.'

'So do I,' said Gillian. She squeezed his arm comfortingly. 'But she'll be back soon. Perhaps she'll phone tonight.'

'She won't phone,' said Richard. He swallowed. 'I asked Fleur to marry me last night. That's why she went to London. She wanted to think about it.'

'I see,' said Gillian.

'Now I wish I hadn't said anything,' said Richard. He raised his head. 'Gillian, what if she says no?'

'She won't say no,' said Gillian. 'I'm sure she won't say no.'

'But she might do!'

'And she might say yes,' said Gillian. 'Think about that instead. She might say yes.'

* * *

Later on that evening, when Philippa had gone to bed, and the two of them were sitting with their coffee in the drawing room, Gillian suddenly said to Richard,

'Don't put Fleur on a pedestal.'

'What?' Richard looked up at Gillian in amazement, and she blushed.

'I'm sorry,' she said. 'I shouldn't say things like that to you.'

'Nonsense,' said Richard. 'You can say whatever you like to me.' He wrinkled his brow in thought. 'But I'm not sure what you mean.'

'It doesn't matter,' said Gillian.

'It does! Gillian, we've known each other long enough to be honest.' He leaned forward and looked at her seriously. 'Tell me what you think. What do you mean by a pedestal?'

'You thought Emily was perfect,' said Gillian bluntly. 'Now you think Fleur's perfect.' Richard laughed.

'I don't think Fleur's perfect! I think . . .' He hesitated, and coloured slightly.

'You do!' said Gillian. 'You think she's perfect! But nobody's perfect.' She thought for a second. 'One day you'll discover something about Fleur that you didn't know. Or that you hadn't noticed. Just like you did with Emily.' She bit her lip. 'And it may not be a good thing. But that doesn't mean Fleur isn't a good person.' Richard stared at her.

'Gillian, is there something you're trying to tell me? Something about Fleur?'

'No!' said Gillian. 'Don't be silly.' She gazed earnestly at Richard. 'It's just that I don't want to see you disappointed again. And if you start off with realistic expectations then maybe—' She cleared her throat awkwardly. 'Maybe you've got a better chance of happiness.'

'You're saying I'm an idealist,' said Richard slowly.

'Well, yes. I suppose I am.' Gillian frowned with embarrassment. 'But then, what do I know about it?' She put her coffee cup down with a clatter and stood up. 'It's been a long day.'

'You're right,' exclaimed Richard suddenly. 'Gillian, you understand me completely.'

'I've known you a long time,' said Gillian.

'But we've never spoken to each other like this before! You've never given me advice before!'

'I didn't feel it was appropriate,' said Gillian, flushing. Richard gazed at her as she made her way to the door.

'I wish you had.'

'Things were different then. Everything was different.'

'Before Fleur.' Gillian nodded, smiling slightly.

'Exactly.'

By Friday, Fleur still had not telephoned. Gillian and Richard paced the house like two nervous dogs while outside the sky hung above them in a grey, humid mass. Mid-morning it began to rain; a few minutes later the white Jeep pulled up in the drive, discharging Antony and Zara in a flurry of shrieks and giggles.

'Tell us all about it!' exclaimed Richard, longing for a

diversion from his thoughts. 'Did you have a good time?'

'Excellent,' said Zara. 'Even though Xanthe Forrester has approximately one brain cell.'

'We went on this walk,' said Antony, 'and got completely lost . . .' He caught Zara's eye and they both dissolved into giggles.

'And we drank cider,' said Zara, when she'd recovered herself.

'You drank cider,' retorted Antony. 'The rest of us drank beer.' He began to laugh again. 'Zara, do your Cornish accent!'

'I can't.'

'Yes you can!'

'I don't have context,' said Zara. 'I need context.'

Richard met Gillian's eye.

'Well, it all sounds lovely,' he said. 'I think I'll be having a chat with Mrs Forrester a bit later on.'

'Where's Fleur?' said Zara, dropping her bag to the floor with a thump.

'Gone to London for a few days,' said Richard lightly. 'But she should be back tomorrow.'

'London?' said Zara sharply. 'What's she doing in London?'

'Oh, nothing much. I'm not really sure, to be honest.'

'She didn't tell you?'

'Not in so many words.' Richard smiled at her. 'Now, how about some hot chocolate.'

'OK,' said Zara distractedly. 'Just let me have a look at something.'

Without looking back, she hurried up the stairs, along the corridor and into Fleur's room. There she paused, took a deep breath and, with a thudding heart, pulled opened the wardrobe doors.

All Fleur's black suits were gone.

'Oh no,' said Zara aloud. 'Oh no, please.' A pain hit her in the chest like a hammer blow. 'Please, no.' Her legs began to shake. and she sank down onto the floor.

'No, please,' she muttered, burying her head in her hands. 'Please don't. Please don't. Not this time. Fleur, please don't. Please.'

By supper, the tension in the house had risen to screaming pitch. Zara sat staring at her plate, eating nothing; Richard tried to hide his nerves with a series of jokes at which nobody laughed; Gillian clattered plates briskly and snapped at Antony when he dropped a spoon on the floor. Philippa ate three mouthfuls, then announced she would finish the rest in her room.

Afterwards, the others sat in the drawing room, watching a film on television which they had all seen before. When it finished, no-one spoke; no-one made a move for bed. The next programme began, and everyone's eyes remained transfixed by the screen. We don't want to leave each other, thought Zara. We don't want to go to bed; we don't want to be on our own. When Antony yawned, and began to shift his legs in his chair, she felt a throb of panic.

'I'm off to bed,' he said eventually. 'Good night everyone.'

'Me too,' said Zara, and followed him out of the room.

On the stairs, she pulled him close.

'Let me sleep in your bed tonight,' she whispered.

'What, swap?' said Antony, puzzled.

'No,' said Zara fiercely. 'With you. I just want . . .' She swallowed. 'I just don't want to be on my own, all right?'

'Well, OK,' said Antony slowly. 'OK!' His eyes began to gleam. 'But what if someone finds out?'

'Don't worry,' said Zara. 'No-one'll come near us.'

# NINETEEN

'Zara! Zara!' A voice kept hissing in Zara's ear, kept hissing and hissing. Eventually she thought she might tell it to go away and pester someone else. She rubbed her eyes sleepily, opened them, and gasped.

'You may well gasp!' Fleur was standing next to the bed, dressed smartly in a red suit which Zara didn't recognize, looking down at her with a mixture of triumph and anger on her face. 'Just what do you think you're doing?'

Zara gaped at her through the dim light of the curtained room. Suddenly she became aware that she was lying in bed next to Antony; that his bare arm was lying across her chest.

'It's not what it looks like, OK?' she said quickly.

'Darling, you're in bed with a fifteen-year-old boy. Don't start pretending you stumbled into it by mistake.'

'It wasn't by mistake! But it wasn't, I mean, he wasn't . . .'

'I haven't got time for this,' interrupted Fleur. 'Get up,

and get dressed. We're going.' Zara stared blankly at her, and an ominous pounding began in her chest.

'What do you mean, going?' she faltered.

'Leaving, darling. There's a car waiting for us downstairs. I met a very nice man this week. He's called Ernest. We're going to join him at his villa.'

'We can't leave,' interrupted Zara. 'I won't!'

'Don't be silly, Zara.' A note of impatience crept into Fleur's voice. 'We are leaving, and that's final.'

'I'll scream!' said Zara. 'I'll wake everyone up!'

'And they'll all come running,' said Fleur. 'And then they'll discover exactly what you and young Master Favour have been up to. How will that look to his father?'

'We weren't up to anything!' hissed Zara. 'We weren't *sleeping* together! We were just . . . sleeping together.'

'I find that very hard to believe,' said Fleur. 'Now, get up!'

The duvet heaved, and Antony's head appeared from beneath it. He peered blearily at Fleur and as he saw who it was his cheeks turned white.

'Fleur!' he faltered. 'Oh my God! I'm sorry! We didn't mean . . .' He glanced fearfully at Zara, then back at Fleur. 'Honestly . . .'

'Ssh,' said Fleur. 'You don't want your father coming in here, do you?'

'Don't tell Dad,' begged Antony. 'He won't understand.'

'Well, if you don't want your father to find out about this, I suggest you keep very quiet,' said Fleur. She looked at Zara. 'And I suggest you come with me right away.'

'I'm not leaving,' said Zara desperately.

'You'd better go,' said Antony worriedly. 'Any minute now, Dad's going to hear something and come in.'

'Sensible boy,' said Fleur. 'Come on, Zara.'

'See you later,' said Antony, snuggling back down into his duvet.

'See you later,' whispered Zara. She touched his head gently. 'See you . . .' But tears had begun to pour down her cheeks, and she couldn't continue.

The car was waiting discreetly around the corner from The Maples. It was a large navy blue Rolls-Royce, with leather seats and a uniformed driver who leapt out as soon as he saw Fleur and Zara approaching and opened the door.

'I can't go,' said Zara, stopping. 'I can't leave. I want to live here.'

'No you don't,' said Fleur.

'I do! It's lovely here! And I love Richard, and Gillian, and Antony . . .'

'Well soon we'll be in a villa in the Algarve,' snapped Fleur. 'Doing terribly exciting things; meeting interesting people. And the life we led here will seem very dull.'

'It won't!' Zara kicked the side of the Rolls-Royce, and the driver flinched minutely.

'Don't do that!' Fleur pushed Zara angrily into the car. 'Sit down and behave yourself.'

'Why do we have to go? Give me one reason!'

'You know exactly what the reasons are, darling.'

'Give me one!' shouted Zara, and she stared at Fleur, waiting for a confrontation; for a slap, even. But Fleur was staring out of the car window and her face was trembling slightly, and she didn't seem to have a reply.

By eight o'clock, they had looked everywhere.

'I've checked the garden,' said Gillian, coming into the kitchen. 'No sign of her there.' She glanced again at Antony. 'You're sure she didn't say anything to you?'

'Nothing,' muttered Antony, without meeting her eye. 'I don't know what's happened. I haven't seen her since last night.'

'So unlike Zara,' said Richard. He frowned. 'Ah well, I expect she'll turn up.'

'You don't think we should call the police?' said Gillian.

'I think that's overdoing it,' said Richard. 'After all, it's only eight in the morning. She might have gone for an early morning walk. She'll probably arrive home any moment. Eh, Antony?'

'Yeah,' said Antony, and looked away.

Half an hour later, Gillian came running into the kitchen.

'There's a car coming into the drive!' she said. 'Perhaps it's someone with Zara!'

'There,' said Richard, smiling at her. 'I knew we were panicking over nothing.' He got up. 'Antony, why don't you make some fresh coffee? And have some breakfast! You look as though you hardly slept last night.'

'I did sleep,' said Antony at once. 'I slept really well, actually.'

'Good,' said Richard, giving him a curious look. 'Well, you make the coffee, and I'll go and see if this is Zara.'

'It's not Zara,' said Gillian, coming back into the kitchen. 'It's Fleur's friend, Johnny. And a strange man.'

'Richard loves you,' said Zara accusingly. 'You know he does.' Fleur said nothing. They had stopped at the first small town they reached, and were now waiting in the car outside the bank until it opened. In Fleur's hand, ready for use, was Richard's Gold Card.

'He wants to marry you,' persisted Zara. 'You could be really happy with him.'

'Darling, you say that every time.'

'This time it's true! This time it's different!' Zara frowned. 'You're different. Fleur, you've changed.'

'Nonsense,' said Fleur tartly.

'Johnny thinks so too. He said he thought you were ready to settle down.'

'Settle down!' mocked Fleur. 'Settle down and become a wife! Be "comfortable"'.

'What's wrong with comfortable?' cried Zara. 'It's better than uncomfortable, isn't it? You liked it there! I could tell!' She peered at her mother. 'Fleur, why are we leaving?'

'Oh, darling.' Fleur turned round, and to her shock, Zara saw that her eyes were glistening slightly. 'I couldn't become a boring little Surrey woman, could I?'

'You wouldn't be a boring little Surrey woman! You'd be yourself!'

'Myself! What's that?'

'I don't know,' said Zara helplessly. 'It's whatever Richard thinks you are.'

Fleur snorted.

'Richard thinks I'm a devoted loving creature who doesn't give a fig about money.' Her hands clenched tightly around his Gold Card. 'If I married him, darling, I'd end up divorcing him.'

'Maybe you wouldn't!'

'I would, poppet. I wouldn't be able to help myself.' Fleur examined her nails. 'I know myself pretty well,' she said. 'And Richard deserves better than me.'

'He doesn't want better!' said Zara. 'He wants you!'

'You know nothing about it,' said Fleur sharply, and she turned towards the window. 'Come on,' she murmured to herself. 'Let's just get the money and get a move on.'

Hal Winters was a tall, narrow-shouldered man with a suntanned face and metal-framed spectacles. He sat next to Johnny at the kitchen table drinking coffee in great gulps, while Richard, Gillian and Antony stared at him in silence.

'Forgive us,' said Richard at last. 'This has been a bit of a shock. First Zara going missing and now . . .'

'I can understand you folks being a bit surprised,' said Hal Winters. He spoke slowly, with a rich Midwestern accent which made Antony grin in delight. 'Fleur telling you I was dead, and all.'

'Actually, now I think about it, I'm not sure she said exactly that,' said Richard, frowning. 'Did she?'

'Some sort of misunderstanding, obviously,' said Gillian briskly. 'What a shame she isn't here.'

'Hear, hear,' said Johnny, giving Richard a beady look. 'And Zara missing, too. What a strange coincidence.'

'Zara was here last night,' said Richard, wrinkling his brow. 'I've no idea what can have happened.'

'I fly back out to the States this afternoon,' said Hal Winters. He looked miserably from one face to the other. 'If I've missed my little girl . . .'

'I'm sure she'll be here soon,' said Gillian.

'My wife, Beth-Ann, was asking me last night about it,' said Hal Winters disconsolately. He rubbed his face. 'When I first told her I'd had—' He hesitated. 'Well, when I told her there might be another child – she was real upset with me. Just about cried her eyes out. But, you know, she came round to the idea. Now she's all for me bringing Zara home to meet the family. But I can't bring her with me if she isn't here, now can I?'

There was a pause.

'More coffee?' said Richard desperately.

'I guess that would be nice,' said Hal Winters.

'I'll go and phone the police,' said Gillian. 'I think we've waited long enough.'

'At last!' said Fleur. She sat up, and the fabric of her jacket rustled against the soft leather of the seat. 'Look! The bank's opening its doors.'

'So how much are you going to take?' said Zara, unwrapping a piece of gum.

'I haven't quite decided,' said Fleur.

'Ten thousand? Twenty thousand?'

'I don't know!' said Fleur impatiently.

'You could be happy with Richard,' cried Zara. 'But you trade all that for, like, twenty crappy thousand dollars.'

'Pounds.'

'Jesus,' said Zara. 'Like it matters! Like it means anything! It just goes into the bank and sits there. I mean, you do all this, just so every month you can look at a bunch of numbers and feel safe.'

'Money is safety, darling.'

'People are safety!' said Zara. 'Money gets spent! But people stick around.'

'No they don't,' said Fleur scornfully. 'People don't stick around.'

'They do!' said Zara. 'It's only you that doesn't stick around! You never give anyone a chance!'

'Darling, you're a child; you don't know what you're talking about,' said Fleur. Her voice shook slightly, and she flicked the Gold Card against her red-lacquered nails.

'OK, so I'm a kid,' said Zara. 'So I don't have a point of view.' She looked out of the window. 'The bank's open. So, go on then. Get the money. Throw Richard into the trash. Throw away the nicest man in the world.' She pressed an electronic button, and the window slowly purred downwards. 'Go on!' she yelled. 'Hurry up, what are you waiting for? Go and ruin his life! Ruin all our lives!'

'Shut up!' shouted Fleur. 'Just shut up! I need to think.' She lifted a shaking hand and pressed it to her brow. 'I just need to think!'

'So, Hal,' said Gillian politely. 'You work in pharmaceuticals?'

'Pain relief's my game,' said Hal Winters, brightening slightly. 'I represent a company which manufactures a high-quality analgesic in pill form, currently the number two seller in the United States.'

'Goodness,' said Gillian.

'Do you suffer from headaches at all, ma'am?'

'Well,' said Gillian. 'I suppose I do occasionally.' Hal Winters felt in his pocket and produced a small, unmarked blister pack of tablets.

'You won't find a more effective product than this,' he said. 'See, what it does, it gets to the *root* of the pain. The *core* of the pain, if you will.' He closed his eyes and gestured to the back of his neck. 'A tension headache generally starts right here,' he said. 'And then it spreads.' He opened his eyes. 'Well, what you want to do is catch it before it starts spreading. And that's what this little beauty does.'

'I see,' said Gillian faintly.

'Hal, every time you tell me about headaches, I feel one coming on,' complained Johnny. 'Is that how you manage to sell so many of your pills?'

'I've spoken to the police,' said Richard, coming into the kitchen. 'I can't say they were very helpful.'

'Dad,' said Antony quietly. 'Dad, I need to talk to you.'

'What is it?'

'Not here,' said Antony. He swallowed. 'Let's go outside.'

They walked through the hall, out of the front door – left open, in case Zara had lost her key – and into the drive. It had rained overnight; the air was fresh and damp. Antony headed for a wooden bench which was out of earshot of the house. He wiped it clean and sat down on it.

'So,' said Richard, sitting down beside him and giving Antony a curious look. 'What's this all about?'

'It's about Zara,' said Antony.

'Antony! Do you know where she is?'

'No!' said Antony. 'I've no idea! But . . .' He reddened. 'Something happened this morning.'

'This morning?'

'Well, last night, really.'

'Antony, I don't like the sound of this.'

'It's nothing bad!' said Antony. 'Well, not really. It just sounds a bit bad.' He took a deep breath. 'Zara was lonely last night. She wanted to sleep with me. I mean, just . . . you know. Share my bed. For company.'

He gazed pleadingly at Richard, who exhaled sharply.

'I see,' he said quietly. 'Well, now this all begins to make more sense.'

'We didn't do anything! Honest! You must believe me! But Fleur . . .' Richard glanced up sharply.

'Fleur?'

'She found us. In bed together. She was . . .' Antony licked his lips nervously. 'She was pretty mad.'

'Fleur was here?'

'It was really early this morning. She came in, and saw us, and just dragged Zara away.'

'I bet she did!' exclaimed Richard angrily. 'Antony, how could you?'

'I didn't do anything!'

'Have you no judgement whatsoever?'

'I didn't think . . . I didn't realize . . .' Antony gazed at his father. 'Dad, I'm so sorry.' His voice cracked. 'Honestly, we weren't . . . it wasn't . . .' Richard relented.

'I believe you,' he said. 'But you must understand how it will have looked to Fleur. She left her daughter in our charge. She trusted us.' He rested his head in his hands. 'I'm surprised she didn't come to me,' he said slowly.

'She just kind of dashed off,' said Antony. He bit his lip. 'Do you think she'll come back?'

'I don't know,' said Richard. He swallowed. 'I very much want to think she will. But she may decide . . . she may have decided . . .' He broke off, unable to continue.

'It's all my fault if she doesn't!' cried Antony. 'Fleur won't come back, and Zara won't meet her dad! God, I've ruined everything!'

'No you haven't,' said Richard. 'Don't be silly. There's a lot more to this than you know about.'

For a while the two of them sat in silence, each wrapped up in his own thoughts.

'You really loved Fleur, didn't you,' said Antony suddenly.

'Yes,' said Richard. 'I did.' He looked hard at Antony. 'I still do.'

'Where do you think she's gone?'

'I've no idea.' Richard stretched his legs out, then abruptly stood up. 'We must go and tell Mr Winters about this.'

'Dad! I can't!'

'You're going to have to. It's not fair on him.' Richard looked sternly at Antony. 'He seems a very decent and honourable man, and we owe him the truth.'

'But he'll kill me!'

'That I doubt.' A smile came to Richard's lips, in spite of himself. 'We don't live in the age of the shotgun wedding any more, you know.'

'Shotgun wedding?' Antony stared at him, aghast. 'But we didn't even . . .'

'I know you didn't. I'm joking!' Richard shook his head. 'You youngsters grow up too quickly,' he said. 'It may be fun, to drink and smoke and sleep in each other's beds. But these things bring their problems too, you know.' Antony shrugged awkwardly. 'I mean, look at you,' continued Richard. 'You're only fifteen. And Zara's only just fourteen!' Antony looked up.

'Actually Dad,' he said, 'there's something else I should tell you. About Zara's age. And about . . . other things.'

'What about Zara's age?'

'About her birthday. Remember? The birthday she had a few weeks ago.'

'Of course I remember!' said Richard impatiently. 'What about it?'

'Well,' said Antony, shuffling his feet awkwardly. 'It's a bit difficult to explain. The thing is . . .'

'Hang on,' said Richard suddenly. 'What's . . .' His voice was incredulous. 'What's that?'

Creeping down the drive, like something out of a dream, was a huge, shiny, navy blue Rolls-Royce. It purred to a halt outside the house, and then stopped.

Slowly, glancing at one another uncertainly, Richard and Antony began to approach it.

'Have they got the right house?' said Antony. 'Do you think it's a movie star?' Richard said nothing. His mouth was taut, his neck rigid with hope and nerves.

From the front seat appeared a uniformed driver. Ignoring Richard and Antony, he walked round the car to the passenger door nearest the house, and opened it.

'Look!' said Antony, giving a squeak of excitement. 'They're getting out!'

A leg appeared. A long, pale leg, followed by a red-sleeved arm.

'It's . . .' Antony glanced at his father. 'I don't believe it!'

'Fleur,' said Richard in as calm a voice as he could muster.

She turned at the sound of his voice, hesitated, then took a few steps forward and looked at him, her mouth trembling slightly. For it moment neither said anything.

'I came back, you see,' said Fleur eventually, in a quivering voice.

'Yes, I see,' said Richard. 'You came back. Have you . . .' He glanced at the Rolls-Royce. 'Have you an answer for me?'

'Yes, I have.' Fleur lifted her chin. 'Richard, I'm not going to marry you.'

A dart of pain ran through Richard's chest; dimly he heard Antony's disappointed gasp.

'I see,' he heard himself saying. 'Well, it's very good of you to let me know.'

'I won't marry you,' said Fleur fiercely. 'But I'll . . . I'll stick around for a bit.' Her eyes suddenly glistened. 'I'll stick around, if you'll let me.'

Richard stared at her speechlessly. Slowly the pain in his chest ebbed away; slowly the tension of the last week began to disappear. A cautious, hopeful happiness began to rise through his body.

'I'd like that,' he managed. 'I'd like you to stick around.'

He took a few steps forward, until he was near enough to grasp Fleur's hands, to bring them up to his face and rub his cheeks against her pale, soft skin. 'I thought you'd gone!' he said. Suddenly he felt close to tears; almost angry. 'I really thought you'd gone for good!' Fleur looked at him honestly.

'I nearly did,' she said.

'So what happened? Why did you decide—'

'Richard, don't ask,' interrupted Fleur. She lifted a finger and placed it on his lips. 'Don't ask questions unless you're sure you want to know the answer. Because the answer . . .' Her eyelashes fluttered and she looked away. 'The answer may not be what you want to hear.'

Richard gazed at her face for a few moments.

'Gillian said something very similar to me,' he said at last.

'Gillian,' said Fleur, 'is a wise woman.'

'Where's Zara?' said Antony, bored with obscure adult talk. He looked around. 'Zara?'

'Zara, sweetie,' said Fleur impatiently. 'Get out of the car.'

Slowly, cautiously, Zara climbed out of the Rolls-Royce. She stood still for a moment like a hostile cat, looking around as though suddenly unsure of her surroundings. Antony was reminded of the first time he'd seen her.

'OK,' she said, catching his eye. 'Well, we're back.' She scuffed her foot on the ground. 'You know. If you want us.'

'Of course we want you!' said Antony. 'Don't we, Dad?'

'Of course we do,' said Richard.

He gently let go of Fleur's hands and went over to Zara.

'Come on, Zara,' he said kindly. 'There's someone inside who very much wants to meet you.'

'Who?' said Fleur at once.

'I think you know who, Fleur,' said Richard, looking straight at her.

For a moment they gazed challengingly at each other. Then, as if in acquiescence, Fleur gave a tiny shrug. Richard nodded, a satisfied expression on his face, and turned back to Zara.

'Come on,' he said. 'Come on little Zara. We've had our turn. It's your turn now.' And putting his arm tenderly round Zara's narrow, bony shoulders, he led her slowly into the house.

# *The Wedding Girl*

## SOPHIE KINSELLA

*writing as* **MADELEINE WICKHAM**

When 'I do' gives you déjà vu it could be a problem…

At eighteen, Milly was up for anything. So when a friend asked her to marry him just so that he could stay in England, she didn't hesitate. To make it seem real she dressed up in wedding finery and posed on the steps of the registry office for photographs.

Now, ten years later, Milly is a very different person. Engaged to Simon – who is good-looking, wealthy and adores her – she is about to have the biggest and most elaborate wedding imaginable, all masterminded by her mother. Nobody knows about her first marriage, so it's almost as though it never happened – isn't it?

But with only four days to go, it looks as though Milly's past is going to catch up with her. Can she sort things out before her fairytale wedding collapses around her? How can she tell Simon? And worse still, how can she tell her mother …?

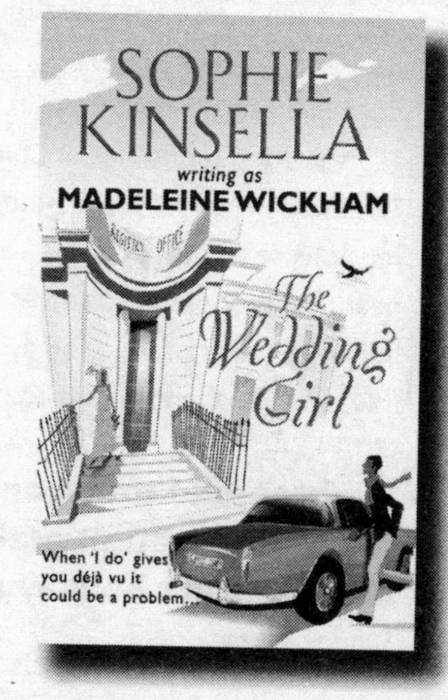


**'Gutsy prose and an excellent ear for social comedy'**
*Independent*

# *Sleeping Arrangements*

## SOPHIE KINSELLA

### *writing as* MADELEINE WICKHAM

*Chloe* needs a holiday. She's sick of making wedding dresses and her partner is having trouble at work. Her wealthy friend Gerard has offered the loan of his luxury villa in Spain – perfect.

*Hugh* is not a happy man. His immaculate wife seems more interested in the granite for the new kitchen than in him, and he works so hard to pay for it all, he barely has time to see their children. But his old schoolfriend Gerard has lent them a luxury villa in Spain – perfect.

Both families arrive at the villa and get a shock: Gerard has double-booked. An uneasy week of sharing begins, and tensions soon mount in the soaring heat. But there's also a secret history between the families – and as tempers fray, an old passion begins to resurface...

**'Lightness of touch and witty observation make this a perfect holiday read'**
*Sunday Mirror*